Praise for *Shadows of the Apt*

'A novel brimming with imagination and execution'   *SciFiNow*

'Epic fantasy at its best. Gripping, original and multi-layered story-telling from a writer bursting with lots of fascinating ideas'
WalkerofWorlds.com

'Superb world building, great characters and extreme inventiveness'
FantasyBookCritic blog

'Adrian is continuing to go from strength to strength. Magic'
FalcataTimes blog

'Reminiscent of much that's gone before from the likes of Gemmel, Erikson, Sanderson and Cook but with its own unique and clever touch, this is another terrific outing from Mr Tchaikovsky'
Sci-Fi-London.com

'I still cannot deny the greatness of Adrian Tchaikovsky's books . . . a glorious success of fantasy literature'   *LECBookReviews.com*

'Tchaikovsky's series is a pretty great one – he has taken some classic fantasy elements and added a unique (as far as I'm aware) twist and element to his characters and the world . . . Tchaikovsky has created a world that blends epic fantasy and technology'
CivilianReader blog

'Tchaikovsky manages to blend these insect characteristics with human traits convincingly, giving a fresh slant to the inhabitants of his classic tale'   *SFReader.com*

Seal of the Worm

Adrian Tchaikovsky was born in Woodhall Spa, Lincolnshire before heading off to Reading to study psychology and zoology. For reasons unclear even to himself he subsequently ended up in law and has worked as a legal executive in both Reading and Leeds, where he now lives. Married, he is a keen live role-player and occasional amateur actor, has trained in stage-fighting, and keeps no exotic or dangerous pets of any kind, possibly excepting his son.

Catch up with Adrian at www.shadowsoftheapt.com for further information plus bonus material including short stories and artwork.

Seal of the Worm is the tenth and final novel in the Shadows of the Apt series.

BY ADRIAN TCHAIKOVSKY

Shadows of the Apt

SHADOWS OF THE APT
BOOK TEN

Seal of the Worm

ADRIAN
TCHAIKOVSKY

TOR

First published in 2014 by Tor

This edition published 2014 by Tor
an imprint of Pan Macmillan, a division of Macmillan Publishers Limited
Pan Macmillan, 20 New Wharf Road, London N1 9RR
Basingstoke and Oxford
Associated companies throughout the world
www.panmacmillan.com

ISBN 978-1-4472-3455-5

1 3 5 7 9 8 6 4 2

A CIP catalogue record for this book is available from the British Library.

Typeset by Ellipsis Digital Limited, Glasgow
Printed and bound by CPI Group (UK) Ltd, Croydon, CR0 4YY

Visit www.panmacmillan.com to read more about all our books
and to buy them. You will also find features, author interviews and
news of any author events, and you can sign up for e-newsletters
so that you're always first to hear about our new releases.

For Scott Young

Acknowledgements

It's been a long road from the gates of Myna to the lair of the Worm. I'd like to thank everyone who has walked it with me.

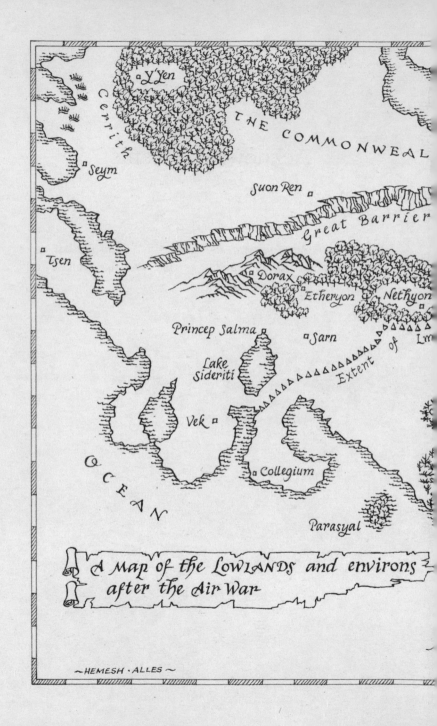

A Map of the LOWLANDS and environs after the Air War

~HEMESH · ALLES~

Shon Fhor

Lake Limnia

Jerez

WASP EMPIRE

Luscoa

Maynes

Szar

Myna

Ridge

rial Advance

Dara'kyon Forest

Tharn

Helleron

Asta

Ruins of Malkan's Stand

Merro

Akta

Tark

Egel

Thord

Iak

Seldis

Araketka

Dryclaw Desert

Felyal

Everis

Toek

Kes

SPIDERLANDS

Siennis

Mavralis

Porta Mavralis

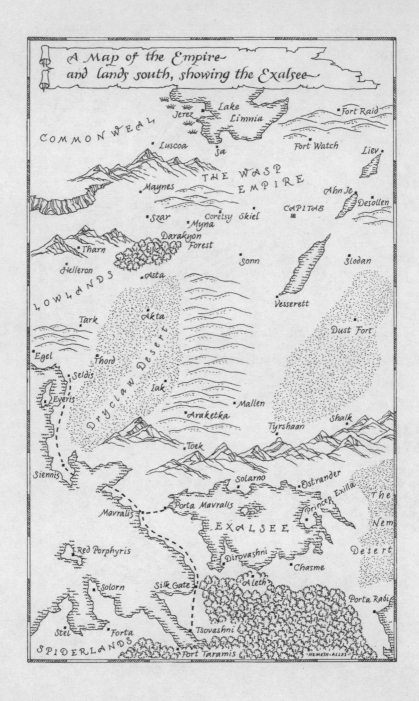

Seal of the Worm

Principal Cast

The Empire

Seda, Empress of the Wasps
General Tynan, Second Army
General Marent, Third Army
General Brugan, Rekef
General Lien, Engineers
Colonel Varsec, Engineers
Colonel Brakker, First Army
Colonel Nessen, governor of Helleron
Honory Bellowern, Beetle diplomat
Major Vrakir, Red Watch
Major Vorken, Slave Corps
Major Oski, Fly-kinden, Engineers
Captain-Auxillian Ernain, Bee-kinden, Engineers
Merva, wife of Edvic, governor of Solarno
Lieutenant-Auxillian Gannic, Engineers
Tisamon, Seda's undead guardian

Collegiates and their Allies

Stenwold Maker, Beetle-kinden War Master, missing, believed dead

Straessa 'the Antspider', officer, Coldstone Company

Eujen Leadswell, Beetle-kinden officer, Students' Company

Castre Gorenn, Dragonfly-kinden, Coldstone Company

Laszlo, Fly-kinden agent, former pirate

Kymene, Beetle-kinden commander, free Mynans

Tactician Milus, Sarnesh Ant-kinden

Sperra, Fly-kinden, agent from Princep Salma

Balkus, commander, renegade Sarnesh from Princep Salma

Sartaea te Mosca, Fly-kinden magician and lecturer

Poll Awlbreaker, Beetle-kinden artificer

Metyssa, Spider-kinden writer

Raullo Mummers, Beetle-kinden artist

Lissart, Firefly-kinden agent, prisoner of Milus

Aagen, renegade Wasp-kinden, now of Princep Salma

Others

Cheerwell Maker, 'Che', niece of Stenwold, magician

Thalric, Wasp-kinden renegade, her lover

Tynisa, halfbreed Weaponsmaster, Tisamon's daughter

Maure, halfbreed magician

Esmail, Assassin Bug spy

Dariandrephos, 'Drephos', halfbreed master artificer and leader of the Iron Glove

Totho, his second, halfbreed artificer

Messel

Orothelin

The Hermit

Part One

Buried Alive

One

It was cold down in the bowels of the earth. The darkness was not the same hindrance to her that it was to her companions, but the cold she could do nothing about.

Worse than that was the *absence*. Born Apt in Collegium, she had no precise words for it. Perhaps the Moths might have done before her ancestors had thrown them out. To a magician, every place had its own feel. There was some additional sense thus engaged that the Apt could never guess at, and that she herself was still learning how to use. Travelling from her home city to the halls beneath Khanaphes, from the great wild expanses of the Commonweal to the tortuous knots of the Mantis forest, all these places had touched her and informed her, even if she had not realized it. There had been a constant voice, and now it was gone – at best. At worst, when she strained that unnamed sense of hers to the utmost, she could hear something else.

A chanting, a susurration from the stone depths. The voice of the enemy. The voice of the Worm.

They were all in the realm of the Worm. In her rage, the Empress Seda had broken the Seal holding that common enemy in its prison domain for a thousand years. Che and her companions had been cast into that dark closed-off place.

It was still closed off, like a woodlouse clasped about itself, but uncurling now, slowly but surely. There would be cracks showing already, weak points that the Worm could pierce to cross,

3

experimentally, into the wide world beyond. Che had thought to do the same, at first. So simple, to exercise her powers as a great magician in this magic-forged place, where surely power was concentrated and free for the taking. She would find out where the fractures were, and she would leave the Worm's realm before its denizens ever realized new guests had arrived.

But that sense, that ability of hers, had fled. She could not breathe water. She could not walk through rock. The medium of this place was inimical to her powers. She, crowned by the Masters of Khanaphes as inheritrix of the ancient ways, had been cut off from her throne and from her inheritance. She was denied the Aptitude that was her birthright, and also the magic that was its replacement. Without those crutches, she fell.

Only one lifeline remained to her. She yet held on to one faint and tenuous connection back to the world, as if fate had considered her exile not cruel enough. Seda was still her sister, in some perverse, bitter way. They had been crowned at the same time. They were linked. Sometimes, unbidden, Che sensed her.

She knew, from this bond, that the doom that had befallen her and her fellows had not touched Seda. Seda was free, still out in the world.

Seda had won.

Faced with that realization, something had broken inside Che. She was aware that she had been down here now – if *down* was even a meaningful word for where she was – for some time, for days, tendays, months even. She was moved, goaded to her feet and forced onwards from place to place. The hands that shoved at her, that grabbed at her and pulled and would not let her just sit down and give up – they belonged to her friends. She remembered them, distantly. She had brought them to this fate, led them here to their banishment. She would not have blamed them if they abandoned her in the dark, just left her behind. Possibly she would have preferred that, but they would not let her be.

They brought her food. It was horrible, uncooked and slimy, breaking into brittle, dry pieces in her mouth. They would not leave her alone until she had eaten. They brought her metallic-tasting water.

Sometimes she was aware that they were hunted, and then they hustled her along from hiding place to hiding place. In the depths that she inhabited – her own personal prison – she could not raise sufficient curiosity to care who pursued them, or why.

Let it be the Worm, was all she thought. *Let it make an end of me.* For surely that hideous, all-consuming monster of legend was more than equal to the task.

In those moments she listened too hard and heard that chanting, ranting echo of it, so distant and yet so potent and hateful, she knew it could do more than make an end of her: it could make an end of all the world. The Worm was a thing apart from Apt and Inapt, from mere kinden and kin. The Worm would devour the world, and Scda had given it the chance to do so.

After unknown ages, there was fire.

Che had lived with the cold and the dark – within and without – for so long that at first she did not understand what it was. The feel of warmth on her skin, the light – so brazen, such a lure to all the dangers of this place – it was like a distant beacon to her, calling her back from the lonely places where she had become lost.

She, who could see in darkness, only realized how blind she had become to her surroundings as she began to return to them.

How long. . .? But she could not know. Some part of her, some internal regulator that marked the hours and days, had ceased to function once she was cast down here. The land of the Worm had no sunrise, no phases of the moon. Timeless, undying, it had lain here for an age beneath an unchanging stone sky. It was beyond the sun, therefore beyond time.

Her eyes were already open, but she opened them anyway, beginning to see rather than just stare vacantly.

She remembered her companions, her friends, fellow inmates of this final asylum. What could be worse than being a lone prisoner of this dungeon? Being responsible for the imprisonment of others. She found their faces as the fire lit them, one by one.

There was Tynisa, her sister in upbringing if not in blood, Weaponsmaster, Tisamon's daughter. Tynisa, whose revenant father was now a slave to the Empress, bound by chains of magic. The girl had always run ahead through all the years of their shared childhood, with poor clumsy Che stumbling in her wake. *So how did it come to this, that she has followed me even to this place?* Che could feel all the sharp points of the Mantis breaking through Tynisa's Spider-kinden facade, and all it told her was how fragile that combination really was.

Thalric next, her enemy, her captor, her victim. Thalric, whom she had wrested from the Empress, transformed from Imperial consort to renegade lover of one Cheerwell Maker, dysfunctional Beetle magician. How could he cope in the realm that she had come to? His limited ability to accept or understand magic must have broken him, surely . . .? And yet here he was, still sitting beside her. The hand that cradled hers was his. She knew its callouses and its lines, the touch that warmed her, the heat in it that could kill.

Further from her: Maure, the halfbreed magician from the Commonweal, no doubt fiercely wishing she had stayed there. She lacked Che's power but far surpassed her in understanding. Seeing her, Che found hope: surely Maure could help her. The woman was a survivor. She must have some way of wriggling free from the bonds of this place.

And last of them: the unexpected, the unasked, the assassin. Esmail, his name was, and he had travelled in the Empress's company. He had tried to kill Seda, and he had succeeded in putting an end to the ancient Moth magician, Argastos. That success and that failure together had led to him being by Che's side when the Empress had unleashed her wrath. But he was a killer by blood and by training and by deed. He had surely earned his place in this realm of the damned.

Her hand clenched suddenly on Thalric's and he started. She

heard him speak her name, soft and almost in her ear, as though wanting to keep her only to himself.

The fire leapt in her eyes, dancing in unnatural hues of violet, blue, corpselight green. The colours glinted on the enclosing walls: a cave? Of course a cave, but she had a sense that they had previously been travelling through vast spaces, caverns whose ceilings were high beyond guessing. Her residual senses recalled waterfalls, lakes that were almost seas, the far constellations of distant cities.

There was a smell of food – of meat cooking – and abruptly Che felt hungrier than she had ever been. On cue, Thalric drew her hand towards a flat rock on which strips and shreds of something pallid and stringy were laid out.

It looked awful, but it was meat and it was hot, so she ate with vigour. Chewy but almost tasteless, it was not what she had been living on since . . . since whenever.

'Someone tell me what's going on,' Che said at last. 'What's happened since we . . . Since whatever. I don't care who, but someone tell me.'

'Now there's the Che we were looking for,' Thalric remarked drily. 'Always with the useless questions.' His sardonic smile was leavened by something uncharacteristic, though: *worry*. Worry for her.

'We've been on our own down here for a long time,' Maure declared, her voice strung taut with fatigue and nerves. 'We've been avoiding other people for most of the time. We . . . this place is huge, a whole world locked away. There are strange kinden here . . . we didn't know, none of us, what they would do with us. So we've been living like vagrants for . . . time. A long time. We wanted just to strike out. I thought I could . . . find a way out.' Her voice shook. 'I can't . . . I have nothing left of my skills. Thalric says they were never real, and I . . . sometimes I think he must be right. This place has killed them, eaten them. And out there, in the true dark, there are things . . . and so little food, so little of anything. And you . . . at first we thought you would come back to us and tell us a way out, but you just . . . there was nothing . . .'

'I . . .' Che's mind thronged with excuses, mystical nonsense about seeking answers, fighting some higher battle. She knew, wretchedly, that they would probably believe her: even Maure, who should know better. The words were in her mouth but she swallowed them down. 'I'm sorry. I couldn't . . . It was too much, and I couldn't face it. I'm sorry.' She took a deep breath. 'But you . . . you've kept us together, all of us. You've found . . . something?'

'People,' said Esmail quietly. 'We found the people who live here.'

'We lived in the wilderness at the start,' Maure explained. 'But it's hard out there. There's just rock, darkness, mushrooms and lichen. When we couldn't last any longer, when we were starving, we had to go to where the fires were. We've been chained to where the people are, since then, where the food is. But never meeting with them, hiding ourselves. Stealing. We've been living by stealing. Esmail, he crept in and took from them, their food, their water . . . It was the only way.'

'But the Worm . . .' Che whispered. This name – and it was not even that ancient enemy's true name, just the Moths' insult for them – had been unspeakable and erased from history, but here . . . what was there to lose in saying it? 'You can't just walk up to the Worm and steal from its table, surely?'

'Slaves,' from Esmail. 'Those we saw, those we took such care to avoid, for fear of their terrible power . . . They're only slaves of the Worm. We have seen the Worm since.'

Che took a deep breath, feeling that her hold on the here and now, rather than the dismal wastes within her, was suddenly failing. *Too much, too soon*, and yet she had to know. She had to understand. 'What's changed? The fire . . . the food . . .'

'Someone found us,' Maure told her.

'He'd been spying on us for days,' Thalric interjected, in what sounded like a jab at Esmail's ability to remain unseen. 'Messel is his name. He's a . . . a renegade, of sorts, but there's a place near here where he has kin. He won't talk about it, but he's not exactly an exile and he's said he returns there sometimes. A slave village.'

Another deep breath. 'You have a plan?'

'We need to know where in the pits we are,' Thalric explained. 'Next, how to get out. This man, this Messel, he had a sort of a laugh when I first said that, but when he realized that we'd got *in* somehow, he shut up real fast. After that, when we asked him again about talking to more of his folk, he was a lot keener.'

'Does your plan go any further than that?' Che asked.

'Why, yes, the plan is: find out how, get out, never mention this place again. Needs fleshing out a little, though. We need intelligence first,' said Thalric, the former agent. 'We're in somewhere completely alien, but there are people here. That means common ground. That gives us something to work with.'

'And the Worm?' Che asked.

There was a long silence. Clearly nobody had any answers.

While the fire burned itself out, they rested. Thalric, Tynisa and Esmail slept, and Che guessed that they had been doing most of the work while she had been refusing to face reality. Now she took hold of herself, still ashamed of the way that she had just given in. *So I have no Aptitude? It's not as if anyone down here's going to ask me to fix their gear train. So this place has no reserves of magic, somehow. Are the Worm Apt nowadays, then? Was there an underground revolution that drove it all out, or . . .?* But it was as Thalric had said: they needed more information. If there were any people here who would not kill them on sight – or worse – then Che needed to speak to them.

Messel had led them to this cave, she was told, and it was deep and tortuous enough that the firelight would not show outside. While the others slept, Maure took Che to the mouth of it, a jagged slash of dark in a broken rockface, where some ancient upheaval had changed the contours of this buried place.

The terrain fell away from them in a tumbled field of jagged stone and shale, and Che's Art let her see out across it, the great desolation of it: as inhospitable a landscape as she had ever seen.

'How can anything live here?' she asked hollowly.

'There's plenty.' Maure's voice still sounded shaky. 'There's stuff . . . lichen-looking stuff over a lot of the rocks, and wherever there's water there are fungi. And things eat the fungi and the lichen, and other things eat them, just as you'd expect. Crickets – there are a lot of crickets. That's what we just ate. Messel brought one down for us.'

The idea of eating cricket meat seemed such a normal and domestic thing that Che almost laughed.

Her Art had limits, but she strained her eyes, seeing something out there that looked more complex, more artificial. There was a chasm, and she thought there was a river, but beyond it, set into the rising cliffs of the far bank . . .

'Is that a town?'

'Cold Well,' said a low, resonant voice, and they both started from a shrouded figure crouching motionless nearby, which even Che's eyes had missed.

For a second Che was reaching for magic that remained stubbornly absent, seeking a defence, a weapon, but then Maure announced, 'Messel.'

He was draped in cloth, cloaked with it, then a long, hooded tunic and trousers beneath, all cut into a heavy and unfamiliar style, the fabric woven from thick grey-mottled fibres. Seeking his face under the cowl, she tried to meet his eyes and failed.

His skin was dead white, save where it was thinnest – where the faint shadows of veins and bones showed through. He was small, surely no taller than she, and thin to the point of starvation. His face was taut over a skull whose contours she could trace, and his long, delicate hands were lessons in anatomy. He had no eyes at all, not even sockets, just a wrinkled expanse of translucent skin from hairline down to his beak of a nose.

'Cold Well,' he said again. 'I was born there.' The voice buzzed within his chest, sounding as though it was meant for a far larger man than this fragile creature.

'A slave?'

'There are only slaves and the Worm.' A thoughtful pause. 'And now you.'

'Messel,' Che spoke his name. He was not coming closer, crouched against the stone with that sightless visage cocked upwards, drawing in his understanding of the world through sound and smell and who knew what hidden Art besides. When she took a step towards him, he scuttled back exactly the same distance, his feet sure on the uneven rocks, silent in motion, then remaining still to the point of invisibility, no matter how good her eyes were.

'Are you . . . the Worm?' She had meant to say 'of the Worm' but the way the words came out seemed more fitting.

He shook his head, his blind attention plumbing unseen vistas. 'Messel,' he said in that rich voice. 'Messel the hunted. Messel who would not work. Messel the kinless, the cursed.'

'And you are of this Cold Well.'

'Once.'

Che let her Art lapse, so that the darkness rushed back on her like a tide, obliterating all she saw of the land beyond. She had the measure of her own sight, though, and after a while her eyes adjusted, and she could see a faint suggestion of light from what Messel had just named Cold Well. Even the prisoners of this tomb felt the chill: there was a scatter of fire over there, though what it was they burned in this place she could not guess.

She turned her face upwards and then clutched abruptly at Maure's arm. 'There are stars! The sky . . . we can just *fly* out?'

A long pause from the other two, and then Maure's subdued response: 'They're not stars.'

'They dwell above. Their lights lure the unwary who tread the air above us, insects, men too. All who are drawn to the lights are devoured,' Messel intoned softly. 'Those that tell the story that says we were not always here, that we came here from another place, a place of light – not my kinden, but I have heard the tale – they say that the ceiling-dwellers were placed there so that none could even search for a way back out. For me, I never believed in such things.' And of course, whether he tilted his head towards the distant ceiling or towards the night sky itself, he would see no stars.

Che felt a hand clasp her arm, and then Maure was leaning into her, trembling slightly. 'There are no dead here, Che,' she whispered. 'No loose spirits, no pieces of the slain. They all go. They all go to the Worm.'

Che shuddered, and for a long time she just sat there, a comforting arm about the halfbreed magician, staring up into that closed and hungry sky.

Two

'It's getting to the point where we're either going to have to risk Imperial displeasure by kicking them out, or arrange for an accident,' Totho commented.

'You think our guests are outstaying their welcome?' Drephos's tone was dry, amused. 'Unfortunately, the Empire remains a source of patronage, even if we are looking further afield for trading partners these days. If that means we must deal with Consortium spies pretending to be merchants, then so be it. Turning them away is not yet an option.'

Colonel-Auxillian Drephos, master artificer of the weapons trade, dwelt in no palace or great hall, nor even in a well-appointed townhouse such as the Solarnese might favour. His rooms were small, uncluttered and poorly lit. A moderately successful merchant's factor would turn his nose up at them. He lived mostly in his workshops, though. He slept only a handful of hours a night, if that, and could see perfectly in the dark. It was a familiar occurrence for Totho to enter the workshops and find his master working through the small hours, surrounded by fragments of clockwork and oblivious to the passage of time.

Of course Totho worked at odd hours too, whenever inspiration struck. The only difference was that he had to bring a lamp with him.

'Well, if we can't officially show our displeasure, what if one of them got his prying hands caught? Poking around in someone else's work can be a dangerous business if you don't understand the principles involved.'

Around them, the machines stood silent, ready to stamp, press, mould and cut. Schematics for half a dozen inventions-in-progress were tacked up on boards all around them. Both of them had particular projects that they were devoting their time to, but the ideas would keep coming nonetheless, to be hastily scribed down for later use.

'If it would make you happy,' Drephos replied indulgently. 'I admit, they have been growing somewhat insistent recently.'

The factories of the Iron Glove in Chasme lay just across the Exalsee from Solarno, seat of the nearest Imperial presence. That sea, and half of that city, was firmly in the hands of the Spiderlands Aristoi, and yet the Empire's mercantile Consortium still paid its visits. The Glove had not been free of them for months now. Oh, they brought sacks of money, new commissions and orders, but they also had other agendas. At least half of those supposed diplomats and artificers and traders who walked in under the Black and Gold took considerable liberties with a guest's access to the premises. They were hunting for secrets, and no doubt seized greedily on any scraps of thought that Totho and Drephos left lying around.

More recently, though – ever since the Glove's two founding members had paid a visit to Capitas – they had been aware that the Consortium, and through it the Empire itself, had something specific in mind.

It did not exist, Drephos had assured them. The complex alchemical formula they asked after had been lost in the confusion of the last war's end. Drephos himself had come out of that war as both a deserter and an invalid. Small surprise, then, if some of his secrets had fallen from the fingers of his broken metal hand, which Totho had since repaired.

And of course they then asked if he could recreate the substance, and he had confirmed he could not. The poison they called the Bee-killer had been the work of two protégés of his

14

who had taken their own lives when it became evident what the Empire wanted their work for. Drephos himself was not a good enough chemical engineer to follow in their footsteps. He preferred working with metal, after all.

At which the Consortium men nodded and muttered and shrugged – and in their hearts they did not believe him.

The latest pack of them had been due to depart a few days ago, but had now stretched their welcome to breaking point, and every night one or other of them had been spotted creeping about the corridors of the workshop, hunting for the supposed secret. And it was certainly there, Totho knew full well. Of course Drephos had the formula for the Bee-killer, the city-devouring poison gas that Totho himself had unleashed on the Imperial garrison at Szar. After all, Drephos's business – his obsession – was with tools of destruction. He had no other reason to exist.

And yet the Consortium asked and asked again, and Drephos put them off.

Totho remembered a conversation with his master, looking out over the city of Szar. It had been the night before the Bee-killer – unnamed at that time – was to be unleashed on the rebels there: a grand statement of the Empire's ruthless use of power, a lesson to all others who dared to rise up. Drephos had argued that the lethal gas was simply the continuation of war, inevitable and even desirable, the furtherance of his craft. Totho had been half convinced. Circumstances had forced his hand, though. They had fought, the two artificers, and Totho had won the fight but lost the argument. He had tested the weapon anyway, on the Wasps themselves. That final show of dedication to his trade, Totho suspected, had healed the rift between him and Drephos as if it had never been. The Colonel-Auxillian was a man to whom moral principles were a closed book, but that cut every way – it made no difference to him who the Bee-killer killed, so long as it worked.

Totho longed to ask him now: *Why have you not given it to them?* He had been ready to resist it, too, to try all those tools of persuasion that had failed to open Drephos's heart or mind the first time.

Now he wondered if his arguments had somehow found a purchase on the man, after all, for the Bee-killer formula stayed locked away, and Drephos brushed the Consortium men off with lies.

Whenever they spoke to Imperial delegations, everyone cheerily agreed that the Empire needed them, and they needed the Empire, but Totho was wondering how much that held true nowadays. The Glove was expanding into other markets now that its reputation was established. The Empire's own Engineers were growing pointedly envious that a pack of mercenaries was outmatching them in the eyes of their superiors. Closest to home, the Glove's guests were becoming visibly frustrated at the denials and evasions, and of course there were plenty who remembered how Drephos had deserted the Empire in its time of need, subsequent pardon or not. It was not as if he did not have enemies.

Totho set to making plans, therefore. The matter in hand, of their unwelcome guests, was almost a pleasant diversion, practically an apprentice piece compared to his usual stock in trade. So it was that, a day later, one of the visiting Wasps was found – far beyond anywhere he had any right to be – caught in the jaws of a steam-press, the mangled pieces of his body imprinted with the hard lines of components as though he was posthumously confessing his spying.

The delegation left that day, uneasily accepting Drephos's wry condolences, but inevitably they would be back.

The Solarno that the Imperial delegation returned to was a city under the hammer, day to day, and yet for all that its shadow spoiled the clear blue skies above, the blow refused to fall.

There were a thousand rumours. After half a tenday, Lieutenant Gannic had heard them all.

This was where the Empire and the Spiderlands had signed their great accord, their declaration of common interests. From

Solarno's gates a combined force had marched out in the direction of Collegium, snapping up every little prize on the way: Tark, Kes, Merro, Egel – Spider satrapies all. The Empire had grander plans: the Beetle city itself.

And they had taken it, Spiders and Wasps together; the great heart of the Lowlands had been stilled. And then, on the back of that victory and before the populace had even been decently pacified, the victors had fallen out. Nobody knew the details – there were a thousand rumours about that as well – but now there were Imperial forces along the Silk Road, and Seldis had fallen to the Black and Gold, and thousands of Spiderlands mercenaries and Satrapy soldiers were on the move.

Solarno sat, jewel of the Exalsee, with its northern districts patrolled by the servants of the Empress and its docklands held by the lackeys of the Aristoi, and a handful of streets in the middle that both sides conscientiously avoided. And . . . and what? And nothing.

In a gloomy backroom behind a machine shop in the lower reaches of the city was a one-eyed Fly-kinden who saw a great deal of what went on. She was a tough, leather-skinned woman with her greying hair cut short, whose past had seen her cross the Exalsee countless times on less than legitimate business, and who had made enough contacts and learned enough valuable secrets to set herself up as a freelance intelligencer.

Gannic sat opposite her on the floor in the Fly style, even though it turned him into a hulking bundle of jutting knees and elbows. He guessed she insisted on seeing her larger visitors like this because she herself could be up and away before they could lever themselves to their feet.

Won't save her from stingshot, of course; but Gannic was a patient man, and he watched the diminutive woman sip her wine meditatively. Every so often her single eye flicked towards him, perhaps wondering who his paymasters were. There were so many to choose from these days.

'I've done some digging for you,' she remarked. 'You ask some interesting questions, for a halfbreed just blown in out of the desert.'

'Enquiring mind,' Gannic told her. He was dressed like a tramp artificer, one of the many who trekked around the Exalsee whoring out their skills wherever the coin was. 'What did you dig up?'

'That a body went into the bay a tenday before you turned up. My friends in the business tell me the deceased looked a lot like your Wasp friend . . . and yes, there's a strong suggestion that the corpse was collected *from* the governor's townhouse, rather than someone stopping the man arriving there in the first place.'

Gannic nodded. 'And the other business?'

'And the other money?'

He regarded her for a moment, knowing that there was no trust in this espionage trade. She could be about to have him killed. She could not know that he was not going to try the same.

He opened a purse and counted out coins – a mix of Imperial and Helleren mint – and then a coil of the gold wire the Spiders tended to travel with. She let the money sit on the table between them, her eye assessing the value. It was more than they had agreed, but Gannic had studied Solarnese etiquette regarding this sort of deal. Holding back information was par for the course, unless the buyer showed good form by being generous.

'The governor, Edvic, absolutely does not deal with the Spider-kinden,' she told him, with a regretful show of spread hands. 'After all, there's a war on.' But she was smiling, and he had paid over the odds, so he waited until she added, 'But.'

'But?'

'But Edvic's wife has a very busy life amongst Solarnese society. Her name is Merva, and she meets everyone. Many of those she meets frequent the lower streets, near the water.' Meaning those parts controlled by the Spider-kinden.

'Merva, you say?'

The Fly smiled. 'No doubt the Wasps would be horrified at the notion, but elsewhere, where we women are more valued, they say she runs the city, and that her husband just sits back and lets her get on with it. Such wisdom is rare in a man.'

He nodded, and listened further as she gave him a concise list of people whom this Merva had spoken to, and the places she had visited. At the end, and again because he knew the etiquette, he slipped another couple of coins onto the table as he stood to leave.

She made a satisfied grunt. 'Enjoy your stay in our city, foreigner. I apologize for the weather.'

Before leaving the machine shop, he considered that remark. Solarno at this time of year was famous for its clement climate. However, the unwary might find worse than rain dropping on them. The woman had probably set him up, and was now telling him that she'd done it – the curious honour of a Spiderlands information broker.

He broke away from the shop quickly, hearing the ambush start into motion. Instead of simply fleeing, he was turning to meet them, hands already out. He caught a glimpse of a couple of Solarnese dropping down from the rafters, and a Spider-kinden behind them, a lean, pale man with a rapier. The pair of thugs had cudgels only – so either they were amateurs or they wanted him alive.

Either way, Gannic had no intention of obliging them. In one hand he had a sleevebow, one of those little cut-down snapbows that were slowly becoming the agent's favourite friend, and he discharged it straight into the chest of the nearest bruiser, stopping him in his tracks and dropping him. The other man went for him, but Gannic skipped back, seeing the Spider descend hurriedly to join the fun.

Gannic's off hand spat golden fire, the Wasp's Art, making them both duck back. For a moment he considered taking the fight to them, perhaps getting a few more questions in this night. As neither of them looked like a flier, trusting to his feet seemed the wiser move. Once he had got them to take cover, he was off and running, reloading the sleevebow as he went.

Gannic had come here for a very specific mission, so the current state of Solarno should only have been of incidental interest to him. The officer overseeing this operation had hinted at some fairly expansive fallback options, though, and to utilize them he needed to work out the true story. The situation here might serve him, if only he could master it.

Once he was sure he had thrown off any pursuers, he followed a roundabout and careful route back up to the Imperial half of the city, seeking out a Consortium factorum, where a man was waiting to hear his report. Despite the trappings, this operation was not being run by the Empire's mercantile arm, and nor was it a job for their secret service, the Rekef – just as Gannic was a capable agent but also something more: a true specialist.

The officer he reported to was a small man with a little patch of beard on his chin in the Spider style. His name was Colonel Varsec, and he was either the rising star or the scapegoat for the Engineering Corps, depending on whether it was praise or blame that was going around. He had come close to execution more than once, Gannic knew. Perhaps this assignment would see both of them on the crossed pikes.

'Let's have it.' Varsec was uncomfortable, unhappy with what they were trying to achieve here, and the range of means that had been given him.

Gannic made his report: the truth behind the impossible stalemate between Empire and those Spiderlands Aristoi who had inherited the Aldanrael conquests. 'What nobody realizes back home, sir,' he explained, 'is just who the power ended up with when the Aldanrael went down – after the Second Army killed their woman in Collegium. There were all sorts of little families who hadn't or couldn't abandon the Aldanrael and, so far, us being here has stopped any of the big boys moving in. So you've got the Arkaetiens and the Melisandyr and the like, who were just hangers-on, and now they're basically running things here in Solarno, and maybe Tark and Kes and points west too.'

'How are the Solarnese taking it?' Varsec prompted him.

Gannic considered what he had seen: the locals going about their business cautiously, with that same hammer hanging impossibly above each of them. 'Cautiously optimistic, I'd say,' he conceded. 'They know there're wheels turning, and that something's got to give, but this place is used to Spiders – meaning there's always some bad news behind the scenes somewhere. They reckon it won't necessarily touch them, if they keep their heads down and get on with it.'

He had been very carefully chosen for this assignment, had Gannic. He was an unusual man. He had slipped through the slums and the tavernas on both sides of the city, listening more than talking, overhearing more than being seen. So far he had not misstepped, as evidenced by his continued good health.

Lieutenant Gannic's rank badge pinned his fortunes to those of the Engineering Corps, the coming power in the Empire, who were just as wary about competition as any Consortium magnate. He was no artillerist or automotive driver, though. He was a sneak for the artificing age. Saboteur was the official label, and there were few enough of them – men with a formidable understanding of artifice, an easy manner and a soft tread.

One other thing, of course, as his mirror reminded him every morning when he shaved: Wasp features in a darker, rounder face, the gift of his Beetle mother. *Rough with the smooth*, he thought, as he wielded the razor. He had the world's two most Apt kinden as parents, and he made a natural agent, for everyone knew how much the Empire loathed halfbreeds. More than that, though, this job – this very particular job – recommended itself to a man of a certain heritage like himself.

'Sir, did you get word back – from the top?'

Varsec's expression was hooded. 'Just two words: "Do it."'

Gannic made an appreciative whistle. 'You want me across the water, or . . .'

'Not yet. Unless our target in Chasme is going to suffer a

sudden change of heart, we need to have our backup plan ready to go. General Lien's getting impatient. Enough eavesdropping and talking to sneaks. Time to act.' Varsec looked anything but enthusiastic about that. *This is going to end very badly*, his expression said. 'Just be careful not to end up like the last man.'

'The last man' had been a Captain Carven – not part of Varsec's operation but a Rekef agent bringing orders from the Imperial governor here: *Start the fires, drive the Spiders from Solarno.* Varsec and Gannic had discussed those words in detail, and were unanimous in their opinion that they were stupid orders. There had been a great deal of pressure from conservatives in Capitas to strike at the Spider-kinden, though, and somehow nobody up there had considered that Solarno was rather closer to Spider reinforcements than it was to any aid the Empire could give it.

Supposedly, this Captain Carven had never arrived. The Spiders had been playing espionage while the principal Wasp entertainment had been living in hill forts and stealing the neighbours' women. Back home the conclusion had been swiftly reached that Carven had been done away with before ever getting in sight of the governor's townhouse.

Except that, according to the Fly woman, his body had been dragged out of that same house and dumped in the bay, to be picked over by fish and water beetles and dragonfly nymphs.

Varsec had guessed that there was a good reason why Solarno had not been riven by civil war: it was not an *Imperial* city at all, no matter whose flag waved over the high ground. *So was that the plan all along*, he mused, *or did Governor Edvic and his wife look at the odds and start a little dance of their own?*

'Personally, I'd rather do without the lot of them and leave the city to stew, sir,' Gannic stated. It was unforgivably familiar before a superior officer, but he knew by now that Varsec didn't care.

'From everything you've learned, that doesn't sound like an option,' Varsec replied. 'We're going to have to get our hands dirty here in Solarno before we can move on.'

We – meaning me, Gannic realized. *And nothing's ever simple where Spiders are involved.* At least by now he'd acquired a good idea of what the Spiders wanted here, too. The little families that had their hooks into this place wanted to keep what they had – which meant avoiding a fight with the Empire, and avoiding calling in the bigger Spider clans.

Between the governor's wife and the local Aristoi, a rather remarkable piece of diplomacy had grown up, or that was what Varsec believed, and what Gannic's investigations seemed to confirm.

'Time to go pay a visit, then,' he decided, and he would just have to do his best to avoid ending up like the late Captain Carven.

Three

The Ant-kinden found it baffling, infuriating and hilarious by turns, Straessa understood. Needless to say, very little of that showed on their faces, but there was always one who stopped to watch whenever the Collegiates were drilling, and with them you only needed a single pair of eyes for the whole city to be spying. She had the impression of being surrounded by gales of unheard laughter at every move, every step out of place, every stumble.

She did not have much to work with here, it was true. Three kinds of soldiers, in brief, and only one of any use. Those actual members of the Merchant Companies who had been able and willing to depart Collegium were her core, but most of that city's soldiers had stayed there, after surrendering their arms. Even under the Black and Gold, Collegium was home, and the exiles in Sarn lived in agony daily, knowing that they could not help their fellows, that they could do nothing to stay the Wasp lash, because they themselves had . . .

She still had to catch herself, to prevent the words *abandoned their city* from coming to mind. *We're going back. We're here to work with the Sarnesh, so that we can free Collegium. We'll do more good if we're free over here than if we're slaves over there.* They were words she had heard from Eujen, from plenty of others. They were all equally desperate to justify themselves.

The second and third batches of her recruits were equally ill at ease with weapons, armour and discipline, but she was not choosy. By simply turning up, they had passed the one test that mattered. Some were inhabitants of Sarn's Foreigners' Quarter, Collegiate expatriates who had made a living here in the Lowlands' most enlightened Ant city-state, but who still remembered their old home. The rest were genuine Collegiates: citizens who had fled before the siege, or who had got out somehow after the city was taken. They were not soldiers but they were hurting. The Wasp boot was on the neck of their beloved home. It was unthinkable, and it moved them to do unthinkable things, such as volunteering to fight.

They were nobody's idea of soldiers: middle-aged men and women with a trade or a shop left behind them, and often family as well. They were driven, though. No drillmaster ever had more willing raw material. Under the stern governance of their Tactician Milus, the Sarnesh had given them snapbows and chain hauberks and swords, and left them to it. At this stage in the war, the Ants were not going to turn away any help at all.

The Imperial Eighth Army had been defeated, that much was fact. The field battle had seemed inconclusive, and everyone had assumed that the Wasps had pulled out with a sizeable slice of their forces intact, but then Ant scouts had found . . .

. . . Something. They had found something, although they were not sharing the details with their allies, which was concerning. Balkus – the renegade Sarnesh attached to the Princep Salma forces – said that they were sure the Eighth were no longer a threat, but what he could glean from eavesdropping around the edges of the Sarnesh linked minds suggested that the precise fate of the Imperial army was a matter of concern.

Eastwards from Sarn, the Empire was still about. The Wasp reserve force sent to support the now-defunct Eighth had been reinforced by elements of the Imperial First and was keeping pressure on the Ant city by its very presence. That meant that the Sarnesh was not preparing for the liberation of Collegium. The Ants were very glad to have allies to fight alongside them, and even more grateful to have the cream of Collegiate artificers modernizing their air power, but their chief tactician would always change the topic when pressed about a return to Collegium.

Well, maybe today will be different. There was another delegation heading to him soon, Straessa knew. And this time Eujen had said he would be going.

'Officer Antspider!' The call came from her blind side, so she had to cast about before she spotted a Fly-kinden boy she vaguely recognized as a Foreigners' Quarter local.

'What is it?'

'Deliveries, Officer.'

'Already?' Her tenuous hold over the recruits had broken and they were out of formation, milling about and pressing closer to hear, but she could hardly blame them. 'Deliveries' meant a courier had run the Wasp gauntlet from Collegium: word from home. 'Reading at Bor's Pit?'

'And soon,' the Fly confirmed, then kicked off into the air to go and spread the news.

'Class dismissed!' Straessa called. 'Bor's Pit – if you want to hear the latest. Time to yourself, otherwise.' They would almost all be there, cramming the theatre offered up by its expatriate owner as a surrogate Amphiophos, providing the seat of Collegiate government in exile. 'Volunteer to let the Mynans know? They like to hear word, too.'

Someone put his hand up for that task, leaving Straessa free to hotfoot it back to her lodgings, because they would be opening the first letter in the Pit in perhaps half an hour, and it was a full street away from where she lodged. That left her just enough time to cover the ground.

Eujen was awake when she got there, which was just as well. They were sharing the storeroom of a machinist whose spare stock had been eaten up by the appetites of the war. It would have been intimate, had they not also been sharing it with a drunken Spider and a pair of printers whose presses had been smashed by the Empire.

He had got himself dressed, although it must have taken him

26

some effort, and his robes were twisted about him, with nothing hanging straight. He occupied the room's only chair as she came in, using a crate as a writing desk, crossing out as much as he put down. A speech, probably, knowing him.

He looked up sharply as she entered. He had recovered a lot of his colour in the last month, although there was still a greyness about his eyes and cheeks.

'Is it Milus?' he demanded. 'Has he—?'

'He hasn't anything, at the moment,' she told him, because Eujen had been waiting for word from the Sarnesh tactician. 'It's deliveries. You said you wanted to be there this time.'

'Right.' He put a hand out for his sticks, which as usual he had managed to leave out of reach somehow. She let him stretch for them because he hated it when she would not let him win these battles against his own weakness. At last he snagged them, and levered himself upright, wrestling their padded forked upper ends under his arms.

That looked easier even than yesterday. Eujen was, after all, one of the lucky ones. He had gone to death's country, to the very border, stared at its grey horizon and then turned back. Instar, the drug that the Collegiate chemists had concocted during the war, had worked its kill-or-cure miracle with his failing body. He would, however, never be quite the same – never quite rid of the injuries or the effects of the drug. He would be stronger, but he would probably not walk again without the crutches, or so the doctors said. There were many who were not even that lucky.

'We're going to Milus tomorrow,' he told her, setting off on the long voyage to the doorway.

'Are you?'

'Whether he wants to see us or not,' he said firmly.

'He has a war to run. He's a busy man.'

'He has hundreds of our people whom he's happy to employ in that war – our own, Mynans, Princeps. Retaking Collegium is the logical first step.'

'Perhaps not to him.' She nodded a greeting to some of the

machinist's apprentices as she and Eujen crossed the shop floor. They worked here all day and most of the night, making parts for all the machinery of war. It made sleeping difficult, at times, but it was the only place she'd found that didn't involve climbing stairs.

'The closest Imperial force is short on siege engines, all the reports agree,' huffed Eujen, already starting to make heavy going of it. 'So it's not going to invest the city any time soon.'

'The Second was short on siege too,' Straessa pointed out darkly: Collegium had been taken with sheer aerial manpower and the new Sentinel automotives that the Empire had acquired. Of course, following the mysterious scattering of the Eighth, the Sarnesh had a handful of Sentinels as well.

Step by step, they came to Bor's Pit, and by that time Eujen's painful progress had drawn a lot of attention. He had become a symbol, she knew. He had been a student agitator back home, then a military leader and briefly a rebel standing up against the Wasps. A great many people looked up to him, despite his young age.

Watching him making his way, though, most of them were fighting to hide their expressions.

The two of them were almost the last to enter the Pit, but someone would always find a seat for Eujen, one by the aisle, and Straessa stood beside it.

There was a constant roll-call of names, personal messages from family and friends under the Wasp yoke back home, but if that was what this was about, there would have been no need for the Pit, the stage and auditorium. There would also be a stack of messages marked for public consumption, those who had stayed telling their stories for those who had departed. *This is how it is now. Remember us.* There would be the latest instalment from the Spider writer, Metyssa – a hunted fugitive still hiding in Collegium – dramatizing the occupation, telling her tales of small courage, humour and tragedy from under the Imperial boot.

'Willem Reader!' came the call from Bor, the theatre owner, and then a pause to see if he was there. Collegium's premier aviation artificer was absent, though, still working on the Storm-readers being built for the Sarnesh. One of his colleagues took custody of the letter.

'Jons Hallend! Pella Mathawl!' And more: each name finding a willing recipient until all the private missives had been handed out and the main show was ready to begin.

'First on the bill, from Mistress Sartaea te Mosca, Associate Master of the College.' Bor had been an actor once, and his voice filled the auditorium, so very different from that of the quiet Fly woman whose words he would be interpreting. Eujen squeezed Straessa's arm at the name, eager for word from one of their friends. Even bad news might be better than the long agony of no news at all.

Sartaea te Mosca moved like a thief through the streets of her own city.

Or perhaps not quite her own city. She had been born in a little place close to the Etheryon, a logging post, but most of her life had been spent amongst the Moths of Dorax, possessed of just enough magical ability to make training her worthwhile. They had looked down on her, turned her out eventually, but more because she had not become the magician they had expected than because of her kinden.

Collegium had been her home now for some years, and when the Inapt studies post had come up at the College she had not exactly had to beat off much competition for it. The College Masters had not cared how meagre a magician she had been, given that they believed in none of it anyway. She had moved into her tiny classroom and begun teaching, without much facility, to students without much interest. The life had suited her well, letting her make friends and host parties.

She no longer taught at the College. All the lecturers were now under scrutiny and, whilst she had hoped that her esoteric subject might pass beneath their notice, the Wasps had Moth allies as well, and they had driven her out by their suspicious regard and by her own knowledge of her inadequacy. Now she stayed on as staff, a house-master presiding over a handful of student dormitories, doing what she could to protect her charges from the harsh world they found themselves in.

She had stayed out too late tonight and there was still a curfew in place. After dark, the streets were the official domain of Wasp soldiers and others bearing their writ. General Tynan – acting governor until someone arrived to replace him – rested a light hand on the city, those under his command were often spoiling for any excuse to display their power. There were plenty of arrests still, and some citizens disappeared or were shipped out east for further questioning and never seen again.

It could have been so much worse, and any day the general might break from his introspection and remember that he could make it so. Sartaea should have stayed behind closed doors, but she had urgent visits to make. It was important to her. There would always be people who wanted word sent out of the city, and she had taken the duty upon herself to help them. After all, she was a tiny speck of a woman, nimble in the air, treading lightly on the ground, and with eyes honed by decades of Moth darkness. The Imperial patrols were a risk she felt qualified to run.

And if she were caught, well, she had made a point of getting to know a few officers in the garrison. There were a dozen sergeants who knew that they could stop at her kitchen in the College and get something hot to eat or drink. She had to hope that those fragile bonds might bear the weight of a Fly-kinden life if the worst came to the worst.

The Reader house was near the College – a good first stop – and she rapped at the shutters of an upstairs window until Jen Reader let her in. The College's librarian would have word destined for her artificer husband, who had been evacuated to Sarn.

After that, there was Poll Awlbreaker the engineer, whom the

Wasps had working for them in their commandeered factories, and whose back, Sartaea knew, bore the trace of the lash to testify just how that arrangement had been brokered. His forced collaboration had bought him some concessions from the Empire, though. His house was unlikely to be searched so long as he kept the work up.

'Any word?' she asked him as he let her in.

He nodded, took a good long look out at the street and then closed the shutters. He was a strong-framed man in his prime, made broad and powerful by artificing work and fighting with the Coldstone Company during the war.

'We've got papers for a single airship heading out for Helleron,' he confirmed to her. 'Space for two passengers and as many letters as you've got. Courier's all set to take them.' Only the courier herself would know the precise detour the airship would need to make in order to drop off its illicit cargo for onward transmission to Sarn.

'Is Metyssa going?'

He made a face and then shook his head. 'I told her she should, but she won't. Two other Spiders, though. They're going freight, nailed up in crates. It's getting harder to pull this business off.'

Sartaea nodded. Being Spider-kinden in Collegium – or anywhere under Imperial control – was a death sentence ever since the inexplicable falling-out between the Second Army and its erstwhile Aldanrael allies. Whatever had happened, a whole second front had opened up down the Silk Road, draining Imperial manpower and resources. However advantageous this was for those fighting the Empire, it had resulted in the summary execution of hundreds of Spiders who had already fled the Spiderlands to make a new life elsewhere.

Metyssa was one such fugitive, Poll's lover and fellow soldier. Her presence, hidden behind a false wall in his cellar, had been more persuasive than the whip in getting him to work the Wasps' machines.

'Has she written anything?' Sartaea asked.

'Oh, you can be sure. For someone who doesn't get out much, she's certainly got a lot to say,' Poll remarked with a strained smile. 'Nothing to the purpose, as usual, but it makes for good reading.' Metyssa had made a living writing sensational stories for the Collegiate presses before the city had fallen. Now she was working on her own vivid account of the occupation, and Sartaea always had to scribble onto it the caveat that none of it was strictly true before passing it on to the courier. It was popular over in Sarn, she understood: each chapter eagerly awaited.

She dearly hoped that Metyssa would have a chance to finish the account. A Spider-kinden man had been unearthed only two days before and shot dead when he tried to run, and the family that had sheltered him had been arrested, their subsequent fate uncertain.

After that there was a string of other visits, a score of patrols dodged or hidden from as Sartaea skipped through the night-blanketed streets of Collegium, striking her tiny blow against the Empire. Last on her list was the home of Tsocanus, an Ant-kinden merchant who lived above his workshop, where he had previously run a brisk trade as a wholesaler to the airship trade. Now he sold, at the poverty-level mandated prices, to the Empire's engineers and Consortium, and even sent his prentices to fix their machines when the Wasps themselves could not be bothered. Like Poll, though, he did it with apparent willingness. His cellars had a hidden room, and there would usually be a handful of Spiders there, or others seeking to evade the Rekef, ready to be smuggled out as soon as an opportunity presented itself.

She arrived there just in time. Had she turned up any earlier, she would have been inside when the Wasps broke in; any later and there would have been no witnesses to what happened.

When she turned the corner she saw the door was already smashed, and her instincts – good Fly-kinden instincts, those – had her back pressed to a wall, frozen in place, her grey cloak pulled about her.

She could hear fighting, inside – or panicky sounds that were probably a handful of civilians who didn't have the wit simply to surrender. Tsocanus was an Ant, though, and even a renegade Ant who hadn't picked up a sword in ten years still had some fight in him. If he fought, so would his prentices, the half-dozen Beetle-kinden who lived under his roof. And then there were the Spiders . . .

For a moment Sartaea te Mosca made a dreadful miscalculation about the odds, thinking, *If there are that many of us, surely* . . . Then Tsocanus himself stumbled out through the shattered door, grappling with a Wasp, hurling the man away with Art-boosted strength before raising what was surely a kitchen knife.

Te Mosca shrank back as the stingshot found Tsocanus, the flash and glare of golden fire that slammed into the Ant half a dozen times making his body dance with the force of it before he dropped.

There was quiet then, and she had a horrible thought that the Ant had been the only survivor. Next they were bringing the rest out: some of the prentices and a bruised and battered trio of Spider-kinden. Sartaea's headcount came up three short, meaning that Tsocanus wasn't the only one who had tried to make a fight of it, and failed.

They were led away, cuffed sharply when they slowed, or just when the Wasps felt like it, and through it all she did nothing, nothing whatsoever. She was one small Fly-kinden woman, and barely a magician at all, and she crouched there, unseen and castigating herself for having only one unworthy thought: that she was lucky that Tsocanus was now dead, as otherwise her name would shortly be on Imperial lips.

'You're off to see the Bastard, then?' asked Balkus, with that irritability that had hung about him ever since he had been unwillingly repatriated to Sarn.

'Want to come along?' Sperra cocked an eye at him. 'It's about the only time I could put you in front of him without you throwing a punch.'

Like so many others, the Ant-kinden Balkus had been injured in the Collegiate fighting, evacuated at the last moment from the city after the student insurrection failed. The physicians had not dared try him with Instar – they saved that for those with a Beetle's sterner constitution. Even now he was weak, shaking if he walked too far. He did walk, though. Sperra knew that he was determined to wrest his strength back from the bolt-wounds that had drained it from him. A full confrontation with Tactician Milus – 'the Bastard' as he and Sperra had renamed the man – was likely to finish him before a sword was drawn. Even now, just back from a few turns about the Foreigners' Quarter, he looked exhausted as he slumped in a chair.

Balkus was a renegade from this very city, which would normally have made his return a death sentence. However, he was also a citizen of Princep Salma, the new city lying half-built in Sarn's shadow. Even though Princep's military assistance had been provided under Sarnesh duress, Balkus's status there lent him some protection.

Sperra was likewise a Princep citizen and former tenant of a Sarnesh inquisition room, the two of them united in their dislike and distrust of their hosts. Whilst Balkus was nominally the military commander of the Princep forces – whatever that was worth – she was just a Fly-kinden, a foreigner in Sarn, someone who at any time could be suspected of knowing too much. The Sarnesh had run her through their machines before, on the off-chance that she knew more than she was telling, and then they had done it again just to be sure. If it wasn't for Balkus, nothing would keep her in this city: Balkus, and the need to keep her adopted city of Princep free.

Right now, the best chance for Princep to have any voice in the war was to link arms with the Collegiates. Whilst Balkus was recuperating, Sperra had been busy winning Beetle-kinden affections. She was one of the regular couriers, making the hazardous trip between Sarn and the conquered city to pick up news and intelligence. She had enough artifice in her to pilot a

34

flying machine, and she was quick, quiet and had a nose for danger.

'Let the fighting belong to the Ants and the Wasps,' she had said. 'Right now, it's a Fly-kinden war.'

'The Bastard won't listen,' Balkus told her. 'I catch just enough, for all they try to keep me out. He's fighting a Sarnesh war for Sarn. He'll keep the pot boiling in Collegium, 'cos it bottles the Second Army up there, but why should he want the place free? The city would be half-smashed in the fighting or by the Wasps when they pulled out, and then what? He has half an Imperial army at large, probably, and all his willing Beetle soldiers and artificers want to go home and pick up the pieces. He's got everything where he wants it, believe me.'

Sperra shrugged. 'He'll push them too far.'

Balkus snorted. 'The Beetles?'

'You haven't seen them. And it's the Mynans as well – and our lot.' She shrugged again, abruptly defeated by the ability of the Sarnesh to prevaricate. 'But you're probably right, this time.'

'And the next, and the next.'

'Maybe not.'

His head had been sagging but it jerked up at that. 'What news? Something you didn't tell the others?'

'I don't peddle false hope to the Collegiates. I've not said anything, because I wasn't sure. Rumours, though. Rumours out of nowhere.'

'So tell me!'

'Can't. Have to go now. Off to see the Bastard, don't you know?' And she skipped back to the doorway of his room. To her delight, he lunged out of the chair after her with a shout – for a moment the two of them again as though the war had never come. Then he was steadying himself with a hand against the wall, but standing, even managing a grin.

'Go tweak the Bastard's nose,' he directed. 'But after that you'd better tell me what's up.'

★

The delegation was five in number, a bizarre cross-section of Sarn's unruly allies. It was accepted that Eujen would take the lead, even though they would have to wheel him there in a chair. Kymene herself would stand for the Mynans, a good number of whom had congregated in Sarn. Sperra represented Princep Salma, and the artificer Willem Reader had broken from his work to accompany them. His services were crucial enough to the Sarnesh that any delegation including him could not simply be turned away. Finally, appearing uninvited at the last moment, the Dragonfly named Castre Gorenn would stand for the Common-weal Retaliatory Army, which was to say, herself.

We just need a Mantis-kinden from the Netheryon for the set, Eujen considered. In truth, nobody knew what the intentions of that newly renamed Mantis state were, despite over two months of Sarnesh diplomacy. The Mantids had attacked the Imperial Eighth and directly contributed to the Sarnesh victory there, but the one certainty with them now seemed to be that all previous alliances and agreements were off. That this included their long-time subservience to the Moth-kinden was currently absorbing the full attention of Dorax as well, to the frustration of anyone who had been counting on their support.

Tactician Milus met them alone, but of course he had the whole weight of Sarn within his head. He outnumbered them by thousands to one. He was in his full armour: dark steel plate heavier than a normal soldier's but undistinguished by finery or any badge of rank. All his soldiers knew who he was, after all.

The interior of the Royal Court buildings was crammed with innumerable little square rooms, gaslit and often windowless, each changing purpose by the hour as the busy Ants ordered their state, their daily lives and the war. They found him in one such, with a map tacked up before him, displaying Sarn and the immediate tens of square miles, out as far as the edge of the Netheryon forest.

'Well, now, haven't we done this before?' He was unusual for an Ant: a confident speaker with a good voice and a sound grasp of expression and body language, who was well used to dealing with other kinden. He carried a presence with him, a tangible strength of purpose that most of his inward-dwelling people lacked. His face was all slightly exasperated good humour as he looked them over: Eujen, young and chair-bound; diminutive Sperra; Willem Reader, a man of ideas who flinched slightly before the Ant's stare; Castre Gorenn, already losing interest and peering at the map instead. Only Kymene met him on even ground. She had led the resistance in her city, freed it from the Wasps and lived to see it taken again. She had enough force of will for the five of them.

'We have been here before, exactly. I believe that we left with the impression that you would be bringing forward your plans to liberate our city.' Eujen's voice was steady, even strong, coming from somewhere the injuries had not touched.

'The Empire is bringing another army up—'

'There is an army in Collegium, if only you will release it from its chains. There is no suggestion that the Empire intends anything other than to forestall a Sarnesh *attack*. Which, I would add, they are achieving with a minimum of effort.'

Milus regarded Eujen placidly. 'You are asking me to gamble with my city in an attempt to save yours. A familiar statesman's trick, but we have no statesmen here.'

'You sell yourself short, Tactician,' Eujen replied implacably.

There was a second of utter stillness that he had learned to recognize: it was when emotions that Milus was not showing were quietly led off to execution. Then the Ant turned his attention to Reader. 'Master Reader, you must be well aware of how much further our preparations must go. Or is your work complete?'

'It is not, Tactician,' Reader admitted, and plainly Milus over-awed him somewhat. 'However, the Second still has minimal air power—'

'It has enough, and you of all people know how quickly the

Empire can move reinforcements in. They could have two score Farsphex out of Capitas and over my city, and us with only a few hours' warning from that Ear device you set up.'

'Well, it wasn't me. It was—'

'It doesn't matter,' Milus cut him off. 'And your being here as part of this business is not advancing the war. Both you and I have better things to do with our time.' Blatantly unspoken was his assessment that the rest of them there did not.

'Then perhaps we should leave,' Kymene stated.

Milus locked stares with her, and it became clear that she was not talking about the delegation but about her countryfolk.

'The Spiders are fighting the Empire. They would take us in,' she went on. 'Gorenn, you'd come, wouldn't you?'

The Dragonfly's head snapped round at her name. 'Of course,' she confirmed immediately, although it was anyone's guess if she had actually heard the question. She had no patience for politics. 'What are these here?'

She was indicating the map, and the conversation derailed instantly, Milus taking up a new defensive position by deciding to humour her. 'Attacks. Attacks made on my people over the last month.' Four sites were marked within the map's extent, the closest of them within a few miles of Sarn. 'Still think we should be sending all our soldiers off to Collegium?'

'What attacks? We've heard nothing,' Eujen demanded, aware that he had lost the initiative.

'Small in scale.' Milus shrugged. 'A patrol, a merchant caravan, a farm. But no signs of how it was done, no sign of the enemy – just turned earth and too few bodies.' He let that sink in. 'So, believe me, I am not sitting here gloating over the plight of Collegium, but I have many demands on limited resources, and my city is not safe.'

'Like the Eighth,' Gorenn remarked, again forcing everyone to change step to keep up with her.

Eujen was about to question her, but then an uncomfortable

understanding came. *Turned earth, too few bodies, no sign of an enemy.* Surely he had heard that – from Balkus, perhaps? – about what they had found when they went to look for the Eighth.

'Be that as it may, these are attacks on *my* people,' Milus insisted, but Eujen could tell from his tone that he had made the connection long before. *And has no idea what to make of it, I'd guess.* 'This war has overwritten most of the rules of warfare that we were used to, and it looks as though the Wasps are still writing it.' He held up his hands. 'I fully understand. You all have homes, too. You want to free them. You want to fight the Wasps – of course you do. There will be a reckoning. The Empire will be turned back and then destroyed. I am dedicating myself and the might of my city to this objective. It must be by concerted action, though, so you must trust us.'

He looked from face to face, as if ascertaining that there was just enough trust left, averaged between them, to get him home.

'And if things change in Collegium?' Sperra piped up, her first contribution.

'What changes do you anticipate? Things seem... stable there.'

'Who knows? New Wasp atrocities . . . or perhaps an uprising.'

For a moment Eujen thought that Milus seemed unsure. Certainly he himself had no idea where Sperra was leading them.

But then the tactician's customary demeanour returned. 'Bring me any such intelligence and of course it will be looked at. The war changes on a daily basis. Perhaps tomorrow it will be me coming to you, ready to head south. Who knows?'

He knows, Eujen decided. He had a great deal of respect for Milus's handling and control of the war so far, but very little liking for the man.

Four

It was a long walk to Cold Well.

Thalric had a lantern of sorts, a twisted braid of luminescent fibres that gave out a pallid, unwholesome light. It barely showed him where to place his feet but, out of all of them, he was no friend of the darkness. Messel apparently knew he held it, and when their blind guide hissed at them Thalric stuffed the bundle beneath his breastplate to hide its meagre phosphorescence. It was a wretched thing, and he was forced to replace it often from the grotesque fungus things that they found in passing.

They had slept down here more than sixty times by anyone's best guess, although Maure cautioned that, divorced from the world beyond, even the passing of time might not be the same. The halfbreed necromancer had little to offer save prophecies of doom, it seemed. Che had found it hard to believe that they could have been trapped in some small prison for so long without escape or capture, but she had misunderstood the scale of their surroundings. The world of the Worm was a *world* indeed. What she had seen from the ledge, with Cold Well spread out in the middle distance, was but a single segment of the Worm's domain, and Cold Well but a single community amongst dozens of similar slave towns. The Worm had its lightless empire.

Messel himself moved surely, crouching low and often with his long fingers trailing over the stone. Some Art led him onwards, and Che began to suspect that he was hearing through the rock itself, interpreting the minute vibrations of distant motion and letting them warn and guide him.

Often they stopped, Messel leading them aside into cracks and overhangs where they could hide. He spoke little, and the supposed threats were often obscure. Once they heard wings, though – vast and slow-beating and strange. Another time, Che saw a hunting beetle, low-slung but as big as a horse, with its mandibles so long that they crossed over one another. Messel led it away, using a sling to rattle stones off its hide until it lumbered after him, then returning after a long anxious time of uncertainty to get them moving again.

Once there was the Worm.

The Worm they did not see, for Messel had found a shallow cave, and they all lay there barely daring to breathe. Messel's manner had become agitated, almost frantic, where he had met all previous dangers with utter calm. This time he crouched alongside them, his hands clutching at his cloak as though trying to wrest some extra concealment from it. From outside they heard the scrape of armour, bare feet on stone, and Che tried to imagine some other race of blind people – but still just *people* no matter how fearsome their reputation. She failed to picture anything so tame. There was something about the quick, rushing movements out there – the way that, when they stopped, they stopped all at once, then set off all together. There were no words spoken at all, and Messel kept them still and quiet for a long while after the unseen Worm had gone.

'Ants?' had been Thalric's suggestion. He, too, had picked up on the lack of any spoken communication in what had sounded to be a band of a dozen or so.

Che had just shaken her head. The motion of them had been something other than Ant discipline, and she felt that the silence was not due just to an Art mindlink. Why she was so certain, she could not say. It was no magical intuition though, for when the Worm had been near she had felt what little sense of magic she retained being deadened, smothered.

They have done something dreadful, she thought. Her knowledge of the Worm was scant, but she had been gifted with a vision of the forces mustering for that final battle that had seen the Worm driven beneath the earth, supposedly forever. They had been a thing to fear even then, but she compared what she had understood from that battlefield to what she had experienced just now and concluded unhappily that there was some new horror added to the Worm, some change that had been made, and not for the better.

Thalric was her crutch as they travelled under the false stars of the Worm's sky. She could tell that he was fighting to understand where they were and what had happened to them. It was a fight he could never win, but he was a survivor. The world had tried to kill him a dozen times, leaving scars on his hide as mementos. He had passed through the hands of so many masters that he had invented a new kind of freedom all his own. And he had stayed with Che through many trials, and he smiled when he looked at her.

And he was a Wasp. That was a strange thing to find strength in, but half the time Thalric looked the world in the eye, and the rest of the time he looked down on it. He had been brought up on tales of his own kinden's superiority, their ability to master anything. He was not exactly a good son of the Empire any more, but when she was at her lowest, feeling as though she was trapped in a pit she could not escape, his barbed wit would bring the world down to her level. He would make some cynical bleak joke of it all, and things would not be quite so bad after that.

They had camped in a crack in the earth that Messel had scouted for them, but it was too exposed for them to risk a fire and so they huddled together for warmth. Meanwhile the man kept a blind watch nearby.

Esmail was already asleep, or at least pretending to be; he seldom spoke, a private, dangerous man who lacked the past association the others shared. The underworld was left to Che, Thalric, Maure and Tynisa to face.

'I don't understand how anyone can have thought this place a good idea.' Tynisa was staring up at those ersatz stars. Sometimes they saw one of the distant lights twitch and shudder, and knew that some luckless flier had been caught by it and was being reeled in.

'They were desperate.' Che wasn't sure why she was defending the magicians of the ancient world, but the words came out anyway.

'I've known plenty of desperate people,' Tynisa remarked, and then: 'I can remember when I *was* desperate, and the things I did, but this . . . Desperate deeds are spur-of-the-moment deeds. This took planning and patience.'

'Power,' put in Maure softly. 'It took power. And when you have that sort of power, then desperation can do very different things.'

'You're missing the main point,' Thalric's acerbic tone cut in, 'which is that the bastards who devised this place were never going to end up in it.'

That silenced them for a moment, ceding him the floor.

'Those old Moths,' he went on, 'your great wizards or whatever you call them – there's nothing inherently *magical* about this story. Change the trappings and it's everyone's. Give someone a big stick, and tell them it's their right, and they'll use it. Desperation just means they'll use it harder. So we all know Moths are useless mumblers who live up mountains and wring their precious grey hands over all these machines everyone else seems to have now. But they were executing your people on a whim a few centuries ago, Che. Give someone power, and at the same time you take away any qualms they'd have about using it.'

'Well, the Imperial subject speaks from experience,' Tynisa said acidly.

'Yes, he bloody does,' Thalric agreed hotly. 'We know there's no slave that wouldn't wield the lash if you gave him the chance. It's only Collegium that thinks there's some mythic moral superiority.'

'You don't believe that,' Che reproached, her eyes searching his face in the darkness. She saw the flaws there, the lines of doubt his association with her had marked out: the certainty in his voice was betrayed by his naked expression.

Still, he came back with, 'Che, since I met you, you've no idea how many stupid things I've had to believe.' And she laughed at him then, feeling the weight of that buried place momentarily lifted off her shoulders.

Later, when both Thalric and Tynisa had put their heads down, Che saw Maure stir, shivering. She reached a hand out, snagging at the halfbreed's sleeve, thinking she must be feeling the cold, but the woman flinched back.

'I'm sorry,' Che murmured.

Maure stared out at that terrible sky. 'No dead, Che. A place of death without any dead. I don't know if you can imagine it.'

'Probably not.'

'I always sensed the dead. Even when I was very young, I could feel them. I got driven out of a lot of places before the Woodlouse-kinden took me in and trained me. No one better for that than the Woodlice. They understand everything there. I wish I'd never left.'

'Why did you?'

'Because I thought I had a duty, to the dead, to the living. I thought I was needed, to mediate between the two. And now I'm in a place where the living live like the dead and the dead themselves are gone beyond, utterly consumed . . . I'm sorry, Messel.'

Che started. She had almost forgotten their guide, but the blind man shifted and shrugged.

'What a world you must come from,' he said softly, an unplumbed depth of longing in his voice. 'As for mine, I have no illusions.'

★

44

At first it seemed that they were travelling to Cold Well simply because, in all this vast, hostile and inbred world, there was no other landmark on their maps. Messel's agitation increased as they closed the distance, though, and even on his face Che could make out a certain furtive look, a need for them to hurry towards some deadline he had refrained from mentioning.

In that place, suspicion came easily.

As they stopped to camp after the second span of dayless travel, she cornered him, dragging him away from the others to the edge of their firelight, aware that Thalric and Tynisa would leap to her defence if she encountered some betrayal.

'So tell me,' she challenged the blind man.

'I don't understand.' He was a remarkably poor liar.

'What's waiting for us at Cold Well?' she pressed.

'You wanted to see . . .' Messel's words petered out.

'Who knows we're coming? You've sent word ahead to the people who live there?' Abruptly she was certain of it. 'What's waiting for us, Messel?'

'Sent to them? No, no,' he insisted. 'But there is one . . . a mentor, one who you must meet. The Teacher, we call him. One who still tells the oldest stories. One who spoke of the *sun* to me once; yes, he did.' The word was given great ritual significance that matched Messel's evident lack of understanding of what such a thing as the sun could possibly be. 'Him, you must meet, if you are to do anything, if anything can be done for you ... He, only he.'

'But he's not of Cold Well.'

'He is of all places – a traveller, a wise man,' Messel insisted. 'And, yes, I have sent word. I have left markings and messages since I found you, only for him. And he is coming. He is coming back to Cold Well for you, only for you.'

She opened her mouth then to gainsay him, to refuse to place her hand in the trap. The echo within her mind called back, *And then what? Where will you go, without him? What have you left to trust, if not this blind guide?*

★

After resting several times, they heard Cold Well before they saw it. The sound rang out across the stony expanses, cutting across the murmur of running water. They heard a disconcertingly domestic sound: hammer on anvil, as from any forge anywhere.

Cold Well was a wound. That was Che's first thought. It was a gash in the earth, jagged edged and organic, and it had been eaten there by human occupation, as though the mere presence of people had corroded the rock like an acid.

Approaching the settlement at one of the points where a narrow track led, switching its way down, she saw how the miners had made this place their own. The walls of the pit were lined with round gaps like eye sockets, level after level of them, the inhabitants carving out their own community from the walls of the grave they had been set to dig. How many? She could see hundreds of openings and no hint of how deep they went or the numbers they housed.

She did not realize how much light there was until she let her Art slip. She had assumed that the locals had as little use for illumination as eyeless Messel. Instead, though, firelight glowed from most of the entrances – the same weird hues as before, nothing so wholesome as wood providing the fuel, but still a sign of warmth and life in this barren wilderness. Deeper in, there were greater fires, too. Che could look down and see vast glowing vats, streams and strips of incandescence that were being constantly renewed as they cooled. They were smelting there, an operation of a size to gladden any Helleren mining magnate's heart.

'What is it they make here?' she wondered, and Messel went still and looked back at her as he was about to start on the downward track.

'Tin, copper, iron,' he explained. 'Salt-coal as well, though some must be brought in. Swords and armour for the armies of the Worm. Food for it in a good year. Sometimes food in a bad year too. We starve, then, some of us.'

They were all holding back at the lip, unwilling to let themselves be drawn into the pit. Che was looking beyond, trying to make out more details of the scurrying figures who were bustling about the smelting works, ascending or descending the steep paths, but the glare of those fires was dispelling her Art.

'I see no guards.' Thalric, relying on the firelight, had made more headway. 'How can you have a slave town with no garrison?'

It was hard to tell what Messel thought of that, but his reply was hushed. 'They come, often. For their tax and for our work.'

'But you're making swords,' the Wasp pointed out. 'Can you not fight?'

'Fight the Worm?' the blind man murmured, as though the concept was something he did not quite understand. 'It has been tried, in earlier generations. Not since then. The price . . . the Worm is many. The Worm is . . .' A shudder went through him. 'The Worm is in all of us.'

That pronouncement transfixed them, all trying to grasp just what horror he intended, but he said no more. Indeed, having spoken even that much seemed to give him pain. His lack of expression was maddening.

'Why have you brought us here, Messel?' Tynisa challenged him.

'Why did you come?'

Her sword cleared its scabbard, but then Maure was holding a hand up. 'Please,' the magician said. 'We have come because we are strangers here, and we seek help. I beg you, tell us now if there is nothing to be had here. We'll just . . .' And her words failed her, because what was it they could 'just . . .'? Where else could they go, in this abyss?

'Help,' Messel echoed, and began moving down again. 'There may be help. I hope we may help each other. What else to hope for, in this place, but help?'

'How much do we trust him?' Tynisa murmured.

'A cursed sight far less than just five minutes ago,' Thalric spat, then glanced around. 'And where's that sneak Esmail?'

Che snapped out of her scrutiny and glanced around. The assassin was nowhere to be seen.

'Just that, sneaking,' Tynisa confirmed. 'He's been here before, remember. He was feeding us from these people's pockets until Messel came. I reckon it was quick in-and-out stuff, and not too far in, even then. But he'll be keeping an eye on us, don't worry.'

'And how much do we trust *him*?' Thalric demanded.

'Enough,' Che decided, fighting a battle with them now that she had already lost against herself. She set off after Messel boldly, knowing the others would follow in her steps.

Messel's progress was halting, stopping and starting at no apparent stimulus as though trying to put off the moment when his arrival was noticed. But now the locals were making their appearance. What passed along the rows of eyesocket-like holes was nothing more than a murmur, but it served to populate each hole in turn. It was only moments before their arrival was the focus of a grand and near-silent audience.

Almost none was of Messel's kinden, whatever that might actually be. Those other faces were more familiar, and Che found herself searching from face to face, cataloguing the inmates of the asylum, matching them with the powers of the ancient world.

The Mole Crickets stood out most, by sheer virtue of their size. Ten-foot tall at the hulking shoulder, white haired and onyx skinned, there were more of them gathered here than Che had ever seen. She knew they had an Art to move and mould stone – even to walk through it as if it were mist – and yet here they were, huge and solemn, prisoners and slaves of the Worm like all the rest.

There were Woodlouse-kinden as well, and in fair numbers. She had seen almost none before – only the Empress's adviser whom Esmail had killed, and perhaps one or two others. Here were dozens of them, tall and stoop shouldered with grey-banded skins and hollow faces. Here, too, were the Moths, with their blank white eyes that were still infinitely expressive compared to the vacant, socket-less faces of Messel's pallid kin.

Here and there she saw others, belonging to kinden she could not guess at, whose alien features were never seen under the sun.

All of them wore similar clothes to Messel himself: cloaks and trousers and long-sleeved tunics of thick cloth. Some had scarves about their mouths and noses, too, or hats of the same fabric, with folded tops.

But she judged that none of these would have use for the light that Cold Well was decked out with. For that, she must seek out more familiar features, for at least one in three of the denizens here was of her own kinden: the familiar dark-skinned and solid-framed people who dwelled almost everywhere in the world above and could endure anything.

Even this, this abyss, this slavery, they could endure. Abruptly it no longer seemed such a virtue.

Messel had stopped, brought to a halt by the sheer force of that massed regard; those he had led here clustered behind him, hands to weapons, unsure whether they would be welcomed or attacked or simply ignored. The air breathed with the sounds of the bellows, crackled with the distant molten metal, rang with hammers. Those at work had not paused for this novelty. They had quotas to make, perhaps, and from Messel's account they had masters who would tolerate no slacking.

And there were young children, Che noted. They crowded around the legs of adults of all kinden –Woodlice offspring, infant Mole Crickets, Moth children and eyeless pale children and more. Many pairs of arms had a child in them, men and women both, and there was a profusion of toddlers. A surprising number of the women showed some visible stage of pregnancy. All the most natural thing in the world, save for how quiet the children all kept, and yet some part of Che's mind was making a calculation, sensing that the mathematics behind what she was seeing here were wrong.

Messel spoke, not loud, but there was precious little competition from his audience. 'Well, will nobody welcome me?' He had his long hands spread, inviting censure or approbation, or anything other than this endless silent stare.

'What have you brought, Messel?' The speaker was a Moth

49

woman, though it took a moment for Che to pick her out from the crowd. She bore a staff, just a plain length of worked chitin, but apparently this was all that was needed to be marked as headwoman of Cold Well.

'Strangers,' he replied evenly, seeming to brace himself.

'There are no strangers.'

'Strangers,' Messel repeated, more firmly. 'From outside.'

A dreadful murmur went through everyone there, as though he had said something terrible, broken some unspeakable taboo. Che saw plenty of heads shaking in outright denial: *there is no outside*. How many generations of their ancestors had been sealed away down here?

And then she asked, out loud though she had not intended to, 'Why are there so few children?'

In the echo of her words, all eyes were upon them.

'Che, they've got the little maggots underfoot all over,' Thalric pointed out tactfully.

'But the older children,' she replied. 'So many babies and . . . look.'

And she was right, of course: that was what had been nagging at her. All those babes in arms, and yet few children who were older than three or four. Even as she said it, she felt a crawling sensation inside her that no matter how barren and bleak this place had shown itself to be, there was an unplumbed depth of terrible revelation just waiting for her.

One thing she had achieved: even to ask the question – the answer to which was surely a constant burden to all here – had established their credentials.

'Outside,' the Moth woman repeated, staring.

This time Che actually heard someone say it: 'There is no outside. It's a lie.'

'Speak to them,' Messel insisted. 'Where is the Teacher? Has he come? He must see them.'

'Wandering,' the Moth replied dismissively.

'No, he must be here,' Messel insisted, too loud. 'I sent . . . he was to come . . .'

'Well, he has not come,' the woman spat derisively, and it was plain such a failure to appear matched her general opinion of this 'Teacher'. 'Bring them after me. I will speak to them. There is no avoiding it. Messel . . .' She hissed, sharp and distinctive, and Che guessed it was to convey the glower that he could not have seen. 'This will fall on your head, the consequences of this.'

Their blind guide spread his hands again. The division between these two was plainly an old one.

The Moth turned round sharply, and the other dwellers of Cold Well got out of her way. She half scrambled, half flew to one of the openings and looked back, gesturing for them to follow. 'And the rest of you, back to your work,' the woman rasped. 'You think this changes anything? You think this is anything to gawp at? Forget these strangers, they will be gone as soon as they came. They are *nothing*.'

Che had hoped that there would be some groundswell of resistance to this dismissive attitude, but already the onlookers were skulking away, vanishing back to their holes or else sloping off towards the gleaming fires of the forges. She tried to catch the eyes of some of her kin, to establish that connection they must surely feel with her, but they would not look at her – indeed they barely looked at each other.

She was halfway after the Moth woman, almost wilting herself under that imperious glare, when Thalric said, 'What about him? He's coming too?'

One of the crowd had not simply gone home. Che looked over and saw a vast figure, a Mole Cricket bigger even than his fellows, each of his arms greater than Che's whole body, and reaching nearly to his knees. He wore a cap of hide and chitin, and the hammer thrust into a loop at his belt must have weighed as much as an ordinary man.

'Go,' the Moth told him, but he shook his head.

'I'll hear this, for my people.'

'Forge-Iron, go. This is a fiction, a nothing.'

He strode over to her, his shadow eclipsing the entire opening that she stood in. 'Let us be peaceable about this,' he said mildly, though even then Che felt the rumble of his voice through the soles of her feet. For a moment he and the Moth were frozen, locking wills, and Che felt the woman's Art sally forth to put the Mole Cricket in his place, but he was immovable, like the rock itself, and at last she sagged and nodded and vanished inside.

The huge man waited until the travellers had followed her in before bringing up the rear.

'Forge-Iron?' Che enquired, looking up into that dark face, meeting his curious gaze.

'Darmeyr Forge-Iron,' he confirmed.

'Cheerwell Maker,' she offered. He accepted the name as though it was something of great value.

Beyond that gaping opening was a chamber barely of sufficient size to fit them all, even with Forge-Iron in the very doorway, and two narrower tunnels twisted off into the rock, canting downwards towards a faint but constant sound of tapping and digging.

Is the whole place a mine? Che wondered. *Do they just sleep in the galleries and chambers, like vagabonds?*

'Where are you from?' the Moth woman demanded, without ceremony.

Che found that the others were looking to her to speak. 'I am Cheerwell Maker. I come from . . .' She wanted to say *up*, but of course the precise direction of the sunlit world she knew was a matter of magical theory rather than pointing. 'Outside,' she finished. 'From under the sun.'

The Moth stared at her bleakly. 'Liar.'

'It's true,' Messel insisted, and she hissed at him.

'Renegade,' she spat. 'Shirker and abandoner, what would you know? They are fugitives from some other hold, some mine or forge whose toil they could not stand.'

'Look at them,' murmured Darmeyr. 'They bear weapons, and they wear . . . and their kinden.'

'Their very tread on the stone is different,' Messel agreed.

'Listen to me,' Che insisted. 'We come from outside here, and we must return there.'

The Moth laughed bitterly. 'Of course. Fly there then, outsiders. Or step there through the cracks in the rock. Or perhaps you will ride the White Death there. Surely you can return there as easily as you came.'

'We came by magic,' Che said, matter-of-factly. 'There was a seal that held this place closed, and it was broken . . .' She stopped. The Moth had both hands up, fingers crooked as though trying to cram her words back down her throat.

'There is no magic,' declared the Moth-kinden with absolute assurance.

In the silence that followed, they digested this.

'Magic . . .' Che began, shaken.

'Magic is a *lie*,' the woman insisted fiercely. 'It is a trick of the mind. There *is* no magic. Only madness lies that way. It is a fool's story.'

Maure held her hand to her mouth in abject horror.

'I can assure you there is magic,' Che stated, wondering at that same moment whether it was herself she was trying to convince. 'Here it is . . . less than it was. There is something wrong with this place. It ebbs, it's true, and sometimes it is hardly there at all, but I still feel it, just. There is magic.'

'No,' the Moth whispered. 'It's a lie. It has always been a lie.' She was shaking slightly, and Che made a sudden connection with her, a moment's clarity, magician to magician. In that painful instant she saw a life of decades lived, inheritrix of a grand magical tradition but born into a place with nothing but the blown dust of exhausted sorcery to fuel her. She saw that the Moth's occasional sense of a wider, grander world was dismissed as a delusion, a lie; it was a path easier to follow than having to face what had been lost.

'Atraea,' the Mole Cricket spoke. 'Ask them.'

The Moth stared at Che with equal parts fear and hatred,

53

obviously desperate to hurt her, to erase her and bury the truth of her, but she stayed her hand.

'What will you do?' she demanded at last. 'Why are you here?'

'Something was broken,' Forge-Iron recalled. 'She said a seal . . . Are you here to mend it? What is it that has broken?'

And, even as Che opened her mouth to answer, his next words were: 'Have you come to fight the Worm?'

'Yes!' Messel crowed. 'Why else are they here? We have all heard the forbidden tales: that our ancestors were imprisoned, punished for their ways, but that there would come our kin from outside, who would redeem us, who would rescue us. What else could they be but that?'

'Lies!' the Moth, Atraea, shouted desperately. 'There is no truth in prophecy. It serves only to lead fools astray. And there is no fighting them, our masters.'

'The Worm,' Darmeyr insisted.

'You must not say that. You must say, "our masters", or say nothing at all. Do you think they will not take even you, if they overhear—!' Atraea was becoming more and more agitated.

'Listen to me. We must spread the word of their coming,' demanded Messel, and Forge-Iron was insisting, 'I *will* say Worm, and I will say they can be fought,' and then he cried out, a yelp of pain that seemed ludicrously high from such an enormous man, and backed hurriedly out of the opening.

Esmail was there, lean and tense against the shadows and the firelight.

'Trouble,' he snapped. 'Get out, now.'

Already they could hear a commotion outside that their argument had blotted out. A gathering wail of dismay was rising from many throats, from all the way down the chasm of Cold Well.

'It is them,' Atraea said, dead-faced. 'Your loose talk has brought this upon us.' And then: 'No, *they* have brought it. What else can it be? These "outsiders" have summoned our doom.'

54

Five

The wife of the governor of Solarno had been out the whole day, and the evening too, and Gannic's informers strongly suggested that she had been meeting covertly with agents of . . . well, his spies weren't *that* good but he'd bet that it was certain of the local Spider Aristoi. They would be constantly weaving, daily patching the accord that they had secretly stitched together to keep Solarno out of the war.

As for the governor himself, he was a Consortium man, a merchant and not a soldier – but either he was the most blinkered buffoon ever to get a colonel's rank badge or he had the rare attitude in a Wasp of being prepared to let his wife get on with things. After all, Spiders would always have more respect for a woman across the negotiating table.

Insane that we ever allied with them, even for as long as we did, Gannic reflected, and not for the first time, but the cautious détente here in Solarno showed that anything was possible.

Since just before sundown, Gannic had been an unannounced guest in the governor's townhouse, hiding from the servants and settling in while the place turned in for the night around him. He was amused to discover that Edvic and his wife occupied separate rooms, but then perhaps that was part of the unique way that they worked together, and certainly it seemed to have served them well so far.

So, time to kick over the barrel. After all, he had his instructions from Colonel Varsec, who was keen to meet the woman who had bridged the Wasp–Spider gap, that everywhere else had ripped apart into open warfare.

The house as a whole had gone to bed by the time the governor's wife got in. Gannic held very still as he listened to her dismiss the last few servants who had waited up for her return, and then she entered her chambers. It was late, she was tired, and Gannic hid himself well. She considerately lit only a single candle before casting off her robe, obviously worn out by the diplomatic demands of her day.

Time to introduce myself. Gannic had inherited the dark-seeing Art of his Beetle mother, and he had to admit that Merva was a fine piece of work, as tall and elegant as any Spider woman, hair of gold and skin perhaps paler than he liked it, but he could imagine her matching the Aristoi pose for pose as they trod their diplomatic tightrope together.

'Now there's a sight,' he said – and watched her freeze, naked before an unseen enemy, exposed and vulnerable. Then she had collected herself, the shift dropping from her fingers and her palms coming up ready to sting.

'I'd keep those hands down, woman,' he told her, and by then she knew exactly whereabouts he was. 'Was it you that killed Captain Carven?'

'Remind me, who was Carven?' she asked, and he watched each muscle tense as she braced herself for the moment of violence, ready to snap out an arm and unleash her Art.

'Firstly, and as a point of etiquette,' he told her calmly, 'my sting's probably a bit on the feeble side but I've a snapbow on you right now, one of the little ones, but good enough at this range. Secondly, I love a show as much as the next man, but how's about you get your kit back on and then we can talk about why there's at least one dead Imperial messenger in the bay – and a Rekef man at that – who I *know* walked into this house alive.'

He saw her consider her options calmly. He had considered

having her remain unclad to intimidate her but, even standing naked before a stranger, she seemed far too self-possessed, and he felt that he would just push her towards a violent retaliation which could lead anywhere – but probably nowhere useful to Gannic.

Slowly she took up her shift again and pulled it over her head, for all the barrier it provided. When her head emerged, her eyes glinted like steel.

'The governor's a lucky man, I'll say that,' Gannic put in. 'But you're playing a dangerous game when you cross the Rekef. That's better, now. Sit down, and keep your hands out flat on the sheets there.'

'So what does the *Rekef* suggest happens next?' she enquired coldly, waiting for that moment of divided attention when she could go for him.

'Sod the Rekef,' he told her cheerfully. 'I'm none of them. If you hadn't done for Carven, I might have had to do him myself.' A pause followed for that to sink in. 'Peace in Solarno, eh? Who'd have thought it? But it turns out that suits my superiors just fine. They've a use for a Solarno that's not demolished and on fire. Captain Carven's current watery grave tells me that so do you – you and your man here.'

She took a deep breath. 'And if we do?'

'Fellow who gives me orders is very keen to talk about how you're keeping this particular plate spinning.' He stepped forwards at last to let her get a look at him. He saw her take in his features, wrinkling her nose at the very thought of being outmanoeuvred by a halfbreed. But she saw the snapbow as well and passed no comment.

'So who gives you your orders?' she asked him cautiously. *If not the Rekef*, was the obvious subtext.

'I am Lieutenant-Auxillian Gannic, lady,' he introduced himself. 'Engineers, believe it or not. Take it from me, a lot of eyes are pointed at Solarno right about now. I'd say you'd be surprised, but I'm not sure you would – not you. So let's get some ground rules straight. Yell out, and I'm going to shoot you. Maybe not to kill, but who can say how good my aim is? And if you or your servants or your man do get the better of me, and I don't show up safe in the morning, then my chief will make sure word is on its way to Capitas by an hour past dawn, to tell them just how you've been playing them. So I suggest you behave.'

Merva gave him a level stare. 'What do you want me to do? Book your commanding officer an appointment?'

'No need – he's ready right now. So how about you get yourself a cloak and we'll go out quiet, the back way. No need to trouble the staff.'

He saw her stiffen, considering the odds, and he lifted the snapbow a little to keep it in the forefront of her mind. 'Let's go now, and slowly – or I'll have to say all this stuff to your widower husband tomorrow.'

He saw himself reflected in her eyes: the brutal halfbreed who might do anything. *I'm not the one who killed the Rekef captain, lady,* he reflected. *Woman or not, I reckon you're more dangerous than me, given half a chance.*

He put the weapon up against the pale hollow of her neck as he bound her wrists, feeling the thought in her mind about whether she could sting without him killing her by reflex. He kept to one side, though, denied her the most obvious opportunities, and then he had her hands tied palm to palm.

They moved through the house like some strange dream, soft footed, an invisible thread linking the small of her back to the barrel of his snapbow. At any moment he was sure she was going to cry out or just run, but she retained a stately calm, as though she was merely sleepwalking.

The side door that Gannic had been shepherding her towards opened just as they got in sight of it, and Colonel Varsec appeared. Gannic stopped, staring at his superior in dumb amazement.

Am I betrayed? Was Varsec about to stage some heroic 'rescue' of Merva? Did that sort of thing even *work*?

Then Varsec stepped inside with a wry look at his subordinate. And behind the colonel was a Spider-kinden woman, a slight little thing with short, dark hair and the face of innocence, save that she had a long knife held to the colonel's neck.

'Good evening, Lady Merva,' the Spider said politely.

'Lady Giselle.' The Wasp woman even managed a cordial nod.

'Perhaps your over-enthusiastic slave will put away his device now?' The Spider smiled at Gannic, who had the snapbow levelled at her face.

Merva did something complex with her hands and Gannic's ropes fell away, leaving her palms directed straight towards him. 'What's the matter, Engineer? Are all your little cogs failing to mesh?'

'Oh, very good.' Varsec grinned at Merva over the knife blade. 'Might I suggest that, since the underhand approach is apparently off the menu, you send for some wine and your husband?'

'And why would I want to do that?'

'Because, right at this moment in Solarno, I am the Empire, or a very large part of it, and the Empire has a deal to make. I want to talk about Solarno's current détente, and after that I want to talk about Solarno and Chasme and the Iron Glove.'

'Three days since the last delegation left, and here they are again,' Drephos mused, watching the bustle of the Chasme docks, but with particular reference to the Solarnese sloop that word said had brought another batch of Imperials to their door.

'Perhaps it's just another order. They still have a few armies to outfit with Sentinels.' Totho was away from the balcony, studying reports from some of the metallurgists by lamplight, despite the bright daylight he could have had for free if he moved his desk five feet over.

'And Solarno hasn't torn itself to pieces yet, either. Everyone was saying it would. Everyone was saying we'd have our own little war around the Exalsee: Spiders and Wasps. There are plenty of troops within an easy sail. So what, I wonder . . .?'

It sounded like a non-sequitur, but Drephos's words always had a logic to them, the trick being to reverse-engineer the unspoken links of the chain.

'They may want an anti-Sentinel weapon, of course,' came Totho's absent-minded reply. 'The Sarnesh captured a few after they defeated the Eighth.'

He read on for another few lines, but Drephos remained silent, and at last Totho glanced up.

'You're concerned over something. Not about their man who had the accident, surely?'

'There won't have been time for that news to have prompted anything,' Drephos said dismissively. 'But something . . . I think our new visitors will be speaking the same old words, however they disguise them.'

'The Bee-killer,' Totho identified.

Drephos let a long pause slide by before he confirmed that, and then only with the briefest grunt. Totho heard his metal hand – that wonder of artifice – scrape on the balcony rail.

'So give it to them.'

That got the man's attention. Drephos turned sharply, stalking back to hunch in the balcony archway, a stark silhouette against the sunlit sky. 'You think so, do you?'

Totho put down his reports. 'In truth? No. But I'm not sure why you don't.'

'I'm undecided.'

'Drephos . . .' Totho stood up and crossed the room to him, trying to make out the man's expression. 'The march of technology, the inevitable broadening of the scope and purpose of warfare . . . Every invention that leaves our foundries has only made your words more true. I confess, the Bee-killer is still too much for me, especially since I was the one who . . . deployed it, that one time. But I've been waiting for you to talk me round. So, what is it?'

The master artificer took a deep breath and returned to the balcony rail, forcing Totho to join him.

'We've worked wonders here, haven't we? With this place?' And now surely Drephos was prevaricating, and that was not like him. Beneath them, Chasme was a sprawling blot on the landscape: workshops and factories; piers and docks; two airfields crowded with a bizarre assortment of fliers; tavernas and boarding houses and brothels. Actual room to live was fitted around all the rest, in alleys and cellars or crammed between buildings.

All of it was lawless. Chasme had always been a pirate town, a pirate *artificer* town, long before Totho and Drephos had arrived. It had been fertile soil for them, though. The rabble of Chasme appreciated good workmanship, and although there were no definite leaders amongst them, the Iron Glove's word spoke loudest. What Drephos wanted, Drephos got.

'What are you thinking? You want this new lot to disappear? I can give the word,' Totho suggested.

'And word would then get back to the Empire,' Drephos noted.

Totho had never been good at talking to people, but then Drephos had never been good at listening, so they were well matched there. Eventually he went with: 'All right, what?'

'There they are.' Drephos's real flesh hand jabbed out towards the docks, but there was such a bustle of business there that Totho could not make out what he had spotted. Since the double invasion of Solarno, many merchants had gone elsewhere around the Exalsee with their wares or their orders, and nowhere had benefited more than Chasme.

'I know you still keep spies in the Lowlands . . . in Collegium.' Another non-sequitur, another twist of Drephos's mind as it gained purchase on the problem.

The stab of guilt he felt at that surprised Totho. 'I don't. Not like that. But I pay for news from there, certainly. Well enough that I've a few who go out of their way to get it to me.' He shrugged, failing at nonchalance. 'What of it?' In the face of Drephos's scrutiny he hunched his shoulders defensively. 'It's not . . . it's not *her*. I'm not . . . for news of her. Just . . . I used to live there . . .'

His words dried up as he realized that his evasions were pointless. Drephos's mind had already moved elsewhere.

'Perhaps,' the Colonel-Auxillian murmured, 'you should listen to spies from closer to home. You've seen how much gold is coming into our coffers?'

'More than even we can use.' Totho shrugged. It was not about the money, for either of them.

'And how much of that is Imperial coin? Less than there used to be, and we're selling much further afield. Even those who can't afford us still send their little delegations. The whole world wants us to arm it. Anyone who we turn away knows that, wherever else they go – Solarno, Dirovashni – they're getting second best. And those ports know it as well. Chasme's growing power – *our* iron fist – has not gone unnoticed.'

'Then perhaps we need to clench it. Or whatever you do with fists. We could outfit an army that could swallow up the Exalsee – if you wanted.' Totho spread his hands. 'What *do* you want?'

'Nothing more than life has provided me with: the tools to move the world. So long as the rest of the world is content for me to move it . . .'

'And the Bee-killer?'

'You're beginning to sound like the Empire.'

'I want to understand,' Totho pressed.

Drephos took a deep breath. 'If it were you asking for it, I'd hand over the formula. You would respect it, use it responsibly,' he said, as if not speaking of an invention the only purpose of which was to massacre thousands. 'The Empire . . .' He shook his head. 'But they are here, I think. Let us pretend they just wish to place orders and enquire after our latest devices. I tire of spies.'

He led the way down, Totho tripping along in his wake, staring worriedly at the other man's back. Drephos was not one for soul-searching: he was a creature of certainties. Now he was talking like an old man.

The Bee-killer ... Drephos had gifted war with countless inventions, from small devices for the more efficient aiming of bombs to grand projects such as the Sentinels or the greatshotter artillery. He had no family, nor love for any other being, no greed for coin for its own sake, only to feed the fires of his projects. Even for Totho, the closest thing to a kindred spirit that he had, he surely felt no more than the distant fondness a man might grant a pet.

And yet his name was linked to one invention like no other, and that was the Bee-killer. The atrocity at Szar was laid at his door: a chemical devised by his underlings and used by Totho against the Empire had somehow become Drephos's great work in the minds of many, many people. And now the Empire wanted to possess more of it.

He wondered if that was it, the vice that Drephos found himself in: a man whose least favoured child has become his heir apparent.

Then they were stepping down into one of the workshops, with Iron Glove artificers and staff clearing out of the way, and the Imperial delegation was being ushered in. There were a dozen of them, and mostly the Wasps and Beetles that Totho had come to expect: not fighting men but Consortium merchants and factors not above a little snooping in their spare time.

In the lead, though, was a different model of trouble. Totho had seen only a scant handful of halfbreeds allowed any authority by the Empire – one of whom was standing beside him. This new man looked to be in charge, though, and he saluted Drephos as though the other man's old rank still held.

'Good day, sir. It's a pleasure finally to meet you,' the Imperial halfbreed said with a bright, sharp smile. 'Lieutenant-Auxillian Gannic at your service.'

Six

'I remain acting governor of Collegium,' General Tynan summarized his newly received orders. 'No new troops to garrison the city. No progress towards the western coast, Vek, Tsen . . .' He stared at the scroll before him as though it was his own death warrant, but one that he had lost the strength to fight against. 'A mealy-mouthed commendation that I have done well, and not even Her Majesty's own seal.'

The Beetle-kinden diplomat, who had been nodding pleasantly up until 'mealy-mouthed', looked sharply at the general. 'These are Her Majesty's orders, nonetheless.'

'Time was,' Tynan spat, 'when a general took orders from the Empress's own hand. No lesser person sufficed. No more: I see the seal of the Red Watch. We all know,' and his sarcasm was heavy and unmissable, 'that *they* are the Empress's voice. Tell me, Bellowern, is she even still in Capitas? I hear rumours otherwise.'

Honory Bellowern, one of the highest-ranking Beetles in the Empire now that he had somehow secured a colonel's badge, put on a stern demeanour. 'Those are dangerous rumours to voice, General.' He cast his eyes about Tynan's staff room, which had once been some Collegiate merchant's ground floor before the Engineers had kicked through a few inessential walls. A dozen officers of the Second Army were easily in earshot.

'*Colonel*, if you wish me to directly order you to answer my question, I will do it.' Tynan had made no secret of his disgust at Bellowern's promotion. The antagonism was not because the man was Beetle-kinden – or not only that. Rather, it was that Bellowern had headed the Imperial diplomatic staff within Collegium prior to Tynan's arrival, and so might have been of considerable use as an intelligencer and liaison when the Second Army appeared at the city's gates. Instead the man had made sure he was out of the city long before the fighting started, returning only now that it was safe to do so and somehow bearing a portion of the glory, which Tynan felt entirely unearned.

'Of course she is in Capitas, General. I saw her myself. Where would she be else?'

Tynan glowered at him, and the first hint of uncertainty entered Bellowern's manner. Tynan had not spoken with a governor or a general's formal cordiality. The Wasp's hostility was palpable.

'Might I ask,' the Beetle ventured, 'whether I have in some way offended?' His change of manner was pointed, as if he had suddenly considered that if Tynan had him shot, he might be unable to raise his objections back at Capitas later.

'You went to Captain Vrakir first,' Tynan pronounced.

Bellowern blinked twice, mastering any surprise he might have felt. 'As it happened, I had orders for Major Vrakir, and he crossed my path on my way to you. It seemed an economic use of my time.'

'Which orders included a promotion,' Tynan noted.

'Indeed, sir.'

'Which promotion also bore a Red Watch seal.' No suggestion in the general's tone of whether it was a question or a statement.

Bellowern was obviously playing it safe. 'Yes, sir.'

'So he's a major now. So when's his colonel's badge due to arrive?'

'I have no idea, General. You can imagine that such matters are not within my compass—'

'I can imagine many things that may or may not be true,'

Tynan told him flatly. 'But thank you kindly, Colonel, for coming so very far just to give me no news worth the hearing. No doubt you'll want to take up your residence from before we took the city.'

'Actually, General, after a little more time with our new . . . with Major Vrakir, I must be moving on. After all, Collegium is an Imperial city now, expertly pacified. I could hardly come here and be ambassador to myself.'

'You are a diplomat. You know these people. I am a general, a battlefield commander.'

'I have my orders. You're welcome to peruse them.' Now even professionally phlegmatic Bellowern was a little sharp. 'They *do* bear the Empress's own seal. You are to hold the city, as you are plainly doing most capably. I have my own concerns.'

Tynan stared at him for a long time, and at last voiced one of those questions that nobody was supposed to ask. 'What is *she* up to?' And, when Bellowern stuttered and stumbled over an answer, 'You don't know. I thought men like you were supposed to know everything.'

After the Beetle had gone, Tynan brooded a while, and his officers knew enough not to approach him. The taking of Collegium had been hard but swift, flawlessly executed. The reputation of the Gears, the Imperial Second Army, was secure. And yet Tynan brooded and mourned.

It was not the taking of the city but its aftermath. He had not been alone as he rode an automotive through Collegium's gates. The Spider-kinden army of the Aldanrael had spilt its share of blood to take this prize, and its leader, the Lady Martial Mycella, had been close to Tynan. Far closer than was wise.

And of course the order had come, from the Empress via the Red Watch officer Vrakir: *Kill all the Spiders.*

Tynan had obeyed faultlessly. He himself had executed Mycella, his co-commander, his lover. He had torn out his own heart to do so, but he had orders. Orders had been his life to that point.

If he had been sent on westwards for Vek and beyond, allowed to do what an army general should, then perhaps he would have soon put it behind him and recovered. The Eighth Army had been broken by the Sarnesh, though, and the garrison force intended for Collegium had been hastily re-routed north to prevent the Ant-kinden from taking the initiative. And Tynan had been told to hold and govern Collegium, and wait.

Sitting there, in the city that to him still reeked of his own betrayal, his soldiers had watched him sink into himself, gnawing on his own regrets. A bitter silent war had sprung up between him and Vrakir, bearer of those fatal orders. Neither man could bear to be in the other's company for more than a few minutes, and the Imperial administration of Collegium virtually existed in two camps because of it: the voice of the general against the transmitted voice of the Empress.

And in the middle were the citizens themselves, at the mercy of a general's depression and the increasing restlessness of his soldiers.

On the far side of the Gear Gate from Tynan's headquarters was the townhouse commandeered by the Red Watch man, Major Vrakir.

He had fewer staff to wait on him than the general. General Tynan commanded the Second Army and governed Collegium for now, but there were many who were waiting for the orders to come that might change that. Anyone who had contacts back home had heard of the Red Watch: its unpredictable, un-accountable habits; the way even the Rekef had to bow the knee to it.

Vrakir had been a regular army officer before the Empress had chosen him. She had taken him to the Imperial Museum in Capitas. She had led him to that hidden room at its heart where she kept the Mantis-kinden idol. She had bid him kill, and then offered him a goblet filled with the victim's blood.

She had asked him if he had not always felt different, detached from those around him. He had not been able to deny it. She had told him the truth. He was Apt, as all Wasps were Apt save *her*. Some quirk of his inheritance, though, some muddying of his blood, had left him with a holdover from the old days. She could make use of him. He was not different, but *superior*.

And he had believed her, and drunk. And so had begun his long road to the edge of sanity.

He was Apt. He understood machines, even if he was not quite comfortable with them – no artificer he – and of course he had never believed in magic. Now, though . . .

He dreamt, and the dreams had meaning. The Empress's will made itself known to him – by nothing so arcane as her words in his mind, but he still *knew*. It was as though he had been told long ago, in childhood, all the demands of state that she burdened him with, and each was only recalled at the proper time.

He had brought Tynan the orders to turn on the Spiders, to murder the man's Aldanrael lover. Only he and the general knew that the supposed betrayal of the Empire by its allies had never happened. But it *would* have happened, he sincerely believed. The Empress had foreseen it.

Even then, with that responsibility on him, he had retained his control. He had faced off against General Tynan with utter confidence in the Empress's orders. Then the Empress had returned to Capitas, though, and she had changed.

There was something terribly twisted, now, in that link he shared with his mistress. Whatever had happened, whatever she had done in the Mantis forest to the north, it had marked her. She had nightmares, and Vrakir shared them helplessly. She tormented herself. She *feared*.

In her dreams she was beneath the earth, and things *moved* there. They crawled and burrowed, they scratched and dug, fighting ever closer to the surface. And it was her fault, he knew, experiencing her dreams. The Empress was to blame, and she had lost something, left something behind, when she fled to

Capitas. She was not whole, and she could not escape her bonds to that lost part of her.

From the earth, such fear, so that Vrakir found himself steadying himself as if the ground beneath him would suddenly betray him. And, worst of all, this was no irrational fear, but very real. The Empress understood entirely what there was to be scared of.

And he sent word for the army's scouts, and he heard their reports: there were isolated farms and mills found empty, only the ground around them disturbed. One entire village had been abandoned, no sign of where its hundred or so inhabitants had gone. The ground was marked with spiral patterns and some of the buildings were cracked as though they had been undermined.

Vrakir fought against sleep, awake even past midnight alone in the empty house he had seized, and still the Empress's nightmares howled in the hollow spaces of his mind.

'I don't understand. Who is it you're meeting here?' Raullo wanted to know.

'No idea.' Sartaea te Mosca sipped at her wine, holding the bowl in both hands. She had brought the Beetle artist to a taverna near the College: the Press House on Salkind Way. The place was still a student haunt, and there was a passage that ran to one of the dormitories, meaning that curfew was negotiable. The windows were even now being shuttered against the dusk, and soon the landlord would lock the Wasps out and pretend to be shut.

Sartaea was an occasional visitor to the Press House in any case, but tonight she had a purpose: word had come that she should meet someone here, no more detail than that.

'It's a trap.' Raullo was well into his wine, but then he could sink quite a lot of it these days. He cut an odd figure in the city, awkward father to a wild and unrepresentative school of painting that had followers amongst locals and Imperials alike and was beginning to spawn imitators. She had brought him along tonight to watch her back in case her mysterious contact turned out to be someone she would rather not be seen with.

'Well, if so . . .' She shrugged. 'There's nothing illegal about meeting someone. Even after curfew, so long as you're indoors.'

'I still don't like it,' Raullo muttered.

'Oh, hush,' she told him, and then there was a scream. It was outside but sounded as though it was somewhere just along their street, and the taverner paused, about to close the last shutters. Collegium had become used to screams after dark, though. Those caught breaking curfew were punished, and if they were women the Wasp soldiers might exact the penalty then and there.

Raullo opened his mouth to pass another comment, but suddenly there was a whole chorus of yells and shouts outside, and the floor beneath them shuddered to the grinding sound of stone on stone. Sartaea and the artist stared at one another, and a few of the patrons stood up uneasily, waiting to see if there would be more. A couple were already inching towards the back room and to the trapdoor that would take them underground and away.

The taverner had been peering round the edges of the window, trying to see, but now he sprang back with a curse.

'What? What is it?' Sartaea demanded of him.

'I thought I saw . . . Something ran past, something . . .'

The sounds of panic were escalating outside; the floor quivered again.

'What are they doing? Is it more fighting?' Raullo whispered. 'Please, no.'

Sartaea abandoned him to go to the window, wings lifting her higher so she could see. She got there just in time to see the house across the street begin to shake, cracks snaking up the walls.

'Save us,' she whispered. The building was coming down all on its own. There had been no explosion, no roar of artillery, but the structure was suddenly falling in on itself, collapsing and dragging the neighbouring buildings towards one another, and there were . . .

Her eyes were keen in the dusk but still she could not quite believe what she saw: figures emerging from the wreckage, swift and sure and together, a long chain of them seemingly vomited up from the earth itself.

Then there was a banging at the door. Raullo stood abruptly, knocking his chair backwards and dragging a dagger from his belt.

'You have to get out!' someone was yelling. 'Out of the taverna!'

The taverner threw the door open before anyone could stop him, revealing a Fly-kinden man there, cloaked and hooded.

'Get out now!' he snapped. 'Something bad's happening all down this street.' As some of the patrons began to run for the rear, he called out after them. 'Not that way! Not *down*! Out of the door and head for home!'

'Who are you?' Sartaea demanded, though she thought she knew him. Was he not . . .?

He locked eyes with her. 'Miss te Mosca . . . some other time. Get yourself out of here, all of you!'

The ground below the taverna shifted. Abruptly the floor was canted towards the cellar stairs. From down there came a scream, then more: some of the patrons had already tried to escape that way.

They'll be crushed! But the screams went on, and Sartaea heard the clash of metal. *No, they're being attacked – but by what? The Wasps?* And yet she knew it was not the Wasps. Some sense, some vestigial awareness born of her paltry magical ability, was screaming at her.

Still, she went to help. It was not in her to refuse it. The cloaked Fly was on her in a moment, wings casting him across the crowded room to bundle her to the floor.

'Get off me!' she yelled into his face, and his name was in her mind even as she did so, 'Laszlo!'

'Out, please!' he insisted, but then Raullo had taken a swing at him, drunken and clumsy, and the Fly's nimble dodge took his weight off her and she darted for the cellar stairs.

They were emerging even as she got there. She saw pale faces looking up at her from the gloom, colourless eyes, sunken cheeks. She locked gazes with one pair of those eyes, but there was no contact, no human interchange, and then they were moving all at once, the band of them uncoiling from the cellar and taking the stairs at a run.

She let out a hoarse yell of sheer panic and reached for her magic to cloak her. Her magic . . .

She had none. In that same stunned moment, her mind turned the word over, 'magic', and found nothing in it, no meaning at all.

Then a hand hooked her shoulder and virtually threw her at the door to the street: not little Laszlo but Raullo's solid Beetle strength. He was out right after her too, far faster than she would have guessed, sprawling across the uneven paving at her feet, and Laszlo behind him, aiming a little snapbow back into the taverna and yet not loosing. She could hear yells of fear and horror from within – some of the patrons had left their exit too late. She could not force herself to go to help them. There was no helping them. Not after that moment of lost blankness when she had forgotten what she was.

Around them, the whole of Salkind Way was tilting vertiginously, some buildings already toppling, as if the Empire had developed some new invisible and soundless bombing orthopter and was punishing its own city.

And she saw them, the lines of them coursing from the broken walls, from the guts of the earth, their movements swift as beasts, human in shape but not in any other way. Some carried bodies between them, but many were dragging living, screaming citizens of Collegium.

'Away!' insisted Laszlo, and she needed no other prompting. From that moment, she and Raullo were running, desperate to put Salkind Way behind them.

Only after they were at the doors of the College library, far enough that no outcry could reach them, did Raullo drop to his knees, wheezing, and she realized that Laszlo had not come with them.

'Who was he?' the artist got out. 'The Fly? Did he make that happen?'

Sartaea te Mosca shook her head. 'I don't think so. He was Laszlo; you know, the . . .' A pause as she considered what she was about to say – 'Stenwold Maker's friend.'

The next morning they returned to Salkind Way, finding it broken and shattered as if the earth had buckled beneath its load, and yet the streets on either side lay completely untouched. There were Wasp soldiers searching the wreckage, so plainly mystified by what had happened that not even the most fervent patriot was accusing the Empire of being behind whatever had happened.

They found no bodies. Upwards of fifty people had just disappeared.

Seven

Darmeyr Forge-Iron lurched outside, dropping down a level. 'Hide them!' he shouted.

'No!' Atraea the Moth snapped back. 'Do you think they will not take all of our people one by one until they find them? *They* are here because of these renegades. Messel and his dreams have brought this upon our heads. Here! They are here!' She was calling out into the great chasm, even as Che craned her neck, trying to see what was going on.

Thalric leapt on the Moth and threw her to the ground, and when she opened her mouth again he slapped her across the face, hard enough to whip her head about. He had his palm out to her in threat, but it was plain she did not realize what he meant by it. Before Atraea could denounce him, before she drove him to kill her, Tynisa had the point of her blade to the woman's throat.

'No more sound from you,' she warned, and the Moth's white eyes glared at her and the Wasp, but she said nothing.

The chorus of wails and cries was passing down the length of the scar that was Cold Well, gathering in volume as more throats joined it. *Not pain*, Che thought. *Not panic or even fear, but grief, sheer grief and loss.* She had never heard anything like it, and the rebounding echo of the rock walls made it all the worse. She felt as though this was the cry of some great beast that was approaching, a creature it would be death even to look upon.

Her Art shouldered aside the darkness, and she saw the Worm.

Just men, of some unknown kinden, save that nothing about them said 'human' apart from their shape. They moved in bands of a dozen or two dozen, and they were swift when they were not completely still. Each body of them was pale, no taller than she and narrower at the shoulder. Their hair and skin were all of the same colourless hue, their eyes so pale that the white shaded into the pale grey of the iris, the mid-grey of the pupils, without any hard distinction. They wore armour of overlapping plates that left their limbs mostly bare and low helms with jagged cheek-guards. For weapons they had swords a little longer than she was used to, but still unremarkable except that most of them carried two. She saw no shields, no bows, no spears, though a few had slings dangling from their long-fingered hands.

She realized that she could not tell their gender, for they had nothing to their faces or their spare frames to tell her one way or another. Even that was a trivial thing: watching them as they coursed in their groups across the levels of Cold Well, the wrongness in every motion cried out to her.

They do not move like humans of any kinden. They did not move like humans at all. They walked on two legs, held blades in their hands, had eyes to see with, but the unavoidable impression was that these were not men: that these human figures were the puppets of something utterly other that was rushing them this way and that. No – rather that the entire group was a single puppet linked invisibly, the slaves of one alien mind.

She felt ill, sick to her stomach just to see it, and Maure was clutching at her arm, swaying.

'It is the tax!' Darmeyr boomed. 'They are not seeking our guests, Atraea. The tax is come!'

Che glanced back at the pinned Moth, seeing her head shake, despite the razor point of Tynisa's blade there.

'It cannot be,' she got out. 'Too early. They have been here already! We have paid our tax!'

'What do we do?' The huge Mole Cricket sounded utterly

75

impotent. 'What can we do? That is what they are demanding. Look – I see the priest. He is coming this way.'

'Priest?' Che demanded. 'What's . . .' The word was familiar from her studies, a holdover from ancient, primitive times: beliefs that even the Inapt would not consider these days. Except . . .

'He is coming here,' Darmeyr said, shaken. 'He will want you to give the order.'

Tynisa made a judgement and stepped back, and then Thalric allowed the Moth woman to get up. Her unguarded expression was piteous to behold.

'We need to get out,' the Wasp said, but Esmail protested, 'They'll see us. They're all over this place.' He hissed through his teeth. 'I should have seen them sooner, but they move so fast.'

'And we need to move fast, too. How far does this go? Can we hide back here?' Thalric demanded.

Atraea was staring at them, and perhaps she was wondering whether this 'tax' of theirs could be offset by handing over the strangers.

'If they find them here, they will blame you,' Messel put in, plainly sensing the same.

'Then hide,' the woman spat, almost in tears. 'Hide, and hear, if you are truly outsiders.'

Che fell back into the cave, retreating further into its depths until they were out of sight of the entrance. In moments they heard the rapid patter of bare feet as the Worm arrived.

'Speaker,' snapped a hoarse voice, an old man's voice.

Atraea's reply was meek. 'Scarred One.'

And Che could not stop herself. She inched forwards, despite Thalric frantically plucking at her sleeve. She edged and edged, quiet as could be, until she could put an eye round the corner and look.

A single unit of the Worm soldiers was entering Atraea's domain, half of them still outside but a chain of men already coiling inwards. None of them looked at the Moth, or at anything else.

Che had no sense that they had any actual presence as individuals at all.

She identified the male speaker at once, though. He was of that same kinden as the rest, but he wore robes of chitin scales stitched into that hardwearing cloth they all used here. He was old, and his features were sufficiently distinct from those of his underlings that he might almost have been of a different race altogether. Most striking were the scars, though: long, curling, puckered lines that had been scored across his face and down his forearms, then left to heal badly, so that the skin had cracked into jagged darts on either side of the original mark, and the whole resembled . . .

And she saw it then, at his feet, a long, sinuous, weaving shape. It must have been five feet in length, and she felt an instinctive revulsion as soon as she saw it. The world was full of venomous creatures, but none had a reputation as bad as this sort, so that sane people killed these creatures wherever they found them. But why? Let the academics of Collegium argue as they would, nobody could say just why. Except Che, right now. She understood why the mere sight of a centipede sent shudders down the spines even of the Apt, and why there were so many stories casting them as deadly killers.

It was the Worm; they were remembering the Worm. The beast there, with its whip-like antennae and curved claws full of venom; the ridged scars that ornamented the old man's hide; the very line of soldiers, just segments of a greater whole, undifferentiated and mindless. Symptoms of the same ancient disease.

'This is too soon,' Atraea quavered. 'You cannot be here for the tax.'

'You will have your people present their tribute,' the old man – the Scarred One – informed her. He sounded bitter, *human*, and he regarded Atraea with the contempt of an owner for his slave.

'But you were here . . . I have marked the time faithfully, I have!'

77

'The Great Lord demands,' the Scarred One said. 'Do not believe that scratching marks on the wall allows you to guess the plans of god. Do as you are told.'

'But what has changed?' Atraea begged him.

'Do not tempt a further tax of Cold Well.' The Scarred One sounded almost bored, like a College bureaucrat dealing with a student who had filled in the wrong papers. The threat plainly went straight to the heart of Atraea, though, for she was bowing and nodding, practically kissing the man's filthy feet.

'I will, I will,' she promised. 'It will be as the Great Overlord commands. Please . . .'

But the old man was turning aside, stepping back past his men. Che shivered to watch them follow him, the entire line of them moving like a single living thing. The centipede itself remained a moment, its front segments lifted from the ground, its trident of a head casting from side to side as if sensing that all was not as it should be. Che froze, fearing that it had sniffed her out somehow, but then the beast dropped back down and coursed fluidly off after the priest.

Atraea was already gone, but they could hear her thin, hopeless voice crying out beyond: 'We must do as they say! Do not defy them, or we will suffer all the more! Please, my people, please!'

'Cold Well goes hungry this season, then,' Thalric murmured. 'I'll admit I've seen the same in the Empire on occasion.'

'You have not,' Messel told him flatly. 'You do not understand. Of course you do not understand.'

There was something in his voice, some dead echo, that affected Che. 'Then make us understand,' she urged. 'Tell us. Show us.'

He crept past her, fingers brushing the stone as he moved to the cave's entrance. 'Then see,' he told them. 'And see what you have been sent to save us from. See the Worm at work.'

They moved to the entrance of Atraea's cave cautiously, but it was Che alone who went so far as to put her head outside, so that she could witness what was going on.

Work at the foundry had stopped. All the people of Cold Well were standing out in the open, as the chains of Worm soldiers passed between them. There seemed to be some manner of census going on, or at least Atraea seemed to be flying here and there, trying to account for people.

Che expected to see goods being brought from the forges: weapons or armour or metal ingots, such as Messel had mentioned. Or else food: Atraea had been worried about something more than simply not making quota, surely? Was Cold Well going to starve in order to load the tables of the Worm?

'Cages.' Esmail was beside her, crouching low; she had not realized he was still at the cave mouth until he spoke to her. She saw what he had seen: there were Mole Crickets and a few Beetles up at the lip of the cliff, overlooking the whole of Cold Well, and they were lowering angular lattices of chitin struts on ropes.

'Containers, for the tax,' Che corrected, desperately. 'Not cages.'

There was activity from further away down the chasm of Cold Well, where the cages had already descended. It was coming closer. She could hear the sobbing and crying start up again.

'Cages,' repeated Esmail grimly.

'But they're so small . . .' Che started, and at last her eyes could hide it from her no longer. She watched as a Beetle woman held up a child of no more than two, tears running down her face. A soldier of the Worm snatched the infant from her and passed it back down the chain towards one cage, in which another two children already crouched, crying, arms thrust through the gaps towards their helpless parents.

'They're just . . . handing them over,' Che whispered. She saw plenty of reluctance, even some fights between parents before the inevitable surrender, but as the Worm passed through the people of Cold Well, they were making that impossible choice. Each family was selecting its least favourite son for the cull, offering up its own flesh and blood to the Worm.

'How can they? They're . . . it's monstrous,' she got out.

'A thousand years of defeat and resignation.' Esmail the killer,

79

the assassin by birth, sounded just as sick and shaken as she. 'They are shackled, body and mind.'

She saw Darmeyr Forge-Iron, who could have broken any of the Worm soldiers in two with his bare hands and hurled the pieces into the chasm. She saw him stare down at them, and his great frame trembled. There was a woman behind him – his mate, no doubt, and as large and powerful as he – and they had three children clustered close at their feet, a girl and two boys, hiding their faces in their mother's skirts.

'No,' Che whispered, but the Worm was demanding, through the scarred priest its mouthpiece, and huge Darmeyr was turning to his children, his expression fixed and dreadful.

His hand fell on the youngest of his sons, and his wife was shaking her head, but it was plain she had no answer to his blunt question: *What other choice?*

So many children here – and so many of the women already growing round again with child, now she looked for it – and yet so few of four years or more. Cold Well had another resource for the Worm beyond weapons or smelted ore.

The chasm was a cacophony of screeching infants separated from all that they knew, of children just old enough to realize what they had lost in being taken from the hands of their parents and shoved into jagged cages by the soldiers of the Worm. Che did not even ask herself what this was in aid of, what need the Worm had for such a sacrifice. There were no reasons that she could ever want to know.

She saw Darmeyr take his son in his hands and hold him up, looking into the child's screwed-up face, and she could not stop herself.

In the aftermath of her cry, which had cut through even that loaded and busy air, she now had the attention of the Worm.

'Go!' Esmail hissed, about to take off along the wall back the way they had come, but the Worm were there also – all of them roused in that one moment, all of them coursing up the sides of Cold Well towards them. 'In!' the assassin decided, pushing Che back into Atraea's cave mouth. 'In, and hope these tunnels go somewhere useful.'

But that's mad; we'll just get lost or— But there was Messel ahead of them, beckoning urgently. An expression had appeared on his eyeless face at last, screamed out by the set of his grimacing mouth: fear, terrible fear. His words of defiance were utterly gone.

'Lead us!' Thalric demanded, and the blind man shrugged past him, disappearing into the rear reaches of the cave and beyond, down into the warren of the mines.

'No light.' Esmail warned. 'Hold to Maker, she can see. Beetle girl, you must go first.'

Logic roused her from her horror and she went rushing after Messel, terrified that he might already have taken one turn too many and be beyond her reach. He was waiting, though, and she caught up with him quickly, with Thalric hanging on to her shoulder, and Tynisa and Maure behind him. A hurried glance showed Esmail bringing up the rear, hands extended like weapons.

'Quick quick quick,' insisted Messel, and then he was gone again, and at a run that Che knew her stumbling charges could not match. She hauled them on at the best pace she could, and every time she thought that she had been abandoned, there the blind guide was waiting for her, his face twisted in fear.

She recalled the speed at which the soldiers of the Worm moved, how long it would take them to return to Atraea's cave and how swiftly they would follow into the tunnels.

And where can these tunnels possibly lead us?

She knew she would barely even hear them approach before they caught up with Esmail, and the thought of even being that close to the Worm, with its horribly vacant human faces, made her weak with fear and revulsion.

Then there was a clatter and a thrashing, and she almost cried out at the sound.

'One of their beasts,' came Esmail's tight, controlled voice. 'Keep moving, whatever you do!'

'They're coming,' whimpered Maure. 'Oh, Che . . .!'

Was that a plea, or recrimination? *You should not have followed me from the Commonweal. I have doomed us all.*

Magic – surely I can find some magic . . . but it was like trying to wring water from stones, and the approaching Worm's mere presence seemed to drive from her mind the faintest understanding of how she might even accomplish what she thought of as magic. That whole sense, that she had grown so accustomed to, had been put out like an eye.

Except . . .

One star remained in that sky, the thinnest thread back to that old life led under the sun. *Seda, the Empress.*

Her enemy, her sister and bitterest enemy, but the Worm was closer and closer, swifter and more sure than they could be in these confined and uneven tunnels, and Che would take anything at all now – anything to save herself and her friends.

She pulled, reaching across that immeasurable distance for aid of any sort, and it was given – a reflexive gout of strength, like a cup of water spilt on the desert sands.

Che took it in her hands and cast it at the Worm, anything to delay them, to buy another few moments without their attentions.

And nothing. Even as she cast it out, she lost the thoughts that would let her make use of it. Wasted – all that borrowed power, all she had; the simple presence of the Worm had deadened it to nothing.

Then she fell. Messel had descended a near-sheer drop of twenty feet without stopping, just crawling down the rock by his Art without ever thinking to warn her. Her wings snapped out as she dropped, and Thalric's too, and the pair of them spiralled down, clutching at each other, into a wide mine gallery.

There were lights here – made of twined fungus like Thalric's, and dim. The miners were all gone, though, summoned above to pay their tax to the Worm.

Messel was crouching, looking up. Maure had flown down,

but Che saw Tynisa being supported by Esmail on the lip of the drop. Neither of them could fly.

'Climb!' she shouted, but she knew the Worm would climb down faster, and Tynisa seemed injured.

'Just drop!' Thalric shouted, and then he was kicking off, wings surging him upwards. Che saw him recoil as he reached the top, saw Tynisa's blade out, the Worm surely almost on them. Then Thalric had grabbed the Weaponsmaster about the waist and just yanked her off the ledge, straining to slow their fall so that they crashed down almost at Che's feet, bruised but alive.

'Esmail—!'

But the assassin was already with them, falling on his feet, knees almost to his chin to absorb the shock of it, then turning to see the Worm moving down the cliff, descending almost as fast as they could run on level ground.

Gather, said a voice, and only a moment later did she realize it spoke directly into her head. It was a man's voice, a tired voice but a strong one.

'To me!' Che hissed, and she dragged Esmail back even as he was weighing a throwing blade in one hand, then she clutched Maure closer with the other hand. The little knot of them drew close, defiant, blades out against the Worm.

A sense of calm touched Che, utterly incongruous in the circumstances but she saw that Maure felt it as well, and even Esmail.

'Very still now,' said that low, deep voice, in words they could all hear. A huge figure had joined them, stepping out from who knew where. Che's eyes were fixed on the Worm as they reached the ground, those slack faces unreadable. She saw one huge pale hand from the corner of her eye, though, bearing a staff of black wood etched with countless tiny glyphs.

Messel's Teacher had come, after all.

The man's other hand, empty, was on the far side of them, so that their entire group fit within the curve of his arms, and Che could sense a vastly focused power at work – not strong but applied with a finesse and skill that could make her weep. It was not turned against the Worm, but focused inwards, drawing the darkness around them, turning the light away, until even the most dark-adapted eye would miss them.

The Worm had stopped, though nothing in all its faces or its bodies betrayed any emotion. Then it set off a little way, and halted once more, then back, as if making tentative searches for an enemy that had apparently been snatched away from it.

Che could hear the laboured breath of the giant newcomer, and she saw the hand holding the staff begin to shake. Without thinking, she placed her own there, and even though she had nothing she could give, the huge man seemed to take strength from that gesture.

Then the Worm was gone, its human segments retreating up the wall as quickly as they had come, heading elsewhere in their determined search.

The staff drooped, and their benefactor let out a sigh as big as himself. 'We must go now. They'll be back here very soon, searching for the trail. Oh, I have given too much, drunk a cupful out of a thimble.'

Thalric was already staring at the man, backing off slightly, and Che turned to see what had so startled him, craning upwards.

He was as big as a Mole Cricket, but without that broad strength, his frame instead a vast, sagging bulk within his patched and ragged robes. He was sickly pale, too, haggard and grey as though he was near death. Once upon a time his pouchy face would have radiated majesty. Che knew it – she could almost see him as he had once been, because she and Thalric had both encountered a great deal of his kin beneath the ancient city of Khanaphes. He was of their Masters, the Slug-kinden who had a claim on civilization to predate all others, who had beaten back the wilderness, raised the first cities, taught the younger kinden about law and craft and magic. Or so they claimed.

Having witnessed what he had just accomplished with so very, very little, she believed that.

'Master . . .' If a little reverence had crept into her voice, she felt she could be forgiven.

'Ah, no,' he said gently, 'not "Master", not from you. We are ill met in this benighted place, but I know a crowned head when I see it. But we must leave here. Please, come with me.' He levered himself upright again. 'No place here is truly safe, but at least I will take you away from the Worm.'

Eight

Capitas was filled to bursting with soldiers. The entire Imperial war machine was on the move, and the Third Army and elements of the First were thronging the streets, trying to resupply while waiting for their orders.

To General Brugan, watching from the Imperial palace, it all had a random, mindless air to it, the mad scurrying of insects whose nest has been turned over. He had a horrible feeling of doubt in his own perceptions. *Was it always like that, and I just fooled myself that I could see any patterns?*

He was the general of the almighty Rekef. He had plotted and schemed for it, done away with rivals, raised conspiracies. He should have been the most powerful man in the Empire, with the Empress under his complete control. That had been the plan.

Yet he could not have guessed what the Empress was. Even now he did not know, save that she was not human, not natural. When she looked at him, or thought of him in a certain way, he loved her, lusted after her. When she forgot about him, he found some place out of her sight and lived in dread of the moment that his name would enter her mind again. None of it made any sense.

He wanted to be mad. If he was mad, and it was all his own madness, then at least that would leave the rest of the world sane. But he knew it was true and he was sane, and everything he had ever believed in now made as little sense as the scurrying of the soldiers below.

She had been gone for a while: some whim of hers taking her westwards to where the Eighth had been fighting. She had not told him why, and he had not dared ask, where once he would have demanded. For some short time his life had been his own, even though the Red Watch men strode through the palace with decrees somehow direct from the Empress's mouth. He believed that as well. He was becoming painfully adept at believing the impossible.

And now she was back, and it had all started again. Half the time he felt that even his own body was somehow running his commands to it past the Empress before allowing him to move his limbs.

Last night she had sent for him again. The lovemaking had been hard enough, torn between the helpless need she generated in him and her own hunger that devoured another part of him every night they grappled together. Afterwards, though, when he had lain exhausted and blood-dashed by her side, there had been no sleep. He had trembled and clenched his eyes shut, hands to his ears as Seda, Empress of all the Wasps, fought with her own nightmares.

There had never been nightmares until her return. Whatever she had done, whatever had been done to her, it had ended badly. Before her journey, she had been the cool, fierce Empress that the Wasps had grown to love: ruthless, elegant and deadly. Now Brugan alone was witness to something new, an undermining of her nature. As she slept, she twitched and cried out, moaned in horror, screamed sometimes.

'I'm sorry,' she had said, last night. Words he had never thought to hear from those lips.

And all through it, the coupling and the torment, her bodyguard Tisamon had watched on, silent and menacing, in the very same room. She would not be parted from the man. Or from whatever lurked within that metal shell.

'General!'

He turned sharply to recognize General Marent of the Third Army. The man looked angry, and it was unthinkable that anyone could address Brugan with so little respect. A Rekef rank overrode a regular army one, as everyone knew. Brugan should draw himself up and stare the man down, enforce his indomitable will on this jumped-up infantryman.

He reached into himself for that certainty and self-possession he had known of old, but it had rusted under the Empress's caustic regard, leaving nothing for him to draw on.

'What is it, Marent?' he asked, horrified to hear a trembling in his own voice.

The army general's eyes widened, and Brugan saw that he would far rather have been shouted at, dismissed, threatened even, because that was the way the world worked. He had come looking for reassurance, and had found only Brugan.

Marent had been a battlefield colonel whose record during the revolt of the traitor governors was such that the choice was either to promote the man or to have him disappear. Right now Brugan was wishing it had been the latter. Marent seemed to storm through life constantly angry with the inefficiencies of everyone and everything else, but that resentment had never quite dared to light upon his superiors until now.

'My Third is still sitting idle, General,' the man reported. 'We were supposed to head for the front two tendays back, but the quartermasters have been feeding me excuses, I haven't any Engineer Corps, siege train or air support, and today . . .' His hands were clenched into fists at his sides as the man forcibly restrained himself. 'Today your cursed Red Watch comes to me—!'

'They're not *my* Red Watch!' Brugan's words were supposed to match the man in rage and volume, but there was a terribly plaintive edge to them he could not control. 'They take orders from the Empress – only the Empress.'

'So they said,' spat Marent. 'And so I asked for an audience with her, to hear it from her own lips. The Empress—'

'The Empress is not seeing anyone,' Brugan finished for him. *Not true. She sees me. Oh, she sees me.*

'And so I have nonsensical orders to sit here, with thirty thousand men clogging every barracks and garrison and camped outside the gates, without even the basics of a support corps. Because – and I quote – I "may be needed".What is that supposed to mean, General?'

'It means you may be needed,' Brugan replied hollowly. 'If she says it, that is what she means. Don't question her.'

Marent stared at him, and for a terrible moment Brugan thought some kind of pity would fight its way onto the man's blunt features. 'What is going on?' Marent demanded. 'Is this what we fought the traitors for? Orders that make no sense, commands from the throne that are vaguer than an Inapt prophecy –' if he saw Brugan's twitch at that, he did not let it slow him – 'a war on two fronts, for no reason that anyone's saying. And the Eighth . . . how did the Sarnesh destroy the Eighth so thoroughly, Brugan? What aren't they telling me?'

He was so self-righteous, buoyed by his own war record and his youth, that Brugan should destroy him, remind him of the Rekef's power, break him for the sheer disloyalty of even questioning the way things were.

But he's right, the Rekef general knew. He could only shake his head, sagging against the stone rail of the balcony, whilst beyond him the city bustled and struggled in a hundred different directions, and achieved nothing.

'What *happened* to you?' Marent said, his voice at last losing its anger in the face of the inexplicable, but Brugan only shook his head further and turned away.

Wasps lost their tempers, it was well known. Every officer had been forced to discipline soldiers who let that temper fly. Every occupied city had learned the dark side of Wasp temperament, to tread carefully and not provoke the Lords of Empire. Each Wasp conquest had paid for its resistance in killings and rape after having sparked the frustration of the invaders. Few from outside the Empire realized the amount of effort that went into directing and controlling that innate rage, from their rigid upbringings to the Imperial expansion itself, a constant channel for a kinden unwilling to be idle and quick to take offence, and whose every adult member could deal death through their Art.

Soldiers and the lower ranks could afford to let loose their anger occasionally – earning a flogging perhaps, but little more. Those who sought promotion must learn to curb their excesses, though. The Empire had no use for a colonel or a general who could not keep a level head, no matter what.

And what of an Empress?

She had been so careful. All those years spent in the executioner's shadow during her brother's reign, and then the careful – oh, so careful – conspiracy to bring him down. And then the frustrations of the war against the traitor governors who would not accept her rule, and her discovery that her privileged position as Great Magician amongst the Apt had to be shared . . . her quest to the broken hold of Argastos, her contests with Cheerwell Maker, her unwanted sister . . . None of these had sufficed to breach her calm.

And then it had seemed that her rivalry with the Beetle girl might become something else, that Seda could now live in peace with her, that they could even combine their strengths. She had entertained such hopes.

It had been that, she thought, that had broken her resolve. Not the betrayal itself, for under other circumstances she would have been expecting it, ensuring her response was deadly but proportionate. She had laid herself open, though, cast off her armour. She had fallen victim to hope, and then the girl had turned on her.

And Seda had struck back, with all the might that she could muster. She had broken the Great Seal beneath them all and condemned Cheerwell Maker to the cold dark below. And all the Seals, all those locks that chained the Worm down in its lightless prison, they had cracked across in that same moment, and she had doomed the world.

Not all at once, not a sudden pent-up flood of squirming evil vomiting forth onto the world's surface, but the Worm was now pushing at the gates, squeezing loops of its substance through the cracks and forcing them wider with its blind persistence. It struck in darkness and left no trace behind, nor path whereby it could be followed. It was growing bolder and it was *strong* in some way that Seda could not fathom. She knew what it was that had destroyed the remnants of the Eighth Army, but she did not know how. Her attempts to scry or divine the truth encountered only a fog.

The Worm, the Centipede-kinden of old, had been magicians, but this was something other. They had transformed themselves into something even worse during the long ages of their banishment.

And she could not forget what she had done. Every night was a reminder. When she could cling to wakefulness no longer, when sleep rose from the stone darkness to claim her, that link opened up once more. The same bond with Cheerwell Maker that had led Seda to the Masters of Khanaphes, and thus to power, was a constant fount of nightmares. In her sleep, Seda *saw* the domain of the Worm, suffering through it as Che suffered. She would wake screaming out, 'Just die! Leave me alone and die!' because that was surely the kinder path, for the girl to meet a swift extinction in that terrible place.

But Beetles endured. Even that fate, they endured. Somewhere in that cold prison, Cheerwell Maker struggled on, her enemy and her sister.

'I'm sorry!' Seda had heard the echo of her own voice, as she started awake. And now, back in Capitas and with her arch-rival consigned to the pit, she truly was sorry. *I would bring you back if I could*, but she knew the girl could never hear her.

If only she could drag Che Maker from that fate, then perhaps, just perhaps, the two of them together could have repaired the Seal.

Now she could look out over her city, her Empire, her world, and know that it was ending. The attacks of the Worm were slow and tentative still, but she knew that their numbers were vast and they were getting bolder.

They seek to make everything like them: that had been poor dead Gjegevey's belief. A world of the homogeneous, an endless writhing carpet of the Worm.

In locking the Worm away those centuries ago, the powers of the ancient world had only bequeathed a worse terror to their descendants. Now Seda was desperately trying find some way to follow in their footsteps, because that was all that was left to her. The Moths and their allies had performed a ritual not seen before or since; it had been the highest and most terrible moment of the Bad Old Days. They had possessed a skill and understanding that Seda had not been given the opportunity to develop. She could only rely on what she had.

So what do I have? What can I do that will put things right? What is my magic good for?

Each night, each morning, the same questions. She was the Empress of the Wasps. Every difficulty would yield to her will, to the might of her armies, to the strength of the magic she had been an unwilling recipient of. *I will not accept that I am helpless.*

All the while she gave those orders that she saw might help, she could not waste her precious attention on trivial matters. Her Red Watch carried out her bidding but understood nothing. Her soldiers and her citizens were growing worried, this she knew. They could not see what she had seen, and if they could only know, how *thankful* they would be that the horrors that visited her were hers alone. She was the shield between them and her people.

Only she could save the world.

She mourned the loss of her Woodlouse adviser Gjegevey. The old man had infuriated her but, now that he was dead, his absence hurt her more than she could bear, and his guidance was what she now needed most. But he was gone, and the turncoat Tegrec was gone – the only other Wasp magician that she knew. She had only her limited understanding of magic to call upon.

She had dredged up all she had read, all she had seen or been taught. Everything the old Woodlouse had patiently explained to her, everything she had sieved from decaying Moth records. Everything vouchsafed to her by her original master and co-conspirator, Uctebri the Sarcad.

He had been a man who had known the uses of power. His people had a rare and terrible understanding, honed over those long years of hiding after the Moths brought them low. Denied their place as rulers, they had learned how to gather power in other ways. They would not have dared to attempt what was in her mind now, though. The sheer scale would defeat them. Gjegevey would have begged her to find another way.

But there was no other way, and there was so little time. *Somebody* had to save the world from the Worm. With Che lost, there was nobody else but herself.

Nine

In the absence of clear direction from the throne, the Imperial forces fought on as best they could. Armies marched south down the Silk Road against the Spiderlands, to be met by inexhaustible enemy troops, treachery, poison and falsified orders. Tynan held Collegium and ground his teeth in frustration, whilst Colonel Brakker held his ground east of Sarn as he waited for the Ants to stir from their city.

And yet around the Exalsee there might as well not have been a war on.

'Colonel, you have a most impressive complex here,' Lieutenant-Auxillian Gannic complimented Drephos. Although he had been insistent about his own inferior rank, he would promote the master artificer to full colonel every time he addressed him.

He had been all attention as they showed him round those workshops and forges that Totho and Drephos judged fit for outside eyes. Plainly he was knowledgeable about the Empire's previous commissions for the Iron Glove, discoursing in a familiar manner on the Sentinels and the greatshotters. He had done his best to demonstrate an artificer's knowledge, but Totho had caught his partner's eye partway through, and Drephos's covert nod had signalled agreement. Gannic was no simple engineer.

They had brought him at last to one of the bigger foundries, where steel ingots shipped in from the Spiderlands were being resmelted into stronger alloys. The noise was tolerable, the machinery going about its practised routine with a hiss of steam and a ratchet of gears. Gannic barely had to speak up at all to be heard.

'Of course, people back home have been taking notice, seeing how fast you've built up your fiefdom here,' he explained. 'Everyone knows how much you've helped in the war effort.'

'Even so.' Drephos's voice was guarded.

'And you've not forgotten your old friends in the Empire, Colonel, so everyone says,' Gannic went on. His eyes flicked between the two of them, his smile pleasant and easy. *Three half-breeds together*, it seemed to say, *so we should be friends*. Totho had known at first sight that the man had been chosen for this role because of his heritage: there could not be many of mixed blood to have attained Gannic's rank.

Drephos held up his steel hand. 'We've already had enough embassies and trading missions and diplomats, Lieutenant-Auxillian,' he observed. 'And spies, for that matter. But you appear to be something new. Perhaps now is the time to set out what it is you're here for.'

Gannic nodded companionably. 'Between you and me, Colonel, you scare them, back home.'

Drephos regarded him expressionlessly.

The lieutenant shrugged. 'There honestly aren't many individuals who have the reputation you do, and now you're out in the world, and at any moment the latest Iron Glove creation could march out of the Sarnesh gates – that's what they're thinking. After all, it's all good stuff, what we've had from you, but who knows what else you have on the drawing board, or waiting in the hangars.' That bright grin broadened. 'The Empire's a little scared of you, I think. The Engineers certainly are.'

It was said so flippantly that Totho snorted, and was about to make some slick rejoinder – about how maybe the Empire *should* be scared, something like that – when a sharp gesture from Drephos's real hand silenced him.

'What is your mission here, Lieutenant-Auxillian?' the master artificer enquired flatly.

'Ah, well.' Gannic crossed over to one of the foundry fires, watching the low-guttering flames as they slowly cindered the last of the coal. The red light touched on his face, the solidity of Beetle-kinden there but also something of a Wasp's hard coldness. 'The Exalsee has been – literally – a backwater for generations. The Spiders never knew what they had here, so left the place as a playground for their failures. And, all the while, what an artifice was born on the shores of this lake! Yes, you two and your Iron Glove have built on it, but where would we be without the innovations of Chasme and Solarno, which they put together all by themselves?'

He looked back to catch Drephos's eye, and the Colonel-Auxillian nodded.

'But backwater no longer: the wider world caught up with a lot of places during the last war. These lands are on everyone's maps. There is even something that in Capitas they call the "Exalsee question".'

'And what is the answer?'

'The preferred answer involves you and your operation here, Colonel,' Gannic said frankly. 'It involves you coming back into the fold, resuming your rank in more than name, and serving the Empire as more than a mercenary tinker.'

'Not an option we are willing to consider.' Drephos's real hand landed unexpectedly on Totho's shoulder, startling him, but now drawing him into the conversation.

'You're concerned about General Lien and the Engineers shackling your creativity? Believe me, Lien knows he can't control you. He hates you, that I'll admit, but if you're with us, you're with us. You could even become the General-Auxillian, if you wanted that badly enough. And you wouldn't have to leave Chasme and all you've built here because this would become an Imperial city, under your governance. I don't think an offer this generous has ever been made in the Empire's history.'

Drephos's grip was becoming painful, and Totho was only glad that the pressure was from the man's living hand. His metal hand, still hanging by his side, would have broken bones by now.

'The Empire's changing, in a lot of ways,' Gannic went on. 'Whatever you remember from just a few years back, believe me, it's not the same. And you can see the opportunity you'd have to demonstrate the fruits of your craft.' His eyes seldom left the master artificer's face. 'Far more than now, in fact. Everything you've wanted to test out could be put to *real* use in battle. You'd have a hand on the tiller of the war. You'd want for nothing.'

'I see,' was all Drephos would say, and then a pause. 'And no doubt, in return, *everything* of mine would be tested in battle, whether I wished it or not. Everything that the Empire believes I have to offer.'

This cannot all be solely for the Bee-killer, Totho thought, and surely there was a core of truth to the absurdly grand offer, for the Empire had been leaning on the Iron Glove too much recently, and no doubt it would want to control the maverick artificers whose inventions it found so useful. But it was plain that the city-slayer weapon, that lethal chemical, had lodged itself in certain imaginations in Capitas. They *wanted* it, and they wanted to *use* it.

And Drephos did not. *Why not?*

'The offer is there, anyway.' Gannic shrugged. 'Think about it, at least. Sleep on it. Weigh it up.'

As confidently as if he owned everything he saw, the Lieutenant-Auxillian walked out, with Drephos's pale eyes tracking him all the way.

The next morning, before dawn, one of the junior artificers came banging on Totho's door, sending him kicking and grappling over the edge of his bed. He had been dreaming of Collegium, and for a moment he thought that he was late for classes there.

Drephos, when Totho joined him, was looking out over Chasme, over the Exalsee, at the first faint touches of dawn.

'What is it?' Totho demanded, still half asleep and feeling off balance and irritable.

'He's gone,' Drephos pronounced.

'You mean you've—'

'*I've* nothing. He's gone.'

Totho stared blankly at the great expanse of water. 'It's early,' he pointed out. 'How do you know? Did you . . .' *send men to kill him?* went unspoken.

Drephos's lack of answer was reply in itself.

'So he wasn't waiting for our response, then.'

'I suspect he could see it in our faces as he asked the question,' Drephos replied acidly. 'Whatever Iron Glove forces we can put under arms, we should do so now. Distribute snapbows and whatever else is in stock to our people. Ready all assembled engines for live testing, and gather anything that can be made to work.'

'You're serious?' Totho queried, for those orders meant essentially shutting down their normal business. The Iron Glove stronghold was no fortress, and there was a limited amount of ordnance that they could call on at any time, most of their grander projects being built to order. Beyond their compound, Chasme was so loosely knit as to be indefensible, but at the same time it was full of hard lawless people at least nominally operating under Drephos's banner. The more Totho thought about it, the more he couldn't see the Empire making an attempt. 'The Spiders would gut them,' he pointed out. 'Whatever line they're walking in Solarno can't last long, anyway, before they come to blows there.'

'Get us ready, Totho,' Drephos insisted, still staring north towards Solarno, towards the Empire.

And in Solarno itself, in a grandly appointed room of a townhouse in the Spider half of the city, Merva the governor's wife was speaking to the enemy.

She and her husband Edvic had been so careful. Securing the governorship had been a joint effort, he fighting for elbow room in the upper echelons of the Consortium, she visiting the wives of senior officers and casting her net: bribes, threats, favours deployed as weapons to get them the jewel they were after. Solarno was considered the crown of the Exalsee; Edvic had taken the governorship, and there had been that accord with the Spiders, and everything had been golden.

Then it had all fallen apart, and for a while it looked as though Solarno was going to become the South-Empire's prettiest war zone.

They had worked so hard, she and her husband and all the minor Aristoi who had become their opposite numbers. A battle for Solarno would serve nobody: not the Empire, not the Spiders, certainly not the Solarnese.

And then the Engineers – the *Engineers!* – had uncovered the plan, just as if they had been lifting the housing from some machine to see why it wasn't working as expected. For a moment everything had begun unravelling around Merva, all her plans falling apart. Then smooth Colonel Varsec had told her simply that, yes, she and Edvic could keep it all, and why not? Except for one thing. The Empire was asking a price to avoid dragging Solarno into the fighting.

This was a large room made for elegant, mobile Spider gatherings, and right now it was almost full. Just across from Merva was a delegation of Spider-kinden – and not just factors and surrogates, but many of the little Aristoi who ran the lower reaches of Solarno. They were young and tough, all of them used to fighting to keep a social station that greater nobles would see as one step from the gutter. The elimination of the Aldanrael had suddenly given them their place in the sun, if they could only hold on to it.

Giselle of the Arkaetien headed their delegation, she was the one who had rescued Merva from Gannic before. She was a girl who seemed barely twenty, dressed in glittering bright armour of chitin and silks that should have made her seem a fop, and yet a simple change in the way she stood and she became a dangerous duellist, the rapier at her hip far more than just for show. At her back stood her peers, into whose uncertain care Solarno had been given when the alliance with the Wasps had met its grisly end. Nobody had expected anything from them save blood.

There were others there too: two or three Solarnese Beetles rich and influential enough to ape Spider fashions and mannerisms; a pair of well-dressed Fly-kinden merchant magnates; a handful of squat, plain-dressing Bee-kinden from Dirovashni; even a gaudy Dragonfly noble from Princep Exilla, one of Solarno's traditional enemies. They had all just heard what Merva had to say. None of them had walked out. None of them had sneered. They exchanged glances, murmured amongst themselves. Evident in their many disparate faces was an admission of the possible.

'Let me tell you what we think,' Giselle stated. 'We know of the Iron Glove. We know of Chasme. That place was a thorn in the side of our kin here in Solarno long before your Empire's halfbreed traitor made his home there. The Solarnese have always dreamt of taking up arms against them.' Some nods from the Beetles there. 'Now you say your Empire, in the midst of its war with our people, has achieved some manner of civic responsibility concerning the pirates and renegades there.'

She smiled prettily before continuing. 'I think you're scared that they'll sell to us. Or to the Lowlanders. I think they're – what was it? – loose artillery. Who knows which way they'll point with each shot? And, if I'm advised right, this man Drephos loves war and the Apt toys of war. A fight between Spiderlands and Empire on his very doorstep would let him sell his toys to all the children, and so make the fight that much the bloodier.'

Merva shrugged. 'The Consortium and the Engineers want rid of him, I know only that much. But I think you're right. He's grown too great, too dangerous, and he cannot be controlled.'

'And these merchants and tinkers can bind the Empire? I hear no mention of the Empress's writ in this.'

The Wasp woman kept her face level. Given their facility with spies, the Spiders almost certainly knew by now that Imperial writ was suddenly in short supply. 'These days the merchants and the tinkers represent a great deal of power at Capitas. There is no more of the Empire available to treat with but this. On the table now is the best deal that Solarno – meaning the Exalsee – is likely to get.' She looked from face to face, and not just at the Spiders, seeing the wheels turning there, seeing the unexpected balance of power. Giselle was their spokeswoman, but there were a lot of interests represented in that room, none of whom had any wish to see the continued growth of Chasme as a new power on the shores of the Exalsee.

Ten

They came again to confront Tactician Milus, finding him this time on the walls of Sarn, apparently supervising the placement of artillery. It was a sham, of course. Linked to the artillerists, Milus could have directed and advised his soldiers perfectly from anywhere in the city. His presence there in person was intended to focus the minds of the Collegiates, and other malcontents, on the danger to Sarn.

Expressions did not come naturally to Ant faces but, when Milus looked down to see Eujen and Balkus at the foot of the steep steps, there was something that clearly had hold of him. Straessa reckoned it was probably amusement rather than pity. She had wheeled Eujen here in the chair, and he hunched there like an old man, no support save a simple walking stick clutched in his hands.

Well, Milus loves to put on a show, and there's more than one way to make a point here. 'You're ready?' she asked the pair of them.

Balkus was looking somewhat concerned at the climb, but Eujen just squared his shoulders, and even managed a small smile for her. *And who would ever have thought he was such a fighter?*

Behind her, Kymene shifted restlessly, wanting to be done with the talking so that she could act. The Collegiates wanted their home back, yes, but they were a habitually patient people, well used to waiting and planning. The Mynans, meanwhile, were virtually in outright revolt at being denied the chance to go off and shed Wasp blood. In contrast, the citizens of Princep Salma, as represented by Balkus, just wanted to go home, seeing that most of them were here in something disturbingly close to slavery at the insistence of their 'allies' in Sarn.

Straessa made an abortive attempt to take Eujen's arm but restrained herself as he braced his hands against the chair arms and then levered himself to his feet.

There was a hiss and a clack from his brace as it took the strain, and she heard the intricate clattering as the gearing at his knees measured the pressure and added its support. Without even putting his hand out to steady himself, Eujen ascended, step by step, with a ticking of mechanisms.

Many artificers had been smuggled out of Collegium, as Sarn had been only too glad to acknowledge. They had been at work on more than just orthopters and weapons of war.

Tactician Milus's face changed only slightly, but Straessa had been watching closely for his reaction, and the suggestion of surprise there was gratifying.

Balkus had no such artificial aids, but his wounds had been less serious and he had been pushing himself almost every day to regain his strength. Adopting the measured pace of Eujen, he tried the stairs next, leaving the two more able-bodied women to follow.

All the Ants up on the wall were now watching as the delegation reached the top, and Eujen had their undivided attention. Sweat was beading on his brow but he kept his pace steady all the way, his progress punctuated by the hiss-clack of the mechanical brace and the tap of his stick.

'Well, now,' Milus said, with a smile, 'you look well, Speaker.' He had begun calling Eujen that recently, possibly to try and strengthen opposition within the Collegiate ranks amongst those who were not fond of the man. After all, Collegiates chose their leaders, but nobody had cast lots to select Eujen as their ambassador to their Sarnesh hosts.

If that had been his intention, it had backfired. Somewhat to Eujen's annoyance, the title had become widespread amongst the Collegiates themselves. The best he had been able to achieve with any disavowals was to have it amended to '*acting* Speaker' in his earshot.

'Thank you, Tactician,' Eujen replied, and Straessa could hear the catch of breath as he spoke. He was leaning on his stick, but only a little. Balkus, beside him, had a hand on the wall top, but it was merely a light touch. The two of them were far more the men they had once been.

I'm still waiting for a new eye, though. There were limits to even Collegiate artifice, but by now Straessa was almost used to her new field of vision. *Focused, that's what I am.*

'You had something you wanted to bring before me?' Milus asked him.

'We wanted to thank you, Tactician – to thank your people.'

The Ant went still for a moment, no doubt reaching out to his kin, trying to second-guess where this conversation was going.

'You have taken us in,' Eujen pressed on mildly. 'You have proved yourselves good allies.'

'This is the preamble to another request to march on Collegium, I take it.' But Milus was nevertheless off balance, and therefore so was Sarn.

'We understand that you must look to Sarn's defence first.' Eujen gestured at the walls, seizing Milus's own rhetorical ammunition. 'But we will be marching south shortly.'

Another pause for hurried redeployment of the tactician's thoughts. 'Define "we".'

'Those Collegiates who will take up arms for their city's freedom,' Eujen explained. 'It is time we started acting on our own behalf. Kymene has agreed to bring her Mynan contingent to our aid as well. I suspect that some of the Princep fighters may join us.'

'This is a strange game you're playing, little Speaker,' Milus growled. 'We both know that you could barely raise two thousand under arms, and many of those no real soldiers. Even if your people still within the city tried to rise up – which I doubt – you would not have the strength to retake your home. So, is this your ultimatum? That I commit soldiers to march with you or . . .? Or what? What will you do if I say that nothing has changed?'

'You mistake us,' Eujen told him, with eminent calm assurance. 'We will march. We ask nothing from Sarn. You have given us shelter and food, a home away from home when we needed it. We are grateful, and we do not wish to impose upon you any longer.'

Balkus tugged at Straessa's sleeve covertly. The renegade Ant had a small smile, and she guessed that he had caught something leaking from the edges of Milus's composure that amused him.

'I will consider your position,' Milus stated, just as though Eujen had made a formal request of him.

'I imagine we will be ready to depart within a tenday,' Eujen informed him. It was as though the two were holding entirely separate conversations.

After they had descended the walls – Eujen making heavier going of that than he had the ascent – they returned to the Foreigners' Quarter to meet with the Fly-kinden – with one Fly-kinden in particular. *And who would have guessed that kinden would become the threads that bound this venture together.*

A modest square of garden was the closest she had to freedom here in the heart of Sarn. The walls that overlooked this little space of green – so meticulously tended that it felt as artificial as a gear train – were patrolled by two Ant soldiers at all times, with half a dozen others ready to jump should the alarm be raised. Escape was not an option: their eyes were on her always. These guards were not to protect her from attack, or even to prevent rescue from the outside, for what help could reach her when she was so deep in their domain? Instead, they were looking inwards always. They had locked gloves to her wrists that were of some cloth that would only smoulder sullenly and not burn, and they had her secured in Fly manacles that wrapped across her back and stifled her Art. But she was dangerous, and Tactician Milus was no fool.

This was where he came whenever the demands of state loosened their hold on him. Not to visit family, not to lose himself in the company of his own kind. Milus was a singular Ant in a culture that normally held singularity in disdain. He played the conformity game well enough to pass muster, and his particular strain of independence had allowed him to walk the treacherously narrow path to a tactician's rank: more an asset than a liability – just.

She looked up now to see him enter the garden. She had been sitting in one corner, in the shade, her back against a windowless wall, and she noticed the two guards diplomatically move to the far end, so that she and Milus could talk without being overheard.

She had no idea what the other Sarnesh made of this little ritual, this privacy that their war leader insisted on. But she knew that he had come to need this outlet, this time spent with her, as a way of expressing that part of himself he did not share with his siblings.

Perhaps the Sarnesh just wrote it off as a necessary evil. After all, she was Milus's prisoner and nobody much cared what happened to her. When he decided that he would question her about Imperial protocols and practices, they let him get on with it. When he put her through torture by freezing again, on the pretence that he was not satisfied with her answers, they reacted likewise. Perhaps in peacetime an eyebrow would be raised, but this war was a direct threat to Sarn, and Milus was the man they needed to conduct it.

She had lived her whole life flitting from faction to faction to maintain her freedom. Even the Empire had not mastered her, not quite. She had enjoyed a life free from conscience or consequence. His idle tortures did not hurt her as much as being denied the chance simply to walk out of here, and he knew it.

She had become adept at reading him, from bitter necessity. This time she judged that he would just talk – with her as his audience whether she liked it or not. That was preferable to so many alternatives.

'Lissart,' he addressed her pleasantly.

'Good morning, Tactician,' she replied, as meekly as she could make herself say it. She saw a spark of annoyance in his eyes, because he preferred a little defiance so that he could break her of it.

'I have a question – something I was hoping you would help me with.'

'Anything, Tactician.'

'First, though, tell me – when you came to me, you were masquerading as an expert on the Inapt and their ways. Was there any truth in that?'

Lissart considered her answer carefully before replying. 'I have some training. I am Inapt. I've worked for Moths and Spiders.'

'There is . . . a weapon,' Milus said. His voice was hushed, and she started as she realized that this was not a game, after all. She had caught him in a rare moment of uncertainty. No wonder he wanted his guards out of earshot, and no doubt he was keeping his thoughts securely locked within his head. *Prisoners, just like me.*

'It seems to strike at random. People disappear. It strikes the Empire and my own people equally. My artificers and scholars cannot explain it.'

'You think that . . .' *You think that it's magic.* But of course he could not think that, although Milus had shown himself an unusually open-minded man when he had been dealing with the Mantis situation.

'I think that my artificers cannot explain it,' he repeated, with a glint of irritation. 'I think that I do not trust the Moths and the Mantids. I think that the Apt powers of the world are currently fully committed against one another, and I know my history books. The Moths were tyrants, in their day, and it's a habit not soon unlearned.'

'Tell me of this thing, this weapon,' she encouraged him, and he did so, giving a concise flavourless report, details without any interpretation: disturbed earth, missing bodies, no witnesses.

Lissart had an esoteric training but she was no magician. Some old stories might have elements of what Milus described, but these were tales to scare children with, down in the Spiderlands where she had grown up. 'Sounds like centipedes to me,' she told him with a smile, and he took her by the throat with one iron hand. For a moment she thought he was going to snap her neck.

Her gloves scrabbled at his fingers, moving them not one inch, and all the while Milus was staring into her face. 'The beasts were seen at several of the sites. At one there was the body of a creature more than ten feet in length, hacked and burned by stingshot. What do you know?'

She choked, and he loosened his grip slightly. 'Just stories,' she got out.

'I will send paper and ink. You will write down everything.' He straightened up, releasing her. 'And, yes, the gloves stay on. You'll just have to manage.'

She watched him depart, and it was not lost to her that the two guards were watching him, too, as he left. It was perhaps the first moment of complete privacy she had been gifted with in tendays.

But still the manacles and the gloves were keeping her here. If only there was some other chance at freedom . . .

'You heard all of that, of course,' she murmured from the corner of her mouth.

'Oh, I heard it.' The whisper issued from the carefully pruned greenery in this shaded corner of the garden. 'And, believe me, it's happening all over. I may not like the man but he's worrying about the right things.'

'Laszlo, there's only one thing that's concerning me.'

'I know, I know.' He had come to her immediately before Milus, slipping adroitly past the guards, but she knew him of old. He was not quite the skilled infiltrator he might take himself for.

He had tracked her here on a path of rumours. Some of the Collegiate artificers in Sarn were aware that Milus had a Fly woman prisoner, a woman with red hair. She was distinctive enough that she had stuck in their minds.

'I don't think I can get you out right now,' he confessed. 'Not with the guards – and those manacles look well made.'

'So much for you, then,' she said, trying to sound nasty about it, but her heart wasn't in it. She was fighting very hard to avoid showing how much hope had leapt in her, just knowing she had not been forgotten.

'No, listen, I'm working on it. I've kind of got mixed up in some other stuff as well, but, believe me . . .'

'Laszlo, just . . .' To have a jagged piece of hope thrust into her hands and then torn away so swiftly was unbearable. 'Just do something,'

'I will. But you need to make sure Milus takes you with him when the Sarnesh march out. And that'll be soon. Things are happening. Just be with him.'

'Oh, he'll take me.' There was a wealth of tired pain in her words that left him silent, and for a moment she had mad thoughts of him putting an arrow into Milus, stabbing the man or getting killed while trying, and then where would she be? Milus was her jailer, but at least he had an interest in keeping her alive.

Then Lazlo said, 'You'll get your chance, I swear to you. I'll get you out and then you'll never need to see Milus again.'

I'll see him one more time after that, she told herself, but that was more than Laszlo needed to hear. So she moved over to the brighter end of the garden, drawing the soldiers' gazes after her, so that he could creep away.

★

It was a Fly-kinden war.

The machine that ghosted to a silent landing north of Collegium was a fixed-wing, and Taki never liked flying fixed-wings. If a Wasp combat orthopter had caught her in the air, she would only have speed to trust to in her escape. Actual fighting would be out of the question.

It was quiet, though, her machine, and, most importantly, it could glide for long distances with its propellers stilled. She had kept up high on the trip south from Sarn, riding the winds whenever she could to conserve fuel, she and her passengers muffled in scarves and overcoats against the chill of the upper air.

Once touched down, she listened intently for the engines of Wasp fliers, but the night was keeping its secrets. She twisted in her seat, looking back at the others.

'Your stop.'

There was little space in the body of the fixed-wing, but enough for two Fly-kinden.

'You know what you're looking for?' Laszlo prompted her. Beside him, Sperra shifted, still half asleep, and leant into the man.

'An army's a hard thing to miss,' Taki told him contemptuously. 'You just concentrate on doing your own job, whatever that actually is.'

'Top secret,' he insisted, and not for the first time. 'I'm a spy, remember.'

'A piss-poor one, if you keep telling people,' she retorted, and was surprised to see a slight twinge of pain come into his smile at the reproach.

'You just remember your job, mistress aviator.'

'Avia*trix*.'

'Whatever.' He untangled himself from Sperra, who made a complaining noise and then woke up with a start as Laszlo unlatched the hatch.

'Already?' she demanded.

'Winds were with us,' Taki said. 'That, and the fact that you have the best pilot in the world.'

Laszlo snorted. 'Good luck in the city,' he told Sperra.

'I thought you were coming in with me.'

'Got other places I need to be, and better roads to take me there.' He hopped down to the ground and then put his head back through the hatch. 'Good sailing, both of you.'

He was gone even before Sperra replied in kind.

'You too,' Taki urged her. 'Come on, out. I want to be on my way west before the Wasps decide we're overdue for a fly-by.'

'He's quite a character, isn't he,' Sperra said, in a thoughtful tone of voice.

For a moment, Taki couldn't imagine what she was talking about. Then: '*Laszlo?*'

'Do you think he really used to be a pirate?'

Sperra and Laszlo had been talking earlier on, but due to the rushing of the wind and the softness of their voices, Taki had caught not even one word in ten. Now she regarded the other woman doubtfully, deciding with uncharacteristic tact to let her own opinions remain unspoken. There was a hope on Sperra's face that was just ready for some jovial bravo like Laszlo to step on. 'Pirate? No more than he's a spy,' was all that she said.

Sperra looked put out at that. 'He's doing good work.'

'So am I. So should you be. Come on, move.'

Still Sperra hesitated. 'You think . . . what they were saying in Sarn, Leadswell and the rest. This *is* going to work, isn't it?'

Taki shrugged. 'Wasn't really listening, except for my bit.'

Sperra was unhappy with that, but Taki finally got the woman out of the hold and did a few quick calculations as to how much room she was going to need to get airborne. The fixed-wing was a flimsy little thing, though, light as anything she'd ever flown. It only took a little lift to get it away from the ground and into the arms of the wind.

★

The summons from Milus came just a few days after Eujen had bearded him on the wall. This time it was a map room in the Royal Court, the unspoken subtext being: *Look how seriously we are taking you.*

The tactician regarded him without expression as Eujen stood there under his scrutiny, the brace and the stick taking his weight between them.

'We've fought the Wasps about ten miles east of here – the former Collegiate garrison force and some of the First Army,' Milus announced. 'Mostly a skirmish of scouts and automotives, but a fair-sized engagement.'

'I assume congratulations are in order,' Eujen advanced.

'The result was inconclusive, but the Wasps have been pushed further back. We think that we can control any attempt to reconnoitre our city, save for a full-scale assault. The reports from the officers in charge suggest that they will not be in a position to make such an assault in the immediate future.'

'That is good news.' Conversational pleasantries, obviously marking time until Milus got to the point.

'I am aware of how many Collegiates you can put under arms, little Speaker. There is clearly nothing you can accomplish in Collegium, even with that woman's Mynans at your back.'

'And yet we are going,' Eujen confirmed. 'Perhaps we, too, wish to test the enemy's strength.' Wondering all the time, *And what else have you heard?* The plan was full of big secrets, sliding into place like blocks of stone, and Milus must have spies and agents listening out for their movements.

'Our recent gains against the Wasps here, however, mean that I can spare at least a nominal force to accompany you south.'

Eujen waited.

'Five hundred men, some light artillery, some war automotives.'

'A thousand would perhaps better demonstrate the leading role that Sarn is taking in the fight against the Empire,' Eujen stated.

For a long time Milus's eyes bored into him, hunting for the awkward, injured student he knew was in there somewhere.

'Very well.' So very grudgingly, and Eujen could see a flare of that un-Ant-like temper, that erratic nature that marked Milus out from his fellows.

'Thank you, Tactician,' he said graciously, thinking, *I have an enemy there. Once this is done, I will have to be careful.*

Eleven

His name was Orothellin, and Che had waited for the cascade of titles that all of his kinden burdened themselves with, but if he had ever possessed such, he had shed them a long time ago.

He had led them from Cold Well, choosing path after path in the pitch-dark caves, and never once coming within sight of another segment of the Worm. There was no magic to it, just an utter certainty of his route, as though every inch of it was second nature to him. His pace was leaden, his bare feet dragging on the stone, and his hoarse, heavy breathing echoed about them.

When they came out into what passed for the open, they were far enough from Cold Well that the lights and the foundries were only a reddish glow limning a distant ridge, and Orothellin gave out a great sigh, swaying so that Che thought he might collapse. A moment later he was on his way again, one scraping step after another. He did not even look back, and for a moment Che thought he was abandoning them.

'Please,' she hissed at his retreating back, 'I have questions.'

He stopped, then turned – not just his head, but his whole bulky body, as though craning over his shoulder would somehow have involved even more effort. He was a shocking sight, his pale, slick skin dirty and lined, and his hair long and matted and streaked with grey. He looked *old*, Che realized. The thought had been slow in coming because she knew his kind lived for many centuries, and those she had met beneath Khanaphes had seemed still in their prime.

'Ah, no,' he mumbled. 'Come with me. No, there is further to go yet. They will search here. Come, now.' His staff creaked as it took his weight, and then he was shambling off again.

Their progress was agonizing, given the thought of the Worm and its swift-ranging pursuit, but somehow their lurching hulk of a guide took them on a winding route that avoided all notice, despite shackling them to his slow shuffle. Messel kept ranging further ahead or off to one side, plainly anxious to be further from Cold Well, but he always came back. Orothellin had become the centre of their world.

At last he found a crack in the rock that seemed shallow but opened out below into a fair-sized cave. The walls were tacky to the touch, and there was a bundle of rags in one corner that must serve as a bed. A pot beside it held embers, and Messel built a low fire to bring some warmth to the place.

The huge man gave out a groan and slumped down onto the ground, the staff clattering at his feet.

'So, my people survive still, do they?' he asked Che.

'They . . .' In her mind again was the tomb complex beneath Khanaphes, with the Masters lying in dignity and state. What would they think to see one of their own like this? 'They sleep. They are almost forgotten. I am sorry.'

'As I knew they would be,' Orothellin said mournfully, a prophet unacknowledged in his own country.

There had been Masters amongst those who had driven the Worm below ground, and no doubt there was a complex story to account for this man being trapped down here, but Che had other priorities, urgent priorities. *Like escape.*

'Please, Master . . .' And, when he waved the title away, 'Teacher, then,' for that was how Messel had addressed the man. 'Tell me . . . that was magic. Of all we have met down here, you are the first who . . . Please, can you help us?'

He regarded her grimly, and for a long time he said nothing, so that she thought he really was falling asleep, but at last he said, 'Messel, keep watch.' A ridiculous request to a man with no eyes, but their erstwhile guide nodded sharply.

'Yes, Teacher,' and he had crawled from the cave, out into the hostile dark beyond.

'So, you really are from the Old World,' Orothellin said. 'I had almost convinced myself that there was nowhere else but here.'

'At least you can believe us, then,' Tynisa stated. 'Those other creatures didn't – the slaves.'

'Believe?' Orothellin echoed mildly. 'Dear girl, I *remember*. I remember the sun and the sky. I remember *rain*.' His voice was hoarse with wonder.

'When did you come here?' Tynisa demanded. 'If there's a way in—'

'I have always been here,' the great man told her. 'Since there has been a "here", here I have been.'

'But that's—' Tynisa started, but Che put a hand on her shoulder.

'It's possible,' she confirmed. 'It's just possible.' *How long ago was it, really? How old is this man?* 'But, yes, we come from above – from the Old World, if you want. Please . . . we need to get back. The Seal . . .'

The huge man gave out a low moan. 'So it has happened at last. They broke the Seal.'

'It was broken from the surface, by the Empress of the Wasps,' Che told him, but of course he had no idea who he meant, or what Empire that was. 'She has released the Worm,' she pressed on. 'She will ally with them, make use of them. She must be stopped.'

'One does not *ally* with the Worm.'

'She will,' Che insisted.

Another vast sigh from Orothellin. 'The Worm does not nego-tiate or deal. It cannot. It has only one goal: for there to be nothing in existence but the Worm. All you see here, all those poor wretches in Cold Well, they are kept solely because their toil and their tax make them more useful to the Worm than their deaths would, but in the end all will be the Worm. That is what the Worm wants. And if the Worm can breach the surface, then perhaps it will not need any of this down here, not for much longer.'

'Then we must stop it – but from up *there*,' Che insisted, hearing the ragged sound of her own voice. 'Please, you have magic. Can you send us out?'

'If he could do that, do you think he'd still be here?' Thalric demanded sharply.

'Perhaps I could have left here a long time ago,' the massive man mused, almost to himself. 'I had power then, but it has bled away over the ages while I have hidden away here. I have a bare shadow of it left, now: so little that my kin would weep.' He shook his head slowly, even that motion seeming to tire him. 'If I could only sleep a little, then perhaps some might be saved up again, and I might accomplish something. But the Worm hunts me always. I have not slept in so very long.'

'How long?' Che asked, voice hushed.

He met her eyes, and she had to fight to hold that weighty ancient gaze.

'I don't think I have slept in a thousand years,' he whispered.

'Excuse me, sieur,' Maure put in. 'I am a magician of some small skill, back in our home. Here . . . I cannot find any strength here.' Her hands were clasped together, wringing and twisting. 'There is nothing . . . even in the great cities of the Apt it was not such a desert as this. But you . . . you hid us. That was not Art nor skill; that was magic.'

Orothellin smiled slightly. 'I am pleased you think so. It was almost the last of my poor marshalled strength. I have that little only because the Worm does not know me. I have evaded its notice for all the time I have been down here. If it turned its gaze on me, I would be as helpless as you. More so: you at least could run.'

'Then there's nothing . . .?' The halfbreed magician trembled, staring at the man's sloping bulk as though she was starving.

'Ah, little one, I am sorry.' He took her hands, losing them entirely within his vast, gentle grip. 'I have no gifts any more. A thousand waking years, what could there be?'

Che saw the woman twitch, eyes wide. The power that leapt between them was a mere spark with no tinder to goad into a blaze, but for Maure it must be water in the desert.

'I am sorry,' the big man repeated. Maure was weeping, though, holding her hands to her face to shelter that tiny mote of strength Orothellin had given her.

The big man turned his sorrowful gaze on the others. 'You see, it is useless,' he murmured. 'I'm all used up. I can't get out, and I can't get you out. I can barely keep the Worm away for a few moments, perhaps not even that any more.'

'Yet the Worms get out,' Thalric objected. 'Why not us?'

'The Worm.' Orothellin made a curious stress of the singular. 'Can you walk the Worm's path? The Worm has ways, but they are its own ways. My poor children,' he said softly, 'to find yourselves in this place. Can it be done? I cannot think it, but I can't know, can I? The Seal has always held until now, no ray of hope in this place, no sun or moon. But perhaps you are right. Perhaps the boundaries between the New World and the Old are crumbling as we speak. Bring Messel back. Let me speak to him.'

Esmail, who had sat silent and unreadable throughout, went out to fetch the blind man, and Che leant closer to Orothellin, glancing sidelong at Thalric, whose expression was still one of fierce suspicion.

'When the Seal . . . when it happened, why did you stay?'

Orothellin raised his eyebrows, as though he could not quite remember. 'In all conscience, I stayed – we stayed, my country-folk and I – because we were responsible for this place and the doom of all who were trapped here. Many of my people escaped at the start, while they still had strength. Of those who stayed, all the others have been found and killed. To my knowledge, I am the last.'

'But Argastos made the Seal,' Che argued.

'His idea,' the great man said, 'but we all agreed, my people included. We are all responsible for this place. We – I – had hoped that I might help. I am dearly afraid that I have not been of much help to anyone, until now.' For a moment he stared desolately into space, then: 'I see how it may be done.' It was as though he were divining, not by the ragged ends of his magic, but simply by thinking through each possibility, over and over. Messel had returned by then, to be greeted with: 'You must be her guide.'

'Not just *her*,' Tynisa said instantly, but Orothellin held up a broad hand.

'One alone might escape their notice. Messel, the Turning Spire, you know it? It overlooks . . .'

'Their city,' the blind man finished grimly. 'If they catch us there, we will have nowhere to go.'

'But she will *see*. Will you go, Messel?'

Che could read the blind man's agitation, eyes or no, but at last he nodded. 'Yes, Teacher.'

'The rest of you . . . here is shelter, warmth, some food.' A nameless expression crossed Orothellin's haggard face. 'And if you would keep watch, then perhaps I might sleep for even a day, an hour . . . it has been so long.'

After Che had gone off with Messel, Tynisa was left with the others, standing guard over the great bulk of Orothellin who lay sprawled at the back of the cave. The man had gone down like something punctured, sagging in collapsing folds until his massive frame was stretched out in sleep, his breathing slow but ragged.

Thalric wanted a fire but, without Messel or anyone from this otherworld to advise them, the others refused. Besides, what had they to burn? Nobody much fancied trekking out into the abyss to gather fungi and lichen, or going tapping the rocks in the hope of striking coal. So they huddled there in the cave and listened out for movement in the chasm of the world beyond, their only lights the distant false stars, and the darkness so absolute that Tynisa was scarcely better off than Thalric himself. Only Maure's heritage gave her good enough eyes to pierce it.

Esmail spoke first, waiting until Orothellin seemed to have fully embraced his long-denied slumber.

'You put great faith in her.' He spoke softly so that any scuffling or displaced stone from beyond would still be heard.

'Of course we do,' Tynisa said defensively. 'Che . . .' And then she paused.

'Now you're trying to remember just when it was you started to put any faith in her at all,' Thalric remarked drily.

'No!' Tynisa insisted, and then conceded, 'Well . . . yes. I grew up with her, we were like sisters. She was always wanting to do things she was no good at. She wanted to be like me. And she was constantly taking things the wrong way, or offending people without meaning to, tripping over her own feet, coming up with big ideas that everyone else could see were foolishness. When exactly did we start listening to everything she said?'

'Khanaphes,' Thalric said firmly. '*His* people's place. Orothellin's, I mean. You weren't there to see what I saw.' His voice shook a little, and Tynisa caught herself thinking, *And when did you start to doubt yourself, Rekef man?*

'The thing is,' Thalric went on, 'she changed. I didn't realize it at the time, but I was watching her at the very point as she . . . grew up.' At Tynisa's derisive snort he added defensively, 'I don't mean it like that. I mean like . . . larva to insect. She was growing, right then. I saw her become something new, and suddenly it wasn't me rescuing her but me following her. By the time she found you in the Commonweal, she was almost there.'

'Almost,' Maure said quietly. When she had first met Che, the Beetle girl had been under attack by the Empress, trapped inside her own mind. 'I don't think she's changed like that. I think she's still making things up day to day, like the rest of us. It's just that you've finally learned to listen to her.'

'Typical Inapt nonsense,' Thalric mocked. 'All light and flowers.'

'Oh, if you believe that, Thalric, then you know very little about the Inapt world indeed,' the magician chided him, and Esmail made a curious noise that Tynisa realized was actually something close to a laugh.

'Still,' she put in, 'we're following her now, though.'

'Only because she's the only one who can *see*.' Thalric's humour sounded forced. It died on his lips, then he came out with, 'I wish I'd stayed in the Empire.'

'I wish you'd stayed in the Empire, too,' Tynisa responded automatically. There was a pause that could have gone either way. 'But you don't actually mean that,' she added.

'Don't tell me what I mean.'

'Do you?'

'No, no I don't.' A shuddering sigh. 'But I do need her to get us out of here. I don't care how she does it. I don't need to understand. But I need it to happen. There's only so much of this darkness a man can take.'

Messel led her, in fits and starts, across an increasingly uneven rockfield that seemed as if some great impact had broken it up into tilted slabs. The man was plainly reluctant even to be there, flinching at nothing, disappearing into crevices at sounds or vibrations that Che could not detect, sometimes staying still for minute after minute, while she crouched beside him. She held her patience in check, aware that he was born to a world of darkness that even her eyes could not penetrate, and that they were travelling in his domain.

She tried twice to ask questions, but both times he virtually thrust his hands in her face to stifle the sound.

At last they stopped, and she looked about them, seeing nothing that she would call a landmark. Had they arrived? She realized that they had not. Instead they were merely resting, the two of them tucked under an overhang after evicting a nest of pallid crickets, their antennae longer than their bodies, who went tapping their way off through the rocks in search of another hiding place.

Watching them go, elongated feelers exploring a world of touch, she recognized the origin of Messel's kinden's sightless Art.

She slept poorly, cold and cramped, and they travelled on soon after, with her guide becoming more and more erratic. She wanted to ask him what he owed the 'Teacher', that he should expose himself to such fear. What was it that Orothellin *taught*?

She remembered Messel at Cold Well, a firm believer in a world beyond, a world that he could never see. Orothellin taught *hope*. He taught the legend of an Old World he could barely remember.

And at last she spotted what must be the Turning Spire. It was a spear of rock stabbing hundreds of feet towards the unseen ceiling, formed with an irregular spiral twist to it. Seeing it, she understood what Messel had meant. If they were caught at its top, with the Worm scaling it after them, then where could they escape to?

She put her hand on his shoulder, feeling him tremble.

'I see it,' she told him. 'From here I go alone. Wait here, and I'll come back to you.' She saw his thin lips move, and she hurried on with, 'I know what Orothellin said, but this is what *I* say. You've done enough.'

'Thank you,' he said eventually. 'The seat of the Worm is beyond the spire. I cannot know what your eyes may see from the top, but you will see it all.'

She wondered what he made of it when she took wing. Could his senses follow her through the air, or did she vanish for him, utterly gone beyond his ability to imagine?

The spire was high, and she was no strong flier, so she let her wings take her to a midpoint, where she clung to the twisted side of it and rested a little before casting herself further upwards. She guessed that few enough of the prisoner kinden here could fly – only the Moths, perhaps. The air must be a barren void empty of life.

During her second rest she saw that this assumption was not true. She saw enough to make her regret her boldness.

There was a moth, far bigger than she, thundering gamely through the air on whatever unguessable errand its small mind had fixed on. Clutching at the stone of the spire, she tracked its progress through the dark expanse. *Large enough to ride, surely,* she thought, and wondered that the locals had not enlisted these creatures already, or perhaps they had and she had just seen no sign of it . . .

Then the moth dropped from the air ten yards before catching itself, weaving madly back and forth so that she could see the desperation in its every movement.

When the great shadow came from above and scooped the insect up and away, she was caught rigid and horrified at even that brief glimpse. Something horrific, something unnatural, a great pale thing with silent wings that looked almost like webbed hands.

It was a long time before she dared ascend further and, when she did, she climbed more than she flew. *If this place were not terrible enough, there are monsters of the air as well,* and with that thought she looked up to find herself near the top of the spire, almost approaching the stars.

She had momentarily forgotten them, those ersatz constellations. The Art that let her see needed no light, and so she saw no light. Where the naked eye saw that glittering array, eerie and almost beautiful, her sight saw the truth: the gleaming threads, the hungry larvae, the drained moth corpses hanging distantly like dead leaves. There was no escape above.

And had they always been there in the Worm's realm, or was this some twist of the Moth ritual, to make their prison even worse? She had a sudden desperate need to be out of here, back to somewhere where her newfound magic was worth something, to some place less inimical to life.

Then she had reached the summit, a bare ten feet below the lowest of those sparkling, murderous threads, and she finally beheld the city of the Worm.

Twelve

Bells sounded across Chasme an hour before dawn, startling hundreds of pirates, mercenaries, tinkers and whores from their beds. Nobody had heard anything like it: the alarm system had been installed by the city's new masters but never needed before now.

Totho found Drephos standing at his high balcony, staring out to sea. All was darkness out there, barely even a moon, but the master artificer had the eyes of a Moth-kinden. Back in Imperial service he had made a practice of walking right up to the walls of besieged fortresses on moonless nights, just to get a personal look at them.

'What's coming?' Totho demanded of him.

'A fleet. At least three score ships of various sizes, with airships as well, and . . .' A hand was lifted for quiet, and they both heard the droning buzz of flying machines.

'I've all our people armed and ready: machines to go into the air and the artillery crewed,' Totho reported. 'But . . .'

He did not need to say it. The Iron Glove had all the technological marvels of the age, and its artificers and labourers could all don a breastplate and hit a target with a snapbow, but they were few. There was no army on the Glove's payroll.

'I have sent some chests of coin into the city. Those who will stand and fight will be wealthy men, if they survive,' Drephos said.

'Tell me,' Totho pressed him.

The Colonel-Auxillian's head snapped round. It was plain he knew what Totho meant, but he said nothing.

'Why won't you give them the Bee-killer?'

'You think *this* is about the Bee-killer? You think they have roused the entire Exalsee against us for that? Have you learned nothing from history, that you think everything must have such simple causes?'

'Tell me,' Totho insisted.

'I have made a mistake,' Drephos said softly. 'Should I have given them all they wanted? Should I have whored our last secrets, spread our legs that final span? Or would they still have come calling with their rank badge and their invitations. Do you think that they would have been happy, in the end, if I remained outside their reach?'

'Tell me!' Totho repeated, and at that moment the first of the Iron Glove greatshotters loosed into the darkness, the range to their targets calculated. The thunder rolled out across the lake, but Totho knew the weapons were not meant to take on moving targets like boats.

'I did not want it to be my legacy, that is all,' said Drephos quietly, so that Totho had to read the words forming on his lips as more engines roared and boomed, brief flashes lighting up the shanties and chimneys of Chasme. 'It was all they spoke of, after Szar: the Bee-killer, the city-slayer, the weapon of all weapons. And it was a failure, inelegant, hard to control, easy to suborn. A bludgeon, not a blade. And it was not even *mine*. The Twins, those Beetles of mine, devised it, and my own input was solely the method of delivery, and even that was never *used*. You just piled up the canisters and set them off, like any common soldier might. So many wonderful things I have created – *we* have created: the ratiocinators, the new alloys, the similophone, and they would cast me in the histories as some demented alchemist.'

The fliers were launching, powering off into the pre-dawn sky. The Iron Glove had a small stable of elegant combat orthopters, and there were plenty of mercenary pilots in the city who would fight for their home – up to a point. Against them would be Imperial Spearflights, and perhaps some of the new Farsphex.

And whatever Solarno itself can launch. The city had its own pilots and machines, even if its formal air force had been destroyed in the joint Imperial–Spider invasion. Totho had heard plenty of rumours of unrest amongst the Solarnese, chafing under two yokes. If there was one issue on which they would see eye to eye with their conquerors, though, it would be Chasme.

It was still too dark to make out much, but he thought he spotted shapes out on the water. Then there were flashes answering the Iron Glove artillery, small shipboard weapons throwing explosives and scrapshot at the docks. There seemed to be precious few ships at anchor there, and Totho suspected that many had already fled rather than become an unwilling first line of defence.

'What should we do?' he asked. Chasme had no walls – it was a straggling mess of a place, constructed piecemeal and slipshod, half out over the water, utterly indefensible. The Iron Glove's own stronghold could be barred against attackers but the place was a factory complex, not a fortress. It had a dozen weak points and far too few defenders.

'Arm yourself,' Drephos told him. 'I see mercenary companies in place to defend the wharves, and our artillery will have more success against their vessels once they have come to rest. The air battle remains open.' His eyes flashed defiance. 'And we have some more toys to call on, which they have not guessed at. Arm yourself and take command of our forces. I myself shall look to the engines.'

Totho had not worn this armour for some time, but he remembered how to don it with a minimum of help. It was black and all-encompassing, its plates fluted and angled to turn away shot and blow. He took up his snapbow and strapped on a belt of little grenades, small enough to throw a fair distance, but with enough power to them to punch in the side of an automotive if he got his aim right.

With the helm on, the visible world would shrink to a narrow slot, so for the moment he left it dangling at his belt as he set out from the Iron Glove complex with a score of his followers. Their own mail was somewhat less than his: helm and breastplate of black steel over chain links so small that they flowed like water. They were veterans of a score of small actions defending the assets of the Iron Glove, and they carried repeater snapbows of Totho's own design, an expensive luxury that had never been viable for mass export. *Some toys we keep just for ourselves.*

Parts of Chasme were on fire; that was what first greeted his eyes. Flames roared and leapt across a broad swathe of the docks: ships and piers and the clustered shacks there all ablaze, constricting the possible progress of the attackers.

Fly-kinden messengers sought him out, dodging and swerving through the air. After a handful of reports, he had a picture in his mind of how the fight was going. The Exalsee forces had forced beachheads at three points, with the superior aerial might of the Empire driving the defenders from cover. Two of these were locked in bloody stalemate even now, the mercenaries – and the outraged Chasme locals – preventing the attackers from pressing further in. There was a solid central thrust that had broken through the cordon and was working its way towards the Iron Glove; it seemed to be mostly made up of Wasp Airborne and Bee-kinden heavy snapbowmen under the drab banner of Dirovashni.

He gave orders with an artificer's economy, drawing together all the forces that could be spared and setting out exactly where they should position themselves. The men at his back, his picked few, would be the anvil to meet the attackers' hammer. *We have more tricks yet.*

Denied targets, the artillery was mostly still now, but the orthopter battle raged on – the sort of war the Exalsee best understood. There would be dozens of Chasme and Solarnese pilots up there who were old enemies, duelling not for anybody else's grand plan but to resolve their own bitter grudges.

Already there was fighting close by, so he led his people to cover, having them spread out as a rabble of mercenaries was pushed back on his left flank. He saw the Dirovashni snapbowmen advancing in professional order; the Bee city had always been a third player around the Exalsee, never quite matching the inventiveness of Solarno or Chasme, but they were solid warriors, that was plain.

Let's make some holes in them, see how solid they really are. Totho braced his snapbow against his shoulder, because these models tended to jolt a little. He had a magazine in place, and spread a dozen bolts across the face of the Bee-kinden advance with a single touch of the trigger. His own mail might have turned the shot, but the steel of Dirovashni was not equal to the task; a handful of the Bees dropped before they even realized what was happening. Then Totho's people were following suit with their repeating weapons, each of them worth a squad of regular soldiers at twice the range, and Totho watched the Bee advance shudder and disintegrate as the attackers rushed for cover.

He let off another spray of shot, hitting little but keeping the enemy at bay, hoping that there were other eyes watching the flanks, because an encirclement was all the Bees could really try at this stage.

The Wasp Airborne tried attacking them shortly after, but Totho and his people were dug in, and their snapbows were more than equal to the task of picking off soldiers in flight. Again the enemy fell back, and those Bees who had tried to take advantage of the distraction were made to regret it in short order. Totho had not lost a soldier of his command.

He recalled leading the defence in Khanaphes, matching modern snapbows against the ignorant ferocity of the Many of Nem. Now his enemies came against him with snapbows, and he was teaching them the same artificer's lesson.

An automotive would be problematic at this point. It was a detached thought, as though this was some classroom problem of military theory. But, of course, the enemy had not brought automotives.

Is this it, then? Can we hold them here until they run out of will, or bodies?

Then a Fly-kinden was scuttling up to him from behind, one arm bloody.

'The complex is under attack! You have to pull back!'

Totho stared at her. *But we're winning . . .* 'Attack from who?'

'Wasp Airborne, and there are Dragonflies as well,' she got out. 'And more on the way. The city's wide open on your right – they've all run away there, the lot of them.'

Mercenaries, of course. And if he had two hundred of these repeaters rather than twenty, then he could have held off the entire Exalsee, but . . .

'Get everyone to fall back to the complex, double time,' he agreed. 'We're still in the fight.'

The gates of the complex were open only long enough for Totho and his followers to get through them, but the skies overhead were already busy. Squads of the Airborne were dropping down wherever there was space, while overhead swooped great dragon-flies, the battle-mounts of Princep Exilla, whose warriors would not be far behind.

The Iron Glove forces pulled back in good order, their superior weapons accounting for any attempt the enemy made to engage them in close fighting. The compound itself was indefensible, though – too many buildings, too scattered. Totho spent precious minutes seeking word of Drephos before the order came: *Fall back to the main workshops.*

That was the centre of their power, where they lived and slept and worked. Neither he nor Drephos had intended to make a stand there, but the walls were strong enough to contain explosions, the windows few and much of the Glove's artillery was mounted there.

Even as he was giving his orders, those weapons spoke almost in unison, the shudder of their recoil resounding through the air and the ground simultaneously.

Beyond the walls of the compound, whole sections of Chasme erupted into incandescence, and Totho could only stare, even as his own people ran for the shelter of the workshops. Their own city. Drephos had unleashed their artillery on their own city.

But it isn't our city now. Even so, he took to his heels to go and find the Colonel-Auxillian, to talk to him, to dissuade him, to . . . Totho did not know what he intended to do.

There were Wasps ahead of him as he came within sight of the main door, but snapbowmen stationed at each window and balcony were stripping them away even as Totho approached, running full-tilt in the perfectly balanced weight of his mail. He loosed a scattering of bolts with his own weapon, tearing down a pair of the Airborne as the men tried to lift off. Then he was inside with the door slamming shut behind him.

'Drephos, where is he?' And, of course, the master artificer was at the top level, directing the bombardment. Where else would he be?

Every step of the way up, Totho was rehearsing his arguments, thinking of the streets of Chasme in flames, the hundreds who eked out their existence there, the senseless waste of human life. Bursting in upon Drephos, half out of breath, finding the man giving his cool, clipped orders to the artillery crews via a speaking tube, Totho's mind reeled and he realized he was wrong.

Drephos looked back at him, and Totho saw the other man waiting for his objections, but instead he just walked over to stand by the Colonel-Auxillian's side.

'This is the end, is it?' he asked, as another salvo of incendiaries fell on Chasme, rooting out the invading soldiers that had tried to use their own streets as cover.

'We have a few tricks left, you and I,' Drephos replied. He was strung taut as a wire, but at least some of the energy now animating him was exhilaration. It had clearly been too long since he had been given free rein with his machines.

A word from him, and the sky around the workshops crackled with lightning, the generators below giving up their stored power like a sacrifice. Totho saw the briefly writhing forms of men and insects who had got too close, saw them char and fall. This weapon was the very latest addition to their arsenal, based on accounts of Collegiate air defence.

The attackers were within the compound in force now. Totho saw Imperials and Spiderlands troops and the motley rabble of the Exalsee, all jockeying to get to where the long-reaching artillery could only overshoot them.

All those people. But Totho reached into his heart and felt almost nothing, for Chasme was no town of innocents. There was nobody who chose that place as home who did not live off piracy or the arms trade, or some other manner of vice. It was a wonder the Solarnese had not destroyed the place earlier, before the Iron Glove had made the city too strong to be threatened by the little powers of the Exalsee.

It has taken the might of half the world to break down our doors. An exaggeration, but not much of one.

'Shutter the windows now,' Drephos commanded, and Totho rushed across to haul the lever that slammed the iron covers over each open portal, sealing them in.

'Something new?' he asked.

'Nothing I'm proud of,' Drephos replied. 'Amateur's work. I beg your forgiveness in advance. I'm pressurizing the fuel tanks.'

Totho's mind spun its wheels, imagining the big vats spread around the compound. Yes, you could detonate them, and that would do some damage, but surely not much . . .

'I understand. What's your dispersal method?'

'I had some bolts installed a while ago, when we were waiting on that steel shipment. When the pressure reaches . . .'

Now that the artillery had stopped, there was enough quiet for them to hear the explosive popping sounds, the inner bolts perforating the skin of the fuel tanks, piercing each in a dozen places, the holes so tiny that the viscous oil vented out in a great

132

cloud of black mist. In Totho's mind's eye he saw it: a choking fog that issued from every quarter and covered the entire compound.

Drephos threw him a glance, and his response was automatic: 'Do it.'

Out there, the attackers would be choking and coughing from the stuff, eyes and lungs alike on fire with it. But not *really* on fire. Not until the last of their lightning banks discharged. Not until the whole world outside the workshops was set alight.

Not until now.

Drephos rammed the switch up, summoning that last dreg of crackling power from their glass cells, and Totho watched the edges of the shutters flare orange, then white, until the very metal itself was glowing. The Glove artificers were backing away from the heat of it.

Our enemies have forgotten who they came to kill.

The roaring of the flames died swiftly, leaving distant screams – and pitifully few of those. The mass of troops who had been crowding into the Iron Glove compound had surely been devastated, eliminated as any potential threat to Drephos.

Have we won, then? And what now?

'Open the shutters,' Drephos croaked. Totho opened his mouth to countermand the order, then realized what wretched hypocrisy was moving him. That it had been done, he was glad, but he did not want to see it. He would force himself; he would face what he was.

Half of them would not open, in the end, their metal warped and softened by that sudden flare of heat. What the rest of them revealed was a blasted wasteland, the familiar outlines of the stores and forges and foundries coated black, and everywhere the flash-charred bodies of the dead and dying. The sound was the worst part: that weak chorus of agony and mortality from those still alive, set amidst the many voices of the inanimate – the burning wood, the metal that creaked and cracked as it cooled, the secondary retorts as flammables burst their casks and drums.

'It would have been the perfect time,' Totho heard himself saying, 'to use the Bee-killer, after all.'

Drephos studied him. 'You're right, although I had not thought to hear you say it. I . . . One of the reasons I had kept that weapon from the Empire was that I thought . . .'

'You thought that *I* . . .?'

The Colonel-Auxillian's face was blank, as the mind behind it – whatever its perfect grasp of artifice – wrestled with its less than perfect understanding of people. 'That you would not approve.'

It was a strange moment, to find that there was something in the man beyond that pursuit of efficiency, and that he valued his junior partner enough to tiptoe around his imagined sensibilities. Totho sagged against one wall, feeling as though he should weep, if only the fires without had not scorched away his ability to do so.

One of the other artificers suddenly lifted his head. 'I hear fighting still.'

Even as he announced it, Totho picked out the sounds himself, wondering how some pocket of the enemy could possibly have survived the firestorm outside.

No, not outside. Fighting within the workshops.

He was bringing his snapbow up, hearing the harsh hammer of a nailbow's firepowder charges detonating. The first two Wasps pushing through the doorway took the balance of his magazine, but then it was empty and he was fumbling for a new one as five or six more spilt into the room. Their nailbows were crude and inaccurate compared to the Glove's weaponry, but they were good enough at close quarters, and most of the artificers there were not even armed.

A trail of bolts tore across Totho's chest, knocking him from his feet and almost propelling him out through one of the unshuttered windows. The impact dented his mail but failed to pierce it, the new magazine spinning from his hands across the floor.

He was scrabbling at his belt for a grenade, actually had his hand on it ready to prime it and tear it free, when Gannic came through the door with a snapbow directed straight at Drephos's head. The sly merchant who had visited them before was now almost unrecognizable. The man wore the mail of the Airborne, his scalp stiff with dried blood: a desperate man wild with the need to fulfil his orders.

'And now you stand down,' he spat, taking one careful step after another. Others of his men had their nailbows aimed at Totho where he sat or at the surviving artificers. They all looked ragged and battered: the Iron Glove staff had plainly given them a hard time, even when taken by surprise.

'You forced entry before we closed the shutters,' Drephos observed. 'Or . . . no, before the fighting started.'

Gannic nodded. 'And chose our moment to make our move, too. We had to wait for your apprentice to come back from playing soldier. My orders are to take the pair of you back to the Engineers.'

'For execution?'

'For conscription,' Gannic returned. 'Your head's made of gold dust, Colonel. And don't think I was joking about anything I said before. You could make the next best thing to general if you play along. The whole cost of our taking Chasme could be written off.'

'"Taking" Chasme?' Drephos enquired carefully, his eyes on the slight weaving of the snapbow barrel as he slid a half-step closer to the other man.

'I'm amazed you held out as long as you did. Goes to show that governors make bad battlefield commanders nine times out of ten, and this is no exception . . .' Gannic's words trailed off into a querulous sound as his eyes registered the opened windows and what lay beyond: the charred wreck of the Iron Glove compound, the fires still blazing across much of Chasme, the wrecked boats at the wharves. Less the city of Chasme now than its broken corpse. 'What did you do?' the Imperial whispered, eyes wide.

'We defended ourselves with whatever tools were available,' Drephos declared. He had moved a little closer now, and Totho saw some of the Wasps notice, but Gannic himself was still staring at the utter desolation outside.

'What did you do?' he repeated. 'The attack . . .'

'Has been repelled,' Drephos said calmly. 'Totho thought we should have used the Bee-killer instead. On reflection, I believe it would have been more elegant.'

At last Gannic's eyes returned to him. 'You had it all along, then.'

'Oh, yes.' For a moment Drephos was looking at Totho, an understanding passing between them. 'I imagine you'll want to take it to show your masters.'

'At the very least,' Gannic told him hoarsely. 'We're going to need to show them as much as possible, to explain this mess.'

'Our cellar here has a strongbox that you will find easily enough. The formula is within, along with various other plans. At least they will see some use, I suppose.'

'That's more like it—' Gannic began, and Drephos closed the final distance between them and got his metal hand about the snapbow barrel.

Had Gannic simply pulled the trigger, it would have ended there, but he tried to tug the weapon free, and Drephos's mechanical grip crushed the steel tube into a clenched mess.

Totho twisted the release catch of a grenade, feeling the priming cord whip free as he tore it from his belt. He counted two seconds – during which the first nailbowman was already shooting – and cast the little faceted shape past the Wasps towards the far wall.

The blast seared through the room, knocking most of the Wasps off their feet, with the edged shrapnel cutting the nearest two apart, and then Totho was lunging for Drephos and Gannic.

The two of them had been blown over by the blast. The Imperial had a sword out, and Drephos had lunged for his throat but caught only the collar of his armour. Gannic slammed the sword down with a yell of rage, and Totho saw the master artificer's delicate elbow joint shatter.

A spray of nailbow bolts pounded him as he cast himself across the floor, reaching for Gannic. The sword came down again, striking the same point with mechanical precision and smashing the joint entirely, so that Drephos rolled free and staggered to his feet.

'The window!' Totho yelled, because, although Drephos was a poor flier, at least his Art gave him wings.

Gannic was in his way, but Totho backhanded the man and was already reaching for another magazine, trying to locate the Wasps who were still shooting. Then Drephos's remaining hand had hooked Totho's arm, hauling him away, the enemy shot impacting around them, striking stone chips from the walls and scoring lines in Totho's armour.

They tumbled backwards out of the window, and fell, Drephos's wings fluttering and flickering as he tried to slow their joint descent. Even so, they hit the ground hard, Totho ending up on his knees with the Colonel-Auxillian laid out beside him.

Realizing they would be within sight of the window still, Totho snapped, 'Come on,' hauling on the other man's good arm. This distance was a long shot for a nailbow's accuracy but, after what the Glove had done here today, the Wasps were probably due some luck.

Drephos lurched to his feet, then sagged against Totho, hissing. Dark stains were spreading across his robe. After two steps he collapsed again, shaking, hunched about his wounds.

'Come on!' Totho was no surgeon, and Drephos was such a piecemeal thing anyway that he would not have known where to start. 'Come on, we've beaten them. We've escaped.'

'Nailbows,' Drephos spat – and he spat blood too, his lips shiny with it. 'Totho . . .'

'I'll get them,' his apprentice promised fiercely. 'I'll kill Gannic. I'll kill them all, the bastards. I'll kill the Empress. I don't care if it kills me, but I'll tear the pissing Empire apart.'

'Totho.' Drephos's hand scrabbled at his breastplate. 'No, Totho. Live.'

Perhaps there was more: live and work, live and build, a whole plan of artifice rooted in Totho's continued survival. If so, it would be lost to posterity. The focus of Drephos's pale eyes slid off Totho's face and into infinity, and he was gone.

Back in Solarno, Colonel Varsec would not even look at Gannic while the lieutenant gave his report.

Chasme destroyed, the Colonel-Auxillian dead. Was that a victory for the Engineers? Did the removal of the competition make up for the loss to the world of artifice? What reception would Varsec meet when he returned to Capitas with that news?

If not for one thing, Gannic reckoned that Varsec would simply have not gone home, instead thrown in his lot with the Spiders, fled across the Exalsee, or who knew what? Except that, in the charred fortress of the Iron Glove, Gannic had found the strongbox, as promised. Until he had located it, he had not truly believed it existed. Inside had been a scroll bearing a surprisingly simple chemical formula. Apparently Drephos had, this one time, not trusted to his ability to invent a thing at need.

The Bee-killer. With luck, it would buy Varsec a safe return home, just enough of a success to make up for the whole wasteful venture: the last secret of the Iron Glove.

Thirteen

It was vast, what she saw. If the chasm of Cold Well had been like a wound in the earth, this was a body in advanced decay, the substrate not mined out but genuinely eaten away as though the mere presence of the Worm was corrosive and even the stone could not bear its touch.

A slope-sided pit hundreds of yards across, declining shallowly but inexorably towards a busy centre – that was what she saw. She thought of ant lions more than centipedes, on viewing it, but the scale was immense, city-sized. And it was a city of sorts. There were buildings there – crude slab-sided constructions that might have been barracks or civic offices or warehouses, or nothing of the sort. They were not packed together like the homes of Collegium or Helleron, though, and much of the Worm's city was open ground that was riddled with pits and openings, so that she knew there must be far more than she was seeing, beneath the surface.

There was much movement but no sign of Apt industry, and of course no feel of magic came to her. Seeing all that scurrying activity without either artifice or ritual brought back the gnawing sense of wrongness she had known when looking upon the soldiers of the Worm themselves. What it did *not* remind her of was an ant's nest, nor yet an Ant city-state. The linking that the Antkinden shared allowed them to act together, in concert – to build great things, to have their ordered and tidy society – but they were individuals beneath it. Even watching the insects that the Ants drew their art from, she could have discerned individual effort and initiative, each ant contributing to the nest's well-being through its best judgment. Not so here, though. Ants would have wept to witness such coordination, but not for joy. The entire city moved like the coils of a single living thing, and so much of it about a business that she could not understand; it looked as though simple coursing, in their lines, from place to place was an end in itself for whatever mind directed the Worm.

She watched a caravan approach, no doubt bearing produce from some place like Cold Well: food, metals, crafted goods, plus the terrible tax that the Worm exacted on its slaves. Huge millipedes, burdened along every segment, hauled the goods, and she saw big men and women, large as Mole Crickets but of a different kinden, guiding the beasts' progress. Then they were unloading outside the city, strings of the Worm's people issuing out to take the load and carry it back in. She heard a shrill and distant squalling and saw how some of that load consisted of cages, and she knew that the same tax had been levied on some other luckless place.

And is that the meat the Worm feeds on? It could not be, though, for there were thousands of the Worm thronging the city below. They would have consumed all the future generations of their slaves long ago if it had been mere sustenance they sought. *Then what . . .?*

Like so much else about the Worm, Che felt that she would far rather be in a position where she would never find out than have to remain in this cursed place. Even as that thought came, she remembered Orothellin, who had stayed: the huge weary man a volunteer in this prison, because to do otherwise would be to leave all the Worm's victims to an unwitnessed fate.

They are not my responsibility. Who can tell me I should bleed for them? A desperate plea, because she wanted out, she so very dearly wanted *out*.

And that was why she was here. The Seal was broken,

and the Worm itself was finding a way out, and so she should look . . .

But her eyes were now following those cages. There were pits, she could see – a ring of round apertures in the rock. Even at this distance, she could just make out the course the Worm took. She could follow the sound of the screams, the sound of the inconsolable forever parted from home and family, and yet too young to comprehend truly. She could watch as they were consigned to whatever fate the Worm reserved for innocence.

They were emptying the cages into those pits. She felt ill with her understanding, thankful only that it was not complete. *What dwells in the pits? What horror is the Worm hiding there? I hope I never know.*

She dragged her eyes away, let them follow the twists and turns of the Worm until she found the midpoint, and there she felt it.

A pulse, a flicker, a touch of magic.

Her heart leapt: *There is a way!* But she was still watching, seeing that vortex of bodies in the lowest point of the city – too far away to distinguish individuals, just the great spiral that all those bodies made up. It seemed they were dancing with a regular ordered step, dancing ever inwards, though, not one of them returning out: a spiral that consumed itself. And she understood.

They were passing beyond this place to the greater world beyond, a raiding party of the Worm. *This* was what she had come to see. Deny it as others might, here they were surely using magic to step beyond – and, if they could, so could she.

Again that brief flare of magic, like a snatch of conversation heard when a distant door is opened. What was it that the Worm was doing? How was it summoning up power in this powerless place?

The spiral was devouring itself at a regular pace. Soon they would all be gone, escaping into the place that she had been banished from, that world of magic that was already seeming like a memory.

With that thought, she understood it: the Worm was not using magic. Whatever they were doing to slip past the jagged edges of the Seal was nothing she herself could comprehend. What she sensed now was the world beyond, the very magic she had been cut off from. As each segment of the Worm crossed over, as the fabric of their prison twisted and stretched to let them through, there was a tiny window opened, letting in a breath of air that had known the sun and open sky.

She could not open that way, even if she could have fought her way through all the Worm to get there. Indeed, she had no reason to believe that the centre of the city here was special, rather than simply convenient for the Worm. She could no more do what they did than she could operate an automotive.

But, with magic, I could find my own way. I could construct a ritual out of whole cloth and cut my way to the sun.

And if I had an army I could put the lot of them to the sword, but I have neither.

But the thought nagged at her, and there was still that regular breath of magic from the Worm's progress, and at last she reached out to it.

So little, so little, but now she had nothing at all and so even a stray thread was something, and she unravelled and unravelled, tugging and tugging, harvesting scrap after scrap from the table of her enemies, marvelling that they could not know what she was doing.

They had no sense for magic, of course. They were as blind to her theft as Messel would be to a heliograph signal, but they had detected her already by some means. When a faint scuffling sound made her look down, there they were, the Worm. A score or so of them were scuttling rapidly up the side of the Turning Spire, Art guiding their hands and feet swiftly and surely. They were no more than twenty feet below her when she heard them.

She cried out, and her instinct was to reach for her magic but, as soon as she saw them, it was gone, her mind losing the ability to unlock the power she had been scraping together. For a moment she just stumbled about atop the Spire as the creatures closed on her, but then at last she remembered her Art, and cast herself up and away into the stone-edged void.

They reached the top behind her, where she saw them scurry around as though still looking for her. Then one or two had slings out, stones whipping through the air towards her, but she herself kept high and put distance between them, leaving the Worm behind.

Too close. But she had stolen a little strength from the rift the Worm was feeding itself through, and she had a plan, if only Orothellin would help, and . . .

A sensation went through her, as though some great retort had sounded and resonated in every part of her except her ears. She faltered in her flight, some instinct checking her wings for a second, so that when the monster swooped past her, she was outside the sweep of its claws and sent tumbling away through the air.

She fought for control – seeing a wheeling glimpse of those great wings of skin, the horrible almost-human face of the monster – but she had never been a skilled flier. Again that thundering vibration coursed through her, making her feel sick and weak.

She saw it plainly as it came in, vast fingered wings spread wide, feet like taloned hands webbed together to form a net to catch her. Its mouth was filled with needle-sharp fangs.

She sought for height, climbing and climbing, but the monster adjusted its heading without effort and was upon her in seconds. Remembering training older than her piecemeal dealings with magic, one hand found her sword hilt and dragged the blade out even as the monster scooped her out of the air with its hook-clawed feet.

Those jaws were her whole world, a beast more horrific than anything she could have imagined – all the worse because it seemed to be some distant, distorted cousin of the human form. *Is this a kinden? Is that even possible?*

Then she had stabbed up with all her might, her blade gashing the creature across its lips and wildly flaring nostrils, bloodying its gums. It jerked its head away without letting her go, twitching upwards in the air.

A moment later it went berserk, wings flapping and twisting madly, spinning without falling, and she realized it had gone too high. The threads of the ceiling-dwellers, the star-mimics, had caught it.

She had a brief glimpse of them sliding down along their threads, unhurriedly, mandibles questing towards this chance meal. Horrible, yes, but they at least seemed more wholesome than the thing that had taken her,

She was now off the creature's mind, which was entirely focused on its own survival, and so she let herself fall from its claws, her wings catching her, bringing her down gently as she looked up at the struggle above.

Seeing it at this distance, diminished almost to a manageable size, she recognized it at last. *Surely not . . .* In Collegium they kept little furry flying pets that must be looked after at all times to keep them from falling prey to wasps or dragonflies. She had once named a duelling team after them.

No flying insects here, save for the moths, she reflected as she dropped. *How lucky we are, in the world beyond.*

It took her some time to locate Messel, to pick out landmarks from the broken terrain, and then of course there was the long trek back to Orothellin. But she had a plan now. She had a little power that she was husbanding, holding deep within her, away from the rigours of this place. There was a way.

'It must be done now,' Che explained. 'This place is just a bottom-less pit for the Worm's power to fall into, I know that now, and it will do the same to all of us. What little I have scraped together will evaporate soon. The Moths built this place well – save that they must have driven the Worm to find some source of strength other than magic.'

'Very true,' Orothellin confirmed mournfully. He seemed visibly younger after the rest that Che's friends had granted him, and she dared to hope that he had somehow regenerated power of his own. After all, he had lived here so *long*, and he could still deflect the senses of the Worm to hide himself.

'Will you help me?' she asked him. 'A ritual to breach this place for just a moment? With the Seal cracked through, and with our combined strength, it may be possible – just for the moment it takes for us to step out.'

'This is not what the Worm does.'

'But it will give the same result. What the Worm showed me was that it is *possible*.'

Che looked about at her friends: Tynisa and Thalric plainly willing to trust her and follow her wherever she went; Esmail suspicious; Maure sunk in misery, her arms clasped about herself. 'I have no other plan, and I cannot do it alone.'

Orothellin sighed. 'I am sorry,' he murmured, and for a plunging moment Che thought he was speaking to her, that he would deny her, or deny that the venture could ever succeed.

But it was Messel who shrugged awkwardly, and Che looked between them, uncertain what was being apologized for.

Then Orothellin said, 'Let us at least make the attempt.' And she forgot about everything else.

'Maure, you're a better ritualist than I am,' she directed. 'Let's give ourselves the best chance. What have you got?'

They made a fire, and Maure set out her candles and her herbs, emptying her pack of all the paraphernalia her trade made use of. She drew symbols in chalk on the rock floor of their cave, descendants of the ancient glyphs of Khanaphes, as passed down from mentor to apprentice over the centuries, their true meaning lost.

Save to Orothellin, of course, who studied them curiously, altering each one minutely when he thought Maure was not looking.

'This will not work, of course,' he whispered to Che, whilst Maure continued working herself into a frenzy of preparation.

'Is she . . .?'

'She prepares as well as anyone can, but we do not have the strength,' he told her sadly. 'That little you have come back with is nothing, while I have next to nothing – the last dregs of my craft from a thousand years ago, all this place has left me with.'

'We have to try.'

He shrugged massively. 'I suppose you do.'

'Ready!' Maure turned, hands clasped before her. Her eyes were mutely pleading, *Please let this work. Please let us get out of here.*

'Form a circle,' Che advised. 'Just . . . kneel down and keep quiet. Unless there's anything you can give . . .?' She cocked an eyebrow at Esmail, who shrugged.

'Come on, then.' She took Thalric's hand in her left, feeling the rough calluses there. He was an Apt man in the circle of a ritual, an utter dead weight, but she would bring him out of this place; she would bring them all out. And then let the Worm beware. She would find some way of locking them back in their tomb – of recreating the Seal that had formerly banished them.

Orothellin sat down across the circle heavily. He took Maure's and Esmail's hands as Che took Tynisa's in her right, the circle joining link by link.

The Slug-kinden, the former Master of Khanaphes, looked over his shoulder at Messel lurking unhappily at the back. 'Never fear,' Che heard the big man murmur. 'I will be here still. I'm not going anywhere.'

Che felt her mind enclosed in the shell that was the Worm's prison, the curved-away world that the Moths' great ritual had made of their underground fastness. She felt as though she was scrabbling at its inner surface, unable to gain purchase on it when she needed to rip and tear her way out. Still, she had some strength to spend now, if she could but muster it. Then perhaps, just perhaps . . .

Maure opened to her: the halfbreed woman had a thimble of power she had somehow hung on to in the face of the Worm, and it came now to Che across the bridge of clasped hands. Within it was that spark she had gained from Orothellin, given to Che guilelessly, desperately. Esmail, too – a weak magician but one whose power was only ever used on himself, and less amenable to being siphoned away. He gave to her willingly, to her surprise. It was the first time she had had any real sense of him as a person since their banishment, feeling the economic strength of purpose that moved him, willing to do whatever it took to get home. From Thalric, nothing, of course. From Tynisa, some wretched thread, but Che's sister had no training, no way to make real use of what little magic she had: the magic of her sword and her badge.

From Orothellin . . . she sensed a great reluctance there, a man who had been holding on to his strength for so long. But it was more than mere habit. Once he had given this all up to send them on their way, she saw how he would be unable to hide forever. The Worm would catch him, tomorrow or in a hundred days, or a thousand. His long, dragging life would at last be brought to an end.

And more: his charges, his students, those he had exiled himself to help. He was abandoning them in helping Che, turning his back on Messel and all the other slaves of the Worm.

Then why help? Che asked him.

Because what have I accomplished in all that time save be a witness to their losses, the price of living with the Worm? You are right. You, at least, should escape this place.

And he gave her all the power he had, a great tide of it like the river Jamail in flood, eclipsing Maure and Esmail's meagre contributions, and Che took it all in, held it in her mind and opened the gates of her power.

Out. We are getting out right now.

Because this place was not a physical place, and it had no fixed connections to the world beyond, there was no gateway to journey to, no portal to unlock. The exit was everywhere and nowhere. It was wherever someone tore a hole, whether that someone was the Worm using the Worm's ways, or whether it was a desperate Beetle magician.

She shaped her power like a knife in her mind, making the substance of the world around her like taut cloth.

Time and strength enough for one strike.

She felt the hands of all of them on the hilt of the knife, Orothellin's most of all, a thousand years of skill to cut just so.

I want to see the sun, and I will see it.

They struck together, and she felt the walls of the Worm's domain stretch and protest, the ancient Moth ritual that had made it was fighting her, even as the power she expended bled out into the abyss.

More! Drawing on them, leaching their strength, clawing at their very breath, feeling that imaginary knife shake and shudder as its tip grated across the walls of the world. *More!* A desperate plea, ransacking everything she had within her, all that unasked and unearned power that had been thrown on her shoulders by the Darakyon, by the Masters of Khanaphes. *It must be good for something, or what was it all for?*

And it was not enough. They began falling back, all that hard-won strength haemorrhaging into the cold void; Che lunged for something more, and in a moment she found it.

Give! she insisted, and only realized afterwards whom she was demanding this of. For one moment her mind touched her sister's – not Tynisa, whom she had grown up with, but that other sister that fate had thrust upon her. Seda, the Empress, her enemy.

That thin cord still linked them, the bond of their shared throne, the mocking curse of Khanaphes.

And Seda gave. There was little enough that she could force through that tenuous link, but what she could, she gave, and Che felt that knife-point scrape and dig—

And cut.

For a frozen moment she felt the sun just beyond her finger-tips, the world she knew, maddening in its proximity, just out of reach.

No, just *in* reach. She could do it. She could step through, force her bulky frame into the light and air, the Worm just a rancid memory behind her. But only her. In that moment of the possible, there was strength for just one to step through.

She had no time. She had them all there, linked in that circle, their minds as open to her as they could ever be. She was holding the knife. She was the judge and arbiter of what happened next. She would live with the consequences.

In that moment, that split instant, she weighed a great many things on the scales of her life, and she understood Orothellin, and the others, and herself most of all.

Then the knife was slipping, and she had a brief wave of despair and loss, at all the possible futures she was confining herself to, and she made her choice.

Part Two

Tremors

Fourteen

'You obviously left most of your wits behind when you quit the College,' decided Metyssa. 'This is what we Spider-kinden would call a stupid idea.'

They were in the cellar of Poll Awlbreaker's workshop, after dark, which meant that it was a question of either staying as his houseguests or breaking curfew in order to leave. Of course, Metyssa was enforcedly his houseguest anyway, but right now her hidden retreat was getting crowded.

Sartaea te Mosca, at whom the jibe was aimed, drew herself up with dignity. 'I have not "quit the College". I am on extended leave from teaching until they stop having Moth-kinden leering over my shoulder. Which temporary cessation of my duties allows me to serve the city in other ways.'

'Such as giving yourself up to the Wasps, apparently,' Poll Awlbreaker grumbled.

'I am not giving myself up. I am merely presenting a petition to the general. I am, after all, a law-abiding citizen with no connection to any form of wrongdoing – or that is how the Wasps see me.'

Poll sighed heavily. 'Firstly, when has that stopped them? Secondly, you don't know what they know. They could have you on a list even now.'

'If they wanted me, they could have taken me. Raullo, you see why this is necessary, surely?'

The artist sat sketching in the corner of Metyssa's cellar, although odds on it was one of his new-style works, the ones that left te Mosca with a sick feeling in her stomach but that she couldn't look away from. His eyes stared out of his pouchy, dark face like prisoners. 'I agree with you: it needs to be done. I agree with them: do it now and you'll get vanished like the rest. According to *her* –' and his finger jabbed at the other Fly-kinden in the room – 'things are about to shift. So just wait.'

Te Mosca glanced at Sperra, the bringer of word from Sarn. 'If what we're told is true, then this must be done *now*. I'm sorry, but I'm afraid that the moment the Empire believes that there are forces actively mobilizing against it, then I might as well tear this scroll of mine up and walk away. Tomorrow isn't too soon. I only hope it isn't too late.' She glanced from face to face, seeing nothing but grim, miserable expressions.

'And, besides, who knows how things will go? Perhaps the general and I will get on splendidly,' she added brightly.

'Who's my contact, then?' Sperra put in flatly. It was a moment before anyone understood her meaning, and she had to repeat herself before Poll forced an answer.

'Sartaea will still be your contact when you're here next, don't you worry.'

'No, it's a fair question.' Te Mosca held up a small hand. 'Jen Reader has volunteered for it, and you have everyone else here to rely on as well. We're not lacking in patriots here in Collegium, although we might be deficient in soldiers – at least at first. The student rebellion has stuck in people's minds. It will take a lot to make people risk taking up arms.'

'They'll see,' promised Sperra.

Sartaea te Mosca managed a smile. 'Probably. And I'd argue that a certain caution is probably no bad thing when undertaking an armed uprising. Have you everything you need?'

'I'm stuck here for another day before Taki picks me up,' Sperra explained, not for the first time, from the sound if it. 'Will you have more letters for me to take to Sarn, Sartaea?'

'I'm sure that someone will, anyway,' te Mosca replied, managing a smile.

When the Fly-kinden woman was brought before him, General Tynan was not entirely sure what he was looking at. She was hauled in under armed guard, so that at first he assumed that she was a dangerous insurgent or Sarnesh agent. After something of an awkward silence, and then some murmured questions, with the woman standing between two soldiers throughout, it was plain that nobody had any idea what it was she was supposed to have done. Certainly, if she was something as simple as a criminal or a curfew-breaker, she would never have got as far as the general himself. He had an entire apparatus devoted to keeping Imperial law in Collegium. The whole point of the Empire's order was that things worked on their own, without his constant intervention.

He nearly decided to lump her in with that particular mob and have her taken away. In the end it was her demeanour that convinced him otherwise. Through all this wrangling, with the tangible threat of the Imperial army on all sides, she had shown no fear. Instead, her expression had been one of polite attention. It was Tynan's curiosity that got the better of him.

'Does nobody know who she is, then?' he demanded of his people. 'Is she even a citizen?'

By that time the machinery of government had finally got its wheels engaged, and one of the quartermaster's clerks who were running so much of his administration turned up with a stern-looking Moth-kinden and some information.

Tynan eyed the Moth without love. This was one of the Tharen ambassadors who had descended on him, unasked and unexpected, shortly after the conquest. Tharn was nominally an Imperial ally, and this collection of arch, disdainful men and women were here, somehow, with the Empress's blessing. They spent most of their time over at Vrakir's headquarters, and thus Tynan saw them as his enemies. While he and the Red Watch major were maintaining their uneasy truce, however, there was no reason that this grey man should not turn up in Tynan's commandeered townhouse.

'Well, then?' he demanded.

'This individual is known as Sartaea te Mosca, General,' the Moth declared. 'She was formerly a teacher of magic at the Great College, but abandoned her post under suspicious circumstances shortly after I and my colleagues arrived. Our belief is that she has been responsible for spreading sedition and anti-Imperial sentiment.'

'A teacher of magic,' Tynan echoed with some disgust.

'I do not imagine she had much to teach,' the Moth sniped, obviously looking to drag a reaction out of this te Mosca, but the Fly woman's composure was equal to the challenge.

'Lieutenant, what does Intelligence say?' Tynan prompted.

'She's on the watch list, sir,' the quartermaster's man reported, meaning that the woman was not sufficiently under suspicion to have been arrested, but she was the next best thing. Whether the Moths' antipathy alone had done for her, or whether others had noticed her being in places she should not, Tynan did not know, but the information told him that there was a formal duty here beyond his personal whims.

'And you, Sartaea te Mosca, why do you say you're here?'

She mustered a fragile little smile. 'I have been deputized by our citizens to bring a petition to you, General.'

'Have you, indeed?' And that statement marked her out as some sort of ringleader, and he could lock her up for less than that. 'And what is it that your citizens are so unhappy about? I've reopened their precious College, have I not? My men keep order on the streets. I even have my chief engineer overseeing the rebuilding.'

Te Mosca cleared her throat. 'Ah, well, there are just a few matters that people are curious about.' The Moth was stalking about behind her, and she was doing her best to ignore him pointedly. 'Such as, for example, the Spider-kinden.'

'What about the Spider-kinden?' Tynan asked flatly.

'How long will an entire kinden be outlawed from our city, under threat of arrest?' Abruptly there was a thread of bravery in her tone. The Moth stopped pacing, staring down at her.

'We are at war,' Tynan informed her dismissively. 'Next matter.'

'I beg your indulgence, General, but you are at war with a state, not a kinden. Collegium is – *was* – home to hundreds of Spiders who had fled their homeland, or who simply preferred to live here amongst the Beetles. So I . . . we were wondering . . .'

Tynan wondered if she knew his own past, how he had been close to the leader of the Spider-kinden before that inexplicable order had come through to turn on them. It was common knowledge amongst his men, but perhaps not in the city as a whole, and he could not imagine that this woman wanted to provoke him.

'Send for Major Vrakir,' he ordered, shocking the entire room into stillness.

'Sir . . .?' one of his aides queried nervously.

'I think hers is a valid question, so we'll go to the source.' *And it's been too long since I hauled him from his pit to remind him of the chain of command.* 'Tell him he's needed.' Everyone knew the Red Watch was answerable to nobody, but ever since Vrakir had brought the order concerning the Spider-kinden, Tynan had been fighting the man at every opportunity. It was as if he had found the resolve to refuse the man, just one order too late.

'What else?' he demanded of the Fly woman, once the aide had set off.

'I have a list, General,' she said, a little more softly.

'A list of demands?'

'A list of names, I'm afraid.'

Something in her tone warned him he was not going to like this – not that he had liked much of it so far. He was already making the relevant adjustments for a fight with Vrakir. The Fly had given him that opportunity, and now he just wanted rid of her. 'You understand that you're going from here to the cells to await questioning, yes? There's too much stink attached to your name to avoid it.'

'It did seem likely, yes.' Was that a faint tremor in her voice? He thought it was. Her veneer of calm was cracking, then, but she was still putting on a brave face. *I've had soldiers who broke sooner. She's doing well for a Fly-kinden.*

'Well, then, what's this list? Perhaps it can be looked at while you're otherwise engaged.'

'I do hope so.' This time there was a definite trembling. 'Only . . . I am aware from what I've heard about Myna and other places that your administration here has not been heavy-handed, by Imperial standards . . .'

He nodded bluntly, accepting the praise to exactly the extent that it was intended.

'Only, by Collegiate standards, it has still been something of a novel experience for us, and I was wondering . . . we were wondering . . .'

'What's your list, woman?' Tynan demanded of her.

'Everyone who has been arrested, taken away without charge or who has disappeared after being in the company of your soldiers, and who has not thereafter been seen, General,' te Mosca declared. 'All those sons and daughters of Collegium, Spiders and other kinden, whose fate remains unknown, and who have families and friends who desperately wish to know the truth.'

He found that, in the silence she left, he had stood up, staring down at this woman who *dared* to question Imperial practice. She met his eyes, this tiny thing that he could have struck down with a sting or broken with his bare hands.

'Do you think that they will like the truth when they hear it?' he demanded of her.

'I suspect not,' she replied quietly, 'but they wish to know, nonetheless, because not knowing is worse.'

He closed his eyes, wavering on the point of violence, of some punitive order that would serve no purpose but to make him feel as though he was again in control of the situation. At the back of his mind: *Is this really what I have become?* He had been meant as an army commander, not to become mired in this civic morass.

'Take her away,' he snapped, and then, as they were marching the woman out, 'Bring me the list.'

Captain Bergild of the Imperial Air Corps knew that most of the Second Army were getting restless. They were a battlefield force pressed to act as a city garrison, and she was frankly amazed that General Tynan was holding them in check as much as he did. She remembered, from her childhood during the Twelve-year War, just how soldiers could be.

Her own pilots were suffering in the same way. They were warriors of the air, and so far no aerial threat had come to attack the Second or its new possession of Collegium. The Sarnesh had yet to venture south, and who else was there?

Instead, Bergild and her people were flying endless long-range scouting missions, like this one, looking for an enemy that wasn't there. Technically the orders were Tynan's, but she had spotted Vrakir, the Red Watch man, about the airfields, insisting that they scout further and further, that a foe was out there, if they could only find it.

The man was going mad, by her reckoning, and, as he was in command whenever Tynan's back was turned, that was a very bad thing indeed.

Then there was Oski, the major of engineers who had formerly been the one non-Air Corps soldier she could really talk to, but he was off doing some secretive business that he was evidently very keen for her not to know about. This left her and her pilots rattling about in their Farsphex orthopters, ranging out over ludicrous spans of ground, looking for . . . anything, really. Anything at all.

If there had been more of them, then perhaps they might have formed an effective scouting force, but the Imperial manufactories were still replacing the catastrophic losses that the Collegiates had inflicted on the Air Corps. And now, of course, there were multiple fronts to supply: both the fighting down the Silk Road and the force that was blocking the Sarnesh path eastwards. The Second Army had to make do.

I remember the last war. The Empire had stretched itself too far, fought on too many fronts, then the Alliance cities had risen up . . . and then the Emperor had died. Leave it to the historians to untangle that mess, but it certainly seemed to Bergild that they were fighting at least one enemy too many, right now.

Always the same question: why did we turn on the Spiders? And Vrakir, who had borne that order, wasn't talking about it. He was just giving erratic instructions to pilots: *Search here! Search there!*

I know, I know, came the thoughts of her wingman into her mind, and she realized that she had been sending at least some of her opinions across their mindlink.

He sent Halden and Lidrec out to sea a tenday ago, as if there was an army just treading water out there. Someone needs to do something.

She conveyed her agreement, but added, *Except 'someone' means Tynan, and enough people believe this 'Empress's voice' business that, if Tynan and Vrakir go head to head, it'll be unhealthy for pretty much everyone else in the city.*

You reckon he's going soft?

She paused before answering, turning that thought over in her mind. Her wingman meant the general, of course, and he wouldn't be the first to suggest it. Most of the Second were still fiercely loyal to their general, and some were even trying to match the tentative manner in which he was governing Collegium – treading around the locals as though they were as brittle as eggs. *Do the Beetles even realize how pissing* nice *we are being to their snobby, jumped-up city?* The muttering dissent was steadily increasing, though. There were always those who felt the hand of restraint as an unbearable weight on their shoulders.

But that sent them off toadying to Vrakir instead and, whilst Tynan might sit around moping, the Red Watch man was as crazy as a Moth mechanic.

None of that talk, she cautioned, aware that her long pause would lead the wingman to draw his own conclusions.

It's because of that Spider he was poking, the man opined knowledgeably.

I said, shut it – look out! And she was sliding sideways in the air because suddenly she was under attack.

She had a brief glimpse of the orthopters as they dropped on her. They moved like lead in the air: bulky boxy machines with repeating ballistae spitting out bolts. There were four of them and, even with the advantage of perfect surprise, they had not touched her. She reached out for her wingman, found that he had been clipped but was still airworthy. Then the two of them were coordinating courses, outrunning the sluggish enemy, which had split up to follow them.

And yet she tracked their lines and saw how they worked together, pushing the limits of their technology, coordinating in the air as well as Bergild and her wingman.

Ant-kinden, she decided.

Sarnesh? asked her wingman.

If these are the Sarnesh, then we seriously over-estimated the threat their pilots pose. Those machines are ridiculous . . . and what would the Sarnesh be doing this far west along the coast? . . . Oh . . . oh stab me . . .

For a moment she and her wingman coasted in silence, after seeing what was below, matching it up with where they were. *Oh, you can't be serious! Vrakir was* right?

Orders, sir?

We get out of here immediately, lose our Ant friends and get back to Collegium. Things just got interesting.

*

161

They kept te Mosca under lock and key for a tenday, confined down in the cellars of the counting house that the Rekef had appropriated for its own use.

They fed her erratically. They did not torture her, but sometimes she was taken out and up to the ground floor, where the business of interrogations and confessions had shouldered out that of money-changing and loans at interest. Shackled across her back to clamp down on her Art wings, she was left in a guard's custody for up to an hour before being taken back down again, as though some missing piece of vital paperwork had inadvertently gifted her with another few hours of pain-free existence. She was wise enough to know that this was all part of the game to her captors: their standard procedure, without meaning and almost without malice.

She was not the only guest of the interrogators. She heard some of the others, for whom that piece of paperwork had most definitely come. Yes, the Imperial hand lay light on Collegium, by the standards of Myna or the half-ruin that was Tark. That meant that fewer were taken up, and perhaps even that more of those put under the machines had done something to occasion it. It did not excuse the methods that the Wasps had built into their culture for rooting out those they believed were their enemies.

And they only gain more enemies from it. Brave words, those, but they rang hollow in her head right then. Oh, she recalled the rhetoric of the College academics, about the inferiority of the Wasp way, how their violence would inevitably lead to instability and defeat, the uprising of their slave cities, the end of their oppression. A convenient line to take for those Beetle scholars not personally keen to cross swords with the Empire, but te Mosca had believed it. She had lived with the cold and distantly contemptuous Moths of Dorax, and she had seen the excesses of Beetle merchant magnates, but in her naivety she had fervently believed that the Empire was an aberration of history and thus could never last.

But here she was in Imperial Collegium, and the Empire's

rough vitality had survived civil war and insurrection and seemed only to grow larger and stronger, until she sat in her dark cell and wondered whether it was not Collegium itself that was the freak, the error that the Empire's conquest was correcting.

At last they came for her and did more than just stand her about to watch the Rekef clerks mark up their scrolls. She was led across what she now thought of as the Imperial district, to where she had first stood before Tynan.

There were fewer officers in attendance there, and Tynan himself was not slouched and brooding, but on his feet and talking to a Fly-kinden officer wearing the insignia of one of their specialist corps. The trailing words of their conversation washed over her, technical details that she could not understand.

Tynan glanced around and saw her; a flick of his fingers dismissed the officer, who gave te Mosca a curious stare as he exited.

'So, it's you,' the general grunted. His eyes passed over her, taking in the grime, the thinness of face, the eyes dark from lack of sleep.

'Good morning, General,' she responded politely. 'I hope I find you well.'

He strode closer, searching for mockery. She was surprised to discover that she was not scared of him, nor of being thrown back in the cell, nor even of the Rekef's machines. Instead she found, from somewhere, a mild and self-contained boldness that plainly baffled him. She had no idea where all that fear had gone.

Tynan opened his mouth, and just then another Wasp burst in, to the general's obvious astonishment. The newcomer wore a uniform with red pauldrons and had some badge she didn't recognize, but his mere appearance was nothing to the horrible feeling of wrongness that washed over her just to look at the man. With a small cry she stumbled away as he advanced on the general.

'*Major* Vrakir, what can I do for you?' Tynan growled.

'I require a redeployment of the wall artillery . . .' Vrakir trailed off under te Mosca's horrified scrutiny. 'Who is . . .? This is the seditionist, the Fly lecturer from the College.'

Tynan blinked slowly. 'She's being released.'

'She's been interrogated?'

'She's being released.'

Vrakir digested that, as Sartaea te Mosca shuffled back from the two men, lest the loathing between them cut her in half.

'The Tharen believe—'

'I don't care what those dust-peddlers say. They can't back it up with anything solid.'

'General, since when—?'

'And, unlike *some*, they can't claim to be the voice of the Empress.'

In the silence that fell, Sartaea had her hands over her mouth to stop even a whisper escaping.

'Well, then, the *Empress* commands—' started Vrakir, but Tynan cut him off with an angry gesture.

'Be *very* careful when you next play that card, Major. Be sure you mean it. Perhaps you should restrict the Empress's wisdom to military matters such as the artillery, your recommendations for which you can bring to Major Oski, who knows more about such things than either of us.'

'General Tynan, I am concerned that your personal dislikes are colouring your command of this city.'

Tynan regarded him with utter distaste. 'Believe me, Major, you'll be the first to know if I let my personal dislikes start influencing me.'

'I am not responsible—'

'Men like you never are. Go and seek out the engineers, Major. Don't come here with your artillery.'

How is it they don't kill each other? Te Mosca knew that either man carried death in the Art concealed within his hands. *How is it that the entire Empire hasn't torn itself apart over private squabbles like this?* And in that moment she saw it: how the Wasps had clawed their way up from chaotic barbarism to make their Empire;

how they had taught themselves that iron self-control; how their strength had turned that rage and ability to kill on the rest of the world.

And is that it? Is that the secret? Will they consume all other cultures and never become other than they are? Or can there be some metamorphosis into something new? If it is too late for the Wasps, is also it too late for the world that they have set their sights on?

After Vrakir stormed away, Tynan's gaze returned to her, and this time she could not keep away a shiver of fear – not for the man but for what he represented.

'What did you see?' he demanded. 'You looked at Vrakir as though he was covered in blood.'

'A fit image,' she whispered. 'I saw . . . something twisted, something wrong. I've never seen the like before.'

'A singular man, is our Major Vrakir,' Tynan agreed heavily. 'Now get out of here, and if you come to someone else's attention it's the machines for you, you can be sure. Stay away from petitions in future. I'd thought only the Beetles were stupid enough to believe in them.'

She had already been backing away, but then she slowed, fighting off the fear, remembering her purpose.

'General,' she said, as steadily as she could, 'on that subject, did you get a chance to consider the petition I brought you?'

He stared at her for a long moment, a sad old man with all the power in the world, or at least this corner of it. 'Did you know, when you came, what was going on west of here? North of here? If you're a seditionist, you should know.'

She was sure her face betrayed nothing, that it held only that mild and polite expression that had got her through Moth-kinden disdain and College meetings alike. *It's started? It really has started! But, then, why . . .?*

He took up a scroll, glanced at it once and then threw it towards her. It was her list, and there were notes against many of the names.

'You won't like it,' he told her flatly.

Her eyes were telling her just that already, seeing those brief words: *dead, dead, slave, sent for interrogation.*

'At least we will know,' she told him softly. 'Thank you.'

'I choose to believe you're a foolish philanthropist who will keep her head down in future, but if you meet anyone intent on sedition, you should tell them that the forces moving against this city are not sufficient to take it. Any citizens of Collegium who might be harbouring the misguided notion of rushing to the streets with sword and crossbow would do well to remember that.'

'Of course, General,' and knowing her luck was stretched as taut as a bowstring, ready to break under the slightest additional strain, she left it at that.

Fifteen

After it was done, and after they realized what it was she had done, Thalric left without a word, scrabbling outside into the cavernous blackness without even his torch.

He had not understood at first, none of them had. He had just put on a wry face and shrugged.

'That didn't work, then,' he said. 'What's next?'

Che could not look at him, for he would read the truth in her face, and she was willing to buy more of his ignorance with any coin she had. Instead she glanced at Tynisa, who was looking more frustrated than anything else: a woman denied an enemy she could fight. Che had felt her trying to force the strength of her emotions down the narrow link that connected her to her sword, as though sheer determination could somehow be transformed into magic. Her contribution in truth had been pitiful. Tynisa would never be a magician.

But trusting, so very trusting.

Che's eyes skipped to Esmail, his closed, narrow face, seeing him already picking apart what had happened, sieving it for meaning as any good spy would.

Then Orothellin; he met her gaze, and his own eyes spoke volumes: *he knew*. He had been with her, at the end. He had a thousand years of bitter life behind him, enough to understand the decision she had made.

And Messel . . . but of course she could not lock eyes with

him. He had realized, though. He could not overlook absences as the others did.

Then, from Esmail: 'The halfbreed's gone. Maure.'

Che felt the realization reach the other two.

'Where did she go?' Tynisa was still working it out. 'Did she . . .?'

'She got out,' Esmail stated flatly.

'Yes,' Che confirmed. 'I got her out. There was only the chance for one. I only had a second to make the choice.'

A silence fell softly, in the shadow of her words.

'But . . .' Thalric said at last, 'it *was* a choice.'

'Yes.'

And how could she have done it, in that vital moment, with the lives and futures of those closest to her riding on her whim? And now they were all three staring at her, waiting for her to justify her decision somehow.

'Of all of us, she was least to blame for being here,' Che whispered. 'She wasn't fighting the Empress. She wasn't a part of it. She was just . . . unlucky enough to be with me.'

Esmail she had no responsibility for. He had been one of the Empress's party from the start. And, as for the others, her lover and her sister . . .

She should have saved one, she knew, but she could not make the choice. That was the truth. How could she have sent either one of them from her side, only to doom the other?

And Thalric and Tynisa had both been in the web with her from the start, connected by invisible threads to the vendetta between Che and the Empress. Maure, halfbreed necromancer, had been the closest thing to an innocent in this whole sorry business.

That was when Thalric left, and she let him go. It was not as if he could go far. He was here in prison with her, after all.

Esmail drew in a deep breath, and only in that did she read his disappointment and realize how much he had been wanting to go home.

'Tell me,' he asked, quite casually. 'Where did you send the woman, the halfbreed?'

Che closed her eyes. 'Away, to the surface. I had so little control . . .' Even as she said it, she realized that was not quite true. 'Somewhere connected to me, somewhere that meant something to me . . .' *Please not to Capitas, to the Empress* – but, no, that was not what her subconscious was suggesting. 'Somewhere safe, I think.'

'Che, you should have saved yourself,' Tynisa reproached her. 'From the outside you could have . . . Well, maybe you could have done something, I don't know.'

Che shook her head. Escaping herself, and abandoning everyone else, had been the first course of action she had dismissed, and not just because she could not have lived with herself afterwards.

'Messel,' she said, startling the man, 'what did you think, when you found us? What did you think it meant?'

For a long time he did not answer, and only when Orothellin murmured encouragement did he admit, 'That you had come to save us. From the Worm. All of us. I always – I had always thought the day would come, when the sunland kinden would return for us.'

'Is there . . .' Che glanced at the Slug-kinden. 'Is there a prophecy? Did you foresee that we would come?'

Orothellin smiled weakly. 'I did not. I am no oracle, nor is this any place for divination. There is no prophecy. But I have done my best to keep alive the idea of the Old World for the people here, and perhaps I have been incautious in the words I used.'

'And yet . . .' Che added thoughtfully. Esmail's eyes flicked from her to Messel and back. Tynisa was just waiting, somehow retaining complete faith that Che knew what she was doing.

'We are responsible,' was what the Beetle girl said eventually, and Orothellin nodded.

'For what?' Tynisa demanded.

'For all of this. The mantle I have assumed, the inheritance that was thrust on me, it includes this place. The imprisonment of the Worm may or may not have been fair and just to the Worm, but the Worm was not alone when it was sealed down here. There were other kinden, like Messel's people, who had been their prey for generations, yes? And there were still more – those from the surface who had tried to take the fight beneath the ground – Moths, Woodlice, my own people. Argastos and those other great magicians, my predecessors, they doomed them all to this.'

'Che, what do you expect to do about it?' Tynisa asked, her faith finally eroding. 'Especially if you can't even do . . . whatever it is you do. This place has been – what? – Worm-ridden forever.'

'But something has changed now,' Che reminded her. 'The Seal is breaking.'

'And that helps us how?'

'I don't know. But it means the Worm is venturing outside. It means that there is some way out that the Worm controls. For the present, they step through it one by one, sliding into cracks in the rocks that I cannot even see, but the Seal is failing, this entire place is falling back towards the real. Eventually, perhaps there will be no separation, and any cave or crevice from the surface may lead down here, and then we can all go home. But only . . .'

'But only if we have a home to go to,' Esmail finished for her. 'And you think that's it? That you can defeat the Worm, even as it masses for invasion?'

'I think that the Worm must have a weakness. It relies on its slaves. Just as the Wasp Empire could not survive if all its slaves could throw off their shackles, so too can we fight the Worm.' The words sounded hollow to her but she was desperate to justify herself.

'And those who will bleed for your vision?' Esmail asked her, watching her face carefully.

Che glanced at Orothellin. 'There was a tax of children when we were at Cold Well. It had come sooner than the people there expected.' The simple fact that such a practice could be 'expected' made her voice tremble a little.

The huge man nodded slowly.

'I'm right, aren't I?' she pressed him. 'Patterns are changing. The Worm is changing its habits. Because of the Seal.'

Again that ponderous nod.

She turned her gaze towards Esmail again. 'The Worm has its eyes on the surface world. It is preparing for a campaign that it has surely dreamt of for centuries. It will want to make best use of its resources. The slaves here are expendable – after all, there are so many more almost within the Worm's grasp.'

'And if it gets what it wants, if it can achieve its final goal, then perhaps it will not need slaves at all,' Orothellin added grimly. 'Nothing but the Worm surviving in all the world.'

'But it needs strength, bodies. I think it is consuming its stockpile here. It will consume its slaves, take their children, devour their bodies. But what if those slaves evaded it? There is a great, dark space around us, and the Worm cannot be everywhere at once. Even if the slaves cannot fight, they can hide. I need to understand, though,' Che decided. 'If I am to do this, I need to know what the Worm is. They call you Teacher. Teach me.'

'There is only so much I can tell,' Orothellin replied, 'but there is another who knows it all. Messel must seek him out for us, and then we will travel to him. Once he has spoken to you, shown you, you will wish you never asked. He is unique. He is half-mad. Most likely he is not to be trusted. But nobody else can tell you all he knows. Messel, you know who I mean.'

'The Hermit?' the blind man replied. 'The Cursed One?'

'Even he. I know you don't want to, but we need him. Che needs to hear what he has to say. She needs to see what only he can show her.'

Messel shuddered, but nodded. 'I will sleep, and then I will go,' he confirmed.

Che sighed, knowing that she too should rest. She ducked outside and went to find Thalric.

He was standing out in the open, staring into the darkness that surrounded him, but that could not hide him from her.

'Thalric.'

He did not turn at her voice. She noticed his hands clenching and unclenching at his sides.

'Thalric, I'm sorry. If I could have . . . No, I won't say that. I could have sent you back, and not Maure. But in that moment, it was just . . .'

'Justice, innocence, I know.'

'And I needed you here with me. It was selfish. You and Tynisa are my strength.'

'Strength?' he demanded bitterly. 'Strength here, with me blind and her crippled? Che, of everyone here I am the one who understands nothing, who can't even use what he was born with. This place . . . I can't understand it. It's not part of the world I'm meant to live in.' She knew he did not just mean the physical, sunlit world they had left.

'Can you believe that it's just about the same with me?'

'No,' he said bitterly. 'Che, I don't know what it is you have gained, truly, but if you call it magic, so be it. You're Inapt and you have your magic, and this . . .' His arms swept about, encompassing all the great chasm that he could not actually see. 'This is all magic, and nothing but.'

'It isn't,' she corrected him. 'It's the negation of magic. And the Worm even more so. When they were near, I could not even . . .'

But he was already speaking over her. 'Che, I was brought up to expect the world to act in rational ways. I learned calculus and basic principles of artifice. I'm no engineer but I know machines – I know that they work, and they make sense. And here, and when those *things* were after us . . . it was gone, Che. There was a hole in my head, and everything I thought I understood just fell out. It was as if I'd learned nothing . . . no, it was as if everything I'd learned had been a lie.'

'Yes, that is what it is like,' she whispered, and she felt shaken. She had thought that this place, locked away from the magic of the world by its Moth creators, had emptied itself of magic, leaving no clay for her mind to sculpt with. That should not affect Thalric, though.

It is the Worm, she understood. *It is not this place, it is the Worm itself. What has it become?*

'You still have your Art,' she told Thalric, although the words came out as more of a question than she had meant.

'For what it's worth,' he confirmed.

'I'm going to fight the Worm,' she told him. 'I want you to help me. I'm going to start a revolution.'

'That's it, then, is it?' he demanded. 'We're here for the duration, fighting in the pits until we die?'

'If there is a way out now, it is over the defeated body of the Worm.'

His face turned, hunting the dark in search of her, and she reached out for him − catching his hand first, then pulling him close, putting her arms about him. 'Please, Thalric,' she breathed.

He held her gently enough, his head bowed over hers. 'We always do seem to end up in dark places.'

The Empress Seda was reinventing magic.

This was her blessing and her curse, that she had been Apt, once.

She had never been tutored by great magicians or had anyone explain to her the shifting laws by which magic functioned. She had worked always from first principles, but hers was a quick and enquiring mind. She had tested her powers, working on the world and on the minds of those around them. She had already accomplished something unheard of with the Red Watch, a corps of the Apt suborned to serve as her senses and her voice, drawing on that ancestral Inapt spark they all kept hidden away. Was it something the Moth-kinden would think of? It was not, but of course they had Inapt servants aplenty that they could rely on.

She was trying to mend the world with broken tools.

But she had learned in logic classes how to test a theory, back when the world had been smaller and made more sense. Such methods made awkward bedfellows with magic, but she had no other way. She needed to be able to measure.

She could sense the Seal always now, her mind attuned to it. She could feel each spreading crack in it, sense every one of the smaller seals and bans as they shattered one by one. Daily, even hourly, her Red Watch brought her word of every Worm incursion, reports coming in from across the Empire and beyond. She had a map that plotted them all, lines weaving and spiralling and connecting. It did not matter that her former self would not even have recognized it as a map.

If she stretched her mind as far as it would go, she could appreciate the pattern; she could begin to measure the approach of the Worm.

Knowing that, she had begun to devise a theoretical countermeasure.

Had she been Apt, then she would have calculated, abacus in hand, and filled pages with her equations, charts, graphs – all impossible to comprehend in her current state. As it was, she had a whole book of diagrams, sigils, glyphs, the ideograms of an Inapt calculus that perfectly described everything she had uncovered about the Worm, its spread, its paths into the world, her projections for its complete emergence.

Had a Moth Skryre looked over that book, he would have understood completely and been horrified and shocked. Perhaps even now there were Moths working on exactly the same calculations, coming to the same terrible conclusions. Although probably not to her *final* conclusion. The Moths had been a race conniving at their own extinction since the revolution. She was Wasp-kinden: she believed that all obstacles could be overcome.

174

With enough strength behind her, she could stop the Worm, renew the Seal, perhaps cut off its bleak and terrible home from the world forever. Her magic had always been one of brute might – those were the cards she had been dealt – and now it was raw strength that the world needed.

She knew that she would get one chance only. If she tried but lacked sufficient power, then what she spent would be wasted, and, once wasted, that power would never come again. Experimentation was therefore needed to work out just what she would be required to do, how far she must go.

'Tisamon,' she directed, 'when you are ready.'

They were in the Mantis room of the Imperial museum, that hidden nook with its walls covered in vines and dead branches, standing before the great worm-ridden idol ripped from its place in the Commonweal as a war trophy, and now returned to its original purpose: a focus for a very specific form of magic.

Tisamon's armoured form remained still, because such things were not hurried. The revenant Weaponsmaster, another of her grand magical triumphs, had his metal claw folded back along his arm as he regarded the slave before him. She was an old Grasshopper woman, some skivvy that nobody would miss or care about, just a worn-out menial at the end of her useful life.

But Seda had one use left for her. This woman was about to provide a great service to magical theory.

She was tied to the idol and, although she had probably been amongst the Apt for decades, she knew exactly what was going on. Seda had ordered her gagged, because her screaming had become a distraction, and still those muffled, desperate sounds issued from her.

I envy you your ignorance of why this is necessary, the Empress considered. *But if you knew how important this was, you would understand. This is for everyone. This is to save the world.*

Tisamon brought the blade of his claw to the old woman's chin, tilting her head back. Seda saw her eyes try to seek out those of her killer, to appeal to some common humanity between them, but of course there was nothing there. His pale dead face had been short on empathy even while he lived.

Still, she almost saw tenderness in him as his off-hand touched the woman's cheek, before forcing her chin up further, baring that wrinkled throat.

He angled the edge of his blade, so that the point was jutting down towards her collarbones, the line of it along her neck, then with a sudden, almost ecstatic motion, he cut her throat.

As he moved, Seda focused on the moment of death, the idol's greedy drinking, drawing that release of power and turning it downwards, inwards, in whatever impossible direction it was that the Worm was approaching from. She felt the infinitesimal give – the tiny reaction to her sacrifice – that validated her calculations. It could be done. It must be done. She could put it all right.

Soon thereafter she had summoned General Brugan to attend her. She was beginning to tire of him, in truth. Something in him had broken when his conspiracy had been undone, when she had forced him to drink the blood of his comrades, and to watch his Rekef supplanted by her Red Watch. She had expected more of him. She remembered first setting eyes on him – so strong, so ruthless and determined. She barely called him to her bed any more. He had become a dull lover, too timorous to be satisfying.

She needed him and his Rekef now, though, because her Red Watch was simply not numerous enough for this task.

'Brugan,' she addressed him. She had chosen the throne room for this audience, hopeful that this reminder of the familiar ways of the Empire would put some steel back into him. He remained kneeling, though, barely able to look her in the face.

'Inapt slaves, Brugan,' she told him.

He glanced up briefly with red-lined eyes. He was drinking more than before, too. Really she should have found a replacement, but there was no time now. His lips moved, and she heard, 'I will have some brought to you.'

'You will,' she confirmed. 'You will set your Rekef Inlander in motion with one aim only, General. I want Inapt slaves. I want every Inapt slave in the Empire. Have them confiscated from their owners. Have the Slave Corps deliver all they can find. All the prisoners we've taken in the fighting with the Spiders – have them brought to me. And take more prisoners, far more. Live prisoners, Brugan. Those cities in our Empire that are Inapt, have them deliver up one in five – no, one in four – and let's hope we don't need to go back for more.'

Brugan was staring openly at her now. 'What . . . Majesty, you can't mean all . . . that's thousands, tens of thousands. . .'

'That is what I mean.'

'What will you . . .? How could we even manage so many together?'

'I leave that to the ingenuity of the Rekef and the Slave Corps, but it will be done. Set up depots for them; bring them all together near Capitas. I have need of them.'

He must have now guessed something of her purpose, for it took a lot to shake a Rekef man like that. He had no capacity left to argue, though, merely bowing meekly to her wishes.

And just hope that it will be enough, was her sober thought. *Because although the deaths of the Apt are worth less, I will use them if I need them. The Worm must be stopped.*

He was not sure how far he had come, or even of the number of days that had passed since that great ruin that had taken away so much of his life.

It seemed to Totho that he had barely seen a familiar sight since then, as he made his stumbling way along the edge of the Exalsee with no clear destination in mind. He had slept beneath the stars, and when he had grown hungry he had shown himself at villages or farms, and the mere sight of him had prompted offerings of food. *Go away*, had been the clear implication and, as the inhabitants did not feel that they could force him, they bribed him. *Go away*, and he had gone, onwards like a clock-work thing, aimless and disconnected.

He had no idea where he was. He felt almost as if he had stepped into some other world, where all the landmarks were changed. He was far enough now that the smoke of devastated Chasme could no longer be seen. Tired, he sat with his back to a tree, staring out over the great expanse of water. There was not a boat, not an airship or orthopter to dot the sky. It was as though he had turned back time to before the revolution, some ignorant, barren world bereft of Aptitude.

He still had his armour, the elegant work of scientifically derived alloys and shapes that would turn snapbow bolts and weighed him down so very little. He had his snapbow and three magazines of ammunition, and no way ever to find more – unless the Empire was able to reverse-engineer the design. He had his belt of drawstring grenades. That was all that Totho now had in the world.

He did not have the Iron Glove. He did not have Drephos, whose loss – to him and to the world – ached and gnawed at him, alongside all those other losses that seemed to have defined his life.

He did not have a purpose, and his past was ash.

Collegium, perhaps? He could not even say in which direction it lay, save that his home was far, far away, both in distance and in time. *What has the Empire left of it?* He waited for the urge for revenge to surface in him: *Go and fight the Wasps! Avenge your master!* But it never came. His loss was so total that it would achieve nothing, and he was a rational man, an Apt man. He was no hero of the old stories, destined to fall beneath a wave of enemies and count it meaningful. *Leave that sort of thing to old Tisamon.*

Sitting there in full armour, his helm in his hands, the snapbow leaning beside him like a lance, he could not know how he looked: exactly like some storybook warrior defeated in his last battle, scorched and bruised and alive beyond his time.

That was how she found him.

He looked up to see her: a woman in a long, tattered coat, a cowl up to shadow her face, staring at him from the lakeside as though she had somehow emerged, quite dry, from the water. She had a sword hanging at her side, but there was nothing about her to suggest any threat other than her simple presence and the fact that she was staring at him so intently. Even so, his hand drifted to the snapbow.

'What do you want?' His own voice sounded hoarse with disuse, as though his throat was still coated with smoke.

She took a step closer, staring at his face. She was a half-breed, he saw, some tangle of Inapt ancestries and, now he thought about, it there was something of the charlatan about her, or what the Inapt would have called a magician.

'It's you, isn't it?' he heard her say.

'I don't know you.' *I have no interest in you. Go away.*

'Your name is Totho, of Collegium.'

Immediately he had the snapbow levelled at her. Nothing good could come of anyone around here knowing his name. 'And just who are you?'

She did not react to the weapon. 'My name is Maure,' she told him. 'We have a friend in common.'

Sixteen

Reinforcements, the word arrived in Collegium, but only a handful of orthopters had come buzzing from the east – certainly not the garrison force that many were still hoping for. Instead, there was a band of engineers, quartermasters and Consortium men come to take stock, and a visitor for the general.

Major Oski, highest-ranking Engineer in the Second Army and highest-ranking Fly-kinden in the Engineers, was there to greet the newcomers, a smart exchange of key words and salutes before he took them somewhere out of the way. He was not a man who readily delegated, was Oski. Instead, he and his assistant tended to turn up all over the Wasp quarter of Collegium and beyond, making themselves useful. Recently he had even been assisting the locals with the reconstruction, although his method of press-ganging them into work details to rebuild their own homes was not earning him much love amongst the populace.

He was very plainly in charge and, as a Fly giving orders to Wasps and other larger kinden, he had cultivated a large voice and an impressive selection of insults. He made himself very much the centre of attention and fervently hoped that any watchers would not notice that his visiting band of artificers and merchants was unusually diverse – only a single Wasp amongst them, nor that they themselves were paying far more attention to his assistant, Captain Ernain.

Ernain and Oski went way back, and were most certainly both in the same degree of trouble if anyone decided to start asking pointed questions, which was the sort of trouble that won a man the exclusive attention of the Rekef interrogators for as long as he could hold out. So far, Oski reckoned that their little sideline had evaded official attention, but he was unhappily aware that the pilot, Bergild, had begun to suspect something. He liked Bergild: she was good, refreshing company in a job where, all too often, you heard the same half-dozen stock opinions do the rounds of every single conversation. So much for that, though, and now he was putting as much distance between them as possible.

Otherwise, if she would not take the hint, he would have to arrange an accident for her. With him as an artificer used to sneaking right up to the enemy to look over their siege artillery, and her as a pilot absolutely dependent on the proper workings of her Farsphex, he knew he could get rid of her with pitiful ease. He very much did not want to have to do it.

He got them all into a Collegiate taverna, then cleared out the locals and the staff until he and his fellows had sole possession of the place. With one keen-eyed Fly sergeant on watch, the rest of them settled in with a few liberated bowls of wine and waited for Ernain to begin.

'Any luck getting Oski transferred back east with me?' was his first question. A man for practicalities, was Ernain. He was Bee-kinden from Vesserett, that grand old city that had just been winding itself up to become a power in the world when it had clashed with the nascent empire that the Wasp tribes had put together. Nobody had known it at the time, but history should have been holding its breath. There could easily have been a Bee empire locking horns with the Lowlands right now, if things had gone differently.

Or perhaps trading peaceably with the Lowlands, all sweetness and light, Oski considered, though personally he didn't believe it.

'Not a hope just now,' a Beetle-kinden put in, a captain in the Consortium wearing informal robes with only a rank badge to separate him from the civilians. 'Believe me, something weird's going on back home. Trying to get any odd orders stamped is almost a lost cause. The Empress . . .'

There was a general mutter around the room, from men who all knew the same story.

'Anyway, the upshot is that a Captain-Auxillian can probably move about, but the Second's chief engineer? Stuck here for now, looks like.'

'The situation here is still strong,' Ernain told them. 'No doubt that's the official line, too, but this time it's true. I hear that the southern front against the Spiders is stalling, though?'

'Just so,' confirmed their one Wasp, garbed as a lieutenant of the Engineers. 'The usual – ambush, assassination, mass poisoning and broken supply lines. The whole business was stupidity from the start.'

'But a gift to us,' Ernain pointed out. Capital treason uttered, then and there, and they absorbed it and nodded cautiously. 'We'll get our moment,' the Bee went on, 'and we'll get it soon, I hope. Sarn will break out, or else the Spiders. But we need to be ready, have everything in place. Tell me we'll be ready.'

Some strong nods, some awkward expressions.

'We're still testing the water in Slodan and Dekiez, and there's simply no ready way to interest the Delves,' the Beetle started to summarise. 'The Grasshoppers are all for it but basically don't understand what we're trying to achieve.'

'And some of us aren't convinced it can work,' added another Bee, an older artificer also from Vesserett. 'This is the Empire we're talking about. It'll end in blood, no other way.'

'In that case, a great deal of what we've worked for will come to nothing, Tiberan,' Ernain replied. 'But, if you're right, we need to have the sword ready to draw. We don't bluff. I know you think this must end in violence,' he remarked to his kinsman. 'And I know that some of you don't believe it ever will –' and this time a look at the Beetle – 'but the truth is, we must all be ready to fight, and *not* to fight. We must be ready for opportunity. When we make our move, the next pages of the history books will be blank, awaiting *our* writing. If we try to scrawl them out ahead of time, we're fools and likely we'll fail. Here, try this. The final version, I hope.' He threw over a scroll to Tiberan, who ran his eyes down it, frowning.

'I don't like it,' Tiberan grumbled. 'Same reasons as before.'

'I know. Are you still with me, though?'

The older Bee sighed. 'You know I am, Ernain.'

'And the rest of you?'

'If we had to go today, just march up to the throne and throw down the gauntlet,' the Beetle said, 'then we'd have a chance of getting out with our skins. If we did the same next month then I think we might be just about as ready as we'd ever be.'

'Margraf,' Ernain addressed the Wasp, 'are we still quiet?'

'There's nothing in my papers or the rumours I hear that suggests otherwise,' the man replied. 'Still, as we all know, things are on the move back home. Right now, it's not my lot you should be looking over your shoulder for. This Red Watch, that's the new name, and where it gets its information from, I have no idea.' *My lot* meant the Rekef, and Margraf held a lieutenant's rank in the Inlander service as well as his Engineer's post. He was regarded nervously by the rest, but he had proved invaluable so far.

Ernain took a deep breath. 'You're the third group of our people I've met with now. I've met with men who were scared of the consequences. I've met with those who were too keen for blood. I've met with Inapt men who told me their omens said the time was right. I've met with those who thought that I was trying to raise the power of old Vesserett from the ashes. All these different people I have talked to, and secured their agreement. People from all across the Empire. People who have been talking and planning since the end of the last war with the Lowlands, since the time of the traitor governors. I want you to go back to your own cities, to your own followers. Tell them it will happen. Every day brings it closer: our new dawn. We're all together in this.'

'So long as we're not together in the Rekef cells at the end of it,' old Tiberan growled, but the mood in the room remained fierce, determined. Oski looked from face to face and hoped that he was seeing the future.

Tynan wondered if this was how a spy felt every day. For an Imperial general it was certainly a novel and unpleasant experience. Here he was, in the city he nominally controlled, creeping about like a conspirator.

Getting the message had thrown him: the name was one he knew, and there were certain words and references there that convinced him of the hand behind it. Still, a lot of time had passed since then. The instant thought: was this a trap, a prelude to assassination? No great imagination was needed to suspect it – lure the general off to a secluded spot, and next moment Vrakir is in complete control of Collegium and the Empress's supposed will is being done without hesitation.

But here he was, nevertheless, and he knew himself well enough to understand that this lack of caution was a result of a dozen different caustic experiences wearing him down – Mycella's death, the unwanted demands of governing, the friction with Vrakir. He was a blunt, plain-speaking man denied the chance to act like one.

So an old friend called, and here he was. He had brought a dozen of his most trusted men who had drawn sword alongside him for over a decade in the Second's campaigns. Choosing them, aware that they were none of them now as close to him as they should have been, he had come to the painful recognition of how his rank and the toll of the years had distanced him. He had no colonel to rely on, no real old friends. *I should bring that Collegiate Fly woman with me; she would serve just as well.*

In this brooding ugly mood he had come to this taverna, cloaked like a stage villain and trailed by a belligerent retinue.

On seeing that it was the man himself, he felt less relief than he had expected. Perhaps he would have preferred a betrayal, if only to give him the moral high ground.

'Marent,' he acknowledged.

'Tynan.' This general of the Third Army had no business being in Collegium, still less sneaking in incognito aboard a messenger orthopter, but here he was. He was younger than Tynan, and when he had done his stint in the Second he had only been a major, but he was a soldier's soldier through and through, a man who won his wars on the battlefield, not behind closed doors.

In his eyes for just a moment, but there for all to see, was a spark of surprise at how old Tynan now looked.

'Do I take it the Third isn't about to relieve us?' Tynan tried to make it sound light, but in truth he wished there was some chance it was true.

'The Third is stuck in Capitas,' General Marent replied disgustedly. 'I've decided that I've received nothing personally nailing me to the spot, but you'll appreciate why I've not turned up here with a standard and a proclamation.'

'Why *are* you here, Marent?' Tynan asked and, seeing the taken-aback look in the younger man's eyes, held up a finger. 'Not that I wouldn't welcome the chance to talk but, in the Emperor's name, man, you're a general now!'

'In the *Empress's* name,' Marent corrected sourly. 'And in her name my entire force is eating its way through the stores at Capitas whilst there's fighting all down the Silk Road and Sarn readies to march.'

'Sarn already marches,' Tynan corrected him. At Marent's raised eyebrows he nodded tiredly. 'Not a full army, but a few thousands heading for us even now. You'd better not outstay your welcome here, or I'll have to make you part of my staff.'

'Just a few thousands, though?' Marent asked him, shaking his head.

'So it seems: maybe three, four at the most. But there's more. There's maybe twice as many marching east from Vek, down the coast, and I reckon we're lucky they lost so many trying to take this place before the last war or there'd be more.'

Marent frowned, calculating. 'Still not enough.'

'We're waiting to see where the rest are coming from, but it'll be time to keep hold of this place the hard way, soon enough.'

'Then it's even worse madness to have me sitting idle!' Marent spat. 'Let me come against Sarn with a full siege train, and the garrison force that's currently tying them up can relieve you, and you can kick in the Vekken's teeth. Why can't they *see* it?'

'The Empress and her Red Watch,' Tynan suggested.

'Correct. For the longest time, no orders at all and now . . . now there's orders all right, a pissing explosion of them, just not the right ones. Quartermaster orders, Consortium orders, but Slave Corps orders most of all.'

Tynan frowned. '*Slave* Corps?'

'She's sending them out all over the Empire and beyond. They've got airships now – the Slave Corps has an air wing, can you believe?'

'What for?'

'Cargo airships down the Silk Road to Seldis.'

'The Empress has a yearning for Spider slaves?' Tynan felt an odd, cold twist inside him.

Marent looked as though he felt the same way. 'I saw the orders. Not just a few Spiders. The Slave Corps is to take a dozen big cargo airships south and load them up with . . . everyone.'

'What do you mean, "everyone"?'

'As much of Seldis's population as they can cram into the bays, quality immaterial.'

'That's insane,' Tynan murmured.

'Yes!' Marent agreed heatedly. 'Yes, it *is* pissing insane, and it's happening, and anyone who looks sideways at the orders gets that "Voice of the Empress" business from the Red Watch, or gets arrested by the Rekef. Yes, it *is* insane, Tynan. Just like everything in Capitas these days. The whole city's working on nothing but habit, and every day another piece grinds to a halt. There's been a mass confiscation of slaves – and which slaves? Grasshoppers, Dragonflies, creatures of no use to anyone! Menials and cleaners and pissing *musicians* rounded up for *her* private use. They're sending to the Principalities, even, offering to buy anyone they want rid of. I was planning to make this trip anyway, back when things were just peaceably mad, but just as I was about to set off, all of this started. Nobody knows what's going on back home, Tynan.'

'Why tell me this?'

Marent stared at him for a long time. 'Because I trust you. Because you're a man of honour, with the Empire's best interests at heart.'

'And I'm a man stuck here in Collegium, where there's nothing I can do, even if it was in my power to help. And even suggesting something should be done is a form of treason. We can't have another civil war, Marent.'

'You tell *me* that? They'd never have won the last one if it wasn't for me!' Marent insisted. 'But what was that for, the traitor governors and all that fighting? And now . . . it's as if we went off to put them down, and we got lost on the way home and found ourselves in some other Empire.'

'And I ask again, why tell *me*?' Tynan insisted. 'Because if you are suggesting that I, a man of honour with the Empire in his heart, would take some *stand* against the rightful Empress . . .'

'Would you?'

In the silence that followed, Tynan could feel the thump of his own heart. *I don't believe he actually said it.*

'I'm not talking treason—' Marent started.

Tynan cut him off furiously. 'How can you not be talking treason?'

'If there were enough of us – army generals, senior men in Capitas – if we stood before her and said, This is wrong, this isn't the way, she'd have to listen to us.'

'And if she didn't?'

'We'd have to hope she did.'

'And you're a better tactician than to plan a fight that's all based on bluff,' Tynan pointed out.

Marent scowled stubbornly but had no answer.

Taki landed the Stormreader neatly, letting the machine hover for longer than was strictly necessary, just because it was so good at it. The Sarnesh had only just produced the first of their new air force, but Willem Reader had made a few small but significant changes to the design while they were readying their factories.

At last Taki let the orthopter touch down and threw up the canopy as the first mechanics arrived. The expeditionary force had a score of flying machines with it, but only three of the new Stormreaders, the rest being either Collegiate fliers rescued from the conquest or older Sarnesh craft that she would frankly not be found dead in.

'Get him rewound and ready to go right out again.' For a moment she almost told them she would be right back, but she had to report in, and she had already flown double duty after specifically being told not to. Rebellion had its limits. 'Next pilots up – let's have an all-Sarnesh scout team this time – and someone show me where the big noises are.'

The force that was marching south had the sort of loose command structure that Beetles seemed to gravitate to inexorably, but that sent Ants into fits. Arguably it had three leaders, and Taki normally reported to the most junior of them, dropping out of the sky with a flick of her wings to land on the woman's blind side, virtually on her feet.

Straessa – known as the Antspider – swore at her tiredly. They were waiting for a team of artificers to repair the rails, as the grand idea for a swift move on Collegium was to have the soldiers march unencumbered while supplies were brought down the rail line. On various occasions, though, both sides had been fairly determined that the line would not benefit the enemy, so their progress had been somewhat haphazard. Fortunately the Sarnesh had devised an automotive that repaired and replaced the rails as it travelled on them, but even that ingenious machine ran into impassable sections on a depressingly frequent basis.

Give me some way of getting an army on an orthopter, was Taki's only thought in reaction to that.

'Chief!' She saluted cheerily, because the Antspider was always fair game to annoy.

'Just "Officer",' the halfbreed woman growled. She was in charge of the Collegiate detachment, but plainly had not wanted to be. She was a victim of the tendency of Beetle leaders not to be soldiers themselves, so that Leadswell and Reader and the rest were all back in Sarn.

'We had reports of fighting from you and yours, pilot,' broke in Kymene, the Mynan commander and nominal overall tactician. 'Report.'

As Kymene was not on Taki's annoy list, the Fly woman nodded more soberly. 'If they didn't know we were coming before, they surely do now. Three Farsphex came to check us out.'

'You drove them off?'

'Downed one, chased the others way. They've not lost any of their skill, but our new craft are the business, Commander.'

'Good to hear it,' Kymene nodded. She had brought with her just about every Mynan out of Sarn, all of them desperate to shed Wasp blood. For them, retaking Collegium was merely a link in the chain that would bring them home. Even Taki, whose interest in non-aviators was minimal, had marked that a fair number of Kymene's followers were not soldiers by trade, just those who had been able to escape the Wasp assault on their city. *Which is likely to make things messy if there's a real fight.*

Again, that was not normally her department, but Taki was well aware that the Imperial Second could swallow up this expeditionary force and still be hungry afterwards. *So let's hope there's a plan.*

'How are *our* pilots performing?' This came from Commander Lycena, leader of the Sarnesh soldiers grudgingly released by Milus to march south. She was a reserved careful woman, plainly more concerned about keeping her own people alive than the eventual fate of the city they were marching on. *Which probably helps balance out any excess enthusiasm on the part of the Mynans.*

'Good, Commander. They work together well. They need to think round the sky more, though. It's hard, I know, with them not having the Art—'

'Perhaps later for the details?' Kymene interrupted. 'What can we expect from their air power now?'

Taki shrugged. 'If word from Collegium still holds, they've not had much more delivered, which gives us parity, perhaps even the advantage. But we've no bombers, and they might have all sorts of other tricks, like those hornets they flew against us last time, so it's going to be a ground war again. Or they might get another twenty Farsphex delivered tomorrow, in which case we have a problem.'

'What other intelligence from Collegium?' Kymene enquired.

'Sperra was in yesterday,' the Antspider confirmed, 'and it sounds as if we've managed to get the Wasps wound up about us, no matter that we don't have enough people here to . . . you know, actually take the walls.' Taki heard the woman's voice trail off pointedly. 'I mean, there is a plan, right? We're not just here because the Wasp artillery's getting rusty?'

Kymene's smile in response was hard. 'Yes indeed, there is a plan.'

Straessa and Lycena exchanged glances, and the Mynan woman held her hand up.

'Yes, there is a plan. No, it goes no further than the inside of my head right now.'

'That's a plan one assassin away from a shambles, then,' Straessa muttered, loud enough for all to hear.

'Then it's lucky that it's not *my* plan, and doesn't need me to work,' Kymene retorted. 'Let us just get within sight of Collegium's walls.'

Seventeen

They were heading upslope, struggling over ground riven with crevasses, littered with plates of shale that slid from underfoot like the loose pages of stone books, a half-dozen suddenly shifting and clattering away to smash below, all hope of stealth gone. That was when the Worm found them.

It was Messel who gave the alarm, Messel whose light tread, advancing on all fours as much as on his feet, had not dislodged so much as a pebble. Abruptly he was turning in the fickle light of Thalric's torch and pointing behind them. 'Beware!'

Tynisa turned, catching her balance on the treacherous stone, and then having to drag her rapier from its scabbard. She had felt the minute twitch as the bond between them had reached to bring it to her hand, and then nothing, as the deadening air of the Worm descended on her.

Thalric cursed nearby, casting his torch down to gutter on the canted stone, and lighting a second bundle of fungus with a flare of his sting. She had already lost sight of Esmail in the gloom.

Orothellin's voice boomed out, 'We are almost there. Onward still!' And Che's reply: 'What good will that do us, now they've found us?'

'Keep moving' won't suffice this time. Tynisa's eyes had wrung all they could from Thalric's light, and she spotted those scurrying

forms rushing at them from the gloom, far faster and surer of foot than anyone not born down here could be.

'We will hold them off,' she declared, speaking for she knew not who.

'If we can outdistance them . . .' Orothellin tried, and then, 'The Hermit, he will be able to lead them off, even make them forget, I swear it! Only . . . drive them back, slay such of them as are here, and we may find sanctuary! Cheerwell, please!'

From that last plea, and the following shower of sharp-edged fragments, Tynisa realized her sister was descending to help – if help was the word.

'Che, you get up there,' she snapped over her shoulder.

'But—'

'Not this time, Che. We'll deal with them and catch you up, but go!' And then, to Thalric, 'How many, do you think?'

His own eyes had picked them out now, and the flash of his sting seared the corner of her eye. She saw one figure fall, burning, and then another stagger, armour glowing with its own molten fire. For a moment the Worm coiled about itself, and Tynisa remembered that she had not seen so much as a bow down here. Then one of them was whirling something about its head, and she cried, 'Slings, Thalric!'

He cursed, and then was gone, kicking off into the dark air to make himself a harder target. Which left only her.

She reckoned there were between a dozen and a score of them, and a handful had held back to spin stones at her, too small and fast for her to see or react to in this gloom. The rest were surging forwards, fanning out. They carried shortswords, two apiece, and their pale, slack faces sent a shudder through her.

Thalric's sting exploded amongst them again, striking one down from their midst and momentarily lighting up the rest – and she leapt.

Footing would have been a problem had she been aiming for those shifting plates of stone, but she struck with both heels against the chest of one of her enemy, sending the man skidding downhill on his back, legs kicking. Then she was following him, propped on hip and one arm, ripping her keen blade across two sets of hamstrings and bringing it up in time to fend off the single sword that was quick enough to reply.

Their formation flowed and then they were after her, which was a relief as she had planned to stop there and hold them, but the flurry of broken shale was carrying her further down towards the slingers. Again Thalric's sting lanced down, striking wide . . . then again, flaring at the stone.

She fell into darkness, too far from the dropped torch to see, a drawback the Worm would not have.

'Thalric!' Most unlikely of allies, given their past enmity, but he was casting his second torch ahead of her so that she scrabbled to a halt in its pool of light, lurching to her feet, blade first, to meet them.

A sudden movement at the back of that chain of bodies and their end segment was a corpse – all too fast for Tynisa to follow but she knew it must be Esmail. For a moment the Worm recoiled, its many bodies reforming, and then she had half a dozen pressing her, the rest hunting off into the dark.

Thalric was overhead now, but his stings were lancing beyond her, trying to kill the slingers who remained the only threat to him. She was on her own.

She had the advantage of reach, and it nearly killed her. She took the initiative, expecting defence, but killed one of them straight off and was immediately swamped by the rest – no holding back, no fear of death, and yet a mindless discipline to them, so that every set of blades sought to drive her onto the points of their comrades.

In that moment she took a couple of cuts, shallow but survivable, and drew strength from her blade to ignore the pain, cutting another throat as she did so, falling back to keep them at the point of her blade.

For a second they were stilled, as whatever mind lurked behind those faces readjusted, and then pain assailed her, got its jaws into her and would not let go.

The crippling injury that she had taken in the Commonweal, which dropped from her as soon as she had need to draw her blade, was abruptly again an inseparable part of her, as impossible to deny as her Weaponsmaster's magic was to believe. The hand of the Worm fell upon her, and she could draw no support from the blade in her hand. It was just a sword, a thing of craft and steel. She was just a swordswoman, and the badge she wore was just an ornament.

She fell back a step and the tightness of that scarred wound caught at her, till she fell.

They pounced on her, but the broken ground came to her rescue, sending her slipping and slithering away from the light faster than they could follow, hunched about the pain of her overstretched hip.

This isn't how I die! But, amid that agony, she could only wonder how she had lived so long. The blackness around her was almost total. She could hear the quick patter of their feet but realized she would never see the killing stroke.

Then there was a flash, like lightning, imprinting those rushing figures on to her eyes – Thalric's sting, gone very wide but still a moment's vision for her, and she cried out, 'Again!'

He obliged, the flash and flare of his stingshot dancing about the oncoming soldiers of the Worm as though he were an artillerist trying to find the proper range. In the second of those brief gifts of light, she saw Esmail in the midst of them, bare-handed, the severed halves of a sundered sword blade spinning away to either side of him as he plunged his fingers through one enemy's breastplate as though it was not there.

Another ran straight onto her blade, and then she was moving and scrabbling as best she could to get out from underneath their blows, but there seemed only a handful now, and at last Thalric was catching them, using each blast to light the way towards the next, missing Esmail by inches.

And they were gone. No more Worm, and she heard Thalric hiss her name as he landed, all three of them once more utterly blind.

'We must move now. Those that came for me are still out there somewhere,' Esmail stated calmly. 'Take my hand.'

She expected to feel something edged and deadly, but when his fingers found her they were flesh and blood, and she leant heavily on him as he hauled her up.

'You're hurt?' from Thalric, hearing her curse.

'I'll live. But what now?'

'Look up,' Esmail told them.

Far above them, across an insuperable void of darkness, was one of Thalric's dropped torches.

'We go up,' Thalric agreed, and then the two of them were helping her as they all clambered desperately for the higher ground.

It fell to Messel to lead them to where the others were: Che, Orothellin and the Hermit, and none of those three needed a glimmer of light. Tynisa allowed herself one uncharitable thought: *If her eyes were like mine, then she'd be out under the sun and Maure'd still be here.*

'This Hermit, or Cursed One, or whatever,' she heard Thalric growl. 'What is he? Why's he so important. Why do we trust him?'

'I do not trust him,' was Messel's reassuring reply, and then, 'but we are here.'

'Last torch,' the Wasp remarked philosophically, 'and I don't reckon this Hermit has the makings of a fire.'

'I'll find something for you to burn,' the blind man offered immediately, and then he was gone, leaving them in the utter dark before anyone could call him back.

'What . . .?' Thalric asked plaintively.

'I suspect not because he suddenly feels the cold,' was Esmail's dry observation.

'He is right not to trust me.'

A lot of silence followed the sound of that new voice.

'How are we supposed to take that?' Tynisa enquired levelly. 'Che, are you there?'

Her sister answered, but Thalric spoke over her. 'Now for the torch.' And then his sting flashed and flared.

Tynisa's eyes were only for Che, seeing her safe there with the towering presence of Orothellin behind her. Thalric saw the new addition first, and he dropped Tynisa instantly, springing backwards into the air with a hand extended.

'Thalric, wait!' Che told him.

'He's one of *them*!' he yelled back.

Tynisa was leaning heavily on Esmail, gingerly feeling out how much weight her hip could take. She could stand again, now, but lodged like a splinter in her mind was the understanding that her body could fail her at any moment.

She looked at the apparition before them. Thalric was right: he was of the Worm.

She saw that same pallid skin and grey-shaded eyes they all possessed. He was old, though, and he bore those spiralling scars she had seen on the Worm's spokesman at Cold Well. His colourless hair was long and dirty, hanging past his shoulders, and he wore a ragged robe of many stitched-together pieces of hide and fur and chitin, its poor fit making his body shapeless. Moreover, a human animation possessed his face, though in a weak and sickly way. He looked ill, like a man pining for some drink or drug.

'What's going on?' Tynisa asked. Their shadows swooped around them as Thalric touched down behind her, no doubt his hand still directed at the stranger.

'He can keep the Worm from finding us, because he is of the Worm already,' Esmail stated. 'Explain, quickly.'

Orothellin sighed. 'He the only one I know who has turned from the Worm.' He shrugged broadly. 'Either you will come with us and talk, and have some trust, or you will go.'

There was a scattering of exchanged glances.

'I'm with Messel,' Thalric grumbled, but it was plain that Che had already made up her mind. After all, how better to learn about the Worm than from this creature here?

The Hermit dwelt within a cave that stank of him: a thin, sour reek, the taint of an unwashed body that was not quite human, even though it had come a long way towards that goal. That the place seemed hostile to human life merely placed it alongside almost everything Tynisa had seen down here so far. It was an oppressive thing to look out of the cave mouth and see a darkness that cared nothing for night and day, enlivened only by those false, murderous stars.

Messel laid a fire, with plenty of nervous glances at the cave's owner, who sat on a rock staring at nothing, as though trying to wish all his uninvited guests out of existence. Orothellin was the only one his small pupils lit on, ignoring all the rest as if they were hallucinations until Thalric had kindled the blaze with sparks from his steel lighter.

The Hermit stretched his hands out carefully, as though rediscovering how close he could bring them to the flames. For a long time further he just stared at nothing, his Worm's face set into a faint frown that was nevertheless a library of expression compared to those of his kin that they had just fought.

At last: 'Someone, say something,' from Thalric.

'I don't seek visitors.' The voice of the Hermit was surprisingly strong, a College master or military officer turned gravelly with age, but not lacking in authority.

'Not even visitors from the Old World?' Orothellin prompted. He and the Hermit, sitting near to one another, had a curious sort of commonality, Tynisa decided. A pair of freaks with no place in this freak-show world.

The Hermit made a disparaging sound. 'Is that so?'

'Place them for me, then,' the Slug-kinden challenged him mildly. 'Where are they from?'

'Do I care?'

'Excuse me, Master Hermit,' Che, of course painstakingly polite. 'What are you to the Worm?'

At that he turned to her, seeming to acknowledge her presence for the first time. 'A loose limb it doesn't realize it's missing. What are *you*?'

Che opened her mouth, and Tynisa saw quite clearly that she had no answer any more. The ready responses that she would have owned to under the sun outside had been stripped from her.

'She is a scholar of Collegium.' The words came to Tynisa quite readily. 'A freer of slaves, caller of ghosts, speaker of words.'

The moment teetered on the edge of solemnity before Thalric put in, 'Too many words, mostly.'

'And the rest of you?'

'Her followers,' Tynisa stated, and Esmail said, 'Her creatures,' at the same time, prompting a surprised look from the others.

Esmail faced up to them boldly. 'I have had many masters in my time. I want to return to my home, to my family. I see no way to do so, but she does. If we must fight the Worm to do so, then so be it.'

Che glanced anxiously to see the Hermit's reaction to that, to see if he had some residual loyalty to the people – or the entity – he had apparently abandoned. For a moment his pale face screwed up, then it relaxed, lines of character springing away into nothing.

'I have lived free of the Worm this long by avoiding its notice, just as Orothellin has. The Worm need only glance my way, recall that I was once a segment of its body, and I do not know if I would have the strength to refuse it a second time.'

'We do not come to ask you to fight. We ask you to teach us. We need to understand the Worm,' Che told him. 'I *know* that your kinden were not like this when they were sealed here.'

'Oh, you know, do you?' The Hermit stared at her. 'And what do you know, Beetle-kinden?'

'They were a power of the Old World,' she replied. 'They were magicians. They sought to remake the world in their image, somehow. That much I know. The other great kinden united against them and defeated them, and such was their fear that your people might return to contest possession of the world again, that the Moths and the others made a terrible choice.'

'Feh.' The Hermit spat into the fire. 'You know more than I.'

'But what I have seen here is not the Worm of those memories,' Che insisted. 'I need you to tell me.'

'Do you?'

She glanced at the Slug, who seemed halfway to dozing off. 'Orothellin says—'

'Does he? And what is she to you, Orothellin. Why bring her here? What's the point?'

The huge man opened one eye. 'Is that a new version of your asking me why I'm still alive?'

'If you choose.'

'I have hope still. Even after so very long, I have not lost hope.'

Another derisive sound from the Hermit.

'And I will help her, help all of them, when they go to fight the Worm. When they go to my poor people here, the slaves and the victims, I will speak for them.'

The Hermit was looking into the fire again. 'And you will come to the notice of the Worm at last, old fool.'

'It seems likely.'

The old man spat and turned away – from Orothellin, from Che, from the world.

Later, when the others were sleeping, Che found herself awake, staring at the ceiling of the cave, calling on her Art to see, then banishing it again, swapping between a world of black and a world composed of shades of grey.

Their host was not with them, she realized. Thalric lay beside her, and Tynisa a sword's length beyond him. Esmail was a curled shape across the fire from her, still keeping his secrets. Towards the back of the cave, Messel lay with his blank face turned towards her; impossible to know if he slept or not.

And yet she heard the murmur of voices, and where now was Orothellin's great mounded form? At that, she knew she must have slept a while, because the big man could not have crept past her unobserved when she was awake.

Careful not to wake Thalric, she inched towards the cave mouth, straining her ears to catch their words.

'You had no right,' she heard the Hermit say.

A sigh from Orothellin, but no words.

'I have been beyond its notice for so long. I do not know what I may become if I do this.'

'I have faith in you,' the Slug-kinden murmured.

'What you are asking . . . I have no words. I would have to take her . . . How else can I make her understand that what she seeks cannot be done?'

'Do you instead fear that perhaps it can be done?' Che heard Orothellin prompt gently.

A fraught pause between the two unseen men, and then the Hermit was saying, 'If I come to the attention of the Worm, if I cannot pass beneath its gaze, if the other Scarred Ones recognize me . . .'

'You have often said that you have lived too long.'

'Easy for you to say!' An old man's bitter curse.

'That's well – for that is what I am saying.'

Hearing those words, Che did not understand what Orothellin meant, but it was plain that the Hermit did. The silence that followed had a different quality, until eventually he said, 'You cannot mean it. You intend to remedy that drawn-out thread you call a life, do you?'

'If not for this, then what?'

'For this *girl*? This Beetle child?'

Another enormous sigh from Orothellin, and Che had the distinct sense that he knew she was eavesdropping. 'The greatest failure of my people was ever their refusal to acknowledge this:

that all things end. And this place, this prison for the Worm, it ends too, and the Worm plans to be outside, and what it leaves behind here will be picked-over corpses in the hollow scoured-out shell that it has hatched from. What have I preserved myself for? Life for its own sake, or a life with meaning? If any of my works are to have meaning, then this is the time . . . the time to give everything.'

'You could at least have the decency to outlive me!' Che heard their host snap. 'You *made* me, you fat waste of breath. You taught me to be this useless thing I am now. You took me from the Worm . . . I am your whim, your experiment.' The Hermit had looked the older of the two, but Che was forced to remind herself that, of course, the former Master of Khanaphes predated this entire world that they were trapped in.

She had it then, their relationship. Only confusion over their apparent ages had misled her.

'It was unforgivable, I know,' Orothellin said gently.

Another long, melancholy silence from the Hermit, until: 'Why can't you just leave well enough alone?'

'The great failure of my kinden is that we always think we know best. Will you do this, for me?'

She pictured the two of them sitting in the darkness, side by side, those two men, and neither with anything similar to them in the whole of this closed-off world: the bloated father; the withered son.

'I will take her. I will show her. And then she will beg me to remove the knowledge from her mind.' The Hermit's tone was suddenly fierce. 'I will bring her to the Worm in all its glory. She wants to understand? I will make her regret her curiosity tenfold. I will kill her hope within the Worm's coils. I will smother it in the pits.'

'If it dies so easily, it cannot truly be hope,' was all Orothellin would say.

Eighteen

What does it mean?

What can it mean, that she saved me?

The question turned over and over in Maure's head like her very own unquiet ghost.

She had been in that dark place, that terrible place of no escape. Che had been conducting her ritual. Maure had given her all – that little all she had to give. She had felt the others, from each according to their ability, and at the end she had sensed Che's desperation and despair: *Not enough!* Not enough, though it was all the power they had in the world. Maure had resigned herself to defeat, even then.

And, somehow . . . this.

She had felt the curtain tear, just for one moment; the world around her had twisted and tensed, furiously unwilling to let even one of its multitude of captives free. But she had been sprung free, nonetheless. Che had freed her.

She had been the only one. She was enough of a magician to know that. No chance that the others had made it out, too, only to be scattered to the four winds. The Weaponsmaster, the Assassin, Che and her Wasp lover, they were all condemned to the dark.

But me she freed. And why?

Maure could not imagine. She had been nothing to Che, not sister, not lover, not even a friend, truly. Merely an acquaintanc an unasked-for follower.

Looking on the sun, now, she wanted to weep. The tears did come, a little, and not for the first time. *There is no sight more beautiful than this.* And that was true despite the fact that her Moth eyes could pierce that lightless abyss. After what she had seen below, blindness down there might be considered a mercy.

So what does it mean? Because that was always the curse of the Inapt: everything had meaning. Nothing was pure chance. The world fell the way it was because human thought nudged and interpreted and read it. Divination saw the web of the future and wove it at the same time, the seer's vision collapsing all the myriad paths the world might take into fewer and fewer, until the truly gifted magician might look towards autumn and know where every leaf might fall. In theory, anyway. It was true that the science had decayed somewhat since the revolution, the toys of the Apt tearing holes in that predictable web with their mechanistic cosmos that was, paradoxically, so much harder to foretell.

But Maure was a child of the old days, of the Commonweal and other places where divination was still a tool to live by, not a sham to gull the foolish with. She searched for meaning. *Why me? Why here? Why* him? *There must be reasons.*

There was a town ahead, or perhaps just a collection of shacks crouching on the shore of the Exalsee. Her companion, Totho, had put on an extra stumble of speed, fixing his eyes on it, ignoring Maure, making it plain that she was just an unwanted woman trailing his footsteps.

He had spoken to her precisely twice since their first meeting. The first time had been to ask what she was eating, as she started gnawing something grey and fibrous left over from the supplies that Messel had foraged for them. Maure had scrutinized the unappetizing fare and confessed she was not entirely sure. For a moment Totho had just stared at her, and she had thought that he would say something more, as though some great revelation as just on the tip of his tongue. Her expectant expression had htened him off, though – he had seen Che's name written there and had shied away from it, turning his shoulder and stomping off once more, trying to leave her behind.

The second time, not long after that, he had rounded on her without warning and just demanded, 'Why are you following me?'

Maure had blinked at him. 'For a lot of complicated reasons,' she told him; then, as he was turning away once more, she found herself desperate to keep him talking in case she could prise that *meaning* from him. 'And one simple one: I don't have the first idea where I am. Following you's better than nothing.'

'You're by the Exalsee,' Totho had spat back.

'Good.' She had nodded, desperately earnest. 'What's an exalcy? Is it like a principality?'

He had just stared. 'It's this.' A gauntleted hand waved across the water that ran all the way to the horizon. 'It's basically the thing people know about this part of the world. How can you not know this?'

'I was never here before!' she snapped at him, feeling the keen unfairness of it all – she, who had counted herself well-travelled once. 'I come from the Commonweal, understand? I have not the first idea where any of this is!'

For a moment she thought that he might even be sympathetic – but, no, it was just that she had now furnished him with an excuse to explain her away. 'What, you're an escaped slave? The Imperials brought you here?'

'No, I told you. Che—!'

He had snapped, lunging for her – she had skipped back out of his way the first time but his armour didn't slow him half as much as she expected and, on the second try, he had one of her wrists in his metal grip.

'You don't know Che!' He had bellowed into her face. 'Shut up about Che! You don't know her and you don't know me! I'll . . .' Looking into that incandescent expression, it was easy for Maure to finish that bitten-off sentence: *I'll kill you if you say her name again.* He must have seen something in her frightened face – a woman only a few years his senior, and just as lost as he was – and he had just flung her hand away and marched on, bunching his shoulders against her inevitable, unsheddable presence, now dogging his heels like some part of his shadow that had become detached but would not just go away.

Totho had been walking for too long, and each step he took just emphasized the fact that he was going nowhere. He might as well tread round and round the Exalsee's vast circumference like a clockwork toy, until he wound down forever. With that thought, the woman's constant trailing acquired a sinister connotation, as if she was patiently waiting for him to drop so that she could rob or dismember his corpse. Certainly there seemed something of the dead about her, impossible to put his finger on, but just as impossible to ignore.

Now there was something ahead that spoke of other people, after what seemed an eternity of lonely journeying with only the maddening, unwanted company of this inexplicable woman. Totho had never been fond of people, as a general rule – a trait born out of their general lack of feeling for him. Nowhere in the world loved a halfbreed.

Or, no, there had been one place, but it was gone.

Just now he felt he needed company: company that was not hers. For company could supply him with something to ease his pain, in exchange for the coins he had in his purse. That was the function of company, if it was not to be the company of his peers.

He saw mostly Bee-kinden there, some outpost of Dirovashni with a couple of piers extending into the Exalsee and a living based on fishing. There was a taverna, though. That was enough. It was a rough, unfinished sort of place – no tables and nowhere to sit but empty kegs. Three Solarnese were playing a game of cards in one corner, and a Spider sat by herself, clad in armour of silk and tarnished scales, a rapier sheathed at her hip.

The taverner was a squat Bee woman, blind in one eye,

and she regarded Totho nervously, already sensing trouble brewing.

'Wine.' Totho threw a coin at her, close enough to make her duck. It was gold, though – a central from the Helleren mint. It would keep his bowl full for a while.

His halfbreed follower was still loitering at the door, but Totho was waving for a refill before she deigned to find a patch of ground to call her own. The taverner assailed her immediately – even the dirt on the floor was for paying customers only.

She had no coin. Perhaps she was someone's slave, after all. That made so much more sense than anything involving Che. Just another halfbreed slave cast adrift on the shores of the Exalsee. He *wanted* her to have some commonplace unhappy story, and all the rest of it to be mere delusion.

'Oi, woman,' Totho waved another coin at the proprietor. 'Let her drink. Why not?' He was desperately hoping that if he treated Maure like a deranged beggar for long enough, she would turn out to be nothing more than that.

That settled that, and he took the chance to drain his bowl and hold it out again. He was not much of a drinker. He had never had the means when he was a student, and later there had always been his work. A drunken artificer was a creature of little use to anyone. Drephos, of course . . . oh, Drephos never touched a drop. He was . . . he had been drunk on his own brilliance.

Totho felt the cracks start, inside, where the armour could not protect him.

A beautiful abomination, Drephos had been: never to be repeated or to be equalled. A man who cared nothing for kinden or the purity of blood, but for merit only. He had put Collegiate Masters to shame with his egalitarian attitudes. If you *could*, if you were a brother or a sister of the engine and the gear train, the refining vat and the forge, then you had worth to Drephos, no matter what else.

And, in the end, even the Empire had broken its rules for

him. Firstly in creating the rank that he had borne, and secondly in storming an entire city for fear of him.

Totho drank because he had been told that men drank to forget, or for consolation, or to dissolve away all those rational, soluble parts that knew guilt and regret. Each fresh mouthful only brought all those things to the fore of his mind, though. He found no oblivion waiting at the bottom of the bowl.

'That's fine armour you have there, friend.'

He looked up to see a trio of Bee-kinden there, soldiers from the look of them – all too similar to the vermin who had marched into the streets of Chasme and never marched out again. They had snapbows slung over their shoulders and axes at their belts, typical unimaginative sorts without an interesting innovation between them. He had no words for them, and his eyes slid back to his wine.

'Where'd a halfbreed get armour like that, I wonder,' the Bee went on.

'Only one place, I reckon,' one of his companions suggested.

Totho looked up at them again, recognizing that familiar mail of Dirovashni make, that industrious city that had nonetheless always managed to fall behind both Chasme and Solarno, never quite good enough.

'Never quite good enough.' Until he saw their expressions, he had not realized he had spoken aloud.

'We've just come from a city, halfbreed,' said their leader. 'Plenty of halfbreeds there, or there were. A whole nest of them. Burned out now. If it were day, you could see the smoke from here.'

Totho shrugged.

'Some of them got clear. Vermin always do escape. You have to hunt them down or else they breed.'

So, this is it, then. Totho reached within himself, feeling how unsteady he was. Even the prospect of action made his head swim. The unassailable confidence of the drunk seemed to have utterly passed him by. *Perhaps it would be best if I just let this happen.*

'Pissing Iron Glove bastards,' the Bee went on. 'I lost too many friends to your kind when Chasme burned.'

And Totho lurched to his feet, empty handed, snapbow still on the floor with his overturned wine bowl. He was smiling as he said, 'Not to my kind. To me.'

The Bee struck him, a mailed fist striking his cheek and knocking him back against the wall. Then the man had punched downwards, trying for his head again but bruising himself against Totho's pauldron, the force still enough to knock Totho off his feet.

Then they were all on him, kicking and stamping, while he cradled his unarmoured head in his arms, feeling the Bees achieve a rhythm between them, unintentional but mechanical, almost comforting as they tried to destroy him, to stomp him into the dirt of the floor.

They could not hear beneath their own shouts and grunts, but he was laughing. He was laughing because he could barely feel the blows through his magnificent armour, kick as they might.

Then there was a new voice, and he realized to his dismay that the woman had got involved.

She was trying to call them off, and they turned on her, and she had no armour, but she too was a halfbreed. Foreign to Exalsee politics, she would not understand why that made her even more fair game than usual.

But she was speaking firmly, almost desperately, and Totho craned up and saw them listening. First she spoke to one of the subordinate Bees, words too soft for Totho to hear, but the man shook his head, frowning in bafflement, taking a step back. Then she was addressing the other, and he heard her say, 'Would your mother have wished to see you like this? Was this what she meant when she said that she would always be proud of you?'

The look on the Bee's face was stunned. 'My mother's dead,' he got out.

'And she would still be proud of you, if you let her,' the half-breed woman declared.

She turned to the last man, their leader, her mouth open to speak, and he struck her across the face, then lunged forward to grab her even as she fell, hoisting her up and throwing her across the taverna, spilling her in amongst the gamblers. She came up with her shortsword drawn, one hand bloody at her mouth.

'Now we'll see what you're made of, bitch!' the Bee spat.

Then Totho said, 'Hey, you.'

He had prepared himself better, this time. He had his helm on, his world narrowed to a slit, and he had his snapbow in his hands.

To his credit, the Bee was quick. He had his own weapon off his shoulder and aimed towards Totho even as he stumbled back. The whole taverna had gone horribly silent.

Totho had his weapon levelled, as did the Bee. The other two were frozen, reaching for their bows, eyes flicking between their leader and his former victim.

'Go on,' Totho got out, though his words sounded a little slurred even to him. He was aware that he was swaying slightly. 'Go on, shoot me. We'll make it a game.'

The Bee's eyes were very wide.

'A game, you and me,' Totho went on. 'You shoot me, and then I'll shoot you after. Give it your best. Go on. I lost friends in Chasme, too. I lost more than that. I lost everything. So let's play our game.'

He shifted his aim slightly, down and to the side. The Bee's teeth were bared, his hands shaking a little, suddenly on unfamiliar ground.

'*Shoot me, you turd!*' Totho screamed at him, and the man brought his snapbow to his shoulder and loosed it at a range of only a few feet.

He had been aiming for the throat but had hurried the shot. The bolt struck the cheek of Totho's helm, snapping his head round and sending him reeling back into the wall for the second time.

He heard a jubilant yell from one of the other Bees that choked to nothing halfway when Totho did not fall, but just levered himself back on to his feet with his snapbow still levelled, one-handed, the barrel weaving enough to threaten just about everyone else there.

He had their full attention, all of them.

He felt he should say something arrogant and heroic, like *My turn!* or something similarly witty, save that he had known true heroes, men for whom killing was an art form and livelihood and reason for being, and they did not quip as a rule. Instead, the words that came from him were an artificer's.

'Not even a dent,' he told them, and their eyes strayed helplessly to the fluted steel of his helm, the Iron Glove's finest metallurgy and smithing in perfect harmony.

The man on the left broke first, barrelling for the door, and when the snapbow inevitably swung wildly to follow him, the others were running as well, and the rest of the taverna's occupants after them, including the taverner herself. Only the halfbreed woman was left, well within the compass of Totho's roving aim.

'We should be moving,' she suggested. 'No doubt they have more friends, and you seem to be a wanted man.'

'We? What we?' he demanded of her. 'Why are you doing this? Why won't you leave me alone?' He had a horrible moment of disconnection when he wondered if she was actually real, or just some guilt-spawned product of his mind. *But the Bees were talking to her, weren't they? Or were they?*

'I can't tell you, because you wouldn't – couldn't – understand, and it wouldn't make any sense to you. And, anyway, I'd have to mention—'

'Che. Che who you can't know.'

'Her, yes.'

His hand twitched, but he managed to fight his finger away

from the trigger. 'Let's go,' he told her. 'We'll go. We'll find some-where.' He wanted to take more wine, but the sheer logistics of trying to transport a keg defeated him. 'You'll tell me . . . I don't care what. Just tell me. Tell me about Che.'

When Maure had finished the whole sorry story, Totho found himself just shaking his head. They were by the lakeside still, but well beyond the Bee village, amid a grove of willows with the light of a half-moon filtering through their branches.

He felt that if he had drunk less he would have made out more of her actual sentences, and yet still not have understood. It was as if someone had told him some bizarre old story, some ancient Moth legend, but substituted names he knew for its orig-inal mythical characters.

'You make no sense,' he complained weakly.

'I told you that you wouldn't understand.'

'But you make no *sense*,' he insisted. 'How can there be some underground world that isn't actually underground? How can a whole kinden, and all those others, just have been lost to history – and now come back? How was this Argastos . . . *what* was he? How can that possibly even be a . . . a metaphor, even? What does it mean?'

'You're Apt. I have no words that you will comprehend,' she said sadly. 'To think I used to seek out Apt men . . . but I never needed them to understand me before. All of it is a metaphor. None of it is a metaphor.'

'Besides, Che's Apt too.'

'She's not.'

He scowled stubbornly. 'She's Apt. She was . . . confused, in Khanaphes. She'd lost people, she wasn't thinking straight. I know . . . knew her, though. She's—'

'A magician.'

At that he just laughed, hearing an edge of desperation in his own voice. 'Don't be stupid, woman. Fine, you obviously do know Che and Tynisa and . . . but you're Inapt and you're cracked. I don't care whether you were born that way or fell on your head, but . . .'

'She is a *magician.*' And this time she was standing, staring down at him as he sat with his back to a tree.

He found one hand creeping towards his snapbow, for all that she could not possibly be a threat to him. 'Sit down.'

'She is the most powerful magician I have ever known, Totho,' Maure insisted. 'She says she was crowned by the Masters of Khanaphes, and I believe it. She is raw, untrained, but she has power . . . she *had* power.'

'Khanaphes,' Totho spat in contempt, and abruptly a vision came to him, a memory he tried to keep locked in darkness, of a great wall of water descending, obliterating an army, defying rational explanation. 'She's not . . . Che's not . . .' He stared into Maure's face, recognizing utter certainty there, for all the gap in Aptitude that lay between them. Something clicked into place within him, an escapement that had been waiting for its moment for years. '*He* did it. He did it to her.' His voice sounded very cold even to his own ears.

Maure backed up a step. 'Who . . .?'

Abruptly Totho was on his feet as well, snapbow in hand. 'The Inapt bastard . . . the Moth boy.' For all that the *boy* had been older than Totho at the time. 'He corrupted her somehow. He took her from me and he changed her so that . . . he *spoiled* her.'

'I don't think—' Maure started and then the snapbow was directed at her face, its aim far steadier now than before.

'Pissing *Inapt!*' Totho snapped at her. 'Always you pissing Inapt ruining my *life.*' He knew he was still drunk, but *here* was that grand confidence in the rightness of his actions that he had always been promised. Here was the courage to do what must be done. 'If I could – if I could invent a machine for it – I'd kill every pissing Inapt bastard in the world! Piss on the Bee-killer, I'd make a Moth-killer and I'd use it. And the world would be a better place!'

She was frozen, staring at the weapon.

'And you know why? Out of your own mouth, that's why!' He was fighting to order the words. 'Either you're such pissing ridiculous liars that every word you say is suspect, or . . . can you imagine what I would have to think if I *believed* any of it? If any of it was true? How you Inapt have screwed the world over and over, fighting stupid wars, burying whole kinden, sitting around and turning into the living dead? Even if it were true, how much better the pissing world would be if we'd never had any of you!'

Eyes wide, she looked at him down the length of the snapbow. 'I suppose that's probably true.' And then, after a strained pause: 'Do you shoot me now?'

He blinked at the snapbow, which had seemed so very necessary a moment before. 'It was just . . .'

'A metaphor?'

He scowled down the tentative smile appearing on her face. 'Don't you joke with me. I am not in the mood.' With that, he felt as though his strings had been cut, and he slumped down beside the tree again. 'I should have brought that wine after all. Why me, eh?' He hadn't wanted to return to the question, but the mere mention of Che, her reintroduction into his life, even by proxy, had kindled a horrible spark in him, for all he tried to extinguish it. Sometimes hope became the worst enemy.

'I don't know.' She shrugged. 'I saw you in Che's mind, back in her past. I know you were a friend of hers. When she sent me back here, when she sent me out, I don't think she could dictate where I went but . . . there is meaning.'

'Or your bad luck.'

She shrugged. 'You Apt believe the world is so random, and so you build your machines to control as much of it as possible. To me, there is so little actual chance in the world. Its patterns are capable of prediction, and so it is not a matter of controlling so much as planning ahead.'

That came so close to making sense to Totho that he just nodded and let her continue.

'She *sent* me here to you,' Maure concluded. 'What else is there? Not to Khanaphes, not to Collegium, not to the Commonweal where she and I met. No – *here*, to you. The line that connects the two of you was strong enough to guide me.'

'There is no line, not any more,' Totho announced harshly.

He saw her expression, clearly wanting to speak but fearful of doing so, and waved her words on.

'Only if you promise not to shoot me.'

'I won't shoot you.'

'I am a necromancer. I can see the ghosts that haunt people, that hang about them – both the dead and the living. I look at you and I see Che there, right there.' And he actually looked around to where she pointed, craning past his pauldron to see what was so very evident to this woman.

He did have a brief moment of wanting to shoot her then, if only to eradicate this incomprehensible knot that his life was caught in. The realization that he had nothing else left, that the knot was the one thing holding him from plunging into the abyss, stayed his hand.

Nineteen

She tried to tell them, truly she did.

Yes, she was Empress of the Wasps, and her word was law, transmitted by her own mouth or by those of her Red Watch. She was entitled to command, and indeed the entire structure of the Empire was set up for that specific purpose. Nevertheless she had felt a burning need to communicate her reasons for what she was telling them to do.

For I do not wish to be remembered as . . . but there were no words to express how they might remember her. Long after her death, her name would be a byword for atrocity unless she could make them understand how *right*, how *necessary*, this whole desperate endeavour was.

So she had called them all to her audience chambers, where she sat on her throne before them with Tisamon's louring presence at her side. The great powers of the Empire had all been represented there. She had summoned General Brugan of the Rekef and General Lien of the Engineers. She had called in Marent of the army and the magnates of the Consortium. She had spoken the names of the luminaries of the Quartermasters and the Slave Corps, and of course they had come as swiftly as they could. Nobody wanted to disappoint the Empress.

There, in the very hub of her power, where she was strongest, she had confronted them. She had worked it all out beforehand, what she would say. She would tell them the truth. They were the Empire, her people, so the truth was something she owed them.

She would tell them it all: the secret histories and the hidden worlds and the terrible deeds done at the dawn of time. 'There was a war,' she would say, for at least they would understand that much. She would detail who that war had been against, not even deigning to mask her intentions behind the derogatory label of 'the Worm'.

She would stand before them and tell them how all the powers of the old world had gathered together to defeat that ancient enemy, and how it had then been sealed away, locked beyond the world, until now.

Her own guilt in its eventual release she would not describe – they did not need to know – only that it was out now, and must be put back in its place.

After that, she had planned to explain precisely the draconian measures that were now their only chance. It had all made such perfect sense to her, regardless of the blood that would be on all their hands once it was done – blood enough to make even a general flinch. They would at least know that the ends justified those or any other means.

When they had come at her call, to throng her chambers with as great a gathering of Imperial power as the world had seen in many a year, she had stood, faced them and drawn breath. She had looked upon their faces, and touched the hard stones of their minds.

Her words had dried up in her throat.

What she had seen there was ignorance. It was not the sort of ignorance that could be educated out of them: they had been born with it, a birthright passed down through the blood of every Wasp save for her. Looking at all those respectful expectant faces, she had abruptly seen herself as they saw her – and as they would also see her once she had finished her earnest recounting.

They would nod, and bow, and be the abject servants of the

throne, and then they would leave. And they would think that she was mad.

The truth of her words – she would speak nothing to them but truth – would curdle into fiction in their ears and in their minds. The grinding mills of their Aptitude would take it in and churn out nothing but scrap for them. And they would murmur to each other that their Empress was insane. And after that perhaps some of them would laugh at her. And, however hard she strove to root out such mirth, she would still hear their laughter. That kind of humour spread like a disease.

For the first time since taking the throne, Seda stared her Empire in the eye and was the one to look away first. She could bear many things, but she found that the mockery of her people was not one of them. Let them hate her; let them fear her; only let them not laugh.

And so, before that great host of the mighty, she had simply given out a handful of uncompromising instructions, baffling in their scope and intent, and let them wonder. Even then there was a miasma of doubt hanging about the room as they thought: *All this, just for that?* They did not understand her, and the distance between them was only growing wider. Even her own Red Watch could not follow her to the terrible places she was forced to walk.

Straessa the Antspider ducked back, a snapbow bolt striking stone dust near her face. By now she reckoned there were far fewer Wasps scattered amongst the buildings of this village than there were solid Collegiate company soldiers at her back, but the Wasps had been very inventive in picking their shooting positions.

And they said I shouldn't be leading this sort of thing any more. And I didn't listen, worse luck.

It was just a little satellite village on the rail line, but the Wasps had obviously picked it as a good place to inconvenience the expeditionary force; no doubt there were all sorts of explosive surprises planned, and so a punitive force had been sent in to root them out. Straessa had vaguely expected to find barricades and a shooting line, but the Wasps had spread out their force and were using the buildings themselves as their cover, making every step into the open a potential last one.

She had got her people within sight of the central square, but then three or four had speedily been picked off, and everything had ground to a halt. She had some fifty soldiers with her, against perhaps half that many Wasps, but so far the Collegiates had scored only a single kill.

She saw movement across the square, what might have been a shape hunched on a rooftop, and took careful aim at that low bulge disfiguring the flat-roofed silhouette, drawing a deep breath and trying to hold each muscle in perfect stillness save for those of one finger.

And loose.

And miss. She saw the figure jerk back, but in surprise rather than pain. A moment later the Wasp was dead, toppling from the roof, and she had a momentary glimpse of an arrow's long shaft in the corpse.

Castre Gorenn, founder and sole member of the Commonweal Retaliatory Army, dropped from a clear sky onto the roof, another arrow already nocked to her bow, the string drawn back even as the Antspider watched. She got a single shaft off before rolling off from her perch, wings catching her and taking her to cover, the bolts of the Wasps darting past her like gnats.

That's one more – no, two, I'll bet. Three in all. And, because she was watching for it, she saw a Wasp leaning out, trying to track the Dragonfly, incensed by the loss of his comrades. Straessa brought her snapbow up hastily, but someone else was quicker, and the enemy death toll went up to four in that moment.

And how many are there in total? A score? Score and a half?

She had no more targets that she could see, although that didn't mean there weren't any that could see her. *Time to make another dash for it.*

A handful of her people had the same idea, all rushing forwards to their next piece of cover. Bolts struck dust at their heels, and one man fell, yelling, shot through the leg, dragged into cover by his comrades. Straessa sent a shot towards where she reckoned one of the enemy was positioned, then braced herself to make the same advance, knowing that some of her people were going to have to go into the buildings and flush the Wasps off the roofs for the rest to shoot at. *And this is just a little village. Collegium is going to be all this and a hundred times more.*

And where the pits is everyone? Is the Empire enslaving whole villages, or did they flee, or . . .?

She ran, just breaking into the open without thought, and not stopping until she was in the shelter of a doorway, whilst some detached part of her mind calmly noted where the shooting was coming from. A second of pause, in cover, to check whether she *was* actually in cover, and then she had leant out round the side of the house, snapbow already tracking upwards. She saw the Wasp there, exactly where she had guessed at, but he was already ducking back, someone else's shot keeping his head down. Then a bolt came at her from another angle entirely – her blind side – and she returned the shot instantly but somewhat randomly – no hope of hitting but it was something for the enemy to think about.

Then there was a shout from her first target, and she leant out again, wincing, seeing Gorenn there again, kicking the man backwards off the roof. The Wasp scout's wings flared, catching him, but one of Straessa's people took him down a moment later, and Gorenn took three swift steps – as though she was simply winding up to jump to the next roof – and then dropped straight down. Straessa found the man who had shot at her last and skipped a bolt near him as he tried to aim, and then the Sarnesh arrived.

She had not been expecting them. Indeed, the Sarnesh had been remarkably stand-offish about their Collegiate allies, with that particular silent sneer that only Ant-kinden could ever master. Here they were, though, and it looked to be at least a hundred of them, swarming across the village, through the streets, into every house.

The Wasps had plainly decided that enough was enough, and they were lifting off and trying to head south with all speed. Straessa saw several picked off promptly, but at least a dozen got clear away. They had done their job for as long as it remained possible, and they were no fools.

She stayed in cover for a while longer, enough to allow the Sarnesh to clear every building – no point taking the risk of one last Wasp sniper with an over-keen sense of duty. At last, though, once she saw the Ants assembling in the square, she came out and called for her own people.

'Good work, all of you,' she shouted to them. 'Wounded being tended?'

'Yes, Officer.'

'Gorenn!'

The Dragonfly headed over, an arrow to her bow still, just in case.

'You did well.' Straessa expected the Dragonfly simply to shrug that off, but the woman nodded gravely. 'What is it?'

Gorenn held up an arm, putting a finger through the bolt hole in her sleeve that had a little blood at the edge of it. 'Good shots, that lot,' she said soberly.

'Get it seen to,' Straessa advised her, and then put her hand on the Dragonfly's shoulder as Gorenn turned around. She wanted to say, *Remember you're not immortal*, but in the end she just squeezed reassuringly and let the woman go.

'Who's officer in charge?' the Antspider called out to the Sarnesh. She was expecting to encounter that stiff-necked disdain, all the more so because she was a halfbreed – an Ant halfbreed at that – but one of them stepped forwards and nodded to her without any obvious antipathy. Of course he wore no badge of rank, and of course he looked just like the rest, more or less. She made sure she kept him in sight at all times, in case they should pull some sort of switch on her.

'Where are the locals, Officer?' he asked her.

'No idea. Run away, probably.'

'I think the Wasps killed them,' he told her.

'You think . . .' A cold feeling rose up in her. *A village like this with, what, three hundred people, more?* 'Why do you say that?'

'My soldiers see signs of violence in many of the buildings – broken furniture, bloodstains. Some of the homes themselves seem damaged. And there was . . . a body.'

'*A* body? Just the one?' But something in the way he said it was making her very uncomfortable.

'Show me.' And, as Gorenn was shamelessly eavesdropping and had not gone to get her scratch seen to at all, she signalled the Dragonfly to come with them.

The place had been a general store, the main room hung with tools and supplies, neither taken by the fleeing occupants nor looted by the Wasps. The Ant officer led her through to the back room, and there she saw it.

Gorenn was a little ahead of her, and she recoiled as soon as she entered, bowstring tugged back and arrow levelled at something low to the floor. Straessa heard the Ant say, 'It's dead. We killed it when we came in here, though it bit one of my soldiers . . . we don't know yet if he'll survive the poison.'

Eyes following the point of the arrow, Straessa could be forgiven for seeing the dead centipede first, almost bisected by a sword-blow and curled up in its last death throes. Then she saw the human body, or what was visible of it.

Her stomach lurched, and perhaps it was only her stubbornness in not wanting to show Collegium up before the Sarnesh that kept down the bile.

A Beetle-kinden woman lay dead there, but not by sword or sting. She was buried up to her armpits in the ground itself, the very stone flags of the floor rippled and twisted about her, as though it had become quicksand. As though something had been dragging its victim down into it. Her arms were frozen as if clawing at the ground, her face tilted towards the ceiling and locked in a twisted, soundless scream.

'You think . . . the *Wasps* . . .?' Straessa breathed in disbelief.

The Sarnesh officer shuffled uncomfortably. It was plain he very much wanted to be able to blame the Empire.

'Not the Wasps,' Gorenn whispered. 'Not the Wasps.' She was already backing out of the room, out of the building, arrow still held to the string, but her hands shaking far too much to have aimed it.

'We withdrew when the Sarnesh arrived, sir,' the scout reported. 'We got the chance to lay some traps on the rails for their baggage train, though.'

'Given current progress, I'd guess they'll find and disarm them quickly enough,' Tynan decided, because the Collegiate artificers had proved quite capable of that so far. 'They're camped within sight of the walls?'

'Yes, sir, but out of effective artillery range.'

If we still had the big greatshotters . . . But, like respectable air reinforcements, replacement artillery had not been forthcoming. Tynan guessed that, as he was already on the right side of the walls of his city, he was not considered a priority.

'General, the village . . . it was cleared of its occupants when we arrived,' the scout added. 'Signs of a struggle, but we saw no bodies. Just like . . .'

Tynan held a hand up. 'I know.' *I know, and I don't want to think of it, because we've all seen too much of that – even inside the city, that once! – and still nobody has any answers for me.* 'And the Vekken?' he enquired, because that was something military and comprehensible.

'At a similar distance to the west, General, and a good space between them and the Sarnesh. The Collegiate orthopters are still providing air cover for them.'

But not the Sarnesh fliers. Although the Ants and the Beetles flew the same model of craft, Bergild's Farsphex pilots could tell whose hands were on the stick just from the flying styles.

'Fine, back to your squad.' He dismissed the scout because his headquarters was crowded at the moment, with friends and enemies both. 'They can only be waiting for an uprising from the populace,' Tynan decided. 'Double patrols, no exceptions to the curfew, and break up any gatherings of more than a dozen. Let's have some keen-eyed lads up on the roofs as well, to keep a lid on it. Prepare a sally force of about a third of our strength. We'll hit the Vekken first.'

'General, no.'

Tynan's head snapped round, to see the eternal thorn in his side.

'Major Vrakir, you have something to say?'

'Do not dilute our forces within the city, sir. They will be needed.'

Vrakir had that curiously set look to his face that Tynan had learned to expect, as though the man was trying to disassociate himself from his own mouth.

'No doubt this is the Empress's wisdom we're hearing?'

Vrakir locked eyes with him. 'Her own words, General. Our forces will be called upon to defend Collegium. There must be no sorties. You've said yourself that they have neither the numbers nor the engines to take the walls.'

'Unless some concerned citizen opens the gates to them, and the longer they sit out there unchallenged, the more chance there is of that happening,' Tynan shot back.

'Even so, General.'

Each time this happened, each time Vrakir came out with some new proclamation, Tynan braced himself, wondering if this was the moment that he would break loose from these ridiculous shackles and call the man's bluff. But then came the thought, always: *Remember what it is you have already done.* And, in the echo of that, he just nodded and gritted his teeth. *Bend over for Vrakir and the Empress.*

He put a hand to his forehead. He had been drinking last night, when the dreams had got too much for him, and the after-effects were proving stubborn.

'So our ground forces sit still, and yet you want most of our air cover pissing off east to escort who knows what, leaving us open to their orthopters?'

'Yes, General. It is necessary.'

'What does she tell you, Vrakir?' he asked roughly. 'Why can't we just smash the Vekken and the Sarnesh, given they've delivered themselves up to us in such convenient numbers?' He had long since given up questioning how it was that the Empress's words reached this man. Secret agents, messenger insects, some tiny ratiocinator engine surgically implanted in Vrakir's skull: all of these he might believe.

Vrakir swallowed, and Tynan raised an eyebrow, seeing that even he was having difficulty forcing the words out.

'Fear death by water,' was all he had in reply.

After dismissing the lot of them, Tynan returned to his quarters in disgust, to meet with his guest.

When she had been brought in – not long before the scouts returned – he had assumed this was the herald of some great insurgency amongst the Collegiates. After all, the Fly Sartaea te Mosca was reckoned to be some manner of agitator by the Moths.

She had denied that, and so he had her placed under guard while he went to deal with more important matters. He had left her food and wine, though, and refrained from putting her in a cell or binding her. He felt that she had become one of those curious unknown quantities – not one of *ours*, and yet perhaps not one of *theirs* either, someone who might prove useful. Tynan was no intelligencer, but governing a city was fast turning him into one.

'Now,' he addressed her, as he strode in, 'what was it?'

She had been sitting at his table and pouring the last of the wine, and now she started guiltily. 'General, no doubt you're wondering what's about to happen with the Sarnesh and the Vekken.'

'Forgive me if I don't actually believe you're going to tell me.'

'I don't know, not exactly, but I know that they have come to retake the city, General. I've come here to give you some advice, if you will take it.'

He stared at her for a moment. 'Is that advice to leave the city?'

'It is, I'm afraid.'

'Then that's not an option. I have my orders.'

'General, I . . .' She bit at her lip. 'I'd be getting nowhere if I said that I was a magician, would I?'

He laughed at her although, by the time he had sat across from her, the sound had something broken about it. 'Is that something you're likely to tell me? Are you the Empress's voice, too?' Even as he said it, he knew that those words should sound like some wild non-sequitur, but instead they seemed to follow on perfectly naturally.

'General—'

'Listen to me, Fly-kinden,' he told her, harsher than he had intended, simply to cover up his unease. 'Your Ant friends are too few to help you, and they can't even join forces to work together against us. Vekken and Sarnesh, they hate each other worse than they hate us! They'll be at each others' throats within a tenday, if we don't destroy them first.' *Which we can't, because Vrakir says that the Empress says* . . . That curious tone in which the Red Watch man uttered, *Fear death by water*, as though he could not believe his own mouth, as though he was a prisoner to some barbed thing inside his head, which was making him say such things.

'They will not fight each other,' te Mosca told him. 'Your scouts will tell you soon, if you have not heard already.'

'Tell me what?'

'Stenwold Maker has been seen in the Ant camps. He will keep them in line.'

'Maker's dead,' Tynan spat back immediately.

'Then show me his body.'

Abruptly he kicked back from the table, as though this small woman was venomous. Her words, Vrakir's words, the scout's report of the emptied village, everything rattled and jumbled in his mind, and for a moment he felt that it almost came together to make some terrible, unthinkable sense, some pattern that his mind was simply not prepared to accept.

'Tell your people that if they rise up, I will make an example of them,' he hissed to te Mosca. 'Every man or woman who takes up arms will be on the crossed pikes, and their families shipped east as slaves. Tell them!' His own threats sounded hollow in his ears.

Taki was proud that at least half of her pilots got into the air ahead of the Sarnesh. Certainly, the Ants had the benefit of their mindlink, but defending Collegium from the Empire had meant that being kicked out of bed and straight into the cockpit had become second nature to her.

Barely half an hour before, a Stomreader scout had skidded to a hasty landing, the pilot leaping out to warn that there was trouble on the way. The Empire was getting reinforcements.

At around the same time, the Imperial Second Army's Farsphex were all lifting off and heading eastwards to shepherd the new arrivals in. That meant it was time for Taki and her comrades to go and pick a fight.

Rising up now from the Sarnesh camp, she craned left and right to see the swiftest of her comrades falling into place around her – Collegiate Beetle-kinden and Mynan airmen, most of them veterans of a dozen aerial skirmishes. The Sarnesh were below, just warming their wings, all about to leap from the earth at the same unheard signal.

Airships, the scout had said, and that covered a multitude of sins. Taki had given very clear orders on how to react if the Empire was trying the same trick as last time – a ship that was basically nothing more than a mobile hornet hive. When the Second had taken the city, Collegium had lost the bulk of its aerial forces to that ruse, although the Imperial pilots had hardly come out unscathed either.

Still, it doesn't make sense to do it twice. Not only because their opponents would be expecting it, but because the overwhelming air superiority the Empire had been countering then simply did not exist now. Perhaps Collegium and Sarn did have a bit of an edge in the air, but both sides had nowhere near the number of craft that earlier clashes had seen. In the end, neither the Empire nor its enemies had been able to match production to the intervening attrition, and now Taki guessed that the flower of the Wasp Air Corps was being deployed elsewhere.

Three big airships, though? Can't just be a supply run. And the only answer to that was: *Better take a look, the hard way.*

She had them in sight: whatever they were, the dirigibles were big enough that she could see the three dots in the sky even at this distance, and she flashed her wingmen to draw their attention.

It was an agonizing wait for the vessels to come into range and, at the same time, the last few hundred yards seemed to dash by far too fast. By then she had had a good look at the airships, seeing some of the largest freighters her considerable experience had encountered, but certainly not the specialist piece they'd shipped the insect hive in.

The Second Army's complement of Farsphex circled and dived about them, already fanning out to take on the enemy. Whatever this business was about, the Wasps wanted to protect it.

Taki's mind spun through its unconscious mathematics, one hand clicking signals left and right at her comrades, detailing plans of attack, the codes all second nature to her now. She knew that the Sarnesh would work to their own agenda, but she had spotted the line they were taking and simply kept her people out of that quarter. The Ants fought together impeccably, as she would have expected, but they tended to huddle as a pack despite

228

everything she had tried to teach them – deadly, but of limited impact in a battlefield as vast as the sky.

Planning done, the burdens of leadership discharged, she again became Taki the pilot, skimming her Stormreader through the sky at her first target, aiming to scatter the enemy and dive at the closest of those airships. *Let's put a few holes in one and see what colour it bleeds.*

After the fight, there were more questions than answers. The Wasp Farsphex pilots had put up a spirited defence, keeping the pressure on the attackers to deflect them from the slow-moving dirigibles. They had lost four, which Taki reckoned was a good catch. One Collegiate pilot had been struck from the air, and the Sarnesh had lost one as well. *That* had been an education – the Ants all over the air for almost ten minutes, as if they had abruptly remembered the drop beneath them, the utter hostility of the surrounding element to a kinden without wings. They had pulled themselves together after that, but Taki reckoned that from now on they wouldn't be so stuffy about taking advice from kinden more at home in the air.

They had brought down one of the three airships by concerted and determined strafing, and that *had* been mostly due to the Sarnesh, who had been able to coordinate their attack runs faultlessly. The other two had lumbered on until they were over Collegium itself, and Wasp soldiers began rising up from the walls, whereupon Taki had finally called off the attack.

She had gone straight back to that one downed craft to get a good look at it before the Imperials tried to rescue whatever it had been carrying. She had been ready for just about anything: soldiers, beasts, more artillery, all the materiel that General Tynan might need to hold off a siege.

What she had not expected was nothing. Nothing at all.

'What do you mean, *nothing*?' Tynan demanded.

'Just that, sir,' Captain Bergild reported, sounding just as incredulous as he did. 'I lost four of my pilots to bring these things in, and they're empty – great big freight-carriers, and it looks as if the Quartermasters forgot to load up before they took off.'

Tynan stared past her for a second as he fought his temper down. 'Get me Vrakir.'

'He's already here, General, awaiting your pleasure.'

'Then he'll be waiting a long time.' Tynan glowered about his headquarters. 'Send the man in. I want to hear this.'

Major Vrakir entered smartly. There was a look on his face that Tynan recognized immediately: the look of a man whose duty it was to bear unwelcome news. Vrakir had looked like that when he had come to order Tynan to act against their Spider allies.

'You've some explaining to do,' the general growled. 'First, I hear your threat from the sea has resolved itself into a fleet of a dozen ships hanging back down the coast. Apparently the land forces practically at our gates don't take precedence over a few hundred Tseni marines. "Fear death by water" indeed.'

Vrakir regarded him impassively, rising to none of it.

'And now your empty airships that we diverted our entire air strength to defend. Is there a nagging feeling in the back of your mind, Vrakir? Did your people forget something back in Capitas, perhaps? Is their plan still sitting back at the airfield, all neatly crated and waiting to fly?'

'I need to speak with you, and only you, General,' Vrakir replied.

Tynan looked at him, thinking, *Is this it then? Is this when we come to blows, the two most senior Wasps in Collegium trading sting-shot across a small room?*

Would I welcome that, if it was?

With a sick feeling he realized that he would. If Vrakir tried to kill him, then he would take that as a fair excuse for killing Vrakir right back. *Is this something Mycella did to punish me, when I killed her? Is this some Art – some Inapt thing – that has hold of*

230

me? Or is it just me? Come on, Tynan, you don't need *anything more than that to want this man dead. You're already an unnatural bastard for having let him live this long.*

He flexed his fingers, shrugged his shoulders. He wore a leather cuirass under his tunic, and it might deflect the fire of a stingshot, if he was lucky. Vrakir, on the other hand, looked unarmoured.

'Get out, all of you,' he murmured.

'General—?'

'All of you, out now. Out into the next room, but wait for my shout.' *Because if he is quicker than me, then by the Empress I'll trust you to kill him before he can get out of this place.* 'You too, Captain Bergild.'

The woman looked as though she wanted to protest, which Tynan found oddly touching, but in the end she left along with the rest of them.

Tynan slid one foot back for better balance, waiting for the first sign that Vrakir might go for him. He was a loyal servant of the Empire, was Tynan. He would not strike first.

Instead, the Red Watch officer reached into his tunic, the least threatening gesture a Wasp could make, and drew out a scroll.

'Orders, General,' he said quietly. 'These airships brought orders.'

'That's a lot of hold space for one piece of paper,' Tynan remarked. Vrakir was pointedly still at attention – a hard pose to launch a surprise attack from, which was probably the original point of it. Unwillingly, Tynan stepped forwards and snatched the scroll that Vrakir proffered.

Tynan retreated again, unrolling it, noting the seals: no strange intuitions of the Red Watch this time. The Empress herself had held this paper and given it her mark.

He scanned the few lines written there, feeling a weird sense that he had done this all before.

'This is . . .'

'We should begin loading immediately, General,' Vrakir confirmed.

Loading, yes, but not with the soldiers of the Second, who were hereby commanded to hold Collegium against all comers. No last-minute escape for Tynan's boys if things go bad, instead . . .

'What is this?' Tynan demanded, crumpling the scroll.

'Orders, General,' Vrakir said again. 'We have three score Slave Corps to deal with the logistics, but we should . . .'

'Major Vrakir, we don't have anywhere like this number of Collegiates in the cells, never mind whether any of them are Inapt or not. This simply isn't—'

'General, the Empress is not looking for criminals or seditionists or rebels. She simply seeks slaves. I will give the necessary orders to begin rounding up the local population. We have lost one airship, but the slavers reckon we should be able to fit almost a thousand in the hold of each surviving vessel, if they pack them tight.'

'What is this all about, Vrakir?' Tynan demanded.

'The Empress's will, sir,' Vrakir replied, while his expression said eloquently, *I don't know. I do not know.*

Twenty

'First,' said the Hermit, 'we must prepare.' He stared into Che's eyes, as though trying to startle into the open the fear he plainly thought should be there.

She met his gaze evenly, if only because his eyes were relatably human. They had less of the Worm's taint than his other features.

'You cannot just go to the Worm. You cannot see what the Worm is, not a stranger like you,' he went on. 'The Worm knows its own, yes, it does. And you are not. You will be—'

'But you have a way,' Che cut him off. She was very aware of her companions watching all this. Despite the gravity of the situation, she was beginning to feel slightly ridiculous with this man prattling on.

Abruptly there was a knife in his hand, a curved blade most of a foot long, and he had latched on to her wrist, dragging her close again when she tried to pull away. He was stronger than he had any right to be.

Hearing the sudden scuffle, she knew that Thalric would have one palm thrust forwards, with Tynisa's rapier whispering from its sheath. Her eyes were on the knife, though, and she could not work her throat sufficiently to tell them to stand down.

Instead, it was Orothellin's voice booming, 'Wait!' the echo of it rolling about the cave. 'It must be this way.'

Che felt the tension waver in its balance, because the old

Master of Khanaphes did not command that sort of authority, and the Hermit's expression offered no reassurance at all.

Her heart was hammering, but she studied the old man, his pallid skin cicatrized with those twisted spirals. 'The mark of the Worm,' she got out.

His smile was vicious. 'As you say. Are you regretting your decision yet?'

Yes. Because what she did here now would mark her permanently, and not just her flesh. She was being inducted into a terrible mystery, the touch of which would stain her forever.

The Hermit's grin was spreading as he saw her falter, and sheer obstinacy did the rest.

'Do it.' She bared one arm for him, right up to the shoulder. *This is the price I pay, or the first instalment of that price. I have set my course and I shall follow it, come what will.*

He rested his blade on her skin, pausing a moment as though working out the precise movement in advance, and then drawing the keen edge across her skin with a twisting circular motion of his wrist.

She hissed pain through her teeth, eyes clenched shut against it, suppressing the cry. The sickness inside was worse, though: the corruption that bled in just as her blood welled out, and she knew she had consented to a terrible thing. But she wanted knowledge, and every tale of the Bad Old Days made clear that knowledge was only had for a price – and at least she had known beforehand what coin she would be paying in.

Then the Hermit was swabbing at the wound – which hurt more than the cut – and considering his handiwork.

'Not quite, no, not quite,' he muttered, and she felt Thalric's hand in hers, giving her something to clench on as the Hermit picked and cut shallow hatches and lines, and then as he rubbed something gritty and stinging into the bloody gashes, his fingers wet to the knuckles with her blood. The burning pain of his work seemed to go on forever, and reach right to her core, the actual wound itself a mere abstraction.

'It mustn't heal. You'll have it for life, yes indeed,' the Hermit muttered. 'And, even then, it won't last you for long. This doesn't make you one with the Worm. You'll not walk in its shadow for long, with just this little scratch, no, no.' Another vile grin. 'Though you'll have this to remember us by, oh yes, you will.'

She could see more than a dozen such scars on his own skin, and that counted only those parts of his dirty, pasty hide that were exposed.

'Now you're ready, eh?' And the grin had become a glower, as though he had been forced to do all this at knife point. 'Now you'll see – and you'll be sorry.'

'Old man,' Esmail broke in, 'give me a scar to match hers.'

'I'm not taking two!' the Hermit spat.

'Perhaps I'll walk that way on my own,' the Assassin replied.

The Hermit chuckled bitterly. 'This one, I'll take her, but if she strays from my heels, that little mark won't save her. She must be marked, yes, but even then her life is bound to me. I was born of the Worm, at least. She can hide in my shadow. You will not pass for the Worm without me.'

Esmail considered this, his face a closed book to Che. Then he blinked and nodded. 'I have made a livelihood of walking where I was not wanted, seeming what I was not. So, there is no magic here, and my old tricks won't work, but the bulk of my training does not need a magician's touch, and I'll take whatever I can get. Cut me, old man.'

The Hermit's eyes sought out Orothellin, who shrugged, plainly uncertain, but in the end Esmail endured the same ritual, gritting his teeth against it as the Hermit worried away at his arm. If he felt the depth of the taint, he did not show it. Perhaps it was only a little more darkness in an almost starless sky.

'What will you do?' Che asked Esmail, after it was done and he was nursing the wound.

He shrugged with his unmarred shoulder. 'If you intend to accomplish anything here, and if I am to be of any use to you – if we are to see the sun again – then I play by whatever rules this place admits to. If there is an Emperor of Worms, I will walk into his palace and cut his throat.'

At that, the Hermit cackled, eyes bulging. 'You'll . . . aha no, no, you won't. She'll tell you, if she comes back. She'll see, and she'll tell you just why you can't. Now come on, girl. It's time we were gone.'

'Orothellin has told me we were magicians, once.' The Hermit had a surprising turn of speed for an old man, moving swiftly over the uneven ground, clambering here and there with the sureness of his Art, making Che work to keep up with him. 'No more, though.'

'I had thought you . . . or the others like you . . . the men with scars . . .' she began uncertainly. 'Are they not . . .?' Ahead her eyes could make out the random clutter of the city of the Worm she had looked out over before. Until it had come into sight, the Hermit had just hunched alongside, practically ignoring her. Now it was as though the sight of his kin had opened a door within him, and the words came out.

'No, magician is not the word for what they are, or for what I was,' he grunted, hauling himself over a ledge, his staff clattering against the stone. He was making no attempt at stealth. 'But we must keep clear of them. That mark on you, as well as my presence, these will let us pass the segments of the Worm – but the head has eyes, yes? The Scarred Ones, they will see you, and know you for an intruder, and then you will die. I will die, too, if they know me. We must avoid them.'

'If not magicians, then what?' Che demanded, out of breath with the constant scrabbling and climbing and bursts of flight.

He stopped abruptly. 'You must not think in such terms. It will not help you where you're going.'

'So give me some new terms. Just tell me . . . I mean, what do you believe of magic? Are you Apt? Do you just think it's nonsense?' It struck her that here, where the magic just drained away like water out of cupped hands, it would be very easy to be Apt.

'Magic is irrelevant. The work of the slaves, their devices and machines, that is irrelevant,' the Hermit pronounced. 'None of it matters in the face of god.'

Che stared at him, and the smile that broadened across his colourless face seemed only just this side of madness.

'And the name for what they are – for what I was – is *priest*.'

'I . . . don't understand,' she confessed.

'No, you do not and you cannot, just as I cannot understand when Orothellin talks of magic. But I can show you, and then you will understand—'

'And regret, yes,' she finished for him testily.

They travelled in silence for a while, as the broken city expanded to fill the dark land ahead of them, but the Hermit kept glancing back, still trailing the threads of their conversation, and at last he said, 'Orothellin told me we were magicians.'

'So you said.'

'But magic failed us. We fought our war, and lost, and came to this place, as you – so wise, yes – as you know. But magic was not enough, and we were imprisoned with our enemies, so many of them, our own slaves among them. And we needed some kind of strength that was not the strength of magicians nor the strength of slaves. So we found god. You'll see.'

They were approaching a caravan of beasts: great armoured woodlice and millipedes burdened down with cages and sacks. The soldiers of the Worm were everywhere around it, but she saw slaves there, too, some bound, others walking freely alongside, no doubt to assist with the unloading. *Why do they not resist?* she found herself thinking, but she had seen this too many times before not to know the answer. *Because collaboration spares them the whip or the tax or something similar. How cheaply lives are sold when slaves make their own shackles.*

If she was to accomplish anything here, that collaboration

would be her greatest foe: the habits of a thousand years of indenture would not be broken easily. Or perhaps at all.

As they crossed into the shadow of the buildings, the Hermit's pace had become more cautious, and he was looking out for other Scarred Ones, holding her back whenever he saw one, skulking by walls, creeping across open spaces, every clumsily underhand movement seeming to scream out to Che that here they were about some clandestine business. And all the more surreal because the Worm was all around. Its foot soldiers thronged the city, many of them heading inwards to join that great and spreading spiral. But whatever power lay in the Hermit's scars, it shielded them from that collective vision entirely.

In her head, where for a long time had been only the echo of her own thoughts, she heard a faint, deep susurration, the muted, distant sound of some great voice, and she shivered. Other than that imagined noise, the city had only a single sound: a thin, constant keening, high and painful to hear, so that she wondered if the Worm, the destroyer, was itself in constant pain.

'These scars—' she started, but the Hermit waved her back, and the two of them hid, crouching beside a wall, whilst another of the Scarred Ones – the *priests* – passed in the distance.

'They are necessary. Without them, my kinden are just loops and segments of the Worm. Our stigmata, they spiral and they spiral, and they lead the Worm's attention away so that the mind may be kept free. The scars bind us to the Worm, but keep us from its domination – just enough to be useful, yes. And you hear the Worm's voice, don't you? I know you do.'

She could see ahead a broad open space – a market square in any other city perhaps, but amongst the Worm there was nothing bought or sold, only taken. There were pits there, the same circular shafts she had marked from afar – too broad simply to be wells – and she realized with a start that the wailing sound originated there, and with that she knew what it was. The Hermit turned sharply away from the pits, dragging her with him when she paused to stare.

'You must stay with me!' he hissed. 'Step from my shadow and every eye here shall mark you.'

'I wanted to—'

'That is not the way.' There was something agitated, almost furtive in his manner as he pulled her away from the pits. 'We do not, we do not . . . here, we will enter the earth. Come. Everything will be explained.'

He had found a smaller shaft, and Che watched a string of soldiers exit from it, coursing from the narrow shaft without hesitation. The reverberation in her head seemed louder, as they closed with that aperture, and the image of it as a mouth in the stone was unshakeable.

'Orothellin says . . .' the Hermit told her again, 'but, no, you will sense it yourself. I feel it myself. We go to the cavern that all roads lead to. History is thick here. The way we were, my people, when first we were sealed down here, you will feel it. I have come here and known just how it was, for them.'

He ducked inside, and she could only follow him, hauled unwilling in his footsteps for fear of the Worm recognizing her as a trespasser.

'You cannot imagine it, you who have always had your *sun*. What desolation they must have known, seeing themselves so humbled, so trapped. How they sought within themselves for some means to survive.' He was picking up pace now, forcing her almost to run after him. Half the time he was on all fours, scrabbling and scuttling. She wondered what would happen if they met a Scarred One, here where there could be no hiding.

'Do you feel it?' he demanded, far too loudly. 'Do you feel my ancestors searching for their purpose? Do you feel their terrible despair?'

And she did. It was like a sour taste in her mouth, the anguish of an entire civilization locked away to rot. Looking back, the Hermit must have seen it mirrored in her face.

'Those feelings are still here, all the images and the emotions

239

that my kinden divested themselves of. When they found the Worm within them.'

'But they were always the Worm – or the Moths called them that . . .' Che objected.

'Oh, the Moths and their clever insults. How could they have known that down here we would find the Worm in truth?' the Hermit hissed.

Then he would answer no more questions, but led her down, ever downwards, through cramped tunnels, steep slopes, and always that wordless voice waxing in her mind – a constant urging, an incessant dirge like no sound she had ever heard before.

And then the Hermit had stopped, and she was looking out into a vast cavern from a high vantage point. *We must have gone as far down as this world allows.* But she had no idea of how the metaphysics and the geology would work, and the sight before her gave the lie to her thought, because the rock below was riven by a chasm that descended further into the depths, into a darkness beyond even her eyes' ability to pierce.

Approaching that plunging drop she saw a handful of figures and flinched back when she identified no fewer than three of the Scarred Ones, the Hermit's former brethren. They had some of the Centipede soldiers, too, but the most prominent figure was surely a slave, a hulking Mole Cricket man who looked as though he should be throwing his captors about the cave. Instead, he stood with head bowed, arms by his sides, utterly resigned to . . . what?

Will they throw him into the rift? was her initial thought. The Hermit's hand clenched on her shoulder painfully as he crouched beside her, and she saw a bizarre war of expressions on his face: disgust, fear and a dreadful hungry anticipation.

There was something coming, and with it came the voice. That colossal echoing murmur was growing and growing inside her head, strengthening into an incoherent ranting, the colossal demands of something infantile and hungry and almost mindless. The soldiers of the Worm and their scarred priests were falling back from the slave, where he stood on the very lip of the chasm.

'What is it?' Che got out, feeling that monstrous ascent within every fibre of her being. 'What's coming?'

'God,' breathed the Hermit in her ear, and then god came.

It uncoiled from the depths. Perhaps it *was* the depths. Che's eyes, which knew no darkness, could not see it, only the cold stark night that radiated out from its great articulated body. It reared high towards the roof of the cave, and a wave of crushing despair washed over her. It was a hole in the world in the shape of a centipede, from its flailing whiplike antennae and the hooked poison claws that crowned its head to the rows of clutching, pointed limbs. Screaming horror seethed visibly off it like dark steam, even as that roaring voice reached an incomprehensible crescendo in Che's mind.

And still it came, segment after sightless segment thrusting that head up to sway over the gathering below.

And Che beheld the Worm.

She forced herself to stare at it, to encompass it within her understanding, to reduce it to something she could name. *Just a centipede*, she told herself desperately, but how far from the truth! It was a wrong made physical. It was a devouring tear in the substance of the world, a writhing, many-legged door to somewhere that made this cavern world seem verdant and filled with life in comparison.

It was not utterly lightless. Small pale specks seemed to swim in its depths, or across its carapace, and Che sought them out, hoping to find something there she could understand.

She found it, and she wished she had not. The substance of the Worm was swimming with faces. They were faces of many kinden, rising and submerging, contorting into plastic screams that only added to the Worm's ranting chorus. And Che remembered what Maure had said, that there were not even fragments of the dead here in this underworld. Now she saw. Now she was witness to where the dead went, both whole and in fragments. They went to the Worm, to drown in its freezing depthless body and be devoured.

'Under the sun, perhaps my people could not have found god,' the Hermit whispered, 'but here, buried in their own despair and self-hatred, they reached within themselves, and this was what they called to. You see it? You see god?'

'I see . . .' Old College lessons were rising to the upper reaches of her thoughts. 'What did they do? What did they call?'

And that swaying head, boiling with a darkness so intense it was harder to look at than the sun, had risen twenty feet or more over the gathering below and, with most of its body yet confined to the depths, had gone very still.

'Our essence, the heart of our kinden, the perfect form of the Centipede, from which we draw our Art and our identity,' the Hermit breathed. 'We reached into ourselves with all our rage and spite, and ripped out all that we were, all of the human, and gave form to what was left, our base nature, our totem as seen through the mask of our bitter defeat: our god.'

The doctrine of perfect forms . . . Of course she knew the theory, how each kinden had a perfect exemplar, a theoretical ultimate from whence all Art was drawn. It was only a theory, though. She was not supposed to be able to *look* at one.

'What does it want?' she demanded.

'Want? It wants nothing but the Worm. It wants what the Worm – my people – always wanted. It wants to be alone in the world, to have a world that is nothing but segments of the Worm, replicated over and over. It has no other desires, no thought, no reason to exist save to continue to be, and to grow greater, and to destroy all that is not of itself. What else could be the result of all of our despair and horror but this insensate, pointless god of ours?'

With that, the god of the Worm struck – savagely swift for something so large – and she saw those puncturing claws seize on the Mole Cricket, who screamed at last, writhed in their grip even as they crushed his body between them. Che listened for some change now to that constant hungry mantra, but there was nothing except that litany of mindless desire, over and over again.

'Why does it want slaves?' she wondered numbly.

'It does not,' the Hermit told her. 'You think god cares? But the priests will sacrifice nonetheless. It gives an illusion of control, but it is only an illusion. This is what you propose to fight, Beetle girl. This is the source of my kinden's dominion – over this world, and soon over the sunlit lands as well. This is the Worm that will eat up the world. Now you see. Now you share our despair.'

She watched the shape of the great hooked mouthparts treading over the ruined corpse of the Mole Cricket, each curved claw a hole in the weave of the world that stretched longer than her body: the blindly working mandibles of god.

'The Worm knows only enough to know that there are things it cannot accomplish. In order to live and last, in order to replenish its numbers and arm its warriors, there is thought and planning needed,' the scarred old man went on. 'That is why I exist. That is why the Scarred Ones exist. They think themselves priests down there, giving homage to god, but god doesn't care. God permits us our petty freedoms because we advance its cause, and its cause is to consume everything, to be everything. When god has devoured the sunlit lands and made all the world like itself, it will have no need of Scarred Ones. When god has eliminated all who are not of the Worm, it will have no need of warriors. It will consume and consume until this thing you see will be the entire world.'

'And the Scarred Ones know this?' Che whispered.

'We do, and yet we serve, because even that conscious servitude is better than becoming a thoughtless segment of the Worm.'

'But . . .' Che shook her head. 'Just existence for existence's sake . . . what could be the point?'

'Why do you think I listened to Orothellin,' the Hermit said grimly, beginning to retreat down the tunnel. 'My poor kinden . . . myself, those scarred wretches down there, we are all that is left of our people. This is what the Moths wrought when they bound us down here. We are what they left us.'

The Hermit was keen to be gone, but Che turned back suddenly, staring down towards the cavern to which all paths led, the seat of the Worm.

Could she possibly destroy it, and destroy all of the Worm? Could she, right now, assassinate the Centipedes' god, and release the world from their curse?

But all the strength she ever had would not be enough to pierce that lightless carapace. The very thought of drawing upon herself that colossal attention sapped her ability even to think about it. As she searched desperately for some possible weakness, it seemed to grow stronger and stronger in her mind. Even if she could bring an army before it, the army would be helpless. The crushing denial of the Worm would stifle the best weapons of the Apt, would see the magic of the greatest magicians fade to a mere dream. The greatest of Weaponsmasters would not have the courage to raise a blade against it.

What, then, could the slaves of the Worm accomplish? What would they have left to them? The strength of their arms, their Art, their skills. Could those possibly be enough to overcome what she had just seen? The Worm did not conquer as the Wasps did, by bettering themselves to overcome the advances of their enemies. The Worm dragged everything down to its own primal level. The Worm did not believe in Aptitude or Inaptitude. The Worm believed only in itself.

I will do this. But her thoughts seemed muted and tiny against the constant rush and rumble of the Worm.

They emerged again into the city, amid that wordless seething of the Worm's human bodies. The Hermit crouched in the tunnel mouth, eyes alert for his former brethren.

'Now you have seen enough,' he declared. 'Now you regret coming here. Now we go.'

'I don't,' she insisted, but inside her was something dying and near dead, the fires of her hope dimmed to an ember.

244

They were halfway clear of the city when she heard it – shrill sounds piercing the constant murmur and scuff of the Worm's movements. A new consignment had arrived. The Worm had been exacting its tax.

She stopped, and the Hermit dragged at her sleeve, but this time she stood firm, watching a train of warriors course between the walls of the city, bearing cages crammed with screaming infants. They were heading for the pits, as she had known they must be.

'We must go!' the Hermit insisted fiercely, but she could not – not until she knew the full scope of what was done here.

She saw the cages opened at the pits, the squalling captives hauled out, one by one and dropped in almost gently – as if to be kept alive for something. *Something that likes live prey?*

'What are they feeding those children to, Hermit? Is it the Worm?'

He managed a sickening, wretched laugh. 'Yes. No, no. They feed them to nothing. Come, we must go!'

The insincerity on his face was hideous. As a Scarred One he had never needed to lie, save to himself.

'I'm going to see.'

'No, you mustn't. I'll leave you here.'

Looking into his pale eyes, reading the twitchings and spasms of his expression, she shook her head, and set off for the pits. Instantly he was at her heels, begging her, clutching at her, and yet unable to prevent her progress.

She passed like a dream through the purposeful bustle of the Worm, all those enemies seeing only a Scarred One's shadow. She came to the lip of the pit, the sounds of wailing, terrified children louder in her ears, the air below reeking of death and excrement.

What will I see? Is this the Worm's stomach? Are these the pens where its beasts fatten themselves? What is the last piece of the puzzle?

She looked down.

Maggots.

That was her first thought, seeing those countless bodies writhing and clawing helplessly over one another, smeared with their own filth, turning their faces towards her to shriek out their need, to demand the human care and comfort that they had been torn from. Not maggots, though. Children, infants, carpeting the floor of the pit. Infants of all kinden, twisting and knotting and fighting, and here and there just lying still, already dead. Many of them were blankly silent, but some – probably the newest arrivals – were wailing at the tops of their voices, demanding their lives back, their parents, that fragile little slice of love that they had known. Their voices, that chorus of loss and loneliness, raked claws deep down inside her.

The Hermit was still trying to pull her away, but she had become immovable, nailed there by sheer horror and revulsion.

'You must go,' he mumbled. 'This was always the way.'

At that intervention, she could break free some fragment of her attention for him, enough to lash out and take him by the throat with a strength she had not known she possessed. 'What do you mean,' she demanded, '"This was always the way"?' For this was exactly what he had sought to keep her from, she realized. Not to protect her but to protect himself, the memory of his already-accursed kinden. He was ashamed.

'Orothellin says . . .' he whimpered. 'He says this was why the Moths and the others warred against us. This . . .'

I should hope so . . . But it did not explain anything. It did not make sense. Her legs were shaky as she stumbled over to the next pit, although her grip on the Hermit did not weaken.

She had expected to witness the same scene, but the children here were older, larger. They struggled and fought with one another, and it was as beasts fought – in sudden confrontations just as suddenly abandoned. Again, some were dead, and there was a curious look to the rest that sent her hurrying on to the next pit, revelation curdling in her gut. They made no sounds here. *Because they have learned it will do them no good*, was the inescapable conclusion.

'Orothellin . . .' The Hermit's voice came to her. 'He says that my people ever sought to make the world in our image. That was what the others could not forgive – what our efforts showed them, of how the world truly worked. Our intolerable truths.'

And the bodies in the third pit were older still, looking not far from grown, pallid and lanky and all too similar to one another, save that here or there she could see some mark of ancestry: darker skin, a larger frame, a Moth's blind eyes. But they were the Worm, all of them, or would be soon. They were the foot-soldiers of the Worm.

'What am I looking at?' she whispered. 'What does Orothellin say this is?'

'That we found a way, long before the war, to break the bonds of kinden. That we took the children of our enemies, and we made them into our own. So that when others fought the armies of the Worm, they knew that they would shed their own blood, make themselves kinslayers, every blow they struck. We called them the New Soldiers, Orothellin says. In those days it was just to supplement our numbers, to swell our armies. He says.'

She wanted him to stop then, but she had called the Worm from dark recesses of his mind and it would come forth, segment after segment, whether she wanted it to or not.

'But now we are the Worm, in truth. Now my people have become a mindless appendix to our god. Only we Scarred Ones can even sire or bear children, the rest are just . . . segments. Segments is all they are. Sexless, mindless, hollow shells they are. But the New Soldiers, oh, that is easier, far quicker than once it was. It took so long to grow a mind to the fullness of intellect. But to grow a body to strength is short work. No wonder they tax the slaves. They will tax them until their wombs are barren. The Worm needs soldiers to swallow the world, to empty all the lands under the sun. The Worm can spend the futures of its slaves, for there are a million new recruits in the wider world.

Already they are being carried down here, the children of your kin. The Worm grows ready to hatch from this place. It will consume everything here, and it has no patience for things it no longer needs.' That divide within the man, his present self-knowledge warring with the thing he had once been, was blazing on his face.

And beyond him rose another face, like a brother to his own, and twisted with its own individual rage. Another Scarred One.

Che was moving in that instant, barging past the Hermit, almost knocking him into the pit where the soulless things below would surely have torn him apart and devoured him. Her sword cleared its sheath with the effortless ease she always imagined Tynisa must feel when her rapier leapt to her hand. She was inspired, driven. She had purpose.

The cicatrized priest had his mouth open, the first howl against blasphemy escaping his lips. The enormity of what he saw had rooted him to the spot. He made no attempt to defend himself or step clear of her lunge. She killed his voice within his throat, all the force she could muster driving that sharp point up to the hilt in his neck, seeing that pallid face contort with agony and outrage, and for a moment attain a sort of humanity.

The Scarred One staggered and dropped, twitching, but now she became aware of a wider disturbance that centred on herself.

The Worm was awakening to her presence.

All around her, all throughout the city, the warriors, the segments, had stopped their concerted bustle. They stood like men waking from a dream, and then their heads began turning towards her. The same eyes looked out from a hundred faces, a thousand, searching for this imperfection in the heart of the Worm.

She caught her breath, the Scarred One's blood on her sword, because what could follow now but utter extinction?

Then the Hermit had seized her wrist, hauled her towards

248

him, and in his other hand was his long knife. For a moment she thought he had suffered some change of heart, fallen victim to the Worm once more, abandoned Orothellin and humanity in one brief step. Then the blade licked across her forearm, scoring a twisting line of pain and blood, a jagged spiral to join the blood-matted gouge on her upper arm.

For a moment after that, absolutely everything in that city of the Worm was still.

The multitude of the warriors blinked, all at once, as though caught in mid-thought and forgetting what they had been doing. They then returned to their busy labours, and she saw that more and more of them were joining that great spiral – that it was growing to encompass the whole city around them, thousands of the Worm's bodies threading through the streets, marching inexorably on that vanishing centre.

Clawing their way towards the sun.

'We must go,' the Hermit insisted. 'More Scarred Ones will come. They will know something is wrong. We must escape.'

This time she did not resist him.

When they had put the city behind them, with its buried god and its child pits, he turned to her. 'You regret now, do you not? You wish you had never asked.'

'I do not.' She faced up to him without flinching. 'Because I know more than ever that it must be destroyed, all of it. You have given me purpose, Hermit.' Perhaps this buried chasm was no proper soil for hope to grow in, but that did not preclude a purpose. She defied anyone to see what she had seen and not take purpose from it. She felt herself on fire with a rage that burned as bright as the writhing silhouette of the Worm had been obscure.

And in the back of her mind she explored what had been returned to her when she had got far enough from the city to escape the deadening hand of the Worm: some faint recollection of magic had crept back into her. She had felt that bond, that tenuous link to the outer world that had always been there, but

249

so faint that only by having it taken away and then restored could she know it was real.

Are you seeing this, Seda? she demanded silently. *Do you understand now what you have done?*

Twenty-One

She awoke thrashing at her sheets, eyes open but seeing only that dark place and stark grey images of horror torn from another woman's eyes.

Seda had ridden the waves of Che's own despair and it had infected her, but it was not the children of the dark world that had touched her. The breeding of slaves was beneath her; let them live or die as they chose.

She had seen through Che's eyes, but her mind had remained her own. She tore herself from sleep with a true understanding of what would happen to the world – *her* world! – and of the rules the Worm was breaking just by existing.

A vast void in the shape of a centipede. Kinden blurring into other kinden. A homogenized world contained within the freezing guts of a mindless ignorant god, forever and forever.

That was the future.

Morning in Capitas. As she stepped onto the floor of her chamber, she thought she could feel the ground tremble slightly, even from so many storeys up. The armies of the Worm were coming. There was no way of knowing where they would strike next. Nobody was safe, and there was no way to retaliate.

Seda could only close the door on them, leave them to their obscenities. Let them practise their rites on their slaves in the darkness. Let them scrape to their god, only let them not open the way for it to come *here*, and devour the sun.

For a moment, a great wave of hopelessness threatened to overwhelm her: the thought that none of it would be enough, that her painstaking calculations were wrong, that the entire concept was misguided. *How do I know this will work?* And, of course, she could never *know*, not until she had done it and seen the results. And there would only ever be one chance for her to stopper this bottle, to bury the Worm forever.

Because it's my fault. I let them out. I must force them back.

But I must be right. I must be sure. Better to go too far than not far enough. I have no time for subtlety.

From the corner of the room, Tisamon watched her impassively, and she strode over to him, trying to read condemnation in his face – trying to read *anything* in his face. His pale dead features regarded her and did not judge. He was her creature, and he was the only one she could rely on. The rest – her generals, Brugan, all of them – they were mortal, fallible, weak. She must make use of them, for want of any better, but they were all poor tools. *How is it that my people have come to this?*

Once she stepped from her chambers, her anguish and desperation were left behind. She was the Empress; people bowed before her and feared her.

In her throne room she dismissed the waiting suitors and advisers and petitioners, all the detritus of state. She spared time only for her Red Watch, spread as it was across the Empire and beyond. In her mind she moved it as she would chess pieces, each member with its particular instructions and mandates coming to its mind inexplicably but irresistibly. It was her voice. That was no idle boast.

After that she summoned a handful of Consortium officers, men of the Quartermaster Corps and veteran slavers, those to whom she had entrusted the minutiae of her plan. None of them truly understood what this was all for and, though of course they did not question her, she suspected they did not even ask questions of themselves. If the Empress wanted an unprecedented concentration of slaves, whole camps crammed full of the luckless Inapt, then why should that raise an eyebrow, beyond the intellectual exercise of arranging the logistics?

They reported to her patiently and carefully, checking their numbers with each other. They confirmed that every airship of any size that the Empire could make use of had been diverted; that vessels crammed with the spoils of the war with the Spiderlands were coasting north up the Silk Road; that the Principalities were selling off their Dragonfly serfs with an open hand; that the Grasshopper-kinden of Sa had been culled, a full one in four currently on forced march towards Capitas. They spoke dispassionately about death rates: those who would not make the camps because of the pace or the overcrowding. They were regretful but only because such waste diminished the value of their service to her.

And she sat and listened to those dry voices, these men whose only war had been fought on paper, or against an enemy already in chains, and she felt a spasm of revulsion go through her that she should need such men, and that she should need this venture.

They will remember me as the mad Empress. History will never forgive me. Even though we win, history cannot condone what it is we do here. But I pay that price, and I make all these others pay that price. To save the world.

Put in those words, it sounded almost convincing.

'It's not enough.'

The words were hers. She could not deny them.

To save a world from the Worm, great sacrifices would have to be made. The Inapt made better gifts to oblivion, but she could not afford to restrict her ambitions. The Apt were still valuable to her, and she had far more of them still at her disposal. Entire cities full of them, if need be. Even if it took ten Apt deaths to equal one of the Inapt, why then, she would just find some place with Apt to spare, and have ten times as many killed.

'Your Imperial Majesty,' one of the Consortium men began, 'forgive us. There are limits to what even the resources of the

Empire may accomplish in so short a time. And there is the matter of feeding the slaves at the camps, keeping them alive for . . .?' His small eyes searched her face for some indication of that 'for. . .?'

And indeed, although she herself knew what for, how could she possibly accomplish it? She could hardly haul each one in turn to the museum for a ritual bloodletting. Could she ask Tisamon to pass amongst so many thousands to cut their throats? Even he – even being what he now was – would take too long about the task. And that was just the camps themselves. She had heard their reports regarding the numbers they were gathering. Surely that would not be enough, for the colossal hubris of the ritual that she was planning. Even the ancient Moths would not have dared what she was intending. The power she would require was unprecedented. Only an unprecedented toll would pay for it.

I could have my soldiers shoot them. Why not turn to the weapons of the Apt one last time? The blood would still flow, and it would be quicker. It could be effected with all the efficiency of these modern times.

But even then . . . and how many am I relying on to follow such orders? Too many, surely. And they would fight back, the Inapt slaves, and a city of the Apt even more so. Can I be sure that such bloodletting is possible, even with every soldier in the Empire at my bidding?

Do I even need the blood? Is that not simply an antiquated concept of savage peoples? What is blood, after all, but a symbol for the real power: death.

Death is all I need.

She dismissed them, the entire pack of them, exhorting them to double their efforts, and for a while she brooded, seated on the throne with only Tisamon for company.

Then she beckoned a servant close.

'Bring me General Lien,' she directed.

The Engineers had done so much for the Empire in recent years. Perhaps they would come to its rescue again.

When General Marent returned to Capitas from his unexpected trip to Collegium, he could readily ignore all those questions that inferior ranks dared ask of an army general. The only voices he would truly have to answer to were the Rekef and the Empress, and neither sent for him. General Brugan was seen less and less at the palace, so that some were beginning to say he was a spent force, and the Empress . . . The Empress was fixated on her own concerns, rumour of which was now rife across Capitas. She had a grand project, it seemed, but the more her people found out about it, the less they understood.

What could she need so many slaves for? Most assumed there would be some elaborate entertainment once the war was done, though even the optimists murmured that surely victory was not so imminent as all that. Others wondered at the creation of some new all-Auxillian army to throw against the Lowlanders, some hundred-thousand-strong suicide detachment in a vast war of attrition.

Marent waded through the questions of his inferiors without deigning to engage, brushing them aside before returning to his troops. Against the fact of a general jaunting across half the world without orders, nobody bothered enquiring as to why he had brought a Captain-Auxillian of Engineers back with him.

Ernain had orders signed by Major Oski to seek out parts and mechanical supplies because that had always been a beloved dodge of the Engineers to enable them to go wherever they liked at a moment's notice. He would have preferred having Oski at his side as he stepped onto the Capitas airfield, but the Second Army's chief engineer was not as free to skip about the world as General Marent.

The Vesseretti Bee-kinden had been the Empire's first major conquest. That meant that by now they were everywhere: Auxillian soldiers, house slaves, Consortium men, labourers. A sturdy-framed and hard-working people, with a good grasp of all the Apt world had to offer, they were valued by the Wasps for their skill and industry. They fetched high prices, and as soldiers were often promoted to the lower ranks. The Wasps had almost forgotten the savage struggle their grandfathers had gone through to subdue the Bee city.

The Vesseretti had not forgotten, though.

Ernain remembered finding his way to his home city during the reign of the traitor governors, when the whole Empire was teetering on the brink. There had been grand meetings, open demonstrations, stand-offs between the beleaguered Imperial garrison and the locals. It had then seemed as though the Bees would throw off their shackles and declare independence.

Ernain's voice had been loud at those gatherings. He had argued against. Vesserett was not so very far from Capitas. Whether the Empress or her rivals prevailed, Ernain had seen clearly that his city would not be able to hold on to its freedom. It was too alone, too cut off. They were not ready.

Instead, the Vesseretti had put away their ambitions and stepped back from the battle line. The turmoil in the city had subsided, and it had been made plain to the Wasp governor that the Bees were – after some considerable thought on the matter – loyal.

That had been the moment Ernain had held his breath: would there be purges? Would the Rekef descend upon his people to punish them for what might have been?

But the governor had understood. He had seen, there and then, that the Bees could have torn down the black and gold flag, and that they had not done so. There were no reprisals. Indeed, after the Empress's victory, in which Vesseretti Auxillian troops had played their part, a few new freedoms had crept into the city, for even slaves could be rewarded for their loyalty. Other city-states had made the same calculated decision, as Ernain was well aware.

The plan had arisen out of the ashes of that civil war. It was not Ernain's plan, not quite, but he had contributed to it. It was the work of many hands, with more hands joining all the time.

In Capitas he presented himself at the house of a Consortium magnate, ostensibly in quest of missing deliveries. It was a flimsy enough ruse – for who would trouble a colonel over such things? – but there was a curious feel to Capitas just then. Great invisible wheels were turning, centred about the palace and the Empress. Nobody was inclined to question small matters such as this.

The man that Ernain met was an old Beetle-kinden, Auder Bellowern, the senior scion of that sprawling clan whose fingers were in just about everything the Consortium ever did. He was prosperously fat, his hair white and wispy against his dark skin. At his shoulder was his body servant, a Vesseretti girl less than half his age, whose company the man vastly preferred to that of his wife. The girl was Alysaine and she was Ernain's introduction.

Around them, the magnate's study was virtually choked with the collected trinkets of a lifetime of avaricious acquisition, a clutter matched in value only by the utter disorder of its display.

The Beetle looked him over, his face avuncular, his eyes all measurement and judgement. 'You're the fellow, then,' he noted.

'Sir.'

'You don't *look* completely mad. I'd expected you to come in foaming at the mouth and babbling Moth prophecies or something.' At a gesture from the old man, Alysaine poured two bowls of wine. Ernain took his with a nod of thanks.

'I wouldn't have expected you to ask a madman into your home, sir.'

'Nonetheless, you are quite mad, Captain. I've been let in on your plans to only a modest degree and I can still see that.'

'Sir?'

'I'm sure you have a great deal of support from . . .' Auder's hand flicked towards Alysaine. 'For her sake, I've listened. Bold plans without any visible means of execution. Even with the support of myself, or a dozen men like me, you cannot win because your plan does not address the heart of the matter.' He nodded towards one of his windows, and Alysaine hurried to unshutter it. Auder Bellowern's house commanded a good view of the palace.

'Matters are in hand, sir. It is simply a matter of awaiting the right opportunity.'

The old Beetle snorted. 'No plan ever worked that relied on waiting.' He shook his head against Ernain's attempted reply. 'Oh, you pin your hopes on the Lowlands, but you've no guarantees. What if the Empire crushed them tomorrow? Where would your plan be then?'

'Intact, sir,' Ernain told him, 'because the Empire will not change unless change is forced on it. What will all those generals do without an enemy? They will find a new one, or they will fall upon each other. Now we are ready to exploit it, the Empire will give us our opportunity.'

'You plan for the long term, then?'

'What other plans are worth making? You know enough, sir. If you passed my name to the Rekef, then you have sufficient information to have me racked and executed, though the plan would persist and prevail even so. Or perhaps you think this is worthy of your support.'

'Of my support – and so of Consortium support,' Auder murmured. He glanced at Alysaine, and Ernain caught a brief sliver of emotion alien to his lined face, a moment of genuine affection. 'I'll not put my name to anything, you can be sure. No Rekef interrogation rooms for me in my old age. If your moment arrives, though . . . if you make your move, well . . . the Consortium will do well out of your new world, I feel. We've chafed at the shackles of the throne as much as any slave, believe me. I wish you luck, Captain, I truly do. May we meet again when you have some more concrete achievement to report.'

★

258

In the light of his study, the lamps turned up high, General Brugan of the Rekef studied the latest reports.

Outside his window, the world was fading to twilight and, though he had ordered the shutters closed, still the darkness seemed to creep in around the edges, to steal into his room and hang heavy about him, as though his eyes were failing before their time.

He ordered the lamps turned up, but his servant assured him they were as high as they could go.

'Bring me more lanterns,' he croaked. 'More light.' To his own ears his voice sounded as his ghost might. How long had it been since he had spoken? His mind raised the spectre of General Reiner, a long-dead rival for power. The man had ruled his agents and spies in near silence, weaving a mystique about himself by his unspeaking presence, but Brugan knew that Reiner's closed mouth had hidden only weakness. And when the man had died – Brugan had not even needed to kill him – all that fraudulent inscrutability had died with him.

Now Brugan found his own voice drying up because silence was preferable to disclosing any of the thoughts that sat rotting in his mind. Thoughts about the Empress. Thoughts about the nature of the world. Thoughts about his own death. Sometimes he imagined taking his own life, because that would at least be a decision he himself could make, an attempt to exert some vestige of control over the world, even in that one small way. But always he failed to turn such thoughts into execution, and recently he thought that it was not fear of personal extinction that stayed his hand, but a fear that *she* would somehow prevent him from carrying the business through – that, in his final moment of action, he would discover he was even less his own man than he had thought. As long as he did not attempt it, he could persuade himself that the attempt was possible. He did not want to discover that even death was no release.

At other times he thought that she would have him killed. He would look up, and every shadow would carry its knife. He would see her dark bodyguard, the pale Mantis called Tisamon, lurking in his sight, cold eyes fixed on him, and never know if *this* was the moment that the Empress tired of him. He had long since tired of himself. He was drained, traumatized. The Empress, their couplings, her rule over him, the failure of his coup: she had left him nothing of the strong man he had once been.

Sometimes he saw Tisamon, and the man was actually there. Sometimes the man was not there, but Brugan peopled the shadows with him anyway. 'More light!' he insisted, and his servants would run to light lanterns and candles for him, but the shadows only multiplied.

He stared at the reports, fighting against the encroaching darkness to read them. Here was matter that any Rekef officer should be gripped by: detailed movements of slaves, Auxillians, un-authorized meetings and journeys, gatherings of men who had no business being together save to plot treason.

His eye settled on one name: Captain-Auxillian Ernain of the Engineers, attached to the Second Army, but whose recent activities should be sounding the alarm even now, however much the man had tried to hide them. And that attempt at concealment was itself the action of a criminal or a traitor.

Brugan stared at the reports. He must act, of course. He must tell the Empress. He must send out his agents to have these people arrested and questioned.

But his hand shook, and the darkness only gathered closer about him, and he saw the gleam of Mantis steel in the corner of his eye, and he did nothing. He was lost in the night, and he could not find his way back to a place where any of his life made sense. He scanned the reports but saw only words, and the more he read, the less anything connected to anything. If the Empress could do those things he had seen her do, if she had become the impossible, then how could he trust any chain of logic? How could any of these suspicions bear the weight of his belief?

He swept the papers from his desk and called again for more light.

★

General Lien was lean and bald, and a man loyal to the Engineers first and foremost. His recent promotion, and the general advancement of his beloved corps, had bought his almost unquestioning support for the throne. He was one of the few who came promptly and gladly when called before the Empress.

Seda had caught him off guard, however. He had not expected to be quizzed on matters technical.

'There are ways . . .' he started, and then stopped again, and she could see him thinking the matter over as an artificer should, breaking down the problem into manageable pieces: the little cogs of mass destruction.

'You have engines, surely?' she prompted. She did not want to know the details, and indeed she could not have understood them if he had told her, but she wanted to know for sure that the Apt had advanced so far in this specialist field to be of use to her.

'They could be devised, Majesty,' Lien told her, and he was still elsewhere in his head, even in the presence of his Empress. He was a leader of engineers rather than a grimy-handed mechanic, but she had brought out the craft in him with her question. 'What timescale . . .?'

'*Now*, General,' she told him. 'Or very soon. I cannot wait for inventions and drawings and tests. Surely your engineers have something for me?' She was thinking of all the work that lay ahead, the slaves, the cities, the unthinkable harvest that she must needs reap in order to reforge the Seal of the Worm.

At that, he looked up with a speculative expression.

'Majesty,' he said thoughtfully, 'have you heard of the Bee-killer?'

Twenty-Two

'Instructions are simple,' Sperra confirmed. 'Stay in your houses. No grand uprising.'

Poll Awlbreaker shook his head. 'Makes no sense.' He looked about the circle of his friends for support, the little band of revolutionaries gathered in the back room behind his workshop.

To Sartaea te Mosca it seemed there were few there as dedicated to action as he was. Raullo Mummers the artist shrugged unhappily, and the Spider, Metyssa, put a hand on Poll's arm.

'I'm not exactly keen about being penned up in your cellar for months at a time,' she told him, 'but taking to the streets will get messy.'

Poll stared at her. 'It'll be war. What were you expecting?'

'I'm expecting the Sarnesh or someone to have a plan that won't get everyone killed.'

'Poll, have faith,' said te Mosca. 'And, believe me, I've seen the Empire close up recently, and things are as taut as a bowstring. The first sign of an uprising, and Tynan will give the order to shoot everyone who takes to the streets.'

'And here you were saying he's a reasonable man,' Poll grumbled.

'For what it's worth, I think he is,' she confirmed. 'But he's a reasonable Wasp with an *army*, and that would be the reasonable response to a mass revolt by the people he's been set to watch over.'

Poll stood up abruptly, frustrated aggression making him clench his fists over and over, unable to be still. 'Have you seen how many the Sarnesh have brought? It's a joke, a glorified lorn detachment, a suicide detail! Even with the Vekken and that handful who've supposedly sailed from Tsen, it's not enough to take the city unless we rise up.'

'By your own logic,' Metyssa observed, 'that means that, if we do, the Wasps can hold off the Ant-kinden with just a small force on the walls and turn most of their weapons against us. Is this that Apt logic you're so proud of?'

'Sit tight,' Sperra confirmed. 'That's all they ask of you.'

'They who?' Poll demanded angrily.

'Laszlo,' Sperra announced proudly. 'I met with him only yesterday. He says he got the orders from . . .'

The others waited, watching her fight over whether to say it or not.

'Stenwold Maker,' Raullo Mummers finished for her, in mock-prophetic tones.

Sperra deflated somewhat. 'Yes, that is what he said, actually.'

'Maker's dead,' Poll said dismissively.

'He's not,' Sperra insisted. 'Laszlo said.'

'I rather fear that if I was writing a story intended to inspire the people of Collegium, I wouldn't admit to the man being dead, either,' Metyssa noted drily. 'What say you, Sartaea?'

The Fly magician hunched in on herself. 'I would like to believe . . .' she said slowly, 'but I very much fear—'

The crash of the front door being kicked in seemed appallingly loud. Poll had a solid door but, when the wood failed to yield to the first impact, there was an explosive splintering as an impatient hand simply blasted at the hinges with a sting.

'Metyssa, get under cover!' he shouted, lunging across his back room for the nearest available weapon, one of his heavy hammers. The others were on their feet now, and Metyssa was dragging a dagger from its sheath.

'No! Hide!' Poll got out, and then the Wasps were swarming

into the room, palms out ready to sting. He launched himself at them, the hammer catching one on the shoulder, sending the man staggering and denting his mail. Then, three against one, they were on him, not stinging but punching and kicking, beating him to the ground with brutal efficiency.

The rest of the Wasps were still ready to sting, fully half of them wearing the closed helms of the Slave Corps.

'Sartaea te Mosca,' one of them announced, staring at the Fly-kinden. 'Your presence is requested.'

'Is it the general?' she asked in a hushed voice.

'"Is it the general?"' he echoed, mocking. 'My, what airs you have. Turns out someone has a use for a few Inapt like yourself, and Major Vrakir was kind enough to put your name forward especially. Been making friends, you have.'

'What is this about, please?' te Mosca asked, her voice quavering slightly, and the lead Wasp punched her hard, a straight downward blow that knocked her flat to the floor to cradle her bruised face.

'Slaves don't get to ask questions,' he spat – and then Raullo hit him with a chair.

For a moment there was chaos, and Sartaea remained curled into a ball, terrified of being stepped on but unable to scramble out from between that tangle of legs. Poll was trying to get upright or to drag Wasps down to his level, and Metyssa was in there with her dagger. Then there was a flash of stingshot, and abruptly all was quiet. The Slave Corps was well used to keeping its inferiors in line.

From her vantage point on the floor, Sartaea te Mosca stared over into the face of Raullo Mummers her friend, gone ashen now and quite still. His hands were crooked like claws about the charred crater in his chest.

She, who had always been so mild, let out a howl of loss that surprised her. If she had been some great magician of olden days then she would have summoned a spell to wipe the lot of them off the face of the earth in that moment. She was barely even a magician of the current age, though, and a Fly-kinden to boot, and all she could do was beat at them with her tiny fists as they laid hands on her. Then they hauled up Metyssa and bound her for transport as well.

'What about this one?' One of them indicated Poll, hanging between a pair of Wasps, his face bruised and bloody. 'Doesn't look Inapt to me.'

'So they'll get some gold amongst the dross, and who cares?' the lead slaver replied carelessly. 'Bring him along. We've got a quota to hit.'

She did not look at the corner where Sperra had been sitting, knowing only that the woman was neither a living prisoner nor a corpse. One of them, at least, had possessed the sense to duck for cover when the Wasps burst in.

Then the slavers were hauling Sartaea away, wrenching her head around when she tried for a final glimpse of Raullo's still form.

All over Collegium the same scene was being played out. Anyone even suspected of being Inapt was sought by the slavers, and soon they simply ceased discriminating, used as they were to fulfilling orders of quantity rather than quality. After all, the Empire had an inexhaustible need for slaves of all types, and they had the Empress's writ. Besides, as a number of Tynan's officers agreed, Collegium was well overdue for a humbling.

Bergild found Major Oski supervising a team of sweating Engineers as they manhandled a leadshotter down the streets of Collegium towards the docks.

'Shipping out?' she called over to him.

He gave her a filthy look, then a second glance. 'You look wrecked.'

'Two straight sorties against the Stormreaders.' She had seen her own face in a dented mirror not long ago: grey with fatigue, as dark about both eyes as though she had some possessive husband to beat her. *Perhaps the war's my husband.*

'Get some sleep,' the Fly advised her curtly, then turned to yell at his charges as the bulk of the leadshotter threatened to crash into a shop front.

'Tried that. No good,' she muttered. 'Where's your man Ernain, anyway. Don't think I've seen you without him tagging at your heels before.'

'Elsewhere. Engineer business.'

'Air Corps is still engineers, Major.'

He scowled at her. 'My apologies, *Captain*. Should have said "terrestrial engineer business".'

For a moment she was just about to go, but she needed to be taken out of herself; the company of pilots, the same constant round inside her head over and over, was anything but that. Oski was the only company she knew outside her comrades. She settled on, 'Keep your secrets, then.'

'No secrets to keep,' he replied, before the business at hand claimed his attention. 'Piss on the lot of you, do I have to—? All right, I'm going to—' And his wings took him over to stand on the leadshotter's barrel. 'Now you steer this thing straight or I will kick each one of you in the head!' A little man, half the size of the Wasps he was abusing, but how else was a little man to get things done?

'You're a funny man, Major,' she called to him.

'What can I say? It's a funny war.'

Then they were in sight of the docks and she swore outright. 'What the pits is *this*?'

'Oh, this?' He turned around on the trundling leadshotter, wings glimmering in and out of being as he caught his balance. 'This is the old man and Major Vrakir having another pissing contest, only I guess this time Red Watch pissed higher, because we're moving all these sodding engines off the walls – y'know, where they're going to do us any *good* – to the seafront. And why not? Artillery crews need a bit of sea air, just like every man, right?'

The docks of Collegium had become a siege front waiting to happen. Bergild watched as several hundred of the Second's soldiers dragged out furniture from every nearby building, to pile it into barricades, whilst leadshotters and other engines were wheeled into position as if to repel an armada. On the rooftops overlooking the docks there were soldiers with piercers and nailbows and repeating ballistae, whilst a pair of huge, articulated Sentinels picked their way between the labouring men with absurdly dainty movements.

'All I can say is,' Oski shouted over the noise, 'that if those couple of hundred Tseni marines out there try sailing in, they're in for one pissing enormous surprise!'

'This is insane!' she yelled back, unable to take it all in.

'You're going to tell that to the Red Watch?' Then he was bending down and, pointing, directing his men to where the leadshotter needed to go.

Bergild opened her mouth, about to embark on a sentence that started with, 'But why don't you . . .?' and had no conceivable ending, then she shrugged.

'Exactly,' Oski confirmed, hopping down. 'That's fine there. Make sure it's braced.' He swung through the air back to her. 'Got just about all my boys here in full clank. Got the artillery we hauled all the way to Collegium. Got a load of stuff like that heavy bastard that the Collies helpfully left on the walls for us, including some real special toys and games. I almost want the Tseni to make a go of it now, just for the laughs.' He looked her over again. 'Seriously, Captain, get some sleep.'

'Tried.' She shrugged. 'They broke out the Chneuma five nights ago, and now we're all buzzing about inside our own heads like flies in a bottle. None of us can get our heads down.'

He shrugged. 'I know what that's like, though for me it's more as if there's only one of me but enough engineering work for three majors and a colonel.'

'So ask for a promotion.'

With that, she raised a smile from him. 'Yeah, well . . .' He glanced over the line of artillery, the soldiers camped out in all the dockside buildings. '"Fear death by water."'

'Say again?'

'Supposed to be what Red Watch said.'

After that the two of them just stared across the unquiet sea.

'I dreamt of Che last night,' Totho said.

'No, you didn't.' Maure barely glanced up from the fire. He had found out that her woodscraft was significantly better than his after they had struck out away from the lakeshore, in case anyone else came looking for refugees from Chasme.

Her reply made him angry. 'So you know what I dream now, do you? That's another Inapt lie you want me to believe?'

She had frozen in place – obviously she was still wary of him. He found his anger came almost without warning after Drephos's death, a roiling well of frustration and impotence constantly churning inside him. 'I didn't mean to—'

'No, I understand.' He stood up abruptly, eyes darting to his armour laid out on a cloak as though they were mourners at its funeral. His snapbow lay alongside. 'So the Apt aren't allowed to dream, is that it? Our humdrum lives don't qualify.'

She had heard the fire ebbing in his voice as bitterness crept in to steal away his genuine aggression. 'Actually, that is what I meant, only not quite, and I spoke hastily. When I would talk about dreams, though . . . my dreams *mean* something. Inapt dreams do, if they can only be interpreted.'

He snorted. 'Dreams mean nothing. They're just our minds stirring all the thoughts we've had. So you come to me babbling about Che, so I dream of her.'

'Just so.'

Her dismissal only aggravated him more, although even he was asking himself, *What do I possibly want out of this conversation? Where am I trying to take it?* 'I wouldn't have—'

'If I hadn't come along to bother you, yes,' she finished. 'And I'd tell you I didn't ask to and that I'm only here because you're

268

still connected to Che, because she's still in your mind like a ghost. But you don't believe any of that, so why are we going over this again? Let's get to this Spider place of yours and then you can go . . . wherever, and I can go wherever else.'

'And where would you go?' he demanded of her.

She looked up at him with those pale, irisless eyes. 'North. If I head north for long enough, I don't think I can fail to hit the Commonweal.'

'Hundreds of miles.'

'Hence "for long enough".'

'You'll be dead or a slave or raped before you even hit the Lowlands.'

For a moment she stared into the fire, breathing deeply, and he thought she was pondering those fates, but belatedly realized that she was summoning her composure to deal with *him* without losing her own temper.

'What do you suggest I do, Totho? Why are you trying to bind me to you?'

'What? I'm not—!'

'Everything you've said has "Stay with me!" shouting out loud between each word. Only I didn't think I was such a catch.'

He knew that should only make him angrier but, confronted with that, the rage refused to venture forth. His own knowledge of how unreasonable he was being caught up with him, and he was suddenly out of easy explanations, vacillating, opening his mouth, then shrivelling before her cool, shrewd stare.

At last she said, 'Che. It's Che, then.'

'You think that, just because you—'

'I'm a link to Che, yes. Or isn't that it? Tell me what, then.' And, when he wouldn't answer, 'What did you dream?'

He blinked at this sudden turn. 'She was in a dark place,' he said.

'Well, that's true. Congratulations, you're obviously Inapt and a prophet.'

'I've been a lot of bad things in my time, but Inapt isn't one of them.' At last he sat back down, feeling somewhat more collected. 'Just that: a dark place. Like when I found her in the farmhouse cellar after the Battle of the Rails. Got herself into trouble again, and it was down to me to save her.'

'And you did.'

'I thought I had, at the time.' He tested his fragile composure and found that it would take his weight. 'But she was playing me, all along. The Moth bastard had her, and she loved him, but it didn't stop her leaning on me when it suited her.'

'Perhaps she thought you were a friend.' Maure poked the fire speculatively.

'A friend. Right.'

'I couldn't even say that much for myself, I don't think,' she said softly. 'Just some hireling magician who did her a favour once, but she got me out of there. And all the country between here and the Commonweal will be a joy to cross, believe me, if I never see the Worm again. Although, if I understand correctly, that's no guarantee.'

'Because this Worm has a way out.'

'Right.'

A long pause followed. Totho took a swig from his water skin, and Maure chewed on some hard biscuit they had acquired.

'If you could help her . . .?' he began eventually.

'I owe her a great deal,' Maure told him. 'If it meant something as simple as me sticking my hand out and hauling her from a hole, I'd not hesitate. Though I'd like to think I'm a decent enough type that I'd do that for most people. '

'But if you could—?'

'No.'

'But—'

'I will not go back to that place, Totho, not even to help Che. You don't know. You can't know what it was like. I don't even know how long I was down there, without the sun, surrounded by the earth, and without my skills – and with all that I ever made myself into just stripped away. I was going mad, Totho. Not even for Che, no.'

'But you *could*.'

She rounded on him furiously, demanding, 'Are you judging me?' and froze, staring at his face. 'You're not, are you?'

'No,' he confirmed.

'I'm not talking about this any more.'

'Fine.'

She turned her back on him, almost theatrically, shoulders hunched as though awaiting a blow.

'She was in a dark place in my dream,' Totho repeated. 'She was in pain, in fear. She was calling out.'

'Your name?'

He stared murderously at her back. 'No,' he spat, at last. 'Not my fucking name. Of course not my name. Why ever should she call for *me*?'

Twenty-Three

There came a night where the following morning – or its sunless surrogate – would see them putting Che's plan into action, to whatever extent that was even possible. In the Hermit's high cave they sat around a fire that burned with salt colours, whilst outside the world of the Worm waited for them, ready to break all their hopes against its vast scale and its uncaring brutality.

Then the Hermit shuffled into the back of his cave and returned hesitantly with a jar of something that reeked like paint. He held it out to Orothellin, who took it almost reverently.

'Is that supposed to be *wine*?' Tynisa demanded.

'Approximately.' The huge man took a draught, his eyes creasing about the sudden tears the taste had pricked there, before handing it over to her.

Tynisa had never drunk much wine, and the mere smell of the stuff made her gag, but everyone was watching her now, Thalric especially. It was like being back at the College, engaged in some ridiculous student dare – only then she herself had always been the one to set the stakes. *And now I have become merely a follower, somehow.*

She took a half-mouthful, and that almost overpowered her. The sharp, acrid taste was so much the antithesis of wine that she felt almost awed to be in its presence. 'Did this . . . did this come from the surface?' she demanded of Orothellin. 'Have you been saving this for a thousand years?' She would have believed it.

For a second the Slug-kinden just goggled at her, but then something happened to his mournful, majestic face and he exploded into a belch of laughter. 'Thousand-year wine? Not even my people would drink thousand-year wine! No, no, the Hermit brews it from—'

'Don't!' Thalric interrupted. 'Nobody cares. You'd only put us off. Let's face it, there's nothing wholesome out there to ferment. I don't want to hear that it's crushed mushrooms and cricket piss or something.' He snagged the jar from Tynisa and tipped it back almost contemptuously. A moment later he almost spilled the lot, Che rescuing it from him just in time as he doubled over, coughing ferociously.

'So much for the Empire,' Tynisa remarked, sounding somewhat croaky herself.

Che sniffed at the jar's lip and recoiled. 'I think I'll abstain.'

'Oh, get some in you,' Thalric managed – or something like it.

'Well, yes, I can see the power of good it's done you.'

Tynisa met her eyes, the two of them grinning at each other just as though they'd never left Collegium.

'Go on, drink. Perhaps it's magic,' Thalric pressed.

Are we drunk, already? Tynisa wondered, but it was not the vile concoction of the Hermit's that had brought on this mood. Rather it was the knowledge of what they were about, the terrible odds, the horrors of the Worm that Che had brought back from that cursed city. What was there to lose, therefore? The worst was already here, and had been squatting and growing in these caverns for a thousand years.

Like the wine, thought Tynisa, and she snorted. In their minds they were making the Worm small enough to manage. They were belittling it, each of them inside their heads, because otherwise it was so large and appalling that they would have given up.

Che tried some of the Hermit's vintage and gagged, pulling a face that Tynisa remembered from years before. 'That's what you do with real wine,' the Weaponsmaster taunted, remembering when Stenwold had first let his niece try the stuff.

'Oh, yes,' Che was blinking furiously, 'it's quite lovely. Esmail?'

For a moment the Assassin was going to remain aloof and preserve his dignity, but then he took the jar and took a long swallow, keeping his face meticulously composed, though Tynisa saw one of his hands crook itself into a claw.

'A little tame,' he decided, each word precisely pronounced, and handed the jar back to the Hermit, who had watched stony-faced through the entire routine, blankly baffled by all of it.

A few days later they walked into Cold Well, and the reaction of the locals was gratifying. Thalric looked at their faces and saw every emotion there that he would have looked for in a slave: guilt, terror, shame, shock. These wretched downtrodden animals had no doubt consigned the memory of their surface-world visitors to their impoverished histories. No doubt they had been telling each other how the Worm had caught those impossible visitors, those imposters, those renegades. They would have nodded at each other, oh so sagely – how right they had been not to fight the Worm.

And here we are, you worthless maggots. How he felt about Che's current venture was hard to say. Thalric looked on these creatures with disdain. Not only were they slaves, they had been enslaved in such a humiliating way as even the Empire had never contrived. Born and dying in the dark, barely more than a herd of sheep with useful skills, kept about in order to breed the next generation of their oppressors.

Che had told it all, spared nothing.

And Thalric had thought, *The vermin are beyond saving,* and yet at the same time something had risen up in him, contradicting and complementing that part of his Wasp upbringing that still saw slaves as something inferior. What the Worm was, what it did here in its lightless places, was an abomination – something more unnatural, by whole orders of magnitude, than anything he had seen in Khanaphes or the Commonweal. Even the horrors of Argastos paled before the Worm the man had been set to guard.

The panic, the scattering of the slaves, was predictable. They had no resources, no resolution, no purpose other than to run about and babble.

So come listen to us. We have your resources and your resolution and your purpose, right here.

There were seven of them that went striding into Cold Well like figures out of some Inapt legend. Che went first, her arm bandaged about the spiral scars she bore there. Tynisa limped at her side, gaunt and silent, balanced by Esmail's slender shadow. Bringing up the rear came the ponderous figure of Orothellin, and at his side the Hermit, picking nervously at his filthy robes. He had never come down here before, nor to any of the other slaves' places. Nobody knew how they would react to him.

Messel was keeping close to the big Slug-kinden as well, to shield himself from the ire of his kin here, but Thalric ranged out wider, taking advantage of his wings now that the fires of Cold Well were lighting his way. If any of the slaves did have more steel than the Wasp gave them credit for and chose to turn it on Che rather than the Worm, then his sting would be ready for them. It would serve as a solid object lesson.

There was a welcoming committee rather reluctantly assembling ahead, a few levels down. Thalric overflew them, realizing that not one of them even looked up. He caught a few familiar faces: the Moth woman – Atraea? – was there in the centre, and that big Mole Cricket smith – something Forge-Iron – and a handful of others: Woodlice, Beetles, another blind Cave Cricket like Messel. Forge-Iron had a weighty hammer in his hand, his clothes sooty from his work. There were a few staves otherwise, and probably some knives.

And yet Esmail saw scores of those nasty little Worm swords all waiting for delivery, the stupid bastards.

'What do you want?' Atraea demanded, her voice shaking. 'You must not come here!' With her blank white eyes it was impossible to know whom she was most frightened of.

Thalric swooped down and found a perch overlooking the meeting, landing delicately enough that still nobody noticed him. He saw Che stop and regard the delegation grimly.

'To get you to fight,' the Beetle girl began.

There was a murmur that passed back through the crowd, one of horror, of incredulity, as though they had never heard the word 'fight' before. Some were already shepherding their children away as if they did not want them to learn such inappropriate language.

Keeping them safe for the Worm, Thalric reflected derisively.

Atraea stepped forward, leaning on her staff. She had one hand about her stomach, and Thalric suddenly realized that she was pregnant – *would have thought she was too old, myself* – and after that he saw how many of the women were, or might be. The thought struck him as depressing beyond all the tales that Che had told. Not so long ago they had been handing over their babies to the Worm, and even then they had been working on the next batch. This was not a community of slaves. It was a factory.

'You cannot be here,' the Moth woman hissed desperately, as though trying to wish Che out of existence. 'You will bring the Worm down on us with your madness. They will punish us.'

'They're already on their way,' Che told her, and Thalric fancied he saw in her face at last a little of his own scorn, at these pathetic specimens. The reaction was certainly the one he expected from such craven wretches, the underland slaves wailing and moaning and lamenting and yet doing precisely *nothing*, not even offering a threat of retaliation against the bearers of bad tidings.

Except, no – here came the big man, Forge-Iron, pushing past his fellows, jaw jutting angrily. 'You have drawn them here,' he accused.

'No, but we are here because we saw them on their way. They are coming to exact another tax.'

'That's impossible!' Atraea insisted. 'They've only just . . . they've been, already been.'

'And you still have children to spare, so they will come again, and again, until you have no more, and you are no use to them. Then they will come for you instead, for your own flesh. They will tax and tax, and take and take, and in the end your fires will be cold ash, your homes just empty caves.'

'And how do you know this?' the Moth demanded.

'He has shown me.' Che indicated the Hermit. 'He *knows*. The Worm is entering the Old World, as your Teacher calls it, those lands beneath the sun that so many of your ancestors sprang from. They will not need you any more.'

Atraea made to speak again, but Forge-Iron laid a broad hand on her shoulder. 'Evastos, fly a circle and look for the Worm.'

A younger Moth – barely more than a boy and therefore one of the younger generation's few, a veteran of taxes that must have stripped away his siblings – flared his wings and rose unsteadily into the air. It was quite the worst flying Thalric had seen in a long time, but then, he had even wondered if the Moths here had lost the Art altogether. Che had mentioned the unpleasantness that hunted above them, the star-makers and their sticky threads, and the appalling flying monsters – the White Death as the locals charmingly called them.

'And if they are coming, what do you suppose we should do?' Atraea exclaimed, although Thalric felt that she was losing the sympathy of the crowd a little. 'We cannot fight the Worm!'

'You must,' Che told her flatly. 'You have no choice.'

There was a chorus of despair and denial already rising up, but Orothellin struck his staff once on the stone and they all fell silent. Thalric blinked: for a moment the haggard, run-down giant had mustered a little of the majesty of the Masters of Khanaphes, his voice resounding with the cavernous echoes of their last stronghold, and tomb.

'Listen,' the huge man said, not loud, yet clearly heard. 'These are the end times. No prophecy, but a promise. The Seal is broken – it has been real, all this time, and now it is gone. The Worm works its way upwards to claim the world that I still remember, just. That world is vaster than you can dream of, peopled by kinden you cannot imagine. The Worm is ambitious. It will scour this place of everything it can use and consume so as to gain its foothold, and after that it will treat the people of the Old World – your cousins – just as it has treated you. And for you – nothing. Oblivion. If you think that would be kinder, then await it. For those who wish a chance at tomorrow – and a tomorrow where none come demanding a tax of your flesh and blood – then take up arms now. Fight, now. Die, if you must, so that others may live, for you will die anyway in the end, and better it be for *something*.'

Silence fell, after that, and Thalric found himself nodding, impressed despite himself. *Give that man a general's rank badge.*

Then the Moth boy, Evastos, was back, already yelling out as he dropped from the sky, 'They're coming! They're coming!'

My cue.

'Fight now!' Che was calling. 'Take up the same weapons you've made for your oppressors, and put them to use. Take up your hammers, your slings, your staves, the blades of your Art! Fight now, because they will take the last of your children, and then they will take your lives! Fight, or be extinguished so that none will know you ever were!'

Thalric had stepped into the air, his Art wings catching and lifting him, already looking for the Worm's soldiers encroaching into the light spilling from Cold Well's fires. Before, when they had fought outside the Hermit's hole, the darkness had been his greatest enemy. The Worm's slaves feared the dark, though, even those of them without eyes. They feared the cold and the isolation. They feared the Worm, and kept the fires burning, and now Thalric could see.

The band of the Worm approaching was made up of a couple of pack millipedes, a score of warriors and a Scarred One, not unlike the group who had come to exact the tax before. It was Thalric's job to strike, to use his natural advantages to kill as many of them as he could. He would give the slaves a little time to overcome their fears and arm themselves. He would also commit them. He was not sure whether Che had quite seen her plan evolving in that light but, by striking first against the Worm, they would be forcing the slaves' hands.

They're dead anyway, so who cares? In this subterranean world there was no place for sentiment.

And here they come. The first of the Worm resolved from shapes in the dark to shapes in the light, the lead soldiers rushing forwards with that constant hurrying tread as they danced to the mind-less urgings of their god. Thalric coursed over them and wheeled, seeing them begin to spread out as they sensed him but could not quite locate him.

There. And Thalric's sting spat fire, and the Scarred One in their midst, the only human mind amongst the lot of them, was down and smoking before he had had the wit to look up.

Thalric had hoped that there would be a few shots' worth of milling panic or blank stillness as they tried to digest what had happened, but the Worm's bodies were on to him almost before their priest had hit the ground. Some of them had slings, and they had the weapons to hand on the instant, fitting stones to them and whirling them up to speed.

At least the bastards don't have bows, and Thalric let his hands speak for him, lashing into them with his sting, his Art searing streaks of gold across them, striking down, burning them, melting their armour. Of all the gifts of the Wasp, this one had always been strong with him, reaching further, striking harder, sapping his strength less. He kept on the move, darting and diving through the air above them, lashing left and right with both hands, feeling his wings eat up his strength. Let the Worm be as coordinated as it might be, let its aura of denial smother all thoughts of

Aptitude in him, but he was no artificer and he needed only what nature had given him.

Then a sling stone struck the armour of his shoulder hard enough to spin him in the air, and the next moment he was skimming the rocky ground, knowing that they would be running for him with those nasty little swords drawn. He tried for height, but then another rock hit him in the chest, knocking him on to his back even though his mail took the brunt of it. He lurched to his feet, hands out and blazing, seeing one onrushing figure cut down in the flash. *How many did I get? Not enough, apparently.*

Then Esmail was with him, darting past to open up a Centipede-kinden as a conjurer would, mail and all, just with a sweep of his hand. Thalric took the chance to back off, hands up and hunting for targets, seeing a dozen of the Worm still on their feet and running full-tilt towards them. Another slingshot skimmed past his ear.

Tynisa was there too, although she was holding back with him, and he remembered how she had fallen before the Worm the last time, how her fighting grace had deserted her and left her crippled. Che was on his other side with her sword drawn, and he wanted to shout at her to get back – except she was rousing the rabble, and the rabble sometimes needed to be led by example.

His hands flashed again to send a further Worm down, seeing Esmail dancing between two of them, another whose Art was equal to the task.

And if something doesn't happen about now then we know this is a lost cause.

He was ready to fall back, to grab Che by the arm and haul her out of the way, to let the others do the dying. But the rabble had apparently made its decision, and not a moment too soon.

Thundering between Thalric and Tynisa went the enormous figure of Forge-Iron, the Mole Cricket. He whirled his great hammer in one hand, and Thalric saw it strike a Worm soldier square on, practically turning the creature to paste. There were now sling stones zipping past towards the enemy, too, and then a ragbag of fighters deigned to present themselves: men and women without armour or any real idea about how to fight, but suddenly the odds were in their favour, for all that they looked terrified of everything that they saw – and of the Worm most of all.

'Now!' Che yelled, and charged forwards, and although Thalric cursed her for it, he knew it was the right thing to do. He drew his own blade and hurried after her and, like the feeblest tide of history, the slaves came as well.

Once the Worm had been dispatched, all of its bodies strewn at the periphery of Cold Well like broken dolls, the slaves stood around, staring. Not one of them seemed to know what came next, and Thalric felt that he could share their apprehension. Did Che really think she could forge anything from this down-trodden dross, even with the threat of extinction as the whip?

Still, Thalric had been a soldier once. 'Strip the bodies!' he shouted at them. 'They have armour, weapons! Things you lack, you wretches! Come on, do yourselves a favour!'

A few did pick up a sword or pluck disconsolately at the mail of the dead, but most just stood there, staring at the corpses, staring at him, staring at each other.

Then he heard a voice, and knew it for Atraea the Moth woman: 'What have you done? You have killed us all!'

'You're as good as dead, anyway,' Thalric spat back, but then Che was there, hands extended to call for attention.

'Listen to me,' she called. 'This is just the start! Now you must go to the other communities nearby, all those other people who have lived under the tax, who have suffered as you have suffered. I know that they are there. You must tell them what we have told you. They must do as you have done. They must rise up against the Worm, if they value their lives, and the lives of their kin. This is their only chance.'

'It is forbidden to travel to other towns!' someone called back, and Che blinked, plainly finding a complication she had not anticipated.

Thankfully, Messel came to her rescue. 'And yet it is done! I have done it. Many of you have done it. The word must be spread – so fly, run, follow paths of stone, but go swiftly!'

'Not swiftly enough!' Atraea insisted fiercely. 'Raise a hand against one soldier of the Worm, and all the Worm knows of it! They are on their way here even now! You have only ensured that everyone in Cold Well will die.'

'Then there shall be no one in Cold Well when they arrive,' Orothellin's voice boomed out. 'You must leave, all of you – strike out into the wilderness, set off for False Hearth or The Shelves. Take all you have, and most especially the food and the weapons that you have already gathered for the Worm.'

'This is madness!' Atraea insisted. 'This . . .' And her jabbing finger found Che. 'This is because she knows the Worm is attacking her people in the Old World. She thinks to sacrifice all that we are just to aid her kin under the sun!'

A silence fell, and Thalric looked from face to face: Mole Crickets, Beetles, Woodlice, all the detritus of this grim place, and not one of them with a thought in their heads, or so he assumed.

Then one of the Woodlouse-kinden women coughed and said, 'So you believe in the Old World now?'

Despite himself, Thalric's heart leapt. *Is it possible? Did one of them just have an idea? Wonders will never cease.*

'That is . . .' Atraea's pale eyes flashed as she stared around, trying to muster support. 'They are using you! That is all that matters. They don't care about you!'

'Do *you* care about yourselves?' Che countered. 'The Worm doesn't care. The Worm remembers the sun. From the moment

282

the Seal was broken, you became nothing to the Worm but a resource, a vessel to be emptied and cast aside. Ask him, he knows – he hears the Worm still though he tries to deny it.' She was pointing at the Hermit, who hugged himself and flinched away from her. 'The Worm doesn't care about you, for all that you have been the fat it has lived off all these centuries of imprisonment. If you sit here like good, obedient slaves then the Worm will harvest all you have, down to the flesh from your bones. But the Worm is already marching. If you make it work, if you run and hide and fight, then it will spend its blood and its time hunting you down.'

The Mole Cricket smith loomed beside Atraea, and she sagged into him, hands about her midriff.

'We will die,' she got out.

'Some of you will, surely. Perhaps I will too,' Che said equably. 'But you mistake me if you think I do this for my kin. I do this because the city that gave birth to me teaches what is right and what is wrong, even if we do not always practise it. We hold no slaves, where I come from, and we value human life, of all kinden. And in the Worm's blind hunger, and with the collaboration of its priests, a great evil has been created here, and it must be fought. Perhaps a year ago you could indeed have said that to live in the Worm's shadow is better than to die on its swords. Now you will die, every one of you, unless you set yourselves free.'

'Gather everything you can take, everything you can carry. Use the pack animals the Worm has so thoughtfully brought you!' Orothellin boomed. 'Fill those cages with something more wholesome for once. Cold Well must be emptied. Take everything you can.'

'Teacher . . .' Atraea's taut, frightened face turned towards him. 'There must be some way . . .'

'It is the end of many things,' the big man told her gently. 'Unless we act now, it will be the end of all things.'

Around them, the people of Cold Well began to move, slowly at first but then with a gathering urgency, preparing for their exodus, whilst others were already setting off to pass word of what had happened across the Worm's realm.

Twenty-Four

Major Oski dropped down beside the artillery crew positioned on the roofs overlooking Collegium docks. 'All right, what now? What's so important? The engines have gone wrong or something?'

'No, sir,' the sergeant of Engineers reported. 'Out on the water, though—'

For a moment, Oski went cold. *But this is nonsense, isn't it? Vrakir's lunacy.* There was a half-moon tonight, and it touched the wavetops as they rolled forever in towards land, and out there . . . Ships? Did he see ships?

For a moment he thought this must be it, that somehow Vrakir had been right. *Is it the Spiders? Have they sent an Armada to relieve Collegium? Why the pits would they even bother?* Then he spat. 'That's – what, is that the Tseni, in their little boats?'

'Yes, sir.'

Oski slapped him across the back of the head, using a flicker of his wings to gain the required height. 'You stupid sod, you got me out of bed for that?'

'Sir, they're moving. It's as if they're getting ready for something,' the sergeant insisted, aggrieved.

'Do I look like someone who gives a piss? Go send for the officer of the watch or something.'

'That's you, Major. You were given the harbour defence.'

'No, I was given the set-up, the artillery . . .' Oski bit his lip, trying to remember exactly *what* he had been told, because he had been so angry with the whole pointless venture that he hadn't exactly been taking notes. 'Listen, there must be a captain, or some army major, or . . . Ah, piss on it.' Besides, he was well and truly awake now and out of bed, so he might as well blow things up.

'Let's shoot at them. What's the range?' He could see better by moonlight than any of them, and he had a better head for figures too. *And a better flier. Makes you wonder how the Wasps ever got this far, really.* The Tseni had come in a host of little metal craft, swift and low to the water. Bergild's pilots had reported that they had repeating ballistae mounted on them, of some superior design that had actually given the aviators some tough moments when they tried to overfly them too low to the water. Nothing that would trouble the ludicrously overstated defences here, though. Oski hopped up onto the engine next to him and saw several hundred very bored Wasps – some sleeping, others keeping the watch. A couple of Sentinels had pulled up right at the water's edge, as though about to embark on a trip around the bay. All those engines, the leadshotters and the ballistae and these new toys he'd lifted from the Collegiates were dutifully pointing out into the great emptiness of the sea, across which the Tseni ships were skimming as though happy to oblige his need for some target practice.

'Right, get this bastard's engine primed,' he instructed. The device he was standing on was something like a ballista, with an explosive bolt in the breech, but there was no string, no arms, and the bolt was all metal. Oski's people had blown up two of these before they had worked out the principles, and it was a diabolical little toy indeed that the Beetles had come up with. The charge of the lightning batteries in the base created some sort of magnetic differential down the length of the engine, which resulted in that metal bolt being thrown . . . *basically as far as you like.*

'Primed and ready, sir,' the sergeant said. 'Only you'd better—'

'Right.' Oski let his wings lift him off the machine, to avoid one of his own feet being sent hurtling at the Tseni fleet at a thousand miles an hour.

There was a curious shiver through the air and the bolt was gone, faster than the eye could follow it. His aim was dead on: one of the Tseni ships instantly blossomed with flame, the explosion seeming to come almost in the instant the engine loosed. Oski grinned broadly and declared, "Hooray for Collegiate engineering," and then someone screamed.

He swore and was airborne in a moment, cornering over the barricades and the lines of soldiers, hearing a growing murmur in response as men began to wake up. 'Report!' he shouted out. 'Someone report!'

'Sir!' A cry from the waterside, on one of the piers. 'Here, sir!' And Oski skimmed over the heads of the soldiers, swinging wide around a Sentinel's great segmented bulk to touch down on the timber of the wharves.

'Report!' he demanded again, seeing a cluster of Wasps staring down at the water.

'Sir, it's the lieutenant, he's . . .' said one, before running out of words, so that another had to fill in, 'He's gone, sir.'

'Do you call that a pissing *report*?' Oski shouted.

'He fell in,' the first soldier started, but the other spoke over him, 'He was grabbed, sir – something in the water got him.'

Oski stared at him. The water – and out here on the pier there was a great deal of it on three sides – was very dark, slapping and slopping at the pylons.

A moment later, fighting broke out on one of the neighbouring wharves. He could not see clearly what was going on, just soldiers kicking into the air, or falling back towards the land, because – he could not see because what, just something moving there that his eyes refused to find a name for. He saw stingshot flash and crackle, caught a glimpse of something shelled, many-legged.

'What . . .?' he got out, and a man next to him went down, shrieking. A pincer as large as Oski's whole body had clamped the luckless soldier's leg, the bone already shattered in its iron grip. As Oski watched, a crab the size of a small automotive began hauling itself up on to the pier, the wood creaking and protesting under its weight.

In a heartbeat he was in the air, seeing stingshot – even snapbow bolts – scatter off the thing's carapace. And, the next thing he knew, the entire wharf front was heaving, the creatures climbing sideways from the water everywhere, snapping mindlessly at anyone luckless enough to be near. Even as he tried to phrase an appropriate military response, some part of Oski's mind was shouting, *What the pits are they doing?* As though there was some naturalist's explanation, some freak migration that could rationalize what he was seeing.

'Back, back from the water! Form a shooting line where you can do some good, you morons!' The order was unnecessary. The entire waterline had come alive, bristling with legs and pincers and stalked eyes as a wave of bafflingly enraged sealife boiled from the surf with a weirdly unhurried inevitability. Some of the creatures were picked apart by bolts from those soldiers already safe behind the barricades, and Oski saw a pair of them just explode into wet shards as one of the leadshotter crews woke up and began doing their job. *Vrakir! Did he bring this on? Is this what he saw? How could he . . .?*

The Sentinel at the waterfront tilted itself, trying to lower its leadshotter enough to do any good, whilst its rotary piercers began chewing up the emerging crustaceans, the firepowder-charged missiles rapidly disassembling the animals into their component pieces. Then the vehicle was tilting further, at an unhealthy angle, and Oski let his wings speed him over, thinking perhaps that a particularly large beast had somehow got underneath the automotive's legs.

Even as he closed in, he saw the entire vehicle jerk forwards by a man's length, an impossible sight as though there was some great magnet beneath it that had just yanked it across the stone of the wharves, halfway onto one of the piers. The Sentinel's legs were scrabbling, digging in for purchase, and yet it was shuddering closer to the sea even as Oski watched.

He spotted them then, the tentacles that had snared it, four or five thick rubbery cables snaking across the automotive's armoured shell. A ripple of muscular contraction shivered through them, and the Sentinel lurched again, its front half hanging over the water, legs waving frantically, uselessly.

Before Oski's eyes, it wavered, caught on the fulcrum of its body, and then whatever unthinkable monster had hold of it just pulled again, as effortlessly irresistible as an earthquake, and the vehicle was gone into the sea.

He swung back towards the Imperial lines, where concerted snapbow volleys were flaying away the slow advance of the sea creatures. Order was being restored, and he was only hoping that the owner of the tentacles wasn't up to the brief walk that separated his new position from the water.

Even as he touched down, another cry went out, and he turned to see something new emerging from the sea.

It was a man – or the shape of it was something like a man – wearing a colossal suit of armour, and almost as broad as he was tall. Before Oski's eyes, the apparition hooked its way out of the ocean, water streaming from its joints. The sword it bore was the most mundane thing about it, and even that was the length of a man, curved forwards to a savage point. Seeing the enormous claws of its gauntlets, Oski wondered that it needed the blade at all.

By then there were a dozen of them clambering to their feet along the waterfront, and behind them the water was seething with more: great plated shoulders breaking the surf, claws driving gashes into the pylons of the piers, as they lumbered and lurched onto dry land.

He did not even have to give the order; the snapbows were already prioritizing these new targets. Bolts were sleeting down on the Sea-kinden even as they advanced, their forward steps ponderously slow. Oski watched, frozen at the barricade, seeing the bolts dance off that armour like raindrops. A couple fell, perhaps struck in the joints or through those narrow eyeslits, but the rest just forged on as though it was only inclement weather: still slow but closing all the time.

'Where's my pissing artillery?' the Fly fairly shrieked, and even as he did so, he saw a ballista spear ram into the shoulderplate of one of the leaders, knocking it off its stride for a moment before it continued its inexorable progress.

The leaders had bigger, better armour than the rest, he saw. Those behind seemed to have something that looked like chitin, for all it was warding off snapbow bolts better than steel would, but that first wave wore more massive suits that looked pale and encrusted, almost like . . .

Stone. Stone armour!

A leadshotter boomed from behind him, and he saw the ball plough into the rear ranks, smashing three of the sea warriors down before bouncing into the water. Another ball ploughed into one of the leaders, and Oski saw the man's breastplate appear to disintegrate in a great cloud of shards and stone dust. He whooped for progress and the power of good engineering, but the sound died in his throat. The target had been knocked flat, but even now it was struggling to its feet, its armour mazed with cracks and hanging with loose fragments, and yet holding together; and somehow the thing inside it was still alive.

'Has someone gone for the general?' he demanded, watching that advance grow closer and closer. *I'm an engineer! I shouldn't have to think of these things!*

'Yes, sir!'

'Prepare to fall back to the building line.' The artillery was really opening up now, two or three engines apiece concentrating on the same target. He saw those gargantuan armoured forms begin to falter, individuals being cracked and broken, smashed to the ground and not getting up, and yet the wave itself did not slow. All the engines he had lined up, and it was not enough. Who could ever have believed—!

'Sir!' A soldier grabbed him by the collar and hauled him back as if he was a child, even as the first monstrous figure reached the barricade. The clawed gauntlets seized on the wooden barrier, all those planks and pieces of furniture that Oski's men had taken hours to nail together, and tore it asunder with one convulsive motion.

At least we've got them outranged, he thought, scooting backwards across the sky towards the rooftop emplacements. But, even as he watched, he saw one of the stone-clad monsters raise a hand towards the retreating Wasps, and heard a series of explosive clacks – distinct over all the other sounds of battle. Bolts, the length of Oski's arm, were being spat out from some piece of clockwork mounted *within* the thing's armour. That was when everything changed for him. That was when he suddenly recast the scene before him: not just a vision from some impossible nightmare, but an invasion, an amphibious assault such as the Empire had never even conceived of.

Oski's military mindset returned then, so that he shook off the shock and began darting from crew to crew, ordering the aiming of their engines whilst shouting to the rank and file to form shooting lines, to get their swords ready, above all to *hold*. They had to give General Tynan time.

Tynan was already half clad in his armour, his slaves buckling on each piece even as he took in the reports. The phrases he heard were fragmentary, unbelievable: an invasion from the sea – not in boats but the sea itself – monsters, men, scuttling beasts, the docks lost already. He had given orders to mobilize every soldier he had in the city, but he was keenly aware that there were several thousand Ant-kinden within striking distance of the walls, and surely *this* was what they had been waiting for.

Further reports were still coming in, but he could not just sit and wait for a complete picture, because every new word that reached him would be critically out of date.

'Are the Ants moving?' he demanded. No word had come back, though some Farsphex scouts were already in the air to go and look. Tynan spat in dismay, still trying to assimilate what was going on, desperate to believe that what he was hearing was an exaggeration, and yet each successive report matched and exceeded the last: casualties, lost ground, destroyed engines.

'Where the pits is Vrakir?' he demanded.

'Here, sir.' And there he was, the Red Watch man, the Empress's voice. To his credit, there was no gloating, no triumph. He looked just like Tynan felt – a man hauled from his bed in the middle of the night and still trying to make sense of a hostile new world.

'Get to the docks and take charge, Major. Leave the engines to Oski, but the soldiers are yours. Your "death by water" has just turned up.'

'Yes, sir,' and the man was off, like a model soldier.

'General, the Vekken are marching. They've been reinforced, sir.' This came from a Fly-kinden landing practically on Tynan's shoulder.

'Reinforced with what?'

'We're not sure, but it looks like Spider-kinden, sir,' the Fly told him, falling over his words in his hurry to get them out. 'And new automotives as well, sir, and some sort of artillery.'

'How did it arrive? How did we miss the ships that brought it in?' Tynan demanded.

'Sir, there were no ships. We've been on watch for the Tseni, or even a Spider fleet. There's been nothing!'

'Plainly there has!' Tynan snapped, feeling the fabric of his control fraying, a bad moment for his temper to start getting away from him. He calmed himself instantly, taking a moment's breath to remind himself who he was. 'The Sarnesh will be on the move as well. Lieutenant Gath, you have the north wall, and make every shot count. Captain Haldric, you have the west against the Vekken and whoever they've got with them. Hold them off. I refuse to believe they've suddenly inherited sufficient engines to bring the walls down, and neither Ants nor Spiders are noted for flying over things. Get some heavies on the wall tops to repel climbers, and put as many bolts into them as you can.'

The two designated officers saluted and were off to their tasks. The mood around Tynan was bizarre: men were confused, perhaps frightened, and yet they were a field army that had been without a fight for too long. Better this than beating and imprisoning Beetle civilians.

Which leads me to another point. 'What about the locals?'

'Nothing yet, sir,' a sergeant reported. 'Maybe it's because of what the slavers have been doing, but all quiet on the streets so far.'

'Sir.' One of the messengers from the docks held up a hand, and at Tynan's nod went on: 'I saw some of the locals take a look at what's coming out of the sea. They were shuttering up and barring their doors, sir.'

Stab me, what if this isn't *a Collegiate reconquest at all?* He thought of those emptied villages, the mysterious attack within Collegium itself, that irresistible suggestion of another, unknown enemy.

'I need a messenger to fly north to Colonel Brakker and the relief force, and also a Farsphex to get word to Capitas. They need to know.' Tynan felt distinctly unsteady now, as though the ground was shaking with the forces of history moving all around him.

The fight for the docks had been fierce, in the end. The Sea-kinden troops had carried the battle all the way to the Port Authority buildings in their first rush, tearing up barricades, casting down engines and killing every Wasp who was fool enough to stand still for too long. After that, the Imperials had recovered from their surprise and begun to fight back. They had a lot of light artillery mounted on roofs offering a good view of the wharves, although how they had known that an attack was coming in, nobody could say. The Sea-kinden had no fliers, and only relatively modest ranged capability. The big shock troops, the Greatclaw Onychoi, were not climbers, and many of them could not even squeeze up the buildings' internal stairs.

They kept marching. The Imperial lines that had been drawn up to halt them were simply not physically capable of it. The Greatclaw warriors in their formidable armour shrugged off snapbow shot and ignored the Wasps' stings and swords alike. Spears splintered from the plates of their carapaces as they struck about them with their curved swords of weighted bronze, or with the claws of their armour and their Art. Each rooftop emplacement became like an island as the tide came in.

Behind the Greatclaws came the others, a hurrying mass of soldiers from the sea, eyes wide at their own daring, braving the storm of snapbow shot; rushing forwards because to stand still would be to die. They were the Kerebroi and their allies, the people of Hermatyre, and for most of their lives they had believed that to set foot on the land was to die.

For many of them, that would be true, but they were paying a debt; their Edmir had asked it of them, and it was a new world.

Rosander, Nauarch of the Thousand Spines Train, didn't care about any of that, for all that it was his people in the vanguard of the invasion. He was here with his Greatclaw warriors because there had been a plan once, to do just this, and he had never quite forgotten it. Oh, he had been shown how foolish an idea conquering the land was, but *this* . . . he had always wanted to know how it would have gone, and now he had been given the chance to find out.

The irony in how that chance had come about was not lost on him, but he didn't let it slow him down.

The Wasps defended each building fiercely on all sides, shooting at the Kerebroi as they climbed the walls, fighting sword against spear to save their artillery. Once a roof was cleared – the surviving Wasps on it casting themselves into the air when it was either that or be overwhelmed – the Smallclaw came in. The little artificers of the sea had not been idle, and the diminutive Onychoi wore light armour of moulded shell and carried weapons that would be familiar to any land-kinden who had seen a snapbow. They set up their own shooting positions, their long bolts raking the Wasps on neighbouring rooftops, whilst their mechanics began examining the artillery that they had prised from the enemy's hands.

Meanwhile, the Wasps were all over, darting about in the air like shoaling fish, in plain defiance of logic. They kept trying to break up the advancing front of the Sea-kinden wave, but their little weapons merely crackled and pattered against the stone of Rosander's mail and that of his picked warriors who wore suits just as heavy. For the rest, reinforced shell was still good enough to fend off the worst of it. Rosander was frankly amazed that these diminutive landsmen put such stock in those little weapons, but then he hadn't yet seen one of them who looked strong enough to wear the requisite weight of armour.

Rosander saw fierce fighting ahead – his line was getting broken up by the sheer maze of the place – and he realized that he had lost track of the shape of the battle entirely. The walls rising on every side made it worse than a weed forest for getting lost, and he saw ahead that a band of Dart-kinden had got ahead of him, engaging the Wasps with nothing but their spears. *Let them die, then*, was the obvious conclusion, but against that was the thought of a decent fight, because the enemy were standing their ground, having found a foe they could hold off. The enemy were still hopping about like mad things, though. They had discovered that the Darts' spears had stinging cysts that could lash out nearly a man's length, so they were constantly repositioning themselves, and using their little bows and that flashing Art of theirs to whittle down the Sea-kinden's numbers.

Rosander raised his left arm and aimed along it as best he could, pitching up to catch the land-kinden as they took to the air. Pressure-driven weapons had been brought to the Sea-kinden from the land almost by accident, but the mechanics of the Hot Stations had not been slow in re-engineering and improving them. Rosander's hand – almost lost within the great hooked mass of the gauntlet – clenched on the bar trigger, and the weapon set in his armour snapped out a handful of bolts, picking one Wasp straight from the air. Each shot was accompanied by a jet of mist as water vented from the battery, and the last bolt barely made it six feet away from him, so that he waved his stone hand in the air.

Immediately, Chenni was there, his top mechanic, clambering up to crouch on his shoulder and open up the compartments in his mail, first replacing the water battery and then feeding in more bolts.

'You've got the land map?' Rosander demanded of her. 'You know where we are?'

'Easily, Chief.' With deft fingers she closed him up again and unfolded the land-kinden document, its fragile material already starting to come apart from too much damp and rough handling. 'I reckon we're – oh, will you look at that!'

Something new had arrived, and for a moment Rosander thought it was one of the land-kinden's beasts, which had been strangely absent so far. Then he looked again, and saw the way its high-fronted segmented body gleamed: no animal but a machine.

'Looks better than your ones,' he grunted.

'Give me a chance to take a look inside, Chief. I'll build you one.'

The Wasps were now fleeing, and he thought the Sea-kinden warriors had driven them off, but then devices at the base of the new machine's front spun into life and scythed the Dart-kinden down to a man, before they even knew what was going on.

'Let's get it,' Rosander decided on basic principles, just as the machine seemed to notice they were there. Certainly it opened its single eye wide once it saw them.

A moment later, Rosander was knocked sideways, his knee crunching onto the flagstones.

'Nauarch!' and 'Chief!' rang in his ears, sounding oddly distant, and his warriors began helping him up.

'Where's the weapon? Someone go and throw it off a roof!' he demanded, but they told him that the machine had gouted fire from its eye.

'Chenni?' he bellowed, in sudden fear, but she was at his elbow immediately, looking bruised but intact.

'Javel's dead,' she told him. 'Pushed his breastplate clean in.'

'Bastard,' Rosander decided, and began lumbering forwards with his followers in tow. By that time the thing was ready for another shot.

The slap of the leadshot knocked him flat, and his left arm was instantly numb. His head was ringing within his helm, and for a few seconds he had no idea where he was or what was going on. Then Chenni was shouting at him to get up, and that sounded like a good idea, and he was lurching to his feet, his bannermen streaming on either side towards the offending machine. His shoulder armour had been struck square on; had it been just stone, it would have cracked down the middle and taken his arm with it. His people knew what they were doing when they built armour, though. They knew that it had to allow some give, to take in the shock of a blow without passing that force straight through to the wearer. There were hollow cells like coral forming lines that dispersed the impact away and, as they laid down the stone, layer by layer, they interleaved wires of the new Hot Stations steel in a branching network that strengthened and reinforced. Now his broad pauldron had shattered into a hundred pieces, but all those pieces were still bound together and holding.

His men were all swarming around the machine now, battering brutally at its armoured sides, and Rosander stumbled over to them, determined to take out his hurt and anger on the thing. It was loosing its weapons, from the front and from the sides, but they were meant to kill lesser things than a Greatclaw Onychoi garbed for war.

'Don't mess around!' he boomed to his followers. 'Tip the thing over! Let's see what its guts look like!'

297

He cast aside his sword and hooked his right hand beneath the lip of curved plates where he could glimpse the machine's articulated legs. It was trying to back out now, but the Onychoi had it surrounded, pounding and rocking it, whilst others joined Rosander in heaving up one side.

He put all of the strength that would fit in one arm into the effort, and there were four or five others of his kind – huge men with a colossal build that none of these landsmen seemed to have – and they were strong, and in the end the machine just wasn't as heavy as he had expected. Abruptly it was tipping over, the warriors on the far side scattering so that the great metal beast slammed down on its side and began to revolve slowly as its legs continued to piston.

The underside was metal too, but Rosander was willing to bet that it was nowhere near as tough. He cocked back his good hand for a strike, aiming for the point where the legs met the body.

Out on the water, the Sea-kinden were still arriving. Great clumsy automotives, just enormous curved shields over their powering legs, were clambering onto the wharves, assisted by dozens of Onychoi, or being lifted onto land by hastily erected winches. They were mounted with big spring-powered bolt-throwers and began crawling determinedly forwards the moment that their metal feet were squarely on the ground, shouldering for room amongst the soldiers and the crabs that were still dragging themselves out of the water.

Rosander strode through this bustling chaos, taking a break from the front line because his arm was bruised from wrist to elbow, and because the bannermen of the Thousand Spines were already stationed at most of the places they had been heading for. He had left Chenni in charge because she had a good head on her and could read the map.

Further out, a submersible was surfacing, the curved apex of its nautilus-shell hull breaking the surface as it jockeyed carefully in towards the docks. As Rosander limped closer, he saw a handful of figures clamber out and take stock. He saw the Kerebroi woman, Paladrya, in conference with the little Smallclaw Wys whose submersible it was, and beside them was a stocky figure, armoured head to foot in light shell mail, with a Sea-kinden snapbow in one hand and a landsman shortsword in the other, shifting his footing to keep his balance until he could just step off onto a pier.

Rosander dragged his helmet off, grinning fiercely. 'Well, now! And you wonder how it would have gone if we'd come for you after all, back then? Wonder no more, landsman!' He laughed, despite his pain. 'What would you do now if we decided we wanted to keep this place, once we win it for you?'

'Oh, I'd find some way to take it back. You know me, Rosander.' Gauntleted hands reached up to tug away the helm, revealing a dark, serious face, its eyes flicking from the Nauarch to the cityscape beyond.

Stenwold Maker had come home.

Twenty-Five

Greenwise Artector had intended to get out, he really had. When the Eighth Army had descended on Helleron, however, it had come howling out of Three Cities territory far quicker than anyone had expected. He had just not been ready.

He could still have slipped out, nevertheless. Sufficient applications of care and money would have allowed it, because money always spoke loud in Helleron. He had been watched, though. The other magnates of the city already knew that he was a man the Wasps would want to speak to. He had faced a choice, in the end: he could have abandoned his family and staff within the city and crept out like a thief, or he could remain, public and noticeable, sending his family and staff away instead. He had sought within himself for that courage, the self-sacrifice he had always believed he was capable of. Somewhat to his surprise, he had found it. He had stayed on until it was too late to leave, just so that his kin, his servants, his entire household could get clear.

Then, with the noose already closing on him, he had vanished.

All the routes in and out of Helleron had sported eyes on the lookout for this rogue magnate. One of the Council of Thirteen that had governed the city would be recognized, and many on the lookout had been former colleagues, former employees – men who knew his face. The airfields were watched, the gates likewise. After that, there were Wasp soldiers on the streets, and his name was first on their list to apprehend: Greenwise Artector, the missing magnate.

Even so, perfect vigilance was impossible to maintain for long, whether it was the hirelings of the rich or the soldiers of the Empire. Helleron was ostensibly a free city where the ruling council – its thirteenth place now filled by a woman who had until recently been the fourteenth most powerful merchant in the city – took careful advice from a colonel in the Imperial Consortium on all matters. The city's trade – its life's blood – ran free, especially that conducted with the Empire to the east. Greenwise could have got out by now, if he had been willing to risk it.

Instead he had decided to take a stand.

He had fallen far from his old haunts. He had gone to the slums, where a man could lose himself and just about everything else. Thankfully he had been making preparations for this day ever since the end of the last war. Helleron's gangs, the fiefs, had not been friends of the Empire, and the Wasps had done their best to eradicate the network of criminal cartels whose inter-locked gears made the city's underside turn. Greenwise, like many magnates, had his contacts beneath the surface, but he had been marked as a man who opposed the Wasps. Criminals, mobsters and murderers, thieves and racketeers, who cared nothing for anything but their own illicit properties, saw in him something worth keeping alive. Not a hero exactly, for they had no use for a hero, but an ally in these hard times.

They had resources and he had knowledge, and together they were making plans. Greenwise wanted to hurt the Empire and, most of all, his former fellows on the Helleren Council. His new friends from the fiefs wanted to do the same by filling their pockets and perhaps shedding a little blood. The Empire hated their chaos, and the Consortium hated any flow of money it did not control. Had the Wasps used a lighter hand last time round, then no doubt the Imperial merchant arm could just have bought into Helleron's cesspool of vice, but the crackdowns had closed that door.

Now Greenwise, with a sword and a crossbow hanging from his person and dressed in clothes that would not have been fit to clean his servant's boots not so long before, was guiding a gang of thieves towards the heartland of the rich. Their target was the townhouse of a man named Scordrey, perhaps the most influential merchant in the city. Nobody was feeling inclined to think small these days.

At the moment Greenwise was working with two fiefs. The Whoresellers fleshed out their pimping with fencing and protection rackets, and the Bitter Men were strong-armers and housebreakers daring or lunatic enough to try and crack a target this big. Greenwise Artector, erstwhile big man about town, was hurrying through the narrow covered streets of Helleron's poorer quarters in company with a pack of Fly and Beetle thieves, a lean and loping Scorpion who was second in command of the Bitters and a halfbreed locksmith and appraiser that the Whoresellers had hired. He himself was along with them because he had kept one of Scordrey's men on his payroll for years, knew three quiet ways into the man's house and had a very good idea of where the strongroom was and how to get into it.

Helleron was a cramped city, and a cunning man who knew the right paths and shortcuts could make the transition from the gutter to the mansions of the rich in surprisingly few steps. So it was that Greenwise and his crew were passing through the slums along the back of a row of refineries, but ahead of them rose the roads where the houses grew larger and the streets were better lit.

There were watchmen, of course, the city's militia, but the Whoresellers had greased a fair number of palms these last few nights, and if any watchman turned out to be incorruptible enough to get in the way, then Greenwise reckoned it would be a poor night for that man. The same would apply if they ran into a Wasp patrol, especially as the Imperial hand lay light on the richer parts of the city – only two or three soldiers at a time.

The ground shook, just a little, but at first Greenwise assumed that some machinery in the refineries was responsible. Nobody else raised the issue, so they were soon on their way.

'This alley takes us to Shoffery Row,' he murmured. 'From there to Servil Street, where there's a tunnel that can take us to Brackish Lots, practically behind Scordrey's house.'

'Handy,' the Scorpion grunted.

'It is indeed. It's how his staff receive deliveries without the great man's view being cheapened,' Greenwise explained, thinking for a moment about the recent times when he himself had lived with such considerations.

One of the thieves twitched. 'Curse me, what was that?'

'What?'

'Anyone feel that, the ground . . .'

'Just some engine . . .' Another, dismissively.

'No, wait,' the halfbreed locksmith broke in. 'That was . . . That was no machine, that was . . . an earthquake?'

'Don't be a fool,' someone said derisively, and the slowest-witted of the thieves wanted to know what an earthquake was. But by then Greenwise was feeling decidedly uncomfortable; something was communicating itself to him via the soles of his feet.

Then the entire city of Helleron seemed to lurch and slump fluidly beneath them, spilling them all off their feet as, behind them, several hundred yards of low-rent workshops and refineries – and at least a hundred homes – just fell into the earth.

Greenwise cried out, but his voice was lost in the colossal scraping and rumbling of stone, the shrieking of metal, wooden beams snapping and cracking like munitions. And the voices: hundreds of voices in a moment's hideous realization, shocked from sleep, caught while at work, ripped from their dreams in the night's quiet.

He went running back towards the broken edge of the city, aware that half of his confederates had already made themselves scarce. Given the shadow life he led now, he should have done the same, but the night was wild with the screams of the injured, the cries of children. He was not the man to turn his back on all that.

And besides . . . he needed to see. Because this was impossible, what had just happened. He needed to bring his eyes closer, so that they could take in and comprehend the ruin of so much in such a fractured moment.

The street was already slipping and canting even as he ran, the earth still about its vengeful night's work, but he scrabbled to that broken edge, intending to find a way down, to help the trapped, the hurt. He could still hear yells and wailing and sounds of horror, but he put it down to the simple mechanical damage. He had not thought to see his city under attack.

The earth was boiling with them. His eyes would not take it in. From the cracks between the shattered buildings they came seething out, a riot of armoured forms like no kinden he had ever known, and moving like nothing human, as though he was watching some spreading, foaming plague – a contagion in human form. They were swarming over everyone down there, and he saw blades glitter and flash, bright silver on the descent, but red as they were lifted once again. They were butchering everyone trapped down there – literally, hacking them limb from limb without the mercy of killing first, then just carrying off the severed pieces.

No, they were not killing them all. He saw struggling, living forms carried away on that churning tide, being hauled back within the earth as they wept and kicked and screeched. The children! They were taking the children.

He staggered back from the brink. Going down to help was no longer an option. Those below were beyond any help a mere human could give.

The street tilted further, and he felt the ground beneath him shift and shudder as though it was being eaten away from below, hollowed out to an eggshell thinness, like ice about to crack.

He ran. He ran towards those grand houses that he had planned to prey on that night. The quiet streets were beginning to fill

304

now: with watchmen, Wasp soldiers, servants, the great and the good tottering from their doors, half asleep, to demand what was going on. He was Greenwise Artector, most wanted man in Helleron, but right then nobody cared.

Ahead of him, suddenly looming from the night, was the town-house of Corda Halewright, a fellow magnate back when the world hadn't fallen completely sideways and gone mad. Greenwise had the crazed idea of banging on her door and begging for sanctuary, because even familiar enemies were to be preferred to what he had just seen. He shouldered past a couple of militiamen who were just staring back towards the devastation, and he staggered on towards that remembered building, feeling the earth jump and shudder beneath him. And slide.

He actually saw it slide. Before him, three of the grandest houses in Helleron were suddenly on a slant, tilting and tilting further as the ground beneath them cracked and decayed, falling away to reveal impossible depth, rifts reaching into the earth's innards, and from those rifts a swift-surging swarm of something that was not humanity but wore its shape.

Greenwise cried out, backing away, even then feeling the flags beneath his feet peel away into the abyss, one after another, until suddenly there was nothing beneath him and he was teetering on the very brink.

A hand took his shoulder, hauling him away from that hungry profundity, landing him on his back, and he saw – his world skewed further with it – three Wasp soldiers step past him, hands out to sting, the gold fire flashing and flashing as they struck downwards at that advancing host. One of them turned, dragged the former magnate to his feet with a grunt of effort and gave him a shove.

'Get out of here!' the soldier snapped, and Greenwise stumbled away, but where could he go? All around him he could see the facades of buildings running with fractures as their foundations were tested and found false. His ears were ringing with the groans of broken stone, with the appalling composite wail of hundreds of people in pain and fear, with the shrilling of children.

Then they were before him, the enemy. Their faces, their movements, everything about them spoke of an abdication from the human race.

He took up his crossbow and a bolt, but that was all he did. Some vital connection between the objects he held was missing in his mind. The principles, the learned motions, all of it was gone from him in that moment, and the weapon fell from his numb fingers.

By the time he reached for the hilt of his sword, they were already upon him and it was too late.

In the lowest reaches of Tharn there were cries and screams, the lightless chambers overrun by enemies who came from deeper still, creeping up through cracks in the rock to kill and steal, all moved by the same great and inhuman hand. Above, the great magicians of the Moth-kinden, the Skryres, stared at their pages of lore and found that none of it meant anything to them any longer. They were left with an understanding of nothing but despair.

Across the sea, Golden Skaetha, glorious heart of the Spiderlands, heart of the web, was riven by earthquakes, thousands crushed and whole dynasties thrown into chaos.

In the cavernous halls of the Delve, where the Mole Crickets laboured in Imperial servitude, the scuttling of claws could be heard in the dark. Whole families of Fly-kinden vanished overnight from the deepest warrens of Shalk and Merro. In the salt mines of Coretsy the miners abandoned their galleries and chambers for the surface, knowing only that the worst had come to pass. In a thousand buried places, what had once been dead ends, closed chambers, blank stone, all were suddenly gaping on to a deeper world that had been hidden and closed off for a thousand years.

Everywhere across the Lowlands and the Empire the ground

trembled – what was solid become abruptly brittle. Apt and Inapt alike had dreams of a suffocating ignorance, of a horrifying presence, of their children turning terrible and alien faces to them.

And in that dark world that had been sealed away for so long, Cheerwell Maker stumbled as she arrived at another slave town, staring up towards the living constellation of the ceiling only because she had no other point of reference for the world she had been banished from.

'It's gone,' she got out, and her companions stared at her. Orothellin and the Hermit would have known her meaning, but her friends had parted ways, the better to spread their ragged revolution. She now had only Tynisa and Messel with her, and neither understood what she meant.

'The Seal has finally given way,' she told them, trembling. 'This place is rejoining the world once more.' The Worm would be casting itself out into the wider world in ever-increasing numbers, and with just one aim in mind.

And as the Worm's half-world moved back into full conjunction with the real, as if she had been deaf all this while, her strangled and tenuous connection with the outside flared and grew in her mind: her link to her sister in Inaptitude, to Seda.

She braced herself for the venom, the loathing that she was used to, but instead that faint contact came with an altogether different sense from the Wasp Empress.

Reassurance.

Seda was telling her that it would be all right. She had a plan.

Part Three

On the Edge
of the Abyss

Twenty-Six

'What are they?' Tynan demanded. He was looking red-eyed after being torn from his bed at midnight and put through a battle that nobody really understood. His officers around him looked worse, though, and the oldest of them was ten years his junior. Oski himself felt about a hundred.

'General,' he said, 'we have no idea, but we basically can't contain them. That armour's so strong some of the men thought they were automotives or something. The bastards go where they want, when they want. We've lost most of our pissing artillery at the harbour, sir – just gone – and they're using it on us, you can believe me. They're not slow with the Aptitude.'

'They're Spiderlands troops, sir?' one of the army majors asked.

'If the Spiderlands had *that*, why didn't they use it when we were still . . .' another snapped back, and then faltered into silence under Tynan's glower.

'Sentinels have proven effective as mobile artillery, and are just about the only things that will keep the creatures back, but we only have about seven left. We've lost three overnight,' Oski went on. 'We have the air, still. We can drop Airborne wherever we want, if only they could accomplish much when they got there. The other troops – the buggers that look like Spiders or Grasshoppers or whatnot – they're not shot-proof. But now the Tseni have landed several hundred repeating crossbows and snapbows at the docks and, wherever we go, we're getting bolts coming at us.'

'Sir.' A lieutenant had finished marking up a map of Collegium with the latest scouts' reports and now stepped back for Tynan to look over his work.

'They've slowed up a lot,' the general noted.

'Yes, sir,' the lieutenant agreed. 'Scouts say they seem to be working to a plan, taking key points – the College, market squares, workshops – and then holding them. We've now lost –' he actually took a breath as though the news was just catching up to him – 'almost half the city, it looks like, sir.'

'We just can't keep them back or bottle them up or anything,' Oski commented wonderingly. 'They're real Sentinels, sir, the old heavy infantry – only like I never saw. If we'd had lads like that, we'd not have disbanded them.'

'"Stone armour,"' Tynan threw at him.

'Sir, you didn't see.'

'What's the latest word on the Ants – not the Tseni, the Ants outside the walls?'

A captain who had been waiting patiently for just this moment stepped forwards. 'Sir, they're moving in, but they're not storming the walls just yet. Sarnesh and Vekken both, they've approached to just outside the range of the wall engines.'

'What are they waiting for?' Tynan murmured.

'Morning.' It was the first thing Vrakir had said since he arrived, standing at the back like a pariah, and yet the only man who didn't look drawn and pale with fatigue.

Tynan glared at him. 'If they'd wanted the walls they could have had them by now. We've not had the men to keep them back. Someone's playing games. Besides, at least when morning comes, we can see properly what we're doing.' It had become plain that darkness was no encumbrance to any of these invaders. 'And the locals are just sitting tight, too. No taking to the streets, no throwing themselves at our stings and snapbows. Precious little welcoming of their liberators, as far as that goes, which suggests that they don't know what the pits the creatures are, either.'

'They couldn't be . . . *them*, could they, sir?' Oski asked hesitantly. Tynan stared blankly at him, and he added, 'You know, from the earth. Those villages . . . and when that whole street went . . .'

Tynan grimaced. 'They've changed tactics, if so. We can't know for sure, but my gut says no.'

'Sir,' the lieutenant in charge of scouts put in. 'Reports say the Tseni are doing a lot of house-to-house, speaking to the locals.'

'Familiar faces,' Tynan finished for him. 'Makes sense. I don't know: maybe there is some far corner of the Spiderlands where they grow these kinden. How would we know?' He did not sound convinced. 'For now, we need better barricades. Redeploy the Sentinels here, and here –' pointing out spots on the map – 'Major Oski, artillery to support, here, here . . . We need to draw a line, to secure at least part of the city. You say we can't stop them? Find a way. Caltrops, explosives, bring houses down on them, whatever it takes.'

'Yes, sir,' Oski said, without a great deal of hope in his voice.

'Sir!' A soldier skidded in, one arm bound up in bandages already leaking blood. Any of the lightly wounded who could still fly were running word between Tynan and his officers. 'Messenger, sir.'

'Well, out with it.'

'Sir, I mean a messenger from the enemy.'

The room went silent. Tynan took a deep breath.

'And what power does this messenger purport to bear word from, soldier?'

'War Master Stenwold Maker, sir.'

All eyes were on the general now. The name, the dead man's name, was like another presence in the room.

'And what,' Tynan asked at last, 'does War Master Stenwold Maker have to say?'

'That he wishes to meet with you. That he has an offer for you and the Second, sir.'

Oski was watching his superior's face carefully, and he saw the slight quirk of the man's mouth, a bleak moment of something close to humour.

'I'll bet he does,' said Tynan quietly and, against the wave of objections that it must be a trap, that he should send someone else or nobody at all, he raised his hands for quiet.

'Where and when?' he asked.

They met after the eastern sky had greyed towards a sullen, red dawn, less of a promise of another day than a threat. The venue was a market square, now clear of stalls, and of bodies, too. Imperial scouts could not swear that it rested quite on the boundary between 'what we have lost' and 'what we have yet to lose', but it was close. Tynan's troops had seized every house on his side, turfed the locals out onto the street, put soldiers at each window. There was a Sentinel a street away and some Farsphex ready to launch.

When he stepped out into that grey light, into that open space, he did so alone.

The enemy had set out lanterns, or some sort of globes that would pass for such – half a dozen bruise-coloured lamps that gave the square the air of some malevolent Inapt festival.

A single figure had broken from the far side of the square, striding forwards like Tynan's reflection. Behind him, the windows did not throng with troops, but with citizens, those whose homes overlooked the square – dark Beetle faces of men and women and children, wide-eyed, fearful. *They don't know if they're being liberated or invaded*, Tynan decided.

His opposite number was not familiar: a Beetle by his frame, certainly, but clad in such armour that Tynan had never seen, looking as though it had been grown more than made. *Proof against a snapbow, though?* It did not seem of a heft and bulk to match the shock troops that his men had faced so far. *Will we get to find out? There's the question.*

Tynan himself was wearing only light armour. Heavy mail would not stop a well-aimed bolt, and he wanted the use of his wings if he needed them.

The man across from him removed his helm with a slight awkwardness that suggested that the armour was not second nature to him, and for a moment Tynan let the unclean, ugly light play across those features, seeking recognition. It was surprisingly slow in coming: this man had been wounded, driven into the sea and spent the intervening months who knew where. He was thinner now, his face written over with new experience in a script Tynan could not read.

But it was him. In the end, that conclusion was unavoidable.

'So, it's true. Here you are, at last,' the general grunted. 'Stenwold Maker, no less.'

'General.' Maker nodded.

'War Master.' Tynan's eyes flicked behind Maker to the hulking shapes lurking between buildings. 'New friends, then?'

'Old friends,' Stenwold replied calmly. 'General Tynan, meet the Sea-kinden.'

'In truth?'

'Very much so. Collegium has always been good at finding allies in times of need.'

'Sea-kinden . . .' Tynan wasn't sure he believed it, for all that it seemed to explain a great deal. 'Since when have there even been . . .?'

'For longer than our histories record, and yet they have been little more than a myth since the end of the Bad Old Days. I feel that is likely to change, after this.'

'And they've given up a thousand years of secrecy just to help you out, have they?'

'They pay their debts,' Maker confirmed.

For a moment, Tynan just stared at him, unwilling to proceed, with all the lost ground that would entail. Then: 'I have snap-bowmen ready to bring you down, War Master. One gesture from me and you're a dead man.'

'As would you be, and the bulk of your army.'

'Probably. What do you want, Maker?'

'We've been here before, you and I.'

Tynan just nodded sullenly.

'When you came to me, outside the gates of my city, you gave Collegium the chance to surrender then and there, and we refused you. I made a speech that was very self-righteous and far too long. Your offer was not accepted, and we fought you at the wall.'

'And you lost.'

'And we lost,' Stenwold agreed flatly. 'And a great many men and women died – yours as well as ours – for nothing. Had we accepted reality and taken your deal, we'd have been no worse off.'

'That speaks of a great deal of faith in myself and my soldiers,' Tynan pointed out with a bleak smile.

'Do you think I haven't heard the details of your time as governor? I have seen many Imperial administrations. Yours is hardly the worst, not by a long reach. And you forget – we have met twice now. I have a sense of the kind of man you are.'

'I used to think the same.' Tynan grimaced. 'So, go on, Maker. Tell me.'

'You and your soldiers leave the city. You give the order now. You're gone by midday, all of you. You surrender control of Collegium peaceably, without reprisals. We let you leave. "We" meaning the Sarnesh and the Vekken as well as my forces here within the city.'

'You think I set the honour of the Empire so cheaply?'

'I hope you set the lives of your soldiers so dearly, General. I have thousands of Ant-kinden outside who can storm the walls, or else we can just take a gatehouse and open the city to them. I have an army of Sea-kinden who are used to very different standards of mercy and warfare from ours. I, on the other hand, speak for Collegiate enlightenment.'

'And you don't want to have to destroy half your city in order to save it, or have my soldiers butcher your people in the streets, or use them as shields against your shot.'

Stenwold nodded. 'Of course I don't. And you? You want to do this? You want to make my city hurt for the crime of wanting to be free, and you're willing to keep putting out our fires with the blood of your soldiers until you have nothing left? I have known men who thought like that – and not just Wasp-kinden either – but I had not picked you as one of them.'

'I am a man who obeys orders,' replied Tynan, although the words tasted like bile.

'General,' the War Master snapped out flatly, 'I will return to my forces now, and await your word. If it has not arrived within the hour, then we will take the rest of the city from you, with the aim of exterminating every soldier of the Second who does not take to the skies and flee.'

'Duly noted.' Tynan's hand twitched, and he saw Maker's face harden, thinking that the general has been about to use his sting. The Beetle would never realize that the reflexive gesture, inexplicable, humiliating, had been a strangled salute.

'We cannot quit the city, of course.' Major Vrakir was the first to speak after Tynan had relayed the ultimatum. The other faces of his officers, the men who had been fighting all night to stop it coming to this, looked less certain, pale and worried.

'Alternatives?' Tynan demanded, the clock in his mind counting down.

'We hold the city as long as possible.' Vrakir again, promptly.

'We're barely holding half of it now!' another major snapped. He had a bandage about his head to cover the gash a Sea-kinden claw had dealt his scalp.

'We make them pay in blood and time,' Vrakir insisted. 'The Empress is relying on us. Our forces to the north of here are—'

'Already under attack,' Tynan finished for him. In the surprised quiet after that he added, 'No, I've heard no report, but of course they are. The Sarnesh were only holding back because of *us* – because a strike north by the Second could catch their city undefended if their main force was off chasing our relief. Now that we're pinned here, they can just push east at their leisure. Last reports had them outnumbering our forces.'

'The Empress's will is plain: no retreat,' Vrakir said flatly.

'This is your "voice of the Empress", I take it,' Tynan needled him.

'Yes, sir, it is.' Vrakir met his gaze without flinching.

Tynan glanced away first, and for a long moment he just looked up at the ceiling, hands clenched into fists, keenly aware of the gaze of all his officers on him, knowing that they were torn as he was torn. They wanted to live. They wanted their men to live. They wanted to continue serving the Empire.

He, Tynan, wanted to serve the Empire. It was all he had ever done. He had never disobeyed an order. And, whilst there had been a time when he could have denounced Vrakir as a fraud, denied his Imperial mandate, that time had now passed. He had been given too many unpalatable commands straight from the Empress's own mouth, and he had obeyed every one.

Out there, the Sea-kinden would be stirring, if that was truly what they were. They were something new, certainly – new and deadly. With their Ant allies they would break the Second, today or next day or in a tenday, and all that remained was to see how much of Collegium the Wasp army would destroy or depopulate in its death throes.

You want to do this? Maker had asked him.

Tynan felt himself poised on the edge of a great fall that no Art could save him from.

'Ready the army for an evacuation of the city,' he said quietly.

The very moment he said the words, three of his officers were already moving.

Vrakir's voice halted them. 'You cannot go against the Empress's wishes, General!'

'I serve the Empire,' Tynan stated. 'The Empire is not best

served by my men giving up their lives so that Collegium can live another tenday under the yoke.'

'That is not your decision to make, General.'

'It is!' Tynan snapped. 'I lead the Second. Not you, not even the Empress. Here and now, in this room, in this city, I am the final voice of Imperial authority. We cannot hold Collegium, and the Sarnesh will be marching even now. Where will they be marching, Major? East, towards Helleron, towards Myna, towards Capitas. The Empire needs this army, but not just to make some mindless stand here.'

'No, General—!'

'Major Vrakir, I will have you locked up if you so much as say another word, and then you can keep the flag flying alone over Collegium after we're gone. Go, muster the men and get them ready to retreat. Lieutenant, get a messenger to fly out to the enemy and let them know I've made my decision.'

This time Vrakir remained silent, though his throat worked and he opened his mouth once or twice.

Tynan felt a great surge of relief, the promised confrontation receding. 'And empty those big airships. I want all our gear – artillery, supplies, anything that would slow us down – stowed in there and ready for getting out.'

'General, those are Slave Corps ships,' a new voice objected: the captain of slavers.

'Consider them commandeered.'

'General, no.' Vrakir once more, but now a new tone had entered his voice, a new stillness to his body. 'They do the Empress's work. The slaves they are laden with are for *her.*'

'She has all the slaves in the Empire at her disposal,' Tynan told him, slightly wrong-footed.

'This is the will of the Empress,' Vrakir stated. It was as though someone else spoke through him. 'The slaves must go to Capitas. A great deal depends on it. This is the Empress's command. There is nothing more important than this.'

'More important than whether we stay or evacuate?' Tynan demanded.

'Yes!' The otherworldly quality was abruptly gone from Vrakir, its work done, and Tynan saw the man visibly catch up with what he had said and latch on to it as his new purpose in life. 'The Empress is not to be denied!'

But, to Tynan's surprise, having twisted in Seda's unseen grip once, it was easier to struggle free now. 'Get the airships emptied. We need them.'

'General, this is treason.'

'I shall answer for it,' Tynan told him, quite calmly. The assembled officers watched, frozen, this long-threatened confrontation coming at just the wrong time. 'Get the—'

Then Vrakir's palm was out, directed at him, killing Art wisping and flaring on the man's skin. Tynan stared into his enemy's eyes, seeing madness there: a man under pressures that no Apt man had been born to. Death too, though – he saw his death there, sure enough.

'Major Vrakir, stand down.' Useless words, for the other man was beyond that now.

'I am the voice of the Empress,' Vrakir stated, each word forced through clenched teeth. 'Obey, or die a traitor.'

Then a lieutenant had feinted at him, a desperate lunge that the officer was already turning into a dive as Vrakir's arm snapped around. And Tynan's wings flurried enough to close the distance, barrelling him into Vrakir so that the pair of them landed hard on the floor with Tynan on top.

He was older, and he had not fought with his fists for too many years, and Vrakir was fiercely mad, capable of anything, fearless of any consequence. There was no time for subtlety. Besides, Tynan was not interested in subtlety just then. His pent-up rage at this subordinate's orders, of what Tynan himself had done at this man's prompting, the betrayals, the wrongs . . .

He had Vrakir's throat grasped in his hands in that brief moment before the other man caught his breath back, and Tynan's Art blossomed with a release that was fierce and primal, a second's worth of youth and strength that he had been husbanding for his old age. The searing flash left the Red Watch major's head almost scoured from his body.

Shaking and unsteady, Tynan allowed himself to be helped to his feet.

'Unless there are any other *objections*,' he said, his voice uneven, 'get those poor bastards out of the airships and get our kit in. We're leaving.'

In drawing up his plans to decamp the whole Second Army as efficiently as possible, he did not wonder about the sudden disappearance of the Slave Corps officers until it was too late.

Twenty-Seven

The clear light of morning uncovered a scene of ruin encompassing a score of Helleron's streets, a blot of rubble, broken earth and the shattered remains of lives that straddled the border between the close-packed tenements of the poor and the grand townhouses of the rich.

The militia were out in force now, picking over the rubble, but old habits died hard and the money that turned all the wheels of the city took disasters in its stride. Far more men were engaged in recovering the property of magnates than were searching for the bodies of factory workers or their families.

What few bodies remained, at least. There had been plenty of eyewitnesses to testify that this had been no mere earthquake. An intelligence had been at work, a human face to the catastrophe.

'An attack,' murmured Colonel Nessen of the Consortium. He was a lean, hungry-looking man, adviser to the Helleren Council of Thirteen and de facto Imperial governor, an authority unchallenged so long as he allowed the magnates to retain their illusions by not formally assuming the title.

'Who from?' Scordrey demanded. The merchant, one of the most powerful in Helleron, had been elsewhere in the city when the earth had broken open. Only servants had died in his house. Already he was speaking about rebuilding, and about clearing away all those fallen tenements, putting the space to some more wholesome use than simply housing the poor.

'Enemies of the Empire; enemies of Helleron,' Nessen prompted. As a Consortium man he was a merchant first, of course, but he had a soldier's basic training and rank badge, and he found the gap between his perspective and that of the Beetle beside him widening even as they spoke.

'Such as who? The Lowlanders are all engaged by your forces, and this isn't exactly the sort of thing Collegium or Sarn would do. Or do you think the Spiders accomplished this somehow? Or the Moths? Some of my fellows have been saying it was the Moths, but we both know that the scale of this thing is beyond the ability of any human agency.'

'It wasn't the Moths,' Nessen replied tonelessly. He knew it was not the Moths, because a very shaken ambassador from Tharn had sought him out under the Moths' rather tenuous alliance with the Empire and had stated that a similar incursion had occurred into the deepest levels of Tharn itself. The Moth had not said who the attackers were, but Nessen recognized fear when he saw it.

'It was an earthquake.'

'We have reports—'

'Looters brawling in the wreckage!' Scordrey declared stridently.

Nessen honestly could not have said whether the man was trying to convince himself or whether he had already succeeded. The Wasp turned away in disgust and headed back to the house the Empire had rented for him.

He got a messenger off to Capitas, asking for . . . He had not known what to ask for. He had only reported, and left it to wiser heads to work out what response could possibly be made to the patently impossible.

Back behind closed doors, he retired to his room to stare at the walls and turn over all the things Scordrey had said, and what Nessen had heard the man's peers say. Their response to the tragedy had been 'highly personal', as his report had stated. They had been apoplectic over the damage to their property.

The loss of life throughout the wider city seemed barely to have touched them. Their general feelings seemed to be summed up as: *There are plenty more.*

Nessen was not a soft man, but he was one who abhorred waste. He had come to see Helleron as his city, and its workers as something akin to his slaves. It was an eye-opening thought to realize that this meant he was more concerned for their well-being than were their own leaders.

He gave his orders, sending a detachment of Light Airborne and a couple of spare Engineers to go and help look for survivors in the poorer districts. He felt it was a valid investment of resources – not sympathy for the bereaved and the injured so much as that the mess offended him.

He had expected his house guests to question him closely about what had happened, for they had picked a tumultuous time to overnight in Helleron. There were two officers travelling with a dozen of the Engineers and a score of soldiers, and they had come to Helleron on the heels of top-priority orders to three of the city's chemical works. The seal of the Empress had been all over their business, and Nessen was wise enough to ensure that, when they had turned up the evening before, everything had been ready for them. The canisters had already been taken from the factories and loaded onto the visitors' airship, and he understood that they would be setting off back east shortly afterwards, bound for some destination he sensed it would be unhealthy to enquire into. Under other circumstances he would be curious and would use his contacts back at the capital to indulge that curiosity, but his lead visitor wore the armour of the Red Watch, and Nessen was astute enough to know when to leave well alone.

He knew that he was not the only one to find this new corps, with its apparent absolute mandate from the throne, to be intrusive, unbalancing and bad for business. Similarly, he knew that anyone saying so would be looking to end up on the crossed pikes in short order. *Best to get them out of my city as fast as possible.*

So perhaps it was a good thing that the Red Watch man had reacted the way he had when he had been told of the night's upheaval: not horror or alarm, nor even surprise. Whatever had laid waste to so much of the city, the Red Watch man clearly knew what was behind it, and he wasn't telling anyone as lowly as a mere governor-colonel.

The other man, the little halfbreed officer who stood in the Red Watch's shadow, had been concerned only for their chemical cargo, some foul sort of stuff that Nessen's contacts suggested was being churned out at three or four other locations as well as Helleron.

Another thing that it's unwise to enquire further about. Nessen was uncomfortably aware that more and more of his life was falling into that category. Something was going badly wrong, back home. Or perhaps it had always been going wrong, and only now was it visible. Now it had gone too far to stop.

After that was all dealt with, after he had patrolled the wounds that Helleron had suffered overnight and seen off the Red Watch with his airship full of reagents, Colonel Nessen finally found that he had time for other apparently urgent business.

After all, he told himself, *how important can it be, if they trust the news to such a messenger?*

What appeared before him in his townhouse wore a uniform, but was no soldier of which he had ever seen the like before. One of Nessen's slaves poured the colonel some wine while Nessen shook his head at this apparition. Yes, there were signs that things were not well at home, but this . . .

'What's the sour look for, woman?' he demanded.

'Colonel, I have been waiting for over four hours.' His visitor was a Wasp-kinden woman got up in the leathers of the Air Corps, on this day of all days. 'I have come with urgent word from General Tynan of the Second, sir, for your eyes only.'

He stared at her levelly. 'And for this urgent word he sends me a woman.'

'No, sir, for this word he sends you his best pilot and the officer in charge of his aerial forces.'

'Well, listen, woman, whatever your name was—'

'*Captain* Bergild, sir. May I deliver this into your hands?'

Nessen felt that he had gone through quite enough today, above and beyond the requirements of a Consortium colonel. To hear that sort of insolence from this . . . whatever this even *was*, was too much. 'I never picked Tynan as a man with a sense of humour,' he snapped, snatching the scroll from her hands and breaking the seal.

A moment later he visibly twitched, reading it again. 'The Second . . .'

'Yes, sir,' Bergild said, with exaggerated patience.

The Second have fallen back from Collegium. The Sarnesh are marching. The war . . .

The war is coming this way.

'You have an answer for me, Colonel?'

His eyes flicked towards her, then back to the message. Tynan was asking for any and all military aid he could provide. 'What does Tynan think I have here? There's barely a garrison, and when the Beetles here get word . . .' Actually, the Beetles here would do nothing, he reflected. They would sit there in their double-sided coats, ready to turn them at a moment's notice. A Helleren uprising was not the problem. *The Alliance cities, however . . .*

'Go and tell Tynan he's on his own.' Nessen stood up abruptly, already planning exit strategies.

Within sight of Porta Mavralis, they had watched the Worm attack. A caravan had been travelling north up the Silk Road – Totho and Maure had almost tried to join it, checked only by a residual caution. They had not realized that their lives rested on so simple a decision.

The caravan had consisted of a dozen beetle-drawn wagons, two score travellers and two dozen armed guards – which seemed a lot. Then again, the Empire was fighting Spiderlands troops not so very far away, and a long-range airborne squad might have slipped over the lines to come down and cause trouble.

Totho and Maure had shadowed them all night, travelling unseen in their wake. Whoever the travellers were, whatever their goods, they were not stopping to set up camp.

They had been going through a pass between hills when it happened: the earth rippling and cracking, wagons sinking up to their axles, turning over, the beetles rearing and twisting in their traces. The travellers and their guards were running back and forth, unsure of what was going on. Totho and Maure had heard their shouts of panic.

The Worm issued forth, some from the earth itself, more from a great rift in the hills. The two of them had watched those swift expressionless warriors dissect the caravan with clinical efficiency, as ants might cut up and parcel out some large beast that had fallen into their jaws. The guards were slain, the travellers likewise; even the draught beetles were just cut apart, without hesitation or sentiment. The wagons themselves were prised open, the human bodies of the Worm showing no sign that they understood the purpose of such things or how they worked. Everything within, along with bodies and the pieces of bodies, was carried back inside the hill, the Centipede-kinden working with horrifying speed and leaving only spilled blood and broken wood in their wake. The entire business, from attack to the site being left picked clean, was a matter of minutes.

Neither Totho nor Maure had made any attempt to help the travellers, but whilst she had fallen back and back, unwilling even to look at the attackers, Totho had stared on, his hands on his snapbow, fingers twitching. Maure had wanted to go to him and drag him back, for fear that the Worm would see him and find her, too, when they came for him, but there was so much anger in Totho that she did not dare.

After the butchery was done, he turned to her, angrily gesturing her back to his side.

327

'That was them, was it?' he demanded.

Maure nodded cautiously, still not coming close.

'Savages,' was his verdict.

'Oh, surely,' she agreed. 'And in ways you can't imagine.' She paused, studying his face. 'Vile, unnatural, utterly without . . . whatever it is that makes us *us*.'

Totho shrugged, his armour plates scraping. 'None of that Inapt business now. Savages, like I said. Not a crossbow amongst them.'

'And yet you yourself didn't stand up and show them the superiority of your Aptitude. I wonder why?'

He sent her a sharp glance, but then looked down at his snapbow, plainly troubled by the thought.

'You think they're Inapt,' she noted. 'They're not. They don't believe in my magic, any more than you do. Less than you do, perhaps. They don't even tell each other stories of when the magic was. But they're not Apt, either. They don't believe in your gears and machines. And when they get close, they can stop *you* believing, too. A world without artifice or magic, that's the Worm's world. A world without anything of the human mind.'

'Artifice doesn't work like that. I can shoot you dead with this snapbow whether you believe or not.'

'Only if you can think how to make it work.'

'It's just pulling a trigger.'

'And yet I couldn't do it. Or perhaps I could do whatever that is just by fumbling at the thing, but I'd not be able to aim it like a bow, and probably I'd just shoot a rock with it, or a friend, or even myself. But you can't imagine what it's like to *not* know all those things you take for granted. And if I have a better idea of how you Apt think, it's only because the Woodlouse-kinden who trained me counted both types in their number.'

She wanted to move on, but he would have none of it. The contained massacre they had witnessed had not affected him in the way that it had her. Or perhaps it had, but he buried his feelings deep. He was obviously not an expressive man – his emotions were bottled up and put under pressure, and when they burst to the surface, they had soured into varying degrees of anger. She knew that the true object of all his animosity was Totho himself, but that would not stop him harming her if she got too close at the wrong time.

'Those things . . . those ignorant . . . whatever they were. She is amongst them, even now?'

Maure only nodded.

'Do you think she's dead?'

'I hope not.'

'*Do* you?' He hauled his helm off and stared at it. 'If I could know that she was dead, I think I'd be free. I could walk away. There'd be nothing I could do. She'd have passed the limits of even what artifice is capable of. But I can't know.' He was a man in dark armour, picked out against the darkness of the sky only because she had Moth eyes. 'She won't leave me alone.'

I know, she thought. *I see her there, the ghost of her that's in your mind. But what can I say? You can't understand me, and you wouldn't let go even if you could.*

'There is no kinden that artifice and Aptitude can't conquer.' He said it to the blank face of his helm, and to the hills and the sky, and to the rift that the Worm had ventured from. 'Progress: how can we have progress if there was some *thing* such as that, which could undo all our work since the revolution.'

'Totho,' Maure tried, 'I know—'

'What do you care? Your magic is nothing – a lie, not even a spent force.' There was no rancour in his tone. 'But I have power. Drephos taught me that. In my own hands, I have more power than any magician that was ever born.'

She saw him differently then, for just a moment, in as vertiginous a shift of perspective as she had ever experienced. For a moment she saw him as he would have been, had he been Inapt; had he been born a thousand years before. She saw the questing hero of Commonweal legend, with lance and bright mail, willing to brave the stuff of nightmares for the woman he loved, invincible in his purity of heart, his nobility of spirit. And herself, of course: the magician who advised him and sent him off on his journey. There were so many stories that followed that old road.

And here they were, a thousand years later; she was the most meagre of magicians and he was a tormented, brooding and bitter man whose aim – if he even had an aim – was not to be reunited with his true love but to show her, to prove her wrong, to win the argument that he had been conducting with her inside his head for years. The woman who rode his shoulders and ate through his mind like a maggot was no more the Che that Maure knew than she was some great Skryre of legend. *And is this what Aptitude has brought the world to?*

And even with that thought, and despite everything, the responsibilities of her role were on her, now that she had recognized how fate had cast her.

'Do you . . . I could foretell your future, cast for omens . . . Advise you.'

He did turn at that suggestion, just enough to look at her past the armour of his shoulder. 'You have nothing to say to me,' he told her, but not harshly, more as a recognition that their worlds were too far apart for any mutual understanding. And then: 'Whoever dwells in that cave, they are just men.'

She woke at dawn, alone, the fire burned down to nothing. There were tracks, heading towards the broken rift in the earth, but nothing in the world could have persuaded her to follow them.

Instead she set off northwards up the Silk Road. The Commonweal was out there somewhere, and she would make it home eventually if she kept putting one foot in front of another.

Nobody knew what was happening, or at least Straessa didn't, and if any of the Collegiate soldiers under her command did, they weren't telling her. Obviously there was supposed to be some manner of signal, and with luck Kymene or the Sarnesh or someone knew what it was, because everyone had advanced to a point where it looked as though they were going to make some mad dash for the city walls, and then they had stood about past dawn, making no attempt actually to fulfil that promise. The Wasps, in turn, made no attempt to come out and do anything about them.

A single one of their enormous airships had risen from the city earlier and lurched off across the sky; Taki's aviators had been ready to take a shot at it, had it shuddered its way over the Lowlander forces with a bombardment in mind. It had kept its distance, though, and despite fierce debate, they had let it go. The Second had plainly remained in command of the city; nobody had wanted to waste time and resources on an enemy that seemed to be going away, and risk an assault by the enemy still very much in evidence.

So, is our being here all a bluff? She could see the impatience down the line. Even the Sarnesh were plainly raring to go; if it was a bluff, and a single one of them knew it, then *all* of them would know.

And now this: the messenger from out of the city, and Straessa found that she knew him. She knew him and was not even particularly surprised to see him. It was that loudmouth Fly, the one who got everywhere: Laszlo.

He strutted out quite on his own, as though he wasn't coming from a city held by the enemy, asking to speak to the leaders of the Sarnesh force. Straessa found herself ranged beside Kymene of the Mynans and Commander Lycena of Sarn.

Laszlo beamed up at them with a face Straessa wanted to slap, and then told them how things were.

An hour later they stood watching as a delegation marched out of the city to meet with them. Behind them, the city bustled with black and gold, but if it was an attack it was the most elegant piece of misdirection Straessa had ever seen. The Second Army was giving every indication of abandoning Collegium to its new masters, as represented by the approaching delegation.

And the city's new masters are us, Straessa reminded herself. Looking on them, however – indeed looking on this whole gathering – she had to work hard to quell her concerns. There was precious little that looked Collegiate in this mess, not even the leader of the approaching forces, for all that he *was* Collegium to a great many people.

She sensed a similar disquiet from her troops, the Company soldiers squinting and pointing and muttering. The Sarnesh Ants were standing stiffly, plainly still all bowstring-taut and mistrustful of the situation, especially given who *else* was turning up around now. The Mynans, though . . .

Kymene broke from the pack, striding forwards.

'Stenwold Maker.' She stopped before him, shaking her head with a rare grin. 'Look at you, old man, back from the dead.'

The face was Maker's, Straessa had to admit. He was carrying less weight and had made up for that by wearing far more armour, of a material and design she could not place, all spiral and flute patterns moulded out of something brown and shell-like.

He smiled at Kymene, but it was not an overly sentimental expression. Purpose burned in Stenwold Maker's face like a furnace.

'We have much to discuss,' he told them all.

'Why can we not attack the Empire as they leave?'the Sarnesh commander, Lycena, demanded. Imperial airships were floating over the city, along with a cloud of Light Airborne. The gates had opened, and already the first automotives of the Second Army were outside the walls, with soldiers marching behind to join them.

'We have much to discuss,' Stenwold Maker repeated. 'But this thing is simple: the Wasps are leaving because I have requested that they leave, and I promised them safe passage if they did.'

'And how long does that last?' Lycena asked furiously. 'Do you think that we shall not have to fight them again, once we march?'

'Of course we will,' Stenwold confirmed, 'but we will fight them as soldiers. I will not have my city turned into a battlefield. I will not have the war fought over the bodies of civilians.'

'Tactician Milus will not be pleased,' she warned him.

He shrugged. 'Tactician Milus can take it up with me himself. Now, gather round, give me leaders from every contingent. You have questions. I have answers. Then we march to meet Milus, who, if I can second-guess him, is already leading the main Sarnesh army against the Wasps who are dug in north-east of here.'

There was much jockeying then, shouldering and elbowing for precedence, and she would gladly have given up her place at the front if only someone had come to demand it. Instead she found herself standing there, feeling as though she had gate-crashed a horribly inappropriate party, while Stenwold Maker introduced his allies.

The Tseni Ants were led by a stern-faced woman with blue-white skin, and Stenwold explained how they were maintaining a presence on the Collegiate streets, keeping order until the Beetles themselves were ready take that mantle from them. Why them? Because, compared to the forces that had won Collegium against the Second, the Tseni were practically familiar faces.

The little contingent of Vekken were meanwhile keeping well away from the Sarnesh. They would also be marching east against the Empire, in a symbol of the newfound solidarity between their city, Tsen and Collegium. Straessa was watching Lycena carefully for her reaction then: surely the Sarnesh would go berserk on hearing that two enemy Ant city-states – and all other Ant city-states were surely theoretical enemies at all times – were now allied to the Beetle city whose affections they had been monopolizing. Her face was blank, though, any whirl of emotions hidden well away inside.

Laszlo was fully reintroduced, as though anybody would not know him, but Stenwold said he was from the *Tidenfree*, and named the little muster of Fly-kinden with him as that vessel's crew, although Straessa spotted Sperra in their number.

Then Stenwold turned to his other allies, upon whom most eyes had been fixed since they turned up.

'May I present Rosander, Nauarch of the Thousand Spines Train; his mechanic Chenni; the magnate Wys; and Paladrya, chief adviser to the Edmir of Hermatyre.' He reeled off the string of titles and names as though they were supposed to mean anything to anyone. 'The Sea-kinden,' he finished.

Straessa looked at them and saw a middle-aged Spider woman, a couple of little bald girls about the size of Fly-kinden, and . . . and a very, very big, broad man in pale crusted armour that made Maker's suit look as if it was made of paper.

'Sea-kinden,' went the murmur, passing back down the ranks, or passing invisibly between the heads of the Ants.

'Explain,' said Lycena, almost desperately.

He did. Concisely, and with obvious gaps in the narrative, Stenwold told them about the Sea-kinden, opening up a secret that had stayed beneath the waves since the revolution.

Listening to his calm, measured account, Straessa had to keep looking at the massive figure of Rosander, because otherwise she would not have believed any of it.

'You, Officer.' Abruptly Maker's gauntleted hand was directed at her.

'Officer Antspider, Coldstone Company.' *Probably.* Whether there was still a Coldstone Company to be part of was debatable, but what else could she say?

Although he might have recalled her as Eujen's friend, if nothing else, there was no recognition in his face.

'Get a pilot off to Sarn to call back the Expatriates. This city's going to need to stand on its own feet just about immediately. We can't spare the soldiers to . . .'

'Administrate it, War Master?' Straessa dropped into the gap, because she was horribly sure that the unwanted word Maker had bitten back on was 'garrison'. *He said 'this city', not 'our city'*, she thought, but maybe she was being too hard on the man because of Eujen's clashes with his ideology. Or perhaps going where Maker had gone could not help but change a man.

'Officer.' At Straessa's elbow was the aviatrix, Taki. 'I'll go.'

'Thank you. Cram everyone who wants to come aboard a rail automotive and get them over here, double time. I don't think we're hanging about,' the Antspider told her. 'Take word to Eujen and he'll sort the logistics. I expect the Sarnesh'll be glad to see the back of us.'

The Fly-kinden nodded, casting a sidelong look at Stenwold Maker. 'Right you are.' Then she was lifting herself into the air and scudding over the assembled heads towards her Storm-reader.

'War Master, regarding your allies . . .' Lycena indicated the Sea-kinden. 'What do I tell the tactician? Do they march east with us? The Vekken, you have spoken for –' no disguising of her distaste there – 'but these?'

Straessa saw the 'No' on Stenwold's face, but the Spider-looking woman at his side said, 'Yes,' immediately, and Rosander, the vast armoured brute, echoed her a moment later. Maker glanced at them, and she noticed his facade crack briefly.

'Paladrya—' he started, but the huge Sea-kinden broke in.

'You once showed me the land, Stenwold Maker,' he rumbled. 'Do you think I put it from my mind, what you made me see? Those horizons you have? I want to see it, Maker. Those of my train who will follow me, I will take as far as you need to go. Chenni has my orders for the rest of my people.'

Stenwold's gaze was still on the woman, though. No words passed between them, but she put a hand on his plated arm, eyes speaking directly to his, and at last he nodded.

'You're cracked,' said the little bald woman he had called Wys. 'Back home for me and mine, for sure.'

Straessa glanced from face to face: Ants of three cities; her own people just beginning to understand that they had won back their home; and the unfamiliar features of the Sea-kinden.

At the last, she looked back towards Maker, and was able to

interpret that hard, driven expression of his in a new way. He was tired. He was a man tired almost to death, but with a long road ahead of him still.

Twenty-Eight

I should have stayed with Che.

Thalric had been a battlefield officer once, long ago, before the Rekef had recruited him. He remembered enough about the soldiering trade to know that quality of troops counted for more than just about anything. He had never seen a worse band of warriors than the rabble he was trying to marshal now. Military historians would have to invent whole new words for how appalling the slaves of the Worm were in war.

Of course this is hardly textbook stuff: the hopeless against the mindless. He had seen quickly enough that standing toe to toe with the Worm was not a game these people could win. Even wielding the weapons that they had made for their masters, they lacked all training and coordination – lacked all virtues, in fact, except for a desperation that turned too readily to panic and fear. Thalric had heard that some people believed sheer rage and righteous fury would win a fight, and he could only assume that those people had never been in one. In a massed battle, training and discipline would defeat random flailing every time, however righteous or angry.

Of course, training and discipline were not exactly what the Worm had, but what they did have would serve. Watching them fight made him feel ill – and his varied career had instilled a strong stomach. The way they moved together, the many limbs of a single presence, was utterly unlike soldiers, unlike humans. It served,

337

though. In close combat the Worm was ferocious, unflinching, never retreating, swift and savage and unhesitating. A part of him watched that dreadful will to slaughter and thought, *perfect shock troops*, even whilst the rest of him was trying not to retch.

But Che wanted these hopeless victims to fight, to make their extinction costly enough that the Worm would leave them alone. After all, the driving force behind those human puppets did not understand vengeance or hatred any more than it could know of love or hope or happiness. If they could bloody the enemy enough, then it would draw back from them through sheer expedience. That was Che's plan. Thalric did not believe it, now. *After all, the bastard's down here, isn't it? Somehow it's at the centre of this place – wherever you go, you reach that city, that's what Messel said. So is it really going to give its slaves the run of the place while its armies are away?* Thalric was bitterly afraid that Che had miscalculated – but not in guessing that the Worm would dispose of its entire slave population, the other kinden that had shared its banishment. No, that was patently the case, but he was less and less sure that either running or fighting would save these blighted failures from the blades of the Worm.

He wanted to tell her he had no sympathy, that those who bent their backs to the lash had chosen their place in life and deserved no more. He wanted to tell her that he and she – and Tynisa and Esmail, if she insisted – should simply find some place to hide that was as distant as they could find from any tendrils of the Worm, and there they should wait until all the slaves were devoured. Perhaps, having gutted its world, save for the four of them, the Worm would seek elsewhere for its nourishment. He wanted to say that this was the only real use that they could find for this host of useless subhumans.

He had said nothing of the sort to her. In his mind's eye he saw the reaction in her face, the disapproval, the knowledge that, by her impossible Collegiate standards, he had failed some test of morality. *But you can't save the world, you can't! Sometimes it's all you can do to save yourself.*

The time would come when this doomed venture turned sour, and even Che would have to admit defeat. Until then Thalric would play her game and hunt for a battlefield on which the Worm could be even mildly inconvenienced.

There had been tactical exercises when he had graduated from sergeant, about pitting an inferior force against one larger, swifter, more skilled. None of them had been quite this hopeless.

Light had been the first problem. Most of the native combatants on both sides could see in the dark. He himself could not, and a blind general was not someone the history books had ever had cause to sing the praises of. He had spoken at some length with Che, and then with his troops, gauging the nature of their sight. Chiefly this revealed that actual light – fires, lanterns, whatever – did not leap out at their eyes if they relied on their Art. And the same would go for the Worm, so that he had a whole chain of beacons up the route of retreat, for his eyes, and to remind the wretched slaves where they had to go.

'They're here! They're here!' A Moth woman hurtled overhead and disappeared back into darkness, and Thalric's troops began milling and trembling.

'Remember what I told you!' he shouted at them, just one step away from, *Do what you're told*, for they were little better than children, at war, and he had no time to explain his logic.

There were no bows in the whole extent of the under-earth, as far as he could work out. The people here did all sorts of clever things with fungus fibres and rock and coal, but there was no wood, and no substitute for it. They had no crossbows, either, and it had been something of a vertiginous revelation that they had been trapped down here since long before anyone thought of that quintessential Apt weapon.

And of course, with that whatever-it-was that the Worm did to peoples' heads, perhaps crossbows would be no great asset anyway. *Another thing that your general here doesn't understand – and what do I recall about tactical decisions made in ignorance?*

What they did have were slings, which Thalric reckoned to

be surely the least efficient ranged weapon after just throwing things. He had to work with what he'd got, though.

'I'm going to give them something to think about!' he called out to them. 'As soon as they're in range, you start on them. Make every stone count.' *If you can even actually aim a sling.* He was unsure about that, and he had no real grasp of their range, not in this dark place where his sense of space was hopelessly compromised.

The host of the Worm was approaching.

He let his wings carry him lightly towards them, lifting higher, hoping one of the appalling hunters of the cavernous sky didn't choose this moment to complicate his life. His furthest fire was just casting its light on to that onrushing tide: a sinuous, weaving inroad of the Worm, the green-blue flames glinting on bronze mail and steel blades.

Neither of which they'd possess without their slaves. How can people connive at their own impotence like that? How could they even give up their own children to the bastards?

The Worm, much like Beetles and other ground-bound kinden, did not look upwards half as much as they should.

He was no strong flier, but he did not spare his sting, soaring across the face of the Worm like a stormcloud, hands crackling with fierce gold light. He had no need to aim, with that dense column rushing below him, and he just let his hands work, a dozen blasts in as many seconds, each one tearing into a target, cutting a jagged wound across the mass of the enemy.

There was no confusion: they knew him immediately, and some of them had slings, too. Not so many, though, compared to how many bodies advanced down there. He kept moving, and he guessed they did not get much practice against a flying target – if these vacant segments did anything as human as practise.

Another staccato burst from his hands, curving back above them, and of course they were not waiting for him, were still rushing towards the hapless mob of his own followers. The dozens he struck down were nothing, less than a scratch on the body of the Worm.

Then the air was alive with hornets. One clipped his foot as he pulled up, and he saw a ripple pass across the face of the enemy, the leading edge of their charging column fraying and coming apart as three score sling stones pelted into them. Those weapons he had dismissed as weak were cutting apart the front ranks of the enemy by sheer numbers.

The slaves here did not go to war, but they must hunt and defend themselves from the savage beasts that had been locked into this asylum alongside them. Slings were all they had, and the animal foes they used them against were also armoured.

Emperor's balls! Thalric thought, seeing that initial salvo, because the entire front line of the Worm advance had just disintegrated. Surely, only around one in five or six stones had achieved anything, but there were close on a hundred slingers stacked up the raked incline where he had placed them, and they were already loosing their next shot.

Had an Imperial advance hit such unexpected resistance, then Thalric reckoned a regroup and redeploy would have been in order, but the Worm needed no such devices and simply pressed on, trampling the discarded bodies of its own fallen whether they were dead or not.

For a handful of seconds, as his own hands kept busy, he thought they might achieve something. It had seemed as though the slingshot was tearing down the Worm as swiftly as they could advance. Then reality asserted itself, and he saw that the enemy were still advancing – advancing swiftly, even – and that the attrition was insufficient to achieve anything against an enemy that had such immense numbers and no concept of personal extinction.

He let his troops loose and loose again, though, because each dead enemy surely counted for something, and then he was skimming over his own lines, calling, 'Fall back! Fall back! Remember the way!' The Worm were really coming on swiftly now and, as soon as the sling barrage stopped, they would become swifter.

Some of his people had already been inching away, and at Thalric's order – *or perhaps it's my permission* – the whole mob of them were scrabbling and running up the slope away from the enemy, and at least a sling was easier to run with than a bow and a quiver. He saw some of them stumble, even fall down-slope, and they would certainly die, and there was nothing he was able or willing to do about it. The majority had good Art for climbing, though, and they were hurtling upslope almost as fast as the Centipede-kinden were pursuing them.

Thalric thanked his parents for giving him wings and over-took the lot of them, rising to where the rest of his force – the non-slingers – were waiting.

'On my mark,' he alerted them. He wondered if the insensate nature of the enemy would mean this sort of set-up would keep working, or whether the Worm would adapt to it.

It doesn't matter. Let it work as often as you like, but we're still pissing into the hurricane.

The Worm was beginning to catch up with the stragglers now, each wretched victim overcome in a knot of struggling figures and rising blades.

'Go! Now!' he shouted.

'There are still—' someone objected and he shouted them down.

'They're dead. If they're in the way, they're already dead.' He dropped down and put his shoulder against one of the great rocks they had piled up here. In all honesty, he barely shifted it, but then one of the Mole Crickets followed his lead, and then others were pushing and prising and levering. And, with barely a prequel, there were tons of stone in sudden movement, des-cending on the body of the Worm. Some of his followers would be caught under that, but the majority were already clear. By Thalric's book that was a considerably better outcome than they were due.

'Now move!' he snapped. 'No going back for them, no sitting around spectating! Get your legs moving, come on. They'll be after us quick enough.'

Che was learning about a chain of command.

The slaves had been trickling in for days, but word was spreading. Some came because Messel or others had warned them to flee, others because the Worm had descended on their villages, taken their remaining children and begun killing the rest. Nobody could say how many communities had nobody left to speak for them, wiped out without witnesses, their lights put out forever.

There were a handful like the Moth, Atraea, who had been headmen and headwomen of their own communities. These Che set to work in organizing the rest. They pooled whatever food there was, found places to sleep, reunited families. Others, those who could move swiftly and surely in the dark, were set to foraging – young Moths and the blind Cave Crickets of Messel's kinden particularly. They ranged further and further, hunting with their slings and gathering fungus and lichens. Some of them did not return.

Darmeyr Forge-Iron and a few others were responsible for recruiting more warriors. None of the slaves had any prior experience, but many were willing, in return for having their dependants fed and looked after. There were plenty of Worm swords, and there was a little armour, and anyone who could use a sling was always welcome.

But there was no time for training. Anyone who could demonstrate to Darmeyr and the others that they had the will and an able body was sent on to wherever Thalric was going next, in the hope of rescuing more from the jaws of the Worm.

The Worm had not found them yet. Che suspected the Worm had not even begun to appreciate what was going on. At some point it would realize, in its blinkered, hungry way, that things were not going as they should.

She did not know what they would do then. No ideas had come to her.

Now she strode through the camp, aware of the attention fixed on her: the woman from the other world whose eyes had seen the sun. Some seemed to treat her with a reverence she found uncomfortable; others scowled at her. Still more did not care, concerned solely with their own well-being, their own fears.

Orothellin had walked amongst them earlier, to calm them. Everyone seemed to know the ancient Slug-kinden, and to call him Teacher. He had been a calming influence in the often-disruptive life of the camp. Now he was gone, though, to help bring in more of the lost, to try and thwart the predations of the Worm. Che was left to manage on her own.

Not on her own, quite. She had Tynisa as her constant shadow, though after her failure on the way to the Hermit's cave the Weaponsmaster was riddled with doubts about whether she would serve any useful purpose when the Worm arrived. She had the Hermit, too, although the ragged old man stayed out of everyone's way, by mutual consent.

Tynisa worried Che, if only because the less credence the Weaponsmaster put in her own abilities, the more she seemed to defer to her sister. She dogged Che's footsteps as though the Beetle was the only spark of hope in the whole underworld. As though Che knew what she was doing.

And I'm still working on that one. No guarantees.

Che stopped to receive the latest news: more arrivals in, word from Messel, movements of the Worm. She did her best to listen, to take it all in and end up with a coherent picture of what was going on. She was terrified that vital information was slipping through the cracks in her mind.

'What will you do if you win?' Tynisa asked her suddenly.

Che almost replied, *I don't think that's very likely*, all very self-deprecating as a polite Collegium girl should be. But that was not what anyone wanted to hear. Instead she hedged, 'Win?'

'If you defeat the Worm.' Tynisa, who had not seen that darkly shining abomination beneath the stone city, sounded almost optimistic about it. 'These people have never known anything other than this. They're slaves born.'

'Nobody's a slave born.' It was pure polemic but, as she said it, Che realized it was true in a way. 'The Worm didn't feed these people, or house them or clothe them. Take away their masters and they will live and thrive.' *Easier here than in the Empire, if only the Worm could be resisted as the Wasps can.* 'The Worm is a parasite on all of them, on this entire world. It takes, and gives nothing – not even the tyranny of order. If we can defeat the Worm, or outlast it or exhaust it, then these people will live very well in its absence.' She glanced up at Tynisa, seeing her frown. 'You doubt me?'

'It's just . . . what then?' the Weaponsmaster finally managed to say, apparently wrestling with the question herself. 'And will this place be cut off forever, or will it join up with what we know, or . . . I mean, if we fit back with the world we came from, what happens when the Wasps come down here and enslave everyone, or Helleren magnates realize there's a whole nation of cheap labour, or . . .'

'You have been thinking this through,' Che noted, as if she was a proud College Master. 'Well, perhaps I will have them cast lots and form an assembly of the underworld. Perhaps it will be they who venture into the lands of the Wasps and Beetles, rather than the other way round. Perhaps everyone will finally learn to live with one another and there will be no more war. Only, let us just find a way to beat the Worm first, Tynisa.' She heard her own voice tremble a little with the words. 'There's no sense in planning for tomorrow when we haven't secured today.'

They thought Esmail was mad. He himself wasn't sure whether the whole exercise was just stupidity or a failure to adapt. His discipline was unknown here in the underworld, though. If he did not test his limits, how would he ever know?

He was being forced to improvise: conditions were adverse.

There had been a community here in the darkness by the name of Old Aderax. Enough Moths had lived there that he wondered if the name was an echo of Dorax, the Moth hold that still existed back in the familiar world. He and Orothellin had gone there to spread the word, lunatic missionaries crying out that the end really was nigh.

By that time their enemies – or perhaps Enemy singular, by Che's version – had become aware that something was amiss. The response had been fierce. Locals, using their Art wings and the dark-seeing eyes of their kinden, had reported a host of the Worm descending on them. Fighting to win had been out of the question, whatever Che might have wanted. Fighting to give the bulk of them a chance to escape – the non-combatants, the few remaining children – had become a necessity.

Old Aderax had been a layered city, a strip mine that people lived in, descending in broad tiers into the pit of its own workings. Esmail had been hoping that the Worm would just swarm them, as blunt and simple as the force Che had claimed possessed it, but the horde of bodies sent against them instead split into snaking columns, each accompanied by a seething foam of their sinuous beasts. The armed defenders who had hoped to delay them had been flanked almost immediately.

That was when Esmail had seen it: of course there were minds directing the assault – not the blind and oblivious Worm-god but the Scarred Ones, the priests, those who had betrayed humanity to buy themselves back from oblivion.

He had identified the one column that would be quickest on the trail of the fugitives and dispatched the defenders to intercept it. The miners of Old Aderax were strong and determined, and many of them were huge Mole Crickets, but he knew they would die, and he knew that they themselves had not quite appreciated this. It was a cold decision, but he made it quickly, without hesitation. Regret he would save for later.

He himself had gone hunting.

His small magics had almost vanished after they had been

banished here, but he was still sensitive to the fluctuations of his meagre personal power. When the Seal had broken, as Che claimed, he had sensed a little heightening of his strength, perhaps as magic began seeping in from the wider world beyond. Whenever he was close to the foot soldiers of the Worm, however, it was gone entirely. The power they had tapped into was a primal, mindless, pre-human archetype that knew and understood neither Aptitude nor magic, and so denied them both, potent enough in its ignorance to enforce the same on all who came into contact with it.

Nevertheless he wanted answers, and most of his training needed no magic, and he had crept and lurked through the near-abandoned galleries of Old Aderax, listening to the fates of those few who had been too slow or too stubborn to leave.

It had been a nerve-racking business, because Esmail could not see in the dark as well as his quarry could, but he was clever and careful, and eventually his moment had come. Secure in the knowledge that the Worm's human bodies had scoured Old Aderax of life, one of the Scarred Ones had gone wandering.

Esmail had struck, descending on the robed figure, dealing a blow that sent the priest insensible to the floor, then pausing, waiting. He had been sure that, had he tried this with one of the husks that formed the army of the Worm, he would even now be running for his life as their entire force came for him, each individual body just a segment of the angry whole. How separate were the Scarred Ones? That had been the test.

A slow count of five as he had crouched against the stone, and no instant backlash. He had shouldered the unconscious body and stolen away with it, avoiding the many-limbed coils of the Worm as it thrashed and clawed at Old Aderax, executing the few it could find there and carrying their bodies away.

There would come a time to feel horror, Esmail knew. Even he, whose heritage should have steeped him in blood, could not go into a place like this creature's mind and remain unmoved.

Esmail had listened to every word Che said, and he knew that the Scarred Ones were about something unspeakable, beyond mere tyranny or cruelty. He clung to his humanity, embraced it. Once he had done what needed to be done, he might face the memories, but until then he must entertain nothing but professionalism.

Orothellin had led the refugees into the darkness, keeping the majority safe by sacrificing detachments of men and women, sending them to lead the Worm's questing tendrils away – and to die, surely, Esmail thought – and Esmail had caught the rabble up eventually. When they saw what he had brought them, they had wanted to tear the priest to pieces. When he told them he had a use for the creature, they had begun to suspect a madness in him.

But he was not mad. He was desperate. He was inventive. He was going to see if his discipline, all that vaunted training, could subvert the will of the Worm.

The refugees from Old Aderax had made a wretched and temporary home out of a scar in the rock, but they would be moving on through the pitch-dark landscape soon. Orothellin had been telling them that they must keep ahead of the Worm, though Esmail was not even sure if that was possible. The Slug-kinden had very clearly decided that anything resembling an organized defence was a lost cause. He was hoping to keep people on the move until the Worm had sent the bulk of its forces elsewhere – meaning to the lands under the sun, the Old World, Esmail's home.

Esmail had thought about that, coldly and clinically as his training required, and decided that, even if he liked the idea, it wouldn't work. He had listened when Che had spoken of the terrible beast below, the avatar of the Centipede-kinden whose blind hunger possessed and drove the legion of bodies that comprised the Worm. It was an impossible thing, a terrible thing that the Centipedes had called up and turned into, at a time when it was either that or extinction.

And Esmail, the assassin, considered his chances. What would happen to the Worm if he was able to kill god?

Had he been given free rein with his particular brand of magic, he would already be walking freely through the foot soldiers of the Worm, seeking his chances, but his old trick of taking on the face of another would now fall away the moment he got close to a single human segment of the beast, let alone to the colossal creature itself.

But not, apparently, the priests themselves. There was humanity enough left in them that they could still become his victims.

This one was a woman, he noted, although he had not realized before. She was pale and lumpen and her skin positively boiled with spiralling scars. Taking that pasty face of hers would not serve, but Che and the Hermit had showed that there was another way.

First, though, he needed to understand.

His remaining little handful of magic, which he had sheltered like a candle down here, would finally see use. The Scarred One snarled at him and spat, and called down curses on his head as he reached for her mind.

She sensed him, and her defences were remarkable, walls after walls, all slamming into place about her, fending him off, turning him away. She was as defended as a magician, and for a moment he was thrown, unable to force his way into her, his strength venting itself against the barriers of her brain.

How has she learned to do this? Why should she need it?

And, with that, he understood. She did not need to fend off roving assassins who might want to pillage her brain, but every day of her life she must shield her mind from the thing that was her god. Mind was the very quality that it abhorred, that it denied in its tools and subjects. The higher things of mind were blotted out even in the presence of its servants. If it detected the decaying human thought left in its unasked-for priesthood, then it would obliterate them entirely.

Knowing that, Esmail attacked again, drawing upon not

strength but sheer finesse, not the hammer but the needle, to pierce through all the little gaps in her armour that the bludgeon of her god could not have penetrated.

He was in . . . and in that moment her whole mind, her history and her nature, were spread before him like an abattoir.

Afterwards, the horror came, and he abandoned the corpse that he had made of her and found some place out of the sight of humanity and shook and shuddered for all the dead in Old Aderax, and for all that he had since learned.

He had seen how they lived, the Scarred Ones: the last true Centipede-kinden. Priests and leaders, as they styled themselves, servants of their insatiable god. But he had seen through their eyes. He had seen how they scratched a living inside the city of the Worm, maintaining their fragile identities against the constant eroding tide of the godhead. He had seen how they were permitted to direct the armies of labour, to organize and provision and supply. He had seen how they were suffered, an irritant that salved the sore it had caused, and so lived on another day. They had become parasites in the corpse of their own history, and they knew that one day the Worm would not need them. The perfect unthinking monstrosity that they had called up in their time of need would consume them, just as it would consume everything else.

They comprehended all of that, did these scarred priests, and yet they did nothing. They cringed and served, and they sacrificed countless lives to an entity that only grew and consumed and made everything like itself, just as the Centipedes had always done, every child of every kinden becoming just a new segment in their composite body. Only now even they would be the victims of their own work, and the only victory they could hope for was that they would be the very last, when all else was gone.

Later, when the trembling had subsided and he had come to terms with what he had learned, he took his Art to his own flesh, keener and more precise than any knife, drawing red, raw sigils to complement the mark the Hermit had already laid on him.

He gritted his teeth and illustrated his skin with careful spirals. His magic would fail him, but those marks, and his understanding, would serve to let him pass beneath the notice of the Worm. Or, if they would not, he would die, but it seemed to him that the Worm meant the death of everything, above and below, sunlight and darkness.

He had failed to kill the Empress of the Wasps when the chance had been given to him, but he could make up for that. He could kill the Worm god.

Twenty-Nine

The Sarnesh army was already on the march eastwards. The Imperial force that had been camped out to dissuade the Ants from just this sort of move was packed up and retreating – leaving a network of traps and buried explosives, and moving slowly enough that the Ants could not just steam all the way to Helleron unopposed. The Imperials had recognized the superiority of the Sarnesh force, however, and that was before Milus's allies were taken into account. The liberation of Collegium was the trigger that released the Sarnesh war machine.

There had been some dissent, back home, silent concerns voiced by other tacticians and commanders. Was Sarn being left too exposed? Should they not hang back now that their city was free of threat? What would this march eastwards achieve?

The destruction of the Empire, Milus had told them. *No more threat from the east. No more strong Wasp power to overshadow us. Total victory. And if Sarn gains from that, if it is we who fill the power vacuum, then so be it.* That had persuaded many of them, and to the rest he had said, *If you do not agree, replace me, for this is my plan.* That was not how Ant cities or Ant armies were run, but he had a strong and charismatic mind that used consensus as a tool to get what he wanted, rather than as a decision-making process. Every time he interacted with the Royal Court of Sarn he put his career on the line: *Replace me or let me do my work.* He had sufficient past success to vouch for him, and he found that the rest of his people were scared. The Wasps had come so close, had smashed their fortress at Malkan's Folly, had enslaved other Ant city-states. In the face of extinction, they had found allowing Milus the reins the least unpalatable solution.

Now he had the army moving east and repairing the Helleron railtracks as they went. Milus was not going to stop at that mythical line that cartographers used to delineate the edge of the Lowlands. There was a city out there called Capitas that was supposed to be the greatest in the world, and he intended to visit it with an army at his back.

Tactician, the Mantids are here.

First order of business: the Sarnesh army alone would not suffice. His people were disciplined, well armoured and equipped, the best soldiers in the world, but the Empire had far more – both their own and their slave soldiers, the Auxillians. Sheer numbers would crush little Sarn on its own.

But Sarn was not on its own. Stenwold Maker was even now approaching with every Collegiate willing to bear arms, with soldiers from Vek and Tsen – of all the madness! – with warriors of kinden that Milus had not even known existed. The old Beetle had come through at last, and Milus was grudgingly impressed, for all that the man's tactical sense plainly left something to be desired.

And now there were the Netheryen, as they had taken to calling themselves. Since the Mantis civil war, or whatever it had been, the forest kinden had been quiet, making no attempts against either Empire or Ants. Now, and at last, they had deigned to send out some ambassadors.

The sight of them, relayed through his scouts, was something of a surprise. He had expected perhaps one sullen warrior, or a knot of them, bitter and resentful and wanting somebody's blood. Instead they had actually mustered something that looked like an embassy. There were about a score of them, and some – older women mostly – who were robed like diplomats, or perhaps wizards, for all he knew. They were still armed, of course, and no doubt they would be effortlessly lethal with their claws and rapiers and bows, if still rather permeable to snapbow shot, for all that.

They had a couple of Moths and, through his vicarious sight, Milus watched the way they stood, interested by the changes. Everyone knew the Moths normally told the Mantids what to do, but that had fallen apart with all the fighting in the forest, and now a pair of Moth-kinden were plainly trailing after the Mantids in a rather submissive manner, like beggars hoping for crumbs.

And there was a monster . . . or a beast, anyway. Milus had heard of the great forest mantids. Chiefly he had heard that they never left the forest, for which everyone elsewhere was duly grateful. Here was one, though, towering over the mere humans around it, stalking with measured, stilting strides, its killing arms folded demurely close to its thorax.

He went to meet them: what man wouldn't who was interested in building his personal legend? He strode forwards without fear, well aware that he was within range of that barbed reach, their blades and the spines of their Art. At the same time his mind was reaching west, through the string of scouts he had left behind, so that he could talk to the King and his court instantly. It was a method of communication that was going to become less efficient the further east he travelled, but right now he could speak to the city with only a handful of seconds' delay.

He faced the Mantis delegation boldly, even staring into the faceted, judgmental gaze of the great insect itself.

'So,' he asked them, appearing casual, in control, 'what do you want?'

Negotiations after that were swift and businesslike, and that was also a surprise to many of his people, if not to Milus. Mantids were mystics obsessed with the past, with grudges, perverse beliefs, taboos. Milus himself had felt the wind change back when they were fighting each other. He had heard all the same reports from his rangers within the forest but, as he himself thought a little differently to most of his kinden, he had drawn slightly different conclusions. *Either they will destroy themselves or they will come out as something changed and honed.* And here they were.

One of the old women spoke for them, but she conferred with the others and even, it seemed, with the insect. The language she used was not that of prophecy and magic. She spoke of borders, recognition, payment. The Mantids had always loathed the idea of slavery – how relations had improved with Sarn, when the Collegiates had persuaded the Ants to give up that institution! – and now this old woman was saying that they would no longer be slaves even to their own past. They had no Aptitude, no industry, no technology, but they were bartering their skill and reputation into becoming a modern power of sorts. For the first time in centuries, the Mantids were looking outwards.

Even Milus felt a chill at that. Who knew where that would steer the history books? After the Wasps were obliterated, their Empire dismembered and its best parts carried back to Sarn in triumph, he could see that this Netheryon might become a problem if not well handled. For now, though, he argued fiercely with the Court back home, negotiated keenly with the Mantids to see how much give there was in them – little, for they had not changed *that* much – and hammered out terms that were just this side of acceptable for all concerned. *As for the future, we can look to that when we need to. And, who knows, if we give them enough of what they want, then perhaps we can make them part of our destiny. We will have to find a word for that destiny that is not 'Empire', though. The word is too debased.*

With that in mind, and the Netheryen issuing from their forest to form up for the march, he turned his mind to the next diplomatic challenge – for here came Stenwold Maker.

Even Ants needed to sleep, and the great regimented host of the Sarnesh force was just setting camp as Stenwold and his immediate escort arrived. The bulk of the Collegiate force would catch up with the Sarnesh over the next few days – some coming from the city itself, others direct from Sarn, using the restored rail lines to make up the time. Stenwold had travelled ahead in the hold of a fixed-wing hauler with an escort of Stormreaders, in case the Wasps were trying anything clever in the air. He had Kymene with him, and Paladrya, Laszlo and a handful of the *Tidenfree* Fly-kinden that the man seemed to have co-opted as his personal retinue.

There was an unfamiliar tightness to Laszlo that Stenwold was concerned about. The ex-pirate had played his role perfectly, liaising between the surface and the Sea-kinden, but there had clearly been some personal business on his mind all this time. With the death of the *Tidenfree*'s skipper Tomasso, Laszlo had become a grimmer man than Stenwold was used to. It was as if he had finally grown up and accepted his responsibilities. Stenwold could only hope that this change in him would not get in the way of the campaign ahead.

In his heart, he could make a solid guess at what was motivating Laszlo, and he knew he should do something, because if the man put any of that pent-up resentment into action, then there would be trouble that Stenwold – and the war effort – could do without. He said nothing and did nothing, though. The invaluable aid that Laszlo and his family had tendered, and the price they had paid for him, stayed his hand.

I will regret it. But Stenwold regretted a great deal already, and the deeds of Fly-kinden seemed a small enough burden to add.

'Kymene,' he beckoned.

'War Master.'

He glanced at the Mynan woman, iron-hard and lean, and still an arresting figure despite the lines of wear and hardship on her. The first time he had set eyes on her, he had been newly released from a Wasp cell, and she had been one of the most striking women he had ever seen – though hers was a statue's beauty, to be admired without being touched. The struggle for her city remained her life and her sole purpose. In that brief

356

time when she had not been fighting the Wasps, she had been fighting her opponents within the Mynan Consensus.

Paladrya walked at his other side, her hand resting on his arm, carefully cowled and shawled against the sun that would crack and burn her pale skin.

Tactician Milus received the three of them in his tent, arrayed in full armour, a man with his hands full of war sparing some of his valuable time for his allies. Stenwold knew him, though: for unlike most Ants, Milus was good at putting himself behind the eyes of others and predicting how they thought. It gave him a tactical edge over his peers. *And it makes him very dangerous.*

'War Master,' Milus acknowledged. 'Commander Kymene, Adviser Paladrya.' That last name, which should have been un-familiar to him, was pronounced perfectly. 'Congratulations on your victory over the Second. It was an immaculately executed campaign.'

'Thank you, Tactician,' Stenwold said, waiting for more.

'I'm told that you might have dealt the Second a stronger blow, had you followed them up.' The mild voice was just as much of an affectation as the un-Ant-like preface: 'I'm told'.

'I'm sure your subordinates have explained my reasoning,' Stenwold replied. *No games, please.*

For a second Milus displayed no expression, and Stenwold could not have guessed what he was about to do, but then he nodded. 'It was your battle to direct, War Master,' he conceded pleasantly. 'I myself might have played things differently, but "if" is the scourge of the tactician. The Second is in full retreat, anyway, and we're closing on the nearer Wasp force that was to have been the Collegiate garrison, as I understand it. I antici-pate that either they'll break or we'll catch them within the tenday. My scouts report that they are currently sabotaging the rails as they depart, but we can re-lay them almost as fast, and once the Wasps are out of the way the road to Helleron should be clear unless the Second head north to intercept us.'

'I take it you have strategies ready for either eventuality.'

'Of course.' Milus smiled slightly. 'Although, as the composition of our forces changes and our numbers grow, they must be modified.' His eyes flicked from face to face: dark Beetle, grey-blue Mynan, the startling pallor of the Sea-kinden woman. 'War Master . . .' His tone seemed to mull the title over and examine it. 'I understand that your Collegiate contingent is sizeable. Your soldiers will prove invaluable in prosecuting this war.' *Sizeable* still meant less than the Sarnesh, of course, and they both knew it. 'Also we have Mantis-kinden, Mynans, the other Ants that you are bringing –' this was said without a suggestion of hostility – 'and a small number of troops from Princep Salma. This is the largest single force that the Lowlands has ever mustered. Even our logistics are going to be stretched tight, keeping such a number supplied and moving fast.'

Stenwold nodded, still waiting.

'We are more than equal to any one Wasp army. Given our varied capabilities, I would stake us against two. Do you appreciate the scale of the military might we have amassed, War Master?'

Put that way, it was an oddly chilling thought. Stenwold looked into Milus's face and read the thought, *What might we not do?*

'Even so,' the Ant went on, 'we are still less than the Empire. If they concentrated their forces against us, we would be heavily outnumbered, and we will be moving closer and closer to their home ground – our supply lines becoming increasingly stretched and vulnerable.'

'I am sure you have plans for all of this,' Stenwold suggested, because it was evident that the man did. *Come on, Tactician, no more games.*

'I do – and they are plans on which I am staking the lives of everyone here,' Milus confirmed. 'And for that reason, War Master, I need something from you.'

Here it comes.

'War Master, I understand how Collegium organizes its affairs. Your Assembly is an admirable system, truly. But an army needs *one* tactician, one man to command all, you understand?'

358

'And you are that man.'

'I must be, if we are to prevail,' Milus replied, with a touch of passion in his voice that Stenwold couldn't pin down as real or just for show. 'For us to succeed against the Empire, against that great wealth of men and machines, we must be unified. You are War Master of Collegium, and I respect that, but this army must have a single War Master. Will you follow my orders? Will you commit your followers to my direction? If not, then we cannot rely on you, and your presence will do more harm than good.'

'I understand,' Stenwold replied smoothly, and he did, but it was one understanding among many. Yes, the Lowlander forces would have to work together, and there was nobody save Milus who could lead them – for the Sarnesh were the army's iron core and they would follow nobody else. He found, though, looking into that solid soldier's face, that trust did not naturally follow. He remembered the complaints about this man from Laszlo, and from his old friend Balkus.

There will come a time when we may have to part ways, he told himself, and knew that the skill would rest in judging precisely when that time was. The irony was not lost on him. He had been preaching 'unity or slavery' for years, and now it was a greater unity he was backing away from, because it looked as though it could become something very like slavery, if he was not careful.

'I told you I could bring him.' Sperra looked almost desperately proud of herself.

Laszlo was not sure what he felt about Sperra. He had worked alongside her in setting up the liberation of Collegium, and she was a clever, resourceful woman who would make a valuable ally. On the other hand, he knew she wanted something from him that was not his to give – or that was how he read her.

And, even knowing that, he still made use of her, and she – knowing what it was that he was plotting – allowed herself to be made use of. He had lost track, in all this, of the precise rights and wrongs.

Have to have a chat with Mar'Maker about ends justifying means, some day. Because philosophy was for Collegiate scholars, if any of them had survived the Wasps with their faculties intact.

'That's good,' he told her. 'Share our fire, Balkus. Come talk to the Bloodfly.'

He exaggerated. The Bloodfly was the inherited title of the feared Fly-kinden pirate leader, but while his uncle and former captain, Tomasso, was dead, Laszlo was not his successor. Solid, practical-minded Gude was currently aboard ship and many miles away, though. Out here, Laszlo led the little contingent of *Tidenfree* crew who were marching with the army. They were his people, and they were here for his purposes.

The big Ant whom Sperra had brought dropped down carefully, the little Fly-kinden giving him plenty of space. Balkus's eyes flicked from his old friend Sperra to Laszlo – a very casual acquaintance – then towards the others he did not know.

'This is Despard.' Laszlo indicated the woman who served as the *Tidenfree*'s chief artificer. 'This is Herve, Mallori, Scriena, Apello.' Hard-faced Flies, all of them, pirates varnished over only lightly with respectable Collegiate citizenship. Shipmates and relatives all. 'How's life for the Princepi?'

He referred to the folk of Princep Salma, Sarn's neighbour, who had been forcibly drafted into the army – or as good as.

Balkus glanced about, though the *Tidenfree* camp lay on the far side of the Collegiates from the Sarnesh majority, buried within the Mynan contingent, where hostile ears were likely to be few.

'Not the best,' the Ant confirmed. 'Right now my former kin reckon we're too much of a rabble for fighting, so they've got us waiting on them hand and foot – digging their privies, cooking their meals, sharpening blades. Which frankly wouldn't be so bad, save I remember what I was told about how quick they were to shove us to the front when we were up against the Eighth. A lot of my bunch think that the Sarnesh see our contingent as just small change for their tactician to spend whenever he needs to.'

Laszlo nodded. He was amazed how calm he felt. 'Tell me about *her*.'

Balkus glanced sidelong at Sperra again. 'Well, she's with the army, all right. Some of mine got a look at her – Fly woman, red hair, prisoner, like I was told. Milus keeps her close, and she's locked up in a rail carriage all the time, as if she's dangerous.'

'Oh, she's that,' agreed Laszlo.

'It's not going to happen,' Balkus told him flatly. 'She's in the middle of their camp. She's under guard. Poke one sentry and everyone in the army will know it. There's no way.'

'There's a way,' Laszlo stated flatly. 'Piss on Milus. Piss on the war effort. There's a way.' He was aware of how the others were now staring at him, as if this was some imposter who had managed to steal the face of their cousin Laszlo.

'Look, I understand.' Balkus's face creased in worry. 'Yes, it's wrong. Yes, Milus is a bastard and something should be done. But the war—'

Laszlo met his eyes, unflinching. 'You sound like Sten Maker.' That was unfair. He knew Balkus and Sperra had gone to Maker to complain after the Sarnesh had virtually annexed Princep Salma, and they had been rebuffed. He himself had received the same treatment concerning Milus's imprisonment of the woman he now proposed to rescue.

The Ant's expression fell away, leaving Laszlo without clues.

'It's going to happen,' the Fly told him. 'If it happens, and Milus and Mar'Maker and the Wasps get to have their war, all the better. I think the Wasps deserve a kick in the parts, myself. I'll lend a boot. But I will have her back, Balkus.'

At last those broad shoulders rose and fell, and Laszlo reckoned it was Sperra who made the difference, her support for him so against her own interest. The smile he sent her, the implicit encouragement, made a liar out of him.

'Tell me what I can do,' said Balkus. 'No promises, though. I have my people to keep safe, and the Sarnesh wouldn't need much excuse to put me in the next cell. But tell me what you need, and I'll see.'

Thirty

The Slave Corps was busy.

Across the Empire, prison camps had sprung up at locations dictated by geographical convenience, the availability of transport or mere quartermasters' fiat. They were hasty affairs, for the Empress's orders had been unexpected, unprecedented. *Bring me slaves, Inapt for preference.* And in numbers, such very large numbers. But Seda's writ was unyielding, and never before had the Slave Corps had such a chance to wield it.

They had started small. They had combed households and slave markets for Commonwealers left over from the Twelve-year War. They had bought Moths and Grasshoppers from the Scorpions – and not a few Inapt Scorpions as well. But the demand had just increased, the figures rising in leaps and sudden skips as Seda refined her calculations.

They had gone into Inapt communities within the Empire, such as the Grasshopper-kinden town of Sa, and simply levied a tax of bodies, a mass conscription of men, women and children. They brooked no argument, for they were drunk on vicarious power. They carried away trains of hundreds, even thousands.

They sent airships to the Principalities, those Commonweal states formerly under Imperial control and now close allies, offering to buy every slave they had, and the ships returned with full holds and set off again as soon as they had unloaded.

Then the conflict with the Spiderlands, which so many others had been decrying, began to pay dividends. A steady flow of prisoners from Seldis and points south became a flood, and the Slave Corps seized on them all, buying or trading or confiscating as the need arose.

And still the Empress demanded more.

At the last they began going to the gates of all the Auxillian cities, Inapt or not, and making their demands. They sent to the Lowlands. They sent to every compass point. The Empress demanded slaves and, while that demand existed, the Slave Corps – loathed and maligned by every other branch of the Imperial forces – was the most powerful force in the Empire.

But they let their enthusiasm to carry out her orders outstrip their ability. They had learned few lessons from the excesses of the Twelve-year War, when the influx of Commonweal slaves had been so overwhelming that almost one in five died of neglect and maltreatment before reaching the Empire. The Slave Corps continued amassing the terrible quantities of bodies that the Empress was demanding, but they would not be able to keep them long. They could not feed them. They could not safeguard them from pestilence. Already the deaths were beginning, choked and starved, plagued and crippled, killed by each other, killed by the brutality of their warders, dying by their own hands.

The senior Slave Corps officers were starting to exchange glances, writing urgently to Capitas to say, *We have so many now – but what next?* No response came save, occasionally, a Red Watch officer would arrive and remind them that it was not their place to question the Empress.

One such prison facility was within ten miles of Capitas. Slaves stripped from the capital itself had been sent there, but recently the place had become full to bursting with Spiders taken in the war, the overflow from other places already starting to go septic with overcrowding and lack of care.

The inmates were crammed almost shoulder to shoulder into wooden cages still rough with splinters. Whether a slave ate or not depended on the charity of those around them, since there was no way for the Wasps to ensure that food and water reached them all. Each morning there were a few more dead, and all too often the bodies could not be removed.

The place reeked of death, of excrement, of the sour reek of human desperation. The Slave Corps contingent there was constantly being rotated out because men had a tendency to desert rather than face what they found themselves contributing to, or else they began to consider un-Imperial ideas about mercy.

One evening there was a visitor.

The figure approached the gates with a swift stride, as confident as a general, although no Wasp-kinden ever looked as he did. The guards barring his way noted the armour of immaculate black and yellow in a style a thousand years old, ancient Mantis-kinden sentinel plate, a multitude of interlocking pieces, elegant and barbed, something from another time.

They could not quite see the face within the helm, even with the visor up. He was pale, they would say later, and he had surpassingly cold eyes.

'I am from the Empress,' he told them. 'I am come for the slaves.'

He was a Mantis, and everyone knew how Mantids felt about slavery. The prison commander was sent for, a Major Vorken of the Slave Corps, a veteran of the Twelve-year War. The visitor waited patiently for him.

The major, as it happened, had been in the capital recently and had seen the Empress. He recognized the apparition before him as her bodyguard, but that raised more questions than it answered.

'What are you here for, sir?' The honorific was a wager: surely no Mantis outranked a major, but to omit it where it was due would doubtless incur harsher consequences than to award it unmerited.

'I am come for the slaves.' Again that cold voice, the intonation identical.

Vorken had been uneasy from the moment he set eyes on this

365

man. Now real alarm was rising up within him. 'The prisoners here are being held by Her Majesty's own order. I cannot countenance any attempt to release or move them without her written instruction.' And surely she would send her unloved Red Watch with such orders, anyway, and not this freakish figure from a history book.

'I am come for the slaves.' Again. 'Do not attempt to impede me.'

The figure was past the gate before the guards could react, the major stumbling frantically back to keep out of the intruder's reach. It was a terrible moment of choice. If the man was the servant of the Empress and acting in that capacity, then any action taken against him was nothing short of treason – crossed pikes for sure. If he had broken from his mistress, though, then letting him meddle with the slaves – perhaps creating some great slave army within march of Capitas itself – would be a betrayal of both the Empire and the corps itself.

Vorken made his call. 'Stop him! Bring him down! Alive if you can!'

The Mantis turned as a score of slavers descended upon him, noted their stings and snapbows, and then continued towards the nearest cage door.

'Bring him down!' the major shouted again, furiously.

Stingshot crackled, boiling off that antique armour without marking it and, though the odd snapbow bolt penetrated, the occupant seemed barely to notice, as though what was inside it was proof against mere steel darts, no matter how vigorously they were thrown.

The helm turned back towards them, and Major Vorken was sure that he saw some spark of disappointment in the way the Mantis held himself.

Then he was moving amongst the men who had attacked him, without seeming to clear the distance in between, cutting them down – cutting them *apart* – with ruthless efficiency even as they realized they were being attacked. A half-dozen were dead in that first wave of blows, and the rest were scattering, shooting back at nothing, wounding only their comrades.

He hunted them down. It was swifter than Vorken would have thought possible. He stalked shadow to shadow, and Vorken lost track of him almost immediately, then located him again with each cry and scream as the man danced through the city of cages before the staring, starved eyes of the slaves.

Then silence. A minute had passed, or perhaps even less.

Vorken took a deep breath. His life had been fraying at the edges since he had realized that the prison camp could simply not continue to support itself any more, that his orders had carried within them the seeds of their own destruction. Now this man had arrived and seemed to be simply the embodiment of the disaster he had known was coming.

Vorken turned slowly and, of course, the figure was there. Its blade, one of those Mantis claws that folded back against the arm, was barely bloody.

'I am come for the slaves.' Pale lips moving, the tone unchanged, as though a score of Vorken's men were not now dead.

'Take them.' Waiting for the death strike.

It did not come. The Mantis had lost interest in him. Instead, he strode to the nearest cage – crammed with two score Spiders in a space where the major would normally have kept a dozen slaves at most.

The blade flashed again, and abruptly the wooden grille of the door was sagging open.

Empress, forgive me, Vorken thought – although he knew she was not the forgiving type.

Then the Mantis went to work. Not to free the slaves. Of course not. Mantids despised slaves as much as they did slavers, it seemed, and despised Spiders more than anyone. But even that could not account for what Vorken was watching. This was not hatred, that most enduring of human traits. This was something beyond the experience of a Slave Corps major, an order of magnitude beyond anything he himself had ever done or ordered.

The Mantis moved on to the next cage. By now the slaves – quicker on the uptake than their masters, perhaps – had begun to shout and cry out for help. Vorken and his surviving men stood silent and paralysed. Help was something they had already tried to offer, although they had not realized that was what they had been doing.

Cage by cage, he was killing them. He was killing all of them, as coldly and methodically as a machine. There were thousands of slaves crammed into Vorken's camp, of all ages, of all kinden, soldiers and civilians both. The Mantis was making no distinction.

After the man had made an abattoir of the third cage, something snapped within Vorken and he moved to intervene. It took a single glance of those freezing eyes to stop him in his tracks. That lone moment when he might force himself to do something passed in deadly silence, then he stepped back.

The hysterical shrieking extended across the whole camp now, a cacophony of human fear and dread producing a composite sound Vorken had never heard before. It almost seemed that his Inapt charges were finding a horror in what was going on that went beyond mere inescapable death.

Vorken knew other Slave Corps officers, and many of the other camp commanders. He gritted his teeth and, hunching his shoulders against the unbearable sounds of massacre, began writing them messages as swiftly as his shaking hands could manage the pen.

Lieutenant-Auxillian Gannic, engineer and saboteur, had expected to be debriefed long before this. After returning from the Exalsee expedition, he had anticipated punishment, or at the very least being sidelined on to some low-priority job. The death of Dariandrephos, whilst anticipated as a possibility, had not been quite the result that had been expected from him.

Instead of a reprimand, he had merely received curt orders from General Lien that sent him off to Helleron and Sonn, where the chemical manufactories were already producing the noxious Bee-killer. Having been kept waiting for Gannic's recovery of the formula, they were now churning it out as fast as could be.

Gannic understood the tactical uses for the stuff – a canister smuggled into an enemy camp, say, or thrown in amidst an army by catapult. Beyond that, somewhere his mind was somewhat loath to go, he was aware of the greater potential – indeed the original test that had been envisaged. Get enough of the stuff together and you could smother a city.

They had a great deal of the Bee-killer by now, and those factories were still working at full tilt.

He had travelled there under the command of a Red Watch captain who had barely looked at him and certainly not disclosed his name. Gannic had heard plenty about the Red Watch, and this man had confirmed all of that: hostile, quick to criticize, never explaining himself, his orders vacillating between patronizing and insufficient. *Perfect officer material therefore.*

Back in Capitas again, with their cargo of death, he was summoned to Lien immediately to account for himself.

The Engineering Corps' only general looked as if he could use a little more sleep, Gannic decided. He braced himself for a tongue-lashing because he had failed to accomplish the Chasme mission perfectly – or even particularly well – and because he was a halfbreed, and therefore paradoxically, whilst less was expected of him, any failure was deemed all the more blameworthy.

Instead, Lien just scowled. 'Report,' he barked. And when Gannic tried to tell him about Chasme and the Exalsee he waved it away.

'I've read about that. Report on the Bee-killer.'

Gannic's unease changed direction and he spent a careful twenty minutes setting out the quantities of the chemical amassed, rates of production, logistics of transport. When he had finished,

Lien remained silent, not even glancing at him. The lean, bald general seemed to be staring into some future that the man didn't like overmuch.

This is where I get slapped down. Indeed, Gannic pressed the question, because a flat reprimand to put him in his place would at least restore his faith in the machinery of Empire. After all, at least he would *know* his place then, however hard he was returned to it.

'General,' he hazarded, 'what's it all for?'

Lien's eyes flicked towards him, but the expected annoyance only flashed briefly and went out of the general's face. What was left was a man looking older than Gannic remembered: a man for whom the wheels of both artifice and state were suddenly spinning too fast.

'There are camps,' the general replied. If he was surprised to find himself explaining matters of Imperial policy to a halfbreed lieutenant, he did not show it. Indeed, he seemed almost relieved to get the words out. 'The Empress is amassing a sizeable number of slaves and captives.'

Gannic frowned, baffled. The question, *To what end, sir?* stuck in his throat. Having his previous impertinence actually answered left him frightened. Being told such things seemed bad for his health.

'But such matters are not your concern!' A new voice intervened, an unsteady voice. 'Give the halfbreed his orders and send him on his way, Lien. She has other work for you.'

Lien did not look at the newcomer, but Gannic could not resist. He saw a man who had once been strong framed but seemed almost eaten away now, as though by a disease. His eyes were certainly fever-bright, and they flinched and twitched as if constantly trying to stare into the sun.

After a long moment of blankness, Gannic found a name to tack onto this sick-looking creature. *Can that really be General Brugan of the Rekef?*

'You're to take an airship loaded with the Bee-killer to Myna, under Red Watch orders,' Lien said bluntly. 'Do everything that's asked of you. Then come back. There'll be more.'

Myna? Gannic turned the city over in his mind. Not a place that anyone felt over-fond of, surely, save for the Mynans themselves. And he had the feeling that *their* views had just ceased to count for anything.

'Do you understand your orders?' Lien demanded of him. Gannic tried to lock eyes with him, but the general shook off his gaze without even acknowledging it.

'Yes, sir.' What else, in the end, could Gannic say?

When she awoke, he was there, and she could feel the blood inside him, full of it as a tick and yet still hungry: Tisamon.

For a moment she thought he had come to challenge her. Never mind what he might have done to amass such power, she was ready for him to turn it on her now, to wrestle for his freedom. If she had shown any weakness just then, perhaps he might have done so. Instead she struck the instant she was aware of him, holding him with her raw power, and then binding him anew with his oaths and honour and, in the process, finding out the truth.

'What have you done?' she screamed at him. 'I need them! I need them to die for *me*! You've wasted them – what if I don't have enough now?'

He weathered her outburst and told her, *I have saved them for you.*

For a moment she misunderstood him, but, yes – the power was still within him. He was not a thief of blood, but a receptacle.

You need them, but you need them dead, he told her. *For you I have done this. I shall slay all your enemies. I shall lay their very essence at your feet. Make use of me.*

For there it was, a growing frustration she had sensed in him: knowing that the whole world was engaged in war and he could play only the smallest part. The great battles that a creature such

371

as he was made for were fought only in the oldest of histories, but so were the great rituals that she sought to emulate.

'Yes,' she agreed at last. 'In this you can serve. You cannot kill them all. Not even *you* could kill them all, or even most of them. I will yet have to rely on the toys of the artificers, to make up the balance. Their deaths shall be sweeter at your hand, though – true Inapt deaths to feed the ritual. But I will need to calculate, to redraw my figures. This changes the measure of my power.' And here her eyes grew hard. 'You will kill only on my command, Tisamon. I know you sought to please me, and I am pleased, but you will shed blood on my word, and not on your own whim. I have no use for servants that will not obey.'

For a moment he bucked against her, straining at the leash, and she sensed the words before he said them, and shouted him down with, 'Don't you *dare* believe that you know better than I what is best for me – or for my Empire! Too many men have thought just that before, and the world is well rid of them!'

Still she sensed resistance, and for a moment she was going to banish him from her presence. But what mischief might he get up to then? Instead, she turned away from him, anger and contempt in every line of her, freezing him to a mere statue with the removal of her attention. Let him stand there and fret, until she let him loose again.

She was going to send for Brugan, but this new development had focused her mind on her grand plan once more, and she found herself reviewing her calculations, considering how best to make use of Tisamon's little mutiny. The magical world around her seemed more alive now than ever, even here in Capitas at the heart of an Apt Empire. A strange spring had arrived – or perhaps it was just that the world knew what she intended, and held its breath.

A feat the like of which has not been seen since before the revolution. Long before.

And a distant echo, though louder than before, calling: *Seda.* Not Tisamon's harsh whisper, but the faint and far-off voice of her unwanted sister, the rival she had plotted to destroy for so long. Che.

How strange now that she felt the Beetle girl to be almost a part of herself. It was through Che that Seda had witnessed the extremity of the horror that the Moths had trapped in that closed-off subterranean world. Without Che as her unwilling advance scout, she would never have known the abomination of the Worm that her own actions were even now unleashing upon the world. *Che, I broke the Seal.*

She could not tell whether she sensed anger or blame emanating from the girl, but she knew she deserved both. *Not often does an Empress apologize, but I have done a terrible thing.*

Yes, there she felt it. She could almost see the girl nodding vigorously.

But never mind, Che. I'm mending it. I'm mending the world. I've found a way. Lend me your power, Che. Lend me your strength, to extend my reach that much further, to be that much more certain of what I wish to do.

Was that questioning she sensed, across the appalling distance between them? Surely Che deserved to know. Even she must see the necessity, for she knew what the darkness held. She knew how important it was that such things be kept from the sun.

At whatever cost. At any cost.

Seda tried to explain. She reached out as far as she could, trying to force her plans into her surrogate sister's head, to bring an understanding there of the scale and boldness of her endeavour. She could not know what, if anything, was understood. They were far apart in so many ways, even with the Seal finally gone from between them.

Trust me, Che, she was reduced to thinking. And how absurd a thing was that, to be asking of the girl. *Trust me. This is the only way.*

And Sartaea te Mosca looked out over the West-Empire and shivered.

They were packed into the big airship like livestock – or perhaps worse than livestock. Animals tended to be valuable commodities, after all, to be transported with care.

The Slave Corps had been in a mad panic, back in Collegium. They had raided the overstuffed cells with whip and club, forcing their prisoners out into the open and herding them towards the airfields. Around them, the city had seemed to be at war again. Every Wasp soldier te Mosca had seen had been in armour, and most had been running somewhere. There had been smoke on the air. *It's an uprising!* she had thought at first. Where there had been Collegiate citizens visible, though, they had looked as agitated as the Wasps, just faces peering from behind half-shuttered windows for the most part. Whatever the Empire had been reacting to, it had not been *them*.

Even so, she had been waiting for the prisoners to turn on their captors. They had outnumbered the slavers by dozens to one. Many even had unbound hands. Surely someone would throw a punch, wrest a weapon from a soldier, do *something*. And yet they were prodded and cuffed through the streets, and nobody rebelled. A few tried to run, but stingshot caught them almost before they had broken from the mass of their fellows. The Slave Corps were professionals, each of them more than able to read the eddy and flow of a body of human stock in trade. They had been maintaining control of superior numbers of lesser kinden for generations.

And there had been another factor, one that cut te Mosca to the bone. There were a few Beetle-kinden in amongst the captives. There was the odd Ant, even a Wasp or two, renegades brought to heel. The demographics of her fellow captives did not represent those of the city they had been sieved from, however. Metyssa was in good company, for there were remarkable numbers of Spider-kinden present, despite the death sentence pronounced on their kind. There were what looked like most of the city's fugitive Moth population. There were Grasshoppers and Dragonflies who had fled the Wasps once before, and had now

374

failed to make good their escape a second time. There were some other Flies, quite a number of other Flies. The Wasps had been testing them, back in the cells. Te Mosca had been given a crossbow, of all things – a small model, though still one that she would have struggled with, had she been Apt enough to do anything with it. Because that was what was gnawing at her: they had been testing for Aptitude. Several Apt Flies had been released. Those who had failed the crossbow test had all remained in the cells, with the Spiders and the others, the scions of the Bad Old Days. The grand majority of the herd of frightened prisoners had been Inapt.

And there had been a knowledge of that, in those Beetle faces that peered out from behind the shutters. And te Mosca had read clearly there: *better them than us.*

The airship had been hard: cramped, stifling compartments with a derisory ration of water and no food. In the daylight the cargo hold had heated like an oven; at night the chill had crept from body to body. The Slave Corps officers had spent much of the time arguing amongst themselves. They were very obviously doing something suspect, and te Mosca did not sense the hand of General Tynan behind all of this.

In her less rational moments she had imagined writing him a letter of complaint. A polite letter, of course, because she was who she was, but she would certainly take him to task. She indulged in such thoughts because she had been crammed in too far away from Metyssa or Poll Awlbreaker to know how they fared, or even if they still lived. As the Inapt seldom travelled well within the machines of the Apt, there had been a sluicing of vomit about everyone's feet, and worse soon enough, as the most basic human needs of the captives went unmet. Around her, others had been dying: crushed, parched, succumbing to their wounds. The Slavers had just left the bodies. As a Fly, te Mosca could at least bear being crammed into a small space better than the larger kinden. And so she had crouched in a corner, knees to her chin, and fantasized about correspondence with the general of the Second Army because it gave her a feeble illusion that she could somehow influence her fate.

And now they were somewhere behind Imperial borders, over lands she had never wanted to visit, and the airship was descending.

She could get an eye to the slats and stare out, and see great expanses of open country: the mosaic of fields, with no sign of any town or city nearby. Nobody near her had any idea how far a vessel such as this might have travelled. They might be just inside the border or over the far side of the Empire by now.

But there was something down there. She could just catch sight of it if she contorted herself at the crack. There was what looked like a camp. During the descent she was naive enough to assume it was for the mustering of armies.

And then the airship had been tied off with its keel ten feet from the dusty ground, and the slavers had come and opened the hatches in its underbelly. They had gone from compartment from compartment, dragging out the captives and just throwing them down, let them land how they may. With Fly-manacles killing her Art, the drop was terrifying to te Mosca.

Looking around after her bruising landing, that terror did not go away.

A hand fell on her shoulder, and she saw that Metyssa had fought her way through the crowd to her. Numbly, she let herself be dragged over to where Poll was sitting, clutching at a twisted ankle.

'Can you help him?' the Spider asked desperately, and of course te Mosca should have become the instant professional, kneeling down to offer what healing she could. But she just stood there, with her mind full of what she had seen before Metyssa had grabbed her. Her only thought was, *No. I can't help any of us.*

There had been cages. A great host of cages, stacked two and three tall as though some Wasp had seen the poorest ghettos of Helleron and been determined not to be outdone. They had been full of human bodies – many of them Spider-kinden, but plenty of others too. Then there had been the rings of people just sitting out in the open, ankles manacled to great metal stakes driven into the hard earth. And, after them, there had been a pit like a strip mine, and she had known without looking that it, too, had been thronging with people, people on top of people.

And even now, the airship was disgorging the last of its human cargo, and more slavers were moving in to shift them towards that great maw in the earth. Te Mosca had a horror, then: a horror of being just one tiny mote in a vast mass of the dehumanized, the disenfranchised, the faceless. She had thought about what it might be like to be a slave, sometimes. She had wondered idly – oh, the luxury of the Collegiate life! – what master her own skills might attract. She was valuable, of course: a scholar and a doctor. No doubt she would be plucked out, bought at a good price. She had imagined how she might nobly change the Empire from within, given half the chance.

Now she saw the reality: here were not hundreds but thousands of people, surely. Each face, each body, had its history, its special skills, its memories, its reasons for being cherished and preserved. And, just as obviously, they were nothing to the Wasps but a bulk commodity, something to be shipped and sold by the hundredweight. The slavers played no favourites. Whatever they sought from this appalling morass of massed captivity, they cared nothing whatsoever about who their victims were. The cages, the pit, they were like some Apt machine designed to strip the individuality and humanity from whoever was thrust into them.

And then there was another officer coming up, waving his hands and shouting. His helm was pushed back, revealing a puffy red face. 'What are you doing?' he demanded. 'What do you think you're up to?'

Plainly he was a superior officer and te Mosca felt a sudden rush of relief, because of course this must be a mistake. All of this had been some terrible error. And – she was not proud of the thought, but it came to her from the meanest part of her being – even if it was not an error for the rest, surely it was an error for *her*. Did they not know who she was?

And then she listened to the conversation between the slavers, the camp staff and those who had come on the airship, and she understood. It was just that the pit was already so full that they could not possibly fit so many new slaves in. The camp commander had a wild expression on his face, a man close to the end of his leash, but apparently for logistical reasons and not humanitarian ones.

'What are we supposed to do with them, then?' the airship slavers demanded.

And the answer was simple: as there was no material for new cages, they needed a second pit. That was when the shovels were passed out to the stronger-framed of the slaves, for Imperial policy forfend that the inferior kinden should have their mass grave dug by their betters.

Thirty-One

Reinforcements were coming down the rail line from Helleron; troops rushed in from all points of the Empire, whoever could be mobilized in time. The Sarnesh were on their way, too, with a pan-Lowlander army and a new tactician.

The core of the force taking a stand against them in the ruins of Malkan's Stand had originally been intended as a garrison force for Collegium and had since become a field army by default. The colonel in charge, a man named Brakker, had arrived not long before with elements of the First Army, and his feints and manoeuvres had kept the Sarnesh confined in their city up until Collegium had fallen. After that, and with Tynan's orthopter messengers even then turning around and refuelling, they had fallen back eastwards. They were operating almost entirely without orders, but the colonel knew that the Sarnesh could not be allowed to march unimpeded towards the Imperial border. He sent daily for more troops and artillery, and asked that General Tynan be allowed to come and take command, bringing the veteran Second with him.

For more than a tenday, Brakker's forces had been on the retreat, but they had done everything in their power to make the Sarnesh advance difficult: poisoned wells, broken up the rail line, littered the terrain with mines and traps. All that while, the Ants' own pilots were flying almost constantly overhead in their ersatz Stormreaders, making strafing runs and clumsily dropping the occasional bomb. Brakker was no tested battlefield officer, but a good logistician and planner, and he did everything he could to slow the Sarnesh, apart from actually taking a stand against them.

Word had come from Tynan. He and his army had been called to the capital – the Second to defend it, he himself to account for his decisions. It was a chilling thought that, even in this moment of crisis, they were all still being judged by the Rekef, by the Red Watch, by the Empress herself.

The Sarnesh had been closing the distance steadily, and once the lost garrison force reached the ruins of the Stand their colonel knew that they would get no better terrain to turn and hold the Ants at sword point for as long as possible. This place had once been the pride of Sarn, an indestructible fortress intended to last the ages, save that the Eighth had brought it low with the newest artillery, and now only craggy ruins were left. Ruins were better than an open field, though, so Brakker started refortifying as best he could, and setting up what little light artillery he had been left with.

Then, with the Sarnesh now absurdly close, the reinforce-ments had arrived down the rails from Helleron: a ragbag of disassociated units with brief orders to hold firm until further notice. The newcomers had real artillery, at least, and a good number of engineers, plus half a dozen Farsphex orthopters to at least dull the edge of the Sarnesh air superiority. The troops themselves included two thousand Light Airborne, who were so new to the uniform that the colonel considered it a wonder that half of them could even fly. To give them some backbone, General Marent of the Third had detached a couple of hundred heavy infantry from his own men and sent them along – strictly without orders, the colonel surmised. Then there were the Auxillians: Ants from Maille and Monas, Grasshoppers from Jhe Lien, all come to join the colonel's own sizeable contingent of Vesserett Bee-kinden and give their lives for the Empire.

Not that this last was likely to be an honour unique to the Auxillians, Brakker knew. *Hold until further notice* was not the sort of order any commanding officer looked forward to receiving.

At least their force now equalled a more respectable fraction of the Sarnesh in numbers, and perhaps the Ants' firebrand tactician might take a moment to consider the potential losses on both sides when he came hoping to prise the Wasps from their makeshift fortifications.

Milus looked over the entrenched Wasps and their allies and laughed briefly.

'What's amusing you, Tactician?' Stenwold asked him. He and Kymene had been trailing the Sarnesh leader as he stalked through the camp, and at last as he came to view the enemy. Even with the Wasps in sight, Milus was not being very forthcoming about his plans.

'Don't you see how the tide's turned?' the Ant asked them. 'For too long the Empire's had the initiative, but now look at them repeating our mistakes. We couldn't hold out here when there was still a fortress to hide inside. What chance have they got?'

'They have the chance to buy time for the balance of their forces,' Kymene pointed out.

Milus made a doubtful noise. 'I don't see any of the Second. It looks as if the Gears are on the run. I'd hoped to find them here as well.'

'You were hoping to be outnumbered?'

Milus smiled pleasantly. 'Tomorrow we will smash the Wasps. I'd rather we smashed as many of them as we can. I'd rather that balance of their forces was as small as possible.'

'You seem very confident. Perhaps you might tell us why so, given that you no doubt expect us to commit our own forces,' Kymene put forwards.

'I *am* confident, and you have agreed to abide by my battle plans,' he told them implacably. 'Have your forces ready for a fight tomorrow, that's all I ask.'

'No night attack?' queried Stenwold.

381

'Not this time.' That smile of his was maddening, and no doubt Milus knew it. 'In fact, we'll give them a couple of hours to watch us getting ready, just to rub it in. I want them to know exactly what we're doing.' He looked at their expressions and then laughed again; the sound was chilling to Stenwold, because *Ants didn't laugh*. Not out loud, not like that. Milus was playing at being a human being for their benefit: jovial Uncle Milus.

'If you didn't trust me, what are you doing here with your soldiers?' the tactician asked them both. 'You have some other war to fight? There are a great many Wasps out there, War Master, Commander. We will devour them piece by piece, but I will still need all our forces. I'm not going to waste any bodies on foolishness.'

But you may waste them on what you consider necessity, Stenwold filled in silently, guessing that Kymene was thinking the same. *And if so, it won't be your own Sarnesh that you waste, I'll wager.*

'Tomorrow I'll give out the battle order, and you'll see what I intend. Master Maker, I have a great respect for you . . . I hear the Wasps call you "General" and you are truly a tactician amongst your people. But a Beetle-kinden tactician all the same, and there are reasons nobody ever heard of such a thing. I know you consider my people simple and direct and predictable, but we understand war and the use of weapons – all manner of weapons. Trust me, and we will carry the battle tomorrow.'

Stenwold would have to be satisfied with that, because the tactician was now pointedly busying himself with the administration of his army, and so any other discussion would have to wait.

With dusk on its way, Milus retreated to his tent in the midst of the Sarnesh camp, and it was there that Stenwold went looking for him, guided in by silent sentries and knowing that unspoken word of his arrival would have reached the tactician the moment he made his presence known.

'War Master,' Milus greeted him. 'Only an hour out of my company and here you are once more.' Again such an utterly un-Ant-like comment that Stenwold was momentarily thrown. He had caught Milus sitting on a folding stool inside his tent, reading by the light of a hanging lamp – not a scout's report or a quartermaster's tally but what looked like a Collegiate novel, some lurid tale. He was quite sure that the whole odd impression had been planned purely to unbalance him, constructed even while he still picked his way through the camp.

'There is one other matter that I wished to speak about with you in private,' Stenwold confirmed, refusing to be discomfited.

Milus shrugged. 'Speak.'

'You have a prisoner, a Fly woman named Lissart. I am aware that she has travelled with the army and is here in this camp.'

For a moment he saw a change: the false expression freezing on Milus's face, the body language grinding unattended to a halt. Then: 'What of it?' and a little more caution, perhaps, in the way the words came out.

'I would like her released.'

'She's a Wasp agent.'

'Nonetheless.'

Milus rolled his eyes, back in full mummery now, but Stenwold wondered just what the Fly girl meant to him, that mention of her had momentarily dragged him out of his charade.

'This is because of that man of yours, is it?' the Ant asked him. 'The awful spy – the one who was in Solarno with her.'

'His name is Laszlo,' Stenwold stated. 'I admit he's far from the perfect spy, but there is a difference between spy and agent, and he excels in the field of action. The recovery of my city owes a great deal to his hard work.'

'And he's put you up to this.'

'Before Collegium fell, he asked for my help, my intervention,' Stenwold replied. 'Since then, he's not pressed hard but I know he still wants her back, and I owe him, Milus.'

No doubt the Ant had a great deal of uncomplimentary things

to say about that sort of thinking, but he kept them to himself and just remarked, 'She worked for the Wasps. I still have a use for her.'

'I'm told you've tortured her.'

Again that momentary stillness, leaving Stenwold wondering, increasingly uneasily, about why Milus cared – about why this conversation was even necessary.

'What of it?' The same careless response, but with a sharp edge ready to be unsheathed. And then, before Stenwold could speak, 'It is a tool of statecraft and of war. Or it is everywhere else except Collegium.'

'Some would say that is what makes us better than the Empire.'

Milus cast the book aside in a single, swift motion, one of incredible contained violence, so that the bundle of pages almost exploded against the tent wall, its bindings splitting at the spine. When he stood, he seemed quite calm, but that brief abandon was all the more shocking for that.

'The goal of Sarn in this conflict is not to be *better* than the Empire. It is to be more victorious, War Master. Any measure to achieve that end is permitted. Sarn will survive, and for that to happen it appears that the Wasp Empire must fall. If the Wasps had come to us at the start and started talking terms, then perhaps you and I would be standing in very different places, but history has given you me as an ally, and for that you should be grateful. I am not interested in the navel-gazing of Beetle philosophers. I am interested in winning.'

'And she helps you in this, does she? Somehow there are still secrets you've not already prised from her?' After all, none of this was exactly revelation.

'She heard a great deal about various Imperial personalities while she was in their employ. She has a good ear for gossip, and I may wish to ask her about whoever we end up against next.' Milus held up a hand. 'Are we two truly on the verge of coming to blows over one Fly-kinden turncoat?'

'You tell me.'

Milus obviously wanted very much to show Stenwold that he appreciated the man's spirit in taking this stand. He got the expression slightly, discernibly wrong, though. 'What would you do if I refused?'

'Be gravely disappointed in you. And I'd remember.'

The conversation balanced on a razor's edge, and Stenwold waited to see which way it would fall.

'Let's get to Helleron,' said Milus dismissively. 'It won't be long. From there this army will become an arrow pointing straight at Capitas, and the Helleren will have better and more up-to-date news than anything the Fly girl can tell me, and they'll sell it more willingly, too.'

Stenwold nodded heavily, aware that he couldn't necessarily trust the man, but aware that even though he needed Milus, so Milus needed him a little, too. That would have to do, and at least he would have something to tell Laszlo.

The next morning the Sarnesh began mustering for the assault, but they were certainly taking their time over it. Colonel Brakker was not sure whether this was meant as a taunt to try and get the Empire to abandon its position and attack, or whether the Ant tactician was having second thoughts about committing his forces. The first seemed vanishingly unlikely and the second too good to be true, but Brakker's makeshift team of subordinates could offer no alternatives.

What it did mean was that he had plenty of chance to study the structure and arrangement of the Lowlander force, and to redeploy accordingly. The Sarnesh had taken the centre for their own, along with what he took to be Beetles and a rabble of other kinden in Collegiate uniforms. There was a big wing of Mantis-kinden on the Sarnesh left, which he guessed would be swift and mobile enough that the fortifications would not slow it down much, and they were so scattered that snapbow volleys would have only a limited effect on them. The enemy's right was more of a plodding anvil to that hammer: mostly non-Sarnesh Ants and the red and black of Myna.

Keeping the Mantids back would be key to holding his position here for any length of time, Brakker surmised; it was no enviable task. He had heard plenty of horror stories about that kinden – how they had annihilated the old Fourth Army near Merro, and the grim, savage fighting that followed the Eighth's incursions into the Netheryon quite recently. And, of course, the Eighth was lost, too – General Roder and his entire army massacred to the last man by the Sarnesh and their allies.

It gave Brakker a cold feeling just to think about it. He had never been intended as a field commander. He thought too far ahead, and too broadly, and it seemed to him that even in the last war the Empire had not been put in quite this position. *Eighth gone, Second – the mighty Gears! – in full retreat, and 'hold until further notice' is the word from Capitas.*

In his heart, Brakker had already begun to fear for the Empire and his kinden.

He would do the best he could with what they had given him. He must hold.

A quick decision, then: who would face the razor storm of the Mantis charge? He would concentrate his snapbows against the solid Sarnesh centre, where they would be most effective – and most especially he would place the new recruits there, where their more experienced brothers would give them heart. The logical choice for facing the Mantids was his Auxillians – the Ants, the Grasshoppers, the Bees. He spared the Maile detachment to fend off the enemy's comparatively weak right, placed the men of Vesserett, of Jhe Lien and of Monas to sell their lives as dearly as possible against the Mantis left.

As he gave his orders, the Auxillian officers glanced at one another. He assured them that, once the Sarnesh were pinned, he would spare Wasp troops to back them up. Even as the words spilt out of him, everyone present knew that they were nonsense. This was not a battle for winning. *Only for holding.*

Then the Sarnesh and their allies were visibly on the move, and the artillery began speaking loud on both sides.

The first orthopter droned overhead, Brakker's own Farsphex rising to meet the superior numbers of the enemy. A moment later the bombs began to fall.

Taki skimmed over the Imperial positions, noting just how much refortification they had managed in a relatively short time. The Stormreader she piloted was sluggish and bumbling, a profoundly unsatisfactory flying experience because of the load of bombs it carried. By Milus's orders the combat flying would be undertaken by the Sarnesh pilots this time, allowing them to chase the handful of Farsphex about the sky and thus hone their skills in what should be a relatively safe air battle. She and the Collegiate and Mynan aviators had been left with the heavier Stormreaders, bombing craft refined by the skills of Willem Reader from the jury-rigged machines the Collegiates had used against the Second Army.

And doesn't that seem a long time ago now? she reflected.

She had wanted to know why they hadn't been bombing the Wasps for all they were worth every day since the Sarnesh began heading east. A Sarnesh pilot commander had explained that they didn't want the Imperials just to run and keep running. Milus wanted his battle. He wanted to start cutting away slices of the Imperial forces. Hence, Taki and her pilots had maintained their aerial presence, even dropped the odd piece of ordnance, but they had held back: a war of shadows and misdirection to draw the Wasps to this place and this fight.

Now she unloaded the last of her bombs – holding only half a dozen, the Stormreaders were far less effective bombers than the Imperial machines that had rained fire on Collegium – and turned on a wingtip to head home for more. She marked out in her mind the arrangement of the enemy, where she might want to come back and spread some love. *Only the centre, though.*

Those were Milus's orders and, like most of the man's plans, not to be questioned.

The Sarnesh were coming on in open order so as to deny Brakker's snapbowmen a chance for a solid charge-stopping volley, but the bolts were flying fast both ways, the closing gap between the two forces shredded by shot. Brakker's men had cover, and so far were getting the best of it, but the Ants would soon turn that around if they could get in close.

Because he was an administrator and not a warleader by nature, Brakker was very focused on the centre of the battle – the part of it that contained himself – and had been assuming that someone would tell him if other parts of it were not going according to plan. When the Mantis-kinden screamed unopposed into the Wasp right flank, he was completely unprepared, unable to formulate an order for one vital minute during which hundreds of his soldiers were killed in their trenches and dugouts.

By that time the Sarnesh were in full advance, pelting across the broken ground as fast as they could in their heavy mail, with felt-backed shields held high.

The Auxillians? Brakker had time to wonder. *Did they chew through the Auxillians so fast?*

He had far too many underlings clamouring for his attention right then, but he needed to see the field for himself, discern how it had all gone wrong. With a strangled grunt, he kicked into the air, Art wings carrying him above the throng.

The Auxillians were still there. The Ants and Bees and even the Grasshoppers were falling back with a discipline and dignity that any drill sergeant would have been proud of, utterly unmolested by the enemy. The Mantids were just rushing straight past them, across the front of their retreating formations, as though they weren't there.

On the other side, the Ants from Maile were pulling out with the same almost dream-like calm, as though they had not noticed that there was a bloody battle in progress. The Lowlander right was already moving in to catch Brakker's other flank.

Brakker opened his mouth to give some order – he had no idea what, but it was plain that something remarkable would be required, the sort of order that went down in the history books.

He never made the histories. A Sarnesh bolt took him in the chest as he hung above his army, and he dropped back into the panicking mass of his men. In moments those Wasps that still could were trusting to their wings, whilst the Auxillians marched implacably away.

Thirty-Two

He had a lamp. The lamp was life.

It gave out a harsh, greenish-white chemical glare, and it would last for a long time but not forever. That indicated Totho's deadline, his allotted time to find Che and get her out of this black and unnatural place.

He was not sure what he had expected, but this was not it. He had thought of caves, winding tunnels where the monstrous Worm-men walked. He had thought that he could catch and question one of them, perhaps. He had thought that all roads would lead him to Che.

In this, he recognized, he was guilty of thinking as the Inapt must think, that there was some pattern directing life, so that these things worked out.

The caves were a world in themselves, vast and overarching. The stone sky was filled with stars in some way he could not understand. Moths battled through the air, and also terrible things, great albino shadows he glimpsed at the very edge of his light. Here was not a warren of narrow passageways that he might search methodically until one of them was found to contain Che. He had thought to find her in some prison, at the mercy of a villain that Totho could slay. He had come to rescue her, after all. Poor, helpless Che was always getting herself captured. It was almost endearing, save that those enemies who caught her seemed thereafter to become the target for her mercurial affections: Moths, Wasps, vile and deceitful kinden all.

But the caves remained a world that was vast and unplumbed, and he knew she must be here somewhere but he had no way of finding her.

He had seen some of the Worm-men. When they had come within the reach of his lamp he had been petrified at first by the fear that the thing he clung to must make him a beacon to the whole of this dark world. Later he had come to realize that their eyes worked backwards: they saw in the darkness, but they could not see his light. It meant nothing to them.

He had killed them initially. He had intended to confront them, or to capture some straggler, but he had forgotten the skin-crawling way they moved all together, the utter inhuman detachment that was in their every look and motion. Revulsion had risen within him instantly on seeing them – the simple fact of having them within sight was more than he could deal with. He had ambushed them with his snapbow and emptied a precious magazine into them, striking down half a dozen instantly at long range and before they knew he was there.

Then they had seen him, and something terrible had happened. He had stood there with his snapbow – he was up on a jutting rise and had been shooting down at them – and his hands had lost their way. The very logic of what he was doing, that deep, ingrained understanding of mechanism, of cause and effect, had gone. His finger had been on the trigger, and had even twitched on it, spitting a single bolt uselessly off into the dark. It was not that the weapon had jammed. It was that he himself had.

They had come for him – were already coming for him – and he might have stood there until he died if they had not been so repulsive and unnatural. That instinct to get away owed nothing to those higher parts of his mind that had come unmoored. Clutching his useless snapbow and his lamp, he had fled them and escaped.

Later, hiding in a cave after driving out the pallid long-legged spider that was its previous occupant, he had tried to understand what had happened. He had panicked, he told himself. The sight of the Worm-men had unnerved him. It had been a human failing, and therefore one that he, Totho the Apt, could overcome.

He had seen things in his life that he had fought to explain away and he had succeeded in each case. Time and the dulling of memory had allowed him to conquer even the sight of the river Jamail in Khanaphes, stirred to sudden flood and scouring one bank of the invading Scorpion-kinden whilst leaving the locals on the other bank untouched. In his Apt heart, he could look back on that sight and know that there had been a rational explanation because he himself lived in a rational world.

When he remembered confronting the Worm, though, he found his powers of self-deception were insufficient to the task. He could deal with attempts to add new and intolerable experiences into his life, but this was an absence, a theft. When the attention of the Worm had turned on him, he had been stripped of all those things that made him *him*.

He ate sparingly of the food he had brought – another constantly encroaching limit to the time that he had. He was suddenly convinced that he would not be able to find his way out of this place if he did not find Che. His journey only went one way. No retreat.

He slept, dreading what dreams would follow. When he awoke again, adrift in time in a strange, cold place, he turned out the lamp and forced himself to face the darkness.

There was other light, aside from his chemical lantern and those distant, mobile stars. Something out there was ablaze. To Totho, fire meant the work of human hands, and he had nowhere else to head for.

He could see people, when he drew closer. Because of the lamp, some of them had already spotted him. In this dark-mirror world, that meant that they were not the enemy. Or not necessarily the enemy. Not the enemy that he feared.

But they were a horrible ragbag of creatures, nonetheless. He had the snapbow ready, and he nearly killed the first of them that he saw. They were Moths. Of all creatures other than the Worm, Moths were those he most did not want to see.

There were others too, he saw shortly afterwards, and the Moths were their advance scouts, their fliers. As he strode into their community in his dark mail, with his lamp in one hand and his snapbow over his shoulder, they stared at him as though he had come from another world or another time. Which he had.

There were Beetles there, and Mole Crickets, and a weird dark-grey velvet-haired people whose Art let them throw nets of gluey strands at their prey or their enemies, and pallid men and women with no eyes at all, who saw through their feet and their long fingers. Confronting them, seeing them study him with just the same wariness of the familiar facing the alien, he felt that he had taken the final step out of a sane world and into some ancient folk story.

They were in the process of leaving, he understood. They were the slaves of the Worm, and the Worm was consuming its slaves, burning them like fuel so that it could make its grand assault on the world that Totho knew. He gained this understanding in fragments and pieces. They were all scared of him, so none of them was particularly coherent. He learned first of all, though, that the Worm was coming: their common enemy.

He asked them about Che, without much hope – did they know a Beetle girl from the surface who had become lost down here? Would they know if she was a prisoner of the Worm? For a long time, none of them realized who he was talking about.

Then, with the Moths floating back in to warn that the Worm was almost upon them, and the evacuation still ongoing, the people of that nameless place fleeing into the dark, one of the blind men approached Totho warily.

His name was Messel, he said. And, yes, he did know Cheerwell Maker.

★

393

Esmail walked amongst the Worm.

He hadn't been sure that it would work and, even now, he couldn't know how long he could pass amongst them in safety. He was limiting his exposure.

The sheer geography of this realm had begun to make his mind hurt. Che had spoken of the Worm's city, and he had thought, *It must be just one of many, surely.* But no, there was just the one, from whence all the Worm sprang, and all roads led towards it. It was the centre of this prison world, and the Worm itself – the physical form the Centipede-kinden had given to it in their desperation – was the centre of that, ergo the centre of this entire world.

He could not imagine how it worked, how everything would have to curve and funnel in to make that true. Perhaps Che could, or some Moth Skryre with a far greater understanding of the world than poor Esmail.

The breaking of the Seal had sent slow shockwaves through the Worm's domain, Esmail surmised. This had been a part of the larger world once, and it was trying to be so again. These caves and caverns, this lightless place of many kinden, had simply been another power in the old Inapt games of state, until the Worm's practices – their aggression, their conversions, their taking of children and repurposing them for their own cause – had caused that great and almighty war of antiquity. Now the under-earth was striving to return to its proper place, and Esmail could see cracks and damage, fallen buildings, entire shattered districts of the great stone city. But of course the Worm needed no buildings, no cities. The Worm had been born out of the Centipede ideal and from the depraved desperation of its people with one need only: that there should be the Worm, forever and forever. The Worm was the centre of its own world. The only things it permitted to exist were those that furthered the existence of the Worm. It needed slaves because they produced new life to become segments to graft on to its extended body; because they toiled and mined to arm and equip its mindless host of soldiers. For a long time that uneasy stasis had been maintained by the Scarred Ones, who had the human intellect the Worm lacked. They had preyed and preserved all at once, keeping a precarious balance of feast and famine.

The breach of the Seal had ended that. Now the Worm, which had been coiled in readiness for a thousand years, was striking upwards at that great mass of the sunlit world, not because it was some manner of birthright from before the war, but because it was different to the Worm. Because it was a world that the Worm was not the centre of.

That was the thought that obsessed Esmail, for what he had gleaned from the scarred woman's mind had suggested that Che had underestimated how the Worm would conquer. Not merely casting the bristling loops of its body up into the wider world, but by warping that world's very nature, simply by its presence. As its armies funnelled into the lands above, so the Worm would twist the very weave of the world around it, dragging at the centre until all the world, and not just this barren prison, led to its jaws. And by then the Worm would need no others, not soldiers, not priests, not slaves. There would be just the Worm.

Esmail had killed, in his time. He had served evil causes. He was well acquainted with the sort of motives that drove the Wasps to send out their armies or drove Moths to intrigue against one another. He understood evil. The horror of the Worm was that it was not evil. Evil implied a choice. The Worm was what it had been made to be, as innocently destructive as a machine.

The Scarred Ones, though . . . they were evil. He was happily killing any that he could creep up behind and cut open. They had been given the choice, and they had made it.

Here in their city he possessed no magic, but he remembered with a professional clarity just how a Scarred One's mind had thought, and he remembered the Hermit's reluctant blessing, and he had cut himself again into the exacting patterns of their mystery. He had taken every word of Che's account and analysed it as a spy should, and now he walked amongst the bodies of the Worm and they did not notice him. Or, if he felt a ripple of unease run through them, he would add another scar to his flesh and quell their suspicions. He avoided the Scarred Ones themselves, who would know in an instant he was not one of them. It was hardly textbook fieldcraft, but it had kept him alive and undetected so far.

And he had seen it all. He had not realized that he came here only because Che's story had seemed too bizarre to be believed, but now his eyes had been opened: it was true in every word.

Or every word but one. He had yet to see that final inner secret. He had yet to confront the Worm inside its den.

The child pits had nearly finished him. He had been a hard man once, but having children, loving children, had fractured some part of his inner armour. He had stared down at the terrified, lonely infants, seen them look up at him beseechingly as though he could do anything for them. He had come so close to trying to help, even though all he would have accomplished would have been to destroy his own cover.

He had looked in each subsequent pit, witnessing each group of children one step further removed from their roots, from their individuality. He had seen, stage by stage, the Worm consume everything that they had been, and leave nothing but its hollow casts behind.

It was after that that he had started murdering the Scarred Ones whenever they gave him the opportunity. He desperately wanted to kill somebody for it, and they were the only ones to whom it was even possible to attach blame. If it had been feasible to go backwards somehow and kill all their ancestors as well, all the great magicians of the Centipede-kinden when they had first thought up this madness, then he would have done that, too.

Not long ago he had made a surprise discovery: he had found out where the Scarred Ones lived. There was a nest of caves beneath the city, unconnected to the tunnels leading to their god. There the true remnants of the Centipede-kinden clung to their precarious existence, hiding and breeding like vermin, like parasites in their own places. He saw them there, and their children – already scarred to keep them from the wrath of the mindless host all around them. He could have stalked in and butchered them, but found that it was not in him, quite, to do so. Besides, they did not all sleep at once, but operated some kind of staggered rota, so that some were always vigilant. At first he imagined that they feared some intruder such as himself. Then he realized that they feared the end of their immunity, that their god would suddenly realize that it had no need for them. Such feeble sentries could not have kept that tide out, but still they watched. It was not quite enough to engender sympathy in him, but it came close.

He had no idea how Che's own work was going – her attempts to gather and organize the slaves. He had been out of contact now for unknown days and uncounted moonless nights. All he knew was that there were prisoners being brought into the city on a regular basis, but no clue as to whether they were captured in battle or were just part of the Worm's attempts to consume its human chattels here to fuel its assault on the world above.

That there were prisoners at all was because of the priests, he guessed. The Worm would have no use for living slaves to be brought to its city, any more than it had a use for the city itself. The priests, though, had concocted their insane, all-denying religion around it, and told themselves that their practices earned them its blessings, and their sacrifices protected them from its wrath. Esmail could see, with utter clarity, that there were no blessings and likewise no wrath.

The priests killed their prisoners fairly quickly. Many they killed themselves in lesser rites – and the bodies went to feed the Worm's own growing mass, or to load the tables of the priests themselves. Far more were being taken down into the chamber that Che had spoken of – the true final point of all roads within this stone nightmare. The Worm was hungry.

He had been steeling himself to follow one such expedition.

397

He needed to view his enemy with his own eyes before he brought this whole edifice down.

In the end, his hand was forced. He would never know if, unassisted, he might have possessed the courage to make that journey deeper into the earth.

He saw the latest band of prisoners brought in. Amongst them was a familiar face.

The big man stood in the centre of this ragged band of slaves, hands extended over them as though still trying to protect them in some way. Orothellin.

Esmail watched that huge, haggard figure even as the Scarred Ones came for him, weaving through the constantly busy throng of soldiers. The big man had mustered a certain dignity for the occasion, and Esmail badly wanted to make himself known in some way: to let Orothellin know that he was not alone in these last moments.

Then, of course, the soldiers were separating the giant out, for who was a better offering to the Worm than this man, this veteran of a thousand years and a symbol of their captivity?

They took him away, Orothellin moving slowly, almost as though he was still half asleep, with the people of the Worm milling around him like children.

The thought suddenly made Esmail sick. Of course, like children. They were all somebody's children. Generations of children stolen and hollowed out and sent to tyrannize and kill their own kin. *And no wonder the ancient world had stood together against the Worm.*

This time, he followed when they took Orothellin beneath the earth. This time, the Scarred Ones did not delay. There was a dreadful excitement about them. *They know who he is. They have been hunting him for a long time.*

And it will buy you nothing from your god, save that the wretched man is perhaps a larger morsel than most.

He crept in their shadow using the skills of a long life in the trade – no magic, but his expertise had always counted more than mere magician's tricks. There were many of them, and soldiers too – had there been fewer Esmail could have won Orothellin a moment's freedom, for all that they were in the heart of the enemy's domain. As it was, natural caution won out and he merely watched. What else, after all, was a spy for? Today he was a spy.

Tomorrow an assassin, he fervently hoped.

They led him, all unknown, to the lair of their god, that same great rift that Che had described, and there the Worm came for Orothellin, and devoured him and his thousand years without thought or appreciation, and went away again.

Immediately afterwards, Esmail left the broken city and found himself some hidden nook in the stone to creep into, and he trembled and stared at his hands in the darkness.

He couldn't do it. He saw that now. Even if the thing was not a god, then it was still too vast, too dark, too terrifying. He had no Art or skill or useless, useless magic that would permit him the hubris of attacking the Worm. His courage went only so far. It could not be done.

Thirty-Three

Everyone had questions, but Eujen had no answers, not real ones. *When are they coming back?* was the one he heard most often. So many citizens of Collegium had marched off with the Sarnesh, and people wanted to know when they would see their loved ones, their relatives, their business partners or drinking mates. Worse, there had been that airship which had escaped ahead of the Second Army's retreat. Nobody had realized at the time just what had been going on – not even the general of the Second, apparently. Only after the dust had cleared did anyone realize that the Imperial Slave Corps had simply floated away with several hundred citizens.

Everyone was mourning someone: dead or missing or marched off with the army. Whole sections of the city were running short-handed. There weren't enough hands to rebuild or to reorganize. Collegium was merely limping through the days.

When are they coming back? people asked about the Merchant Companies. Eujen himself wanted to know that. What news he received from the troops showed that nobody there knew, either.

And there was that other trouble – the attacks under cover of darkness that scoured isolated farms and mills and villages and left no witnesses – or sometimes left a row of houses untenanted without warning or explanation. Everyone had somehow been assuming that it was some game of the Wasps, some pastime of Tynan's Second, but the Wasps were gone, and it was getting worse, and so they came to Eujen and asked him what he intended to do about it.

He had not been appointed the leader of the city. There was no real Assembly. That sad rump that the Wasps had permitted to 'advise' had since been disbanded, and those who had sat on it were all doing their best to explain that, really, they had been given no choice, and of course they had worked against the Empire in so many, alas invisible, ways. At the same time, nobody was about to say they needed another governor to rule the city with a tyrant's rod. Their intricate system of government had been taken apart, and nothing brought in to replace it.

Eujen, a student who could walk only through the intervention of artifice, had been the de facto Collegiate Speaker in exile in Sarn. Now he found that people were still looking to him for leadership, when there was so very little he could do.

So he did the little that he could. He found other people who themselves could only do a little. He got them together and talking to each other. He combined all those small contributions, building one on another until he had something that looked as though it would at least keep the wheels turning for now.

He started with his friends and associates, with a keen realization of, *So this is nepotism, then*. He found people who had been useful in Sarn, College Masters, his parents. He moved on to people they knew, for his parents had their mercantile contacts; scholars knew other scholars, who in turn knew someone who . . .

Eujen himself did nothing save point people at other people, and point people at problems, and he waited for someone to look at him and demand to know what gave him the right.

When the people he was pointing at each other had differences or came to blows, he intervened. To his lasting amazement, they listened to him bluster, nodding soberly. If he voiced a thought, that opinion of his seemed to manifest almost as a physical thing, with weight and impetus.

Nothing was working. Everything was still falling apart.

Except, each morning, it was all still falling apart just as the day before, barely any worse at all. He was a dam against the entropy that would lead to collapse, anarchy, starvation.

He had no militia, of course – the Merchant Companies were off with Stenwold Maker, what was left of them, and his own Straessa had gone with them. There was a contingent of Tseni Ant marines on the streets, though, and one day they just started doing what he said, their leader apparently recognizing in him some authority that was otherwise wholly fictitious.

Then the Spider ship had sailed into harbour, as civilized as anyone could have asked for.

There had nearly been a fight over that – not even involving the Tseni so much as the locals who remembered the Spiderlands' armada and alliance with the Empire, however that had turned out. There was only one ship, though, and it put ashore a single ambassador, an elegant woman who wanted to speak to Stenwold Maker. Of course to Stenwold Maker, who else?

She would have to make do with Eujen Leadswell, she was told.

Their meeting was strained but cordial. Eujen the student had sat there, pretending to be the important Collegiate diplomat whilst wincing at the spasms of pain afflicting his back and legs, and the Spider woman had apparently pretended to take him seriously. There had been an offer, in the midst of all the talk, and Eujen's scholarly mind had cut through the expressions of mutual need, of shared history, of regrettable recent developments, to see that the Spiders wanted a truce, a safe port, perhaps even an alliance in due course. He had heard that the fighting down the Silk Road was fierce, and more than that, he had heard that the vast reaches of the Spiderlands were beginning to show the strain of current times. There had been catastrophic earthquakes in Skaetha, the golden city at the heart of the Spiderlands' web. He had heard of a high death toll amongst the highest echelons of the Aristoi, divisions between the families, an inability to address the Empire's encroachments. Their pragmatism in coming to Collegium was almost disarming.

He would have to consult the Assembly, he had told her, and they both pretended that there still was such a thing, rather than merely a large group of people Eujen knew distantly who could each make small things happen. He would offer her and her crew accommodation in the city, but there might be some wait before she received word of any decision.

He saw the tiny wince in her expression, suppressed just a moment too late. Time was a precious commodity along the Silk Road.

Minutes after the meeting, Eujen was hurrying through a letter to Straessa because, resent it as he did, he really needed to know what Stenwold Maker thought.

His letter caught up with the Lowlander army at the gates of Helleron. The rail lines from Malkan's Folly eastwards, which the Imperials had used to send in their reinforcements, were intact, and the entire force was able to close the remaining distance to the Lowlands' eastern borders in remarkable time, using automotives rushed in from Sarn. Straessa had wondered if destroying those rail lines, if the worst came to the worst for the Wasps, should have been the job of the Auxillians whom Milus had apparently suborned. Certainly it seemed an obvious way to slow the Lowlands down and yet nobody had done it. More cracks were showing in the Imperial facade.

By the time they reached Helleron, the Empire had already abandoned the city, plainly all too aware of the place's shifting loyalties. Everyone had been expecting sly Helleren merchant lords appearing to swear smoothly that the Wasps had been their guests under protest, but a whole district of the city was in ruins, and the faces of the citizens looked stunned, unsure whether this was liberation or just a new invasion.

When the magnates did come, Milus kept them waiting, and then presented them with his demands: ammunition, fuel, supplies, automotives – with no suggestion of paying for any of it. Those who demurred, he had arrested. At the same time, Stenwold was sending Collegiates into the city to make contact with lower-level merchants, men and women who would normally wait for the nod of their betters before dabbling in this sort of politics. Enough of them were sufficiently quick off the mark to ensure that supplies were quickly rushing in on credit, because on credit was still better than free, and because being friends with Collegium and Sarn suddenly looked good.

Even now, after a pause of just a few days, Milus's people were getting ready to move out.

Eujen's missive was carried there by a civilian pilot with a swift fixed-wing who had tracked the Lowlander army by simply following the rail lines. Finding Straessa in that throng should have been harder, save that – just like Eujen himself – she was looked on as the solution to every problem, large and small, and so everyone knew where to locate her.

She took the missive eagerly, because it gave her an excuse to shake off the little mob demanding her attention. *About time, Eujen,* she thought. *Beginning to think you'd forgotten about me.*

The seal broken, she found the contents were not exactly as personal as she had hoped, but still she found herself smiling fondly, skimming over Eujen's patient setting-out of the Collegiate situation, as orderly and clear as if he thought he would be graded on it. Given that he had marked the contents for the urgent attention of Stenwold Maker, she wasn't sure why he hadn't simply bypassed her altogether. Perhaps he still felt too wary of the man to approach him directly, even in writing.

And then, just as she was despairing of Eujen entirely, came that last paragraph:

I badly want to hear the news that Maker and Milus, between them, have brought the war to some manner of satisfactory conclusion. Every child of Collegium, of whatever kinden, is

*badly missed and badly needed. I miss and need my Antspider
most of all. I will muddle on here, and do what can be done, but
I am waiting each day for the news that you are coming back to
me, and most of all for you to bring that news in person.*

And this letter is to go before Maker, apparently, she considered
with a wry smile, picturing him losing his thread, forgetting the
chief purpose of his writing. *He never did remember to read things
through.*

She excised that last paragraph deftly and went in search of
the War Master.

He was to be found with his pirates – or that was what Laszlo
had claimed the pack of Fly-kinden were. Straessa had her doubts,
principally because the thought of being cooped up on a ship
with Laszlo for any period of time felt like the prelude to homi-
cide. The pack of them had seemed just a vagrant band of
travellers, save that they had the ear of Stenwold Maker. Now,
as she approached, she saw them in a different light. Maker was
sitting at their fire, discussing something in earnest, and there
seemed no suggestion that he was just handing down orders to
them. Instead, from their cautious nods, their thoughtful looks,
it seemed they were assessing some sort of proposal he was
putting forward – but something with no guarantee of accept-
ance. After that, she also noted just how well armed they all were,
and began to wonder, *Pirates, really?* And if that was the case,
what were they doing here?

And there were others, too, she saw. Sperra was there, whom
Straessa had met before the liberation, and that big renegade
Sarnesh from Princep as well, and that weird pale Sea woman
who seemed to be at Maker's elbow much of the time, and all
of them apparently conspiring over something, thick as thieves.

She waited awkwardly at the edge of their circle of firelight –
when she tried to take a step closer, which might have allowed
her to make something of their low murmurs, one of the Fly
women gave Straessa a filthy look and shifted a crossbow slightly,

so that it was not quite directed at her. The message was clear enough.

But I'm an officer in the Coldstone Company with an urgent message . . . only she felt that wouldn't count for much with this crowd. Perhaps not with Maker either, right now.

Then she could hear distant shouting from across the camp, and a moment later another Fly – one of the Collegiates whose name Straessa should really know – dropped down right in the middle of Stenwold's gathering, almost getting herself killed several times over. She was urgently insisting, 'War Master! You have to come now!'

Stenwold stood up immediately, and a moment later he was following the Fly as she set off, Laszlo and his crew of pirates trailing after them.

Hearing a clatter of steel, Stenwold quickened his pace, feeling a multitude of old wounds tugging at him. He was keenly aware of Paladrya at his elbow, unarmoured and almost unarmed, horribly vulnerable if the camp erupted into fighting. *Is it the Wasps?* But he knew it was not. He was pushing on between the Sarnesh tents, and the Ants were not forming up, not rushing to repel an assault. They were all alert, though. Whatever drama was playing out was in all their minds. He sensed their eyes on him, the word of his approach rippling out ahead of him.

In front he saw a brief flurry of motion, heard more swords clash – a shout of pain, raised voices. One was a woman's, louder than the rest. A voice he knew.

'Hammer and tongs!' he swore and started running abruptly, lumbering along with the dumb force of a ram, hoping Paladrya could keep up. Behind him, Laszlo's people whirled in the air like a trailing tail.

Kymene! Then he saw her, held by half a dozen Sarnesh, wrestling with them furiously. There were a lot of Mynans there with drawn blades, facing off more Ants, and more arriving moment to moment from both sides, save that Sarn had so many more to draw on. Kymene was spitting, shrieking like a madwoman at – yes, at Milus. Of course, at Milus. The tactician was standing aloof, a few paces away from her, his own sword still in its scabbard. His expression was one of mild, almost scholarly interest.

'What is going on here?' Stenwold demanded, finding a pair of Ants moving to block his path. He slammed into their shields, but they braced against him and fended him off with that surprising strength of their kind.

'Stenwold!' Kymene shouted, and then got out something more that he missed, save that it was to do with her city.

Then the Ants were letting him through at some unheard order from Milus, and he stumbled forwards, aware that the *Tidenfree* crew was now holding back and, he hoped, Paladrya along with them.

'Release her!' Stenwold demanded. 'This is insane!'

Milus gave a wintry little smile. 'I am afraid I cannot allow attacks on my person, War Master – whether from enemies or supposed allies.'

'Attacks?' Stenwold looked at Kymene, seeing her scabbard empty – disarmed by the Ants or had she actually drawn on the tactician?

'Stenwold, Myna is rising!' Kymene shouted. 'We have to march for Myna, now!'

He blinked at her. 'Well, of course—'

'That is not the plan,' Milus pronounced. 'I have one destination for this army, Master Maker, and you know that. It is Capitas.' The cool boldness of that statement was sobering. 'We will cross into the Empire south of the Darakyon. We will not detour north for the Alliance lands. When the Empire is on its knees, *all* its cities shall then be free. I play no favourites.'

A good speech. Stenwold had to admit that it *was* compelling logic. If Milus believed Capitas could be taken, then the Empire could be shattered all at once. *Unless the garrisons from the north head south to take us while we're committed . . .*

'Stenwold!' Kymene insisted. 'My people are taking to the

streets now! There is an uprising in Myna *now*! You know how large the Wasp garrison there is – if we do not go to aid them, they will be slaughtered!'

The horrible twisting feeling inside Stenwold was nothing less than impotence, because Milus's logic still held. There would have been a time for the Mynans to throw off their chains, but this was not it. 'Kymene . . .' he said helplessly, and she read the thought on his face.

'Ask him!' she spat, fighting with her captors again, almost breaking free. 'Ask this flat-faced Ant bastard what he's done.'

Milus's expression admitted nothing, but Stenwold sensed the mass of assembled Mynans reaching the point where they would just lay into the vastly greater number of Sarnesh to get their leader back and, at all costs, he had to stop that.

'Enough!' he yelled out, using his Assembler's voice that had silenced dissenters in the Amphiophos for a decade. 'Release her. She's hardly about to attack anyone with her bare hands.'

The pause that followed was plainly Milus weighing the options, and then abruptly Kymene was free, shaking off her captors, her eyes still glowering bloody murder at the tactician.

There was something in Milus's face, something that all the Ant stoicism in the world could not quite hide. It was an admission that there was more to this business than his smooth words might suggest.

'A messenger arrived, half dead, from my city,' Kymene hissed between gritted teeth. 'He came in a heliopter that had been riddled with shot, and almost crashed it coming down. He told me that my people were rising against the Wasps.' She drew a ragged breath. 'He was asking where we were. Why we weren't at the gates to help them.'

'I don't understand,' Stenwold admitted. 'Help me, Kymene. What's going on?'

'*He* sent people to Myna.' She jabbed a finger at Milus, as though it could kill. 'While he was making deals with the Auxillians to sell their Wasp masters, he sent men to my city. He said that his army was coming, and that now was the time. Ask him, Maker! Hear him deny it, then come listen to my poor aviator's tale.'

Stenwold glanced between her ravaged features and Milus's infinitely composed ones. *But why would he . . .?* came to his lips and was instantly banished, because he thought that he was starting to see.

He settled on simply 'Tactician?'

The Ant met his gaze without a shadow of guilt, surrounded by tens of thousands of his kin who would implicitly understand and approve of all he had done. 'It was necessary to clear the way to Capitas.'

'Because of the garrisons in the Alliance states,' Stenwold filled in for him. 'You needed them occupied.'

'And any other forces still positioned north of our route. I am hoping for widespread revolt across the Auxillian cities as we near Capitas, too. The aim of this war is to win, War Master. The Wasps are a formidable adversary, you must admit.'

'And Myna is our ally,' Stenwold replied heavily. Kymene was shuffling from foot to foot ever so slightly, as if counting every minute in the blood of her people.

'The Mynans will win their freedom eventually, whether now or after the Wasps are defeated,' Milus explained dispassionately. 'I will not allow the Empress more time to strengthen her defences, nor divide my forces to attend to secondary objectives.'

'You think the Mynans will fight for you now?' Stenwold demanded.

Milus shrugged slightly as if in a brief token of regret, not for what he had done but at being inconveniently discovered. 'There are not so many Mynans. It is unfortunate, but apparently unavoidable.'

Stenwold eyed Kymene. Milus was correct: there were simply not so many free Mynan soldiers with the army. *Enough to save the people of Myna from the Wasps' wrath? Probably not.*

He remembered all his promises to Kymene before the war,

regarding solidarity and unity. He himself had stood beside her when the Empire came to knock down her walls and bombard her city.

When the Empire had come against his own city, she had stood beside him. She had led her people against Tynan's Second Army. They had died to keep Collegium free, so that they in turn might be freed. Their pilots had kept his city's skies safe. Their soldiers had shed blood before the walls, and then on the walls. They had never even asked him for sworn promises, because Kymene had trusted him to keep them.

He remembered Myna long, long ago, that distant day when the Wasps had first arrived. The day he and Tisamon and the Sarnesh renegade Marius had learned about the Empire the hard way. Where had Sarn been then, apart from disowning its only son who had tried to warn them about what was coming?

And indeed it was coming. And had it not been for Myna, I would never have known.

'You will march without the Mynans?' he enquired, for clarification.

'Apparently,' Milus confirmed.

'Then you will march without Collegium.'

Milus studied him for a breath. 'Reconsider,' he snapped.

Stenwold was very aware of the many, many Sarnesh gathered around him. Many of them might well be shocked and disappointed at their leader's strategy, but they would even now be subsuming those feelings into a core of loyal obedience. They were still Milus's to command, any fugitive personal feelings notwithstanding.

'You have sent to Myna, inciting an uprising on the pretence that you will come to relieve them. You have given them false hope, without which they would surely have bided their time. You have killed thousands as surely as if you had held the blade yourself.' He reached desperately for the sort of arguments that would sway Collegium. 'How will people speak of Sarn, after this?'

'As the victor!' Milus declared. 'For once, Maker, cast aside that blinkered College philosophy. The Wasps will spare nothing to defeat us, so we cannot spare ourselves any trick or advantage to beat them. What did you think, all those years ago, when you started rattling swords against the Empire? Did you think that you could lecture the Wasps into surrender? Did you think that they – or anyone! – would look over towards your sanctimonious city-state and fall to their knees in awe of your moral superiority? Victory is all that matters, Maker. Why have you been fighting to keep them out of the Lowlands for so long, if you didn't want to beat them?'

'What I have been trying so hard to keep out of the Lowlands is right here in front of me!' Stenwold spat, the words outstripping any ability he might have to check or tailor them.

'And yet I am what you have!' Milus shouted back, his thinning mask of calm cracking apart. 'Who beats the Wasps for you, if not I, Maker? Who brings down the Empire you have been preaching against for years? How will that war be won, if not by my strategy? You *need* me, Maker. You need me more than you need Myna. You need me because you need to beat the Wasps. That has always been what you have wanted. You will not throw it away now.'

Stenwold stared at him, and he was aware, just for a moment, of a brief shiver that seemed to run through the assembled Sarnesh forces, as though Milus's thoughts had abruptly yanked them viciously back into line. *All those 'I's and 'me's and not a single 'us'.*

'I will go to Myna,' he said, finding that, now the Ant had at last lost his temper, Stenwold himself was able to be quite calm.

'Then you concede the war to the Empire!' Milus hissed at him, and abruptly the Sarnesh were closing in – many of them evidently unhappily, but still they were all closing, ringing Stenwold and Kymene and the Mynan soldiers, and at that moment it was anybody's guess what the Ants were about to do.

'Will you prevent us diminishing your ranks by simply killing us all?' Stenwold asked quietly. 'And will you still hope to hold on to the Collegiate detachment then? And the Vekken? The Sea-kinden? The Tseni?'

Milus's expression was murderous, but he summoned up restraint from somewhere. 'Regarding the other Ant cities, Maker, you are too far behind the times. Believe me, we understand each other.' That was an unwelcome revelation. 'But of the rest . . .' He paused, lips moving minutely as though testing out the words. 'If we lose before the gates of Capitas, then Myna cannot hold anyway, even if you take your soldiers there now and cast the garrison out.' He was smiling now, and that was even more unwelcome. 'It's true, Maker! Fault my logic: Myna dies either way!'

Stenwold opened his mouth, glancing sideways at Kymene, trying to weigh numbers and odds and realizing that he simply did not have enough information to make the call. Every warrior he took from Milus's army was one fewer sword against the Wasps, even as it was one more towards the salvation of Myna. If there was some perfect solution to the equation it was beyond his ability to recognize.

And what of my own kin, the people of Collegium. Would they even agree? Surely most of them would back Milus, because they need to defeat the Empire. They do not need to free Myna.

But then: 'Stenwold,' Kymene hissed, and he knew: *I need to free Myna.*

'I will take Rosander's Sea-kinden, if they will follow me,' he said into Milus's face. 'I will take Maker's Own Company. That will have to be enough. The rest will remain in the command of their officers with your force.'

He sensed Milus at the tipping point, angry enough to give rash orders that Stenwold would not even hear before they were carried out, yet at the same time he remained a rational, pragmatic man. Stenwold could not hope that any better nature would win out, but merely that what he proposed would be recognized as the tactician's best chance at overall victory. *And what a mess we'll face when this is over, if it ever comes to that.*

Milus's nod was small, but the Sarnesh were abruptly stepping back, no longer crossing swords with the Mynans. The Ant leader's face was stony, but then wasn't that what his kinden were known for?

Stenwold caught a glimpse of Laszlo, though, as he turned. The Fly was staring at him desperately, and only a short while before Stenwold had been passing him assurances about the fate of Lissart, Milus's prisoner. *There is nothing I can do. No matter how hard we try to do the right thing, we still do wrong things alongside it. I am sorry.*

A company soldier was pushing forward then – the Antspider halfbreed, the officer from the Coldstone. 'Master Maker, there's a message from Collegium,' she was insisting. 'It needs . . . you can't just. . .' She was thrusting the partly torn scroll forwards, virtually into his face, and he took it from her automatically, letting his eyes skip listlessly across it, before shaking his head.

'They'll just have to sort it out for themselves,' he stated flatly. 'I don't think I'm in a position to speak for Collegium any more.'

Thirty-Four

The Second Army had now reached Capitas, having commandeered every transport in Sonn to make the last leg of the journey as fast as possible. Behind them, Tynan knew, there would be Imperial soldiers giving their lives just to slow the Sarnesh advance. It cut bitterly that he could not bring the Second to their aid. Every day the thought occurred to him: *You have disobeyed one order by abandoning Collegium. Why not another?* And yet he had not turned back. He had received a missive demanding his presence before the Empress, borne by an unsympathetic Red Watch captain who apparently looked down on a mere army general.

The meaning was plain. Word of his parting of ways with Vrakir had flown ahead of him. *That, or she really does know.* Tynan's world seemed to be fraying at the edges, the impossible bleeding into it. Who could say, any more?

He called up his underlings – Major Oski of the Engineers and a handful of others he trusted to keep order. The soldiers of the Gears ringed them round, the veterans, the survivors, a great mass of fighting men worn out by their long retreat, but all staring now as their commander made his farewells.

'I will be entering the city alone,' he told them. It was a ridiculous statement, for a general needed an escort, a personal guard. He would not give a bent coin for the lives of any who accompanied him, though, and so he would preserve his followers, and walk without companions into the trap. For a moment, he saw in his mind the image of Stenwold Maker leaving Collegium, walking towards Tynan's camp to save his Spider-kinden lover, with an honour guard behind him that the man had plainly been trying to shake off as he stepped out through the gates.

A brave leader inspires brave followers. The difference was that Tynan's orders were obeyed, and that the Wasps had the discipline to do as they were told. There would be no wasted heroics from the men of the Second, though he knew that, if he asked for volunteers, there would be no end to them.

But it's better this way. And had he not been waiting for this moment since that first time he had fallen back from the Beetle city? He truly was the man who had lost Collegium. He was owed a rebuke from the throne, and if that came with a brace of crossed spears, then he would accept it.

'It's been a privilege to command the Second,' he told them, lifting his voice so that it echoed over the heads of his men, and his words were passed back and back further by the murmurs of his soldiers. 'And you and your new commander will have to do your best, because the Lowlanders must be driven back from the Empire's borders. The fate of the Empire is in your hands!'

'In your hands, Tynan!' snapped out a new voice, and then there came an arrowhead of soldiers pushing forwards. For a moment there were hands thrust out, swords drawn, snapbows levelled, but Tynan recognized their leader and shouted for calm.

'General Marent, what is this?' And the humiliating thought, *Is he here to arrest me in front of my own men?*

The leader of the Third Army looked about him at the assembled host of Tynan's followers.

'Do not go into Capitas, Tynan,' he stated, and he too was pitching his voice for the crowd.

'Explain.'

'General Tynan, the Empress's Red Watch is waiting to arrest you as a traitor,' Marent stated.

Tynan nodded soberly. 'I had thought as much. That doesn't change—'

'Yes, it does!' Marent snapped, his tone sending a ripple of anger through the men of the Second. 'Tynan, do you think men like yourself come so cheap that the Empire can do without you now?'

'If we do not follow our orders, then men like me are worthless, Marent,' Tynan told him stonily.

'It is because you killed a Red Watch man,' Marent stated. 'You silenced a voice of the Empress. That alone is sufficient to turn the Empire's most able general into a traitor!'

Tynan could feel the temper of his soldiers rising, their loyalty to him leading them on dangerous paths. 'Quiet, you fool!' he hissed. 'Every word you speak is a danger to you and to everyone who else hears it.'

Marent shrugged. 'Tynan, my hands are red with the same blood.'

Tynan stared at him.

'How do you think I know all this? They sent a man to me to tell me I might have to command my soldiers *against* the Second Army. That man's dead now, but not before he told me all he knew. And, yes, I'm sure *she* knows, but I have an army, and so do you, and we have more real soldiers between us than the rest of Capitas can muster. And we're not alone.'

'Treason, Marent. You're truly talking treason.'

The General of the Third had the honesty to lower his gaze at that. 'I am loyal to the Empire,' he said quietly. 'The Empire needs you, Tynan. We have nobody finer to take the field against the Lowlanders. And I would happily proclaim that the Empress has been misled by evil counsel, that these Red Watch men are like the Rekef under Alvdan, the rot at the core that must be cut back. I would be the gladdest man alive to strip them away and find the Empress behind them, innocent of their evil.'

Except that . . . said his expression, and Tynan nodded wearily.

'I know,' he said, 'but I have my—'

'You do *not* know!' Marent insisted. He seemed to have forgotten his audience, now. 'Tynan, you have no idea what has been done in the Empress's name while you have had the fortune to fight a clean war against an honourable enemy. The slaves, the prison camps . . . I have heard such news that even I don't know what to believe. And her voices, her Red Watch, her Mantis bodyguard, wherever you hear of some insanity, always they are there. Tynan, we can't . . .'

'Marent—'

'No.' The younger general looked up again, his face set. 'They will kill your general!' he shouted out for every ear to hear, the voice of an officer whose commands can be heard through the tumult of battle. 'They will execute him as a traitor! Do you men believe the charge?'

The angry roar of the Second Army must have been audible deep within the city.

'Do you believe he should give himself into their hands?' Marent yelled.

Again that fierce denial.

More quietly now, Marent said, 'Tynan, if you bear the Empire any love, then you will keep camp here, and you and I will hold the bloody city to ransom if we must, because they *need* us. Piss on their Red Watch and their orders. If this city isn't to be the prize of the Ant-kinden then they will need your soldiers and mine, and they will need *you* to lead our forces.'

Tynan closed his eyes, and there was a host of voices in his mind: every commander he had served under as a young man; every order he had received; every subordinate who had taken Tynan's own words and gone off to a soldier's death because it was necessary; all of his understanding of the way the Empire functioned. *Because we obey orders. That is our strength. That is what we have had to learn. Empress to generals, generals to colonels, and so on down to the lowliest Auxillian and beyond – even to the slaves themselves.*

And does that make us all slaves, save whoever sits on the throne?

He wished – bitterly wished – that fortune-telling was real, just this once, so he could call up some shabby conjurer and have his future told, because all the tomorrows from this day were an unreadable grey mystery to him, and yet he must make his choice.

And at the last, in his mind, he heard *her* – not the Empress but that other *her*, Mycella of the Aldanrael, whom he had betrayed and murdered in obedience to his orders. How often, after that fact, had he bowed his back to the Empress's demands, thinking, *If I could not break this bond for you, what other cause is worthy of it?* But now he asked himself what Mycella would advise, and he knew that no Spider-kinden ever born would put her head into this noose.

'I stay,' he said, and was then not sure whether the words had truly passed his lips. 'I stay!' he repeated, this time loud enough that the first half-dozen ranks heard him clearly, and the cheer they raised as good as told the rest what he had decided.

Major Oski had been making ready to creep out of the Second Army camp – because fabricating an excuse to visit the capital had suddenly become more difficult following Tynan's recent decision – when the man he had been going to see simply walked into the tent that the Second's Engineers were using as their headquarters.

Oski stared at him, nodding at the visitor's salute.

'Captain-Auxillian Ernain reporting for duty,' the Bee-kinden said, expressionless.

'Right, right.' Oski nodded, glancing sidelong at the handful of other artificers who were there. 'You've been out there a while, Captain. Let's find us somewhere, and you can report.'

'Of course, sir.'

Oski retreated to stores and ousted the quartermaster lieutenant who had been quietly dozing there, citing a pressing need to count the snapbow ammunition. 'You should knock off that "sir" and "reporting for duty" malarkey right off. From you it sounds more suspicious than outright insubordination.'

Ernain grinned a little. 'I forget how comfortable I became here with the Second.'

Oski flitted back and forth about the storage tent, then did a quick circling flight of the exterior, low to the ground, looking out for eavesdroppers. He was still casting nervous looks around as he dropped back in. 'Well, report then,' he told the Bee-kinden. 'So is it happening? I've heard nothing here. Ignorant as a Commonwealer, me.'

Ernain nodded soberly. 'No more than I'm ignorant about what the pits you've been doing. You lost Collegium?'

'You would not pissing *believe* how that turned out,' Oski spat. 'Seriously, don't get me started. Only good part of it is that Red Watch bastard didn't make it out. Tynan killed the sod himself, if you can believe it.'

'About time,' Ernain acknowledged.

'After that it's been a pissing forced march all the way. Never knew a man so glad to go to his own execution . . . except suddenly that's on the back burner.' He eyed Ernain cautiously. 'So how does that fit with your plans, eh?'

Ernain looked away, studying the tent's shadowy interior. 'What's your opinion of General Tynan, Oski?'

The Fly-kinden shuffled a little. 'Honestly? A good man. Gives sensible orders, cares for his men. Is that a problem?'

'No. When the time comes, I'd rather confront Tynan than someone I didn't have a feel for. Certainly I'd rather go up against Tynan than Brugan of the Rekef, or *herself*.'

Oski shuddered. 'You've got that right,' he agreed. 'So . . . soon?'

'The Lowlanders are on their way,' Ernain said softly.

'Oh, you do *not* have to tell me that.' Oski glanced up sharply. 'There's been . . . contact? Only there was some word about Auxillian desertions already. I wasn't sure that . . .'

'There's been word come to us, yes. Their Tactician Milus has a good mind and good agents.'

The Fly's eyes went wide. 'He knows about you?'

'No, but he's guessed that someone will be doing what I'm

doing with the Auxillians, the Empire's slave cities. He makes a lot of promises.'

Oski made a doubtful noise. 'I'm not sure an empire of the Ants will be any kinder to live in than a Wasp one – a whole extra barrier between *them* and *us*. But of course he promises that's not what he wants, no doubt.'

'Of course.' Ernain smiled slightly. 'It's going to be soon, Oski, yes. And as it's Tynan, I'll be relying on you to get me to him.'

'Ah, right,' the major muttered. Well, I reckon I knew that one was coming.' He waited for Ernain to say more, but the Bee just regarded him steadily until he had to hold up his hands to ward off that scrutiny. 'All right, yes.'

'Say now if I can't rely on you.'

'You ask me that?' Oski demanded, aggrieved. 'Look, I like Tynan, yes. I've served under worse officers, believe me. And I'm no Auxillian, it's true. Citizen of the Empire, me. But yes, what you need done, I'll do.'

Ernain laid a hand on his shoulder. 'You'll hear soon. Just remember how much work and planning has gone into this; how many people will be doing their part, great or small, to bring our new world about. And how many people will be executed if this fails.'

'I know, I know,' Oski told him. 'Come on, how long've you been away, that now you don't trust me?'

For a long moment Ernain's expression was unreadable, but then the smile came back, a little sheepishly. 'I'm sorry. You're right, we're in this together, just as we always were.'

'Don't you forget it.' Oski took a deep breath. 'Now you get yourself over to the mess and eat, and do all the stuff soldiers do when they get back to camp from a long journey, and make sure you've got a good story, too. They'll ask.'

Marent's command tent was close to full when Tynan entered it, the crowd there a strangely disparate group, and he thought: *So these are who the Empire must rely on.* Even taking himself and

420

Marent into account, it was an uncomfortable thought, a symptom of the cracks that were beginning to show in the Imperial hierarchy. Where were the generals? Where was the painstaking chain of command that would answer all questions and absolve all guilt? Where was the Rekef, even? Tynan had never thought he would miss the secret service, but its absence here was like a missing tooth. *Unless someone here is a Rekef man, and just hasn't bothered to mention it.*

He and Marent were the two highest-ranking officers, nominally sharing command, and he could only be thankful that the two of them just about saw eye to eye. The moment they met some problem that made them pull in opposite directions, this entire venture would fall apart.

Over from Capitas was the aviation artificer, Varsec. Apparently General Lien himself was not willing to be seen meeting with rumoured traitor generals, but at the same time had not been able to countenance being kept in the dark. Dapper goateed Varsec was already enough of a maverick that no doubt Lien could disavow him should the need arise. The man's somewhat haunted expression suggested that he was well aware of that fact.

The Consortium colonel sitting next to Varsec was Nessen, former governor of Helleron for a fairly brief space of time, now performing a role for his corps similar to the one Varsec had for the Engineers. Tynan regarded him narrowly, remembering the difficulties the man had given Captain Bergild when she came to warn him of the Lowlander advance. Yet another man who would not bear the weight of too much trust, he guessed.

There were two others he did not know: a major in the uniform of the Slave Corps and a handsome Wasp woman sitting demurely by herself and wearing clothes that looked southern and Spider styled. The distance between her and the others was notable, and Tynan was surprised to examine his own reaction and realize that it was that gap, rather than her presence, that struck him as wrong. He had stood beside a female co-commander for too long, it seemed, and fallen prey to non-Imperial ways of thinking.

'This is Merva,' Marent said, while making a hurried round of introductions. 'She's been sent by her husband, the governor of Solarno, to deal on his behalf.'

'Solarno still has a governor? I thought the Spiders had taken it,' Tynan grunted.

'The Spiders also have it, sir,' Merva said carefully. 'We are in a unique position there.' She kept her eyes lowered, but Tynan had the impression that she was adhering to protocol only out of reluctant necessity. *Must be an interesting posting for a woman, that close to the Spiderlands.*

'Did Edvic not have any subordinates he could send?' Colonel Nessen demanded. 'This is ridiculous.'

'He sent me, sir.' This time she did look up, with a brief flash of fire. 'I have his full authority to deal—'

'Don't be stupid, woman—'

'Quiet, Nessen,' Tynan snapped. 'So she speaks for Solarno – another city heard from. Who's the slaver?'

Nessen blinked, surprised and angry, but the Slave Corps man beside him saluted and said, 'Major Vorken, sir.'

Tynan glanced at Marent. 'Why do we need him?' He had no love for the slavers, and nor did just about anyone in the regular army. They were notorious as a mob of undisciplined, slipshod profiteers, holding lower standards than real soldiers and at the same time making more money.

Marent's expression was oddly pensive. 'Because I want you to hear what he has to say. Major, your report?'

'Sir.' Vorken stood, shoulders back, head high, giving his best impression of a good soldier. Tynan listened somewhat idly to his talk of camps, the Empress's orders for the mass acquisition of slaves. He had heard something of the practice before now, and it had seemed a small enough eccentricity of the crown. He had not quite appreciated the scale of the endeavour, he now realized, as Vorken went on to give numbers of camps, estimates of slaves per camp. Tynan thought through the mathematics of it. *How can anyone keep that many slaves fed?* But next Vorken

422

was reporting just that: his own corps' essential inability to manage so many slaves in such concentrations. He told it straight, staring at the inside of the tent, unapologetic and hiding nothing. He gave a concise outline of the conditions in the camps. Tynan had assumed that was it – wasteful and unpleasant, but hardly unprecedented, for he had heard of similar excesses during the Twelve-year War.

But then Vorken began to recount the night that his own prison camp had come to an end. He kept his voice as steady as he could, but it shook a little even so, and this from a man who had made a living out of trading in flesh and misery. He got through it, though, until the slightly raw sound of his voice became almost impossible to listen to as it sawed manfully though the massacre of thousands.

'One man?' demanded Nessen. 'It's not possible.'

Vorken met his gaze. 'With my own eyes, sir. And I have heard similar from other officers. At least one other camp has been emptied by the same means. By the same *man*. And others . . .'

Varsec coughed. 'I think I can reveal that the Engineers have had orders regarding some of these camps. Involving the installation of certain machinery, to await the Empress's command.'

The image that news conjured up silenced everyone for a moment.

'I won't go into the technical details,' Varsec's voice had sunk to a hollow whisper, 'but there can be only one purpose for it all, I'm afraid. More efficient than what Major Vorken has just described, but with the same end result.'

Nessen was staring. 'You mean the Bee-killer?'

Varsec twitched slightly, then nodded. 'Of course, you were in Helleron. We had you brewing it up. And in Sonn . . . and elsewhere. Once we got the formula, she did seem to need an awful lot of it.' He sounded somewhat sick. This was a long way from the clash of orthopters that he had made his speciality.

'Enough.' Tynan clapped his hands together, to capture their attention and break the tension. 'Marent, you knew most of this ahead of time, I'm sure, for you to gather us together like this.' *Tell me how far you intend to go.*

The general of the Third nodded unhappily. 'It's this simple. You and I have already made the decision. There is a rot at the heart of the Empire, and it is *her*.'

'Be very careful what you say, Marent,' Tynan warned him.

'While she holds the throne—'

But Tynan lifted a hand immediately to silence him. 'No more.'

'Tynan, you've just heard—'

'No.' Tynan shook his head. 'Because where you're going . . . we've already seen that. You won your general's rank badge in the war against the traitor governors. Do you think a war against the traitor generals will be any better? That way lies the end of the Empire.'

'Tynan—'

'If for only one reason: who takes her place, Marent? Even were she just to die right now, of no unnatural cause at all, what would we do? How many would step forward to put a hand on the throne and tear off a piece? How many would rally a city or two behind them, and demand the recognition of the rest? It would be the end of it all, Marent. The Empire would shatter. She is our Empress, however mad, however flawed, because at least, whilst everyone is agreed on that, the Empire still exists.'

Marent took a long, deep breath. 'I would pledge my sword and my soldiers to you, General Tynan. All the Empire knows you.'

The silence within the tent was keen and brittle, the others studying Tynan, waiting for the first stones of history's landslide. Nessen looked horrified, Varsec thoughtful, the slaver was almost expressionless, his major's rank shielding him from the burden of having a say. Tynan found himself looking to Merva and seeing such a calculating expression there that he wondered how much time she had really spent with the Spiders in Solarno.

'No,' he said simply. 'I am a soldier, therefore I will defend the Empire and throw the Lowlanders back where they came

424

from. When our borders are secure, when the war is done, I will submit to the judgment of the throne. If you ask me to defy the Empress to save the Empire, I will, but the same logic compels you afterwards. If we love the Empire so much, we must bow the knee to it when the danger is past, and accept the consequences of our defiance. And she is the Empire – all the Empire we have.'

'But what about Vorken's report – the camps, what she's doing there?' Marent demanded. 'It's gone beyond madness. She's gutting the Empire, herself.'

And he's right, and yet . . . anarchy. Cast down the Empress – the very thought sent a cold shudder through him – *and we will fall apart. The deaths of thousands of slaves, yes, but . . .* He glanced at Vorken, met the man's stare – reading there not a demand for help but something closer to defiance. *Has he . . .? Surely not the Slave Corps taking a stand, after all this time?* For a moment he was desperately spinning the wheels of his mind, trying to find some way out of the maze that would leave him with an intact Empire and an intact conscience at the same time, but there was nothing. He was no great statesman, no philosopher. *So where's Stenwold Maker when you need him?* A dry thought. *If I'd caught him in Collegium, would I have him with me now, in chains, to advise me? Would he see a way clear that I cannot?*

But I cannot. That is all there is to it.

'I am a soldier,' he repeated. 'I will fight this war, and no further. Because the moment we try to seize the Empire, we will lose it, all of it. And then the Lowlanders will just pick over our bones when we've finished killing each other.'

Marent's mouth twisted unhappily, and Tynan wondered just how far ahead he had planned into the reign of Emperor Tynan the First. He had no counter-argument, though, and neither did any of the others.

Thirty-Five

The soldiers of the Worm were right behind them, and Totho could feel them catching up. Their presence was like a blanket laid over his mind, stifling those parts of it that understood the weapon he carried and the artifice that had gone into its construction. At the same time, there was almost no light – just his lantern and a few brands carried by the fleeing refugees. *If I could achieve range.* But at the distance he would need from his enemy to know his own mind, he would have no target but the vast canvas of the darkness itself.

He heard the first cries from the blackness behind, indicating the slowest of the fugitives falling to the blades of the pursuit. Ahead, others were breaking off from the flight – the boldest, the most desperate, those who had dependants still fleeing. Totho caught mad, wheeling glimpses of their faces as they gave up their chance at life: great solid Mole Crickets towering over him, the runners dodging about them as though they were features of the landscape; stocky Beetle-kinden wielding stolen Worm swords; Moth-kinden slingers who perhaps would trust to their wings to carry them away at the last.

Messel, he saw too. Messel was now stopping, a sling in his hands. A blind man with a sling. It seemed to summarize everything that Totho had so far seen of this insane, terrifying place.

'Move!' he yelled. 'Messel, go! I need you to take me to Che!'
A Beetle man pushed past, a screaming child laid over his shoulder.

Totho reached for the eyeless man's shoulder but Messel just stepped away, sensing, somehow, where his hand would fall.

'Go.'

'Come on, you witless imbecile!' Totho shrieked at him. 'Move, you blind bastard!'

Messel's teeth were bared, and Totho saw that he was shaking with fright. He had his sling whirling, though, and the fighting sounded very close. 'I am doing her will,' he spat.

'Who – Che?' Totho demanded. 'You, this . . . Do you even . . .?'

A vast Mole Cricket woman barrelled past towards the fighting, bellowing out what sounded more like a dirge than a battle cry. She had a great metal hammer in one hand, already whirling in a wide underarm stroke, and it made contact even as she passed Totho, sending one of the Worm's bodies flying, broken and loose jointed, into the darkness.

'Please, Messel!' Totho insisted. 'Che needs to . . . I need to get to Che. I . . .' He swore furiously, setting his lantern down then and skidding it across the stony ground towards the onrush of the Worm.

He saw only a brief glimpse of their charge before he went fleeing into the dark, scrambling, battering his mailed shins against the rocks, then understanding fell back into his mind, his distance from the Worm just sufficient for it, and he turned and levelled his snapbow.

He saw them approaching there, just shadows dashing past his lamp, and he loosed and loosed, emptying the weapon, then slotting another magazine into place and emptying it again, every shot a hit, every hit a kill – and sometimes more than one, as the bolts tore through more than one body. But he ran out of bolts before they ran out of Worm, and when his weapon clicked empty, they were still coming. Then one of them kicked his lamp, quite inadvertently, and that bright, hopeful flare was plunged into darkness.

He could see the few brave torches of the fugitives, and he made for them, skidding and stumbling into their ranks, desperate to find Messel, to drag him from the fray and abscond with the man so that the knowledge lurking behind his eyeless visage might be preserved. Then someone drove a blade at him and Totho staggered back under the impact, the now-useless snapbow dropping from his hands.

The Worm were on him, three or four of them, but he got his own sword out as their blows fell on his armour, one arm up to protect his head. *Should have worn the helm. Not as though there's much to see down here, anyway.*

He lunged, with one of the enemy virtually falling onto his blade, the bronze scales of its armour parting with minimal resistance against his keen steel.

He was no swordsman, not really, but he had fought. He had been trained in the Prowess Forum, and marched with the Empire, and held the bridge at Khanaphes.

He had no sense of the rest of the world, right then, hacking at everything that presented itself in the hope that it was an enemy. His edge bit home over and over, though he took half a dozen blows for each one he struck. They rattled and banged against his indomitable mail, a constant shock and jolt that he almost found himself becoming used to.

Given a few moment's breath, after killing his seventh, he donned his helm. He had been a fool to go without it. In his head was still that yawning abyss where understanding had once sat, but he had now completed his shell that was hard proof against the weapons of the enemy. They were faster than him, and they were so very many, but he let them break like a tide against his carapace, body after body of them as the Worm tried to bring him down. Its coils were all about him, laying hands on him, stabbing and hacking and sawing, but he lopped at wrists and thrust at faces and cut and cut and cut, and the soulless husks fell away, and tripped him even after they were dead.

Then the last fugitive lantern, which had been burning on its side where some desperate slave had dropped it, went out.

He found it made no difference. He had long ago lost any ability to dodge or to ward off the enemy, and they were all around him, leaping onto the razor of his blade, dragging at him, pulling him down.

His sword lodged deep in one and left his hand, but by then he had barely been able to swing it. He felt hands on him, crawling for weak points but not understanding how the mail was made: a blade trying to pry between the lames of his shoulderguards, nails scratching impotently at his helm but missing the eyeslot.

Then nothing, a sudden cessation of movement, so that he lay half covered by the fallen, sightless and alone.

Or not alone? It was dark, so how could he know what was creeping softly towards him. Bizarrely, this sensation of uncertainty inspired a deeper dread than the actual fighting had. How much better to *know* that they were trying to kill you.

'Do you live?'

A voice. A human voice. Though his enemies had looked like men, he could not imagine them aspiring to anything so familiar as speech.

'Stranger, do you live?'

A voice he had heard recently. Messel's voice.

'Just about,' he replied to the darkness. 'I lost my sword. Get these bastards off me.'

He held still, feeling dead flesh slide and shift away, cringing from the unlimited blackness on all sides. At last he sat up, feeling a thousand small bruises, but no more.

That's good mail. And he properly understood that it was, and why, and realized that the enemy were gone for now. *And my armour and my sword, they are an artifice the enemy cannot take from me. I do not need to understand their metallurgy or their forging to benefit from them.*

'We got the lot?' he asked.

'They are dead. You and I live. I stood in your shadow as you fought. Your last enemy, I slew myself.' Messel sounded slightly awed. 'You are truly her champion.'

'I . . .' It sounded wrong, spoken like that. 'I came to rescue her.'

There was a choking sound, and for a moment Totho could not identify it.

Messel was laughing awkwardly. He probably did not get much opportunity to do so.

'Rescue?' the blind man wheezed. 'From what? From all of the Worm? From my world?'

'I thought she would be . . .' *Someone's prisoner, or something, not queen of the new revolution.* 'That's why I came, anyway.'

A pause long enough for Totho to worry that Messel had just crept away, until at last he demanded, 'Get me light,' just to prompt a reaction. 'A lantern, Or just something that will burn. I have a lighter here.'

'You are a magician?'

'Piss off,' Totho snapped, and then, a little more gently. 'I . . . you don't need to be a magician to set stuff on fire, believe me.'

'To have got here at all, you surely must be a magician.' There was a strained tone to the man's voice.

'There was a cave, and your Worm bastards had been in and out of it. I wanted to go and get Che out, so I went in after them. No magic, just my feet.'

He heard a sharp, ragged breath, and then something prodded him. When he snatched at it, he found a handful of leathery stalks.

'You walked into the lair of the Worm? From the *outside*?'

Totho waited until after he had coaxed a flame from his steel lighter and applied it to the stalks. The tough fungal growth took light only stubbornly, leaving him staring dumbly at the little gadget in his hand, its function and use rapidly fading from his mind.

Which means . . .

'They're back!' he spat, but Messel was already tugging at his arm.

'Now is the time to run!' And he was swiftly away on the trail

430

of the fugitives. Totho ripped his sword from one of the bodies around him and then stumbled off in Messel's wake, running straight into a world of darkness and trying to keep up, the blind leading the blind.

'It's not working,' was Thalric's harsh assessment. 'Yes, we're managing to get plenty of people out before the Worm-kinden turn up. But fight? A rebellion? I've seen them, Che. They can't fight. They have no training, no discipline, borrowed weapons and precious little courage. Most of them have been afraid their whole life. They're just slaves, Che.'

'And you know about slaves,' she said bitterly.

He shrugged, needing to add nothing.

'But . . . Myna,' she persisted. 'They threw off the Empire.'

'And there were still some there who remembered a time before we invaded, and they are a warrior people, like the Ants, like my kinden. This lot? They're hopeless, Che. Even the ones that have some heart are just getting themselves killed. And it's worse than that. We've gathered a whole load with us here, yes, but we've not saved them from anything. We're running out of everything. If the Worm hadn't required its slaves to find their own food, everyone here would have starved long ago. But this is like living in a desert, down here. They've scoured this place bare already, and there are almost no stocks left.'

They were in the midst of a great sprawling slum composed of the Worm's slaves, people who had fled their homes with whatever they could carry, or nothing at all. A host of them stretched into the darkness on all sides, and behind Che their numbers scaled a cave-pocked rock face as well. They were desperate, all of them. Had they stayed where they were, then the Worm would have harvested most of them to aid it in its push towards the wider world, but it now seemed she had just delayed the inevitable.

She looked from Thalric's face to that of Tynisa, who had been brooding over her own thoughts. 'Give me options, then,' she urged them.

She had been hoping for Tynisa to suggest some piece of Mantis-kinden aggression, some mad strike at the heart of the Worm. Instead, her foster-sister just shook her head. 'I can't fight, Che,' she murmured. 'Whatever this Worm does, it . . . I'm hurt, Che. The wound comes back, whenever they're near, and I can't get free of it. I don't know what to do. I'm sorry.'

Thalric grimaced. 'As for me, I don't know about your . . . end of things, but it's the same problem. Yes, you can defeat a more numerous army, especially as these Worm-kinden aren't exactly tacticians and don't have much variety of troops. You need something more, though: better equipment, better training. If we could get them coming after us, and control where they went, then . . . traps maybe. These wretches are good for a rock-slide, but that needs very specific terrain, and we only get one shot at it in any engagement. And anything more complex than that . . . we have no artifice to rely on, because of their . . . that thing they do. What they take from us. And I've tried. I've even tried to make sharpshooters from our slingers, to kill off the scarred bastards. Except *they're* not actually leading the fight. I get the feeling they can guide matters, add some strategy, but sometimes the Worms fight even better when they're not there.'

'Perhaps we can . . . attack their city,' Che whispered. 'That is where their master is, the mind behind them all. If we could . . . somehow . . .'

'Che, Esmail's just returned from there, and he says it can't be done,' Thalric cautioned. 'He also says the place is crawling with them. All the Worms who aren't hunting us or actually . . . heading up, whatever . . . are there, in that city. Which means that if we tried to go there, we'd basically end up fighting all the locals plus every single one of them who's already trying to find us. Which is almost all of them. And it's not as if this pack of bolt-fodder could pull off a sneak attack, even if the enemy couldn't see in the dark . . . even if they ever actually slept, which Esmail says they don't. And most of our fodder here aren't even combatants, by any stretch of the definition.'

Che was staring at him desperately, and she realized that this was the limit: that she had thought him sufficiently resourceful in ruthless ways she herself could not countenance, and that he would always have a plan. He just looked at her, a man who had left his hope behind, his face gaunt and pale in the unhealthy firelight.

After having slept, cold and shivering on the hard stone, surrounded by the quietly mounting misery of those she had wanted to save, she woke and had no new answers, except to know that the pressing needs from before had only become more pressing.

Then Messel arrived. She saw him heading through camp with a knot of people trailing in his wake – new arrivals – asking questions and being pointed towards her. It was strange, for to start with she had been almost unable to distinguish him from the rest of his eyeless kinden. Now she couldn't imagine not knowing him. It was just a matter of looking beyond that absence.

'Cheerwell,' he hailed her. He looked grimy and ragged and worn to a nub, but terribly animated, as though something within him was on fire. 'I must speak to you. Something remarkable has happened.'

'I could use something remarkable,' she replied sadly. 'Sit with me, Messel, please. Tell me.'

Tynisa and Thalric were just stirring, but the blind man's next words startled them fully awake.

'There is a name . . . a man you know. Totho, he called himself.'

Che felt her world shift sideways abruptly; things she thought she had understood suddenly uncertain. 'How can you know that name?'

'I was with him,' Messel told her. 'He came here searching for you.'

'That's impossible,' she told him flatly. 'He's no . . . he's nothing that could come here. There's no way . . .'

'He *walked*,' Messel insisted. 'He entered a cave he had seen the Worm use, in their raids.' His hands clutched at the air, as though groping for understanding. 'Cheerwell, the Seal, you said it cracked . . . and then that it was broken.'

'Yes.'

'If only we had the Teacher,' Messel muttered, for Esmail had brought back the news of Orothellin's death. 'I do not understand the way things were, in that time he spoke of, before this place was made as it is. But . . .'

'The domain of the Worm – of the Centipede-kinden – was underground,' Che said slowly. 'That means . . .'

'I understand "underground", from the Teacher's stories. But at that time there was no seal, and the Worm walked in and out of its domain, and he said that there were those of the Old World who walked in also – ancestors of some of us here. What now, with the Seal gone?' Messel asked at last. 'If the Seal kept us from the Old World, what keeps us from it now?'

Che stared at him, knowing that Thalric and Tynisa must be wearing kindred expressions.

'You mean . . .' the Wasp said, 'we can get *out*.'

Che took a deep breath. 'Everyone can get out. Every single person can get out. If we can get people to some caves, any caves that carry on through into the world. It doesn't defeat the Worm. It won't save the lands above. But it can save the people here, for now. Messel . . . did Totho say where he came in?'

'I know the place,' the blind man told her. 'There *are* caves there. They go . . . when I was there, they went nowhere. Now . . .'

'Where is Totho?' Tynisa asked.

Che froze, an appalling dismay falling upon her. *Why did I not even think to ask?* For surely Totho was not amongst the handful that Messel had been trailing.

Messel's hands twitched, and he explained.

He and Totho had been with a fleeing band of refugees. The Worm had been behind them, gaining pace, but it had still seemed as though they might break away, at some cost – that some at least of the fugitives might escape.

Then the second Worm column had been sighted ahead of

them. Messel did not know if this was some actual plan of the Worm, or just unfortunate chance. At that point, of course, it had not seemed to matter.

'Some fought,' he recounted sadly. 'Most . . . just remembered how life had been under the Worm. That it had still been life, despite all. And they gave up: some the Worm killed, and others the Scarred Ones took away, to their city.'

Esmail had said that the priests of the Worm seemed to be sacrificing more and more to their uncaring god. Che imagined that they must see the end of their own world here, with the Worm focused more and more on its intended new conquests.

'And Totho?' she pressed.

Messel shrugged. 'He did not break free with the few I managed to get out. I cannot say what his fate was.'

She sent for Esmail and the Hermit, and they came reluctantly. The Assassin had been brooding since his recent return from the city of the Worm, and his news regarding Orothellin had hit the renegade Scarred One hard. Neither looked impressed when Che told them she needed their help.

She explained about Totho. That did not help much.

'So this friend of yours, whom I wouldn't know from a stranger, might have turned up down here and might have been captured, and might be in their city right now, instead of just torn apart and already feeding their fields, or their bellies,' Esmail summarized in disgust.

'Esmail, please,' Che said simply. 'The two of you can go to that place safely. Or I'll go myself, but I need one of you to take me.'

'And she's needed here,' Thalric interjected, over her shoulder. 'Because at least some of the people will listen – and listening to Che's the only thing that'll save them.'

Esmail moved to make some sharp retort, then bit it back. 'Is it true that you can get out? That we can all get out?'

'I hope so,' Che told him. 'We have nothing else, now.'

435

The Assassin closed his eyes, considering. 'If I – we – go, he may not be there. He may even be there but hidden from us. Even if we find him, we will not be able to get him out.'

'Cut the scars into him and hide him. At least try,' Che insisted, a surge of frustration welling up inside her. She had intended to say, 'please' like the good Beetle girl she had been brought up as, but instead she found herself standing up, with some unspoken word echoing about them. Esmail's eyes were wide as he scrabbled back.

'What?' Thalric demanded, and Tynisa's sword was already clear of its scabbard. But Che was still trying to work out what had just happened, what she had done. Esmail was regarding her in a different way, now – respect and fear together.

'You have it back,' he murmured. 'For just a moment . . .'

'I have what?' Che asked, almost plaintively.

'The crown, the mark of the Masters that I saw on Seda . . . and on you, before we came down here. The magic came back for a moment.'

It was true that they were far from the Worm – or so she hoped – and so its deadening, levelling smog was not robbing her of the ability even to consider magic. Still, this place was parched dry of power, choked off from the world beyond, a dead place drained of its strength by the Moths and their Seal . . .

Their broken Seal.

Che felt an odd flutter. *Like a disarmed duellist finding a dagger in her belt.* That door was open only a crack, but did she perhaps have more options than she had realized? The Worm's cavern realm was open to the world once more, and she could reach out for the magic that still existed outside. But, more, the *Seal* was gone. All that magic tied up in one place to keep the Worm locked away, and now the great knot of it was undone, all that magic was freed to . . . to do what? To drain away, even as all the magic had? Or could she still grasp for it?

'Will you do it?' she asked Esmail.

'I cannot promise that I can accomplish anything, still less

436

save your friend,' he told her, 'but I will go. I will search for him.'

'And you?'

The Hermit had stood silent through this whole exchange, merely glowering at her. 'Me? Return to that place? To my people? Forget myself that much, eh? Would I come back, I wonder? Now that *he's* dead, should I even care?'

'Please . . .'

The old man shook his head angrily. 'I would lose myself. Then I would be gone. Without Orothellin, what am I but a broken-off piece of the Worm. I will not go. Let this fool go back to that place. I will not go.'

That night she tried to dream. She lacked the props she had once used to retain the pictures that issued from her sleeping mind, but she simply concentrated, meditated and absorbed the slow filtering of magic that was permeating this world for the first time in a thousand years.

Who else here, after all, could make use of it?

To her reopened mind, the cavern world was a continuum strung from the bright flare of the outside down towards the obscuring murk of the Worm itself. Up above, beneath the sun and moon, she could touch Seda distantly and feel the Wasp woman trying to reach back towards her.

Che, I need your strength! I am so close! I can defeat the Worm!

And then there was a sense of some great plan in motion, forces of ritual like great stone slabs sliding into place, leaving Che terrified and appalled and yet unable to say exactly why. The details did not come through.

And, besides, she was seeking a different communion. She was trying to find Totho.

I know him so well, after all. We were friends for so long. If he is down here, and living still, then surely I can find him.

But she hunted and hunted, gaining transient glimpses of other groups of slaves – fleeing, dying or squatting in filth and misery

437

as they waited for their end. Even if Che got her current charges out of this charnel world, they represented only a fraction. So many more would die; so many more were already dead.

But there was no sign of Totho, and so she turned her attention to that coiling blot at the heart of the world – where the Worm dwelt.

By now she was deep in dreams, her revelations progressively less reliable, more likely to be the product of her own wishes and needs. When she did find a momentary contact with a familiar personality – the callused edges of his innocence, his earnest striving, his bitterness towards the world – it was a fleeting thing, and she could not know for sure if she had found him after all.

More likely he was dead. More likely he was smothered beneath the cloud of the Worm's influence, and she could not reach him at all. Or else his own stubborn Aptitude prevented her from touching him.

Or perhaps I just don't know him as well as I should do.

Thirty-Six

The Red Watch man – he never revealed his name – entered the governor's residence in Myna as though he owned it.

In truth, just getting here had been a struggle. Myna itself was in chaos, the streets fiercely contested between the Wasp garrison and the local forces. *It's as though they know what we're about to do*, Gannic thought. The reality of what they were planning – what his vaunted technical expertise would propagate – was something he was doing his best not to think about.

There were lines drawn now. The governor had been sent his orders, and the garrison forces had done their best to corral the bulk of the Mynans into a single district, pushing them up through the tiers of the city until they were crammed into its highest areas. By then, there were no intact flying machines left in native hands, and the Imperial Spearflights and Farsphex could drop incendiaries on the locals to their heart's content. Except that orders forbad it.

In actuality, a great part of the city was not safe for either side. Insurgents were constantly breaking out and setting traps and ambushes for Wasp forces, or being caught and killed in turn. Keeping the Mynans bottled up was a constant struggle.

The great governor's palace, which had once dominated the city for more than a decade, had been torn down by the ingrate locals after they had driven the Empire out during the last war, but they had yet to replace it with anything else. Their interim government had been keeping the Empire's seat warm in a structure still only half complete when the Wasps returned, and that building had been methodically destroyed during the retaking of the city. Instead, the garrison had fortified its own district, turfing out all locals and barricading all the streets. In between those two districts of concrete loyalty, the Wasps had a fair run of the streets, but their control was piecemeal.

The airship, with its lethal cargo, had been shot at by ballistae when it arrived over the city – and Gannic was by no means sure that all those incoming bolts had been Mynan. It was a fearful chaos down there, and the thought of what might have happened, had some explosive cracked open the hull, did not bear thinking about. When at last they had the vessel anchored to the ground, he breathed a sigh of relief.

He had thought, without much hope, that he might be able to hand over responsibility to the local engineers. The Red Watch man kept close to him, though, leaving the airship under heavy guard and snapping at any of the garrison men who tried to get in his way. Gannic remembered the way the Rekef had always worked. Yes, the name had inspired fear, but its presence had been subtle – everywhere and nowhere: could be your superior officer or the man next to you on parade, or even your own slave. The Red Watch was nothing but a fist backed by the Empress's writ. It was great power given to little men. Gannic, a little man himself, knew how that would feel. *Oh, what I'd do if only I . . .*

The Mynan governor was an old soldier with grey in his hair and a jagged scar on his face, seconded out from the army as a reward for long service, but given the poisoned chalice of this city because he was a warrior still.

'So, what have you brought me?' he demanded. He seemed less awed by the Red Watch than the rest were.

'Orders, Colonel,' the Red Watch man told him. 'The Empress's voice. May we speak in private?'

The colonel's expression was wary, but a flick of his fingers sent his junior officers out of the room. 'This Myna business, it's absurd,' he commented. 'They're fighting like madmen. The whole city's up in arms, all of a sudden. I don't have the forces to keep them bottled up. I've sent to the Szaren garrison for reinforcements. I sent to Capitas, too. Apparently you're who they sent in response.'

'It seems that way,' the Red Watch man confirmed. 'Other reinforcements will not be necessary. The Empress has decided to settle the Mynan question once and for all.'

Gannic had thought the colonel would take this as typical Capitas bombast, but the man looked thoughtful. 'My men say you've a whole load of metal barrels on that boat of yours.'

'Yes, Colonel.'

'I was fighting near here in the last war, you know. Some bad pieces of business in this region. You hear all sorts. Some kind of madness-weapon in Tharn, they say. And then there was the Szaren garrison. What was it they called that stuff the Colonel-Auxillian had?'

The name made Gannic start guiltily, and the Mynan governor did not seem surprised, only disappointed. 'So you're here with orders for me to win the war that way, are you?'

'No, Colonel. My orders are to relieve you of your position and have you return to Capitas.'

Gannic wasn't sure whether he or the colonel was more startled by that statement.

'Are you mad . . .?' The governor – *former* governor – tailed off because the Red Watch man now had a hand directed towards him, palm outwards.

'Effective immediately. Show him the orders, Gannic.'

Unwillingly dragged into the dispute, Gannic took the scroll from the man's other hand and hurried over to the governor, making sure not to get between them.

The colonel pointedly ignored the threatening palm, breaking the seal on his orders and perusing them as calmly as he was able. 'I see,' he observed. 'And Her Majesty's commands will of course be 'obeyed.' His eyes flicked up. 'I shall depart for Capitas to clear this mess up myself. I note that, in my absence, you are acting governor. Congratulations.' Gannic had never heard a more bitter word uttered. 'One question,' the colonel added. 'Why?'

'Because she knew you would not go through with it, in the end,' the Red Watch man told him flatly. 'Sometimes the Empire needs special servants to carry out special tasks.'

'Is that what you are?' The ex-governor's tone was dripping with disgust.

'This is insane. Why don't they fight?' Castre Gorenn complained.

The Lowlander army had reached Sonn, the predominantly Beetle city that was one of the Empire's great centres of industry.

In actual fact, there had been fighting. The local garrison force, or whatever, had come out and destroyed the rails west of Sonn and then fortified themselves as best they could outside the city. They had fought doggedly and well, but the Lowlanders had outflanked and heavily outnumbered them. The Sarnesh had got in close because the Wasps had not been willing or able to retreat from their positions, and that had been that. At the time nobody had understood why they had not retreated back to the city.

Now it seemed that the good people of Sonn had ideas of their own.

The army of the Lowlands was currently mustering, division by division, in the city's rail yards, embarking on the carriages of rail automotives about to head east with all the speed of the Apt age. The local Beetles had only seemed apologetic that the Empire had already stripped them of their great lifter airships.

'You remember Helleron, Gorenn?' Straessa enquired, watching the Collegium contingent begin to climb aboard.

'Disgusting place,' the Dragonfly spat. 'But much like this one, yes. Like twins that were separated.'

'Well, you might not know, but Helleron got a bit of a reputation after the first war,' the Antspider explained to her. 'Basically, for kissing the arse of whoever turns up with more soldiers. Now, I remember hearing that the Wasps were putting a lot into modernizing this place, Sonn – factories and the like, and all built with Helleren knowhow. Every tramp artificer from west of here was guaranteed a good salary, if the Rekef didn't take them up and torture them to death, you know.'

Gorenn made a rude noise.

'At the time, I remember, everyone was saying how this meant that Helleron wouldn't even pretend to think about it when the Wasps came knocking again and, sure as death, that was the right call. But there was something Eujen said. He was all for the exchange. He said that whatever Helleron learned from the east, the Sonnen would learn just as much from the west.' There had even been a rumour that the Sonnen had been ordered to destroy the rail line east of their city and had mysteriously failed to do so, as a gesture of appeasement towards Milus. In return, aside from some requisitioning of supplies and automotives, their city had been left almost unmolested.

Meanwhile the soldiers of the Coldstone Company were starting to file aboard, shouldering their kit. Gorenn looked around her, past the throng of soldiers, to the locals themselves. They were mostly Beetles, with some Flies and even a few Wasps standing in carefully passive poses. There was a remarkable lack of black and gold, as though everyone had been stockpiling spare clothes of neutral hues.

'Thing is,' Straessa went on, 'the Wasps were basically as fed up with Helleron's weathervane thing as everyone else, and so they wanted their own tame Helleron right here in the Empire. And that's what they got, I reckon. Perfect in every detail – right up to the surrendering.'

Gorenn let out a brief yap of laughter at that but, when Straessa turned to nod her on to the carriage, the Dragonfly looked sad.

'What's the matter?'

'It's . . . is this it? Is this the world, now, outside the Commonweal borders?'

The Antspider blinked. The Gorenn she knew was bright, hard, almost insanely optimistic. The Commonweal Retaliatory Army, she had called herself, and had appeared to believe it. Straessa had not seen this solemn Dragonfly face before.

'We fought the Wasps,' Gorenn said softly. 'It was hopeless. We fought and we fought. My whole family . . . everyone I knew. But we fought, because that is what one does. That is how it is in the stories. That's how it's always been. And now you clever Apt have invented a new way of being invaded, a clever way that means you do not have to fight. Like all your Apt things –' she waved a hand at the automotive that they were about to board – 'it makes your lives easier and more comfortable, and at the same time it robs you of something of worth that you do not know enough to miss.'

'*We're* fighting,' Straessa reminded her, giving her a shove to get the woman into the carriage.

'Are we?' Inside, Gorenn turned back to her. 'I don't know what the tactician is doing. Fighting is part of it, yes.'

There was one carriage reserved for Milus himself, guarded by his soldiers and only accessed with his direct orders. The tactician spent most of his time elsewhere, however, sitting amongst his troops, just one anonymous Ant amongst many. He would be able to receive reports from every soldier in his army, keep an eye on all the others – the Mantids and the Lowlanders and the like – and take reports from the scouts who were checking the integrity of the rail line ahead. Sometimes he spoke face to face with Ants of the other cities, such as Tsen and Vek. It was the first time that military leaders of different Ant-kinden city-states had done so in living memory.

The interior of Milus's private carriage had been stripped bare – no comforts here, and certainly not anything too flammable. Some machinery had been installed – a few unique pieces brought by Milus himself, but also a good deal of equipment that had been freely available in Imperial Sonn. The artificers who tended it were specialists, equally at home with the anatomies of metal and flesh.

Lissart shivered. Her world was reduced to this. She had fought and fought to preserve her freedom, defying every master who would lay a hand on her. She had defied the Empire, and she had fled poor Laszlo, and all in the name of not being bound by the world or anyone in it.

The other tenet of her life – that she was cleverer than the rest – had been the one to break under her small weight and to land her here. She had hooked on to Milus as a useful source of amusement – why should she be not be able to play some dull Ant with titbits of knowledge about the Empire and the Inapt? Everyone knew that Ants were plodding unimaginative creatures, and that it took a dozen of them to have an idea between them. She had out-thought Wasps and Spiders and Fly-kinden. Ants should have been no challenge. She had not reckoned on Milus, however.

He had seen through her. He saw through most things. Having now had a proper opportunity to study him from the unenviable vantage point of being his prisoner, she knew what he was. Ant or not, he was a kindred spirit to her. He walked through the world as though he was the only solid thing in it, as though everything else was just a kind of mist that he could shape as he liked. She knew him better than the other Ants who shared his mind, because he never let them into the main parts of it. He was a singularity amongst his kinden: a man who could feign sharing and yet hold himself private and aloof.

He had got information from her, at first. He had found new ways to torture her – utilizing the cold machines that she was staring at even now. Then the information had run dry, the Sarnesh war effort expanding beyond her knowledge of the Empire. But the machines had not stopped. He had come sporadically, when his busy schedule allowed it, and made her scream for him. He had taught her what he wanted, what would spare her the worst – not complete acquiescence, but a carefully judged

445

combination of defiance and surrender. He liked her to fight him.

Only because he thinks I can't win.

But, right now, she could not win. They had long ago found the limits of her fiery Art, and now her hands were kept locked away in gloves, as her wings were suppressed by the Fly-manacles across her back.

When they moved her into this carriage, she had been desperately on the lookout for some sign of hope, but she had not even spotted Laszlo in the brief moments before she had been bundled in here.

She found she had faith left in him, though: that he had not forgotten her. It was a tenuous thread to cling to, especially as he was such a fool, but she had little else. Until now.

Now she had company. She might have preferred company that wasn't a Wasp, but anyone was better than nothing.

He had been taken by force, judging from the bruises and the cuts, but he was wearing Lowlander clothes.

'My name is Aagen,' he explained to her. 'I come from Princep Salma.'

She was enough of a rumour-gatherer that this name rang bells. There had been a Wasp who was ambassador to Collegium, but had perhaps been killed or perhaps deserted, and perhaps was right here in front of her.

'That didn't work out, then?'

'It did until the Sarnesh walked in.' He was bound as well, hands behind his back and strapped together to stifle his sting. 'Who are you?'

'Te Liss.' She wasn't sure why she had fallen back on her Solarnese name, but telling her real one never felt right.

'You were . . . what? Why are you here?'

The official answer was, *Because I was an Imperial agent.* But she went with, 'Because Milus is a bastard,' which seemed truer.

'I was supposed to be assisting the tactician. I told them that

446

'I did not flee to Princep because I wished to betray the Empire. I simply wanted . . . I wanted out. I wanted to be . . . somewhere they wouldn't make me choose sides,' Aagen told her.

'Well, I know what that's like,' she agreed. 'Just like I know that people like Milus don't see things that way, whatever side they're on.'

'We're on the Sonn–Capitas rail now,' Aagen said softly. 'That's my home, ahead of us. A huge Lowlander army, moving east as fast as the automotives can haul them, a string of carriages a mile long, with thousands of soldiers, supplies, munitions, this deep into the Empire . . . It's unthinkable. Where can this lead?'

'I assume your presence here means that Milus wants your help with that question,' she observed.

'They just came and took me from the Princep camp . . . just grabbed me and marched me off. Nobody stopped them – it's not as though the Ants have much use for us in Princep. I think Balkus would have . . . but he would have died. I'm amazed they didn't take him as well, but Ants follow orders, and maybe Milus didn't think to give that one yet. I didn't think that Milus would . . .'

'I think he'd do any cursed thing he wants,' Lissart said. She was thinking rapidly, trying to find some use she could put this man to. If she used her Art to heat her gauntlets up, could they burn through the straps that secured his hands? Could he use his sting, then, to free her? Could she get out, with or without Aagen? Once she had regained the skies, the bulk of the Sarnesh army would cease to be relevant.

Then the carriage door opened, and Milus and a handful of his specialist artificers stepped aboard.

'Now, Aagen,' the tactician said mildly, 'we were discussing the defences of Capitas. You're an engineer, after all, so I'm sure you've got a useful professional viewpoint on them. Special focus on weak points, if you please.'

The Wasp took a deep breath. 'I will not betray my own people.'

'You already have, plenty of times,' Milus told him. 'This is no different.'

'To me it is, Tactician.'

Milus smiled. Lissart recognized that smile, and in fact he glanced at her at the same time, as though automatically linking her with what he was about to do.

'You'll tell me,' he said pleasantly to Aagen. 'You'll see that we Sarnesh are the coming kinden. Just as you Wasps picked up so much from your conquests, so we're learning from you now.' He patted the nearest machine, which was an interrogation rack taken straight from the Rekef chambers in Sonn. 'It'll be a taste of home for you.'

Paladrya was suffering from the sun, therefore spending most of her time below decks. Stenwold had been surprised that Rosander's Onychoi soldiers could weather the land as well as they did. He remembered his first excursion with Paladrya and the Sea-kinden into Collegium and Princep. They had complained about everything – the food, the cold, the heat, the dry air.

Or, no, *she* had not complained, but she had suffered, just as she suffered now, her white skin reddening and cracking where the light caught it, so that she went about veiled and cloaked like a theatrical ghost.

Rosander's people seemed far better able to cope, and eventually the Nauarch of the Thousand Spines had explained that their armour had been specifically designed for the land campaign. Stenwold had thought about that, and about how much warning the Sea-kinden had honestly received, after he had made his unexpected arrival at sunken Hermatyre to plead for their help.

Rosander had been about to invade the land once. Stenwold did not dare ask whether this armour, with its internal pockets and channels of water, had been left over from that attempt, or whether the Thousand Spines had simply never forgotten that dream.

In which case I am very glad I gave you this outlet.

Right now he stood at the airship rail along with Rosander and a handful of his men, watching their little fleet scud across the sky towards Myna. This was another memory made flesh. 'You remember . . .' he said, and the huge Onychoi nodded vigorously.

'Oh, I do. You took me up into the skies and showed me your land world and said, "Will you conquer all this?"' He laughed. 'And of course I was shocked – whoever thought there was so much *land*, eh? But I tell you this, Maker – once I went home, to where life is sane and nobody's in constant danger of falling to their deaths, I never forgot. I dreamt of horizons, Maker.' Rosander grinned into the wind, showing neat yellow teeth. 'And so here we are.' He did not seem to care about the web of politics that had diverted them here to Myna, so long as there was a fight at the end of it – and that Stenwold could certainly promise him.

The airships had come from Helleron. Stenwold had tried to obtain them by negotiation and credit, but his separation from the main Collegium force had been very quickly known – Milus's work no doubt – and his personal credit was less than nothing. The Helleren merchants had not even taken the time to meet with him.

So he had taken his force, Collegiates and Mynans and Seakinden all, and simply appropriated what he wanted from the Helleren airfields, acquiring a small fleet of airships to carry the soldiers and their supplies and as much water as could be loaded aboard. He directed any objectors to take matters up with Rosander. It was not exactly the finest hour of Stenwold Maker, diplomat and scholar, but by then he had run out of patience with the entire city of Helleron. And was running out of time as well.

Leaving Rosander at the rail, the former War Master of Collegium retreated below to the shrouded undersea gloom of his cabin to find Paladrya.

'Myna will be in sight soon,' he told her. 'We're almost there.'

She smiled at him, though a little uncertainly. She had said before that she felt that the Stenwold she knew was just one of many sharing Stenwold's skull. The War Master was an intractable, intimidating companion, far from the man she had met once in the cells of Hermatyre. *I think I liked you better when you were a fugitive,* she had joked – or half joked.

He took her hand. 'This is almost over, but I cannot abandon Kymene and Myna.'

'You've told me: this was where it all started,' she confirmed. 'Your friends are fortunate in you, Stenwold.'

He shrugged, sitting down beside her. 'There have been plenty of my friends who wouldn't say so. That makes the survivors all the more precious.' He noticed her concerned look and shook his head. 'But I won't stay. I don't think Collegium needs me any more . . . in fact, I think that having a relic like me stomping around and trying to run things will do far more harm than good. I'm not suited to peace. Or at least not peace on land.'

When he had returned to Hermatyre, he remembered how the two of them had hedged and edged about one another, neither quite sure where they were. Two veterans of different conflicts, both of them marked by their own privations and grown old in different worlds.

In the end, the ruler of Hermatyre, Aradocles, had summoned them to a meeting of his advisers at which nobody else had turned up, and they had found themselves alone, in the Edmir's private chambers, with a banquet laid out. Paladrya's young protégé had been wise beyond his years, apparently.

For Stenwold, the morning after that night had been one of terrible soul-searching, not because of anything so irrational as guilt, or because he had any regrets, but because he could no longer pretend that he did not love Paladrya. In the face of that, he very nearly abandoned Collegium and the dry land to its fate.

Duty, though – its cords still bound him. Even now he was doing what he knew needed to be done, paying his debts, severing his ties one by one. Myna, he felt, was the last of them. After that, everyone he owed anything to would be paid in full or dead.

For a long time they lay together quietly, Paladrya curled into his chest as though sheltering behind him from some great storm.

Later they sent for him, one of the Maker's Own soldiers hammering at the cabin door. Myna was in sight, and the Mynan airmen in their Stormreaders were already fending off a questing band of Spearflights sent to investigate. The time had come to land as close to the walls as possible, and to disembark. Stenwold Maker was returning to Myna.

Thirty-Seven

There were several hundred of them in the slave pit, when it was dug. More arrived all the time, day and night. Even with their wings shackled, plenty could climb. Even without that, they could have simply stood on each others' shoulders. The Slave Corps were at the rim constantly, watching. There was a sense of frustration about the lot of them: professionals not being allowed to do a professional job. Looking up at their faceless helms, te Mosca could still read emotion in them. The slavers who just came here to deliver a fresh load of live human meat were brusque and hard: it wasn't their problem what happened after they left. The camp guards had probably been like that too, at heart. They were men who had chosen a profession that was a filthy word in Collegium. Surely, of all the villains of the Empire, the Slave Corps harboured the worst.

And yet she looked up at those men silhouetted against the bright sky and she saw them as just that: men. Some were still and some were vicious. Some threw stones at their charges for sport. Some took women from the pits for their own uses, and nobody stopped them.

And yet, though they tried to seem impassive, they were troubled: she saw it in the way they stood. There was a slow panic creeping through the Slave Corps. It was insignificant compared to the misery and squalor and fear of their charges, but it was there. The slaves kept coming in, and none was permitted to leave save through the slow death of neglect. They were being overwhelmed with their chosen commodity, like a glutton being force-fed with luxuries until he burst. Something in the Empire had gone dreadfully wrong, and these men had become the touchstone of it. Even the Slave Corps was asking the question 'Why?'

Te Mosca wondered why as well. She had an active mind, a good imagination. It was not a facility designed to give her much joy, here and now.

Today the hungry mouth of the pit was given a change of diet. Today it fed on Wasps.

When they came to the brink, te Mosca thought they were more persecutors come to see the waste of life and potential this place represented. Then they were flung in, first a few and then by the dozens. They were women, uniformly, and most of them wore white robes. Asking around, te Mosca discovered they were some sort of sisterhood, the Mercy's Daughters. They had followed the Imperial armies, giving respite and medical aid, but apparently they had not been an approved part of the Empire's hierarchy. And now they were here, as expendable as the rest. Yes, they could have stung, perhaps; they could have fought. But they had been beaten and whipped, and some bore ragged scars or open wounds on their palms, to show what the slavers did to those of their own kind who resisted them.

And yet te Mosca watched, and she saw that these Daughters were plainly known to the Slave Corps, and she saw that disquiet take a deeper root and grow in their captors. It was as though they were waiting for the next orders, which might demand they consign themselves to the pit.

That night, as the slaves huddled in their great host, elbowing and pushing to keep away from that part of the pit which had become their overflowing and stinking latrine, Metyssa spoke.

At first the Spider storyteller was just speaking to those closest to her: Poll Awlbreaker and a handful of others from Collegium. She had been talking for some time before even te

Mosca realized it. Metyssa had a low voice for a woman – slightly husky – and it did not carry well against the constant murmur and moan of the prisoners.

Except that that undercurrent of complaint was slowing and falling silent around her, as more and more tried to listen. Te Mosca pushed between the tight-packed bodies – a Fly-kinden's meagre blessing – until she could hear what the woman was saying.

She's calling on them to rise up, she assumed at first. *She's inciting them, somehow.* But there was nothing of the call to arms in Metyssa's voice. There was no dirge there, either. Her voice was bright and crisp. She was telling them about Collegium.

Not the real Collegium, of course. Not the city pocked with bomb craters; the city labouring under the boot of the Second Army; the city picked to pieces by war after war, siege after siege, until it had run out of all the resources required to keep out the foe, up to and including simple defiance. The stories Metyssa had sent to the expatriates in Sarn had never been the bleak truth, after all. They had been daring tales of a resistance that never was. They had been the stories of prisoners rescued, of lovers reunited, of rooftop chases and heroic deeds. She had populated them with distorted mirrors of the people around her. Locked in Poll's basement, denied the sun and the air for fear that her very kinden would see her arrested and killed, she had cast herself as the dashing swordswoman. They had been Spider tales, full of energy and life, of trickery and convoluted plots.

To te Mosca's ears, at first, there was nothing sadder that she could possibly hear than a doomed woman telling her shining stories to her companions in oblivion.

And yet they listened. Pressing close on all sides they came: men and women culled from the Collegiate streets; captives ripped from the broken principalities of the Commonweal; slaves bought or just confiscated from their settled lives about the Empire; citizens of Imperial dominions taken up in their scores because of their Inaptitude; Spider-kinden prisoners of war. A wave of quiet

454

rippled piecemeal across the pit as they jostled each other into silence, until the only sound was Metyssa.

She spoke for an hour that night, and an hour the next morning. Te Mosca had been frightened that the Wasps would single her out but, so long as the prisoners were quiet, they didn't care.

The next night she spoke for two hours – and now she was improvising, not just repeating the stories she had written for the expatriates. She added characters, she tangled their relationships. She told of their *lives*. That was the thing: she told of people who lived in some other world where things had gone differently. She took her imaginary protagonists to other places – her approximations of lands that her fellow captives had known. Nobody tried to correct her, even though she was fabricating most of what she said from whole cloth.

And the day after, a Slave Corps sergeant hauled Metyssa out, because she had caught his eye, and two of his colleagues – unranked soldiers as far as te Mosca could see – kicked him half to death and made him send her back. Only then did anyone realize that her stories had attracted a wider audience.

Still the new slaves came. Soon enough there was another shovel detail working on a third pit. But te Mosca would lie awake at night, once Metyssa was sleeping, and hear distorted snatches of story being passed about elsewhere: in the other pits, in the cages, between the guards.

She saw, then, how it would go: that the story, that invisible agent, would go from ear to ear amongst the slavers, and it would win them over. It would make them see their captives as individual and human, and they would be unable to go on with their work. They would turn against the evil that was demanded of them. They would open the cages, and step back from the lip of the pit. In te Mosca's mind – famished and thin and filthy as she was – she could plan it all out, the liberation of thousands by the words of one Spider woman. It was a tale fit to be a legend of the old days, when armies were charmed by song, and monsters were tamed by a few magic phrases.

Then another airship arrived, but there were no slaves on this one. It brought an officer with red pauldrons who immediately took command from the lead slaver. It brought engineers as well: nervous, careful men who spent a long time unloading great metal canisters from the hold, treating them as though they were glass.

Then the Red Watch man secluded himself with the slaver chief, while everyone else stood around staring at the man-high barrels.

And the work began.

Slaves were picked out: the largest and strongest. They were made to dig, again, cutting channels into the side of each of the pits. Others were sent to clamber about the stinking territory of the cages, whose reek of decay and refuse was strong enough to overwhelm even the pits' own stench.

They were putting barrels up on the cages, over the top of them. They were placing barrels at the mouth of each channel into the pits. Some of the slavers were joking about everyone getting a drink when they popped the bungs, but most of them just stood and stared at the canisters with a terrible fear and awe.

Poll Awlbreaker it was who identified the lines the engineers ran from barrel to barrel as fuses, and then had to explain to the massed Inapt what that meant.

And there was a name being passed from lip to lip – a name caught like a disease from the more agitated of the slavers. To most there it meant nothing, but there were enough Imperial slaves or former citizens to enlighten the ignorant.

'Bee-killer,' they said, and they stared at the canisters. And the Red Watch man would come out periodically and examine their handiwork, all the slaves hard at work, and he would nod and smile.

After sunset, Tynan received the latest scouts' reports. The Lowlander army was moving on through the night, according to the pilots. They were keeping up a good, fast pace, with their own scouts and counter-saboteurs clearing the land ahead of Imperial ambushers, and with automotives repairing and replacing the rail lines that the Wasps had torn up.

Some detachments of the Imperial army had tried to get in their way, but without proper coordination and without sufficient numbers. Other forces had been diverted off to the Three-city Alliance states, where there was a full rebellion going on. Large elements of the Empire's forces were hopelessly entangled in the fight with the Spiderlands, unable to return in time to be of any assistance.

And still the situation did not add up. There were definitely garrisons and armies that were simply not moving, or were dragging their feet about it, as if avoiding the fight. Officers whom Tynan had personally sent to and entreated for aid were not replying. Some Wasps had already given over their Empire for lost. Perhaps they were plotting out their little fiefdoms. It was the reign of the traitor governors all over again.

He had spoken with Marent and the others – his co-conspirators, rebels against the Empress on behalf of the Empire. Their little alliance of like minds was fragmenting. Nessen, the Consortium man, had been unsteady. Varsec the aviator was away; hopefully mustering a good aerial response. Tynan had sent Bergild along with him, because he guessed the pilots would be loyal to their own, above all.

Vorken the slaver was receiving his reports, too, from his own reprehensible branch of the services. He was corresponding with the camps. Tynan did not know what he was doing there, whether he had a plan, but it at least kept the man out of the way. He had expected a similar courtesy from the woman, Merva – ostensibly here to represent her husband back in Solarno – but she seemed to be enquiring about everything. He had a feeling there was more to her presence than had been vouchsafed, but he had men watching her, and there was no more he could do than that.

By all estimates, the Lowlanders seemed likely to arrive in

mere days. The assembled Imperial forces would be hitting them as soon as they were in range of the artillery – including a handful of greatshotters already positioned and aimed down the rail line. Despite all they could do, Tynan knew that the battle for Capitas would begin shortly after that. The thought brought a bitter taste to his mouth and a queasy feeling to his stomach, but he was self-aware enough to think, *I suppose they'd just ask us how we like it, since we did it so often to them, and to so many others. We always said it was our manifest destiny, the proof of our superiority. But what do we believe when Capitas lies in ruins under the Ant boot, eh?* He shook himself and added, *Another reason why we'll not let it happen.*

It appalled him how quickly everything had caved in towards this moment. *Did we never actually put something in place for this?* But, of course, Imperial policy was all expansion and conquest. If someone had stood before the Empress – or her predecessor – and suggested they plan for the Empire's defeat, for an enemy army to penetrate to the gates of the capital, that luckless speaker would have been on crossed pikes within the hour. *Curse it, if one of mine had said it to me, I'd have had them flogged, most likely.*

He had retreated to his tent, poring over the updated plans of the defences, earthworks and artillery emplacements, the best paths of attack for their vaunted Sentinels, their indestructible war machines.

Except the Lowlanders destroyed some when they retook Collegium, and when they wiped out the Eighth as well. There were no absolutes in war. *Even an old man like me needs to remember that.*

'General.'

He looked up sharply, seeing Major Oski there.

'All in order, Major?'

'The artillery? Yes, sir, absolutely. Everything we've got is all . . . lined up.' The little man was ill at ease, sufficiently so that Tynan straightened up from the map table, abruptly suspicious.

'What is it, Major?'

'Someone here would like an audience, sir, if that's . . .' The Fly-kinden glanced back. 'There's someone you need to speak to.'

'Do I?' Tynan flexed his fingers, still uneasy, but if this was an assassin he guessed that there wouldn't have been all the introduction. 'Let's see him, then.'

The man that stepped past Oski was a Bee-kinden, an Auxillian engineer with a captain's rank badge whom Tynan thought he recognized as one of the Fly's assistants. The moment the Bee stepped in, though, it was plain that something was wrong. The dynamic between them was all skewed, with the major deferring to the captain.

Rekef? But, no, it wasn't like that – and who'd ever heard of a senior Rekef who wasn't a good Wasp?

'What is this?' he demanded.

'Sir, this is Captain Ernain.' Oski appeared to be trying to make himself invisible. He was frightened, Tynan saw, and not just for himself. He was carrying far more anxiety than the normal life of a Fly could account for.

'General,' Ernain addressed him politely. 'I've come here as the head of a delegation.' His eyes flicked briefly to Tynan's hands, but his expression remained calm.

'Whatever it is, it can wait,' Tynan said, without much hope. This was unlikely to be a wrangle over pay or conditions.

'It cannot.' No *sir* and no *general*. 'I see that you and General Marent have called in every soldier you can. It's a mighty force assembled out there.'

Tynan waited, as if poised on a knife edge. He had no sense of the assassin from Ernain but then, if the man was good enough, there would be no obvious sign. *Still, only a sloppy assassin strikes up a conversation.*

'A lot of Auxillians out there,' Ernain added, as if as an afterthought.

That hadn't been something Tynan had wanted to hear because, yes, a great many of those hauled from their posts to the gates

459

of Capitas had indeed been soldiers of the lesser kinden, those who were not citizens. Tynan had heard some rumours about the Empire's slave soldiers deserting – even abandoning their Wasp masters in the midst of battle. The details had been sufficiently vague that he had drawn no definite conclusions, but now . . .

'And what delegation are you here to represent, Captain Ernain?' he asked softly. 'The Auxillians in this army, perhaps?'

'Not exactly,' Ernain replied. 'However, I would like to report that I and other Auxillian officers have received communications from the enemy. From Tactician Milus of Sarn himself.'

'And what does Milus say to you, Captain?'

'Walk away, and know freedom.'

'I see.' Tynan was already calculating. What proportion of the force here was Auxillian? *Too many, and from so many cities.* What could he do to restrain them if they attempted to desert or, worse, join the enemy? *He could do so reasonably effectively unless, for example, he had a Lowlander army to fight at the same time.* What showing could he still make against Milus if the Auxillians were gone? *Almost certainly not enough of one.* 'And what has your response been, to this kind offer from the Sarnesh?'

'We've not made one, not yet.'

So we come down to haggling now, like Helleren merchants. 'And what do your Auxillians here want, Captain? Shall we cut to the core? I have a battle to plan.'

'I do not represent the Auxillians here – or not them alone.' Ernain did not seem in a hurry to get to the point. It must be a luxury for a slave soldier to make a general sweat. 'You remember the war with the traitor governors?'

'Of course I do.'

'I'll recall to you one of the most remarked-upon features of that war: the lack of other rebellion while the Empress was restoring order. All those cities, all those other kinden . . . and there were so few signs of unrest. Oh, some, I'll grant you, but there were so many cities that might have thrown out their garrisons – whether loyal or traitor – and fought for their own independence.'

Tynan was feeling like a man creeping along a ledge who suddenly realizes he has no idea of the drop that he teeters above. 'Get to the point.'

'We did not rebel,' Ernain said flatly, and with that 'we' he was suddenly a man of a different stature, speaking words of greater weight. 'However, we did begin to talk. Amongst ourselves, with each other, with our allies. A surprising number of allies – and some Wasps amongst them, even. About the future of the Empire. And about change.'

'Captain, I have a Lowlander army on its way—!'

'Yes, you do!' Ernain declared. 'A Lowlander army on its way to Capitas! And it may destroy all you have here and tear open the Empire's heart, anyway, but it most certainly will do so if *we* go.'

'What do you want, Captain?' Tynan snarled.

'*Change.*' There was a fire in Ernain's eyes. 'Vesserett wants change. Maille wants change. Jhe Lien and Sa want change. Thirteen cities and countless individuals now make their stand and speak through me. Because now you see the lie that is Empire: you need us. You need us to fight and die for you, but why should we? And right here, right now, you cannot force us.'

'"Change" is not a demand, Captain,' Tynan told him fiercely. 'I'm afraid you may have to be a little more specific.'

Ernain reached into his tunic, and Tynan extended a hand towards him, ready to sting. Oski lurched forwards, mouth open to intervene, and got the general's other palm in his face for his troubles.

'Easy, now.' What Ernain had there was no weapon, but paper, just a few sheets of creased paper.

Ask any man on the wrong end of a death warrant whether paper can kill you or not, Tynan considered, but Ernain was holding the sheets out towards him, so he snatched them and stepped back.

461

'And remember,' the Bee told him, even as Tynan unfolded the sheets, 'even if you refuse us, and you beat the Lowlanders anyway – and if ever there was a general who could, I'd say it's you – you'll have thirteen cities in open revolt before the last shot is loosed. In open revolt *together*, and where will you ever get men enough to put that down?'

Tynan had been skimming his eyes over the written words, but he seemed unable to quite take it in, as if the sheer affrontery of it was more than he could swallow. 'What is this?' he demanded. 'You want freedom?' Because that part he could understand.

'There were some who thought we should take this chance to demand it – to offer ourselves as mere mercenaries rather than soldiers of the Empire, to go back to homes with no black and gold flag and no garrisons. But some of us looked further, and saw we would simply end up fighting one another, like as not. Or we would become divided and then fall to your people once again. Or perhaps to the Sarnesh, or whoever the next great power happened to be. This is no time in history to be a city alone.

'And, besides, we're not like Myna, where the older generation still remembers the time before the first occupation. We'd rather not be free only to starve. None of us was born to anything other than what we have, not even the oldest. And you know what, General? It's our Empire too. We've built it just as much as your people have. We have a stake in it now. We've marched with its armies and we've constructed its ziggurats and its engines. And even we, even we conquered slaves, have reaped the benefits of Empire, once you Wasps had finished with them. But now it will change. The Empire will recognize us – or we will abandon it and it will fall.'

'This is insane . . . you're talking about . . .' Finally he was starting to assimilate what he was reading. 'An Assembly, like in Collegium.'

'And everyone is entitled to their say,' Ernain confirmed. 'Army generals, Consortium, Engineers, and also city governors. City governors who will not be Wasps – or need not be. Who knows? There are certainly some out there who have gone native enough. More of them than you'd think. And everyone to be citizens of the Empire, regardless of kinden.'

'This?' Tynan demanded, the paper crumpling in his hand. 'This is your price for the battle tomorrow? You think I can bring this about?'

'I think that a few minutes with a pen and some paper would give us the signatures of you and your fellow commanders, and there could be copies of this document with your name on it speeding across the Empire. To save time, I've brought the copies.'

'You think you can hold me to ransom – hold us all to ransom – over this, Ernain? You think that change can come by holding a knife to our throats?'

Ernain smiled slightly. 'What I think, General, is this. I think that of all the commanders I have served under, you are the best. Not in the sense of the best military mind, but the best man. I think you will read this, and you will think on it, and you will start to see something other than greedy Auxillians exploiting you in your hour of need.'

'What will I see?' Tynan asked him, trying to muster a dismissive tone, but not quite managing it.

'You will see that we are right. If I am correct in what I see in you, you won't need me to tell you that things can't continue as they have been. Look where that's brought us, after all.'

He turned to go, and Tynan threw in, 'You forget one thing, Ernain.'

'I forget nothing, General,' Ernain replied over his shoulder. 'Because of course, someone must tell the Empress that it is no longer her Empire.'

For the Lowlanders, progress eastwards was faster than an army should be able to travel, with so many of the slogging infantry packed onto automotive carriages and hauled down the line. It was still something of a stop-start business, though, as the rail-laying automotives ahead had to slow to negotiate more difficult terrain, or as Imperial saboteurs and local forces fought desperate rearguard actions to give their main force at Capitas more time to assemble.

Out there, tearing up the dry ground, was a veritable armada of automotives – everything that Milus had been able to requisition from Helleron and Sonn. They were driven by the Sarnesh, manoeuvring together with their faultless coordination and forming a broad wing on either side of the rail line, ready to intercept any attack. Their aviator siblings were performing the same service overhead.

Straessa was passing along the Collegiate carriages, checking on her followers. Nobody was particularly happy: being cooped up in a rail automotive for days on end, barely a chance to stretch your legs, was nobody's idea of what a good time was about. It wouldn't have been the Antspider's first choice for what soldiering was about either, but apparently war had moved on in a number of efficient but uncomfortable ways.

Some of her lot were trying to sleep, despite the light cutting in through the shutters and the constant jolt and sway that plagued them day and night; the rails were just bad enough to ensure there was no smooth rhythm to it. In one carriage, a dignified old Beetle woman she recognized from the Faculty of Logic appeared to be giving a lecture to whoever might be interested. In another someone had a cheap printing of some of lost Metyssa's great Collegiate cycle – that lurid, exaggeratedly dramatic account of the occupation that some there had lived through, and that others only heard about second hand – and was reading it aloud for the benefit of his fellows. They were all doing their best to stave off the tedium of the journey.

And just as she was starting to think that it was this waiting that was the worst part of the whole experience, someone gazing through a window called out, as she passed, 'Are those ours?'

Straessa hunched down, peering out. Her blood went cold.

She could see the Sarnesh automotives scattering, splitting off in faultless harmony, manoeuvring at top speed to react to the newcomers. But she could already see it would not be enough. She had endured at least one nightmare about these mechanical monsters.

The Empire had finally sent its Sentinels against the rail convoy.

There were five of them, that familiar and feared design of overlapping plates, like tall woodlice save that they moved at a gallop towards the great, helpless flank of the train, curving in the course of their charge so as to keep up with the automotives' speed. Even as Straessa watched, she saw the flash and smoke of their leadshotter eyes. A Sarnesh war-automotive was abruptly lying on its side, frustrated steam venting from between its armour-plating. Another shot struck close to the rail, raising a gout of dust and earth. Some of her soldiers had snapbows already to the windows, but there was absolutely nothing they could accomplish. Straessa opened her mouth to give an order, but realized that nothing in her experience or any military theory had prepared her for this. There was absolutely nothing she could do. Their only defence was the rail automotive's speed, and the train of carriages was so long that they were the grandest target in the world.

She saw an explosion burst and bloom about one of the Sentinels, a Stormreader pulling into a tight turn to come back for another pass. The Wasp machine had not slowed.

She was so busy watching that, that she missed the shot that actually impacted.

It struck the far end of the carriage behind hers, and sent a whiplash of destruction all along the train. The carriage taking the brunt was flayed open, punched off the tracks and sent end over end, spilling soldiers and supplies. Straessa's own carriage was yanked off the track itself, slewing on its side over the uneven ground, occupants slamming against the walls. Two other cars, in either direction, were derailed whilst the automotive itself continued driving up the track, even with the brakes applied as hard as could be. The carriages behind rammed their siblings that still lay partway across the track, shunting them to a grinding halt.

And the Sentinels came on, shouldering aside the nearest Sarnesh automotives contemptuously.

Straessa found herself sprawled on her back against the shutters of a window that would now only open on to bare ground. Every part of her ached but nothing seemed broken. For a second, feeling that the carriage had at least come to a stop, she stared with her single eye at the sunlight coming in through what was now the ceiling.

Then she was shouting. 'Out! Get out and get ready to fight. Grenades if you've got them! Get out or we're all dead in here!'

She curled herself into a ball to avoid being trampled to death by people following her orders. Those who could were evacuating sharply, piling out at either twisted end of the carriage or hauling themselves up out of the skyward-facing windows. Most seemed to have a snapbow at least. *Which is better than me.* Straessa had not even been carrying hers as she checked on the troops.

With luck, by now the Sarnesh are doing something useful. She levered herself up, wincing at the all the bruises she was going to have. *Come on, get moving, woman!* Blearily she stumbled from the carriage into the abrasively bright daylight after her soldiers, dragging her rapier from its scabbard.

She almost fell under the Sentinel as it charged past, slamming into the next skewed carriage, sending the entire car spinning about its midpoint. She heard screams from those caught in its wake. From somewhere nearby another leadshotter boomed.

Straessa took her chance and ducked past before the machine could return, looking frantically for her people. They had formed up into approximate maniples of ten to twenty, but were keeping a lot of space between each other, which seemed good sense. *Not sure why they need officers, really.* They were also already shooting, using what cover the carriages and the rocky terrain gave them, and she saw Wasp Light Airborne dropping down and coursing overhead.

Another Sentinel was coming up, following the rail line, its articulated body bunching and flexing as its legs pistoned furiously. For a moment she actually raised her little sword against it, in desperate defiance, but it was already breaking off, heading almost head to head against one of its brethren. She saw that it had been painted with a long streak of black on its segmented flanks. *One of ours!* For the Sarnesh had a handful of the machines taken from the vanished Eighth Army, just left vacant and untouched by whatever disaster had destroyed the Imperial force.

She assumed that the two Sentinels were going to strike each other head-on. Before they got that close, though, the Sarnesh machine loosed with its leadshotter and she saw the ball skitter off the Imperial vehicle's armour, doing no damage but deflecting its course so that, when they collided, the Sarnesh ran its prow into the flank of its enemy. Straessa flinched back from the tremendous impact, seeing both machines lurch away under it, the Imperial limping, with a couple of legs on that side trailing, and the Sarnesh brought almost to a stop by the collision, then slowly building up speed as it sought a new target.

'Antspider!' Gorenn dropped down beside her, an arrow ready on the string as always.

'Report!'

'Holding them off, Officer! There aren't so many of their soldiers,' the Dragonfly informed her, scanning all around. 'Machines are fighting machines. They've been stopped, I think. We're throwing them back.'

'Was that it, then?' Straessa frowned. 'Just a desperate shot and then they're spent? There must be more.'

Gorenn shrugged, but Straessa's mind was working feverishly, starting with, *Now what would I do . . .?* A moment later she was darting away down the track towards the emptied carriages. There were soldiers all over – Ants forming up with silent precision, Mynans charging past with swords and snapbows – but she was looking for people who were instead keeping still, trying to be overlooked. But in such a milling crowd, stillness itself was out of place.

There . . . Curse it, I was right, and she was picking up speed, hoping Gorenn was following her. She had seen a Beetle-kinden crouching at one of the carriages still on the tracks, and no doubt the Sarnesh thought he was one of hers. He was a stranger, though, and wearing no uniform, and he was working on something at the carriage's underside. *Because if I myself was organizing this, I'd sneak a few artificers in to set some charges.*

He saw her even as she was running at him, eyes wide as he realized he'd been detected. He had no snapbow, but he brought out a shortsword quickly just as she reached him, and then they were furiously steel against steel. Straessa knew she was better, but her bones and muscles were protesting the treatment with each blow, whilst the Imperial Beetle was desperate, strong and good enough to keep her at bay despite her longer blade. She tried three times to pierce through his guard, even going as far as her old trick shoulder thrust, which hurt a lot more than it had last time. She managed to pink him in the shoulder, a bare half-inch of blade, but she nearly got his own sword in her face in return, and then he tried to lunge past her point so as to grapple with her.

She got her sword into his thigh, but there it stuck, and his greater weight bowled her over, and then she was struggling with him for his own sword, as he raised it over her like a long dagger, trying to drive it down past the rim of her breastplate.

We're in the middle of my own cursed army! Why is nobody helping me? She tried to draw breath to cry out, but she was losing ground inch by inch, and she felt that the attempted yell might see that blade plunge straight through her. His face was so close to hers that she could see the veins about the edges of his bulging eyes as he fought to kill her.

She slammed her forehead into the bridge of his nose. Or that had been the idea. In fact she slammed her forehead into his hard cheekbone, dazing herself, but he started back, losing force on the blade so that, when she pushed, she toppled him off her. With a cry, he went for her again before she could struggle upright, and an arrow skewered him almost ear to ear, leaving him sitting back on his haunches, transfixed head tilted philosophically at the sky.

'Took your time,' Straessa hissed, taking Gorenn's hand and letting the Dragonfly do most of the work of pulling her up.

'Didn't you hear me yelling at you to give me a clear shot?'

Straessa blinked at her. 'No . . . no, I didn't. Look, go and round up a bunch of ours, get them to go check down all the carriages for other sods like this one, or for explosives, right? I reckon that's going to be our best contribution for now.'

Gorenn nodded briskly, flared her wings and was away.

There were two more saboteurs caught and killed, and a dozen set explosives to disarm, but the Collegiate artificers were up to it. The Empire's gambit had failed, on that front.

The carriage that had actually taken a leadshot hit was irreparable, and the entire army lost a day's progress while the combined might of its artificers got the other cars back on the rails and ready to travel.

Two hundred and four Collegiates and twenty-three others had died in the attack. The work on the carriages gave their comrades time to bury them, and to mourn.

Thirty-Eight

There was one corner of the world left where Totho could think.

He was packed into this cave with the slaves, jostling shoulder to shoulder in the lightless, airless press of them. He had fought with his blade until it had been ripped from his hand. He had fought on with his gauntleted hands, but they had dragged him down. When they could not kill him, battering at his mail with their crudely forged swords, they had dragged him to their sightless city and thrown him down here with the others, those wretches who had been caught but not yet killed. The only way out was the same shaft that he had been dropped down.

Nobody was fed. Nobody was given water. Several had died already.

Totho had allowed himself to be buffeted back and forth, sometimes almost falling over save that the constant sway of bodies kept him upright, until he had found this corner, this last black outpost of understanding. A nook at the far back of the cave, as far from everything else as he could ever get.

The Worm's deadening influence did not quite stretch there, as though it was so deep into the rock that it was thrust into some other place where sanity still reigned, and Totho could crouch there with his armour scraping against the walls, fending off the moaning, weeping mass of composite humanity, and think Apt thoughts.

Only wedged there into that corner did he have options. They had not taken his mail, so they had not taken his weapons. He had one last trick, if only he had the final courage to use it. His belt of grenades remained, and it had been easy enough to feed a single pull-cord through them all. One bold wrench and the privations of this place would be gone. He would not have to worry about them any more. He guessed that the blast would kill just about everyone else here, too. It would only be a shame that his captors would not die as well, though perhaps the contained force might crack the rock, tumble down some part of their domain into the pit that his explosives would create.

He thought about it further. Over and over, he thought about it, but he did nothing.

Where are you, Che? He had been so sure that he would find her, but he was a prisoner, and she was not here beside him. She was dead, perhaps. Or she was free.

If he had known what the Worm would do to his mind, he would never have come down here. With his Aptitude intact he felt that the world was his to face and to master. But here . . . crammed into his tiny space, throat and nostrils choked with the sweat and excrement and fear of all those doomed souls, all his Aptitude could give him was a way to die.

And he knew, horribly, that if he took one step forwards, even that would be gone from him. He would have nothing.

His thumb found the cord, hooked into the metal ring there, tensioned it. He had linked the triggers to all the grenades: the simple mechanical exercise had been almost calming. Just one solid pull.

It was safe to say, he reckoned, that this was not what he had been looking for in coming down here. But, in all honesty, after Drephos died he had become unmoored in the world. Che had been the only landmark left for him to steer by, but what a treacherous course that had proved to be. She had never been any good for him.

He looked up, eyes wide against the darkness, and spotted the light. It was merely a faint, pallid luminescence, but it was light. A few of the slaves appeared to have seen it too – he could make out the odd face turned upwards, the dim radiance touching them fleetingly. The rest seemed blind to it, as though it did not exist for them.

But then he remembered Drephos – who had possessed eyes like a Moth's – telling him how his vision had adjusted to darkness, leaching the colours from things, but sharpening the shapes, seeing the world in greys by some medium that owed nothing to light itself – the dark-adapted eye saw no light or radiance, torches and lanterns did not betray their owners to it.

Someone up there had a light, and Totho knew that it could not be any of his captors.

He lurched forwards, feeling doors slam shut in his mind, but in that moment not caring, shouldering his way into the human morass, fighting through it as though it were quicksand, shoving and kneeing and striking his way through the whimpering, unresisting throng.

'Here!' he shouted. 'I'm here!' as though the glow was for him, as though it could possibly be for him.

He saw a man there, crouching almost upside down at the mouth of the shaft, held there by the Art of both feet and one hand, with a kind of lantern held out into space – little more than some burning embers in a metal cage.

Some of the other slaves around him were staring mutely, although many were just ignoring everything, eyes empty as wells, denying what they heard and anything they might see.

'Tell me you're Totho,' the lamp-bearer said. He was an odd sort of man, of no kinden Totho could immediately identify.

'Yes,' he answered.

'Cheerwell Maker sent me.' The stranger peered down, studying the dense mass of bodies below.

'Get me out.'

'I . . .' The man glanced up the shaft. 'I'm not sure that I can. Up above the city's crawling with them. They'd see you the moment you got out of here. I need to think. Now I've found you, I need to think.'

'They come here,' Totho said. 'The creatures that rule here, they come and take people. I've not been here long and I've seen more than a dozen go already. They just climb down and seize on victims at random.' There was a moaning starting up, amongst the slaves, as though even speaking those words might incur the next visitation. 'They can climb well – even on the ceiling. They get everywhere. How much thinking time do you need?'

'I really don't know if I can get you out. I'm sorry,' the lamp-bearer admitted. 'I promised Cheerwell I'd try, though.'

'Can you come down here?' Totho heard his own voice shaking. The dreadful sound the other slaves were making was swelling in a wordless, inhuman chorus of fear, of people who had been robbed of everything, their hope last of all. 'I need . . . I need . . . Please, there is something I need to tell you, to show you. If it comes to the worst. Please.'

The stranger ducked his head back, and for a moment Totho thought he would just go, abandoning all attempt at a rescue. Then he was back, and his Art seemed to be almost as strong as the bodies of the Worm, because he crouched flat against the ceiling, creeping in jerky, awkward motions, following as Totho pushed and cuffed his way back towards his corner, hunting for it with the inner senses of his mind that told him when he was reaching that tiny pocket where the world again made sense. Where he could explain.

He looked up, and started away from the man's upside-down face. The dirge of the slaves was rising into a full wail, and they were pushing and fighting not to be directly beneath the shaft.

'The Worm's heard that racket,' the lamp-bearer guessed. He made no move to put the light out. Apparently he had come to the same conclusion as Totho about the limits of the Worm's sight.

'Or they were just coming anyway,' Totho replied. 'To do . . . to take us . . . wherever they do.'

'Oh, I know where they're taking their captives,' the stranger hissed. 'The Worm and its warriors, they don't care. They don't have any use for live prisoners. Up above, there are some scarred old men, though, some filthy, cowardly creatures who live in the Worm's shadow. And the Worm is their god, and they give it offerings because they hope it will spare them. But it won't. And neither will I.' The quiet venom in his words was startling.

Now Totho saw the shadows as the Worm's creatures crept out, clinging to the sheer stone and staring downwards, here at the behest of the stranger's 'scarred old men', apparently. *Sacrificed to a god, though? Is he serious? What does he mean?*

'Stranger,' he hissed.

'Esmail,' the man told him.

'Esmail, then. You're Apt?'

The man looked at him, baffled. 'No. Not that it matters. If I were anywhere else you'd call me a magician, perhaps, but that means nothing here. I'm living on pure skill and self-mutilation.' This close, Totho could hear a quaver in the man's words that matched his own hollow fear.

'There's something . . .' He was watching the warriors of the Worm pick their way overhead. Every so often one would strike down, snagging a slave, and then half a dozen would converge to draw the struggling, shrieking individual up between them, whilst the rest of the host remained silent now, not wanting to draw attention, not wanting to be the next chosen. 'If they come for me . . . there's something I need you to do. An Apt thing.'

'Well, that makes two reasons why I can't do it,' Esmail hissed.

Totho told him anyway. He explained it as simply as possible. He said nothing about mechanical principles or about the chemistry of the efficient little explosives. He focused on the simple physical action required. *It's as simple as pulling on a string.*

'Then you do it.'

Totho shook his head urgently. 'You don't understand. You

can't. One step . . . one step forwards and I lose it. I can't . . . I won't be able to . . .'

Then the creatures of the Worm were retreating, taking their chosen sacrifices with them, and Esmail was backing off.

'Forget all that,' he snapped. 'I'll get a rope. I'll find some way out, if there's a way to be found.' Then he was carefully making his way back across the ceiling, one limb at a time, teeth gritted with the effort, following in the trail of the Worm.

There was no forced marching of the slaves of the Worm. Many were injured or ill, or simply weak from hunger. Some – the lucky few – had children to slow them down. The great mass of them crawled across the barren and bleak terrain, torches and lanterns scattered randomly amongst them. They were making the best time they could, but it was painfully slow. Originally, Che had been using whatever Moth-kinden were willing to act as her eyes, spying out the ground ahead and to either side, wary of the approach of the Worm. That had not turned out well. The great mass of movement, the constant comings and goings in the air, had attracted the attention of the monsters they knew as the White Death, and several Moths had been snatched in mid-flight. Now Che was having to rely on scouts on the ground – anyone with good enough eyes for the pitch dark and who could run fast. Still most of her volunteers were Moths; it seemed almost surreal that their people – so isolated and haughty up above – were some of her most willing helpers here.

She had no idea of the level of the Worm's awareness, whether it was relying on the eyes of its creatures, or whether the sheer movement of so many would communicate itself through the stone to the creature as it lurked down in its hole. The topography of this realm was baffling, and she knew that a simple straight journey must in some way also follow a curve to accommodate the simple fact that all roads led eventually to that blighted city. The very thought made her head ache.

Then the scouts began returning, some of them running, some risking a dash through the air. The Worm was on its way, a great snaking column of its human segments, following the path of the refugees and gaining on them with every step.

'How far are we from these caves?' Che demanded of Messel.

'At this speed? Many hours,' he told her.

'Lorn detachment?' Thalric suggested. 'Whip the rest into a decent pace, and some poor bastards'll have to stay back and do what they can. Messel, we need terrain we can use. Find us a slope, some useful overhangs – let's get some rockslides set up.'

The blind man nodded rapidly, and then he and the Wasp were off, trying to round up fighters out of the mass of moving people.

'They're not going to get much faster,' Tynisa murmured in Che's ear. 'Not without leaving people behind.'

'We won't leave anyone behind.'

'You can't save everyone.'

Che glared at her. 'You're starting to sound like Thalric.'

'Maybe he makes sense sometimes. Che, there's only one way to slow the Worm, and it involves people dying.'

A sacrifice to the Worm. Che shivered. 'It won't come to that,' she insisted hollowly. And meanwhile she had kept driving her mind ahead, hunting options, trying to feel out what she herself might be able to accomplish.

So little magic here, but more than there was. What can I gather? What is my strength worth?

If the worst came to the worst, she would use it all up, every grain, in the hope that she could break through. In the hope that it was possible for her to create her own doorway. She had had a moment's doubt as the great mob of slaves set off. Should she just have them hold still while she tried to exercise her powers? Could she not simply tear apart this stone world and let them out into the sun?

She had conceived an image then, as though it was a vision

of the future. An image of herself, Che, kneeling and fighting with this intransigent, uncooperative nature of the world, surrounded by starving, desperate slaves, as the Worm arrived. With no idea if she could ever achieve what she sought, she chose to keep moving. At least it offered the illusion of progress.

Thalric sought her out later. 'Che, I need your help.'

'What's wrong?'

'I need your eyes.'

The scouts had identified an ambush point up ahead, where there seemed some chance that a few stragglers could delay the pursuing Worm. Thalric himself did not trust their assessment, because he had no respect for any of the former slaves.

'I've been all over it, but it's like looking at a picture through a keyhole. I can't keep track of the lie of the land properly. I need you to tell me I'm right.'

She flew ahead with him, leaving Tynisa in nominal charge of the great shambling mass of travellers. What the scouts had found was a path that ran between a rock-strewn slope on one side and the upcurving edge of the world on the other: a jagged, fractured cliff that offered a handful of sizeable ledges.

'So we get people up on the ledges, we get the Moles to fetch rocks up to them. That's our deadfall for when the Worm soldiers arrive. We have some fighters stationed up the slope – slingers and swordsmen. They'll get charged, but the footing's poor and the Worm's going to have a lot to worry about. So, tell me, have I got the right of it? Only it's like trying to fix an automotive while blindfold, doing this.'

'You'd trust my judgement?'

'Don't get too excited. I just trust it more than theirs.' But there was a fond humour in his tone.

'I think it will work. But we'll need to get everyone through before the Worm can catch us,' she decided.

'Then we need to get them to hurry, don't we?'

As his wings ghosted into life, she put a hand on his arm. 'Thalric.'

477

Wings still out, a barely visible film in the air about his shoulders, he waited.

'Thank you,' she told him.

'For sticking alongside you? Not as if I had much choice.' But, still, not said bitterly.

'For everything.'

'Che, what is it?'

And now she was scaring herself, because a sense of dread was upon her, unaccountable, irresistible, rearing its head within her mind. Her fear had communicated itself to Thalric. She saw him go tense, and his face twitch with tension.

She pulled him to her, held him tight. Still there was nothing, only that unreasoning feeling, that certainty of doom. *The magic is seeping in. Unasked prophecy. Unasked and useless.*

But there they were: she saw more scouts returning, could read the panic on their faces.

They gabbled out their news as soon as they located her, as though desperate to be rid of it. There was another column of the Worm, ahead of them, and closing in.

It took them far too long to gather all the fugitives together, and then Che could only tell them one thing: that they would be going no further. For there was nowhere else to go.

When Thalric had chosen this place, he had picked it as a good point to mount a brief stand, an attempt to gain time for the fugitives by making the Worm pay a little, by providing a distraction. The Worm was hungry and, despite the best efforts of the Scarred Ones to direct it onwards, an offering of a few tenacious defenders should occupy its attention for a little extra time.

That was no longer an option. The Worm was closing in on all sides. Mindless or not, it had sensed its prey.

The rise that Thalric had picked for his putative defenders was now under Che's command, heading up the slope as far as she could go with the non-combatants, the injured, the young. The rest of the slaves were below, preparing for their last stand. Thalric assumed that they would buckle almost instantly, would beg their

478

former masters for mercy. If that happened, then the massacre here would see hundreds dead in the first few minutes.

Already some of the slaves had just abandoned them, heading off on their own in the bleak hope that they might evade the enemy and escape the coming slaughter. The Hermit had been amongst them, leaving without a word, just heading off into the dark. He, at least, would be able to walk past the forces of the Worm. The rest . . . well, perhaps their chances were still greater than for those staying here.

Having led them all into this hopeless trap, Che could hardly begrudge the desertions. Thalric had railed, but only because he reckoned that those with the initiative to run would probably also prove the most spirited fighters once backed into a corner.

They were all backed into a corner now.

They were doing what they could. They were breaking rocks and hauling them up on either side. Several hundred Mole Crickets were using their Art to shape the stone, creating obstacles, walls, hoping to funnel the Worm's advance and to slow their charge. Moth scouts were keeping track of the enemy's steady, relentless advance. There was so little time.

'If you have anything, now's the time,' Tynisa told her. Che glanced at her in surprise. Had her foster-sister sensed the fickle gains that magic had made here since the breaking of the Seal?

No, she was just desperate, and in her desperation she had turned to Che. Somehow, clumsy, awkward Che had become the last forlorn hope even of Tynisa, who should know better.

But she's right. If it can be done at all, then now's the time. Once the Worm gets here, I can't say if its influence will reach this far up. All my hopes might be snuffed out the very moment they arrive.

So here she sat, surrounded by the fools that she had gathered here, by the industry of those who had faith that somehow they would survive what was coming. Here she sat with Tynisa beside her, whilst Thalric marshalled his slingers and his makeshift soldiers and the strong but otherwise useless, who would be pushing rocks down onto the enemy.

Che opened her mind as best she could, penetrating the parched drought of this place, through her own fear, and called out to her other sister, to Seda the Empress.

At first: nothing, just the echo of her own thoughts and the unmuted cacophony of those around her, their frightened words, their cries – adults and children both – and the crack and slam of rock on rock, Thalric's barked orders . . .

Seda . . .

And, distant, almost inaudible, and yet in no way drowned by the real sounds around her, Che caught the response.

I am here, Che. The faraway voice sounded strained, as if under as much pressure as Che herself.

Seda, I need your help. I need to break out of here. The Seal is gone, so it should be possible. Please . . . Even as she expressed this thought, Che was doubting herself. She could not think through the logic that would allow such a violation of this place, and now that its mundane relationship with the wider world was being restored, such a piece of magic would surely become less and less possible. The opening of one door meant closing another.

Che, you cannot, Seda insisted. *Che, I would save you if I could. I know you must hate me for casting you into that place. I am sorry. If I could bring you out from it, then I would. But I must think of the world, the whole world. Che, I need your help.*

The suggestion dragged a wretched laugh out of Che, startling Tynisa beside her. *What help could I possibly give you?*

Your power, all your power, everything you have. It should have sounded false, coming from the Empress of the Wasps, but Che heard a terrible sincerity there. *Che, I have damned the entire world by breaking the Seal, but I can put it right. I can put it all back where it should be. I can banish the Worm.*

Che clutched at the stony ground to steady herself. *It cannot be done.*

It can. Believe me, I have spent so long constructing the ritual, but it can. The Moths did it once.

You intend to . . .

I must restore the Seal. I must separate the worlds again.

Che looked around her, at the great mass of humanity that had followed her this far, and no further, who even now were choosing to believe that she, Cheerwell Maker, had some last-moment plan to save them. *There are people here, hundreds, thousands, whole kinden.*

I know. I have seen them, through you. The expected Wasp invective did not come, only regret. *I am sorry, Che, but there is no hope for them. There is only hope for the real world, the true world, and only then if I can gather enough strength to force this ritual into being.*

The Moths had far more, a thousand years ago, than we do now. There isn't enough strength in the present-day world, Seda. And Che was aware that, with that thought, she was conceding something: that Seda's plan had merit. That the sacrifice of Che and Thalric and Tynisa, of Messel and his whole kinden, of all the thousands here, would still be the correct response. The world was wider than their existence, after all.

There is. The steely resolve in Seda's words startled Che. *I have found a way. It can be done, and I will do it, with or without you. But they are cheating me, Che. They are denying me the strength I need, destroying my plans with their idiot sentiment. I need you. I am asking you to help me save the world, Che.*

And the Empress's mind opened further, and Che understood.

In the throne room at Capitas, Seda had banished all others save for General Brugan. The Rekef general crouched at the doorway, as far as he could get from the throne itself, where Seda slumped. His agents came to him, whispered their reports and then fled. There was something about the air in that room that made even the Apt fearful: it twisted and crackled as Seda fought to keep hold of the power she was amassing.

And still the deaths come rolling in, and still the tower builds higher. But not enough, not enough. She could feel cracks in the foundations, inevitable when she was forced to rely on others. Tisamon was on his way back from clearing another camp, but the orders she was sending to the Slave Corps were not being obeyed, the bloodletting that she was demanding was not happening. They were strangling her. *How dare they question?*

'I am the Empress,' she insisted to the cavernous space around her. She heard her own voice: just a frightened Wasp girl's after all. 'I am the Empress!' she shouted, challenging the echo. She saw Brugan twitch and cringe, desperate to go and yet unable to leave without her permission.

She had sent Red Watch men out to teach the recalcitrant slavers what it meant to obey. Of all the vile wretches under her command, how was it that the Slave Corps should suddenly decide to grow a spine and a conscience?

Well, it was too late for them to interfere. She had sent soldiers headed by her Red Watch to every camp, for all that their departure leached some of the strength from Capitas's defence. Her chosen would await her order; they would hear it like a spur in their minds. They would ensure that she had her blood, her death, the currency of her magic.

Che! she called into that howling void that separated them. *I need more. Even now they challenge me, they snatch lives from my grasp. I cannot do this alone any more, please!*

You . . . how can you even consider condemning so many people to death? In Seda's mind the Beetle girl sounded stunned.

Che, I have no choice. Where else can I draw power now but from the blood, the lives? If there was any other way to stop the Worm, don't you think I'd have tried?

But she could sense the condemnation as clear as if the girl was in the room with her – Collegium's daughter seeing only the usual Imperial excess.

No, Che, believe me. I do nothing lightly, but we have to stop the Worm. Do you think the magicians of old did no worse, when the need demanded?

I cannot believe it. Che sounded shaken, sickened. *Not the Moths, not the Spiders. Not even the Mosquito-kinden themselves. They did not even think on such a scale.*

There was more magic then, Seda reminded her sadly. *And, even then, you know they did terrible things. And if some Moth Skryre had needed the power, to preserve their world, they would have snuffed out your city and all your people . . . all their slaves. You know it.*

A long pause, then: *No,* said Che. *I do not. Because when my ancestors rose against them, that was the time. Before the great days of magic had quite ended, they could have ruined the world rather than lose it, and now they are in their mountain retreats, and we are our own masters. So I believe they chose not to, at the last.*

Seda could feel herself shaking with some emotion. She thought it was anger at first, perhaps even shame, grief, horror at what she was even now setting in motion. For a moment she felt that she might see herself in Che's mirror, as the monster she had become. And yet she had no choice, she reminded herself. The Worm was her responsibility. All emotions, whatever they might be, were banished back to their cage. She had no time to indulge them. *Che* . . . but she had lost her connection, and she went reaching down and down, hunting for that one fugitive mind that she could reach: her nemesis, her sister . . . the only one who could help her. The only one who could understand.

Then Brugan let out a mewling sound of fright, and she knew Tisamon was back, striding over to her side with his blade still dripping blood. She would have to send him out again, she knew. The deaths must keep coming, and he was the only one she could rely on.

She could feel the worlds grinding against one another, and she began to apply her pressure, using all the finesse and skill she could muster, committing the vast reserves of tainted magic that she had accumulated in the hope that there would be more to follow. A ritual that the Moths would have envied even in their glory days was what she was about: a magic from the old times, to remake the Seal and bury the Worm.

'Majesty.' Brugan had taken another message, it seemed. 'The army.'

'What?' she demanded through gritted teeth. 'Just report, General. You can still make a proper report, can't you?'

'Generals Tynan and Marent are ignoring your orders, Majesty,' Brugan told her, his voice shaking in case her wrath might light on himself, even in passing. 'They remain beyond the gates. They will not be summoned.'

I have no time for these irrelevances. But they betray me. They already betray me. With so much magic, fragments of prophecy were clouding the air like gnats – all the futures save the one thing she needed to see. *Will I succeed? Will Che lend me her strength?*

'Majesty.' Brugan stopped because he did not dare to contradict her, and so what use was he as an adviser?

'Tisamon,' Seda sighed. 'It must be you, it seems. The general has lost all claim to call himself a man of my kinden. Go forth and kill Tynan and Marent and all they conspire with. Bring their blood. The blood of generals will surely have more power than that of ordinary men.'

And then she heard the faint scratch of Che's voice. *Seda? Do you hear me?*

Che? Tell me, Che. Tell me you see that this is necessary.

And that distant, bitter response. *Yes. I see what must be done. I will do it. I will help you.*

Thirty-Nine

Taki brought her Stormreader in fast over the walls of Myna, thinking how it didn't seem long since she'd been here last. That time, she had left with the city under bombardment and the Wasps taking the streets one by one, reasserting their control after the Mynans' brief and fragile period of freedom. Now . . .

Oh, they did a real piece of work on this place. Great swathes of the city were in ruins, some just deserts of rubble, other buildings standing without roofs, without their full complement of walls, eyesocket windows staring out over so much devastation.

Could have been Collegium, she reflected. *Stick a lake on it, could be Solarno.* Then she was shifting her Stormreader violently in the air because someone was shooting at her.

She was not supposed to have come here with Stenwold and Kymene. She wasn't of Maker's Own Company and, if she had given a curse about chains of command, she should have been winging her way towards Capitas even now. But she was firmly of the position that she did absolutely what she wanted, and telling her to do things that she didn't want was a quick way to see the back of her, whether the orders came from a Sarnesh tactician with a nasty glint in his eye or from Stenwold Maker himself.

What she remembered most in all the war, though, was defending Collegium in the early days, when the Empire's aerial strength had been so superior, and when she and her fellows had been using every ounce of skill and Collegiate ingenuity just to survive each day and night of the air raids.

So many of the men and women who had fought alongside her had been Mynans. They had traded in their ragbag assortment of machines for Stormreaders, and they had given the inexperienced locals their backbone, their fighting spirit. And they had died, her fellow pilots, her peers and her allies and her friends. So many of them had given their lives for Collegium, without hesitation.

And this was what they had dreamt of: the return to Myna. Some of those airmen and women were with her even now, coursing swiftly through the sky, throwing themselves against the Spearflights and the Farsphex of the enemy. Others were with them only as names and memories, but it was for them that Taki had come too.

She turned the Stormreader on one wingtip, neatly as ever her old *Esca* had handled, her rotaries severing the tail of a clumsy Spearflight and sending it spinning out of her course. There were mindlinked Imperial Farsphex pilots here, but they were still too few to prevent the airships coming in, with Taki and the Mynan pilots driving them away. The flower of the Imperial Air Corps had fallen over Collegium, and the replacement pilots and machines had been scattered across too many fronts.

She let her orthopter swing wide to see how the airships were getting on. One was coming down some way outside the walls, and she guessed that its envelope had been holed a few times and its crew had not wanted to risk a drop. Another was actually descending onto the wall itself, and she saw Imperial troops desperately flying and scrabbling to get up there and oppose the landing, like a siege from an upside-down world.

The Sea-kinden were in that vessel, she saw. There was no mistaking their colossal armoured forms leaping down onto the wall – warriors from a world where falling was seldom something to be feared. At least one misjudged and dropped from the walls like a rockslide, but the rest were already fighting, shrugging off snapbow bolts and stingshot and carving joyously through the Wasps. Rosander's pale-plated form shone out at their head.

And we're in. Taki slung her machine through a cloud of Light Airborne, rotaries blazing to scatter them, catching a brief, messy glimpse of one luckless man torn apart by the barrage.

The Imperial air counter-assault was getting more determined – she reckoned they'd put everything they had into the air by now, pulled back anything that might have otherwise been bedevilling the locals. The airships were coming under fierce assault, and one was listing badly as it tried to get to the ground, the cells within its canopy venting gas through holes large enough for Taki to see even at this distance. There had been a suggestion that they simply drop the relief force where the local uprising had made its stand, but it was plain that the Imperials were not going to let these lumbering dirigibles get that far.

Another airship had coasted over the wall and was descending onto the rubble with absurd care, even while the Farsphex strafed it, disgorging Mynan soldiers who were willing to jump the last few feet because they had been waiting for this moment for too long. Stenwold Maker would be down there, too, probably holding on to the rail and staring out at the battle to come. The Wasps would not be slow with their response.

'Gannic!' the Red Watch man was yelling. 'Gannic! Where are you?' Even though the halfbreed engineer was virtually in front of him. 'Halfways bastard, what were you doing?' The man's face was purple with anger, eyes crammed full of suspicion.

'Sleeping, sir. What's happening?'

'The Lowlanders have got here,' snapped Red Watch. 'We move now. I've got the garrison mobilized already, you sluggard. We're taking our special cargo up to the enemy right now.'

'Yes, sir.'

Red Watch was already storming off, leaving Gannic to stumble in his wake. 'We're moving in the artillery. We can sling this stuff up onto the top level, let it crack open and obliterate the whole pack of them. If the artillery doesn't manage to get there, then you'll take squads in, carry the stuff, plant it and set it to explode.'

And get out. You forgot to say, 'Get out,' Gannic thought, but did not say.

Red Watch seemed to have overheard even the thought, because he rounded furiously on the silent Gannic. 'This mission is top priority, orders from the Empress herself,' he snarled. 'I didn't want to have to rely on you. You're not one of *us.*' It was not clear whether he meant the Watch or the Wasp race as a whole, or some other more arcane qualification. 'Understand, though: this must succeed. Nothing can go wrong. There can be no deviation. We are here to execute a city, in the Empress's name. Do you understand?'

'Yes, sir,' Gannic got out.

'And if that means you have to stand over these things with a hammer and hit them until they blow, you'll do it.'

'Sir, you can't just . . . after Szar last time, there are failsafes. They have to be—'

'Whatever they have to be, you do it. You make sure it's done.' Red Watch waved away the technical details, the hours of careful thought put in by Gannic's fellow engineers.

Then Red Watch was off to intimidate some of the garrison officers. 'Get moving! Get moving up the tiers. We need to stop the locals getting out. I want all of your snipers out on the streets. I want that relief force slowed down to a crawl. Get me your Sentinels and put them in the Lowlanders' way. Anything to give us more time!'

'Sir!' Gannic got as close to tugging on the man's sleeve as he dared.

'What is it?'

'Sir, you said up . . . you said the Mynans are . . . they're on the top tier of the city.'

'That's where we've got them penned,' Red Watch acknowledged.

488

Oh ... 'Sir, this gas is heavier than air. Once it's done its work on the Mynans, it'll . . . come back down, to us.'

'It's gas. Don't be ridiculous,' Red Watch pronounced firmly, and strode off.

Oh, no, no no, don't say he knows that little about artifice. Gannic glanced around at the mustered force of the Myna garrison, marching to the orders of their Empress, and not one of them understanding what was about to happen. He felt like waving his hands in the air and shouting, *You're all going to die! You're heading straight to your deaths!*

And he would be the one who would kill them, along with all the Mynans, a city-full of Mynans crammed together in that part of the city they naively believed that they had won back. They had not been bombed, nor had the Airborne dropped in to break them up and scatter them, and they had not asked why. They did not know that the Empress had a purpose even for their defiance. A terrible, terrible purpose.

He could walk away, he realized. He felt the fulcrum moment of his life, the point when he could say 'no' – even just to himself – and walk away, and not be the man who murdered an entire city.

But the Red Watch man would hunt him down, or the Empress would send some other to do it, or the Rekef or . . . And Gannic was a creature of the Empire. Where else could he go?

But as soon as the canisters are in the air, I'm running.

The air was still being contested, the Stormreaders tilting and stooping, outnumbered by the Imperial craft. The majority of the Wasp pilots were operating in old Spearflights, though – yesterday's machines no match for today's. Each time Stenwold looked up, there seemed to be fewer of them.

He had tasked the pilots with getting the word through to the Mynan enclave that help was coming, but there was no way of knowing if they had succeeded. The ground forces, their airships abandoned behind them, were just forcing their way onwards through the city, scouting ahead as best they could and trying not to stop for anything.

The Empire was plainly committed to foiling them in that last objective. Light Airborne had begun dropping on them soon after they started off, squads of Wasps finding rooftops or empty storeys to shoot from, fleeing when they were challenged, but always coming back for more.

The attackers' response to this was simply not to let this tactic delay them at all, moving through the war-ravaged streets of Myna as swiftly as they could, so that by the time the Wasps had set up their ambush, their enemies were already passing on. If the Imperial troops had been a regular field army, then this would have become an exercise in accumulating casualties. The Mynan garrison was larger than most, but it lacked the same keen edge of battlefield veterans. The attackers' speed and simple determination to press ahead caught the Wasp garrison off guard and out of position. The airborne squads were picked off in the air as they tried to get in place, or sometimes found that the fleetest of their enemies had already staked out their hiding places.

By this time, the pilots had reported seeing a large Imperial column heading towards the Mynan enclave, travelling with auto-motive-hauled siege engines. Nobody liked the sound of that.

'Pick up the pace,' came the order, directed at soldiers already making the best time they could, and then the first barricades were sighted – mounded banks of rubble hastily shovelled into place by the Wasps to keep the Mynan relief from crossing their own city.

Stenwold and Kymene had gone forwards to see what the Empire had achieved in the time they had grudgingly allowed it.

Not so much, was the opinion, but it was plain that the Empire had made a serious stand there. He saw the spears of heavy infantry, a handful of repeating ballistae and leadshotters.

'Worth going round?' he asked Kymene.

'If it was, would they have devoted so much to this?' A rhetorical question. 'The street to their left, you see it? That curves back round behind them, though. Scouts say it's all bombed to pieces – craters, rubble, hard going – but we'll take it at a run, fast as we can. There'll be snipers there, most likely, but let's hope not many. Meanwhile . . .'

'We'll hold their attention,' Stenwold confirmed. 'You think Rosander's up for it?'

This last was for Paladrya's benefit, in her notional position as Sea-kinden liaison. In truth, Rosander was plainly like the sea itself, a force not to be commanded or channelled.

'He's not turned away from a fight yet,' she confirmed. It was an unavoidable truth that the plight of Myna had not affected the Nauarch of the Thousand Spines, nor was he remotely inter-ested in the political differences between the Empire and its enemies. He was concerned instead with stamping his mark on the land, in being the first and only man of his people to defeat the land-kinden at their own game. He was enjoying himself and, every time his hugely armoured Onychoi lumbered into battle, Stenwold was grateful once more that they were on his side. *It could have been so different.*

'You stay back,' he cautioned Paladrya.

'And you? Will you stay back with me?'

He grimaced. 'The Maker's Own need me to direct them. They'll be marching right there in Rosander's wake, to hold whatever ground he takes.' For the Onychoi simply did not under-stand about securing their conquests – they just went forwards – and if the Wasps flew back down behind them, they would never know.

'Well, then I come with you,' Paladrya told him.

'You don't even have armour—'

'And you've been to such pains to tell me how these snap-bows wouldn't care if I did,' she pointed out.

To Stenwold's annoyance, Kymene smirked at that. 'She has you there. And, besides, with the way they're deploying their Airborne, being at the rear's no guarantee of remaining safe.'

'Well, then.' Stenwold threw up his hands. 'Let's be at it. Stay safe, Kymene.'

'Tell that to the Wasps.' She was off then, shouting to her followers, the black and red armour of the Mynans feinting a rush towards the Imperial position – drawing their siege engines out of line – before flooding off to one side, keeping up the pace even when they hit the broken, bomb-scarred wasteland beyond.

'Rosander, they're all yours!' Stenwold yelled. Then: 'Maker's Own! Form on me, maniples ready to advance!'

He saw several flights of Airborne lift up from beyond the barricade, obviously about to go after Kymene, but then the Sea-kinden were in motion, a great armoured wedge of them advancing like the tide towards the Imperial lines. The Airborne were abruptly in confusion – Stenwold had the sense of conflicting orders, a difference of opinion on where to commit their forces. If he had been in charge, then he would have sent the Airborne off anyway – only a fool let himself be flanked – but the onrush of Rosander's warriors was a fearsome and alien sight. The Airborne scattered, swirled, and dropped back down at last. By then the artillery was loosing – a leadshotter smashing one Onychoi into bloody fragments, ballistae bolts bursting and flaring as they exploded, with mixed results. Stenwold saw at least one man get knocked flat by the impact, but simply lever himself up again, heavy mail crazed with lines but obviously holding together.

Then Stenwold's feet took him forwards, snapbow in his hands and Paladrya at his back, and with the soldiers of the Maker's Own on both sides. There was almost none left now of those who had earned their battle cry and motto by going with him to meet Tynan's Second Army that first time. He bellowed it out anyway, 'Through the Gate!' and heard it taken up all along the line, a ferocious, bloodthirsty roar such as nobody had heard from the Beetle-kinden since their revolution.

The Onychoi charge did not slow. Some of them died – struck through the eyeslits or throats by snapbow bolts, their strong armour punched in by the fists of leadshotters or torn open by the explosive spears of ballistae – but their thunderous approach ignored it. Perhaps they were moving with such momentum that they could not have stopped if they had wanted to.

The Wasp infantry met them at the crest of the barricade, levering at them with spears, turning them back and prising them over, the shifting, sliding slope of loose stone denying them footing. The Onychoi fell back, scraping down on their backs, lurching sideways off balance. The Wasps were not even trying to pierce that indomitable mail, but only to keep them back, to buy time. The expressions on the defenders' faces spoke eloquently that they understood they could not win, only lose over a longer period of time.

The Sea-kinden's own bolts were tearing into the defenders, and Stenwold's people were shooting now – picking them off because they had to hold the top of the barricade to keep the Onychoi at bay.

'They're fighting behind!' Paladrya yelled in Stenwold's ear, and he saw that it was true. The Airborne were shooting at a new enemy – Kymene had made the distance even faster than he had expected.

He saw the first flash of black and red as the Mynans surged into view, and then the defence of the barricade collapsed. The Airborne took to the skies, fleeing to some other bottleneck. The infantry tried to run, but by that time Kymene's force was behind them, and the Mynans were not inclined to take prisoners or show mercy.

The Onychoi finally gained the top and went skidding and scrabbling down the far side, and Stenwold could only imagine what the Wasps could think in their last moments, faced with these warriors from beyond any civilized nation they could imagine, strong and resilient beyond belief. He found himself rushing at their very heels, not a foe left there for him to fight, then he broke off to find Kymene again.

'They'll throw something else in our way,' she told him, 'but we have a clean run to their column, the scouts say. If we move fast, they won't have the time to set another blockade like this one.' Her troops were marching off, double time, already scanning the skies for the next band of Airborne.

'Come on, Maker!' Rosander's voice boomed nearby. 'What are you waiting for?'

'Nothing. I've waited long enough for this.' Stenwold saw Kymene's odd look and knew that she would not understand. Yes, this was her city, but he had seen it fall twenty years before, and he had not been present the last time the Mynans had fought free of their conquerors. This time it would be real for him. This time he would personally see Myna free, and perhaps lay to rest those decades-old memories.

He was not young, and he had plenty of old injuries to drag him back, but somehow he kept up the pace, though Paladrya had to steady him whenever he lost his footing on the rubble. On all sides the broken facades of Myna gazed at him hollowly, spurring him on with their mute reminders. Occasionally the snapbow bolts sang out – he saw men and women go down and get dragged into cover by their comrades, but they fell singly, and the Wasps could not slow the rest enough. He had the sense of the Empire's brutal hold on this city disintegrating.

At one point he found himself struggling over another barricade, his feet slipping on the broken pieces of Mynan homes, but it was built lower than the last and the Empire had not stayed to defend it. The liberators were driving the enemy ahead of them like leaves before a storm.

'Maker!' Kymene was shouting, and he looked up and saw movement ahead – not an organized force placed there to delay them, but the main Imperial column, a great mass of men and machines seen in slices between the half-fallen buildings. They were reforming, and he saw Airborne all over the sky searching for roosts from which to shoot, whilst others were milling in the streets. He saw the articulated bulk of a Sentinel clatter into view before it made a scraping turn to face the oncoming enemy.

Rosander was already in motion, tireless, inhuman. The

494

warriors of the Thousand Spines pushed themselves to the front and strode forwards into what must surely be the final battle for Myna. Stenwold saw a ripple of shock course through the Imperial lines at the first sight of them.

Kymene kept advancing, sending her soldiers into the buildings on either side to break up the Wasp shooting positions, and Stenwold pushed forwards to keep up with her, the Maker's Own spreading out to his right, shooting at any Wasp target that presented itself. The sky was still busy, but the Airborne were being thinned out rapidly, those who could not find cover being picked off by the Collegiate snapbowmen. *When did we become veterans?* Stenwold wondered. But, of course, his own city had been through a lot in the last few years. The Empire had forged the merchants and tradesmen of Collegium into soldiers, and now the Beetles had come to show them their error in that.

Beyond the diminishing Airborne, the remaining flying machines duelled and danced – not a Spearflight to be seen now, just Stormreaders and Farsphex, and it looked to Stenwold as though his own pilots – veterans too – were carrying the day.

A crash sounded from ahead, and he saw a Sentinel plough into the Sea-kinden at full speed, scattering them, crushing a handful beneath it. Its single eye spat fire, the leadshotter ball carving a bloody trough through the Collegiate lines. Then the Onychoi had converged on it, prising and levering at its armour as it tried to shake them off. The cover over its main barrel gaped again, and a Fly-kinden in Maker's Own colours darted past its face, shoving a grenade into the opening. The flash of the explosive gutted the machine itself but was so well contained by its armour that the surrounding Sea-kinden were barely shaken by it.

He heard Kymene's clear voice yelling: 'For Myna! We will rise again!' and he was just about to throw in his own, 'Through the Gate!' when she cried out in pain.

He saw her fall, leg pierced by a snapbow bolt, and a handful of her men cut down with her, Wasp snipers above suddenly making their presence known.

'Kymene!' He was immediately labouring over the uneven ground towards her, knowing that he would be too late. 'Paladrya, stay back!'

He had no idea whether she would or not, but he was closing on the Mynan leader, seeing her clutch at her holed leg while trying to inch herself into cover. A bolt skipped off the stone by his foot, and another cut past his shoulder.

'Back, Maker!' Kymene yelled at him, her face pale with pain. A squad of Mynans was pushing into the building to dislodge the snipers, and others were rushing to protect their commander, but they were still too far off. Stenwold had almost reached her, one hand stretched out, waiting for the moment when the next bolt would find her, to snuff her out even as her city was being won.

Something struck him a hammer blow to the skull, and his world flew apart.

The Red Watch man seemed to be on the point of apoplexy when he heard the news. 'How can they have reached us so fast? How much further to the Mynans?'

Too far, Gannic thought. Lugging the artillery had done it. The Lowlanders – or whatever those *things* were, because they didn't look like any Lowlanders he had ever seen – had lacked anything resembling a siege train. If the Imperials had just holed up in the garrison, then they could have held out for tendays against a rabble of infantry, but Red Watch's tactical genius – or his skewed priorities, rather – had brought them all out into the open like this.

'Hold them off! Throw them back! Keep up the advance! The Empress wills it!' Red Watch insisted, and Gannic saw his own despair mirrored in the faces of the other officers nearby. *There is no way*, he thought. *You can't have it all.*

Some of the mid-ranking garrison officers, a couple of majors and some captains, were organizing what defence they could, and were plainly ignoring the voice of the Empress for the foreseeable future. They were sending their best snipers forwards to give the enemy's sides and rear something to think about, and were trying to throng the buildings on either side with Light Airborne so that the advancing force would get caught in a crossfire. *Too little, too late.* Too many of those buildings were ruinous shells that gave precious little cover, and besides there were Mynans already rushing inside them, braving the shot to fight over the best vantages. *And then* they'*ll be shooting down on* us.

It's time to leave, I think. But before he could put that thought into practice, Red Watch had hold of his shoulder. 'Into the orthopter!' the man was shouting, and Gannic just stared at him blankly.

'What, sir?'

'The orthopter, the Farsphex!' And, yes, in the direction of Red Watch's shaking finger, there was a Farsphex, summoned here by who knew what signal. 'Get in. You can drop the Beekiller directly on them from the air.'

Gannic stared at him in utter astonishment. 'Sir, I'm not a pilot.'

'It's got a pilot. You can be the . . . what, the bombardier! Do it!' Red Watch cuffed him across the head with a gauntleted hand. 'Do it!'

'Sir, have you seen the *size* of the gas canisters? The Farsphex aren't kitted out to drop anything that big.'

'Then you'll set the thing off and just roll it out of the side hatch!' Red Watch roared into his face. 'Go! The Empress commands!'

'Sir . . .'

Another blow fell. 'Do it, you traitor!'

'No, sir, the Mynan—!'

'We will hold the Mynans!'

Gannic held up his hands, desperately trying to fend off the man's fists. 'The *other* Mynans, sir! They're here!'

At last the Red Watch man stopped and looked round. They had been advancing along one of the main thoroughfares of the city, offering a good straight run up the tiers of steps leading all the way to where they had the Mynan population bottled up. Except the bottle had broken. The locals had realized that help was on the way, and they had not been content to sit around waiting for it. A veritable avalanche of angry Mynan soldiers and citizens was flooding down from the heights with vengeance in mind.

'Trigger them now!' Red Watch spat out. 'The canisters . . . set them off now. Here and now, all of them.'

'In the middle of our own soldiers?' Gannic shrieked at him. 'Are you insane?'

For answer, the Red Watch man grabbed him by the arm and began hauling him towards the laden automotives, shaking him fiercely every time he tried to resist. The man *was* insane, that seemed undeniable, but he possessed all the strength that madmen were supposed to have.

So sting, Gannic told himself. *Sting him. Stab him. Do something.* And yet he did not. Even considering what Red Watch was going to make him do, even with the enemy on all sides and any chance of escape rapidly vanishing, he found that he was more frightened of the consequences of disobedience right now than of obedience a few minutes later.

Do it, then fly, he told himself. *Fly and don't look back.*

Then Red Watch was down, a javelin-like bolt skewering his chest, and Gannic tumbled to the ground with him. He scrabbled up only to see the monstrous armoured shock troops of the Lowlanders virtually on top of him. The Imperial lines had broken, unable to contain them. They were all around him, hacking and shooting.

He found that he was still stumbling towards the automotives, as though the Red Watch man had left some posthumous hook in his mind that he could not escape.

He had a second of clarity, caught halfway there, locking eyes with a Beetle-kinden soldier down the length of the woman's snapbow barrel. He opened his mouth to make his excuses, to beg some kind of exception – *I'm just an engineer* – and then she shot him. The bolt struck him through the shoulder, throwing him to the ground. A moment later a vast armoured form loomed over him, blotting out the sun.

Gannic shrieked, and a curved sword descended and made an end of him.

After it was done, with Mynans rejoicing on every side, Rosander took off his helm and sucked in a deep breath.

'Enough,' he decided. 'This has to be enough. The bastard was right. It just goes on and on.'

His armour was now a great stone weight around him; it had felt as light as air when he had donned it first. He was hot. He was thirsty.

He was happy, though. He would return to the sea and his warriors would tell the tale: how the Thousand Spines had invaded the land.

And we'll be back, no doubt. All that nonsense of secrecy that Maker had cooked up with Hermatyre was well and truly broken open now. *A world of opportunity.* It seemed likely that land and sea were both going to have to make plenty of adjustments.

But we're Onychoi. We'll profit. He felt fiercely proud of his people – not just their fighting spirit, but the engineering and artifice that had allowed them to export it so far. *Chenni's going to laugh, when she hears.*

He lumbered off to find the Lowlander leaders, with the Mynans making sure to get well out of his way.

He found Kymene quickly enough. With her leg being attended to by a surgeon, she was taking reports from her people, but he wasn't much interested in her. Instead he kept on looking until he found Paladrya sitting huddled outside one of the buildings.

'Where's your man? Inside?' he boomed. 'I need to speak with him.'

Rosander was not by nature sensitive, but something moved within him as she looked up, red-eyed and trembling, so that his voice was almost gentle when he asked her, 'What is it?'

Forty

Che looked out, with eyes that knew no darkness, and saw the Worm.

Had I ever realized they were so many, would I have done this differently?

Because, of course, this was not all the Worm's bodies. Far more than this were now funnelling inwards through their city, climbing the gradient leading into the wider world above, seeking to bring the Worm's gift to all the world.

The Moths did an evil thing when they sealed this place away. She wondered if they had ever known – when Argastos and the rest forged the Seal – just what abomination they were opening the way for. Had they any idea what the desperate Centipede-kinden would do, cut off from the outside world and desperate for any means to survive?

And they had failed, in the end. Save for pathetic remnants like the Scarred Ones, they had given themselves over to something that cared nothing for them, and it had merely hollowed them out and consumed them.

Now those shells that were rushing towards the slaves' prepared positions were not even born of the Centipede. They were the children of the Worm's slaves, the stolen generations remade in their old masters' image, force-grown, hollowed out and sent to butcher those who had brought them into the world.

The first sling stones were flying on both sides. Che saw the twin heads of the Worm's advance ripple with casualties which the main body just moved on over. They barely slowed.

She was here at the highest point of all, the last place the Worm would reach, once all her followers were dead. She was here because this was where the magic would last longest. Here where she might have been able to accomplish something. Here where she had found the limits of her Inapt strength.

There was not enough magic in the whole of the Worm's world simply to open a door where she pleased, but even if there had been, she could not see her way to it. She could not find the logic unique to ritual that would bring such a result about. She was not enough of a magician, anointed heir to the Khanaphir Masters or not.

She looked back over the host of those who had followed her here – the fighters who were even now bracing themselves against the onrush of the Worm, slingers, rock-pushers, the untrained and awkward who had been given swords and told to stand. She looked over the far greater number who hid behind them: the weak, the young, the old, the desperate. She felt so very, very sorry.

There seemed no other option now, no better use she could make of her power and her time. She could not save these people. They would die, and nobody in the world beyond would ever know that they had even lived.

But there was something she could achieve while she still had time before the Worm took her. There was yet a cause she could give herself over to.

She understood Seda's plan now, the terrible details, the ocean of blood the woman would drown herself in. She understood why – the inexorable logic to save the world from the Worm.

And I know the horrors of the Worm, of all people. Seda had called on her, all enmities put aside. What little Che still possessed, she needed.

Seda, she sent out, *do you hear me?*

And the distant response, Seda's voice strung as taut as a bow. *Che? Tell me, Che. Tell me you see that this is necessary.*

Che felt sick at what she must do, the betrayal of so much, but what else was there? There was a point when all pretence was stripped away, and she could see herself just as she was, and know the limits beyond which she could not go. *Yes, I see what must be done. I will do it. I will help you.*

There, I've said it. Had she doomed herself and Thalric and Tynisa and all these people, or were they doomed already? *I think that this graveyard of a world is the one place that even I cannot make worse with my mistakes.*

Esmail was a planner by nature. He was used to having time to prepare, absorbing all the information he could raid from the minds of his victims, then to plot his entrance, his exit, his fall-back. He was also used to having his magical abilities to hand, and to facing an enemy that acted and reacted in something like a human manner.

He winced as he sliced a new scar on his arm with one finger. The locals had started to notice him again.

And the city was still crawling with them. Despite the host that was pursuing Che, and the army still spiralling its way out of this world up to the sunlight – and surely even now mustering in some unthinkable halfway place for its grand assault – the city still seethed with the silent host of the Worm, amidst whom paced the huddled, fearful figures of the Scarred Ones, masters and prisoners all at once.

He could not get Totho out. He had kept watching for an opening that would never come. If he tried to extract Totho from that pit, then every eye in the city would be turned on them, and every blade shortly after. Esmail was barely maintaining equilibrium by passing himself off as a Scarred One, using the mindset he had stolen, using the scars he had copied, but only because he was doing everything possible not to draw attention to himself. A single slip would undo all his work.

He had considered waiting for Totho to be dragged out and ambushing the priests as they led their new sacrifice towards the caves. It would be an ambush in the midst of a great host of enemies, though, sheer suicide that no amount of skill could save him from. And surely that moment of truth was coming – Totho was still within, but the hall down below must be emptying rapidly. The Scarred Ones had not been slow about their sacrifices.

He did not want to return to Che admitting failure, but he was a professional, an agent's agent. Sometimes a job simply could not be done. She would have to understand.

The bitter part was that she *would* understand. She would not rail and shriek and demand that he do better, as some employers had. Her disappointed misery would be harder to bear.

Then he felt a change in the crowd about him, and realized that his introspection had closed him off dangerously from keeping track of his surroundings. Through that throng of vacant bodies, a single man was making a direct line for him: one of the scarred.

Discovered! But, if so, the Centipede-kinden had not yet alerted the host of warriors all around him. Esmail considered running, but none of the Scarred Ones ever ran. The bodies of the Worm were constantly rushing, as though appalled by what they had become, but the priests maintained a sedate pace. To flee would be to announce that he did not belong.

So kill him. He could slide his cutting-Art fingers into the intruder's belly as they approached each other, then help the corpse to sit down, robes bunched about the wound to soak up the blood. He could only hope that the murder would not register in the attention of the Worm, so that he would have a chance to get clear before the death was discovered. It would not be the first time he had pulled just such a trick.

Just moments before he sent himself striding forwards into that fatal clinch, he realized that he knew this man. It was not just some old Scarred One about to meet a well-deserved end; it was the Hermit.

Seeing him there, after the man had refused to accompany

Esmail to the city, brought the Assassin up short. *Has he changed sides? Is he about to betray me?* Those were the instant thoughts, followed by, *So I should kill him, anyway.* But the same logic prevailed: if the man had rejoined the Worm, then he would have a hundred swords already within striking distance of Esmail, and no need to risk himself.

The Hermit stopped at what he probably thought was just outside striking distance, though Esmail could still have cut his heart out if he had risked a full extension of his arm. Eyes half buried in wrinkles studied the Assassin dispassionately.

'You do it well,' he murmured. 'I didn't think it was possible, but you carry yourself just like them – just like *us*. I never even knew we stood like that, until I see you doing it now. You're an artist, truly.'

'And you're my audience, apparently,' Esmail replied softly. The Scarred Ones were always murmuring. None of them seemed to dare speak as loud as the Hermit was right now. 'Why are you here?'

The old man looked insulted at first – after all, surely this was his place more than it could ever be Esmail's – but then something else descended on his face, some weight of shame, and he muttered something, losing the words entirely. Only when Esmail leant closer with an exasperated hiss did he get out, 'For *him.*'

'Orothellin.'

The Hermit nodded unhappily. '*He* believed in her. He wanted to help her, the Beetle girl, and he's dead now, the fool. After so long, he finally risked too much, and let them catch him. I should hate her for that – without her he'd still be alive – but it just goes round and round in my head, the way he wanted to help. So in the end I'm here because of *him*, because what else have I got?' A tear was tracking through the grime, finding the path of least resistance down the lines of his face.

And Esmail saw it, and cursed himself for not thinking quicker, because abruptly he had a plan: he had now the tool to accomplish the task he had been set.

'*You* can do it,' he said. '*You're* what I need, to get this man out that Che wants.'

'You've found him?'

'Oh, yes. He's stuck in with a load of others, and they're emptying the pot fast, but if we're faster we can get him out. I'll need you to do to him what you did to Che – cut him up like you did her, then keep close to him until he's out. I can't do it – even at my best. Without my magic I just can't be one of you. But you . . .'

'And he'll just let me carve him up, will he?' the Hermit demanded, a little of his old fire returning.

'I reckon he'll take what he can get,' Esmail shot back. 'Now, come on . . .'

And he was already too late, even as the plan had finally become possibly, because here he was. Here came Totho, hauled from the pit by a knot of struggling Worm soldiers, with a handful of other prisoners alongside him.

'How quickly can you do your work?' Esmail hissed. He was thinking through permutations – attacking, holding the assembled might of the Worm off somehow, then trusting to his heels whilst the Hermit somehow got Totho clear. 'I can win you maybe a few minutes, if I'm really, really lucky.' He was watching the prisoners being hauled away between the crumbling vacant blocks of the city, calculating where he could make best use of the ground to win as much time as possible for the Hermit to . . .

'Esmail, you remember,' the old man said wearily. 'That first marking, it cannot be done quickly or it will fail. There will be no time.'

'No, it . . .' Esmail was already moving, shadowing the soldiers of the Worm and their prisoners, noting the placement of the scarred priests as they led the convoy. He could see Totho fight one arm clear, saw the hand poised near the captive's belt helplessly for a moment. *Something to do with pulling on a string, he said*. Whatever it was, the knowledge of it had evaporated along with Totho's Aptitude.

'Esmail, there's no way.'

'Then they'll put them somewhere else before they . . . We'll have our chance . . .' Esmail tried desperately.

'You know where they're taking those poor wretches.' The Hermit sounded almost gleeful. 'You know the only use they have for live adult bodies here.'

The sight came back to Esmail: that vast, blinding questing head, the segment upon segment of clutching legs, the poisoned claws the size of a man. He had looked upon the thing the scarred priests worshipped and he had known that he could never do so again. He had never truly known fear until he had beheld the Worm.

And now he heard himself saying, 'Then we go after him. We ambush them on the way down, or . . . we take him from the Worm's jaws, if we have to.'

He glared at the Hermit, and saw a wondering, pitying expression on the old man's face.

'Oh, lead on,' the turncoat Centipede advised. 'You go ahead and show me what you'll do. At least someone will know, after you're gone, just how mad you were before the end.'

And at the last, the work was done, and all the prisoners were returned to the pit.

Sartaea te Mosca stood there, just able to see because most of the rest were too tired to stand when the slavers weren't actively whipping them. She stood proud of a sea of slumped shoulders and bowed heads, and watched.

The engineers had finished laying their fuses: that had been a complex and delicate job, and she had been given plenty of time to observe their faces. Unlike the slavers, they did not wear full-face helms to make themselves creatures of anonymous fear. They were young, many of them, and they were frightened. One of them had been weeping, even as he worked. None of them had wanted to look at the prisoners.

They had known what they had, in those great metal drums. The Bee-killer was to the Empire what a hero of the Days of Lore was to the Mantis-kinden: everyone knew the name; everyone was familiar with the deeds. And, just like those Mantis heroes, the Bee-killer's deeds were death, the death of vast numbers in such a brief time.

Why don't the others rise up? Te Mosca wondered. There were so many prisoners, and the channels cut into the edge of the pit should make escape even easier. *We should rush them! Someone should yell out some battle cry, and we'd all go surging out and knock down all the Wasps, and be free. Why doesn't someone do that?*

And she stood, a tiny figure, knowing herself to be so small as to be helpless before the Wasps. She knew whoever might give out such a cry would die for it. She knew the stings and the blades and the sheer physical strength of the Wasps – she felt them like a razor at her neck, like a knife close to her eye. And she said nothing. And they all said nothing. Starved, beaten, half-naked, sick, dying; there was no will left for defiance amongst the slaves.

Te Mosca wanted to call to the Wasps: *I am a Master of the College! I trained in magic with the Moth-kinden! I have healed wounds and saved lives! I am* someone! *I matter!* But, standing in that great assembly of the doomed, she was less and less convinced in that last article of faith. She was only valuable to the world in one way: one more life to be snuffed like a candle.

Then Metyssa was speaking again. Her voice shook and trembled: she was hunched in on herself, hugging her bony knees, head down, and yet somehow her voice still floated free. She began to tell them about the end of the war.

She told them how it came to pass: how the great Imperial war machine came to be dismantled; how peace came to all the lands of the kinden. She told it as though it was some fable from long ago, just the sort of story the Inapt grew up on. No rooftop

508

chases or derring-do now, but a gentle story of a world grown sane. A story where soldiers put away the toys of war and went home to their wives and mothers and lovers. In her story, Collegium and Myna were rebuilt in their old glories, and the Commonweal was free of the shadow that oppressed it. Rival Spider families clasped hands as friends, and Ant cities spoke of treaties and shared works for the benefit of all. And it was magic, te Mosca knew. She had never realized that Metyssa had any magic in her, but she felt it stir in the Spider now. It was a strange, weak storyteller's magic, released at the end of all things as if it could change the world.

But the world had grown old and turned away from such childish things as magic. Even te Mosca could not find much belief in such things within her breast. Captivity had made her like one of the Apt, seeing nothing in the world but their cold and inexorable mechanisms. Metyssa spoke on and on, until her words seemed to be the only sound in the world, but it made no difference. None of it made any difference any more.

Then another voice cut across her, ignoring her as though she was nothing. 'Now's the time,' the Red Watch man snapped, like someone late for an appointment. 'She needs it all now. Ready with the detonator?'

A handful of the engineers had been at work on some mechanism a short distance from the pit – te Mosca had seen it when the digging was going on. Now she became desperate to see it again. It had abruptly become the most important thing in her world. She tugged and nagged and badgered Poll Awlbreaker until he let her onto his shoulders, and from there she saw the instrument of all their extinctions.

It seemed a very little thing: just a box, really. A box with thick cords that issued from it, leading to all the canisters. Poll had said there would be firepowder within them, and charges at the barrels, all timed to break open at the same killing instant.

The Red Watch man stalked to the lip of the pit and looked

in: to te Mosca's knowledge it was the first time he had actually set eyes on the people he was arranging to murder.

'Remarkable,' he declared, in tones plainly intended to carry all the way across to the cages. 'It's hard to think they could have any value at all, isn't it? And yet they have one use left . . .' And he was left frowning, because he had obviously anticipated an attentive audience, of slavers and slaves both, and only those within arm's reach – and te Mosca – were really listening.

For Metyssa was still talking, ignoring their tormentors – ignoring the whole Empire and all written history to date, it seemed – and spinning her hopeless, impossible fable of some world where things had happened differently.

The Red Watch man made a start on another few platitudes, for apparently this was an occasion worthy of a speech to him, but he petered out each time, and at last he demanded, 'Shut that woman up!'

'What does it matter?' the lead slaver asked him in a low growl. 'Let her talk, why not? It won't change anything.'

The man with the red pauldrons stared at him. 'I do not want to hear her voice. I do not want to hear any of their voices. They are not permitted to mar this moment. Silence her.'

For a long moment the two Wasps stared at one another, and then the slaver dropped into the pit with a handful of his people, and they kicked and slapped their way to Metyssa. That was surely the moment to take them, if there ever was one, but by then even te Mosca had stopped believing in it. The Wasps were so fiercely full of vitality, the slaves so feeble and wasted.

The lead slaver stood over Metyssa, and even in his shadow she kept talking.

'Do it!' the Red Watch man shouted at him. But the slaver just stared, and the story rambled on, telling of homes and hearths, of better days and bluer skies. And then the Wasps were on the wing, back out of the pit without a blow struck.

'Just do what you came for,' the slaver spat. 'Piss on your speeches. Just get it over with.'

Red Watch ground his teeth and flexed his fingers at that, but it was plain that the mood of the slavers was frustrated and ugly. They had always been the least disciplined branch of the army, and te Mosca understood that accidents had happened before, with officers who had pushed them too far.

And so the moment of truth narrowed to a single point in time, and the Red Watch man snarled, 'You do it, then. I give you the honour. Fire the detonator, the Empress commands you.'

The lead slaver kept staring at him for a few heartbeats, and then sloped over to the detonator, scattering the engineers. 'What is this for?' he demanded. 'I've carried the whip for twenty years. I know my trade. What could this possibly be for?'

'When you donned that uniform,' the Red Watch man told him flatly, 'you swore to obey. I am the voice of the Empress. You do not get to pick and choose which orders you follow because you disagree or do not understand. Now make it happen!'

And te Mosca was struck by a strange certainty that he himself could not work the machines – that the fog of the Inapt mind was on the Red Watch man. Which meant that all of this was magic: not Metyssa's petty little magics of wasted words, but the greatest magic of all.

She could almost see it in her mind, what they would all be a part of: just as the fuses led to the cannisters, so this and a host of other massacres led into the Empire, to fuel . . . to fuel . . .

She supposed that it did not really matter to her, what it went to fuel. Her consent was not being asked.

And yet she was not dead, and the detonator had not been triggered, and when she looked again at the lead slaver, he was staring at the Red Watch man and saying something. Behind the mask of his helm there were no lips visible to be read, but it might have been as simple as, 'No.'

The Red Watch man went storming over, shouting at him, 'I am the voice of the Empress!' over and over, bringing his hands up to unleash his sting. The slaver ducked away and a scatter of gold fire danced about the detonator, catching one of the cords and sending it flaring and crackling, a trail of sparks snaking away towards the lip of the pit.

Then one of the engineers lunged forwards and drove a dagger down past the Red Watch man's collarbone with a strangled cry, forcing him to his knees. And once he had stabbed, the engineer stabbed and stabbed again, his face a mask of hate and despair.

With a distinct and solitary bang, one of the canisters sprang open, slave to that single lit fuse, and a seeping yellow death began to unfurl lazily into the pit. In moments people were choking and retching, scrabbling over each other to get away from it.

The lead slaver lost one second of contemplation staring at them all before he gave the order.

'Get them out! Get them all out!'

Seda stood in her throne room, preparing to muster her power. Poor cowering Brugan would be the sole uncomprehending witness to the greatest act of magic of the post-revolution age.

In a way, it was an unparalleled act of self-sacrifice as well as the far more overt sacrifice of so many others that she had planned and partly accomplished. She had felt the billowing surge of magic after the Seal finally gave way, and knew that the unravelling of that monstrous knot in the silk of the world had gifted back so very much. She, Seda the Empress, could be the foremost magician in a second dawn, challenging the Moth Skryres in their mountain halls, beating the old world at its own game. She was weaving all that power back into its knot. She was tying it where neither she nor Che, nor any other magician, might unpick and steal it. She was dooming herself to be no more than Seda the Empress, the Inapt ruler of an Apt nation, whose magic amounted to a scattering of tricks and sleights of hand.

But she knew her duty – both to her people and to the world. She would relinquish her bright future to accomplish that task, and she would extinguish the futures of as many others – Apt and Inapt, slaves and free – as it took.

Tisamon had gone stalking off to kill the latest band of conspirators to rise against her. She was used to that – ask Brugan if she was not used to that! – and if Tynan was a tool that had broken in her hand this last time, well, the Empire had got its full use out of the man. She was tempted to spare his family, after his death, but that would send a poor message to other would-be rebels. There would be no insurrection of the traitor generals, and Tynan's blood, and that of all who got in her way, would feed her grand ritual.

Speaking of which, now was her time. She could feel the Worm closing in on the world, with all its stolen numbers. *Time to put you in your place.*

All around her, her plan was falling into ruin, her subjects rebelling against her use of them, even the reviled Slave Corps shying back from what she needed them to do. For every faithful servant, another handful were betraying her commands. Did they not understand that she was trying to save the world?

It was no good: she could not do it alone. Perhaps she could not do it at all, but there was that one faint last chance.

Che, she called out.

A resigned reply came back: *I am here.* Poor idealistic Beetle girl, but at least she had recognized the way of the world at this late stage, when Seda needed her.

We must be strong now, Che. We must be strong together.

I know. The girl sounded so sad that it physically hurt Seda.

You would have killed me once, the Empress reflected. *I would have killed you, too, if I could. Before Argastos . . .* There had been that brief, utterly unexpected, handful of moments when the two of them had joined forces against the old Moth sorcerer. For Seda it had been a revelation. Her siblings had all died years before, save for her tyrant of a brother who had threatened her with execution every tenday until she and her Mosquito magician had done away with him. She had not expected to find a living sister so late. Che had been her rival, her opposite. Who could have known that, now the girl was lost to the underworld, Seda would miss her?

I wish it could be different, came the faint whisper of Che's thoughts. There were a number of things she might have been referring to, but Seda chose to believe that the Beetle's thoughts ran along the same lines as her own.

Me too. Are you ready?

I am.

I will remember you, when this is done.

I don't have much time. Make the connection.

Seda could sense a battle unfolding behind Che's thoughts, the sort of fight for survival that could not be won, which was being waged only because the drive to live was stronger than reason.

She reached out, drawing up the power that Tisamon had already reaped for her. Other atrocities were being enacted across the Empire – far fewer than she had wanted, but when she had Che's power, the other half of her whole, perhaps she could still accomplish what she intended, despite the treason of the white-livered Slave Corps, despite Tynan and Marent, despite all of them.

She drove through to Che, past the layers of earth and magic and impossible geometries, and made the link.

Forty-One

Straessa glanced out of the open window of the leading Collegiate carriage. It was a difficult choice – either stifle in the dark with the shutters closed, or choke in the dust with them open. The Sentinel attack had decided her, though: she wanted to see what was coming and to have as much warning as possible.

Next to Straessa, Castre Gorenn sat hunched over her knees and looking ill, because the Inapt never did travel well by machine. Recently, when the Dragonfly was still well enough to hold a conversation, she and Straessa had been talking about the fight to come and what might follow: whether victory at the gates of Capitas would indeed bring down the Empire, or whether Milus would want to press on and stamp his mark on every corner of the Wasps' domain. Straessa was aware that her people were losing their stomach for a prolonged campaign. Going on the offensive into enemy territory was very different to defending your own city, both logistically and philosophically. The Collegiates were inevitably thinking of the home that so badly needed them.

'I'll put it to the vote,' she announced, making Gorenn look up.

'About leaving?'

'We'll do things the Collegiate way. If enough want to go, then once we've got Capitas, we'll go.' Straessa was aware that the nearby Company soldiers were taking an interest, which would mean the entire Collegiate contingent would know within the hour.

'And you think Milus will let you?' the Dragonfly asked darkly.

'What's he going to do? Kill us and prop us on sticks to keep the numbers up?'

Gorenn shook her head. 'I am not sure just what Tactician Milus might do. There's something wrong with him.'

'He's an Ant.' Straessa shrugged. 'There's something wrong with all of them.'

'That's not what I mean. He's not like the others. He's a . . .' The Commonwealer struggled with the concept. 'He's a wrong Ant.'

'Surely you can't be talking about our beloved tactician?' another voice spoke.

Straessa started at the interruption, although Gorenn just looked up greenly. A slight, small figure had slipped into their carriage, stepping nimbly down the cluttered aisle, between the close-packed feet of the Collegiate soldiers. It was Laszlo, Maker's friend.

'What do you want?' she asked him. She had been about to add 'pipsqueak' or some other derogatory comment about the Fly's size, but he had a dangerous look to him and she felt an uncharacteristic attack of tact coming on.

'Talk with you, privately, Officer Antspider.'

'Find me "privately" anywhere on this thing,' she complained.

'Next car down's mostly baggage and ammo,' he replied immediately. 'Let's get going.'

It was easy enough for him, with his wings, but Straessa felt as if she stepped on every single individual foot on her way out of the carriage, collecting scowls and curses from her subordinates for every one.

On reaching the baggage car she found Laszlo flitting about the cramped space to make sure that nobody would be listening in. She watched him sceptically, wondering exactly what sort of bizarre secret agent business he thought he was about, now that Maker had left.

At last he turned to her. 'You speak for Collegium, right? For the Collegiates here?'

'Interesting philosophical point,' she began but he stopped her with a look.

'Stuff that. They look to you. You're their skipper, right enough. So listen up. I'm calling in my marker.'

'You're doing *what*?'

'You owe me.'

This conversation had gone in an unexpected direction. Straessa felt her footing shift, as though she was about to fight. 'And how's that, Master Laszlo?'

'You know exactly what I've done for your city, while the place was under Wasp rule. I was Mar'Maker's man, who came and went into the cursed *sea* for your lot. Take me away, and your city'd still be painted black and gold.'

'As you say, you were Maker's man,' Straessa pointed out.

He shot her an appraising look. 'Woman, I'm a son of the *Tidenfree*, a free corsair. My family cast their lot in with Collegium for gain, and we were paid. I didn't put my life on the line for your philosophy, and my skipper, Tomasso, he didn't get himself killed for it either. You remember him coming to save your own skin, back when the Wasps had your College surrounded? Well, that's another weight on the scales, because he didn't make it out – died getting Maker to the water. You owe me, halfbreed. Your city owes me. Like I say, I'm collecting.'

'This is to do with Milus, isn't it?' She recalled how the Fly seemed to have some personal grievance with the tactician.

'Up to him, that is. He wants to stay out of it, all the better.'

She hissed with annoyance, but this man plainly wasn't going to go away, and she had an uncomfortable feeling that there was indeed a debt to be paid somewhere in the story he had told.

'Look,' she started, but he interrupted again.

'You remember Sperra, the Princep girl?' he prompted. 'You remember she did her bit for your city, as well?'

Straessa nodded, on firmer ground now. Sperra had done the Sarn-to-Collegium run plenty of times, carrying information both ways.

'This is her marker too. And it's not such a grand thing. And maybe I was hoping that tweaking the tactician's nose was something you mightn't be averse to, after all.'

'So tell me,' she said at last. 'What do you want?'

Balkus stared into space, his mind locking horns elsewhere, fighting to get past the wall of Sarnesh contempt that his former kinsmen had built to keep him out. One simple question, that was all he had, but they ran him around and fobbed him off and ignored him, over and over. His only weapon now was persistence.

Had they truly been united in their dismissal of him, then all the persistence in the world would get him nowhere. He was in a unique position, though, as a renegade travelling within an army of the loyal. He could see them with their own mind's eye, but viewed from the outside. He could see the cracks. Not grand cracks, certainly – no sign of the Sarnesh falling apart because, of course, Ants didn't do that. The hard hand of Tactician Milus had started some tiny, hidden murmurs of dissent, though. These were kept quiet, passed privately mind to mind, but they were spreading enough for Balkus to detect them.

And through that he had his answer, passed to him hurriedly by a woman who would not touch minds with him again. He opened his eyes, his expression bleak.

'Aagen,' he declared softly, 'is dead. Died under interrogation, they said.'

Beside him, Sperra shuddered. Sarnesh torture was something she was no stranger to. 'That's it, then. We're next.'

Balkus wanted to say, *You can't be certain*, but he had a horrible feeling that she was right – the next time Milus wanted someone

to take out his frustrations on, who would be better than a renegade like Balkus, after all? And as for Sperra . . . Sperra would
probably end up in the same trap because she'd try to save her
friend.

'Makes you wonder whether helping the pirates is a good
idea,' he murmured, trying to pitch his voice so that the other
Princep soldiers – or servants, as the Sarnesh treated them –
wouldn't hear.

'No, it doesn't,' Sperra said, far too quickly. 'We're doing this.
It's not as if Milus needs an excuse, if he wants us.'

'Sperra—'

'Are you backing out on me now, Balkus? After all we've gone
through?'

He looked down at her unhappily. What he wanted to say was
some criticism of Laszlo – how it was plain that the pirate had
his eye on that girl that Milus had hold of, and just as plain that
Sperra seemed to have her eyes on Laszlo. But she would deny
it hotly if he made such an accusation. She would deny both
assertions at once, no matter how ludicrous that made her seem.

'We should never have got mixed up in this,' he said. 'Once
the Empire got past Malkan's Folly, we should just have upped
and headed west.'

'To where?'

'I hear the Atoll Coast is lovely.'

'You don't believe that. About heading out.' She had her determined face on, her little fists clenched.

'You know, I do, I really do, but I'll admit it's a tad late now,
when we're within spit of Capitas.'

Then Laszlo came, ghosting into the Princep carriage. Sperra
stood instantly, grabbing for his hand.

'It's ready?' she asked him eagerly. Balkus winced.

'All ready,' Laszlo confirmed. 'The Collegiates are on board.'

Balkus grimaced. 'You're sure about this, are you? Not going
to end up with a Sarnesh snapbow bolt in our ears for our
trouble?'

519

'Oh, we've given it a lot of thought,' Laszlo confirmed. 'Despard's already got everything in place. Just make sure . . .'

'I'll tell our people how it's going to be,' Balkus insisted. 'We'll be ready, don't you worry.'

The first explosion hit the track-laying automotive – just a flash within its workings, and then a gout of flame had sent it skidding off course, one wheel shattered, artificers jolting and tumbling out of it.

Instantly the Sarnesh were responding, ready for the Imperial attack that this must surely presage. The automotives spread out on either side of the rails picked up speed, the train itself slowed, all of this coordinated with perfect grace and not a word spoken aloud. Orthopters began to fly in widening circles, hunting out the enemy troops they knew were out there.

The next series of explosions coursed down the train itself: small, precise detonations targeting the couplings between carriages, going off singly or in strings. By now Milus was loud in the minds of his subordinates, tailoring the Sarnesh deployment, having the carriages brought to a standstill as quickly as possible. Even under his firm command, there was a great deal of confusion. The other contingents did not know what was going on and, rather than just sit tight and trust the Sarnesh, many of them were putting their own conflicting plans into action. The Vekken were stepping away from the rail line, forming up in a solid block of armoured soldiers bearing interlocked shields that would be utterly helpless against a good snapbow volley. The Collegiates had braked their own carriages and were spilling out with a typical lack of discipline. The entire army was spreading out, much to Milus's frustration. Every so often another little charge would crack open, inflicting some more damage to yet another carriage. Nothing major but it would all need to be repaired.

Alarm calls kept going up all along the line, each new explosion spurring yet more of them. Some of the non-Sarnesh were occupying valuable Ant time by demanding to know what was going on, which was apparently a question they were incapable of simply answering through the use of their own senses. Milus brought more and more of his soldiers into active service, forced to waste them in corralling and keeping tabs on the various other groups of soldiers who were apparently set on making his life as difficult as possible.

One voice seemed particularly loud in calling out such alarms, and though this fact bypassed him at that time, it lodged somewhere in his mind for later analysis. Not a voice that should be drawing attention to itself, that was certain.

He had his artificers busy already: repairing the track-layer, replacing the couplings, checking for other explosives. It was routine work, and it would all be fixed with the efficiency he would expect of his fellow Sarnesh. But it was lost time: time given as a gift to the mustering Imperial forces at Capitas.

Then one of his artificers managed to see far enough beyond the repair work to report: *Tactician, this was not a trap set by the Wasps on the line.*

Explain, Milus directed.

Those devices were set on our own machines. It would have been extremely difficult to sabotage the carriages without being aboard the train itself.

Immediately Milus brought more of his soldiers into the plan, having them search for strange faces: Imperial agents. *Unless it's someone we brought from bloody Collegium . . .* But then came a fresh report, *Tactician, your carriage is on fire.*

For a moment he did not quite make the connection. He had been moving forwards towards the track-layer, his eyes watching them winch it up for a new wheel whilst his mind saw fragments of a dozen different perspectives. Then he registered the image: the prison carriage was ablaze, gutted from within. The fire had started whilst the explosives were going off. It had gone unnoticed for vital minutes while his people were responding to the existing emergency.

Lissart!

He had a squad of soldiers there in an instant, and Milus himself was running back down the line towards it. The heat from the ruined carriage kept the Ants at bay, but they could peer through the windows and discern no human form within.

Nothing could have survived, one of them declared, and that only infuriated Milus the more.

You idiots! This was a trick! he shouted out the thought, the roar of his mind encompassing much of the army. *This was to rescue her, my prisoner! It was all a trick and you fell for it! Where are those Fly-kinden? Maker's Fly-kinden? Find them for me now!*

As he stopped before the carriage, seeing its roof half lift off with the ferocity of the blaze – even though it had been lined with metal to stop exactly this sort of damage – he was aware that some of his followers were reacting poorly to his tirade, but he had no time for them and no tolerance for disobedience. *Find them!* he insisted. *Aviators, quarter the ground here. Find me a party of Fly-kinden fleeing the rail lines. They can't have got far.* He did not pause to examine his own reaction, even in light of the way his own people were shying away from it. Lissart had been his, and she had been taken. Milus did not brook defiance, most certainly not from mere Flies.

By then his mind had returned to that little note of discord: the one who had been doing so much of the shouting, summoning the Sarnesh to this and that fresh explosion. Oh, certainly there had been a lot of voices, but one of them should not have been interfering in Sarn's business, distracting the attention of the Ants to each new blast. Not direction, but *mis*direction.

The renegade with the Princep force, Balkus, Milus noted. *Bring him to me.*

Tactician . . . and then no report. For the first time one of his subordinates was thinking twice before breaking news to him.

Tell me, he growled.

The Princep force has joined the Collegiates. They are refusing to give up the renegade.

For a moment Milus became so incandescent with fury that the entire Sarnesh army just stopped, eyeing each other, all suffering an identical stabbing pain in their minds born of their commander's frustrations. Then he had mastered himself, the hard man of war once again, and was striding double time towards the assembled Collegiate troops.

There were the Princep rabble, right in the middle, and that traitor Balkus amongst them. Milus surveyed the mass of Beetles and halfbreeds and assorted malcontents wearing Merchant Company colours, and by the time he had finished his assessment there were orderly ranks of Sarnesh soldiers at his back, more than enough to force the issue.

'Who commands here?'

There were obviously some differences of opinion about that, but what could he expect from Collegiates? Then that half-Spider creature got pushed forwards, the one with the eyepatch.

'Tactician?' she said, trying for casual politeness but obviously as tense as a bowstring.

'Give me that man,' Milus ordered her, jabbing his finger at Balkus. 'He's needed for questioning. He's not Collegiate. Give him up.'

'He is somewhat Collegiate,' the halfbreed told him, bracing herself. 'The Princep contingent has asked for our protection. Honorary citizenship.'

'Officer,' Milus addressed her. 'We have just been attacked by traitors from within your ranks. Fly-kinden in the pay of the Empire. The same ship's crew that your man Maker brought here.'

The halfbreed shrugged. 'They're none of ours, Tactician. I can't vouch for what Master Maker saw in them, him not being here, but they weren't ever ours.'

He blinked at her. 'I have reason to believe that that renegade has knowledge relating to what has happened here.'

The woman glanced down for a moment, as though summoning her courage, and then looked him directly in the eye. 'Where's Aagen?'

'Who?'

'You know who, Tactician.'

'He was a Wasp agent,' Milus snarled.

'He was a Wasp,' she contradicted him. 'He was a citizen of Princep Salma. I understand he died on your torture machines.'

'Spare me your Collegiate scruples.'

'Tactician Milus,' the halfbreed said formally, 'Collegium hereby confirms that it will not relinquish up to you the Ant known as Balkus nor anyone else, because we do not trust what you will do with them.'

At a thought from Milus the soldiers behind him had their snapbows levelled, the front rank dropping to their knees to give the men behind them a clear shot. The Collegiates were armed too, and most of them responded with creditable speed. One Dragonfly woman had an arrow trained steadily at Milus's left eye, and an expression that suggested she would be only too happy to let loose the string.

The halfbreed – herself the target of a good many bows right then – grimaced. 'That depends,' she said, as though he had actually worded some manner of proposal to her. 'How badly do you want to win the war, Tactician?'

Milus was very aware of the Vekken and Tseni contingents watching curiously, not taking sides but plainly not impressed.

Tactician, repairs are complete, an inopportune report came from one of his artificers who had not been keeping up with developments.

The long seconds dragged by. Milus fought a battle inside his head, and enough of it leaked out that he felt the little currents of dismay and uncertainty creeping through his soldiers.

'Back on the train,' he ordered, turning away from the entire fraught confrontation as if it had been nothing. 'Time to move.'

Returning to the carriage, Straessa found her seat again and managed to get herself settled before her hands started trembling.

'Oh, stab me,' she whispered, staring at them. 'Oh, stab me. Oh, that was too close, Gorenn. That was too close. I am so sorry. I am sorry for every thing I just said and did. I nearly got every one of us killed. I am such a pisspoor officer. I am so sorry.'

For a long time the Dragonfly regarded her solemnly, studying the Antspider's pale face. Straessa was waiting for condemnation, the 'this isn't how we run things over in the Commonweal', but in the end what came out was, 'Your people are lucky they have you.'

Straessa managed a strangled laugh. 'Right, sure they are.'

The Dragonfly's face twisted unexpectedly into something that was almost anger. Whatever she was seeing, it was invisible to Straessa, save as a tortured reflection in Gorenn's shining eyes. 'I was young, back then, when the Empire invaded our lands,' she began, with a catch in her voice. 'Too young to fight at the start of it, though I'd killed my share by the war's end. War forges a people, or breaks them, and you see the quality of their metal when you bring it under the hammer. When my people had to go to war, they broke. I saw people leading armies who had no right to. I saw princes and nobles shatter under the strain, and the sharp pieces of their bad decisions kill hundreds of others. When my people were placed under such pressure, we could not hold our shape. You, though . . . like you say, you're no soldier. None of your people is a soldier. You come from no warrior kinden. You are people of peace and money and being clever. And yet you have been forged. You have been made strong by the hammer. You, especially. I watch you and I wish there had been a woman like you to stand before the Wasps in the Twelve-year War.'

Straessa stared at her hands, not knowing what to say.

'I did not know what it would be like, to serve with the Apt,'

Gorenn went on awkwardly. 'It has not been easy. I have made many adjustments, as you have seen.'

Straessa, who had seen nothing of the sort, wisely said nothing.

'You, though, I understand,' the Dragonfly finished, and it was only with the dragging silence after those words that the Antspider realized that that was it, and that it was intended as a compliment.

'Ah, thank you,' she managed, and then the automotive was in motion at last, and they were back on the road to Capitas.

Straessa left matters for most of an hour before she let herself wander back down to the Collegiate baggage car: a little more difficult now to squeeze her way down the aisle, but then an army did travel with a remarkable amount of kit.

'I hope you're happy,' she murmured, after making sure that nobody else was within earshot, 'because frankly that was pissing terrifying. "It's not such a grand thing," you said. My *arse* it wasn't.'

There was a little shuffling of luggage from down by her knee, opening up the space that the Flies had prepared earlier. There she could see Laszlo, his artificer Despard and the rest of his crew, all sitting elbow to elbow in relative comfort in the baggage fort they had made.

'Nonsense, you loved it,' he told her, although his expression was serious. 'Well done, though, you and the Princep lot.' Laszlo and the rescued girl had slipped in under cover of the Collegiate detachment in the midst of the Princep Salma soldiers.

'They'll come searching here,' Straessa said. 'Once they start thinking that maybe you didn't just leg it, they'll search all over.'

'We can move around. This isn't our only bolthole,' Laszlo assured her.

Straessa looked past him at the Fly with the shock of red curls. 'She's the why, is she? You're . . . what was it?'

'Lissart,' the woman said. 'Apparently I'm the why.' To Straessa she seemed too tense and twitchy still, scarcely more at ease beside Laszlo than she had presumably been in Milus's keeping.

Then, again, perhaps being imprisoned and tortured would do that.

'Why haven't you all just gone, anyway?' she asked the Flies. 'I reckon you could vanish easily in this country, let the Ants search as much as they like.'

'Oh, we've got work to do still,' Lissart told her, cutting off Laszlo even as he opened his mouth to speak. 'We're not done yet.'

Forty-Two

Are these the people I would have chosen to decide the fate of the Empire?

Tynan's command tent was full, even cluttered. The Lowlander army was close now – projected to arrive some time before dawn, and it was close to midnight now. Any moment his scouts might burst in and announce that Tactician Milus had made better time than predicted, and that the battle would happen now.

And Ernain would take his Auxillians, stripping away a little short of half the Imperial army's strength. *The lesser half*, most Wasps would say, but half was half. Numbers weren't everything, but they were something no general would go without if he had the chance.

And even with those numbers there are no guarantees.

At first he had been furious. How hard it had been to keep himself from having Ernain and Oski, traitors both, arrested or even executed. Making angry decisions was not a trait a general allowed in himself, though. So Tynan had let them go, and he had read over Ernain's new model Empire, and he had pondered.

Then he had sent for them all, so they had come, and others with them, elbowing each other for room in his little tent.

Here they were, jostling for their place in the history books: Nessen, former governor of Helleron; Merva, the Solarnese governor's wife; Varsec the aviation expert, except that now he was dancing attendance on General Lien himself, the lord of the

Engineers having finally been drawn from his lair beneath Severn Hill. Major Vorken the slaver was still skulking about at the back, a large and powerful man cowed into submission by the fact of his inferior rank.

A Beetle-kinden had arrived, too, apparently unbidden: Honory Bellowern, whom Tynan recalled as the Imperial diplomatic aide in Collegium, but who was now apparently engaged on the business of his wealthy and powerful family. He carried the seal and authority of its patriarch, the venerable Auder Bellowern, on whose word large sections of the Empire's economy might start and stop.

And there was General Marent, of course, and there was Ernain of Vesserett – Tynan couldn't think of him as just *Captain* Ernain any more – with Major Oski at his side. Quite a gathering, all told.

'Marent,' Tynan said, reaching out for a man he hoped would back his strategy. 'Your words: there's a rot at the heart of the Empire. We've heard what Vorken and Varsec have had to say about the slave camps. We know that I'm currently disobeying a direct order just by preparing to defend Capitas from the Sarnesh, rather than hand myself in. We've seen that things have gone wrong, terribly wrong.'

'Yes,' Marent replied forcefully, his stern gaze daring anyone present to disagree. There were plenty of unhappy expressions, but none that gainsaid him.

'You tried to suggest, then, that we needed a new head wearing the crown.'

Utter silence as that ultimate treason was revisited. Tynan looked round at the newcomers, noting Lien's narrowed eyes, Honory Bellowern's politic lack of expression.

'Have you reconsidered your position, General?' *It's not too late*, Marent was saying.

'I have not,' Tynan told him. *Best to make that plain from the start*. 'However, it's safe to say that we're not the only ones who have been thinking on those lines, who've noticed that things are falling apart. The Empire has spoken, or at least significant parts of it.'

'What do you mean?' Nessen demanded. 'Rebellion?'

'Not yet,' Tynan said. He felt ferociously tired. 'Not armed uprising, anyway, but something . . .' He nodded at the Bee-kinden, whom most of his guests must have been wondering about. 'Ernain here has brought an ultimatum.'

He talked them through it, then, just as Ernain himself had stood in this very tent and explained it all to him. Looking from Wasp face to Wasp face, he saw their anger – at being black-mailed in the Empire's greatest time of need, but also just at the suggestion itself. He saw, on many faces, the very problem that Ernain and his followers were making a stand against. *How dare these slaves, these lesser kinden, dictate to us?*

'Put one in ten on the crossed pikes and they'll soon come to their senses,' Nessen said when Tynan finished. Nessen: the man who had never even commanded an army.

'No, they will not,' Tynan told him heavily. 'They are ready to leave, right now. If we attack them they will fight back, and no doubt the Lowlanders will reward them for it – Milus has his agents in amongst them, making promises.'

'This is his doing?' Marent asked. There was a terrible vulner-ability in his face, wholly unbefitting a general. *I probably looked the same when that Bee-kinden bastard put this to me.*

'It is not,' Tynan confirmed, and only just prevented himself from saying, *No, it is ours.* 'This has been brewing for a long time, at least since the traitor governors. They have looked at the Empire, and they have come to exactly the same conclusion as we have: that it must change. The only difference lies in the degree of change.'

'The *only* difference, Tynan?' Lien demanded. 'You're talking . . . *everything.*'

'Oh, no, no, General.' Honory Bellowern's smooth voice. 'Not everything. Only little things. The top of the ziggurat, that's all. The base and all its levels can remain mostly undisturbed.' Most

530

of the Wasps were staring at him now, and he swallowed a little nervously and then went on, 'So a little self-rule for those cities who – let us face the truth – have been more stalwart in their support of the Empire than many whom the Empire put in place to govern them. A few more free men working harder for coin than slaves will for bread. And, in place of all that pressure of government resting on a single point, an Assembly of the great and the good, all working towards the benefit of the state. The Empress has her advisers, does she not? And if those advisers had been more than mere decoration, had been given real authority to check the excesses of the throne's power, then perhaps we might not be in this position even now.'

'Tynan.' Marent was sounding slightly choked. 'Am I to take it you support this?'

Tynan closed his eyes, picturing the Lowlanders nearing with every heartbeat, but more than that: he saw thirty years of Imperial history, the waste of the Twelve-year War, the profiteering of the slavers, the Rekef infighting, how swiftly the traitor governors had arisen, how brutally the power of a single man or woman could be exercised when they had literally nobody to tell them 'no'. *And is this any better? Is Collegium really a model of efficient governance?*

The mocking thought followed: *Measure them by the Imperial yardstick: who will be at whose gates tomorrow?*

'I do,' he said. It was said so quietly, and yet everyone was craning forwards to catch the words.

There was an instant outburst of horror and argument, but Marent shouted them down.

'Tynan, I would have followed you to the throne, and knelt to you as Emperor,' he declared. His eyes were hollow, accusing. *Why could you not have said yes to the crown?* Then the words came out of him like gall, vomited forth as though the taste of them sickened him. But they were: 'I will follow you in this. Your judgement, Tynan, over all.'

'No, no, listen,' Nessen insisted, sounding terrified, almost in tears. 'Yes, the Empress is clearly mad, but there's no need to undo all we've built, all we have. It was our mistake ever to allow a woman on the throne. Women aren't made for such things.'

There was some nodding at this, despite Merva's immediate complaint, which Nessen blithely ignored. But Tynan was shaking his head.

'I have seen a woman command an army as ably as any man,' he told them, feeling something tug and strain within his heart at the thought. 'And I have seen a man sit on that throne and make decisions as ruinous as anything Seda has ordered. Alvdan was no paragon.'

'Then it's the family that's rotten, not the institution!' Nessen argued hurriedly.

'No,' Tynan said with enough finality that it shut the man up. He took a deep breath. 'Listen to me. We are most of us soldiers here, and those of us who aren't at least understand how an army works. It needs one commander: a general to order his officers, who in turn command their men. Perhaps I would take advice from my specialists, from my chief of engineers, my lead scouts, but my word is law, and it is final. That is how an army works.

'But an Empire is not an army. It is not some little tribe in the hills, where a chief knows every one of his village by name, and it is not a military force where an instant's indecision is sufficiently disastrous that one man must take charge. We have an Empire of so many cities, of so many hundreds of thousands of subjects. To give one man – or woman – power over *that*, unchecked and absolute . . . Who would not become a tyrant, a monster? Marent, you'd see me take the crown? Let me stand where my every meanest whim means life and death across all the Empire and I'd make Alvdan seem a glorious warrior hero, I'd make Seda seem the very hand of mercy. Have you never stopped to look around you at our neighbours? The Ants have their kings, but they are constantly in each others' minds, accommodating one another's points of view. Others rule by council or assembly, or just a network of feuding nobles for the Spiderlands. What other state has this madness of an absolute and hereditary ruler? Name it for me.'

'The Commonweal,' from Varsec of the Engineers.

'That's it,' Tynan agreed. 'The wretched, disintegrating chaos and poverty that is the Commonweal. Nobody else, but them and us. So, yes, I am in favour. I will sign Ernain's declaration. And not just to save the Empire here, or because of his threats, but because that way lies a future that might just endure.'

'But . . .' Major Vorken of the slavers put in awkwardly, 'the slaves, the slave cities . . .? They cannot be proposing to do away with slavery, surely.'

'There are slaves and slaves.' It was the first time Ernain had spoken. 'Criminals, war prisoners, those purchased from the Spiders or the Scorpions, they are slaves, certainly, and we rely on them, after all. Let the Collegiates live that particular dream. But, as for the people of my city, and of the other cities, we will not be born into slavery. We Auxillians will be soldiers as you are, not slave conscripts. We will be citizens of an Empire that is *ours*, as it is yours. Yes, there will be adjustments. Yes, some that are slaves now will be free servants or artisans or soldiers in the future, but I'm not some bleating Collegium scholar telling you everyone has a right to be free. We all know that isn't true – and so does most of the rest of the world.'

'And what of those cities that you don't speak for?' Marent put in thoughtfully.

'If they don't come round, if they don't see that this is the best for them?' Ernain shrugged. 'Then they deserve all they get.'

'Well, then.' Tynan looked around at them. 'I have Marent with me. I have Bellowern, so I suspect that means that a great deal of the wheels that would need to spin to make this work are already in place.' And now Honory was nodding slightly at that, the weight of his clan and its many, many dependants and adherents in that small gesture. 'But what of the rest of you?

Here's our experiment in government. You are my assembly, here and now. So speak.'

He saw Nessen shaking his head, shrinking back, a man not in favour but not brave enough to speak out. Vorken had already stepped back, his expression tense and conflicted, quite out of his depth.

'General,' Merva of Solarno said, 'this is probably where I mention that Ernain's people have already spread the word as far as Solarno. The Spiders there are aware of this proposal, as is my husband. Solarno will take what is offered.'

'The *Spiders* will join the Empire, will they?' Nessen demanded.

'Those families who have made their power base in Solarno may,' she agreed, 'so long as it would become their Empire too.'

'What say the Engineers?' Tynan asked.

'I have always been a man of progress—' Varsec started.

'Quiet, man,' Lien snapped at him, but the colonel just looked at his superior for a moment, and then went on.

'Progress is what an engineer should wish for. If a thing does not work, you redesign it until it does. If a thing could work *better*, it's the same. And if you do not advance in this way –' now he was shouting over Lien's orders to be silent – 'if you become fond of yesterday's designs even though they no longer function, then you will fail. Only by changing and bettering ourselves can we survive.'

'Says the same man who brought mindlinked pilots into the army!' General Lien snapped.

'And they have served us well, Lien,' Tynan stated. 'And, yes, some of them are halfbreeds, and some of them are women – my own chief of aviators even – and yet they still serve the Empire.'

'No,' Lien protested. 'Tynan, this is treason and, worse, it is a fool's treason. The Empress has her . . . irregularities, perhaps, but I have faith in her. The Engineers will not sign. I will return to Capitas and prepare to man the wall artillery against the Lowlanders.' As he turned away he bellowed, 'Varsec!'

He left the tent, striding out into the night air, and Tynan wondered, *Can we do it without him? What would the Engineers do – elect their own Emperor if we deposed Seda?*

'Lien!' he called, but then he heard the clatter of steel from outside, and a scream.

Did someone stab him? Instantly, Tynan was pushing his way out of the tent, too. He saw a cluster of men fighting in the fire-light, trying to keep something from approaching him. Even as he watched, that single figure scythed through them, cutting down anyone within reach of its blade, shrugging off or stepping aside from stingshot and snapbow bolts.

The Empress's Mantis.

Tynan's blood ran cold just to see it, but the armoured figure was already picking up speed, cutting down any soldier luckless enough to get in its way and coming directly for him.

The first wave of the Worm's soldiers had fallen on both sides, buried beneath the rockslides that Thalric had prepared. They had used that weapon to the very best of their ability, leaving scores of the attackers crushed and broken. But that was it, for there was no more they could throw down. Now the slingers were working, casting stones into the advancing mass of the enemy as fast as they could, but it would not hold them back long. Nothing would hold them for long.

'Are you ready?' Che asked Tynisa.

'As I can be,' her foster-sister replied. She was standing up straight, right now, sword in hand and feeding off the strength it lent her. The tide of the Worm would not have to advance far before she was a cripple once more and Che was again just a Beetle girl with delusions.

If this is my last act, let it be the right one – but she had gone beyond the ability to judge.

She reached out – with her arms and her mind both – searching for that connection with Seda, that conduit through which the Empress would absorb her power. The cries and shouts of the fighting, Thalric's exhortations to the slaves, trying to shout some backbone into them . . . she did her best to blot it all out. Concentration was everything, as she tried to focus on that ephemeral sense that had been gifted to her, when she had lost her Aptitude.

She had a feel for the great funnel that was the Worm's world, where it squatted hungrily at the lowest point that all roads led to. From above – and it was not truly *above* but her mind insisted on that comparison – filtered down the fine rain of magic, leaking back into this void of a world after so long. She gathered it to herself. She was the only true magician in this whole world. All the power here was hers by right.

She could feel Seda beyond the broken Seal, reaching towards her, gravid with the strength she had stolen from the lives of slaves, from the ambient power of the sunlit world that had always seemed meagre to Che until she had been banished down here.

Further! she told the Empress. *Please, I cannot bridge the gap! Hold out, Che!*

There was a faint tremor running through her internal world, the edge of the Worm's influence brushing her as the attacking warriors gained another step before the raining missiles of the slingers drove them back down the slope again. Tynisa was shifting from foot to foot, wanting to retreat further up, but knowing that she could not move Che.

Almost, she thought. The ghostly extent of Seda's power was like a beacon to her, a blazing lamp being lowered into this dark place.

Almost, again, and Che composed herself, finally separating herself from the distractions of the world around her, shrugging off her fears for Thalric and Tynisa, her guilt, her self-doubt. For one crystalline moment she found a clear, calm place within her from which to muster the magic at her command. In that moment she saw everything.

She touched fingers with Seda, felt the Empress stretching desperately for her power, ritual half complete, ready to recreate the Seal and lock away the Worm forever – or until some other misguided magician should shatter it anew. The lives of thousands of slaves already slain, and thousands more that she had ordered to be slain, all hung about her, bloating her with curdling, stolen strength that prised at every seam of her, demanding to be used.

Che pulled.

She took hold of Seda, accepted the proffered connection, and she pulled, dragging at the other woman's power, the threads of her ritual, her very being and body. Instantly the Empress was fighting against her, and she would have been effortlessly stronger had she not overextended herself so far in driving a connection down to this lightless pit.

Che pulled and pulled, burning the fickle reserves of magic that she had harvested here, pitting her will against the Empress of the Wasps, and even in the midst of this she heard Seda's appalled, agonized voice.

Che, we must remake the Seal! Why?

Because some things come at too great a cost, Che told her. *Because the ends do not justify the means.* And she sank the hooks of her mind into Seda's unwieldy half-made ritual and tore it apart, and then abruptly there was no resistance and Tynisa was dragging on her arm.

The armoured Mantis drove forwards, and Tynan sank two burning darts of stingshot into its chest without even slowing it. He lurched aside, tripping over the lines securing his tent, seeing one of his officers lunge in with a sword and get his throat cut for his trouble. A moment later, Vorken the slaver was in the Mantis's way as Tynan's tent emptied, getting a blow in across the attacker's pauldrons that was hard enough to stagger the intruder, then diving past with a flurry of wings. The Mantis lunged after him, opening his leg from knee to ankle, and then turned back to take on the next challenger.

It was Marent, Tynan saw, as he struggled to his feet. The

general of the Third feinted at the Mantis, his off-hand blazing fire, but the Mantis twisted past both steel and sting effortlessly, the barbs of one forearm raking across Marent's face.

Tynan put another bolt of his Art into the Mantis's side, putting it briefly off its stride. Marent, half blinded, was still trying to go on the offensive, though, hacking down at the lithe, mailed form.

That metal claw drove down into his chest, effortlessly penetrating through armour and bone without meeting any obvious resistance. Marent made a choking noise and died.

A dart of loss pierced Tynan's composure, and he let fly with both hands, bolts crackling and streaking around his enemy, most just seeming to glance away from it as the figure turned to him, taking one long step that put Tynan well within reach of its blade.

The blow never came. Instead, the Mantis lurched sideways as though the ground had betrayed it. Its helmed head whipped about, hunting for an enemy Tynan could not see, and then it . . . *receded* was the only word Tynan could think of to describe what he saw. Without actually retreating from him, the Mantis seemed to fall away suddenly into some unseen gulf, dropping into the shadows as though they were an abyss of immeasurable depth.

Tynan's knees hit the ground, his legs abruptly too weak to support him. 'Marent?'

'He's dead, sir, sorry.' It was Oski, now kneeling by the other general's body. 'I think we've lost at least twenty of the watch as well, the ones who got in that thing's way.'

'Vorken?' Tynan spotted the slaver already under the care of a surgeon. 'Who else?'

'General Lien, alas.' The aviator, Varsec, crouched by him.

Tynan looked at him narrowly. 'Is that so?'

Varsec's face was guileless. 'I believe there was something to sign, General. I appear to be ranking officer of the Engineers.'

On such a shifting foundation do we build. 'Ernain?' A sudden cold moment, what if Ernain, too, had got in the Mantis's way?

There was the living Bee-kinden, though, and Tynan allowed Varsec to help him to his feet. 'Bring your cursed paper here!'

They signed and signed, copy after copy, those of them who were left. If the Empire was permitted to write its own histories after tomorrow, these same names would go down in those records: Tynan, Merva, Nessen, Varsec, Vorken, Honory Bellowern, Ernain, Oski. After that, and after Ernain had dispatched his precious declaration to the cities that had entrusted him with this task, there remained just one duty, and it was one that Tynan could not delegate to anyone else.

He did not enter Capitas alone, but with some several hundred soldiers of the Gears, and he accumulated more as he approached the palace: Engineers, Consortium men, Slave Corps, Light Airborne, newly freed Auxillians – all the pieces of the Empire, not quite knowing what they were supporting but trusting in Tynan or in the other men who had given them their orders.

There followed some fighting at the palace gates, but surprisingly little – a holdout handful of the Red Watch tried to stop him, but they were just a dozen against all his force, and they died swiftly and fiercely.

He was expecting some other force to ambush him within those corridors of power, or perhaps the murderous Mantis to reappear and finish his work, but Tynan reached the doors of the throne room without incident. There were plenty of servants and courtiers and soldiers within the palace, and yet nobody seemed to have orders, and everyone looked to everyone else, and Tynan just marched on.

He threw the doors open and strode in, and the Empress was not there, only the shaking form of General Brugan, who had once been a soldier to be reckoned with and now stared wildly at Tynan with the eyes of a lunatic.

'Where is she?' Tynan demanded of him. 'Where's the Empress?'

'She . . .' Tears were running down Brugan's face, which twitched and jumped as though maggots were running just beneath the skin. 'She's gone, just gone . . . She fell, far, far away . . . Help me get her back, Tynan. We have to get her back.' His hands scrabbled at the carved wood of the throne.

Tynan regarded him impassively for a moment and then lifted a hand, not knowing whether it was necessity or revulsion or mere pity that moved him. The crackle and flash of his sting echoed about the chamber, and Brugan's body rocked back against the throne and then slid to the floor.

No Empress? No Empress and no confrontation, but here was Tynan in the heart of Empire, and nobody to contest the declaration he cast before the throne. He would have to trust to men such as the Bellowerns to ensure that everything held together now, while he got on with his real job.

Soon afterwards the word came: the Lowlander army had been sighted.

Forty-Three

Stenwold woke up.

For a moment, standing there, he had a sense of a great whirl of sound and motion, nearby and yet unseen, as though it was in a further room, in some space separated from him by the thinnest of membranes and yet utterly invisible, undetectable.

He was in Myna. He remembered now.

Before him the gates rose solid and whole, and he felt waves of memory wash over him. He remembered watching them through a telescope while they shuddered under the impact of the Wasps' ramming engine, but that had been a long time ago, in a world now lost. Those gates had fallen, and then the wall . . . years after, when the Empire had come again . . .

He looked left and right, seeing that remembered wall intact now, re-edified and restored to be the perfect mimic of the way everything had been, before it all started.

There was nobody else there, just Stenwold before the gates of Myna.

Again he sensed a wave of commotion just beyond his reach, the clatter of metal, a woman's voice – a woman he knew? – making demands. Atryssa? Arianna? No, another woman he knew and loved. A face ghosted brokenly through his mind, of a woman who looked like a Spider-kinden but wasn't, not quite.

Besides, they were dead, the others. The thought seemed obscurely wrong. As he stood here before those unbreached gates, how could they be dead? Time had respooled itself, surely. All the pieces were back in their box.

He turned from the gates slowly, feeling the city about him blur slightly each time it moved, as though his image of it took a second to catch up. Myna rose up before him in its tiers, towards that top airfield where . . . Again those layers of memory interfered with each other.

There was nobody else in sight. He had the city to himself.

The Consensus building was in its proper place again – no sign of the hideous ziggurat the Wasps had replaced it with after they took the city the first time, nor the mess of scaffolding that was all the second Consensus hall had amounted to before the Empire had knocked it right back down again.

Is this a second chance? he wondered. *What happens if I just walk away? If I open those gates, what will I see? A Wasp army? Or just the view out towards the hills of the Antonine?*

Or nothing?

Instead, he set off into the city slowly, uncertainly. Each step seemed to be over the edge of an abyss until it landed. The Myna of his memories shivered and danced, always on the point of fracturing.

Here there was only silence. Somewhere else a woman was crying.

Hokiak's Exchange was still there, although he felt somehow that the geography had been twisted in order to lead him to it, the city's layout subtly corrupted by his imperfect recall. The old sign swung gently in a wind Stenwold could not feel.

If I go in, will I find the old man there? And then a sharp memory. *But he's left. Last time, he was gone. And the Consensus was in ruins and then the walls . . . the walls came down.* For a moment the image threatened to overwhelm what he was seeing, buildings become vacant, decaying shells; the skies alive with fighting orthopters; incendiaries from the greatshotters unfolding their bright blooms, Sentinels on the streets. The ground beneath him shifted, and he knew that way dissolution lay.

He clung to the peace of his past, that moment before Stenwold Maker the idealist scholar had become Stenwold Maker the driven statesman, chief of all the enemies of the Empire. Rather keep Myna like this, before the Wasps came. He was too tired and too old to go through all that again.

He walked on through the still and soundless city, searching for a way out that had nothing to do with the city gates. He let his feet lead him where they would.

A townhouse stood within sight of the gates. He remembered it well: far better than he remembered many more recent things. *Where it all started.* For a long moment, for a time that he could not measure, he stood before it while, just a hair's breadth away, there was such panic and shouting, hands dragging at him, the clatter of surgeons' tools.

He went in.

Seda stood up slowly. Tynisa watched her.

The Empress of the Wasps stared about herself at the terrible enclosing dark, barely kept at bay by the lone fire that Tynisa needed in order to see. Below them, past the great huddled mass of non-combatants, the thin line of armed slaves surged back and forth, still desperately trying to keep the Worm from breaking through. The slaves yelled and screamed, cried out in shock and agony, shouted encouragement to one another. The Worm remained silent, incapable of words.

'What have you done?' Seda demanded.

Beside Tynisa, Che did not answer. *I don't think I really believed that would work,* said the expression on her face.

The Empress was backing away from her, though there was precious little space – not far to go without climbing a sheer wall or approaching the Worm. 'What have you done, you stupid child?' she cried out. 'My ritual—'

'I could not allow you to complete it,' Che told her simply. 'I could not be a party to such magic. I hope that, in dragging you

543

down here, I have saved at least some of the lives you sought to squander.'

'Squander?' Seda shouted at her. 'I was saving the world from the Worm.'

A fragile smile made its way on to Che's face. 'And I was saving the world from you.'

For a moment Seda just stared at her, face twitching with shock and incomprehension, and then fury gripped her hard enough that her entire body jolted, and she thrust out a palm at Che to burn her from the face of the world.

Tynisa lunged forwards – ready for this moment she had known must come – and her rapier's point opened up the Empress's hand, severing two fingers. The appalled Wasp fell back with a cry that owed more to outrage than to pain, and Tynisa drove in to finish the job.

Her blade struck steel that deflected her thrust, and she dropped back immediately, making space and keeping her sword between her and the newcomer. For, of course, he was here.

Tisamon had come to the aid of his mistress.

In the poor light he was just an armoured shadow, his claw a crooked extension of his barbed arm. As Seda hunched backwards, cradling her ruined hand, the revenant of Tynisa's father stepped closer to her, protectively.

There was so little space to fight in, here at the top of the slope. They had discussed this chance. Che would be trying to get her mind into Tisamon, to prise him apart and disperse him, creation of magic that he was, but Seda would be opposing her, move for move. They were locked together, each the other's equal in strength and skill, but while they struggled silently, magic to magic, their Weaponsmasters fought the real duel.

Tynisa lunged in, angling her blade to take Tisamon under the arm, then circling the point over his arm as he brought it up to parry her, pushing next for his throat. He swayed back, just enough to be out of her reach, inviting her to overextend.

She took a pace back, saw him follow her up, darting inside

her reach and going for her throat, always his favourite strike, but a poor choice against a skilled opponent. She passed back and to her right, feinting at his eyes, at the cold, pale face within his helm. He was dead, long dead, but there was magic in her arm and in her sword. A killing blow from her might not destroy him, but it would be enough to bring him down. After that she needed only a moment to bring an end to Seda, and that would free her father forever.

Abruptly he blurred into motion, striking high towards her head, then stepping around her parry, steel claw darting for her shoulder, her side, her injured hip. She felt no pain from her old wounds, the sword sustaining her as it leapt almost joyously to her defence, matching move to move and always the point directed to him, so that each parry was nothing more than the most economical shifting of her hand, only the angle changing, never the intent.

She struck against his shoulder, then his side, scraping mail both times, and never opening herself up. She was inside his shorter reach most of the time, but her own blade was constantly holding the centre line, standing in the way of his strikes. He was relentless in attack, near perfect in defence but, try as he might, he could not hook his claw around her guard to get to her.

She knew him. He was her father and she had fought him so many times, for practice and for blood. When they had first met they had nearly killed one another. They had crossed blades in the sewers beneath Myna, in the Prowess Forum of Collegium, in the darkness of Argastos's domain in the Netheryon. She retained that connection with him, that understanding of his style and his limits. Dead, now, he had lost his feel for her, locked inside his armour and cut off from the man he had been.

He lunged for her hip again, trying to exploit an injury that did not slow her, and she twisted aside deftly, caught his blade when it flicked up for her face and bound it back behind her, punching him across the jaw with the edged knuckle-guard of her sword. She contacted only metal, but he staggered with the blow, and a moment later she had stepped around him, leaving her sword behind to catch his following strike, and Seda was before her, backing up frantically.

Then a blazing white agony struck through Tynisa, surging out from her hip, and she fell to one knee with a screech of pain, sword dropping from her hand with the utter, unexpected shock. Tisamon would not hesitate, she knew. His blade would be descending even now. She tried to fling up a hand to ward off the blow, in a hopeless, futile gesture.

It never came. She looked back wildly, trying to find him. He was gone. The deadening influence of the Worm had rolled over them, a momentary gain in ground by the attackers, and Tynisa's magic had been snuffed out. As had Seda's. As had Tisamon.

Tynisa gave out a rasping cry and reclaimed her sword – no Weaponsmaster's call to have it instantly to hand, but just fumbling it from the floor with shaking hands. Seda's face was stricken – how long had she been relying on her magic, and now it was gone, as though she had never been special at all.

Tynisa limped forwards, teeth gritted, willing herself to finish this.

A moment later and the pain was gone, her sword flooding its strength back into her. And she turned instinctively, bringing her hilt up so that the diagonal of her blade intersected Tisamon's darting strike. The revenant was back.

The slaves were fighting harder than they had a right to, was Thalric's assessment. Even with all their dependants at their back, and nowhere else to go in the world, he would have thought they should have crumbled by now. Instead, the Worm had rushed them again and again, and the volleys of slingshot had beaten into this attacking force, slowing them, tripping them over their own dead, so that when they reached the first line of slave-held swords the speed of their charge had been checked. There were mounds of the dead, now – dead from both sides – whole charnel barricades for the Worm to clamber over. It was all mounting up, impeding the enemy, making them slow down and wasting their numbers.

Of course, it's still a hopeless fight, Thalric acknowledged. *I'm not exactly going to get a chance to go around and tell everyone 'Well done,' am I?*

He had been leaning heavily on his Art: aloft much of the time and battering down on the Worm with his sting – each shot just a tiny effort, but he was feeling the drag of it now. There were just too many of the enemy, and they didn't care if they died. Or perhaps the problem was that there was only one of the enemy, and they could kill these husks forever and still not win the war.

The Mole Crickets were proving surprisingly effective, too, he considered. Of course he knew them back from his Empire days – big, slow, dull brutes, fit for mining and with a surprising turn for artifice, but seldom much use as warriors. Then, again, they were scarce in the world above, but here he had them in the hundreds, a hulking second line armed with clubs and hammers and the great reach of their long arms. The swordsmen in the front row were just concentrating on staying alive and fending the Worm off, whilst the big Moles reached forwards between them and hammered and crushed and slapped.

But we'll run out of sling stones soon, I suppose, Thalric reflected. *How ridiculous, to be trapped in this hole in the ground, and yet meet your end because there aren't enough stones in the world.*

He let himself drop down again, trying to conserve his strength. Below, down the slope, the lines shifted and wavered, and still the wretched slaves somehow held – the slingers thinning out the Worm even as they came so that what reached the defending lines was just manageable. There was a simple mathematics, though, of attrition and exhaustion, neither of which appeared to be problems the enemy suffered from.

It's been an education, Thalric admitted. *But they're still slaves*

547

all the same, and when that line breaks there'll be no recovering from it.

With that in mind, he began working his way back, keeping an eye on the ebb and flow of the fight. It was not from some desperate need to preserve his own skin, but he wanted to be closer to Che. When the inevitable worst happened, and these doomed defenders were overwhelmed, he wanted to get her out somehow. They would trust to their wings and risk the White Death and the carnivorous stars, and they would find some way out of this place, just the two of them.

He looked back up the slope, and saw fighting there too. For a moment, by the light of their single fire up there, he could not see who was crossing blades with whom, and he let his wings lift him up and carry him over, utterly bewildered. Then he saw them: who else could it be, really? After all, the world had ceased working to comprehensible rules some time ago, so why not these players acting out this scene one last time?

Tisamon, Tynisa, and the appealing thought: *I could just go, right now. I don't have to get involved in this little knot any more.*

But he did. He did if he wanted Che. He let his wings carry him towards them. He launched himself forwards and a sling stone from the Worm's ranks struck him solidly in the shoulder and brought him down.

Forty-Four

Esmail and the Hermit trailed the prisoners across the Worm's vacant stone city, the Assassin taking care to step virtually within the other man's shadow. Even then, and despite the fresh scars on his hide, there seemed to be a growing hostility amongst the Worm's warriors. Those empty faces were turning his way more and more, as though catching him out of the corners of their eyes.

No, not just me – the Hermit as well.

Ahead of them, the band of Scarred Ones and their guards were picking up speed, the robed Centipede-kinden becoming more and more agitated.

'What is going on?' Esmail hissed.

'Just keep moving,' the Hermit shot back, and then, almost to himself, 'I fear . . .'

'You fear what?' demanded Esmail. 'Tell me.'

'What is there here to fear, save one thing?' was the Hermit's hurried response.

Abruptly there was a choked cry from the group ahead, and Esmail's lantern caught a fine mist of blood glittering in the air. The group barely slowed down – and soon it was moving faster than before. A corpse was left in their wake, though – one of the captive slaves, though thankfully not the man that Esmail was here to free.

'Someone couldn't wait for the sacrifice?' he wondered aloud.

'Just keep moving,' repeated the Hermit, a real edge of urgency to his voice.

There was definitely a disruption to the pattern of movement across the city. The steady spiralling that had dominated the general flow through the streets kept breaking up, individual segments of the Worm finding themselves outside it, waiting blankly as though about to receive new instructions.

'Seriously, will you tell me—'

There was another scuffle ahead. No cry this time, but Esmail saw a blade flash, the group moving on as before.

'They'll not have anyone left to offer up,' he commented, and then he saw the body clearly.

Sprawled there, abandoned and now claiming that common kinship all human corpses shared, it took him an additional moment to understand why it was so wrong. It was a Scarred One, a priest – one of the elite.

'A falling-out between your people?' he asked of the Hermit.

'No.'

'What, then? He didn't knife himself.' The old man's reticence was maddening.

'It's all coming apart at last.' The response was close to a whisper. 'He was killed by the Worm, by its warriors. They saw him, truly, for the first time in his life. They saw he was not of them, not really of them.'

A chill came over Esmail. 'The Worm is rejecting its kinden?'

'The Worm has no kinden, save these husks,' the Hermit whimpered. 'We only played at being priests, and it overlooked us. Now our god is turning away from us. Can you imagine?'

'I thought you didn't believe in it?'

'I don't. Not any more. But I know how it must feel,' the Hermit said hoarsely. 'It's the end of everything.'

An unpleasant thought caught up with Esmail. 'Wait, doesn't this mean that *we* . . .'

'Yes, even we,' the Hermit agreed. 'They will penetrate our deception, yours and mine both, soon. It will be soon.'

'Then we . . .' Esmail saw the prison party vanish into one of the caves, down a steeply sloping tunnel that could lead only to one place. Immediately he was heading after them with as much speed as he could muster, desperately trying to blot from his mind the image of what he would find down there.

At the cave mouth his courage failed him at last – not the courage required simply to go on, but that additional strength of mind that would be needed to face the Worm itself.

'We'll catch up with them in the tunnel,' he decided. 'We'll kill them there, then we'll . . . Then we'll . . .' His plan had no second act. 'You can scar him up quickly.' Despite what the Hermit had said about the time that process would take, and the time they didn't have. 'We'll . . .' And he was running, then slowing for the Hermit to catch him, horribly aware that ahead of them the prison party was still speeding up, the stately stride of the priests shattered into outright panic. They were now desperate to appease their god with their offerings, to earn themselves a place back in its good graces.

Don't they know? thought Esmail wildly. *Don't they understand that it doesn't care?* Certainly it had let them live in its shadow thus far, little parasites it could not be bothered to scratch at. But it was vast and inhuman, and how could its priests think it capable of entering into any bargain or contract that they might conceive of?

He wondered if it was his presence that had set off the Worm's instincts: a foreign agent masquerading as one of the kinden that had created it. *Or perhaps it's just that it's the end of the world, and nobody's getting out.*

He should have caught up with them by now, he knew, but the Hermit was slowing him – the old man growing more and more reluctant to follow in Esmail's footsteps, until the Assassin realized that some old hook of his former life was still lodged in him – the awe, the dread, the sacrilege of it was tripping him up and holding him back.

Then it was too late, because they were there. Esmail was

stumbling out into that vast cavern, seeing the group of warriors and priests and their victims right ahead, poised before that sudden drop, the abyss of the Worm.

They had a prisoner forward already . . . no, they were already throwing some others over the edge, just giving them to the pit as if desperate to attract their god's attention, to reaffirm their non-existent bonds of mutual understanding with it.

The next man was thrust forwards, bleeding from their swords until he chose the drop over the steel. But he did not fall, for the vast darkness of the Worm surged into view and caught him between its pincering claws, its whiplike antennae thrashing like mad shadows about the ceiling. Esmail had frozen, his eyes fixed on the one armoured figure amongst the prisoners: Totho. *How the poor Apt bastard must be shaking.*

As he watched, he saw Totho strike out at the nearest priests, knocking them to the ground. The warriors encircling him got him at their blades' points, but he was ignoring them, glancing briefly over at Esmail and his lantern's light – so obvious to his surface-dweller's eyes and yet something that the Worm simply couldn't see.

Tynisa's rapier point scored a line down the side of Tisamon's helm, caught his return strike on her guard and cast him off, taking a step back to make distance her ally again.

Her leg buckled as she did so, the pain flooding back in double measure, lashing her for every step she had taken since the last time. Tisamon faded to a shadow even as he drove for her, and she stumbled sideways, seeking Seda. She had to bring this fight to a close quickly, or one of these sudden shifts would tear her apart.

Or the Worm would get here and kill them all. But, then, that was going to happen anyway, sooner or later.

Seda was standing with her good hand thrust towards Tynisa, but her face was crawling with conflicting expressions, and her eyes clearly saw something other than the crippled swordswoman before her. Tynisa could only assume Che was inside her mind, fighting the Empress furiously, taking up every ounce of her concentration.

The Wasp's sting spat, nonetheless – Che's hold on the Empress failing as the Worm's influence smothered her magic – and Tynisa dropped to one side to avoid that wavering aim, the resulting shock of pain feeling fiercer than death. Then she was lurching back to her feet, screaming out a war cry to fight back the waves of weakness that threatened to drag her down. Abruptly her strength was back and she sprang forwards, desperate to close the distance before . . .

He was there again, claw scything down onto her, and she skipped out from under it, tried a jab towards Seda but then had to drag her rapier back to deflect Tisamon's next blow. He fought her back by three hard-won steps, battering at her guard, the meticulous precision of his style disintegrating, as though he was infected by Seda's own panic. She scored half a dozen strikes against his mail, failing to penetrate the ancient Mantis crafts-manship. The inequality of the fight was weighing on her, knowing that he only needed one good hit, and every step she took would be paid for when the tide of the Worm closed in on them again.

Thalric struggled to his feet, feeling something grind agonizingly within his shoulder. The Worm had so few slingers, it seemed dismal luck that one should have gone for him. For a moment, surrounded by the slaves, caught in the push and pull of the conflict that yanked and jarred him painfully, he could not think what he had been doing. Then it came back to him, and he tried his wings.

The Art had barely flickered before his shoulder was screaming at him, and he staggered, feeling the fight around him start to unravel, the inevitable triumph of the Worm on its way again.

He had to get to Che. He had to get to her and . . .

Of course now he would not be able to go with her. His own escape route had just been snatched from him.

He began pushing through the throng, good shoulder first, forcing his way upslope as fast as he could, as though he could outstrip the conclusion he had just come to. *No escape, not this time.* He had stayed alive a long time, had Thalric. He had outlived a mad Dragonfly set on vengeance, the rejection of the Rekef, capture by his enemies and an entire bloody siege dedicated to his personal extermination. He had even survived so far in this night-black place, but now it looked as though his legendary resilience and luck might just have reached their limits.

Someone crashed into him from behind and he let out a bark of pain and found himself falling. A moment later hands had caught him, and he was hauled up to stare directly into an eyeless, nightmare face.

'Messel!' he got out. 'Help me. I need to get to Che – help me up there.' His tone was somewhere between command and plea.

The blind man got an arm around him wordlessly and started pulling him upslope. He had brief, contradictory glimpses of the fighting up there. Tynisa and Tisamon crossing blades. Then Tynisa was falling, and her father was gone. Then they were back again, the girl recovering from the stab of her intermittent injury just in time to defend herself. It was as though he was watching the moments of this battle out of sequence.

Che and Seda seemed almost motionless in comparison, even as the duel jolted and surged between them. Thalric gritted his teeth and forced himself onwards, with Messel helping clear the way.

Forty-Five

Straessa awoke each time the rhythm of pace of the rail auto-motive changed, which in practice meant at least once an hour. Now they were slowing, and the irritable thought crawled through her mind: *What now? Ambush, sabotage or mechanical failure?* Outside the window the sky was grey with dawn.

Then there was someone shouting at the far end of the carriage, coming closer, and it occurred to her that she was nominally at least partly in charge around here, and so she should know what was going on.

By the time she had sat up, the shouted words had forced their way to a lobe of her brain that was sufficiently awake to understand them.

'Awake! Get up! Get your kit! Clear out!' A Sarnesh soldier was pushing his way down the aisle. 'Ready to fight, Beetles! Come up! Out and muster ready to march.'

'Wait, wait – we're here?' Straessa protested, snagging at his arm. He stared at her, curbing his annoyance on seeing that she was an officer of some sort.

'Well, the Wasps won't exactly let us ride the line all the way to their terminus,' he told her, 'so we're now as close as we'll get. On foot for most of us from here on in. Collegium gets the left flank, between the Mantids and the non-Sarnesh Ants. We're centre and right. Get your people out and ready to march, then stand ready for further orders.'

Straessa applied her mind to that, trying to think like a Sarnesh tactician. Probably they were counting on the non-Ants to give way before a determined Imperial push, resulting in the sort of slow revolution you usually got in a clash of infantry speeding up, allowing the Sarnesh to execute some sort of flanking manoeuvre or similar. *Nice to know they rate us so highly.*

By that time most of the Collegiates sharing her carriage were in motion, starting to pile out even as the vehicle slowed to a gradual stop. Straessa fought her way free of them and headed off after the Sarnesh messenger into the further carriages, encouraging the rest of her contingent to get moving. She cast a guilty look about the baggage car but there was no sign of the *Tidenfree* crew at all.

She was still kicking her soldiers awake when she heard a distant boom, feeling the ground shake as, no doubt, the more powerful enemy engines felt out the range. She didn't waste any time in contemplation, though, but just began shoving Company soldiers out of the doors all the faster.

Outside, when she finally got there herself, was a study in qualified chaos. The other officers and sub-officers were forming the Collegiates into maniples, but lots of people had got out of place or gone in search of new friends over the long journey. Straessa waded in, looking for her own unit, telling anyone she saw who looked lost just to find a maniple that was short of someone. In their midst, Balkus was organizing the little Princep Salma detachment to support them: stretcher-bearers, surgeons, ammunition runners.

Right, so where's the rest of them? The Netheryen Mantids had an easier time of it simply because they had no battle order to speak of, just a great loose-knit mass of them armed with bows and spears, blades and the hooked arms of their beasts. They stood very still, though, far more so than the bustling Collegiates. Straessa recalled that this was the first time they had come to a war on their own terms, without just providing a mailed fist for the Moth-kinden. The thought lent them both a professional quality and also a vulnerability. The Mantis-kinden were doing something new, which in itself was new.

On the Collegiates' other side she saw the Vekken and the Tseni, and somehow they were standing side by side and not killing each other. Sarnesh soldiers were there, too, talking to the Vek contingent and getting them to space out rather than form the traditional solid Ant block which would offer nothing but bait for artillery at this distance.

She clutched at her rapier hilt to steady herself, secure in the knowledge that she could whip the blade out as swift as thinking, and she had the skills to put it to good use. The thought was very clear in her mind, a source of strength and reassurance for the brief moment before she looked at all the soldiers around her, with their snapbows in hand. Her own was slung over her shoulder, and that was the weapon she needed to feel confident about. There was precious little room in this latter age for the sword. Those days of duels and champions and blade-skill were diminishing. Only the Mantids still pined for them. The rest of the world had moved on.

'Chief.' Gorenn dropped down beside her. 'We're over there.'

'Thanks.' Straessa looked the Dragonfly over. 'I suppose we've arrived, then. Doesn't seem real, does it?'

Gorenn gave her a grin that could have meant anything. 'Heart of the Empire, Officer Antspider.' She followed Straessa as the halfbreed went from maniple to maniple ensuring everyone had their kit and was ready to march when the word came.

'You've got enough arrows?'

'We're positioned next to the Mantids. I know where to go to beg more. Straessa . . .'

Gorenn's tone was different, and the Antspider turned back to find her staring out towards Capitas, the greatest city in the world. Straessa's own words echoed in her head: *I suppose we've arrived, then,* and she shivered, thinking just how far they'd come.

'Wasn't that long ago I was just a student cheating at the Prowess Forum and playing artist's model and sword tutor for spare coin,' she said. 'I'm half expecting someone to tap me on the shoulder any moment and tell me I'm late with an essay.'

Then there was a Sarnesh at her elbow. 'Officer, Milus wants all the detachment commanders assembled so he can give out the battle order.' And the man was already on his way, heading for the Vekken.

'Keep discipline for me here,' Straessa told Gorenn. 'Looks like I get to find out how this is all going to work. Though why he can't just tell me through any Ant who's passing by, I don't know.'

'Don't take any shoving from the Sharnesh,' the Dragonfly cautioned her.

'Sure as death, I won't.'

'Good.' Gorenn nodded, and then her wings flashed from her shoulders and she was off.

Straessa adjusted the hang of her snapbow, and then loped off towards the Sarnesh, looking for Milus and his officers. In the end she found the tactician at the head of the rail automotive, accompanied by a Mantis woman and representatives of the other Ant cities.

'Good of you to join us, Officer,' Milus said flatly.

Straessa made no rejoinder. Now was not the time to put the man's nose out of joint. 'What's the order, Tactician?'

There was the crash of another impact, a plume of dust flying not too far short of the Sarnesh lines; the ground shook underfoot.

Milus outlined his battle plan with swift efficiency, his voice loud enough to carry as far as it needed to, and not a jot louder. He explained that the right wing of the assault would be the automotives; that current indications suggested that the Lowlanders should have air superiority by a small but comfortable margin, so that the wall could be bombarded without loss of life once the Farsphex were downed. He went over the ground defences that the Wasps had set up and noted the specialist automotives the Sarnesh had brought to level the earthworks and stake fences. He explained that there would be Sarnesh officers along with every detachment, so that Milus's commands could be relayed – and obeyed – immediately. He noted the heavy weight of artillery lined up on the city wall ahead of them without emotion, and detailed each of his subordinates to be sure of which amongst their soldiers had the Art to fly or climb. 'Volunteers, if you can. Give the order, if not.' He seemed to look straight at Straessa as he said it.

The first Sarnesh Stormreader streaked overhead, followed by a handful more. Another greatshotter shell landed with a gout of flame, close enough to the Tseni to knock a score of them over in the impact.

'To your soldiers,' Milus instructed them. 'March on my signal.'

General Tynan stood atop the walls of Capitas and watched the Lowlanders approaching out of the pre-dawn.

The Second Army and most of the Third were spread out before the walls, making best use of what entrenchments and fortifications they had been able to put up. Beneath his feet the wall quivered every time the greatshotters spoke, and soon enough the rest of the artillery would join them. The Lowlanders were coming in an open formation, though: the Ants spread out in a loose cloud that would firm up into a solid fighting line as soon as they hit the enemy, and the Collegiates in the small maniples they had used when he had come against their own city.

'Their left's the Beetles,' Major Oski noted. 'A screen of Mantis-kinden beyond them. Their right's mostly automotives.'

One of the wall leadshotters boomed, a ranging shot falling short of the enemy – but not too far short.

Out in the city behind them, another sort of battle was taking place. Ernain's supporters – the Bellowern clan of Beetle-kinden and all those others who had committed treason to secure a new tomorrow – were spreading the word even now, adjusting the hierarchies, making room for the new order. They were relying on Tynan to win victory for them today, so that their tomorrow could come.

'I reckon they've got superior numbers,' Oski remarked. 'We've got more engines but that Engineer, Varsec, he said they'd have more to put in the air, and just as good. Which means that having more engines – or even walls – isn't going to win it for us.'

'They're slowing,' Tynan noted.

'Well, they're thinking that some over-keen fellow down the wall just told them what the best range of our wall artillery was,' Oski pointed out.

'They're still taking strikes from our greatshotters.'

'General, we have precisely two greatshotters, and they're big and immobile enough that their orthopters won't be able to miss 'em if they want to come and drop a bit of ordnance.' He nodded down behind him to the two huge engines, barrels even now being winched lower to deal with the advance of the enemy. 'I wouldn't want to be on the crew there, is all I'll say.'

A Farsphex roared overhead, close enough for Tynan to feel the breeze of its wings. Others were lifting off from airfields across the city, along with a rabble of Spearflights and even some of the lumbering old box-shaped heliopters the Empire had effectively abandoned. The enemy orthopters, their Stormreaders, were already waiting in the sky, and now they began stooping for the attack.

'It's been an interesting campaign, General,' Oski remarked, although his voice shook a little as he said it. 'I'd say the usual about honour to serve and all that, but I reckon you've not quite forgiven me for me being one of Ernain's people.'

'Ask me again tomorrow,' Tynan replied softly, watching the flying machines scatter across the sky, seeking out their chosen opponents, spinning and darting and gyring over the city, or else out across the extent of the Lowlander army.

'Right,' Oski said, 'time to start some serious artillery business.' He clapped his small hands together briskly.

'I thought you said they were out of range.'

'That's on the assumption that our over-eager artillerist wasn't specifically shooting short, to my orders, sir. If they aren't going to wait for the aviators to have it out before they come trooping in, I don't see why we shouldn't get a few low blows in at the same time.'

As the Imperial artillery opened up, much of it was still out of range – clearly Milus was no fool. The wall's extra elevation and the unexpected reach of some of the pieces still landed a fair few missiles amongst the front ranks of the Lowlanders, though – exploding into whirling storms of shrapnel or spraying sticky fire over anyone luckless enough to be nearby.

At Straessa's shoulder, her Sarnesh liaison issued flat, emotionless directions, and she passed the orders on, drawing the leading edge of her maniples back and trusting to the rest to make space, just as they'd practised.

Those orders would have originated from Tactician Milus, of course, and she was bitterly aware that he was well out of the range of the enemy engines. He was sitting in the automotive carriage he used for his headquarters, out of sight in case the enemy had sent out assassins or snipers, and yet with thousands of other pairs of eyes through which he would watch the fight unfold.

The Mantids to her left had spread out further, and she saw their far edge begin to creep round like a long, curved horn towards the enemy, inching around their flank. There were not enough Mantids that they could cause serious damage to so large an Imperial force, but their reputation preceded them. They had taken their toll on the Empire's armies more than once, and the Imperial commander would already be trying to redeploy in case they tried one of their traditional damn-the-odds charges. Straessa reckoned those charges weren't part of the plan for today, not given the new calm sense of purpose the Mantids seemed to display. They had diminished themselves, almost, from the killers of legend to something more like mere soldiers. But soldiers often lived, whereas killers of legend always met a tragic fate.

'How's the air battle going?' she asked.

Castre Gorenn gave her an odd look. 'Lots of machines going in all directions. You're asking *me*?'

'Someone?' Straessa called hopefully. 'Anyone?'

'They're doing their best to hold things up,' one of her soldiers told her. 'But we're already trying to get some bombs on their wall, so they can't just keep giving us the runaround – they'll have to make a stand. I think we're winning.'

'Keep an eye on them.'

'Antspider!' someone yelled, and already the Sarnesh who stood behind her was rattling off instructions. 'Airborne incoming. All snapbows up.'

'Snapbows to the sky!' Straessa shouted, 'and get those pikes up!' She heard the instruction passed outwards by the officer of each maniple.

Ahead of her the sky was black with Wasps. The bulk of an Imperial army was always its Light Airborne, and here there were thousands of them, a vast cloud of flying men and – and, yes, their insects too, the creatures held on a fraying mental leash by someone with the Art to speak to them. The Empire clearly didn't intend to wait for its orthopters to be whittled away.

The Airborne boiled forwards, coming in high enough that they would be clear of enemy shot until they chose to close the range. They were like a stormcloud. Coming from the east, they blotted the morning from the sky.

'Gorenn, give me range.' With only one eye, Straessa knew enough to defer to the Dragonfly's keener sight.

'Wait . . .' Castre Gorenn had an arrow to the string as she peered upwards. 'Wait, now . . .' Then her arrow was gone, the string abruptly no longer taut beside her ear even as the Wasps started to descend. And she whooped, 'Now!' as loud as she could.

'Loose!' Straessa endorsed her, but her maniple already had – and the rest were taking that as their signal. To the left, the Mantis archers had already let fly their shafts, and many of them were already taking to the skies to meet the Wasps in their own element.

The return shot came sleeting down at the same time. A bolt struck Straessa's helm like a hammer blow and, all around her, Company soldiers were dropping, picked out from the Collegiate host more by chance than by any decision by the enemy.

'Stretchers!' Straessa shouted. She did not have to order a second shot, for everyone still able to was putting bolts into the Wasps as fast as they could.

Captain Bergild brought her Farsphex back towards the walls, taking as narrow a line as possible, feeling the net of her pilots spread out around her, dancing only to her tune. Of course, the Sarnesh had their own link, and she could see it in every move they made through the sky, all of their Stormreaders moving like game pieces to a single mind's masterplan.

The Imperial Spearflights and clumsy heliopters were mostly gone already, only the best of them surviving the first savage moments of the battle. She reckoned that the Imperial craft were outnumbered three to two, and the Ant pilots were pushing furiously to get at the walls and the greatshotters.

And yet we're holding them. Or almost. And whilst 'almost' wouldn't serve in the long run, it would give time for more Imperial reinforcements to come to Capitas's aid, whilst the Lowlanders were all here already, as far as she could work out, with no reserves to call on at all.

There were more of the Ants, but they were less experienced pilots, without the true feel for the air that an aviator needed. Worse, their mindlink kept them in contact with their forces on the ground. Whoever was giving the orders was not doing so with a pilot's eye. Bergild and her people could improvise, lead them, fool them. She was pulling out all of her tricks for this battle, because what else had she been saving them for?

Another of her pilots was abruptly gone, canopy torn open. A further handful were trying to get a bombing line on the centre of the Sarnesh detachment, to change the enemy priorities a little, perhaps. Their Fly-kinden bombardiers were already looking for targets, but the enemy numbers weren't allowing them enough time to themselves.

Then one of the greatshotters was silenced, a Stormreader dropping down to hover virtually overhead for a second as it unloaded its bombs. *A Collegiate, not a Sarnesh*, came her instant speculation. The Beetles were more experienced pilots and they flew as individuals, dodging through the airborne melee with no regard for anybody else's plans.

Prioritize any craft making for the other 'shotter, she instructed, but the response was instant: *Captain, they all are.*

Hornets are in the air, came the warning, and she ordered, *Get clear of the wall, quickly.*

They had fewer insects than they'd used to clear the skies over Collegium, and there had been no vile-smelling paste to mark out Imperial machines as 'friends' – not that it had helped much before – and so Bergild could only try and call her pilots back and get them out of reach as a cloud of angry hornets spiralled up from the cages they had been penned in. They would not last long, she knew – and they were a desperate measure because of the danger they would pose to the city itself and the men on the wall, but at the moment that last greatshotter represented the only reliable superiority the Empire currently held.

Another try at bombing their centre, she decided, selecting half a dozen pilots for the job. *Get their attention again. And you*, she detailed another handful, *get yourselves over their automotives and start to break them up. The rest of you, split up and hunt down the Collegiate . . .*

Her commands fell away into a great yawning chasm of uncertainty.

Her hands were still gripping the stick, but something was abruptly gone from her, and she could feel a kindred void in all her fellows.

The machine confining her lurched in the air and, amidst the rising panic from her pilots she could only think, *What am I doing here. What is all this for?*

I have no idea how any of this metal works.

Something had reached up and obliterated any understanding that she might have had of her work, her lifelong trade.

Her Farsphex lurched to one side as she twitched and fought with controls that no longer made any sense to her. The densely peopled ground wheeled about her madly. She could not even get out of the cockpit. She could not release the hatches. Her last few moments gave her a view of a spinning sky that was raining flying machines, each one spiralling out of control, tumbling earthwards as though gravity had finally come to its senses.

Bergild screamed.

Straessa saw the walls shake and at first she thought it was an illusion, a heat-shimmer brought on by the sunrise. Then the Sarnesh messenger at her back made a peculiar, almost plaintive noise, and she realized it was real.

Her people were ceasing to shoot, at first just a few but then more, then all, until only Gorenn in their midst was still sending her arrows up at the Wasps . . . the Wasps who were no longer shooting downwards but milling around in the air, pulling back towards the Imperial lines.

'What's going on?' Straessa murmured, but too quietly for anyone to hear, because she had no expectation that anyone had an answer. She stared down at the snapbow in her hands – an unfamiliar weight of metal that did . . . something. It was a weapon, that much she knew, but one she had no idea how to use.

Out beyond the Sarnesh contingent, all the automotives had ground to a halt, save one that was ploughing about in a determined circle. The only other machines in motion were the orthopters and, as she watched, she saw them fall from the sky, each in its own graceful, doomed arc, and that seemed only natural because she could not see how such things could possibly have got airborne in the first place.

Then the walls of Capitas shuddered again, rippling like a curtain, and her hands grasped her telescope, and then were unable to do anything with it.

'They're cracking.' Gorenn sounded deathly afraid, far beyond the very understandable fear that Straessa was fighting down. 'The walls . . .'

'The ground . . .' said someone else.

The Imperial forces out there were moving. Those who could fly were getting within the city's boundaries in the air. The rest were abandoning their positions, fleeing while they could. Straessa saw the ground heave and twist, and heard herself ask, 'Is that because of *us*? Are we doing that?' She would have believed just about anything, right then.

'No,' came the hollow, shaky voice of the Sarnesh. 'That's not us.'

'There's something coming up from the earth,' Gorenn declared flatly.

'People,' someone else with sharp eyes suggested.

'Not people,' the Dragonfly corrected, staring out at those human-shaped forms boiling out of the riven ground that had consumed the Empire's earthworks, already butchering those Imperial soldiers too slow to get out of their way. Around them, the ground seethed with the segmented forms of centipedes of all sizes.

'What are they? What do they want, if they're not ours?' Straessa demanded plaintively. None of them could not know that – between them, by their repeated contact – Che and Seda had bored a path of least resistance between Capitas and the Worm.

Forty-Six

Milus stared out across the rapidly disintegrating battlefield, stepping from mind to mind as his officers in turn relayed to him what they were seeing. There was a constant chaos of reports, an army's worth of shock and bafflement. In the back of his thoughts his pilots were screaming as they died.

The ground before Capitas had just caved in, as though undermined. In fact, he had even prepared a plan to sap the walls if more conventional means failed to take them, but this . . . Their walls were bowing forwards, the foundations rotten and eaten away. Men and engines were tumbling from the top as the great curtain of stone swayed and then cracked across, immense sections of masonry just falling away. He watched the enemy's capital city simply opening up to him like a flower. He had never seen a city's defences fall so swiftly.

His officers were asking him for instructions, and there was a rising tide of fear trying to force its way through his army. *Something* incomprehensible had swept over them: the use of all their weapons – snapbows, automotives, even crossbows – was suddenly denied them, whole sections of their brains just failing to connect. The more level-headed scouts were reporting that the Wasps seemed to be suffering under the same impossible effect.

Be calm, he instructed them. He himself was calm, and that helped. He was not seeing a violation of the way the world worked. He was Milus, and he had different eyes to the bulk of his kinden. He was seeing an opportunity.

He studied the Wasp response – they were pulling back to the broad gap in their walls, seemingly stripped now of all discipline and order. It was a fighting retreat because the broken earth was swarming with bodies, a ravening horde of some kinden Milus had never seen, laying into everything nearby – which meant the Wasps themselves.

Sheltered back here, he could consider carefully. A tactician had no business being on the front line, and no need either. In his mind the concepts of Aptitude were therefore still strong, but whenever he tried to communicate with his engineers and his artillerists he was met with blank incomprehension, a desperate reaching for an understanding that never came.

No matter. We're still the best soldiers on the field. Sling your snapbows and draw swords.

Orders, Tactician? came from a hundred minds, but they were steady now because he himself was steady.

They wanted to go in, he knew. They wanted to get inside the Wasps' city, but also to clear the way of that crawling mass of intruders erupting from the earth. There was something about them that made the skin crawl: they had a human shape but it was animated by something else entirely.

Hold, Milus decided.

There was some surprise at that, some resistance even. He rode out the backlash of queries and demands, eventually just bludgeoning them with his authority, *I have been given command here!* repeated over and over until he had beaten them all down. He knew that there were parts of his army who were not happy with some of his decisions and some of his priorities, but he knew that they would do as he said. Out here, beyond the reach of the Royal Court, *he* constituted Sarn. Anyone who disobeyed him was a renegade to their city, and that was a door that only opened one way.

Our enemies are fighting one another, he told them with some satisfaction. *I don't care what these things are. Let them kill Wasps. Let them kill all the Wasps they want, and let the Wasps kill them back. Whoever's left standing will answer to us.*

Tactician, they're still coming out of that hole, one of his scouts reported. *No end to their numbers. They're spreading this way.*

Then kill them once they get close enough. Keep your shields up and interlocked, and turn them back towards the city. Channel them, but no more than that. They're just a weapon, like any other.

But, Tactician, from another officer, *what's happened to us? Our bows . . .?*

Metaphysics can wait, Milus replied sternly. *Shields up and hold, and let them shed blood for us.*

Tynan did not want to hear casualty reports just then. He reckoned that perhaps a third of his ground-bound troops were still out there fighting to get clear of this new foe. He had lost dozens of wall engines . . . but what matter when his own artillerists seemed unable to use them any more? The sky, by now, was completely swept clean of orthopters from both sides.

It's the end of the world. In his head, a mad little voice was saying that this was something out of the old Inapt legends, back from the myth days of monsters and magicians. Impossible things were happening and, worst of all, they were happening to his city.

The Light Airborne had fared best – already in the air and mobile enough to get wherever they wanted. Their officers had made the right call and pulled them back from their attack on the Lowlanders to throng the breach with bodies, on the ground itself and all up the jagged edges of wall on both sides. Beyond them, the infantry and support of the Second and Third armies was in headlong rout, fleeing for the compromised safety of the city.

And the enemy . . . the *enemy?* Tynan had thought these must be some new Lowlander ally at first, but the foe that he had been *expecting* to fight was not taking advantage of the sudden disintegration of the Wasp position, and instead looked to be keeping well clear of whatever was happening here. The earth-kinden – whatever they were – just kept erupting out of the ground, a great boiling host of them like maggots pouring from a wound.

Like worms, said an old, old part of his mind steeped in the stories they used to frighten children with.

They threw themselves at the retreating Wasps with a shocking speed and savagery, and no sense of self-preservation at all. Their beasts, that scrabbling tide of centipedes, were underfoot every-where, the smaller lunging upwards to sink venomous fangs into legs, the greater ones rearing up to coil about their victims, rending armour, driving down at men's faces with claws agape.

By now enough officers had contacted him that Tynan could start giving some kind of orders but his mind was still scrab-bling for what orders he could possibly give. His mouth was getting the words out, though, as decades of military experience took over, shunting his stunned surprise to one side.

'Get me a perimeter across the wall!' he snapped. 'Use all the infantry you can, spears and heavy armour.' *Why did we let them take away our Sentinels?* Not those useless machines but the elite heavy troops who would have stood off this tide until dusk, if they'd had to. 'Airborne, get yourselves over them – I don't see them flying, and I don't see them with bows. I want a storm of stingshot into their heads as they come in, and I want strong stingers flanking the breach and backing up the infantry. Con-sortium!'

'Sir!' Some clerk or other, but coming at his order.

'Get into the city. Get every man of our kinden . . . get every *adult* of our kinden, men and women, everyone who can sting. *Everyone* comes to defend Capitas. Go get your people to spread the word.'

The clerk stared at him, wide-eyed, but was off into the city the next moment.

The breach was meanwhile filling up with heavier troops,

freeing up the Airborne who had seized it first. Tynan saw a great solid block of Vesserett Bee-kinden – solid armour, axe and interlocking hexagonal shields – take up their positions and brace, with Wasps stationed ready to sting over their heads. *Ernain's lot,* he thought suddenly. *Stab me, but I'm glad we've got them.*

'They're still coming, sir!' Major Oski dropped down beside him. 'The ground keeps just pissing them out and pissing them out. There's no end to them.'

Thank you for your contribution, Tynan thought, but before he could actually say anything, one of the Airborne dropped down beside him.

'General, they're climbing the walls. We've got stingers up top, but not enough.'

Tynan nodded, looking back into the city. Sure enough, here came the first wave of stunned-looking Wasp-kinden – artificers, Consortium book-keepers, intelligencers, factory overseers, wives, mothers, surgeons, whores – all the little cogs that made empires and armies run.

Well, today they're all soldiers. 'Go, get any Wasp not in uniform up on the walls and sending stingshot downwards. Men, women, slave, free – I don't care.'

'Yes, sir.'

'Sir?' It was Oski again, and when Tynan rounded on him he shrugged helplessly. 'Sir, I don't seem to be able to *do* my job, with the . . . with the . . .' He waved his arms towards the surviving wall artillery that was sitting idle and devoid of meaning. 'You need a messenger or something?'

'Good man, Major.'

The surging tide of earth-kinden and their sinuous beasts went crashing against the breach, barely held in check by the Wasps and Bees stationed there. The air above them crackled and sang with a storm of stingshot.

And Oski was right: they were still coming.

★

'Sod me, just look at them,' Straessa breathed, horrified. To say that she had never seen anything like it would be sheer understatement. The sight of the soldiers of the Worm venting up from the earth, clambering over one another, a great coiling mass of human bodies driven by one hungry purpose – it was not something that anyone should have to see.

'Tactician says to hold,' the Sarnesh man told her.

'Oh, no fear,' she assured him. 'I don't see me wanting to go any closer to *that*, thanks.'

'Antspider.' The voice was Gorenn's, though it took Straessa a moment to recognize it. Something completely unfamiliar seemed to have gripped the Dragonfly woman.

'I know,' Straessa assured her.

'No, you do not. This is wrong,' Castre Gorenn insisted.

'You don't need to tell me. I never saw anything more wrong in my life,' Straessa agreed, increasingly aware that she and the Dragonfly were speaking at cross-purposes.

'What is going on?' A new voice – that of Balkus forcing his way through the Collegiate troops to get to her. 'What *are* those things?'

'Why would anyone expect me to know?' Straessa demanded of the world in general.

'Listen, Antspider.' Balkus looked frightened – in a way that even the wrath of his fellow Sarnesh hadn't made him look. His nailbow hung on its strap, a useless deadweight. 'Most of my lot are saying that we either run away or we charge.'

'What?'

'My Inapt, which is most of us Princep lot – Roaches, Moths, Spiders, all that – they're going crazy. They want out, or if there's no out, they want to get stuck in.'

'Orders are to hold,' came the emotionless tones of Milus's mouthpiece.

'Sounds good to me,' Balkus admitted, 'but I'm not joking when I say that my lot won't just sit still for long.'

'*Orders* are—' the Sarnesh started again, but Gorenn cut across him.

'Straessa, we have to fight them.'

'Are you insane?' the Antspider demanded.

'You don't understand what you're looking at,' Gorenn insisted.

'No, I don't, which is why . . .' Straessa tailed off, looking past Gorenn at one of the Mantids, one of those whipcord-lean old women who seemed to make most of their decisions. 'What does she want?'

'She wants us to attack, because it's our duty,' Gorenn explained, as though everything was so very self-evident.

'Orders—' the Sarnesh intoned.

And Straessa snapped at him, 'Will you just shut your yap while I work out what's going on? Gorenn, please?'

'Officer, those out there –' the Dragonfly's tremulous gesture took in all of the seething mass heaving its way clear of the earth – 'they are the enemy. The real enemy. The true enemy. The *only* enemy.'

'How can you know that?' Straessa wanted to know.

'How is it that you do *not*?' Gorenn shouted back in her face. 'How blind are you Apt, that you cannot *know* in your bones, in your hearts, in your . . . *everything* that you must oppose what we see there?'

Straessa just stared at her thinking, *Yes, you are right. All of me is saying just that, except for my brain, which has the casting vote. The brain just doesn't know what the pits is going on, frankly.*

'I'm going,' Gorenn informed her. 'I'm going, and the Mantids are going, and if your people want to come, Balkus, then they won't be alone.'

'There are thousands of the bastards,' Straessa said weakly. 'You'll be pissing into a storm.'

'At least we'll be pissing *somewhere*,' Gorenn declared, and the bizarre discrepancy between her furiously sincere tone and what she had actually said was the final straw for Straessa. It was official: the world was either mad or ending. Either way, why not?

'Let's go!' she bellowed, in her officer's voice. 'Pikes front, swords out, trust to your mail. We're going to kill some what-ever-the-pits-they-are!'

'No!' the Sarnesh liaison protested. 'Orders—' And then Balkus punched him in the face, as hard as a big Ant can punch, and the man went down.

'I'll get my lot.' He drew a pair of shortswords from his belt and weighed them in his hands. 'Maybe that turd Milus will die of apoplexy as a bonus.'

'Right.' Straessa looked past Gorenn towards the Mantis woman. 'I'm trusting you pissing Inapt bastards,' she warned. 'I seriously don't understand just what is going on right now, but you're telling me we have to fight because it's the right thing to do? Well, Collegium's played that card enough times in the last few years. So, fine, let's go at it.'

In his command carriage, Milus stood up suddenly, watching the left flank of his army ripple and bulge and then break forwards, in a weird mirroring of the Capitas wall. Then they began march-ing – the Collegiate maniples pulling closer to one another and presenting a bristling face of pikes towards the earth-kinden that were already spilling their way.

His liaison had been struck down! And what were the Beetles *doing*? Had the loss of their Aptitude stripped away their reason as well?

And then the Mantids were on the move as well, setting the pace and bringing the Collegiates to a steady jog to keep up. And the whole left side of his battle order was abruptly oper-ating on its own recognizance, and no longer under his control.

He swore fiercely, his displeasure crackling across the face of the Sarnesh force.

All others hold! he insisted, aware that there were those amongst his own who dearly wanted to attack as well, moved by some urge, some revulsion at what they were seeing that they could not account for and yet could not deny. Milus's hold over his army was weakening, so he browbeat them, he forced his mind

574

upon them: *You are mine! You have no say! You are just bodies who march to my plan, or we lose everything!*

Then the Vekken went. Through the eyes of his soldiers he watched, open-mouthed, as the dark-skinned Ants formed up into that same solid block of shields that he had been trying to dissuade them from all the way from Collegium. Suicide, of course, to march that kind of close-packed formation directly into enemy shot and artillery. Except that there was no shot or artillery, and this traditional Ant fighting formation was perfect for taking on superior numbers in close combat. Milus stared as they set off, keeping a brisk pace to catch up with the Collegiates.

Hold! Have the Tseni hold! There was a furious argument going on between his liaison and the Tseni commander – the woman demanding to know what Milus was doing and expressing a growing lack of faith in her allies.

Milus smelt smoke.

His head snapped up, his mind abruptly returning to the interior of the carriage. *Smoke . . .?*

There was a wisp of it coiling about the carriage ceiling. Yet the carriage itself was detached from any automotive, and there was no machinery that might have overheated or caught light.

The smoke was rising in leisurely coils from the wooden floor at one end of the carriage – and now he was reminded just how much of his surroundings were just wood, after all, and therefore flammable. He stepped a little closer, hunching down. Yes, between the planks of the floor there was a dull red glow.

'So this is your revenge, is it?' he murmured. *Lissart, of course.* The little firebug had not fled, after all. 'More fool you for staying around.'

Wood would burn, but not fast, and the fire had only just started. He stormed towards the door to the carriage and flung it open.

There was a brief tug of resistance halfway through the motion, as of a broken thread.

Facing him was a placard nailed to the carriage rail, hastily

575

painted white letters stating, 'A present from Despard.' His eyes had time to register those words, though not to understand them, when the explosives went off virtually underneath his feet, flinging him back into the carriage.

A second later, the fire Lissart had set hit the fuel barrels the Flies had hidden beneath the carriage, and the resulting fireball lifted the entire carriage off its wheels and tore it – and Milus – apart.

Forty-Seven

Stenwold glanced back at the silent vacant city as he paused in the doorway of that remembered Mynan townhouse. The sky above, which he had assumed to be morning, was greying over to evening already. He could see no sun up there, only a uniform layer of ragged clouds.

Bad weather on the way. But, if he was true to himself, he knew it was not that, not really.

He shivered. If he listened very hard, he could just discern distant voices, and hear that woman, whose name he could not quite bring to mind, calling out his name.

I'm sorry, he thought. She sounded further away than previously, blown on the wind. He could only just make her out.

Paladrya. That was it. *I don't think I can come back to you.*

He pushed at the taverna door, half expecting it not to give way, for the entire building just to be solid stone, preserving its secrets from him.

But it swung open, and he stepped into that remembered taproom. For a moment his mind supplied the bustle of a Mynan taverna of two decades before but, no, it was as abandoned as the rest of the city. Abandoned but clean and intact, as though the Wasps had never arrived.

Here was where the soldiers of his Ant friend Marius had sat awaiting the start of the siege.

But I wasn't here. I was upstairs with my glass, staring out at the gates. Not knowing we had been betrayed. Not knowing that day would hammer me into shape like a smith. What would I have become, if I had not been there? What would the world have become?

A worse place, I hope. But, at this point, he realized that he had no guarantees. *They named me War Master, an old Moth title from the Bad Old Days. Surely I only ever wanted to prevent war?* But his mind was loose on its bearings, and he could not swear to that, after all.

Stenwold went up the stairs to where it had all started.

He was waiting there, sitting at one of the tables just as when their little band of fools had made their plans. Dead fools now, all of them, Stenwold's oldest friends, and none older than this one.

'Hello, Tisamon,' he breathed.

The Mantis was looking him over, a curiously unreadable expression on his face that at last resolved into the smallest of smiles.

'Hello, Sten.'

Stenwold went to take a seat across from him, noting how dark it was, already, out of the windows.

'You're looking well,' he ventured awkwardly. It was true and it was not true. Here was the young Tisamon, lean and deadly, but with the old Tisamon clearly visible beneath the skin: the lines of care, of soured hope and self-recrimination all traceable there like veins. And beneath even those was the shadow of the skull, telling of the death that had claimed this man and not let go.

'It's good to see you again,' the Mantis said, and Stenwold was startled to see tears glint in his eyes. 'It's been so long, but I knew you'd be here, eventually.'

'Here . . .?' Stenwold glanced around, still trying to come to terms with what he was seeing. The room seemed to blur as his memories fought to impose themselves on it. Surely there was a Wasp army out beyond the gates, about to attack. Or was this occupied Myna where Kymene's resistance was on the streets? Or just a bombed ruin again?

'I don't understand,' he admitted at last, sounding lost even to himself. 'Why am I here?'

'Sten,' Tisamon said softly. 'It's always been Myna for you, surely you can see that? Ever since that first time, when you saw the Wasps capture it. Myna *made* you. For you, it's always been about Myna. Where else would you go, when . . .'

When . . . 'There is no when,' Stenwold declared, feeling an unnameable emotion begin to rise inside of him. *Is it grief, if the person you're mourning is yourself?* 'There's life, and there's death. There is no . . . this.'

Tisamon's smile grew fond. 'Then perhaps this is just you, in the end . . . in your mind. Does that make it any less true for you?'

'I . . .' The Apt part of Stenwold told him he should argue, but it seemed like a lone voice at the Assembly. 'You died, Tisamon.'

The Mantis nodded. 'I know.'

'A long time ago, now. They say you killed the Emperor.'

'I didn't, but it pleases me that they say so.' A rare smile appeared, cut right from Stenwold's happier days.

'So why are you here? Myna was never anything special to *you.*'

Tisamon was looking at him, still smiling, his eyes bright with old pain. 'Sten,' he said, 'you didn't think I'd go on without you, did you?'

For a long time, Stenwold just sat there, looking at his friend, then he looked down at his hands, which had built and destroyed so much, and at the last he smiled back.

'I suppose not,' he conceded, and pushed himself heavily to his feet. 'Shall we?'

They descended the stairs together and stepped out into the night-silent street. Up there, further up the layered tiers of the city, there was an airfield. Where else would they be heading, but somewhere that promised an infinity of destinations?

Stenwold clapped Tisamon on the shoulder. 'Come on, let's go.' He felt twenty years younger.

Above, the stars were coming out.

This time, when the Worm ebbed away again, the crippling pain did not go. It took a step back, like a duellist itself, assessing her condition and ready for its next strike, but when Tynisa lurched to her feet and fended off Tisamon's immediate strike, she still felt that stabbing hurt deep within her.

Her own time, as opposed to everyone's collective time, was running out.

She feigned a retreat and twisted inside his guard, gripping the lip of his helm with her off hand and trying to wrench it free, to expose some part of him that she could pierce, to look upon her father's face. He went with the motion, dragging her into the spines of his arm, which scored red lines across her body. Then his claw was driving back towards her, crooked underhand like a dagger.

She blocked the thrust, forearm to barbed forearm, then grappled at his wrist, getting a hold for long enough that she could drop back on her good leg, turning his attack into an over-extension, smashing him across the helm with her knuckle-guard twice, back and forth, then driving the point of her pommel in between shoulder and neck. She felt the fine mail there give slightly, and for a moment Tisamon was down on one knee, but then he had driven his arm-spines into her side with all the force he could muster, knocking her over and following up instantly, so that she had to roll over the jagged ground to avoid his first thrust, then backwards into his legs to dodge the second. He stumbled over her, and she was slithering out from under him immediately, jabbing back at him and feeling her sword's tip scrape metal yet again.

She forced herself to her feet – her sword dragging her up more than anything, and saw him stalking her sidelong, assessing her condition just like the pain itself was doing, clearly planning his next attack.

She realized that she was between him and Seda.

He must have grasped it at the same time, breaking from his carefully poised stance in an almost awkward rush for her, but she had already passed out of his reach, just one halting step ahead of him, leading with her blade towards the Empress.

Then the pain returned and she crashed down with a wrenching cry, one hand to her hip to find that old wound torn open again, the blood soaking into her leggings. She flailed at Seda, but the Empress was just out of reach, staring at her in fear and rage, hand out and trembling.

Tynisa lurched towards her, just as the crackling bolt of gold fire scorched down her leg. The rapier – leaden in her grip now that the Weaponsmaster's bond had been severed – lanced the Empress's calf, toppling her backwards. This time, Seda's scream was pure pain.

Then Tynisa's agony made its measured retreat once more – though barely far at all now – and she rolled onto her back bringing her blade up, trusting that it would seek out Tisamon's attack.

He stood directly over her, right arm drawn back to administer the blow, left hand extended forwards to slap her blade aside. But his head was cocked as though he was listening.

'What are you waiting for?' Seda demanded. 'Kill her! I command it!' Again she thrust her arm out towards Tynisa, fighting furiously against all Che's efforts to stop her.

Tynisa inched out from under Tisamon's shadow, waiting for him to move, wondering if she now even had the strength to make a strike at him that would have any chance of piercing his guard and his armour.

Then he stepped back, in a single neat little motion, and lowered his blade. It was a movement almost unbearably familiar to her from all those practice bouts. Tisamon had concluded his lesson.

As she watched – as they all watched – he reached up and pulled off the helm. Beneath, his face was pallid and bluish, but still *him*. Whatever those pale eyes looked out on, though, was not his daughter or any other thing in that buried world.

His lips moved slightly, though no words came out.

'Kill them!' Seda yelled at him desperately, and his eyes focused, seeing not the Empress, but Tynisa.

He smiled slightly – in benediction? Who could say? Then he turned to go, and was nothing but a fragmenting pattern of shadows, gone as if he had never been.

Seda let out a scream of anguish, of lost control, and Tynisa forced herself onto one knee, trying to get her legs beneath her before the Worm regained the initiative and destroyed her with that pain. She locked eyes with the Empress, and spotted the very moment that the raging Wasp woman cast off the shackles Che had been trying to lay on her.

The stingshot punched solidly beneath Tynisa's ribs and slammed her back to the ground.

Thalric partly crawled, partly ran and was mostly hauled on by Messel, pushing through the panicking, milling non-combatants, catching fleeting, clashing moments of what was going on ahead. Che simply stood there, seemingly doing nothing, and Thalric could not follow the duel between Tynisa and her father at all, save that every time he saw her, Tynisa seemed weaker and weaker, whilst the armoured behemoth that was Tisamon never changed.

And then for a moment, just as he and Messel broke free from the crowd and lurched out onto that shrinking patch of clear ground that the refugees had given Che, he saw Tisamon leave for good. No uncertainty there: not just dancing in and out of sight as he had before. The man turned, and the light of some other place and time played across his face, and something seemed to drop away from him – no, something returned to him, some innate part of Tisamon that even Thalric could tell had been lacking.

And he was gone, and Tynisa was levering herself up.

Thalric saw Seda kill her.

Che was shrieking her sister's name, and Thalric saw the Empress's uninjured hand turn towards her.

Now or never, he thought and, shouting his body's objections down, he called up his wings no matter how badly it hurt, and hurled himself like a missile, to knock Che clear.

The stingshot struck him in the chest, but he had his Commonweal mail on, which scattered the fire away so that he felt only a solid impact. Then he was up, with Che squirming out from beneath him, and his own hand was directed straight at his Empress. His shoulder was a festering knot of raw pain and the whole miserable underground world was wheeling about him, fit to make him sick. *But I've had worse,* he knew. *Ask all the bastards who've tried to kill me if I've not had worse.*

He looked into the face of Seda and spat, 'Die.'

'No,' she said. Her smile was manic, too wide, unhinged. 'You are mine, Thalric, and you cannot kill me.'

And she was right. Looking into her face, that beautiful, delicate face, he fought to send his Art against her, and could not. She was the Empress of all the Wasps, and he had shared her bed, and if she could not win him to her cause, she could still master him enough to be safe from him forever.

Then something punched into her leg, close to where Tynisa had stabbed her, and Seda dropped to the ground with a hoarse yell of incredulous pain. Her hands spat fire – a searing bolt clipped his shoulder and sent him skidding away from Che. A second stingshot burst near Messel, driving him back even as he was reaching for another sling stone.

Messel. Thalric already had the plan in mind as he saw the man. The eyeless cave-kinden was an unlikely saviour, but he had one advantage over the rest of them.

Thalric threw himself forwards – yet another jolt of bone-jarring pain, but who was counting? – and spun himself about with a jagged flourish of his wings so that he ended up feet first in Che's fire.

Three quick kicks was all it took to rain its burning pieces down on to the cowering slaves below, and plunge them all into unrelieved blackness.

He heard Seda's voice lifted in terrible fear of that all-consuming dark, and then her sting was flashing, lighting brief slices of the underworld and looking for enemies. Thalric only hoped that Messel was bold enough to stand up and take a shot. He himself was too busy dragging himself downslope for the little cover that might grant him. *And please, Che, be smart enough to do the same!*

She was not.

He saw none of it, only that one moment Seda was lashing about herself in a frenzy of stingshot, and the next moment the Empress of the Wasps keened out a last hideous sound . . . and then there was neither Art nor answer from her.

The battle below surged on, and Thalric could hear it getting closer. Then people were stepping on him, and he clawed his way back upslope, calling out Che's name.

'Here.' He heard her, and because he had to see, because he had to know, he loosed a handful of stingshots up into the air, piecing the scene together from the after-image left by those flashes.

There was Che, cradling Tynisa's still form, her shortsword dark with blood. Beyond her, sprawled like a toy, lay the corpse of the last scion of the Imperial line, Seda the First.

Thalric crawled over to her, groping blindly until Che took his hand.

'I forgot you could see in the dark,' he got out.

'It's just about all I still have,' she told him, pulling him close.

'Tell me what the battle looks like,' he asked.

After a moment's pause, she said, 'It doesn't look like a battle any more.'

He stared blindly out into the darkness that held the end of them both, now, and everything else besides. 'Ah . . . Well, then, I have a few complaints about the way this whole business has been handled. When should I take them up with you?'

She was holding him very tightly and trembling now, whether for dead Tynisa or for what she could see before her. 'Can it wait for tomorrow?'

'Surely.' With his next ragged breath he let go of something he had been holding on to for a long time. It might have been hope. 'Che?'

Her lips found his.

The Worm carved its way closer, filling the sightless black with the screams of its victims.

Totho stared up into the face of god.

He stared at the night-black silhouette of that vast pronged head, seeing its antennae scour the edges of the cavern. It chewed over its current victim, mouthparts rending and tearing that ragged fragment of humanity between them with unthinking, destructive hunger until the face-swarming pitch of it had overwritten it all, all that its victim had been, now simply absorbed to become one more tormented visage floating on the surface of the void.

There seemed to be a lot of room in his mind for thought. Normally Totho's brain was clogged with Aptitude, but now it had been hollowed out, all thoughts of importance were crushed by the weight of this . . . this thing before him.

A writhing wound at the world's heart. Almost blind, mindless, ignorant, and so much the very centre of its expanding kingdom that it could abide nothing but its own ignorance. And it was an ignorance that it forced on all those in its presence; that it sent out along with its human puppets, for them to carry to the ends of the earth. He had witnessed this monster's servitors venturing out into the world he knew. The blind man Messel had told him that the Worm was moving out from its lair into the wider world.

He could not now grasp the delicate thoughts of an artificer, but he could understand that here before him was the death of all Aptitude – and of magic too, if magic actually existed – the cessation of human thought, a despot of conformity and blinkered tyranny that could not brook anything challenging its monotonous, meaningless world.

One of the priests reached out for him, and Totho casually backhanded him, smashing his gauntlet into the man's scar-ravaged face. The warriors closed in, swords levelled, and he let a couple of them strike at him, watching the blades scrape off his mail, before he just pushed his way through them.

He looked up again at that eye-twisting divinity that had robbed him of everything he had believed in. Its reach was finite, though, for it could not rob him of the things he had never believed. Staring up at the fathomless dark of its substance, he knew it could not be what it seemed. There was no magic, and the world ran by firm rules – even if he could not bring them to mind any more.

He continued studying the segmented shape that towered over him, looking past all the boiling darkness that seethed out of it, taking in the rippling legs, the hooked fangs. He held firm to his long-nurtured loathing of the supernatural, his deep-ingrained faith in a mechanistic universe, and his eyes pierced the veil that cloaked the god of the Worm. Strip it to its base shape, and there was nothing remarkable about it but its size. *It's nothing but a big centipede.*

'Is this it?' he demanded, his voice ringing unnaturally loud throughout the cave. 'This is your master? I challenge it! I set my armour against it.' He rounded on the aghast priests. 'I cannot tell you how this metal was made, but now that it is made, it goes on working. You cannot deny it. You cannot dent it with your stupidity. It is not subject to your belief.' He saw their baffled expressions. They could not understand what he meant.

He stepped forwards, and the slight shift in the monstrous centipede's swaying motion showed that it was aware of him.

586

He looked over at Esmail, seeing the man creeping closer. *There's a time for subtlety. This is not it.*

The priests were crowding him now, shoving him forwards towards the lip of that chasm. He let them. One hand drifted towards his belt. There was something very important about his belt. He knew it, he knew it, and yet he could not quite understand it. Something was there, and had there not been a plan . . .?

Then Esmail was amongst the warriors of the Worm, shouting for Totho to get clear. His hands carved them apart, shearing through flesh and armour, dropping three in that first surprise rush. The others turned to fight him, swift and relentless, and he led them about the enclosed confines of the cave, cutting their swords in two with bare-handed parries, or darting in beneath their blows to hack at their bodies. He was outmatched swiftly, but he never let them catch him.

'Go!' he was shouting to Totho. 'Run!'

At the same time, someone barrelled into the priests, striking out at them with a staff. It looked just like one of their own, and Totho could make nothing of that – the intruder seemed almost berserk, though, smashing randomly around and scattering them, freeing Totho up for a moment. Perhaps he, too, expected Totho just to run.

Totho's thumb found the string at his belt. He could not remember what it was for, only that it was important.

He remembered his conversation with Esmail, back in the prison.

It's as simple as pulling on a string.

Why had he said that? What would that accomplish? He could no longer remember. Pulling on a string did sound simple, though. One hardly needed to be Apt for that, surely?

His hand was on that string, just one pull required, and yet he could not do it. The necessary link between impulse and action had been broken. He was betrayed by his own Aptitude, which had guided everything he had ever done. Now that its crutch was gone, such a simple move was beyond him.

That vast head struck down, blotting out his entire world, but it seemed confused by the struggling melee before it, instead hammering at the rock, smashing one of the priests into a pulp, then drawing back.

Esmail was coming back round, the warriors right on his heels. 'Go! Go!' he was shouting, but only because he did not understand how important all this was. *Not for Che, not for Collegium, not for freedom, but for artificers everywhere. This obscenity must go.*

Then the Worm lunged again, and this time its hooked claws pincered his body and lifted him up.

The mail held. For a few impossible seconds, the god of the Centipede-kinden strove against the metallurgy of the Iron Glove and could not break it, though Totho felt his cuirass twist and groan, felt the latching between breast- and backplate snap under the force. And still his hand was at his waist, paralysed by ignorance. The dark radiance that the Worm blazed with enveloped him, but he felt the solid physical clutch of its fangs, and knew he was right. The lord of the underworld, the god of sacrifice and slavery, was no more than a vast beast.

Then someone was clinging to him, and he looked down into Esmail's stricken face as the other man brought the lantern down across the Worm's head, flaming pieces shattering across its broad carapace, which burned for moments like flaming oil on water before the darkness began to conquer the flames.

In the guttering light of that fire, Totho locked eyes with Esmail and saw understanding there – at last *someone* who understood. And Esmail had never been Apt: those parts of his mind that this monster was stifling had nothing to do with the urgent instructions Totho had coached him with.

To Esmail, it was just pulling on a string.

The Assassin caught the ripcord that dangled from Totho's belt, which Totho had carefully fed through all his little devices there, in that tiny corner of the prison where he had last been able to think.

He let go of Totho, falling away back towards the ledge, the cord ripping free. Totho stared down, seeing him vanish into darkness towards that unseen shelf.

The mandibles of god increased their grinding pressure and he felt the two halves of his armour shear, each of them still intact despite it all, but the pressure of their displacement beginning to tear him apart.

The Worm lifted him high towards the cave's ceiling, fighting against the resistance of the armour, the products of artifice that it could not suppress.

The thing about artifice, was Totho's last thought, *is that it works whether you believe in it or not.*

The string of grenades that looped through his belt erupted all at once and tore him in two, killing him instantly and ripping apart the head of the Worm.

Forty-Eight

Straessa backed off, her blade sliding out of a corpse that was suddenly, horribly, not the figure she had just stabbed.

The fighting had stopped, all in that very same moment, and now the Collegiates around her who were not concerned with the wounded were drawing back from the sight before them. A grim hush was falling, broken only by the moans of the injured.

Across the field, on the far side of that choked rift, she could see the Wasps were falling back too, recoiling in revulsion from the mess of bodies that now clogged their breached wall.

'Gorenn, tell me . . .' She did not mean, *What am I looking at?* She knew what she was looking at, and yet she desperately needed some clarification, some comforting lie that would let her address this sight, categorize it and turn it into something she could put behind her. 'Please, tell me . . .'

The Dragonfly stood stock still, staring out at that massed atrocity with a fixed expression. She had no arrows left in her quiver, Straessa noticed. In her hands was the same Collegiate shortsword that almost everyone there had ultimately resorted to.

Gorenn had no words, no words at all.

The enemy had just dropped, all at once, like manikins with their strings cut, across the whole of the battlefield, so that the chasm they had been surging from in such numbers was now glutted and blocked with the tangled mass of dead. But not *their* dead.

'Get me a Sarnesh here!' Straessa pleaded. *Please, someone tell me what we do now.* 'What does Milus say? Is he seeing this?'

It was a strained, ghastly minute before an Ant-kinden woman staggered over, her eyes full of the sight before them. 'Milus is dead,' she got out.

'Lucky bastard,' Straessa said, with feeling. 'So where does that leave us? What do we do?'

By now she could see that the Wasps were returning to defend their wall, albeit reluctantly. At the same time she became aware again that the snapbow slung over her back was something more than just a weight of metal: it was a weapon, fit for her hands and her mind.

But nobody was yet moving across that hideous charnel field. Nobody had the heart. The Sarnesh woman was shaking her head. There were no orders.

Before them lay a carpet of fallen children.

There were dozens of different kinden among them – Beetles, Woodlice, Moths, Mole Crickets, and some Straessa could not even name. Not one of them looked to be more than eleven, and most were younger, far younger. They lay still amongst the wreckage of arms and armour crafted for far larger bodies. There were thousands of them; tens of thousands. They were uncountable.

Straessa felt something within her close to breaking point. At no time before had she ever wanted less to be in command of anything, or to bear any kind of responsibility than now, facing *this.*

She could not even understand it. She could not know what the sight meant. She thought Gorenn might, from her expression, but the Dragonfly was not putting it into words.

So what the pits happens now?

'We've got it all back?' she asked the Sarnesh woman. 'Automotives, artillery, all that?'

The Ant nodded numbly.

So what? Do we just . . .? We came here for a reason, didn't we . . .?

It was the thought of trampling across that vast mass of dead children, of grinding them beneath the tracks of the automotives, of climbing that mound of small corpses that had banked up before the breach.

I don't know if I have it in me to do that, or to order anyone else to do it, but someone has to issue some sort of order. We can't just stand here till we starve.

What would Eujen do?

The thought was inexpressibly calming. Eujen would know exactly what to do.

'Fetch me a messenger. I need someone to take word to the Wasps.'

'I'll go,' Gorenn volunteered immediately, but Straessa shook her head.

'I think sending a Commonwealer over to them would give entirely the wrong message,' she decided. And, when the Dragonfly made to protest, she added, 'It's not you. I just don't want any dumb Wasp having flashbacks to what you did to them in the Twelve-year War, right?' It was the world's weakest joke, and Straessa could barely muster the ghost of a smile, but Gorenn returned it, in just about the same degree, and nodded in resignation.

In the end, it was Sperra who went. She had not fought in the battle but arrived afterwards, seeming a strange mix of defiance and misery. But when Balkus explained what was going on, she volunteered. She had run enough messages between cities before Collegium was liberated, after all. What was one more?

And at least she could fly. Nobody was about to tread that body-cluttered distance lightly.

By then, Straessa had the full attention of all the Lowlander contingents: Sarnesh, Vekken, Tseni, Netheryen, Princep and Collegiate. Staring round at them all, she thought, *How mad are you all, that you're going to let me do this? Don't you know who I am? They didn't make me chief officer even when I was the only officer left in the entire Coldstone Company – that's how unreliable I am.*

'Go and tell the Wasps,' she said, her voice stumbling over the words, 'that the army of the Lowlands will offer them terms . . .'

And in the dark of the underworld the sounds of fighting and massacre went abruptly silent.

'What is it?' demanded Thalric. 'What's happened.'

Che held him very tight, so that he could feel her shaking. She had no answer for him.

Then the wailing started as the slaves surveyed what had become of the enemy, and began recognizing faces.

Esmail was left in pitch darkness after the flash of Totho's explosives had blazed across the cavern above him. The force of the blast was enough to knock him flat, and everyone else as well, but he was prepared for the onslaught of dark-adapted Centipede warriors descending on him, taking advantage of his blindness.

Yet they did not come. Only silence came, and silence and darkness were, for a stretched-out moment, his only companions.

Until at last the cries began, fearful and incredulous. They started as a terrified murmur and rose to shrieking denial, to rage, to utter babbling madness. At least one voice rushed past him, and then receded as it pitched over the brink, surely at the owner's intent.

And then his name was called: 'Esmail!'

'Who . . .? Hermit?'

'Come here. Come here, man.' There followed the sound of a solid impact. 'Not you! Get back!'

Esmail limped over, feeling half broken by his fall. 'I need light. Can you hold them off?'

'Easily,' the Hermit grunted, which surprised Esmail at the

time because he still expected the Worm's warriors to be present.

He had tinder with him, and some dry mushroom stalks, and flint and steel, but it took him a long scrabbling time in the dark to get anything ignited. There was meanwhile the occasional whack of the Hermit's staff, and the babble of distressed voices did not let up, but no pitched battle flared up. Esmail was utterly bewildered until he finally got the torch lit and cast a look around.

He saw at once that the Hermit had herded a little knot of Scarred Ones together, and was keeping them hemmed in under the threat of his staff. But of the warriors . . .

He saw the bodies, and what they had become. He understood.

Totho . . .

There was no sign of the Lowlander, just as there was no sign of the Worm, but these corpses gave testament as to its fate. Artifice had triumphed in the end. The new world had undone the follies of the old.

Esmail felt weak, and then another thought struck him: what he would see when they ventured above into the city. *So many* . . .

But there was no other way out. He could either subject himself to that or go blind and let the Hermit guide him, and it was the thought of the old man's scorn at such cowardice which decided him.

'What about these?' he demanded, staring at the Scarred Ones, because he dearly wanted to kill them all. He held them responsible for their own actions, and for the actions of all their kin back into the depths of history. His own kind was now but a memory, a footnote, poised on the very brink of extinction, but if ever a kinden deserved complete annihilation, it was the Worm, for all they had done, and for all they had brought into and taken from the world.

But the Hermit was of their kind, too, and when he said, 'Leave them. What do they matter now?' Esmail deferred to him. He felt he owed the old man that much respect for having been able to break those bonds himself and thus become something resembling a human being.

Or at least as much as I do, anyway. Weary, hurting, disgusted, Esmail led the way back up to the city.

It was just as he knew it would be. Every street, every space, had been taken up by that vast spiralling progress: the warriors of the Worm off on their crusade to master the wider world. The sight made him sick, that slew of the half-grown, the ultimate victims of the Worm's madness, extending as far as his torch-light could reach in every direction, and then everywhere he went.

But then his head jerked up in surprise, because that vast stone city was not silent.

For a second he stopped, heart hammering, trying to work out what it was that he was hearing, that shrill, drawn-out, squalling sound from the centre of the vast maze of stone. Then he locked eyes with the Hermit.

'The child pits.'

And they were there, of course, the most recent taxes that the Worm had exacted, the last few crops of children who had not yet lost their kinden and been turned into the Worm. The pits where the final phases of metamorphosis had been penned were still and corpse cluttered, but the youngest still lived – though for how long, if Esmail could not do something? He stared down helplessly, seeing that seething vat of need and hunger and despair, and just trembling at his own utter lack of power. What could he do?

Then he knew what he could do.

Soon after that, he had rounded them up – the other survivors. He was surprised at just how many there were, despite the toll the Worm must have taken on them towards the end. He had all the surviving prisoners, those who had not been led down for sacrifice. More than that, he had the Scarred Ones, the last enclave of the Centipede-kinden – old and young, adult and child, men and women – standing in a frightened, unruly group before the child pits, staring with loathing at Esmail and the Hermit.

'Get them out,' Esmail ordered. 'Get them all out. Feed them. Carry them if you have to. Keep them alive.'

When one of them stepped forward to question why they should do what he said, Esmail killed him with a single blow of his hand.

'Listen to me,' he told them, without a grain of mercy in his tone. 'I hate you all. I would gladly see each one of you dead, and you deserve it, each one of you. What? No warriors to kidnap and kill for you? No great army to live in the guts of, and perpetuate, and pretend you had no *choice*? The man standing beside me is living proof that you had a choice. If you do as I say now, this one token act of atonement, then perhaps – just perhaps – your miserable kinden might be permitted to survive. Defy me and I will kill each and every one of you myself. And I can. And I will. Just give me an excuse.'

Slowly, fearfully, the former priesthood of the Worm began to move. They moved stubbornly, bitterly, and yet they moved to his bidding. In a way he was disappointed that he was not able to make more of an example of them.

Forty-Nine

Epilogues

The camps emptied, one by one, those where the Empress's will had been thwarted. Imperial citizens returned home to cities that were suddenly more than mere vassal states. Slaves returned to slavery, because change comes gradually and unevenly, and three generations of Imperial history cast a long shadow. Spiders were sent back in long chains to their southern cities. They were all of them currency and bargaining chips in the delicate game of diplomacy that the nations of the kinden were playing in order to extricate themselves from a war that none of them abruptly had the desire for; in order to step back from the brink.

And a band of Collegiate prisoners was eventually remembered and permitted to board an airship to head for home.

In those camps where the orders had been obeyed, where the Empress had been granted her harvest of lives, the burial details waited for the poisonous haze of the Bee-killer to recede. So closed an episode of Imperial history that nobody living now understood, but everyone would remember.

Sitting at the end of a pier on Collegium docks, Laszlo sat staring out to sea, his feet swinging over the water. Looking down, he could see the great metal carcass of an Imperial Sentinel that had been dragged into the water during the retaking of the city, now nothing more than a hazard to shipping.

A great many things were happening in the world, but relatively few of them held any interest to him just then.

Lissart had gone, of course.

She had thanked him. He had saved her from Milus's clutches, and then he had given her the opportunity to have her revenge. He had somehow thought that would bind her to him, that she would look at him and see something similar to what he saw, when he looked at her.

'There'll be another time,' she had assured him, but when he had begged her to tell him where she planned to go, she had demurred. 'That would spoil the surprise,' had been what she told him, but he'd known that she had not wanted him coming after her, just as he had known that he would not have been able to stop himself from doing so, if she had given him any hint.

She was at large somewhere in the world, that duplicitous, untrustworthy arsonist of a girl, and here he sat staring out at the sea and mourning her already.

'Hey, loser.'

He looked up irritably, not feeling in the mood for Despard's jibes. The *Tidenfree*'s chief artificer had always possessed an abrasive sense of humour.

'Gude wants to know,' she insisted. 'We can't just sit around at anchor here forever.'

'Go away.'

'Let me put it another way, Laszlo. The *Bloodfly* wants to know. You're going to tell *her* to go away?'

'If I have to.'

Despard uttered a derisive noise and lit off again for the ship along the quayside. It looked just like a swift little merchantman, but it had been one of the most notorious pirate vessels of its day, and would be so again. With or without him.

Stenwold Maker, Laszlo's friend and patron, was dead. Why

would he stay in this war-bruised city? And yet he had no other destination. Liss had not given him a hint of one.

'Laszlo?'

Another voice. He looked up to see Sperra, the woman from Princep. She was regarding him uncertainly but, before he could turn away, she had sat beside him, in the manner of someone conquering their own fears.

'What are you doing here?' he asked her. 'I thought . . .'

'Princep can manage without me,' she said, desperately trying to appear casual. 'I just wanted to see how you were doing.'

He studied her for a long time. He knew full well that she had taken a shine to him, and he also knew that, on occasion, he had taken advantage of that to get her and her Ant friend to do things for him. He was not proud of that.

But, still, here she was and with an obvious purpose, for all that she would not speak it. One word from him and he would be rid of her, and he could see her bracing for it, ready to risk the hurt, but hoping for the small chance that he might say something different.

'What next for you?' he asked her, instead.

She shrugged. 'I don't know. What about you?' Relentless in her willingness to be put on the rack.

He glanced over at the *Tidenfree* again. 'You know, I was thinking of a spot of piracy.' He took a deep breath, aware that he was doing something right for the wrong reasons – or perhaps the other way around. 'How about you? Only Despard's always after more help with the engines, and I think you know some medicine too . . .? Always handy, that.'

There was such naked hope in her expression that he felt wretched for her, and, yet, who knew? There might be no Lissart in his future, or he might rid himself of his longing for her, and a man at his time of life should be realistic. There came a day when you had to stop chasing dreams.

'Come on,' he suggested, 'I'll introduce you to the crew.'

★

'Willem,' Eujen said, reaching for his stick.

Willem Reader, aviation artificer, made a hurried gesture. 'You needn't get up.'

'I'm going to, though.' Eujen felt the gearing of his supports finally engage and, with a little help from his stick, he was standing within a relatively short period of time. 'It's good to see you.'

'I was beginning to wonder if the Sarnesh would let me leave,' Reader agreed. 'There were quite a few of us, in the end, who were asking just who the enemy was, that we were still helping them get ready to fight. I know it's thanks to you and everyone else here, putting on the pressure, that they finally decided to act like civilized human beings again.'

'In all honesty, it was your wife leading the charge.' Eujen nodded at Jen Reader, who hadn't let Willem out of her sight since his return. The Beetle woman gave him a tired smile, which Eujen returned with, 'And, of course, congratulations on your election, Madam Assembler.'

Jen shrugged. 'I decided that if they still weren't going to give the chief librarian a seat by right, then I'd cursed well earn one the hard way. And, believe me, Master Leadswell, I'm not just going to sit back and cheer while in the Assembly. There's plenty I think needs changing around here.'

'But perhaps not the surroundings?' Eujen suggested. Around them stretched the ruins of the Amphiophos, the shattered wreck of Collegium's seat of government. Here the bombs had fallen, in that terrible night of fire that had led to the Imperial air force's undoing. Here the neutered Assembly had met under Wasp rule, to be dictated to by their conquerors. Grass was beginning to grow between the stones. 'I think we should keep it like this. An aid to the memory, so to speak.'

'Well, Master Leadswell, the man of the hour!' Without warning, Sartaea te Mosca was there at his elbow. She was still painfully thin from the camps, but being back in Collegium had gone a long way to restoring her. 'What a grave face, Eujen. Are you tired of your honours already, the very same day as the Lots voted you in?'

He grimaced with embarrassment. 'I'm not the only one who . . .'

'Oh, yes, certainly yes.' The Fly-kinden woman grinned shyly up at Jen. 'Quite the new broom. A whole new Assembly, so many fresh faces.'

'Well, those who did get elected are going to have to do some work for once,' Jen pointed out. 'That probably put off some of the old faces. Did Awlbreaker stand, in the end?'

'Poll? No,' te Mosca confirmed. 'He said he would rather fix machines than cities. They voted in Metyssa, though. Plenty of people remember her stories, from when they were stuck in Sarn waiting to come home, and from when . . .' For a moment she faltered, then hoisted her smile back up with a visible effort. 'Let's just say she's remembered. Willem, the College Masters are now gathering. Shall we go and join the Gownsmen?'

The artificer grimaced. 'What's left of them.' Replacing vacant College posts was proving more difficult than voting in the elected members of the Assembly. 'We're not quite back the way we were, are we?'

Eujen shook his head. Across what had once been the Assembly hall, the new government of Collegium – magnates, veterans, adventurers and mavericks – was finding itself a place where it could gather: on the broken tiers of the old seating, on the rubble, on the ground, under the sky.

'Time to put the world to rights,' he decided.

Te Mosca smiled slightly, watching the Readers part company: he heading for the College seats, she for the Townsmen's. The Fly's expression was thoughtful, philosophical, a mirror to all the turmoil and change that these last years had witnessed. Then she looked up brightly. 'I suppose I should follow my own advice and take my place. Oh . . . and, Eujen?'

'Hm?'

'Congratulations, Master Speaker.'

The young scholar managed a pained smile. 'Given the work ahead, I can't imagine what I can have done to deserve such a fate, but we'll have to make the best of what we've got.'

This had been an arena once, a place for gladiators and wild beasts to tear each other apart to sate the bloodlust of the mighty.

How appropriate, Tynan considered.

Looking around him, all he could see was division. Here, closest to him, were men representing the armies and garrisons and barracks – mostly junior offices, for many of the generals and colonels were sufficiently unsure of how this might play out that they were keeping tight to their little fiefdoms and preparing for the worst.

Beyond, he could see little knots that represented the various corps, each with their numbers prescribed by Ernain's cursed declaration – Slavers, Engineers, Quartermasters and more, plus a big crowd representing the various factora of the Consortium. The majority of those were Beetle-kinden, and mostly under the domination of the Bellowerns.

And beyond *them*, thronging the raked seating, were the others: the unthinkable; those he had let in to sully the wheels of government.

He broke away from the army seats and strode in their direction, scanning that offensive *variety*, seeing them as all the Wasps must see them. Here were representatives from every city in the Empire, and plainly many of them not at all sure that they hadn't been lured here only to be murdered. He saw Grasshoppers and Bees, Ants and Mole Crickets, Flies and Beetles, even a couple of skinny little Skater-kinden from Jerez who somehow now had a say in the future of the state. *We must be mad. We must all be completely mad.* And yet, even on those seats, there were some Wasps: men – and a very few women – who had somehow won over the very people that they had ostensibly been oppressing. It was a new world of opportunity, and simply for that reason it was the anathema of the old regime.

Another man was coming to meet him halfway. *Ah, symbolism.*

'Ernain,' he nodded. 'Is it Captain, still?'

'Just not "Captain-Auxillian", General,' the Bee-kinden agreed. 'Second thoughts?'

'More than you can believe.' Tynan looked past the other man to the little band of Spider-kinden who had come in from Solarno and points south. The word was that the Aldanraic States – as the new term went for the land between Kes and Solarno – were still somewhat undecided as to what nation they belonged to, but then that was typical Spider-kinden for you. The thought brought a slight, sad smile to Tynan's lips.

The various families controlling those cities had sent mostly women to this gathering, he noticed, and to Tynan that showed that they were serious. In their midst he caught Merva's Wasp features as she nodded soberly to him. *Whoever would have thought it would go this far?* she seemed to be saying.

'The numbers are interesting,' Tynan observed. There were still far more Wasps here than any other kinden, but the rabble of others could just about balance them, if they were all pointed in the same direction. *And of course there's no guarantee that we Wasps will all see things the same way, either. Chaos! Surely it will be chaos.* 'I think the Consortium bloc is going to be deciding a great many things.'

Ernain nodded. 'Only if you're thinking of us as your enemies, General. Who knows: maybe we both want to stick it to the Consortium.'

Tynan managed a brief, cut-off laugh and, in its wake, he saw a businesslike look in Ernain's eyes.

'Are you ready?' the Bee-kinden asked him.

'Why me, Ernain?'

'Because I trust you, and the cities will follow my lead for now. Because your own people trust you – you're the closest thing they have to a hero. You negotiated an end to the war: a graceful surrender that preserved their dignity and the lives of their sons. And because an Assembly needs a Speaker, even an Imperial Assembly.'

'How can we be an Imperial Assembly without an Empress?' Tynan demanded, knowing that this battle was already lost.

'You yourself said that there was no actual body. The Empress is . . . gone. Not dead, but gone. In her absence, we shall govern in her name.'

'Until she returns in our hour of need?' Tynan asked sardonically.

'Perhaps. It's worked out well, don't you think?'

Tynan looked out across the sea of faces, the sea of kinden, all those frightened people who wanted him to tell them how this was going to work. 'Just so long as she never *does* come back,' he remarked grimly.

Months after, in the remote reaches of the Tharen mountains, a cloaked figure struggled through the high passes to reach the door of a reclusive community that almost nobody knew of, even amongst the Moth-kinden.

The door was opened by a Wasp who had given up the life of a soldier a decade before. For a long time he stared at their visitor, not quite believing his eyes.

Soon after, he was conducting the visitor through the lamplit halls, past all those others who had turned away from a military life and sought the peace of the Broken Sword.

'I must ask,' the Wasp said finally. 'Your . . . scars . . .?'

Esmail paused a long time before answering. 'A small price to pay,' was all he said, in the end.

Soon after, he entered a room where a Dragonfly-kinden woman waited, with three children gathered nervously about her skirts.

Esmail had come home.

The road from the Exalsee to the Commonweal was a long one, and Maure never made it back. Instead, misadventure took her into the Empire in all its turmoil, stepping between the gears of government even as men such as Tynan were trying to fit them into place. She fed herself and kept herself free through her old trade of necromancy, calling up the dead and laying them to rest, easing grief and sorrow at a time when there was more than enough of both.

What surprised her was how easily it came back to her. At first she thought herself mistaken – overestimating herself after that long spell in darkness when she had nothing at all – but in the end she had to conclude: *No, this is real.*

All over the Empire, the Lowlands and beyond, other magicians were waking up to the fact that the magic, all that magic that had been locked away to maintain the Seal, was slowly coming back.

As for Maure, she headed northwards every day that she could, and in the end crossed over the Empire's far northern border to the rotting forests where the Woodlice live, those who had trained her, and who knew no strife, nor drew any great distinctions between Apt and Inapt, and who had the greatest libraries in the world, and there she made her home and lived for a long time.

A year after the war, and finding that life in both Collegium and Solarno was no longer to her taste, te Schola Taki-Amre took an experimental orthopter, powered jointly by Nemean fuel oil and new metal gearing, past the west coast of the Lowlands to brave the storms and the open sea in order to either discover new lands or, alternatively, to circumnavigate the world.

She never returned.

Three years later

They had left the broken Amphiophos forum just as it was, so that the city's Assembly met under the open sky, and thus remembered, and managed to conclude its important business remarkably quickly when foul weather threatened. Around that open space, which had become known as the Assembly Gardens, the three years since the war's end had cultivated the offices and staterooms and archives that the city could apparently not do without, under the firm guidance of Jen Reader as head of the restoration committee.

And there was still restoration to be done, for the war had left the city with plenty of scars. When people complained, Reader simply told them, *Be glad you're not living in Myna.* Everyone knew how much work the Mynans still had ahead of them.

For the last few tendays the whole city had been alive with speculation. The recovery of Collegium – of the Lowlands as a whole – was sufficiently advanced that the Assembly had voted to hold the Games once more. The last time had been just before the first war, and the intervening years had burdened the Collegiates with other priorities that they were only now able to shed.

The Games themselves were still a tenday away, but today would be a test of Eujen's abilities as Speaker. He was aware that he would need to do well. The Lots were not so very far off, and any embarrassment now would be raked up when the time came for people to consider whether they still wanted him around. The fact that he was thinking in such terms vaguely disgusted him, but at the same time he felt considerably more sympathetic to those who had gone before.

He lodged near the Amphiophos these days, but even the short walk still took him some time. He made it anyway, every working day. It was a point of pride for the only Assembler who had to remember to wind his legs up every evening. It reminded him, and all who saw him, never to take things for granted.

The offices of the Amphiophos were bustling today, filled not just with the city's representatives and the host of clerks and bureaucrats and errand-runners who made the wheels of government turn, but with a glut of foreigners. Everywhere one looked there were strange faces, the diplomatic staff of a dozen states come to Collegium to discuss the world's ills.

'Master Speaker.' A Fly-kinden man of middle years found him the moment he had stepped inside.

'Arvi.' Eujen had taken the previous Speaker's secretary on because, he had reasoned, at least someone at the heart of government should know what he was doing. 'Our delegates?'

'Most of them already in the Gardens,' the Fly confirmed with pride, as though he had personally herded them there.

Perhaps he did, Eujen mused. 'I'll rely on you to make the introductions.'

'Of course.' Arvi led the way, a little man with his head held high.

Stepping outside again, into that sprawling walled garden where the Assembly now met, Eujen had to stop and stare. He knew a fair few of the faces, of course, but never before had they all been together in one place.

He spotted the Vekken ambassador in deep conversation with a Sarnesh woman and the Tseni who spoke for the Atoll Confederation, or whatever that new business along the west coast was calling itself. Three Ants of different cities earnestly conspiring together, and Eujen wondered whether this would be the start of the united Ant nations that everyone was so worried about, and decided that he would bet against it. *Not just yet, but who can say about tomorrow?*

A pale woman, heavily cowled, took his hand, nodding formally. She seemed a Spider-kinden save for the colour of her eyes. Arvi made the introductions a moment before Eujen could recall her name. 'Paladrya of Hermatyre.'

'Welcome again to Collegium,' Eujen addressed her graciously, before his eloquence fell flat with 'I hope it's not . . . I hope it doesn't bring back too many bad memories.'

Her smile was private, solemn, and said nothing of her lost link to this city. Arvi had already scheduled a meeting between herself, Eujen and the head of the Helleren Mint to talk about the currency problem. Shortly after the Lowlander cities became aware of the existence of the Sea-kinden, they became aware that the Sea-kinden could essentially produce enormous quantities of one hundred per cent pure gold, and the College economists were predicting the collapse of the mint unless somebody thought of something spectacular. *Tomorrow's problems ...*

Passing on, Eujen exchanged curt, standoffish nods with the Moth delegate from Tharn. The Moths were a great deal more outgoing these days, seeming to have regained a drive and purpose that they had long been lacking. Eujen was not sure this was a good thing. Nobody wanted Collegium's former masters raking up ancient history, and surely ancient history was what the Moths were good at. And yet, at the same time, it was becoming fashionable amongst the broader-minded Collegiate magnates to put a Moth on the payroll as a kind of oracular consultant. Alarmingly, there were even claims that this was money well spent.

So who is Tharn speaking to these days? Eujen saw the Moth turn back to his conversation with the somewhat shabby-looking, greying Dragonfly – that princeling from the Commonweal who had supposedly been some sort of brigand not so long before. Beside them stood a lean, elegant Spider-kinden Arista who was probably from the so-called Aldanraic States that somehow managed to involve themselves in Lowlander, Spider and Wasp politics without ever committing themselves to anyone.

'Master Speaker, this is Master Ceremon, translator to the Netheryen ambassador,' Arvi announced, before Eujen could think too much about that.

'Translator to the . . .?' Eujen blinked at the Mantis-kinden man before him. 'Ah, yes, of course. And is your . . .?'

A slight shift in Ceremon's stance, a slight motion of the eyes, led Eujen's attention up to the thing that lurked behind him, half lost against the greenery and fallen stone, and standing so still as to be nearly invisible. Eujen managed a stiff, startled nod towards it, seeing the same motion mirrored into the hungry intent of those faceted eyes. He wasn't sure whether sending a man-eating predator along to a conference of powers meant that the Mantis-kinden hadn't quite understood modern diplomacy or that they understood it all too well.

After that, it was a brief clasp of hands with Balkus, for Princep Salma, and then Kymene, here on behalf of the Alliance. The Mynan veteran had lasted a year in heading her city's new consensus before she had become sick of the bickering and factions. Her diplomatic style was scarcely less aggressive than her war record, and Eujen hoped she would be able to keep herself in check.

'Nobody's here from the Second Empire yet,' Arvi noted.

'I think we won't hear from them,' Eujen confirmed. Those Wasps who had been unable to abide the new order within the Imperial Republic – a label that was giving the College's historians conniptions – had mostly ended up in that slice of the Commonweal that was still nominally under Wasp occupation, and where they lived in daily terror that the Dragonflies would come and take it off them once and for all. That their expatriate leadership consisted of former men of the Red Watch who claimed still to speak for the long-lost Empress Seda was a concern to more than a few in both Collegium and the Empire they had fled.

But they had stayed away, to nobody's great regret, and instead there were more, far more delegates for Eujen to meet: a lean grey Woodlouse-kinden who reminded Eujen of his friend Gerethwy; the jovial corpulence of the Helleren magnates; Spider-kinden representatives from at least four of the factions in what nobody was quite calling a Spiderlands civil war just yet, despite the number of desperate refugees washing into Collegium harbour every day; even a silvery-pale Beetle-kinden in pearlescent armour who refused to shake hands or have any physical contact with anyone, and apparently came from the depths of some lake in the North-Empire. *There is not time*, Eujen thought regretfully. *Give me a day with each of them in turn before we have to get down to business.* But, looking across that gathering, he knew that business was already well underway. Just by bringing all these disparate faces together, Collegium had achieved something.

We were once so inward-looking. Now we send out invitations and the world comes.

'What about the Wasps?' Eujen asked, and then corrected himself hastily. 'The Republic?'

'They have arrived, but they wanted to speak with you before they make their formal entrance. I suspect they're aware of just how many old enemies are gathered here.'

'And when were you going to tell me this, Arvi?' Eujen asked him.

The little man gave him a condescending look. 'If I'd told you earlier, you'd not have taken the time to be seen here shaking hands with other people, Master Speaker, which is quite necessary for any man seeking re-election. Master Drillen—'

'Yes, yes,' Eujen cut him off. 'But now I know, so you'd better take me to them.'

'I believe there was something about a gift, also. Bonds of trade and diplomacy and the usual,' Arvi added airily. 'Your bodyguard was dealing with it.'

'She's not my bodyguard.'

Straessa, who was emphatically not Eujen's bodyguard, and who had refused to be made War Master of the Merchant Companies, was waiting for him in one of the Amphiophos's meeting rooms. Eujen still found that he expected her to be wearing the old uniform, the Company sash and the buff coat. She sported her formal robes, though: the Master Armsman of the Prowess Forum had to know how to dress for the occasion, after all. Looked at like that, the rapier at her side became merely part of the costume, the eyepatch just the same.

She hugged him very close for a moment, almost to the point of pulling him off balance, then set him straight. It was to remind him that she owned him in a way that the Assembly never could, despite all its demands.

Beyond her, and obviously slightly thrown by this familiarity, was a handful of delegates from the Imperial Republic, and Eujen recognized three out of four of them: Colonel Vorken, formerly of the Slave Corps, General Varsec, head of the Engineers, and Honory Bellowern, a diplomat and no stranger to Collegium's streets. The fourth, a Wasp woman, was a stranger, although something about her seemed maddeningly familiar.

'Arvi said something about a gift?' Eujen murmured.

'Look up,' Straessa told him. 'Imperial artists have been busy.'

Hearing that, Eujen feared the worst. A lot of what the Wasps had produced in the last three years had been a fascinating insight into a culture trying to come to terms with what it had become. He knew that there was still a strong nationalistic undercurrent in Republican culture, which all too often surfaced in angry, ugly work trying to portray the Wasps in their supposed pre-eminent place amongst the kinden of the world, fallen only as a result of some imagined conspiracy.

This was different, though. Halfway over to greet the ambassadors, Eujen stopped to gaze at the broad canvas mounted on the far wall.

'They call it *The School of Artifice*,' Straessa explained. 'It's . . . I think it's where they see we have something in common.'

The canvas showed a gathering within an open chamber that resembled the ruins of the Amphiophos that Eujen had just left. The figures depicted were engaged in earnest discussion, with boards and charts and half-assembled machinery providing the focus of their interest. There were a lot of Wasps amongst them, but no more than half. The artists had been generous and diplomatic.

Many of the people there he could not identify, but the man with the one armoured glove was surely Dariandrephos, and the other halfbreed with a snapbow partly disassembled was that second-in-command of his, who had been a student at the College in his time. There was Varsec himself – given some prominence and depicted in spirited debate with fellow aviators Taki and

Willem Reader. There was a selection of other College men and women as well – people whom Eujen had known, and who were mostly dead now. He saw Rakespear, Greatly, Tseitus, and the madly bearded man towards the back gesturing at the stormy sky beyond must be intended as Banjacs Gripshod, for all the likeness was poor. At last Eujen's attention was drawn to a figure sitting by itself in one corner, though: a Woodlouse-kinden youth with a complex gear train anatomized in his lap. It was uncanny how they had captured the likeness of Gerethwy.

'You had them do this,' Eujen accused.

'I had them add him, yes,' Straessa confirmed, looking up at the likeness of their fallen friend. 'I sent them Raullo's sketches. He deserved to be in that company, I think.'

Eujen nodded soberly and squeezed her shoulder, then turned a bright smile on the patiently waiting delegation.

'Welcome to Collegium,' he addressed them. 'As you see, I'm somewhat speechless at your gift. It's remarkable. Would you like me to make introductions, out in the Amphiophos?

To his surprise, it was the woman who stepped forwards. 'That would be much appreciated, Master Leadswell,' she told him. There was an awkward pause then, words that she was slow in saying, and with the other three eager to move on, but at last she got out: 'I believe you knew my son.'

He placed the resemblance then, just too late for it to do any good. 'Averic, yes,' he agreed. 'He was a good friend to me.' A sudden rush of emotion passed over him, aroused by faces and voices now wholly consigned to time. 'Averic came here because he believed that our people could learn to meet in friendship, not in war,' Eujen went on, for all of their benefits. 'I came to believe the same thing. Come, let's meet the others now, and talk about the future.'

Later, much later: it was past midnight after a long day of small matters. Arvi had set out the agenda himself – *the finicky little power behind the throne*, Eujen reflected meanly – and the first day's business had been neither weighty nor contentious: minor trade business, the College making places available for more students from beyond Collegium, the Republic asserting a right to send its spare military men to serve as peacekeepers in the Spiderlands, which nobody was going to contest. After all, if they were over *there*, then they wouldn't be sitting idle and getting ideas over *here* . . .

Until the city's clocks had struck twelve, Eujen and Straessa had been exchanging anecdotes with General Varsec and that Spider Arista from the Aldanraic States. But, now that it was just the two of them and half a bottle of wine, Eujen was beginning to think about that walk home, and how much easier it would be with Straessa to keep him company.

Then Arvi burst in on them, or as close as he ever came to doing so. He knocked, but only in passing as he barrelled in through the door.

'Master Speaker!' he exclaimed.

'What are you even doing up?' Eujen demanded of him, carning a reproachful look that eloquently conveyed the message, *Do you not know how hard I work on your behalf?*

'There are some new delegates arrived,' the Fly reported. 'Or they claim they're delegates.'

'Can you not find rooms for them and let it wait until morning?' Eujen asked plaintively.

'Well, left to my own devices I certainly could, Master Speaker, no matter who they say they are,' Arvi said primly. 'However, the Chief Officer of the Coldstone Company says, no, you must come see them immediately.'

'Gorenn?' Straessa demanded. 'What now? Does she think they're Wasp spies or something?'

'Please, Master Speaker?' Arvi pressed, and Eujen nodded and began the difficult process of getting to his feet.

He found them in one of the smaller clerk's rooms, watched over by a couple of Company soldiers and the Dragonfly, Gorenn, for whom the war, Eujen sometimes thought, had never quite finished.

He saw three visitors there, looking like beggars dusty from the road and wearing just coarse, heavy garments of crude cut. Nothing about them said *ambassador*, except . . .

One was a Wasp man, broad shouldered, scarred, bearded, perhaps forty years or so but still strong. Beside him there was a Beetle woman, a few years Eujen's senior at least, her hair cut unfashionably short, and there was something about her he could not place – more in the way that Gorenn was keeping her distance than anything Eujen himself could see.

The third stranger had no eyes. Eujen blinked, seeing a leathery face without even sockets, and yet plainly he had the man's focused attention.

'Good evening to you all,' he managed politely. 'Welcome to Collegium. I am Eujen Leadswell, Speaker for the Assembly.' *The Collegiate Assembly, I should say. We're not the only one, after all.*

'You seem very young for it,' the Beetle woman remarked frankly.

Eujen spread his hands, conceding the point. 'These are unusual times,' he told her. 'Now, I was told that you are delegates . . . Don't I know you?' *It must be my day for women who look slightly familiar.*

'Master Leadswell, my name is Cheerwell Maker. This is Thalric, my husband, and this man is Ambassador Messel of the Underworld Assembly. I understand that you are holding a meeting of powers here. He has come to take his place amongst your guests and to speak for his people – all his many people. And I have come home.'

Glossary

Characters

Aagen – renegade Wasp, now of Princep Salma

Alysaine – servant of Auder Bellowern

Argastos – ancient Moth mystic

Arvi – Fly-kinden secretary to Jodry Drillen

Atraea – Moth-kinden leader of Cold Well

Auder Bellowern – Imperial Beetle Consortium magnate

Averic –Wasp student at Collegium

Balkus – renegade Sarnesh Ant, now of Princep Salma

Bergild –Wasp Air Corps captain with the Second Army

Brakker – Wasp colonel with the First Army

Brugan – Wasp general of the Rekef

Castre Gorenn – Dragonfly archer with the Coldstone Company

Ceremon – Netheryen Mantis, consort of Amalthae

Cheerwell Maker (Che) – Inapt Beetle magician, niece of Stenwold Maker

Chenni – Rosander's chief engineer

Dariandrephos (Drephos) – master artificer and leader of the Iron Glove

Darmeyr Forge-Iron – Mole Cricket slave of the Worm

Despard – Fly artificer, *Tidenfree* crew

Edvic – Wasp governor of Solarno

Ernain – Bee engineer captain, Second Army

Esmail – Assassin Bug spy

Eujen Leadswell – Beetle student and leader of the Student Company

Gannic – Wasp lieutenant with the Engineers

Honory Bellowern – Beetle diplomat

Gerethwy – Woodlouse student at the College

Giselle – Spider Arista of the Arkaetien

Greenwise Artector – Beetle magnate of Helleron

Gude – Fly helmswoman of the *Tidenfree*

The Hermit – renegade Scarred Priest of the Worm

Jen Reader – Beetle College librarian and wife of Willem Reader

Kymene – Mynan commander in exile

Laszlo – Fly agent and occasional pirate

Lien – Wasp general of the Engineers

Lissart – Firefly agent, prisoner of Milus

Lycena – Sarnesh Ant commander

Madagnus – Ant-kinden chief officer, Coldstone Company

Marent – Wasp general of the Third Army

Maure – halfbreed magician from the Commonweal

Messel – Cave Cricket, renegade slave of the Worm

Metyssa – Spider-kinden writer, in hiding in Collegium

Merva – Wasp-kinden, wife of Edvic, governor of Solarno

Milus – Sarnesh Ant tactician

Nessen – Wasp colonel, governor of Helleron

Orothellin – ancient Slug-kinden master, trapped by the Seal

Mycella of the Aldanrael – Spider noblewoman, Tynan's lover

Oski – Fly engineer major, Second Army

Paladrya – Kerebroi adviser of the Sea-kinden

Poll Awlbreaker – Beetle artificer of Collegium

Raullo Mummers – Beetle-kinden artist of Collegium

Rosander – Sea-Kinden, Nauarch of the Thousand Spines Train

Sartaea te Mosca – Fly lecturer and magician

Seda – Empress of the Wasps

Sperra – Fly of Princep Salma

Stenwold Maker – Beetle-kinden, War Master of Collegium

Straessa – the Antspider, officer of Coldstone Company

Taki – Fly aviator of Solarno and Collegium

Thalric – renegade Wasp, former servant of Seda, now lover of Cheerwell Maker

Tisamon – dead Mantis Weaponsmaster raised by Seda

Tomasso – Fly-kinden pirate and merchant, captain of the *Tidenfree*

Totho – halfbreed artificer of the Iron Glove, second-in-command to Drephos

Tynan – Wasp general, Second Army

Tynisa – halfbreed Weaponsmaster, Tisamon's daughter

Varsec – Wasp colonel with the Engineers

Vorken – Wasp major with the Slave Corps

Vrakir – Wasp Red Watch major

Willem Reader – Beetle Collegiate artificer

Wys – Smallclaw artificer and trader

Places

Capitas – capital of the Empire

Chasme – pirate city on the Exalsee

Cold Well – Mining Community under the Worm

Collegium – Beetle city-state

Commonweal – Dragonfly domain north of the Lowlands

Darakyon – Mantis forest, formerly haunted

Dirovashni – Bee-kinden city on the Exalsce

Dorax – Moth retreat

Exalsee – large lake north-east of Spiderlands

Helleron – Beetle city-state

Hermatyre – Sea-kinden city

Kes – Ant island city-state

Khanaphes – ancient Beetle city-state

Malkan's Folly/Malkan's Stand – battlefield, former site of Sarnesh fortress

Myna – Beetle city-state, formerly part of the Empire

Netheryon – Mantis hold

Princep Salma – city founded by refugees of the last war

Sarn – Ant city-state, ally of Collegium

Seldis – Spider city

Solarno – Beetle city on the Exalsee

Sonn – Beetle city in the Empire

Spiderlands – large domain south of the Lowlands

Tark – Ant city-state

Tharn – Moth retreat

Vek – Ant city-state, recently at peace with Collegium

Vesserett – Bee-kinden city in the Empire

Organizations and Things

Amphiophos – Collegiate centre of government

Aldanrael – Spider Aristoi house

Aristoi – the Spider-kinden ruling class

Arkaetien – Spider Aristoi house

Assembly – Collegiate ruling body

Coldstone Company – Collegiate Merchant Company

Consortium – Imperial mercantile arm

Engineering Corps ('the Engineers') – Imperial army corps

Farsphex – Imperial model of orthopter

greatshotter – Iron Glove-developed artillery

Imperial Second Army – 'the Gears', commanded by General Tynan

Imperial Third Army – commanded by General Marent

Iron Glove – artificing cartel led by Drephos out of Chasme

lorn detachment – soldiers sent on a suicide mission

Maker's Own – Collegiate Merchant Company

Prowess Forum – Collegiate duelling school

Quartermaster Corps – Imperial army corps

Red Watch – Imperial corps, the mouth of the Empress

Rekef – Imperial secret service, divided into Inlander and Outlander

Slave Corps – Imperial army corps

Spearflight – Imperial model of orthopter

Stormreader – Collegiate model of orthopter

Tidenfree – Fly-kinden pirate ship

Twelve-year War – Imperial war against the Commonweal

extracts reading groups
competitions books new
discounts extracts extracts
competitions extracts
books new reading groups
books extracts discounts
events books extracts events
extracts reading groups
new titles reading groups
interviews events new
events extracts books
discounts events
new books events interviews
events new new
discounts extracts discounts
www.panmacmillan.com
extracts events reading groups
competitions books extracts new
books